"No primroses..."

"Forward," the young lieutenant said. Sidroc had heard the word too many times—mostly shouted, and emphasized by shrilling whistles—for it to spur him on as it had when he'd first joined Plegmund's Brigade. What was it but an invitation to get himself killed? Even the redhead seemed to realize as much, for he spoke quietly, as if to say the patrol needed to go on but shouldn't make a fuss about it.

Beside him, Ceorl started cursing under his breath: harsh, monotonous, vicious cursing, all in a tiny voice no one farther away than Sidroc could have heard. "You know they're there, too, eh?" Sidroc whispered. Ceorl looked astonished, as if he hadn't realized what he was doing. He nodded abruptly and went back to his oaths.

"Clearing," the guide said, first in his own language, then in Algarvian.

"Well, go on across it," the young lieutenant said. "We'll follow." That made good sense. Unkerlanter soldiers were far less likely to blaze a peasant than soldiers in the uniforms of their foes. Even so, the guide gave the redhead a look full of hate and fear as he started across the muddy open space.

The guide had got about halfway to the trees on the far side of the clearing when he trod on a cunningly buried egg. Afterwards, Sidroc realized that was what must have happened. At the time, all he knew was the sudden roar and flash of light as the sorcerous energies trapped in the egg suddenly released themselves, all channeled upward to be as deadly as possibly. The luckless guide didn't even have the chance to shriek. He simply ceased to be.

TOR BOOKS BY HARRY TURTLEDOVE

The Two Georges (by Richard Dreyfuss and Harry Turtledove)
Household Gods (by Judith Tarr and Harry Turtledove)
The First Heroes (ed. Harry Turtledove & Noreen Doyle)
Between the Rivers
Conan of Venarium
Gunpowder Empire
Curious Notions
Into the Darkness
Darkness Descending
Through the Darkness
Out of the Darkness
Rulers of the Darkness
Jaws of Darkness

(Writing as H. N. Turteltaub)
Justinian
Over the Wine-Dark Sea
The Gryphon's Skull
The Sacred Land

JAWS OF
DARKNESS

HARRY TURTLEDOVE

A TOM DOHERTY ASSOCIATES BOOK
NEW YORK

This is a work of fiction. All the characters and events portrayed in this book are either products of the author's imagination or are used fictitiously.

JAWS OF DARKNESS

Edited by Patrick Nielsen Hayden
Maps by Ellisa Mitchell

A Tor Book
Published by Tom Doherty Associates, LLC
175 Fifth Avenue
New York, NY 10010

www.tor.com

Tor® is a registered trademark of Tom Doherty Associates, LLC.

ISBN 0-765-34318-5
EAN 978-0-765-34318-5
Library of Congress Catalog Card Number: 2002040948

First edition: April 2003
First mass market edition: March 2004

Printed in the United States of America

0 9 8 7 6 5 4 3 2

Dramatis Personae
(* shows viewpoint character)

ALGARVE

Ardalico	Sorcerer and major in Unkerlant
Balastro	Algarvian minister to Zuwayza
Bembo*	Constable in Gromheort, Forthweg
Blosio	Brigadier in Unkerlant
Delminio	Constable in Eoforwic, Forthweg; Bembo's partner
Evodio	Constable in Gromheort, Forthweg
Folicone	Constabulary sergeant in Eoforwic, Forthweg
Fronesia	Spinello's mistress in Trapani
Gradasso	Lurcanio's adjutant in Priekule
Ivone	Grand duke; head of occupation in Valmiera
Lurcanio	Colonel on occupation duty in Priekule; Krasta's lover
Mainardo	Mezentio's brother; King of Jelgava
Mezentio	King of Algarve
Mosco	Officer sent from Valmiera to fight in Unkerlant
Norandino	Captive on the island of Obuda
Oraste	Constable in Gromheort; Bembo's partner
Orosio	Captain of dragonfliers in Unkerlant
Pesaro	Constabulary sergeant in Gromheort, Forthweg
Polinesso	Brigadier in Duchy of Grelz
Rambaldo	Major in northern Unkerlant
Raniero	Mezentio's cousin; King of Grelz; deceased
Sabrino*	Count and colonel of dragonfliers in Unkerlant
Spinello*	Colonel in northern Unkerlant
Tampaste	Brigadier; commander of Spinello's division

FORTHWEG

Beortwulf	Captain of rebels in Eoforwic
Brivibas	Vanai's grandfather; scholar; deceased
Ceorl	Soldier in Plegmund's Brigade
Conberge	Ealstan's sister in Gromheort
Ealstan*	Bookkeeper in Eoforwic; Vanai's husband
Ebbe	Ealstan and Vanai's neighbor
Ethelhelm	Singer and drummer
Hengist	Hestan's brother; Sidroc's father
Hestan	Bookkeeper in Gromheort; Ealstan's father
Hilde	King Plegmund's queen
Jadwigai	Kaunian girl; mascot of Spinello's regiment
Leofsig	Ealstan's dead brother
Penda	Exiled King of Forthweg
Plegmund	Former King of Forthweg
Pybba	Pottery magnate in Eoforwic
Saxburh	Ealstan and Vanai's daughter
Sidroc*	Soldier in Plegmund's Brigade; Ealstan's cousin
Thelberge	Vanai's Forthwegian alias
Vanai*	Kaunian in Eoforwic; Ealstan's wife
Werferth	Sergeant in Plegmund's Brigade

GYONGYOS

Arpad	Ekrekek (ruler) of Gyongyos
Borsos	Major; dowser; captive on Obuda
Frigyes	Captain; Istvan's company commander
Horthy	Gyongyosian minister to Zuwayza
Istvan*	Sergeant on the island of Beceshely
Kun	Corporal in Istvan's squad
Lajos	Soldier in Istvan's squad
Szonyi	Soldier in Istvan's squad
Tivadar	Istvan's former company commander; deceased

JELGAVA

Ausra	Talsu's sister
Donalitu	Exiled King of Jelgava
Gailisa	Talsu's wife
Kugu	Silversmith; deceased
Laitsina	Talsu's mother; Traku's wife
Talsu*	Tailor in Skrunda
Traku	Tailor in Skrunda; Talsu's father

KAUNIAN EMPIRE

Mikulicius	Poet of Late Imperial times

KUUSAMO

Aalbor	Sorcerer aboard *Habakkuk*
Alkio	Theoretical sorcerer in southeastern Kuusamo; Raahe's husband
Eino	Colonel; commandant of captives' camp on Obuda
Elimaki	Pekka's sister in Kajaani
Essi	Sorcerer aboard *Habakkuk*
Ilmarinen	Theoretical sorcerer in southeastern Kuusamo
Joroinen	Juhainen's uncle and predecessor; deceased
Juhainen	One of the Seven Princes of Kuusamo
Kaleva	Sorcerer in southeastern Kuusamo
Leino*	Sorcerer aboard *Habakkuk*; Pekka's husband
Linna	Serving woman in southeastern Kuusamo
Moisio	Kuusaman minister to Unkerlant
Olavin	Elimaki's ex-husband; a banker
Pekka*	Theoretical sorcerer in southeastern Kuusamo; Leino's wife
Piilis	Theoretical sorcerer in southeastern Kuusamo
Raahe	Theoretical sorcerer in southeastern Kuusamo; Alkio's wife
Siuntio	Theoretical sorcerer; deceased
Uto	Pekka and Leino's son

DRAMATIS PERSONAE

LAGOAS

Brunho	Commander of the *Habakkuk*
Fernao*	Theoretical sorcerer in southeastern Kuusamo
Gusmao	Lagoan minister to Unkerlant
Pinhiero	Grandmaster of the Lagoan Guild of Sorcerers
Ramalho	Sorcerer aboard *Habakkuk*
Viana	Sorcerer in southeastern Kuusamo
Vitor	King of Lagoas
Xavega	Sorcerer aboard *Habakkuk*

UNKERLANT

Addanz	Archmage of Unkerlant
Akerin	Peasant in Leiferde; Alize's father
Alize	Peasant girl in Leiferde
Andelot	Lieutenant; Garivald's company commander
Ansovald	Former Unkerlanter minister to Zuwayza
Bertrude	Peasant in Leiferde; Alize's mother
Dagulf	Peasant from Garivald's village
Drogden	Captain in Yanina
Garivald*	Guerrilla in Duchy of Grelz
Gilan	Soldier in Leudast's company
Gurmun	General of behemoths in Grelz
Hagen	Sergeant in Leudast's company
Kiun	Sergeant in Leudast's company
Kyot	Swemmel's twin brother; deceased
Leudast*	Lieutenant commanding company
Merovec	Major; Marshal Rathar's adjutant
Munderic	Resistance leader in Grelz; deceased
Obilot	Guerrilla in Duchy of Grelz; Garivald's lover
Rathar*	Marshal of Unkerlant
Recared	Captain commanding regiment
Rivalin	Soldier in Garivald's company
Sadoc	Underground fighter who fancied himself a mage
Sigulf	Brigadier in Grelz
Swemmel	King of Unkerlant

Syrivald	Garivald's son, probably deceased
Tantris	Peasant from Garivald's village
Vatran	General in southern Unkerlant
Waddo	Firstman in Garivald's village, probably deceased
Ysolt	Rathar's cook in the field

VALMIERA

Amatu	Count who betrayed Skarnu
Bauska	Krasta's maidservant in Priekule
Brindza	Bauska's bastard daughter by an Algarvian
Brusku	Soldier in the pro-Algarvian Phalanx of Valmiera
Gainibu	King of Valmiera
Gedominu (1)	Skarnu and Merkela's son
Gedominu (2)	Merkela's deceased former husband
Krasta*	Marchioness in Priekule; Skarnu's sister
Merkela	Guerrilla fighting Algarvian occupiers; Skarnu's wife
Palasta	Young mage
Raunu	Skarnu's ex-sergeant; guerrilla
Simanu	Count and collaborator with Algarvians; deceased
Skarnu*	Guerrilla fighting Algarvian occupiers; Merkela's husband
Smilgya	One of Krasta's servants
Sudaku	Soldier in the Phalanx of Valmiera
Tytuvenai	Guerrilla—a *nom de guerre*
Valmiru	Krasta's butler
Valnu	Viscount in Priekule

YANINA

Broumidis	Colonel of dragonfliers in the land of the Ice People
Iskakis	Yaninan minister to Zuwayza
Scoufas	Major of dragonfliers in southern Unkerlant

Tassi	Iskakis' wife
Tsaldaris	Dragonhandler in southern Unkerlant
Tsavellas	King of Yanina
Yiannis	Soldier attached to Plegmund's Brigade

ZUWAYZA

Hajjaj*	Zuwayzi foreign minister
Ikhshid	General in Bishah
Kolthoum	Hajjaj's senior wife
Lalla	Hajjaj's former junior wife
Mustanjid	Prince of the pro-Unkerlanter Reformed Principality of Zuwayza
Qutuz	Hajjaj's secretary
Shazli	King of Zuwayza
Tewfik	Hajjaj's majordomo

JAWS OF
DARKNESS

Great Northern Sea
EQUAT
Cape Hadh Far's
West
ZUWAYZA
BISHAH
NAJRAN
SAMAWA
Wadi Ugeiga
JURDHAN
Bay of Ajlun
SAB ABAR
GLOGAU
UNKERLANT
WIRDUM
EOFORWIC
WIHTGARA
HWINCA
TRICAR
VOLKACH
WALDSOLMS
OYNGESTUN
GROMHEORT
GOZZO
SOMMERDA
PEWSUM
UBACH
WRIEZEN
GOLDAP
COTIGGORO
LAUTERTAL
HWITERNE
MIDLUM
LEHESTEN
FORTHWEG
ALGARV
COTTBUS
THALFANG
TANNRODA
KUNHEGYES
GYONGYOS
DERLAVAI
ORTAH
ASPANG
TRAPANI
GYOVARI
HAGENOW
BALATON ISLANDS
YANINA
HOHENRODA
PRESSECK
ANDLAU
SULINGEN
OSSIACH
PATRAS
PIANKENFELS
MANDELSLOH
MAUROMOUNI
LOHR
PIRMASENS
DUCHY of GRELZ
Mamming Hills
RYBUM
Narrow Sea
HESHBON
LAND of the ICE PEOPLE
Barrier Mountains

SIAULIA

Garelian Ocean

OR

North

East

South

DOBELE
GARINDA
LGAVA
ALVI
SALACGRIVA

VALMIERA

VENTSPILS
KAUTISKIS
PRIEKULE ZARASAI
ADUTISKIS
JUVENAI
JUBARKA
MERKINE ERVILKES
KUNARELLI PAVILOS NAKLAVA DUKSTAS
ALSVANGA
MARQUISATE of
FELTRE KVAROLI
RIGOVENI ROCKS of CLUI
EMUKA
SIGISOARA
SIBIU

Strait of Valmiera

Bothnian Ocean

LAGOABI
SETUBAL
YLIHARMA
KUUSANO
ZKIHLANKI
OBUDA
SORENO
Vaato Jarvi Hills
KAJAANI
Naahtali District

MIZPAH

2003 Elisa Mitchell

One

Ealstan added up a long column of figures. The young book-keeper let out a sigh of relief when the answer turned out to be what he'd expected. Bearing the ledger into his employer's private office, he told Pybba, "Those Algarvians are going to make us rich."

"Good," the pottery magnate rumbled. "We'll give 'em some of their silver back, too, and not the way they expect." Pybba wasn't only the biggest pottery maker in Eoforwic—and, for that matter, in all of Forthweg. He was also one of the leaders in the underground struggle against the Algarvian invaders who occupied his kingdom.

"What *do* you suppose they want with fifty thousand Style Seventeen sugar bowls?" Ealstan asked. The question had bothered him ever since an Algarvian colonel marched in to place the order.

Pybba's broad shoulders went up and down in a shrug. "Powers below eat the redheads, whatever it is." His eyes flicked down to the bottom of the column. He nodded. "That's not a bad pile of change, eh? Why don't you go on home now? Your wife'll be waiting for you, I expect."

"Aye, she will. Thanks." Ealstan was glad to have leave to head for his flat.

Pybba showed no sign of going anywhere. His bushy beard was shot with gray, but he went home later and came to work earlier than anybody he employed. "Go on," he growled now. "Get out of here, before I change my mind."

Odds were, he wasn't joking. Ealstan set the ledger on his own slanted worktable, then got out while the getting was good. Twilight spread gloom across Eoforwic, though the occupied capital of the Kingdom of Forthweg seemed sad and gray and gloomy enough even at midday.

A couple of tall, lean Algarvian constables swaggered past Ealstan. Their arrogant stride made them stand out as much as their coppery hair and their short tunics and pleated kilts. Forthwegian men wore knee-length tunics like Ealstan's; Forthwegian women wore loose tunics that reached their ankles. Men and women alike were stocky and swarthy, with dark hair and eyes and strong noses.

Some of the people on the street were almost certainly of Kaunian blood, too. But most of the Kaunians left alive in Eoforwic these days were sorcerously disguised to look like their Forthwegian neighbors. The Algarvians hated Kaunians as ancient enemies, and sacrificed them in droves to use their life energy to fuel potent sorceries in their war against Unkerlant to the west. Few Forthwegians cared what happened to their blond neighbors.

Ealstan was one of those few. Vanai, his wife, was a Kaunian. She was also the one who'd devised the sorcery that let her folk masquerade as Forthwegians. These days, she went by Thelberge, a Forthwegian name. Her own would have been plenty to betray her.

Not so long after winter yielded to spring, she would have their first child. Ealstan frowned a little as he walked along, wondering if the baby would need a spell cast over it every few hours for years to come. He hoped not. Some half-breed children looked altogether Forthwegian.

After a few paces, his frown deepened. Since she'd got pregnant, Vanai's protective spell hadn't been holding as long as it did before she found herself with child. If it happened to wear off while she was away from the flat . . .

His fingers writhed in an apotropaic sign. "Powers above, prevent it," he said softly. They had so far. He had to hope they would keep on doing it. Vanai was careful. She knew the risk, too, of course. But she couldn't see the illusion that fooled everyone else. The greatest danger lay there. She couldn't see it stop fooling people, either.

Such worries dogged Ealstan about every other night on the way home. They made him walk faster, a lump of dread in his throat, as if an Algarvian constable were about to lay hold of *him* for being a Kaunian. His laugh held no mirth. He wasn't a Kaunian. To the Algarvians, he was that even more suspicious creature, a Kaunian-lover. But being a Kaunian-lover didn't show.

Here was his own street. Here was his own block. Here was his block of flats, a dingy building in a bad part of town. He and Vanai had stayed here ever since coming to Eoforwic from Gromheort and her village of Oyngestun in the east.

He went up the stairs into the cramped, dark lobby. He paused there, at the brass bank of post boxes, to see if anyone had sent him a letter. His family back in Gromheort knew where he lived. He didn't think Vanai had any living family, not any more.

She has me, he thought, and hurried up the stairs to his flat. The narrow stairway had a familiar reek: stale cabbage and stale piss. Sometimes it disgusted him. But he'd lived here long enough that sometimes, as tonight, it just felt homey.

Back when he and Vanai first moved in, before she'd crafted the spell that let her look like a Forthwegian, she'd stayed holed up in the flat all the time, like a trapped animal. They'd worked out a coded knock, to let her know it was safe to unbar the door and let him in. He still used it, more from habit than from any other reason.

He knocked and waited. When Vanai didn't come to the door, he knocked again, louder this time. She fell asleep a lot more easily than she had before she got pregnant.

When she still didn't come, he knocked once more, louder still. He frowned and took from his belt pouch the long brass key that could work the latch from the outside. If the door was barred, of course, working the latch wouldn't matter one way or the other. He turned the key and pushed at the door, not expecting to be able to get in. But it swung open.

"Van—?" he began, but checked himself. He tried again, calling, "Thelberge? Are you there, sweetheart?"

No answer. The flat was quiet and dark, no lamps lit, as if nobody'd been inside since well before the sun went down. Fighting back alarm, Ealstan hurried into the bedchamber. Vanai wasn't lying there sound asleep. She wasn't sitting on the pot, which she also needed to do more than she had before quickening.

He'd already seen she wasn't in the front room or the kitchen. He went back there anyway. "Thelberge?" Fear made his voice quaver.

Only silence answered. Little by little, Ealstan realized he hadn't known what fear meant. Now he did.

My neighbors, he thought wildly. *Maybe my neighbors know something.* Trouble was, he hardly knew his neighbors. For one thing, they kept coming and going—this block of flats wasn't the sort of place where people settled down to live out the rest of their lives. And, for another, because of who and what Vanai was, she and Ealstan hadn't gone out of their way to make friends. If anything, they'd gone out of their way to keep to themselves.

But he had to try. Thinking about the alternative . . . Ealstan didn't want to, he wouldn't, think about the alternative. Imagining Vanai in Algarvian hands . . . He shook his head. He *wouldn't* think about that.

He knocked on the door to the next-door flat closer to the stairs. Silence. He knocked again. "Go away," someone inside said—a woman's voice.

"I'm your neighbor," Ealstan began, "and I'd like to ask you—"

"Go away," she said again, "or else I start screaming."

"Powers below eat you," he muttered under his breath, but he went away, to the flat on the other side of his. Wondering what would go wrong now, he knocked on the door there.

This time, at least, it opened. A gray-bearded man stood in the doorway. His narrow eyes had all the warmth of chips of ice. "What do you want, kid?" he demanded. "Whatever it is, make it snappy."

"I don't mean to bother you," Ealstan said, "but have you seen my wife today? She was supposed to be home when I got back, and she's not. She's expecting a baby, so I'm worried."

"Haven't seen her." His neighbor shook his head. "Sorry." He didn't sound sorry. He sounded as if he never wanted to see

Ealstan again. And when he slammed the door, Ealstan had to jump back in a hurry to keep from getting his nose flattened.

He stood in the hallway cursing softly, wondering whether even to bother knocking on the door across the hall from his. At last, with a sort of despairing shrug, he did. "Who is it?" came from inside: another woman's voice.

"Ealstan, your neighbor from across the hall," he answered, wondering if she'd open the door.

To his surprise, she did. She was somewhere in her late thirties—which, to Ealstan's nineteen, made her seem almost grandmotherly, though little by little he realized she wasn't really *bad* looking. She eyed him with frank appraisal. "Well, hello, Ealstan from across the hall," she said when she was through, and breathed brandy fumes into his face. "I'm Ebbe. What can I do for you, dear? Want to borrow a cup of olive oil? You should have knocked a long time ago."

Did that mean what it sounded like? Ealstan had more urgent things to worry about. "I don't mean to bother you—" he began, as he had to his other neighbor.

"Oh, you're not bothering me at all," Ebbe broke in. Aye, she'd been drinking brandy, all right.

Rather desperately, Ealstan plunged ahead: "Have you seen my wife today? She should have been waiting for me when I got home, but she isn't. I'm worried—she's expecting a baby."

"No, darling, I haven't seen a soul today—till *you*," Ebbe answered. "But why don't you come on in anyway? If she's not there, maybe I'll do."

Ealstan fled. Back inside his own flat, he barred the door as if all the Algarvians in Forthweg were after him. He wondered if Ebbe would come knocking in turn. To his vast relief, she didn't.

But that relief quickly passed. The Algarvians in Forthweg weren't after him. They were after Vanai—and he was horribly afraid they had her.

He ate barley bread and olive oil and salted, garlic-tangy almonds for supper, washing the food down with harsh red wine. Then, instead of talking and laughing and probably making

love with Vanai, he spent the longest, loneliest, most miserable
night he'd ever passed. He might have slept a little. On the other
hand, he might not have, too.

When dawn came, he made a breakfast much like his supper.
Then, yawning, he started back to Pybba's pottery. Someone—
more likely several someones—had scrawled a new graffito—
HABAKKUK!—on walls and fences. Dully, he wondered what
the nonsense word meant. Nothing in Forthwegian, Algarvian,
or classical Kaunian; he was sure of that.

Pybba glared when he got to work. "You're late," he rasped,
as he did most mornings whether Ealstan was or not. Then he
took a longer look at his bookkeeper. "Powers above! Who hit
you over the head with a rock?"

"I wish somebody had," Ealstan answered. He wasn't late.
Anything but—he and Pybba had the offices to themselves.
"My wife wasn't home when I got there. She still isn't. I think
the redheads have grabbed her."

"Why in blazes would they want her?" the pottery magnate
demanded. "You two didn't just have a fight or something?"

"No," Ealstan said flatly. "Why would they want her? She's
Kaunian, that's why." He'd never told his boss that. Pybba
hated Algarvians, aye, but he had no great use for blonds.

Now Pybba stared at him, eyes big as the saucers he turned
out by the tens of thousands. "Oh, you fool!" he cried. "You
great stupid fool!"

Habakkuk—the first Habakkuk, the nameship of what would be
a growing class—glided east along a ley line not far from the
island kingdom of Sibiu. The hobnails in the soles of Leino's
boots dug into the great vessel's icy deck. The Kuusaman mage
smiled—no, he grinned. He was as proud of *Habakkuk* as if
he'd invented her. Along with a good many other Kuusaman
and Lagoan mages, he had.

Ships had sailed the seas for centuries uncounted: ships, aye,
but none like *Habakkuk*. Ships had been wood and canvas, riding wind and wave. Then, as magecraft and manufacturing
grew more sophisticated, they'd been iron and steel, traveling
the ley lines of the world's energy grid in defiance of wind and

wave. Now . . . Leino took another step. His hobnailed boots bit into the icy deck again.

Habakkuk was a thing of ice, ice and a little sawdust for strength. Leino and his fellow mages had planed the top of an iceberg flat, down in the iceberg-ridden seas bordering the frigid austral continent. They'd hollowed out chambers in the ice, chambers that held men and supplies and—the point of the exercise—far more dragons than any ordinary ship could haul.

Magecraft had shaped the *Habakkuk*. More magecraft propelled it along the ley lines. And still more magecraft kept it from melting away to nothing as it sailed these warmer (though still far from warm) waters farther from the land of the Ice People. Leino wondered what the natives of the tropical continent of Siaulia would think if the *Habakkuk* ever had occasion to sail there. Most of them had never seen any ice in all their lives, let alone a great floating mountain of it that refused to disappear even in that blood-warm sea.

High overhead, a dragon screeched. Leino glanced up not in fear but in wariness, lest it prove an Algarvian beast diving to the attack. But it wasn't; it was painted in the Kuusaman colors of sky-blue and sea-green, which made it hard to spot for a moment against the drifting clouds. Down it spiraled: long, snaky body; short, clawed limbs; great batwings now gliding, now beating; long neck and fearsome, big-eyed head. So much ferocity, all governed by a brain the size of a plum—and by the dragonflier who sat strapped into his harness at the base of the beast's neck.

Leino's shiver had nothing to do with the ice on which he trod or with the chilly quartering breeze. Facing the impersonal forces of magecraft was hard enough. They would kill you only if you abused them or made a mistake with them. Dragons, now, dragons might kill you out of malice or simply because they forgot what a command meant. With plum-sized brains, they were better at forgetting than remembering. Leino didn't think there was enough silver in the world to make him train to become a dragonflier.

But his countryman aboard the descending dragon handled his dangerous job with nonchalant competence. He brought the beast down right where a gang of handlers waited for it. One of the handlers chained the dragon to a stout iron stake fixed deep in the ice. Another tossed it chunks of meat yellow with crushed brimstone or scarlet from a coating of powdered cinnabar, both of which helped the dragon flame strong and far. The dragonflier unhooked himself and went off to report to his superior.

Leino went below, too. The stairways and the corridors were cut from ice. So were all the chambers opening onto the corridors. The doors and their fittings were ordinary doors and fittings, and some of the chambers had wall hangings inside to lend more privacy to what went on in them.

When Leino walked into one of those chambers, the four mages already inside looked up and nodded to him. "Good morning," Leino said in classical Kaunian. Two of the other wizards were Kuusamans like himself, the other two Lagoans. They shared the great island off the southeastern coast of the Derlavaian mainland, but did not share a language. But every educated man who hailed from eastern Derlavai or the island could use classical Kaunian, the common language of sorcery and scholarship.

"And a good morning to you," answered his countrywoman Essi. She pointed to a teapot above a spirit stove. "Get yourself a cup, if you care to."

"I think I will." Leino smiled. "Being inside all this ice makes me want to have something warm inside myself."

Essi nodded. "We all feel that way now and again." Like Leino, like Pekka his wife—of whom she reminded him more than a little—she was short and slim, with golden skin, coarse black hair, and a broad, high-cheekboned face with dark, narrow eyes set at a slant. A steaming mug of tea sat on the table in front of her.

"Aye, so we do." That was Ramalho, the senior Lagoan mage of the pair here. He'd worked with Leino on the *Habakkuk* down in the land of the Ice People. Lagoans sprang from Algarvic stock: Ramalho was tall and fair and redheaded, though a flattish nose said he might bear a little Kuusaman blood. He went on, "Of course, there is warmth, and then there is warmth." He took a swig from the flask on his hip. His coppery ponytail bobbed at the base of his neck as he drank. He'd done that down in the austral continent, too, but never to the point where it interfered with his work.

After pouring himself a mug of tea, Leino sweetened it with honey and took a couple of big swallows before it started getting cold. Then he sat down at the place waiting for him at the table. "Shall we begin?" he said.

"We could have begun some little while ago, had you got here on time," said Xavega, the other Lagoan mage.

"I am so sorry, Mistress," Leino said, inclining his head to her. "I did not realize you had an urgent engagement elsewhere."

"Really, Xavega, it was no more than a minute or two," said Aalbor, the last Kuusaman mage in the chamber. He was in his early forties, a decade or so older than Leino, and was more inclined to be patient than sardonic.

Patience didn't help here, not least because Xavega had so little herself. She glared first at Leino, then at Aalbor. "I might have known one Kuusaman would stick up for another."

"Oh, let it be, by the powers above." That wasn't Aalbor—it was Ramalho. "Have you never been late in all your born days?"

Xavega glared at him, too. "Things should run properly," she insisted, by which she no doubt meant, *The way I want them to run.*

Leino sighed. He didn't point that out aloud, and wondered why. Well, actually he didn't wonder—he knew. He took another sip of tea to make sure the knowledge didn't show on his face: Xavega was too pretty for him to want to antagonize her too badly. She had hair the color of burnished copper, fine, regular features, large green eyes, and a lush figure that seemed all the more spectacular to him because he was used to the sparer build of Kuusaman women. He was married, aye, and happily so, but he owned an imagination that worked perfectly well.

"Let it lie," Ramalho repeated, a little more sharply.

"Oh, very well," Xavega said with poor grace. "Some people, though . . ."

Now Leino had all he could do not to laugh out loud. Every

time Xavega opened her mouth, she showed him how absurd his fantasies were. She was one of those Lagoans with no use at all for their eastern neighbors. Over the years, Lagoas and the land of the Seven Princes had quarreled a fair number of times, as neighboring lands will. When the Derlavaian War broke out, some few Kuusamans had wanted to fight Lagoas and not Algarve. *Fools,* Leino thought.

He stole another glance at Xavega. Odds were she'd never look at him, but he still enjoyed looking at her. It might even have been better that she did despise him. He was in less danger of landing himself in trouble this way.

"Do you suppose we might actually work the magic we all came here to work?" Essi asked.

"Oh, very well," Aalbor said, imitating Xavega's petulant tone so closely that Leino, Essi, and Ramalho all laughed. Xavega sent the senior Kuusaman mage a glare more venomous than any she'd given Leino. As for Leino himself, he sighed. However luscious Xavega's body might be, in getting it one also had to deal with her mind. That came close to making it more trouble than it was worth.

Before the three wizards from Kuusamo began to incant, they joined in a small, not quite sorcerous ritual, reciting, "Before the Kaunians came, we of Kuusamo were here. Before the Lagoans came, we of Kuusamo were here. After the Kaunians departed, we of Kuusamo were here. We of Kuusamo are here. After the Lagoans depart, we of Kuusamo shall be here."

That little chant was in Kuusaman, not classical Kaunian. Mages from the land of the Seven Princes had prefaced sorcerous operations with it for centuries. Leino had trouble imagining working deliberately planned magic without it.

Ramalho and Xavega knew what it was, of course, even if they didn't understand it. As he usually did, Ramalho raised an amused eyebrow. Xavega said something in Lagoan. Leino didn't speak much of the neighboring kingdom's language, but both the sound of the words and Ramalho's dismayed expression made him doubt she'd paid Kuusamo a compliment.

Aalbor returned to classical Kaunian: "Let us begin." All five mages pulled off the amulets they wore and held them in their hands. Leino's, like those of Essi and Aalbor, was of silver set with moonstones and pearls. Xavega and Ramalho used gold charms with lodestones and amber to feel for and tap the power of the ley lines. Lagoan sorcery was of the Algarvic school, more closely related to that of Sibiu and Algarve itself than to that of Lagoas' island neighbor.

But the style and substance of the amulets and the charms the mages used to activate them were only means to an end. However much the means differed, they could and did work together toward the same end. As Leino drew sorcerous energy from the ley line and applied it to keeping the *Habakkuk*'s icy structure solid and secure, he felt the energy also flowing into Essi and Aalbor, into Ramalho—aye, and into Xavega, too. They channeled it to the ship, sensing what was, comparing that to the pattern they all held in their minds of what should be, and correcting the discrepancies they found.

They weren't the only team with such a responsibility. Keeping the *Habakkuk* afloat took a lot of magecraft. Leino shook his head as that thought occurred to him. It wasn't strictly true. Ice floated. But keeping the *Habakkuk* afloat as something more than a slowly melting lump of ice took a lot of magecraft.

At last, Leino and his comrades looked at one another. *Have we done all that wanted doing?* they asked one another without words. *Have we shored up the ship for another day?* Again without words, they agreed they had. *Will anything go wrong because of something we have failed to do?* That was a clear negative.

Xavega was the first to speak aloud, with unmistakable relief: "We are finished. We have finished." She pushed back her chair and strode out of the chamber. Almost of their will rather than his, Leino's eyes followed her. Like other Algarvic peoples, Lagoans wore kilts. Xavega's showed off quite a lot of elegantly turned leg.

With another sigh, Leino got up, too . . . and poured himself a fresh cup of tea. It wasn't what he wanted—well, it wasn't all of what he wanted—but it would have to do.

∽

Four hundred years before, King Plegmund of Forthweg had been the mightiest monarch in eastern Derlavai. His armies went from triumph to triumph in Algarve to the east and in Unkerlant to the west. Even nowadays, his name was one to conjure with in Forthweg.

And the Algarvians had conjured with it, recruiting Plegmund's Brigade from Forthwegians who still wanted to go to war despite their kingdom's defeat. Sidroc wondered what he would be doing if the redheads hadn't organized the Brigade. Something boring with his father Hengist back in Gromheort, he supposed.

Whatever else he was down here in the Duchy of Grelz in southern Unkerlant, he wasn't bored. One of the Algarvian officers who led Plegmund's Brigade blew a piercing blast on his whistle and shouted, "Forward!"—in Algarvian, of course.

Forward Sidroc went, on snowshoes because some of the drifts were higher than his head. His sigh briefly raised a young fogbank around his face. In Gromheort, whole winters would go by without snow on the ground. In Unkerlant, it sometimes seemed a day couldn't pass without a new blizzard.

"Mezentio!" Sidroc shouted as he slogged forward. "Hurrah for King Mezentio!" He yelled in Algarvian, not Forthwegian. Plegmund's Brigade might have been named for a Forthwegian king, but it used the occupiers' language. Yelling in Algarvian also lessened the chances that a redhead would take him for an Unkerlanter and blaze him by mistake. He and his countrymen looked more like the enemy than they resembled their allies and paymasters.

The Unkerlanters holed up in the hamlet ahead didn't intend to be run out. They had a couple of egg-tossers in there, and hurled death back at the men of Plegmund's Brigade and the Algarvians with them. The eggs burst when they struck, releasing blasts of sorcerous energy and sending fragments of their metal eggshells whistling through the air like flying scythe blades.

When eggs started bursting close to Sidroc, he flopped down on his belly in the snow. Chunks of sharp metal screeched past above his head. Not far away, somebody shrieked and then started cursing in Forthwegian. Cursing was something not subject to military discipline.

"Urra!" shouted the Unkerlanters in the village. "Swemmel! King Swemmel! Urra!" Their word for *king* wasn't much different from Sidroc's; he understood it. The Unkerlanters sounded raucous and drunk. Sidroc had some spirits in a flask on his belt, too. He wish he were drunk stupid and mean. He didn't have enough in the flask for that, worse luck.

"Forward!" the Algarvian officer shouted again. "We have to keep moving. We have to drive them back. Herborn *will* be ours again."

Herborn was the capital of the Duchy of Grelz. Herborn had been the capital of the Algarvian puppet Kingdom of Grelz till Swemmel's soldiers recaptured it a couple of months before. They'd captured King Raniero, too—the cousin Mezentio had put on the throne of Grelz: captured him and boiled him alive.

"Mezentio!" Sidroc yelled, and got to his feet again.

"Mezentio!" Ceorl snowshoed forward beside him. Like more than a few men who'd joined Plegmund's Brigade, he'd been a robber, a bandit, before. The Algarvians weren't fussy about such things, not even a little.

Eggs fell on the village, too, kicking up fountains of snow. Sidroc whooped when some of the thatch-covered roofs caught fire, sending columns of black smoke into the gray sky. Unkerlanter soldiers ran through the streets. They were awkward and bowlegged on their snowshoes, just as Sidroc was on his. He raised his stick to his shoulder, thrust his right index finger out through the open seam in his mitten, and rammed it into the stick's activation hole. The beam leaped forth from the other end. He hoped it bit an Unkerlanter.

Swemmel's soldiers were blazing back at the men of Plegmund's Brigade and the Algarvians, too. Puffs of steam rose from the snow where their beams missed Sidroc and his comrades. The screams that rang out said not all the beams had missed. Sidroc did his best not to think about that, even when a beam zipped past his head so close, he smelled thunderstorms for a moment. A few inches more to the left, and . . . Sidroc shook his head. *I'm* not *thinking about that, curse it.*

He spied more movement in the village. He raised his stick again, then lowered it, swearing as vilely as he could.

Sergeant Werferth saw that movement, too, and also knew it for what it was. "Behemoths!" he shouted in Algarvian, and followed that with his own foul Forthwegian. Werferth was no youngster looking for adventure like Sidroc, nor a ruffian two jumps ahead of the constables like Ceorl. He'd been a sergeant in the Forthwegian army before the Algarvians smashed it. As far as Sidroc could see, he'd joined Plegmund's Brigade simply because he liked being a soldier. He would never make officer's rank, not in the Brigade—he wasn't an Algarvian. Of course, he wouldn't have made officer's rank in the Forthwegian army, either—he wasn't a nobleman.

But Sidroc didn't have much time to worry about Werferth. The behemoths, now, they were really something to worry about. They lumbered forward, each one with enormous snow-shoes on its feet, each one with a surcoat that made it harder to spot flapping over its chainmail, each one with its great curved horn sheathed in iron to make it all the more sharp and deadly—and each one mounting a crew of armored Unker-lanters who served either a heavy stick or an egg-tosser that made the behemoth deadly far beyond the reach of its horn.

Sidroc threw himself down in the snow again. A footsoldier *could* blaze down a behemoth—if he put a beam right in its eye. What were the odds? Not worth betting. He tried to knock over the Unkerlanter footsoldiers who ran forward with the beasts. He had a better chance of that.

"Where are *our* behemoths?" he shouted. Eggs burst around the Unkerlanter animals, but only a direct hit was likely to slay one. The best way to fight behemoths was with other behemoths.

"Where *are* our behemoths?" That was Ceorl, and that was alarm in his voice. The summer before, Algarve had lost far more behemoths than she could afford to lose, trying to smash the Unkerlanter salient around the town of Durrwangen. Since then, the redheads hadn't had enough to meet the Unkerlanters' onslaught—which was one great reason Swemmel's soldiers had pushed so far east since the battles around Durrwangen. The Algarvians had come up with a fair number of behemoths for the counterattack aimed at Herborn—which was one great reason Mezentio's soldiers had been able to head west again.

If, however, they didn't get some behemoths right here pretty soon, some of Mezentio's soldiers and a good many Forthwegians who'd been rash enough to join them were going to have a very thin time of it indeed.

An egg burst right on top of an Unkerlanter behemoth. All the eggs it had been carrying for its tosser burst, too: a great flash of light, an enormous clap of thunder. Only a hole in the ground—a shallow hole in the ground, for it was frozen hard—showed where the beast had been. The Unkerlanters who served that egg-tosser couldn't have known what hit them. Sidroc cheered. He didn't raise his head to do it, though. Plenty of King Swemmel's soldiers remained alive.

Flame enveloped another behemoth and its crew. This time, Sidroc saw the dragon that flamed the beast. It was painted in green, red, and white: Algarvian colors. He cheered again. The redheads had been short of dragons since Durrwangen, too, though not to the same degree as they'd been short of behemoths.

But the Unkerlanter behemoth crews who served heavy sticks also blazed at the Algarvian dragons. Their beams were strong enough to burn through silvery belly paint and the armoring scales beneath. A dragon slammed into the snow. It thrashed for a long time before it died; its great tail sent a couple of Unkerlanters spinning, smashed and broken, to their deaths. The dragonflier, though, had surely died at that first crushing impact.

With most of the enemy behemoths dead, Algarvian officers blew their whistles. Their imperative cry rang out again: "Forward!"

Sidroc would sooner have stayed where he was and let somebody else take the chances. But, along with the other troopers from Plegmund's Brigade—and along with the Algarvians, too; no denying the redheads had spirit—he scrambled to his feet and went forward. Even as he did, he wondered why. He didn't particularly care about clearing the Unkerlanters from the village ahead. He didn't even particularly care about retaking Herborn; he'd seen enough battered Unkerlanter villages and towns and cities to last him the rest of his days.

What do I care about, then? he wondered, blazing at an Unkerlanter in a snow smock not much different from his own. The Unkerlanter toppled. Sidroc whooped and slogged on. *Why am I giving these buggers the chance to do to me what I just did to that poor whoreson?*

He whooped again when Ceorl blazed an Unkerlanter. He didn't even like Ceorl, and he knew full well the ruffian had no use for him when they weren't up against Swemmel's soldiers. Oddly, that gave him an answer of sorts: *I can't let the fellows who are in this with me down.* If he stayed behind, they'd think he was a coward, and their opinions were the only ones that mattered to him these days. His mother was dead, killed when the Algarvians took Gromheort. His father remained back in Forthweg, and had no real understanding of what he was doing here. He'd killed his cousin Leofsig in a brawl. He'd brawled with Leofsig's brother Ealstan, too—and Ealstan, from what he gathered, had run off with a Kaunian tart. Leofsig and Ealstan's father and mother and sister hated him. Who was left, then, but the men alongside whom he fought?

More Algarvian dragons swooped down on the Unkerlanters. Behemoths died under the eggs they dropped and from the flame that burst from their jaws. The handful of behemoths that survived had had enough, and lumbered off toward woods beyond the village. The trees helped shelter them from dragon attacks.

"Forward!" shouted the Algarvian officers, and forward went the Algarvian footsoldiers and the men of Plegmund's Brigade.

They overran the village King Swemmel's troopers had defended so fiercely. Some of the redheads had weapons Sidroc hadn't seen before: small pottery jugs that they flung at their foes, and that burst like miniature eggs. "I want some of those. When can we get 'em?" he asked Sergeant Werferth.

"When the Algarvians have enough to spare for their poor relations," Werferth answered. Sidroc swore and kicked at the snow; the sergeant was bound to be right.

Some soldiers pushed on down the snow-covered road toward Herborn. Others—the less lucky—were ordered into the woods to go after the last few Unkerlanter behemoths and the footsoldiers with them.

Werferth had never been given to wild flights of optimism—what veteran sergeant was? But now he said, "Maybe we really will drive these sons of whores out of Herborn. Looks like we've got a lot of 'em in a pocket here."

"I wouldn't mind," Sidroc said. "But what'll the Algarvians do for a new King of Grelz? Who'd be daft enough to want the job after what happened to the old one?"

Before the sergeant could answer, the Algarvian officers' whistles started screeching again. But instead of yelling, "Forward!" as they had since the drive on Herborn began, the redheads shouted, "By the left flank! Crystallomancers say there's an Unkerlanter attack coming in. We have to hold. We can't let Swemmel's men out of the box we've shoved 'em into. By the left flank!"

"By the left flank!" Werferth echoed loudly. Then he sighed. "Something's gone wrong somewhere."

Sidroc only shrugged. "Not like it's the first time." He too turned to the left.

Count Sabrino had fought as a footsoldier during the Six Years' War, which ended almost thirty years before the Derlavaian War broke out. That put the colonel of dragonfliers well up into his fifties these days. He was more than twice the age of most of the men in the wing he commanded. When the wing worked hard, as it was working hard now, he felt the weight of every one of those years, too.

I'm still strong, he thought as he spooned up boiled oats with onions and carrots and chunks of meat cooked into them. Like every Algarvian fighting in Unkerlant, he'd long since given up asking what the meat was. Better not to know. *I am still strong, curse it. In a standup fight, I can take most of my men.*

But that wasn't what left him feeling like an antiquity in the museum back in Trapani. The youngsters he led could get by with irregular meals and not enough sleep—and much of that at odd hours—and stay fresh. He couldn't, not any more. A hard stretch of flying left him feeling as if he were moving underwater. He had trouble trusting himself to make the right decisions when he was too worn to see straight.

Captain Orosio, one of his squadron leaders—the only one who'd been with the wing when the war was new—gave him a sympathetic look when he complained. "My guess is, your wound's still troubling you, sir," Orosio said.

"You're a gentleman," Sabrino said, and gave Orosio a seated bow. By his pedigree, Orosio wasn't much of a gentleman, or he would have been a colonel with a wing of his own. Sabrino flexed his shoulder. It *did* still pain him; his wounded dragon had come down behind Unkerlanter lines, and he'd got blazed escaping Swemmel's men. "Aye, you're a gentleman, but it's more than that. I can't stand having my life turned upside down a new way every day as easily as I could when I was your age, and that's all there is to it."

"That's not so good, sir." Orosio lacked much of the spirit of fun that most Algarvians had. Serious and sober as usual, he went on. "War does what it wants to do, not what you want it to do."

"Really?" Sabrino did his best to look astonished. "I never would have noticed."

He hoped Orosio would laugh. He feared Orosio would believe him. He never found out either way. Before the squadron leader could react, a crystallomancer stuck his head into the tent, nodded to Sabrino, and said, "Sir, Brigadier Blosio from army headquarters would speak to you."

"Would he?" Sabrino said. The crystallomancer nodded. With a sigh, Sabrino got to his feet. "The next interesting question is, would I speak to him?" He didn't scandalize the young mage any further, but got up and followed him off to his tent.

It had been cold inside the mess tent. As soon as Sabrino poked his head out the flap, the Unkerlanter winter stabbed icy knives into the marrow of his bones. *This wouldn't have bothered me so much when I was half my age, either,* he thought bitterly.

Dragons crouched in the snow, chained to the iron spikes that kept them from flying off and doing something stupid on their own. Dragon handlers moved among them, keeping them fed. This wasn't a proper dragon farm, not the way the manuals back in Algarve said one should be organized. It was the best worn, overtaxed men could do. Ever since Cottbus failed to fall in the first winter of the campaign against Unkerlant, the whole war in the west had been one improvisation after another, each seeming more desperate than the last.

The crystallomancer ducked into his own tent. With a sigh of relief, Sabrino followed. A brazier in there warmed the air all the way up to frigid. A certain pungency in the air said the brazier was burning behemoth dung rather than charcoal: one more improvisation.

Sabrino sat down on what had probably been some Unkerlanter peasant's milking stool and peered into the crystal. Brigadier Blosio's image looked out at him. Sabrino took some consolation in noting that Blosio looked miserably cold, too. "Reporting as ordered, sir," he said. "What do you need from my wing?"

"You know how our drive for Herborn has cut off a good many Unkerlanter soldiers," Blosio said, as if doubting Sabrino knew any such thing.

"Aye, sir," Sabrino answered stolidly. "Still a good many in front of us, too. We just tore up some behemoths trying to come through a peasant village and smash in the head of our column."

With a typically extravagant Algarvian gesture, Brigadier Blosio waved that away, as if it were of no account. He explained why: "They're trying to break out and smash through our columns."

When the Unkerlanters surrounded Herborn, the Algarvians and Grelzers had tried to do the same thing. They'd failed. Sabrino asked the obvious question here: "What do their chances look like?"

Blosio's shrug was as unrestrained as his wave had been. "Neither one of our columns is as strong as one might wish, and we've cut off a lot of Unkerlanters. But we have to do what we can, you know."

"Oh, indeed." Sabrino nodded. "In case you're wondering,

sir, my wing has twenty-one dragons ready to fly." Had the wing been at full strength, it would have had sixty-four. It hadn't been at full strength, or anywhere close, for a couple of years.

Brigadier Blosio shrugged again. "That's how things are, Colonel. And they're not getting any better. Trapani is ordering some of our dragons taken out of the west and brought back home to Algarve. The way things are now, the Lagoans and Kuusamans are pounding our southern cities flat from Sibiu because we've hardly any beasts to put in the air against them."

"That's . . . not good, sir." Count Sabrino reckoned that a commendable understatement. "The way things are now, the Unkerlanters are pounding our armies here flat because we haven't got enough beasts to put in the air against them."

"We have to try there," Blosio said.

"We have to try here, too." Sabrino knew his protest wouldn't change anything. And Blosio had a point: King Mezentio couldn't very well let Algarve itself take a beating. For one thing, people back home might sour on the war if they kept getting hit without seeing their countrymen hit back. For another, the eggs the Kuusamans and Lagoans dropped hit manufactories that made things the army needed, and also slew the mages without whom Sabrino's men would have had no eggs to drop and the Algarvian footsoldiers would have had no sticks with which to blaze.

"Then go out and try to put paid to that Unkerlanter counterattack," Blosio said. "That's the best thing your wing can do for Algarve." He gave map coordinates.

"Aye, sir," Sabrino said resignedly. He wasn't sure Blosio heard him. The brigadier's image vanished from the crystal. It flared for a moment before becoming an inert globe of glass. Sabrino nodded to the crystallomancer. "Thanks." On second thought, he didn't know why he was thanking the young mage. Because of the crystal, Sabrino now stood a better chance of getting killed.

Out into the cold again. He shouted for his men. They knew he was giving them no great gift—only the chance to die before their time. But knowing that, they affected not to. They scram-

bled onto their dragons and fastened the harnesses that held
them safe as if they were going on a lark, not into battle.
Sabrino also strapped himself into the harness at the base of his
dragon's neck. He knew he could die if any little thing went
wrong. How vividly he knew it was another reminder of his
years.

He also knew his dragon, like most Algarvian beasts, hadn't
been getting enough quicksilver. Its flames wouldn't reach so
far as they would have with more of the vital mineral in its system. Had Algarve taken the Unkerlanter city of Sulingen, had
Algarve seized the vital cinnabar mines south of Sulingen . . .
Had that happened, Mezentio's men wouldn't have been
pushed back into Grelz.

A dragon handler slipped the chain that held Sabrino's beast
to its stake. The colonel of dragonfliers hit his mount in the side
of the neck with his goad. The dragon screeched furiously,
flapped its great, leathery wings, and bounded into the air.
Looking back over his shoulder, Sabrino watched the rest of the
dragons in the wing—all of them painted in varying patterns of
green, red, and white—following him.

He murmured the charm that activated the crystal he carried
with him, so he could give his squadron commanders the map
square the wing was ordered to attack. They passed it on to
their dragonfliers. So did Sabrino, with gestures and pantomim-
ing. *Maybe I'll go on the stage after the war is over,* he thought,
and laughed at himself. He laughed doubly: by all appearances,
the war would go on forever.

The landscape below did nothing to contradict that. It was a
chiaroscuro blend of snow and smoke and soot. All the villages
and a lot of stretches of forest had been fought over two, three,
four times. Whoever finally won the war, the Grelzer peasantry
would be generations recovering from it.

Fresh columns of smoke rising into the sky would have told
him where the heavy fighting was even without the coordinates
he'd got from Brigadier Blosio. He urged his dragon toward
those columns. *Urged* meant hitting it with the goad, harder and
harder, till it did what he wanted. Every once in a while, a
dragon would have enough of that and flame its flier off its

back. Dragons were trained not to do that from the moment they hatched, but everyone who had anything to do with them knew they were too stupid and too vicious to be very reliable.

Sabrino's dragon obeyed now. Captain Orosio's image, tiny but perfect, appeared in the wing commander's crystal. Orosio said, "By the powers above, sir, that's a cursed broad front the Unkerlanters have opened up. How many of them are there, anyhow?"

"I asked Brigadier Blosio the same question," Sabrino answered. "I gather we're supposed to find out by experiment." Orosio said something pungent and abruptly broke the etheric connection.

As soon as Sabrino spotted swarms of Unkerlanters trying to force their way north and east through a wavering line of Algarvian defenders, he ordered his dragons to the attack. They swooped low on an advancing column of behemoths, dropping eggs among them and flaming down several. Sabrino's dragon didn't have to be urged to attack. Restraining it, making it attack when and where he wanted it to, was harder, but he managed.

It was when he made the beast gain altitude for another pass at the enemy that he gasped in horror. The column of behemoths his wing had assailed was one of dozens, perhaps one of hundreds, all with footsoldiers moving with them and in support of them. The Algarvians hadn't cut off a few brigades. They'd tried to surround a whole army, and a pugnacious one, too.

A man who hooked a salmon would eventually pull it to shore. A man who hooked a leviathan would be hauled out to sea and never seen again unless he threw away the line in a hurry. But who would do that soon enough?

In any case, his countrymen couldn't throw away the line. King Swemmel's soldiers gripped them too closely for that. All they could do was hang on tight and hope for the best. They wouldn't hold back this Unkerlanter attack. Sabrino could see as much. That meant they wouldn't recapture Herborn, either.

Which raised an interesting question, or a couple. Who was fisherman here, who fish? And who'd caught whom?

꙳

Skarnu had discovered it was much harder to join in the underground fight against Algarve with a small baby in tow. He'd been fighting the redheads since the war began: first as a captain in King Gainibu's army and then, after Algarvian behemoths and dragons shattered the Valmieran forces, in what wasn't quite battle but could nonetheless have got him killed at any moment.

Gedominu started to cry. Merkela plucked her son and Skarnu's out of the cradle. She checked to see if he was wet. Her grunt said he wasn't. She undid the top three toggles on her tunic and shrugged it off her shoulder to bare a breast. That was what the baby had wanted, sure enough.

"He's hungry," Skarnu remarked.

Merkela nodded. The motion made some of her blond hair flip down onto the baby's face; she brushed it aside with her free hand. "He's getting bigger and stronger every day," she said. "He needs to get bigger and stronger. Even if we lose the fight against Mezentio's whoresons—"

"Powers above forbid it," Skarnu exclaimed, and his fingers twisted in a protective gesture that went back to the days when Valmiera was a province of the Kaunian Empire and Algarve a woodland full of barbarous tribes.

Merkela went on as if he hadn't spoken: "Even if we lose, Gedominu will carry on the fight against the Algarvians when he grows to be a man." She stroked the baby's head, which looked bald but in fact had a thin fuzz of fine blond hair even paler than hers or Skarnu's. "He's sucking in hatred for the redheads along with my milk."

She was implacable as an avalanche. Gedominu was named for her husband. The old farmer—he'd been twice Merkela's age—had taken in Skarnu and his veteran sergeant when he could have turned them over to the Algarvians after the Valmieran army surrendered. Gedominu (the man, not the boy) had gone raiding against the redheads himself. And he'd been taken hostage and blazed after one of those raids killed an Algarvian cavalryman with a trip line.

Skarnu wondered whether he would have ended up in Merkela's arms even if the Algarvians hadn't killed her husband. She was a farmwoman and he a marquis, but that had nothing to do with the way they were drawn to each other. He didn't suppose her wedding vows would have had anything to do with it, either.

But she wasn't just his lover. Before she'd got pregnant, she'd fought alongside him. Count Simanu, who'd been in bed with the redheads, was dead largely because of the two of them. And now . . .

Now Skarnu stared at the walls of the cramped little flat he and Merkela and Gedominu shared. It was a far cry from the mansion in which he and his sister Krasta had lived before the Derlavaian War broke out. And it was almost equally far, in a different way, from the farmhouse whose mistress Merkela had been. With a sigh, Skarnu said, "Ukmerge isn't much of a town."

Merkela's lip curled. She spoke quietly so she wouldn't bother Gedominu, but didn't bother hiding her venom: "I never wanted to live in Pavilosta when I went there on market days, but Ukmerge makes Pavilosta look like it was one of the king's pleasure palaces."

Even had he wanted to, Skarnu would have had trouble arguing with that. Pavilosta was a pleasant little market town, or perhaps village; it still kept much of the air of the countryside that was its reason for being. In Ukmerge, they made shoes. The town stank of leather. People either worked in one of the two big shoe manufactories or sold things to those who did. And the folk who filled the manufactories also filled grim blocks of flats like this one.

Gedominu let Merkela's nipple slide out of his mouth. She put a cloth on her shoulder, then raised the baby to it and patted his back. He rewarded her with a belch and a little sour milk. She laughed at him when he spit up. Wiping his mouth, she said, "You thought you were going to ruin my tunic, didn't you? You thought so, but I fooled you." Gedominu replied with a series of noises from the other end. Merkela laughed again, ruefully this time. "You can't stay ahead of a baby, no matter how hard you try."

"Give him to me. I'll change him," Skarnu said; he'd discovered she scowled at him if he left her to do all the work with the baby. As he cleaned Gedominu's bottom and put a fresh cloth around it, he went on. "As long as we stay ahead of the Algarvians, that's what counts."

Merkela shook her head. "We've got to do more than that. That was good enough when you pulled me off the farm before the redheads grabbed me—powers below eat your cursed Count Amatu for betraying me to them. It was good enough when we got out of Erzvilkas after their mages tracked us there. But it's not good enough any more. Now I want to hit back again."

"So do I," Skarnu said. "But the underground isn't very strong here in Ukmerge."

Merkela's lip curled again, this time with contempt as complete and automatic as Krasta could have shown—which was saying a great deal. "Shoemakers," she sneered as she set her tunic to rights. "They don't care whether they're making shoes for their own people or for the Algarvians."

That was an unkind judgment on the folk of Ukmerge, but also, Skarnu feared, an accurate one. The shoe manufactories had missed hardly a day's work after the Valmieran army abandoned the town and the Algarvians marched in. Ley-line caravans carried endless crates of marching boots west to Algarve for King Mezentio's soldiers to wear. As Merkela said, the shoemakers got paid no matter who wore what they made.

Gedominu looked up at Skarnu and smiled. Skarnu smiled back. He could hardly help it. His son hadn't been smiling very long. Every time Gedominu did, it was as if he'd discovered the idea of being happy for the very first time and wanted everyone around him to be happy, too. Then, smiling still, the baby proceeded to ruin the cloth Skarnu had just pinned into place around his middle.

Skarnu said something rather more pungent than the odor wafting from Gedominu. Merkela laughed and asked, "Do you want me to change him this time?"

"It's all right." Skarnu shook his head. "I haven't even washed my hands yet." He cleaned the baby off again, then tossed the sodden, stinking rag into a pail that held a good many others. The pail, fortunately, had a tight-fitting lid.

Skarnu shut it and then did wash up, wondering all the while if Gedominu would make yet another mess.

Someone knocked on the door. Skarnu and Merkela both froze. Knocks on the door, these days, were all too likely to mean trouble. Skarnu had acquired a small stick from some highly unofficial sources. As a footsoldier, or even as a farmer hunting vermin or after small game for the pot, he would have despised it. But it could knock over a man at short range, and what more did somebody on the run need?

"Who is it?" he asked. If he didn't like the answer, he'd find out exactly what the little stick could do.

"Tytuvenai," said the man on the other side of the door. That wasn't a man's name; it was the name of a town not too far from Ukmerge. Underground leaders often called themselves by the names of the towns where they harassed the Algarvians. It made them harder for the redheads to identify. Skarnu knew a fellow who'd called himself Tytuvenai. The man in the hallway asked, "That you, Pavilosta?"

"Aye." Warily, Skarnu opened the door. If "Tytuvenai" was an Algarvian captive, King Mezentio's men would get an unpleasant surprise. But the fellow from the underground stood there alone. "Well, come in," Skarnu said, and closed the door after him.

"My thanks," "Tytuvenai" said. He nodded to Merkela. "Hello, milady. I've heard somewhat of you. You've tweaked the Algarvians a time or two yourself, if even half what they say about you is true."

"They deserve worse than tweaking," Merkela said with a scowl. "By the powers above, they deserve worse than what they've given our Kaunian cousins in Forthweg. And I want to give it to them." Merkela had no compromise in her, not when it came to the Algarvians and not when it came to anything else, either.

"What are you doing here?" Skarnu asked his unexpected guest.

"I have some news that might interest you." "Tytuvenai" seemed unperturbed at Skarnu's suspicions. Anyone who wasn't suspicious these days, of course, was likely either a fool or a dupe.

"Go on," Skarnu said.

"Good news and bad news, actually," the other man from the underground told him. "The good news is that Count Amatu, whom I gather you got to know better than you wanted to, is no more. He met with an unfortunate accident in Priekule not long ago."

"That *is* good news," Skarnu exclaimed. It was such good news, he went into the cramped little kitchen, got out three glasses, and poured peach brandy into them. After he brought them out, he raised his and said, "Here's to Amatu's untimely demise. If I'd known he would go over to the Algarvians, I'd have killed him myself and saved whoever else it was the trouble."

They all drank. Merkela asked, "What's the bad news, then?"

Instead of directly answering her, "Tytuvenai" swung his gaze back to Skarnu. "The bad news is, he was killed coming home from Marchioness Krasta's mansion."

"From my sister's mansion," Skarnu said, and "Tytuvenai" nodded. Skarnu knocked back the rest of the brandy in his glass at a gulp. "I don't know why it surprises me," he remarked, and then shook his head. "It *doesn't* surprise me, curse it. For years, she's been sleeping with that Algarvian colonel who's come after me. Why *wouldn't* she invite Amatu in for tea?"

"One of these days, you'll have your revenge against your sister," Merkela said. "May it be soon. May it be strong."

"Aye, may it be so," Skarnu said. He would never forget the shocked betrayal he'd felt when he saw Krasta's name and Colonel Lurcanio's linked in a news sheet that had come down from Priekule to Pavilosta.

"Now that the Lagoans and Kuusamans are flying dragons out of Sibiu and from their own island, they'll knock that mansion into a pile of rubble," "Tytuvenai" said. "Here's hoping, anyway." With a nod to Skarnu and another to Merkela, he left as abruptly as he'd arrived.

Skarnu barred the door. "So may it be, just as he said it," Merkela said.

"No." Skarnu shook his head.

"What?" Her stare was fierce and angry, like a hawk's. "You have no sister. We've been through this before."

"I know," Skarnu said impatiently. "But I still don't want dragons dropping eggs on the mansion. It's not just Krasta's. It's mine, too. One of these days, after the war is won, I want to bring you there, you and Gedominu, too. He's my heir, after all."

Now Merkela's eyes widened. He'd never said anything like that before. She knew he was a marquis, but he usually played it down. She started to laugh. "Me, a peasant whose folk have been peasants since dirt, in a nobleman's mansion in Priekule? That's daft."

Skarnu shook his head. "Not when I love you. And not when you've fought for Valmiera. If that doesn't make you more noble than my precious sister, I don't know what would." He took her in his arms. They'd started making love again, cautiously, a couple of weeks before. There was nothing cautious about it this time.

Along with his partner Oraste, Bembo tramped through the streets of Gromheort. Looking around at the grimy, battered Forthwegian city, the plump Algarvian constable said, "Curse me if I'm not glad to be back."

"What? Here?" Oraste was a man of few but strong opinions. "You're out of your stinking mind."

"Not me," Bembo said. "Not a bit of it. Tricarico was even gloomier than this place is, and all my friends are here."

Oraste snorted. "Like you've got friends. The only one of us who's ever got leave since they sent us to this miserable place, and it wasn't good enough for you. Are you an idiot or just an ingrate?"

"Aye, rag on me as much as you want, but I was there and you weren't," Bembo said. "Seemed like everybody was too worried and working too hard to have a good time." He nodded, liking the taste of the words. "That's just how it was, sure enough."

"If a tart laid you for free, you'd complain because you didn't like her negligee," Oraste jeered. "Speaking of which, even looking at Algarvian women had to be worth going home for. These Forthwegian dames are built like bricks, and the long tunics they wear might as well be tents."

"Well, that wasn't so bad," Bembo said. He'd done a lot more looking than touching, but he wouldn't embarrass himself by admitting as much to his partner. "Did I tell you Saffa had somebody's baby?"

"Only four times now, or is it five?" Oraste returned. "If you ask me, you're just jealous on account of she didn't have yours."

Bembo walked the next block in wounded silence. Oraste had been teasing him, but that blaze hit entirely too close to the mark. He wouldn't have minded had the pretty little sketch artist had his baby, or at least done something with him that made it possible for her to have a baby. But she hadn't wanted to do anything of the sort, not with him. That she'd done it with someone else was all the more galling.

Most days, his definition of an ideal tour on the beat would have been to have nothing to do but cadge food and drink from the bakers and taverners on the streets he patrolled. Today, though, he was glad to hear a noisy quarrel ahead.

So was Oraste. He pulled his bludgeon off his belt and slapped it into the palm of his hand. "Let's see what's going on," he said, anticipation in his voice. He liked breaking heads. He'd complained Forthwegian women were built like bricks. So was he. Unlike Forthwegian women, he was just about as hard as a brick, too.

Two men stood in the middle of the street screaming at each other, caring nothing if they got in the way of wagons and carriages. The first thing Bembo noticed was that they looked very much alike, save that one of them had a typical proud, hooked Forthwegian nose, while that of the other fellow was shaped more like a tuber. The second thing he noticed was that he'd seen and spoken with the fellow with the ordinary nose before.

He didn't know whether Oraste noticed the same thing. If his partner did notice, he didn't seem to care. "Get out of the roadway, you idiots, before you get mashed flat," Oraste growled, assuming the Forthwegians would speak his language. Maybe he meant a wagon would squash them if they didn't move. Maybe he meant he would. Bembo knew which way he would have bet.

The Forthwegians did understand Algarvian. They also understood what a constable bearing down on them with a bludgeon was likely to mean. Before Oraste could do anything they would regret, they hurried back onto the sidewalk.

"Now, what's going on here?" Bembo asked. Being partnered with Oraste often made him take the role of sweet reason. He resented that: it wasn't one for which he was well suited.

"My brother is a traitor," said the Forthwegian with a nose like a tuber.

"My brother is a liar," said the other Forthwegian, the one who looked familiar.

Before Bembo could say anything, Oraste used his bludgeon to point at the fellow who'd spoken first. "Every son of a whore is a liar. Not everybody's a traitor. That means you start. Who are you? Who's he? And if you two are brothers, how come you're calling each other nasty names?"

Those were all questions Bembo would have asked. He wouldn't have asked them as if he intended to murder the Forthwegian if he didn't like the answers. Maybe that made Oraste a better constable than he was. He didn't much care.

"I'm Hengist," the Forthwegian with the bumpy nose answered. "He's Hestan. Why is he a traitor? I'll tell you why. Because his son ran off with a Kaunian slut, that's why."

"I have no idea where Ealstan is," Hestan said. "All I know is, he left Gromheort two years ago, and I haven't seen him or heard from him since."

"Left? He ran off after he had a fight with my son. My guess is, he thought he murdered Sidroc," Hengist said furiously. "And what were they fighting about? Sidroc got hit in the head, but he finally got reminded or remembered. They were fighting about a blond bitch named Vanai, that's what."

"Futter your son!" Hestan shouted, sounding even angrier than Hengist. "Talk about murder—Sidroc murdered my Leof-sig and nothing happened to him, so now he thinks he can put a noose around Ealstan's neck, too."

"Hold on. Slow down," Oraste said. "Who's who again? Too many names all at once."

But Bembo had heard all the names before. He pointed to Hestan. "This is the fellow who was talking with that Brivibas bugger when I recognized his voice in spite of the magic that made him look like a Forthwegian."

"So?" Oraste said. But then, a couple of beats behind Bembo, he began to catch up. "Wait a minute. That long-winded bastard was what's-her-name's granddad, wasn't he?"

"That's right." Bembo nodded. "One of our officers who came through here not so long ago was looking for that Vanai twist, too. He'd had her when he was garrisoned in Oyngestun, and he wanted to take her west with him so he wouldn't have to sleep all by his lonesome. But she never got pulled into Gromheort, remember? She'd skipped Oyngestun before we cleaned out the place."

"Aye, that's right," Oraste said. "I forgot how all the pieces fit together." He glowered at Hestan. "What's this nonsense about murder you were spewing."

"It isn't nonsense," the Forthwegian said. "*His* son"—he spat at Hengist's shoes—"beat mine to death with a chair in my own dining room."

"Why didn't he hang for it, then?" Oraste demanded.

Hestan didn't answer right away. When he didn't, Bembo did: "I recall that. Nasty business. This Sidroc item had just signed on with Plegmund's Brigade, so nobody much cared what he did."

"Aye, he's loyal to King Mezentio," Hengist said, "unlike some people I could name."

Bembo was less impressed than Hengist had thought he would be. "Most of what's in Plegmund's Brigade is stable scrapings, you ask me," he said.

Oraste's big head went up and down. "That's the truth. Half of 'em'd be in gaol if they weren't in Unkerlant." Hestan

laughed. Hengist looked as if he hated Bembo and Oraste both.
But Oraste wasn't finished: "Still and all, this fellow"—he
pointed at Hestan—"hangs around with Kaunians, and his kid's
likely a Kaunian-lover, too. I say we run him in, see if the bigwigs think he's worth keeping."

"Suits me." Bembo pointed to Hestan. "You can come along
quiet-like, or we'll make you unhappy and then you'll come
along anyway." He jerked a thumb at Hengist. "As for you, pal,
get lost before we haul you in, too."

Hengist turned to go, but not without a parting blaze: "His
precious Leofsig escaped from a captives' camp. He bribed of-
ficials to look the other way."

"Did he, now?" Bembo eyed Hestan in a speculative way.
He'd never been allergic to cash on the side, or under the table.

But Oraste said, "He won't get away with that, not with us."
Oraste had been known to take a bribe every now and then, but
only every now and then. More often, he preferred making people he nabbed suffer, whether by beating them or just by letting
the law take its course instead of giving them the chance to get
out of their trouble.

Since Bembo couldn't very well take a bribe if Oraste
wouldn't, he grabbed Hestan by the arm and said, "Come
along, you." He'd intended to sound fierce. He suspected he
sounded petulant instead.

Hestan said, "I never thought I would wish anything ill on
my brother, in spite of what his son did to my family. But
now . . ." He shook his head. "Powers below eat him, and may
they crunch his bones doing it."

"Aye, he's a piece of work, all right," Oraste agreed. "Somebody ought to give him a good kick in the bollocks."

The Forthwegian gave him a curious look. "You're arresting
me, but you sound like you hate him."

"Don't let it worry you," Bembo said. "Oraste hates everybody." Oraste scowled but didn't deny it; it was as near true as
made no difference. Bembo felt that way himself a good deal of
the time. It was an easy attitude for a constable to take. Constables saw the worst of people—when people were at their best,

they didn't need constables. And Algarvian constables in Gromheort not only saw the worst of people, they saw the worst of people who hated them as occupiers.

"I haven't really done anything, you know." Hestan, somehow, still managed to sound mild and thoughtful. "Even if your superiors decide that everything my *dear* brother says is true—which it isn't—I haven't done anything much."

Bembo thought him likely to be right. But he said, "That's for them to decide, not for us."

"Well, I can't tell you what to do, that's certain," the Forthwegian said. "But wouldn't you rather have the silver I end up paying stick in your belt pouches? Otherwise, it will just end up with people who have too much already."

That sort of argument made perfect sense to Bembo. He sent Oraste a look of appeal. Oraste said, "If Bembo here and me take you into that alley and beat you to death, you don't pay anybody anything."

Hestan licked his lips. Some constables made threats like that to run up the price. Oraste meant his. Hestan had the sense to realize as much. He spoke carefully: "I've never harmed Algarve. The most I've tried to do is keep my family safe." His laugh was bitter. "Look how well that worked out. One son dead, one vanished off the face of the earth."

"One son who's a Kaunian-lover," Oraste said. Odds were, he reckoned murder a lesser crime.

But Bembo said, "Come here." He drew Oraste aside, all the while eyeing Hestan to make sure he didn't take off. He spoke in a low but urgent voice: "We can't just kill this fellow. He's a big blaze. There'd be riots, maybe. Our heads could roll. And he's got the loot to pay his way free once we hand him over. Don't you want some?"

He didn't usually have the nerve to argue with Oraste like that. Because he argued this time, his partner seemed more than usually impressed. "Oh, all right," Oraste said gruffly. "But we'll squeeze him till his eyes pop."

"Well, of course," Bembo said. After that, it was just a matter of haggling over the price.

Two

Every day the sun rose on Vanai, she thanked the powers above for one more day of life. After two Algarvian constables in Eoforwic seized her when the spell that let her look like a Forthwegian wore off before she could get back to her flat, she'd expected to be shipped west and slaughtered right away. The redheads saw the Kaunians of Forthweg as no more than a convenient source of life energy to fuel the sorceries they used to fight their ever-more-desperate war against King Swemmel of Unkerlant.

But all they'd done so far was throw her into the Kaunian quarter in Eoforwic. It was as if they were saying, *We don't need you in particular right this minute. Now that we've got you, you're not going to get away again.*

Or maybe they were saying something worse. Maybe they were saying, *We can wait till you have your baby. They we'll slay you both, and get twice the life energy from you.*

She walked out of the flat in which they'd stuck her—a flat, ironically, bigger and finer than the one she'd shared with Ealstan, and she had it all to herself—and went down to the street. Not too many people showed themselves in the Kaunian quarter these days. Some of those who did had hair like hers: formerly dyed black but now showing its blond roots. They'd been caught trying to live their lives like anyone else, too.

She walked toward the edge of the Kaunian district. It wasn't far: only a couple of blocks. But it was clearly marked and strongly guarded. A constable pointed his stick at her and snarled, "Get away from me or you're dead, you stinking blond whore."

He wasn't even one of Mezentio's men. He was young, stocky, swarthy, black-bearded, big-nosed—a Forthwegian among Forthwegians. He even looked a little like Ealstan, whom she loved with all her heart. But this fellow didn't love her. The Algarvians found plenty of Forthwegians ready, even eager, to help hold down the Kaunians. That let the redheads send more of their own soldiers off to fight the Unkerlanters. *How convenient for them,* Vanai thought.

"Go on, get away!" The Forthwegian was so young, his voice cracked. But he was easily old enough to blaze her down. "Or else keep coming." He sounded as if he wanted her to.

"I'm leaving," she said hastily, so as not to give him an excuse to do just that. She turned and retreated, letting out a sigh of relief as she put a building between her and the hothead. She'd had guards, Algarvian and Forthwegian, growl at her before, but never an encounter like this.

I could escape, she thought. *I could. It would be easy, if . . .* She still knew the spell that would let her look like a Forthwegian. She should have known it. She was the one who'd devised it, reconstructed a botched charm in a cheap, stupid book called *You Too Can Be a Mage* into sorcery that really did something. She always kept a bit of dark brown yarn and a bit of yellow with her, in case she got the chance.

But the guards wouldn't growl and snarl and curse if she approached the edge of the Kaunian quarter while looking like a Forthwegian. They would blaze without warning. They'd done it before. No Forthwegians were supposed to be inside the district, and no Kaunians were supposed to go outside it unless they were ushered forth to go to their doom.

Since the redheads had stopped letting Kaunians out, Vanai had wondered what she would do inside the quarter. But the Algarvians didn't bother with Kaunian-manned manufactories. Maybe they should have. Had they been as efficient as Swemmel of Unkerlant claimed he was, maybe they would have. Or maybe not. They valued the Kaunians only for the life energy they gave up on dying, not for what they might accomplish alive. And so, whether the Kaunians worked or not didn't seem to matter to Mezentio's men.

A young Kaunian who'd never dyed his hair nodded to Vanai and said, "So you got caught on the outside, did you?"

"Aye." She nodded, then rested a hand on her bulging belly. "I think carrying a baby made the spell wear off faster than it should have. Whatever it was, the spell gave out and I got nabbed."

"Too bad for you," the young blond man said. "Being a Kaunian these days isn't much fun."

"Being a Kaunian in Forthweg never was much fun," Vanai answered. "But you're right, of course—it's worse now." She paused in some surprise. "I'll tell you one thing, though: speaking my own language again feels good." She'd used Forthwegian, not classical Kaunian, whenever she talked with anyone but Ealstan out in Eoforwic, and more and more with him once she assumed her Forthwegian disguise.

"Sure enough." The young man scowled. "We can even write in our own language in here. Why not? The penalty for writing in classical Kaunian is death, and the redheaded barbarians are going to kill us anyhow." He laughed without any great mirth, but then scowled again. "Couldn't you speak Kaunian with your man?" He pointed at her abdomen.

"Some," she said. "But he was—he is—a Forthwegian."

"Oh." The young blond fellow looked revolted for a moment. Then his face froze. He walked away from Vanai as if she didn't exist.

Back in Oyngestun, her home village, both Forthwegians and Kaunians would have reacted the same way to the thought of a union between their people. Here in Eoforwic, in what had been the capital and most sophisticated city of Forthweg, such marriages and other alliances had been more readily tolerated back before the Algarvians overran the kingdom. So Vanai had heard, anyhow. Maybe the fellow she'd been talking with had been dragged here from a little village of her own. Or maybe, like some Kaunians, he was as blindly prejudiced against Forthwegians as so many Forthwegians were against Kaunians.

She wandered aimlessly through the Kaunian quarter for a while. When the Algarvians first herded the Kaunians they hated into this little district, it had been disastrously crowded: It wasn't any more. A lot of Kaunians had already been shipped west—and only the tiny handful of them lucky enough to escape their captors had ever come back to Forthweg. A lot had slipped out of the Kaunian quarter sorcerously disguised as Forthwegians before the redheads started getting wise to them.

Vanai took a certain somber pride in that. Even though she'd been caught, she'd helped a lot of her people go free. But, on the other hand, even though she'd helped a lot of her people go free, she'd been caught. It all depended on how you looked at things.

A bell began to clang in a little square a couple of blocks away. She hurried toward it. So did plenty of other Kaunians, men, women, and children, spilling out of blocks of flats and houses. Seeing all those blond heads around her, Vanai was very conscious of belonging to a separate people. Not for the first time, she wondered what it would be like to live in Valmiera or Jelgava far to the east, where almost everyone was of Kaunian blood.

Whatever the Algarvians were doing to the Jelgavans and Valmierans, they couldn't possibly stuff them into tiny districts and have their neighbors help keep them there. She was sure of that.

And they couldn't possibly set up feeding stations in the middle of the district. That bell might have summoned cattle on a farm. The only difference was, Kaunians knew how to queue up.

"Here," an Algarvian said when Vanai got to the head of the queue. He gave her a chunk of barley bread, a chunk of crumbly white cheese, and some salted olives. It wasn't fancy food, but it was enough to keep her going till the next time the bell rang. She'd feared the redheads would starve the Kaunians they'd trapped, but that turned out not to be so. The Algarvians didn't care if Forthwegians starved. But if Kaunians died of hunger before they could be sacrificed, they were wasted as far as Algarve was concerned. And so they got something close to enough to eat.

Vanai was just spitting out an olive pit when more bells began to chime, these not in the Kaunian quarter but all over Eoforwic. She needed a moment to understand what that meant. Then someone close by spelled it out for her, exclaiming, "Dragons! Unkerlanter dragons!"

King Swemmel's dragonfliers didn't come over Eoforwic very often; the capital of Forthweg lay a long way east of land Unkerlant still held, and Swemmel's forces had trouble sparing dragons from the more urgent fight against Algarve. But every once in a while they would load eggs under some of their stronger beasts and pay a call on the city and the ley-line junctions it contained.

The day was cool and cloudy, with a threat of rain. That made the Unkerlanter dragons, painted rock-gray, all the harder to spot. Only after Vanai watched eggs fall from beneath a dragon's belly and heard them burst not far from the Kaunian quarter did she realize that standing in the street and watching wasn't the smartest thing she could do.

She ran into a block of flats and then down into the cellar. Even if an egg landed on the building, that was the safest place she could go. She wasn't the only one to see as much, either. Plenty of other Kaunians had got there ahead of her. She wondered whether they lived in the block of flats or had fled there from the street, as she had.

"I hope every one of those eggs comes down right on an Algarvian's head," an old woman said.

"Powers above, make it so," Vanai exclaimed.

"I wouldn't even mind too much if an egg came down on me," a man said. "Then the redheads couldn't use my life energy."

"No!" Vanai said. "I want to outlive them. I'm going to have a baby. I want my baby to outlive them, too."

"That's right." The old woman nodded vigorously, though Vanai could hardly see her in the gloomy, shadow-filled cellar. "That's the best revenge. They lose their life energy and we keep ours."

That would have been the best revenge. The only trouble was, Vanai hadn't the slightest idea how to make it real. If the Algarvians seized her, if they took her from the Kaunian quarter and threw her onto a ley-line caravan and sent her to the barbarous wilds of Unkerlant and slew her . . . how could she fight back? She couldn't. She knew it too well.

Unkerlanter eggs kept thudding down. Every so often, one nearby would make the ground shake under her feet and the block of flats shake over her head. King Swemmel's dragon-fliers still didn't come over Eoforwic all that often, no. These last few raids, though, they were coming in larger numbers than before. Vanai hoped that meant they were doing more damage than before, too.

She heard a different sort of thud—not the harsh roar of a bursting egg, but the sound of something large hitting the ground after falling from a great height. "They blazed down a dragon," the old woman said.

"Too bad," Vanai said. "Oh, too bad."

"Their eggs might kill us," the man said, "and we're sorry when they die."

"Of course," Vanai told him. "They're *trying* to hurt the Algarvians, and that's the most important thing." Nobody in the crowded cellar presumed to disagree with her.

Snow blew out of the west, into Colonel Spinello's face. Winters in the north of Unkerlant were less savage than in the south, though still bad enough. The Algarvian officer had fought in both, and had standards of comparison. He also had a wound badge with a ribbon to show he'd been blazed twice, and puckered scars on his chest and his leg to prove he hadn't got it by paying off a clerk.

If anything, he welcomed the snow. It meant the ground got hard enough for proper maneuvering, and he was convinced that gave the advantage to the brigade he commanded. Unkerlanter warfare was that of the bludgeon, not the rapier. Yet the rapier could be more deadly, slipping between a man's ribs to pierce his heart and kill him while hardly leaving a mark on his body.

"Listen to me!" he called to the soldiers within earshot—and they *did* listen to him. He was a bantam rooster of a man, not very tall but proud and swaggering even by Algarvian standards. When he spoke, men paid attention . . . and so did women. Just for a moment, he let himself think of Fronesia, the mistress he'd acquired while recovering from his latest wound in Trapani.

But his mistress was a distraction now. The Algarvian capital was a distraction, too. "Listen to me," he repeated, louder this time, and more troopers in the muddy, half-frozen trenches and holes in the ground turned their heads his way. "We've got to take Pewsum back, boys, and we're going to do it."

He pointed ahead, toward the battered Unkerlanter town a couple of miles to the west. When he'd first taken command of the brigade, Algarve had still held Pewsum; he'd made his headquarters in the village of Ubach, a few miles farther west still. King Swemmel had spent a lot of lives pushing the front this far; Spinello hoped to spend far fewer repairing it. He shook his head. He *had* to spend far fewer repairing it, for he couldn't spare that many Algarvian lives.

"We *need* Pewsum," he went on. "We need the ley-line caravan depot there, and we need the junction with other ley lines running north and south." Algarvian soldiers weren't peasants too ignorant to write their names. The more they knew about what wanted doing and why, the better they fought.

"We've got some behemoths." Spinello waved at the big, white-draped beasts. "I had to yell and scream and jump up and down to get 'em, but I did it." Some of his soldiers grinned, but he wasn't kidding. The north had been the quiet front in Unkerlant for quite a while; most Algarvian behemoths had been moved down to the south, where the fighting was harder. "We've got some dragons laid on, too."

That drew whoops from the men. Dragons were even harder to come by up here than behemoths were. A trooper shouted, "And we've got our luck, Colonel!"

"Well, of course we've got our luck," Spinello answered. "She's standing right here next to me."

The soldiers cheered as fiercely as if they were attacking right then. The pretty young Kaunian girl named Jadwigai—who looked quite fetching in a broad-brimmed Algarvian hat and a heavy cloak over her tunic and trousers—blushed and smiled and waved to the men.

They cheered again, harder than ever. They'd brought her along with them after overrunning her village in western Forthweg when the war against Unkerlant was new and triumphant. The brigade had always fought well since, and Jadwigai had become a sort of mascot for it. Nobody'd ever tried to force her into Algarvian-style kilts. Nobody'd ever tried to force himself on her, either. Had anyone been so rash, his own comrades would have put paid to him—and, odds were, gruesomely.

Spinello sighed, fog trickling from his mouth and nostrils. Fronesia was a long way away. He wanted Jadwigai. He'd had a Kaunian to keep his bed warm, a girl named Vanai, when he was stationed in the Forthwegian village called Oyngestun. Jadwigai was even younger and even prettier. But Spinello kept his hands to himself. He didn't want trouble—and he did want to keep the brigade fighting hard.

He added, "And we'll have some . . . special sorcery to help us when the attack goes in."

That was all he said about that. He glanced over at Jadwigai. Did she know that the Algarvians who treated her like a princess slaughtered Kaunians from Forthweg by hundreds, by thousands, by tens of thousands, to power the magics they hurled against the Unkerlanters? How could she not know? But if she did, she kept it to herself. What went on in the mind behind that blue-eyed, smiling face? Spinello couldn't tell. Not being able to tell excited him, too.

The brigade comes first, he thought, and then, *curse it.* He turned to Major Rambaldo, one of his regimental commanders, and asked, "What is the time, Major?"

Rambaldo pulled from his belt pouch an egg-shaped windup clock smaller than his fist, a triumph of the watchmaker's art. After glancing at the glass-protected dial, he answered, "Sir, it is the very hour set for the attack."

"Then put your clock away and keep it safe—and yourself, too, of course." As Rambaldo stowed away the little mechanical treasure, Colonel Spinello drew from his own pouch a less complex tool: a brass whistle. He took a childish delight in loud noises, and the whistle certainly made one. A moment later, he made another all by himself, shouting, "Forward, you lazy whoresons!" at the top of his lungs.

"Stay safe, Colonel!" Jadwigai called in good Algarvian, and blew him a kiss. He waved his hat to her as he went forward. He would have thought more of her good wishes had she not sent kisses to other soldiers who went past her. He shrugged. That was how things were. She didn't belong to him. She belonged to the brigade.

"Mezentio!" Spinello yelled. "Algarve!" He still favored his wounded leg a little as he trotted forward. He could use it, though, which counted for more. A lot of Algarvians with wounds of one sort or another were back in active service these days. The kingdom needed them too much for them to stay back a moment longer than they had to.

Major Rambaldo, he of the fancy clockwork, trotted along beside Spinello. He was half a head taller, and correspondingly longer of leg. He was also whipcord lean, where Spinello was stocky by Algarvian standards, and so seemed to be hanging back when he could have gone faster. "I wish we'd hit them yesterday, or even the day before," he said, not breathing hard.

"We wouldn't have had the behemoths then," Spinello answered. "We wouldn't have had the dragons, either, or the Kaunians to kill." With Jadwigai out of earshot, he spoke frankly.

Rambaldo's shrug was a work of art even among Algarvians, who could say more with their hands and bodies than most folk could with words. "The Unkerlanters wouldn't have had the extra day or two to dig themselves into Pewsum, either."

Spinello grunted. An Unkerlanter detachment new in a place might be easily routed out. A day later, the job got harder. Two days later, it could become impossible. He'd seen as much in Sulingen and at the Durrwangen bulge and a good many other places besides. He hoped he wouldn't see it again here.

Eggs burst in front of the advancing Algarvians. Moments later, eggs burst among them; Swemmel's soldiers in Pewsum had no intention of being dislodged. Algarvian behemoths lumbered forward to deal with the Unkerlanters' less mobile egg-tossers. And then the terrible beam from a heavy stick blazed through white surcoat and armor and flesh of three behemoths in quick succession. The rest milled about in dismay before pulling back out of range. The heavy stick's crew didn't bother burning down individual footsoldiers with it; that would have been like smashing cockroaches with an anvil. Feeling very much like a cockroach, Spinello scuttled forward, cherishing whatever cover he could find.

Dragons painted in Algarvian green, red, and white swooped down on Pewsum. That horrible heavy stick waited for them, and swatted first one and then another out of the sky. Then more eggs burst around it, and it fell silent. But the dragons couldn't silence all the sticks and egg-tossers around Pewsum, any more than the behemoths had, and Spinello's brigade stalled just outside the town, taking casualties and unable to advance any farther.

Huddled in a hole behind what was left of a stone fence, Spinello cursed the stubborn Unkerlanter defenders. "Well, you were right, Major," he called to Rambaldo, who sprawled not far away. "Now we have to see what else we can do about it." He raised his voice to a shout: "Crystallomancer!"

One of the young mages attached to the brigade hurried up. "Aye, sir?"

"Put me through to the mages at the special camp," Spinello said. "We're going to need the strong magic."

"Aye, sir," the crystallomancer repeated, and took the glass globe from his pack. After activating it, he pushed it to Spinello: "Go ahead, sir." Spinello spoke to the wizard whose image appeared in the crystal. The mage nodded. Then he vanished. The crystal flared and went inert. Spinello gave it back to the crystallomancer.

"Will we get what you want?" Rambaldo asked.

"We'll get what we need," Spinello answered, and the regimental commander nodded.

The sorcerers at the special camp had had such requests many times before over the past two and a half years. Swemmel of Unkerlant preached efficiency; the Algarvian mages practiced it. Rounding up however many Kaunians they needed and slaying them didn't take long.

Peering out from behind the stone wall, Spinello watched the ground shake in Pewsum, as if it were being visited by its own private earthquake. But the magic the Algarvians powered with Kaunian life energy was potent beyond any mere temblor. Not only did buildings shudder and collapse, but great fissures in the ground opened and closed, gulping down men and even an Unkerlanter behemoth. And lambent purple flames shot up from the ground, engulfing still more enemy soldiers and beasts.

Spinello's whistle screeched, along with those of the rest of the Algarvian officers still able to advance. "Forward!" he shouted, and sprang to his feet himself. "Now that the mages have staggered 'em, let's knock 'em flat!"

With a cheer, the brigade went forward again. The men had confidence, no doubt of that. Some of them shouted, "Jadwigai!" along with "Mezentio!" and "Algarve!" Again Spinello wondered what the pretty little Kaunian mascot thought. She was close enough to Pewsum to have seen, even to have felt, the magecraft. How could she *not* know whence it came? But if she did, how could she stay friendly to the Algarvians who kept her? Could she pretend so well, just to stay alive? Spinello didn't know. He wondered if he ever would.

He also discovered, not for the first time, that counting on the Unkerlanters to stay stodgy was no longer a paying proposition. No sooner had his brigade burst from cover and rushed toward Pewsum than King Swemmel's mages unleashed against them the same sorcery the town's defenders had just suffered. The Unkerlanters didn't kill Kaunians. They got rid of their own old and useless and condemned. But life energy was life energy. The spell wreaked as much havoc on the Algarvians as it had on the Unkerlanters.

Spinello fell to the ground as it shuddered beneath him. Algarvian soldiers shrieked as violet flames devoured them. Not twenty feet from Spinello, the earth opened up, swallowing Major Rambaldo. An instant later, the crack slammed shut, crushing him and his fancy, ever so expensive windup clock. Spinello staggered to his feet once more, but he could see at a glance that the assault on Pewsum had failed.

He hung his head and kicked at the frozen dirt. Algarve had seen too many failures lately, some small like this one, some very great indeed. When, he wondered, would his kingdom start seeing successes again?

Leudast had spent a lot of time commanding a company while still a sergeant. He was far from the only Unkerlanter underofficer who'd done that. Unkerlant often gave responsibility without giving rank to go with it. That saved the paymasters money—it saved them more than just the monthly difference between a sergeant's rate and a lieutenant's, too, for everyone's pay was chronically in arrears.

But now Leudast was a lieutenant himself. It would have taken capturing a fugitive would-be king to get a born peasant bumped up to officer's rank, but he'd done exactly that. Mezentio's cousin Raniero, who'd styled himself King of Grelz, had gone into Swemmel's stewpot, and Leudast wore two little brass stars on each of his tunic's collar tabs.

He still commanded a company.

Marshal Rathar had promised him five pounds of gold for capturing Raniero. He hadn't seen any of it yet. If he lived through the war, maybe he would. As a born peasant, he knew better than to complain. If he let people see he was unhappy, he didn't know exactly what he'd get, but he had a good idea it wouldn't be the missing five pounds of gold.

At the moment, he stood inside a peasant hut not much different from the one he'd grown up in, save that one wall and half the thatched roof had burned away. With him stood the other lieutenants and sergeants commanding the companies in his regiment, and Captain Recared, the regimental commander. Recared looked preposterously young to be a captain; the previous summer, before the great battles in the Durrwangen salient, Recared had looked preposterously young to be a lieutenant.

"You know what we have to do, men," Recared said in the abrupt tones that marked him not only for a city man but for an educated city man to boot. "We've stopped the redheads' drive on Herborn. They're not going to take it back from us, no matter how much they want to. And they've stretched themselves thin trying, too. Now we see if we can bite off the columns they used for their push."

"We'll hurt 'em if we do," Leudast remarked. His own accent said he came from the northeast, not far from the Forthwegian border, and sounded particularly out of place down here in Grelz.

Recared smiled at him. "That's the idea, Sergeant—uh, Lieutenant. The worse that happens to the Algarvians, the better for Unkerlant."

"Oh, aye, sir." If anything, Leudast knew that better than his superior. He was one of what couldn't be more than a handful of men who'd fought the redheads since the first day of the war against them. Most of the soldiers who'd served King Swemmel on that now long-vanished day were dead or captured or crippled. Leudast had been wounded only twice, and put out of action for a few weeks of the slaughter around Sulingen. If that wasn't good luck, what was?

"All right, then," Recared said. "We've got plenty of behemoths. We've got plenty of dragons. And if we need sorcery, we'll manage that, too. When I shout, 'Forward!' we shall go forward. We shall not halt until I shout, 'Stop!' Gentlemen, I do not intend to shout, 'Stop!' "

Leudast and the rest of the company commanders looked at one another. Slow grins spread over their poorly shaved faces. One of their number, a sergeant, said, "Curse me if that's not an Algarvian kind of thing to say. Makes it into a riddle, like." The others nodded.

Recared said, "The Algarvians have taught us some lessons in this war, no doubt about it. But that time is passing. By the powers above, it is. Now we're the schoolmasters, and we'll give them stripes for not learning."

The lieutenants, all of them but Leudast, nodded again. He and the sergeants looked blank. They were peasants, and knew little of schoolmasters.

"Let's go, then," Recared said. "We can do it. We will do it. Nothing is more efficient than victory."

King Swemmel had been trying to make Unkerlanters efficient throughout his reign. As far as Leudast could see, the king hadn't had a lot of luck. Also as far as Leudast could see, saying the king hadn't had much luck was about the least efficient thing one of his subjects could do.

He pulled his cloak more tightly around him as he left the

farmhouse. He'd known hard enough winters in the north of Unkerlant. Down here in the Duchy of Grelz—the Kingdom of Grelz no more, not after what had happened to Raniero once Swemmel had his way—the wind seemed full of icy knives.

"Do we hit the redheads, Lieutenant? The redheads and the traitors, I mean?" Sergeant Kiun asked. He'd been a common soldier when Leudast's company captured Raniero, just as Leudast had been a sergeant. But Kiun had been the one who'd recognized that Mezentio's cousin wasn't just the Algarvian colonel his uniform proclaimed him to be. He'd been promised a pound of gold along with his promotion. He hadn't seen it yet, either.

"Aye, we do," Leudast answered. "High time we finish breaking out of this box they've tried to put us in." He'd had to break out of Algarvian encirclements before, and counted himself lucky to have escaped with his life. But this was different. For one thing, he and his comrades weren't altogether cut off; the redheads hadn't been able to slam the lid down on the box. And, for another, there was more power here inside this box than was out there trying to contain it.

Egg-tossers began hurling their loads of death at the Algarvians. Watching the bursts kick up snow and smoke in the distance, •Leudast nodded to himself. He'd seen heavier poundings—especially down in Sulingen, where his countrymen and the Algarvians had hammered at each other till the redheads finally broke—but he'd also seen what the Algarvians were capable of in this particular fight. They'd never flung so many eggs at the Unkerlanter trenches.

Dragons painted Unkerlanter rock-gray swooped down out of the sky, dropping more eggs on the redheads and flaming men and behemoths they caught in the open. Few gaudy Algarvian dragons rose to challenge them.

Captain Recared blew his whistle. "Forward!" he shouted. "Swemmel and Unkerlant! Urra!"

"Forward!" Leudast echoed. Only then did he remember he'd finally got his hands on an officer's whistle. He shrugged. Shouting would do. "Forward! Urra!"

And forward they went, all of them shouting so they

wouldn't blaze one another by mistake. Some of them didn't go forward very far, but stopped beams as soon as they broke from cover. Some of the shouts turned to screams. Red flowed here and there on white snow, flowed and quickly began to freeze.

Back when things had gone well for the Algarvians, they'd always had a knack for flanking Unkerlanter units—sometimes squads, sometimes whole armies—out of position. Even after things started going not so well for them, the redheads had kept that gift for showing up exactly where they would make the most trouble. If they hadn't had it, King Swemmel's soldiers would long since have run them out of Unkerlant.

Leudast wished his countrymen showed a similar knack. No matter what he wished, the Unkerlanters seemed to lack it. As far as he could see, Unkerlanter forces too often hit the Algarvians where they were strong and tried to bull through instead of hitting them where they were weak and going around. Had he been a general, that was what he would have tried to do. Maybe the Unkerlanter generals *were* trying to do it. If so, they didn't have it down yet.

On the other hand, if you hit anything hard enough and often enough, it would eventually fall over. The Unkerlanters had more egg-tossers and dragons than their foes. And they had many more behemoths. Behemoths on snowshoes were cursed awkward beasts, going forward at an aggressive waddle and kicking up little clouds of snow at every stride. But they went forward, which was the point of the exercise. Wherever the Algarvians tried to rally—and, with their usual skill and dash, they tried again and again—eggs from the tossers most behemoths carried, and beams from the heavy sticks the rest bore on their backs, smashed up strongpoints.

"Mezentio!" Leudast had heard that defiant war cry more often than he could recall. This time, it came from a tiny village near the edge of a forest of snow-covered firs. The enemy soldiers holed up in the village blazed at the advancing Unkerlanters. Misses boiled steam from snow. Hits sent men sprawling bonelessly in death. "Mezentio!" The shout rang out again and again.

But it didn't sound right. Algarvians yelled their king's name almost as if they were singing it. These soldiers simply shouted it, the same as they might have shouted, "Swemmel!"

The very same as they might have shouted, "Swemmel!" . . . Leudast stiffened. He shouted, too: "Those aren't redheads! Those are fornicating Grelzers!"

Men who'd served the Algarvian puppet Kingdom of Grelz couldn't very well shout, "Raniero!" any more, not after Swemmel had boiled Raniero alive. A lot of the soldiers who'd chosen to wear dark green tunics instead of rock-gray had sneaked away from the fighting, doing their best to pretend they'd been nothing but peasants or shopkeepers while the Algarvians occupied Grelz. Few who tried to surrender to Swemmel's soldiers succeeded. None had joy of it afterwards.

But here some stubborn souls still did what they could to help Mezentio's cause. "Forward!" Leudast shouted again. This time, he remembered to blow the whistle. "Let's give the traitors what they deserve."

Kilted soldiers slipped away through the trees: the Grelzers were buying time for their Algarvian comrades to get away. Maybe the men who'd followed Raniero and the dream of Grelz as a kingdom of its own realized how little their lives were worth with the duchy back in Swemmel's hands and the king's inspectors sure to be hunting them down. Or maybe the Algarvians were simply selling out their erstwhile allies.

Leudast didn't care why the Grelzers fought. He just wanted to be rid of them as fast as he could so he could go after the escaping redheads. His men converged on the village from three sides. Some of them had a shout of their own: "Death to the traitors!"

By the way the Grelzers blazed, there weren't very many of them. They didn't look like holding up the pursuit for long. But, as the men from Leudast's company came close to the tumbledown shacks in which the enemy fought, they got a nasty surprise: What looked like small pottery jugs flew toward them and burst like miniature eggs when they hit the ground. Several soldiers howled as flying shards scored their flesh. Others hesitated, and the attack wavered.

"Come on, curse it!" Leudast shouted. "I don't care what sort of toys they've got—there can't be more than a dozen of them!" He got up and went on toward the hamlet. If his men didn't follow, he wouldn't last long.

Follow they did. The Grelzers proved to have only a few of those small, throwable eggs. Leudast would have liked to ask them where they'd got the few they did have, but, by the time the fight was over, no Grelzers remained alive to ask.

His broad shoulders rose and fell in a shrug. If the Grelzers had this particular toy, the Algarvians would, too. He was liable to find out more about it than he wanted to know. He shrugged again. "Are we going to let those Algarvians get free of us? We'd cursed well better not!" He plunged into the woods after the redheads. Again, his men followed.

More often than not, Marchioness Krasta worried about no one's feelings but her own. Thus, when her maidservant, Bauska, came into her bedchamber one morning to help her decide what to wear that day—in Krasta's mind, always a vitally important choice—she greeted the woman with, "How's your little bastard doing?"

Bauska's lips tightened. She'd had a daughter by one of the Algarvian officers billeted in Krasta's mansion on the outskirts of Priekule. Carefully, she said, "She's doing very well, milady."

"Well, good." Krasta hadn't intended to be cruel, so she added, "I haven't heard her howling in the night lately. That's something."

"Two-year-olds don't cry as much as newborn babes, no," Bauska agreed.

"I suppose not," Krasta said. "Did you ever hear even a word from the father?"

Bauska shook her head. "Nothing since he went off to Unkerlant to fight."

"Too bad." Krasta sighed. "Mosco was a handsome chap, I'll give you that." Mosco had been a good deal handsomer than Colonel Lurcanio, whose adjutant he'd been. He'd also been a good deal younger than Krasta's own Algarvian lover. Every so often, she thought Bauska had got the better bargain. Bauska didn't need to know that, though. Neither did Lurcanio.

"Perhaps the gray silk tunic and trousers, milady?" the maid-servant suggested, taking them from one of Krasta's cavernous closets.

"Powers above, no!" Krasta shook her head. "Do you want me looking like an Unkerlanter soldier?"

"Milady, if you put on King Swemmel's crown, would you look like him?"

"Of course not," Krasta said indignantly. "He's dreadfully ugly, from everything I've heard, and I'm not."

"Well, then," Bauska said.

"Well, then, what?" Krasta snapped. She was impervious to logic, as any number of schoolmasters who'd tried to instill it in her might have told Bauska. "What does that have to do with anything? Get me another outfit and be quick about it, before I box your ears."

She meant it. Bauska must have known she meant it. The gray tunic and trousers disappeared as if they had never been. Dark blue trousers and a gold tunic met with more approval. As if to prove she could make her own choices, Krasta shrugged on a rabbit-fur jacket and went downstairs, pushing past Bauska without another word. Had the maidservant not got out of her way, Krasta would have pushed right through her. Bauska must have known as much, because she did move.

Down in the front hall, Krasta pointed to another servant. "Tell the driver to ready the carriage. I shall go into Priekule be-fore long."

"Aye, milady." The servant went off to do her bidding.

Before the war, hardly anyone had ever said anything but, *Aye, milady*, to Krasta or done anything but go off to do her bidding. Even now, hardly any Valmierans presumed to go against her wishes. But Valmierans, these days, weren't the only folk with whom Krasta had to reckon. She was re-minded of that as soon as she went into the west wing of the mansion.

The Algarvian occupiers had taken over the west wing with-out so much as a by-your-leave. They'd made it plain that, if

Krasta proved difficult, they were capable of taking over the whole place and throwing her out. Up till then, no one had ever dealt with her on those terms—who would have dared? The redheads dared, and they, unlike her countrymen, had the power to enforce their wishes.

Desks and cabinets full of papers filled the elegant salon of the west wing these days. Algarvian military bureaucrats sat behind the desks, doing what they needed to do to keep Priekule running the way they wanted it to. Krasta had never inquired about the details. Details were for servants and other commoners.

But one detail she did notice: Fewer Algarvian military bureaucrats sat behind the desks this morning than she'd ever seen before. More and more these days, the endless grinding war in Unkerlant pulled Algarvians out of Valmiera and off to the distant, barbarous west. Bauska's Captain Mosco had been one of the first sent away from civilization, but many, many redheads had followed him since.

Those who remained eyed Krasta with a leering familiarity that would have earned them slaps in the face . . . had they been Valmierans to be despised rather than Algarvians to be feared. As things were, Krasta swung her hips a little more than usual when she walked past them. They looked, aye, but they couldn't presume to touch because she belonged to their superior.

Captain Gradasso, the adjutant who'd taken over for the departed Mosco, wasn't at his desk in the antechamber in front of Lurcanio's office. Krasta beamed at that. She would have had to try to make sense of his archaic Valmieran, so heavily flavored with the classical Kaunian he knew embarrassingly more of than she did. As things were, she walked straight into Lurcanio's lair.

Gradasso wasn't in there, either, as he often was when not out front to block importunate visitors. Krasta's Algarvian lover glanced up from the papers that covered his desk like snow drifts in a hard winter. *How tired he looks,* she thought. Lurcanio was in his fifties, close to twice her age. He was a handsome man; more often than not, *distinguished* came to mind when she thought of him. Not now. Now the only fitting word was *weary*.

"Good day, my dear," he said, bowing in his chair. His Valmieran, unlike his adjutant's, was fluent, flavored only by a slight Algarvian trill. "You've come to say farewell before you venture forth to the shops, unless I miss my guess."

He read her far better than she could read him, which never failed to annoy her. "Well, aye," she admitted, not quite daring to lie to him: a telling measure of how much he intimidated her.

"Enjoy yourself," Lurcanio said. "I wish I could find such an easy, pleasant escape."

Honestly puzzled, Krasta asked, "Why can't you?"

Lurcanio sighed. His mustaches—graying copper—were waxed so stiff, the exhalation didn't trouble them. "Why, my sweet? Because, unlike you, I have to work for a living. I have duties to perform." He waved at the blizzard of papers in front of him. "Who would take care of them if I went off whenever I chose?"

Krasta didn't recognize a rhetorical question when she heard one. "Why, Captain Gradasso, of course. What are servants for?"

Colonel Lurcanio sighed again. "First, an adjutant is not a servant. Second, they are *my* duties, not his; he has his own. And third, at the moment he is performing his duties far from here."

"What do you mean?" Krasta asked.

"I mean that he is on his way to the Duchy of Grelz, if he hasn't got there yet," Lurcanio answered. "Powers above grant that he stay safe. For the time being, I have his work to do as well as my own. I may eventually be assigned another adjutant. On the other hand, I may not."

Where she was sensitive to little else, Krasta understood every nuance of rank. "That's an outrage!" she exclaimed.

"It is war." Lurcanio's shrug was less extravagant—less Algarvian—than usual. He got up, came around the desk, and took Krasta in his arms. As he kissed her, his hands roamed her body. She wondered if he would want her to flip up his kilt; she'd done that a couple of times here. She wouldn't have minded doing it again—the danger of discovery often excited her. But Lurcanio let her go. With a last pat, he said, "Go on. Enjoy yourself. Be glad you can." He returned to his paperwork.

Krasta needed no more urging to do what she already intended to do anyhow. Before she left, though, she went around behind the desk, bent beside Lurcanio, and teased his ear with her tongue for a moment. If he preferred work to her, she wanted to remind him of a little of what he'd be missing. Then, laughing, she hurried away before he would grab her.

Her driver smelled of spirits. He often did. Krasta didn't worry about that overmuch. Even if he was drunk, the horse remained sober. "Take me to the Boulevard of Horsemen," she said. When she went into Priekule, she most often went to the street with the capital's finest shops. The driver nodded. He probably would have taken her there even had she said she wanted to go somewhere else, because he was used to heading there, waiting for her, and drinking while he waited.

As it had ever since the Algarvians marched into it, Priekule looked sad and gray. Buildings needed paint and a scrubbing they weren't likely to get any time soon. A lot of the people on the street seemed to need paint and a scrubbing, too: they shambled along, lacking the will or the energy to do anything more. Some of the Valmieran women, by contrast, wore altogether too much paint, and wore either trousers that might have been painted onto their backsides or Algarvian-style kilts that barely covered those backsides. Some of them had caught the redheaded soldiers they were obviously after, too.

Krasta sneered. She'd caught a redheaded soldier, too, but she didn't usually let herself think of it that way.

Now that she was here, she wondered why she'd come. To get away from the mansion for a while, she supposed. But the Boulevard of Horsemen wasn't what it had been. Shop windows displayed mostly junk, and often old junk at that. The only shops with plenty of new items on display were the booksellers, hardly Krasta's favorite haunts. Just because she could read and write didn't mean she felt she had to very often.

But then she saw Viscount Valnu flipping through some volume or other inside a bookstore. She tapped on the glass. Valnu looked up. His smile illuminated his long, bony face. He fluttered his fingers at her, then did a proper job of waving, urging her to come in.

She did, though she felt at least as out of place as she would have walking into a brothel. "Where are my spectacles?" she exclaimed, careless as usual of the proprietor behind his counter. "Don't I have to have spectacles?"

"Not you, darling," Valnu murmured in a husky voice that enchanted women—and also Algarvian officers of a certain inclination. He kissed her on the cheek. "You *are* a spectacle, so you don't need to wear any."

"You should talk," Krasta said: He was wearing a kilt himself, one that showed off as much leg as those of any of the slatterns on the street. "What are you doing here?"

"Eating beans," Valnu answered. "What else is there to do at a bookseller's?" He started to put away the tome he'd been looking at.

Krasta took it from him before he could slide it back on the shelf. "*The Kaunian Empire and the Barbarians of the Southwest*," she read from the front cover, and started to laugh. "Don't let your redheaded friends know you look at such things."

Viscount Valnu laughed, too. "It shall be my deep, dark secret, believe me." He rolled his blue, blue eyes, as if to say no one could possibly take him seriously.

And then Krasta remembered something that had shaken Priekule—had certainly shaken her—not long before. "Don't let your redheaded friends know about Amatu, either," she said, this time in a lower voice. Amatu, who'd gone over from the Valmieran underground to the Algarvians, had been ambushed and murdered on his way home from a supper with Krasta and Lurcanio. Valnu had known beforehand he would be there.

The viscount's smile never wavered. "You'd better keep quiet, my dear, or you'll go the way he did," he said.

"That could happen to you, too, you know," she answered with a smile of her own. "If I had an accident, Lurcanio would learn everything." That was a lie, but Valnu couldn't prove it.

He condescended to raise an eyebrow. "Maybe we should talk further."

"Aye." Krasta nodded. "Maybe we should."

Marshal Rathar wished he were back at the front, still commanding the Unkerlanter armies battling to drive the Algarvians out of the Duchy of Grelz. There, he was lord of all he surveyed: who dared go against the wishes of the second most powerful man in all the Kingdom of Unkerlant?

One man dared, and no one in Unkerlant, not even Marshal Rathar—perhaps particularly not Marshal Rathar—presumed to disobey King Swemmel's express command. And so Rathar found himself back in Cottbus, far from the fighting, all too close to the king. The maps in his office—the maps whose moving gray- and red-headed pins showed the fight going well in the south and not badly in the north—did little to ease his spirit. If anything, they reminded him what he was missing.

Running a hand through his iron-gray hair, he glared at his adjutant. "I feel like a caged wolf, Major, nothing else but."

Major Merovec shrugged. "I'm sorry, lord Marshal," he replied, not sounding sorry at all. He'd spent the whole war in Cottbus, in the vast royal palace. Rathar didn't doubt his courage, but he'd never had to show it. He went on: "The king will surely be glad to have your advice."

Swemmel was never glad to have anyone's advice. Major Merovec and Marshal Rathar both knew that perfectly well. They both also knew how deadly dangerous saying anything else would have been.

A young lieutenant whose clean, soft rock-gray tunic and clean, soft features said he'd never done any real fighting, either, came into the office and saluted Merovec and Rathar. He said, "Lord Marshal, his Majesty bids you sup with him this evening, an hour past sunset." Having delivered his message, he saluted again, did a smart about-turn, and strode away.

"A signal honor," Major Merovec murmured, "and a signal indication of the king's trust in you."

"Aye." Rather against his will, Rathar found himself nodding. Supping with Swemmel meant being trusted enough to hold a knife (no doubt it would prove a small, dull, blunt knife, but a knife nonetheless) in his presence. Considering how the guards searched everyone granted audience with the king, considering how Rathar had to leave his marshal's sword on hooks in the antechamber before passing through, Swemmel had chosen to show him favor. By evening, the palace would be buzzing with the news.

Rathar shrugged. *Maybe I misjudged him,* he thought. *My guess was that he recalled me from Grelz to keep me from winning too many victories, to keep me from getting too popular. I don't want his throne, curse it. But if I tell him I don't want it, he'll only worry more that I do.*

When he walked through the hallways of the palace on his way to supper, courtiers bowed low before him. They were smooth, sleek, confident creatures these days, altogether unlike the frightened lot of two and a half years before. When Cottbus looked like falling to the Algarvians, a lot of them had fled west. For good or ill, they were back. To those of lower rank, being second most powerful in the kingdom seemed little different from being most powerful. Rathar knew better, but also knew no one would believe he knew better.

Pretty women dropped him curtsies as he went by. Had he put forth a little effort, he supposed he could have had a good many of them. His passions didn't run toward seduction, though. The only woman but his wife with whom he'd lain recently was Ysolt, his headquarters cook. That hadn't been a seduction: more on the order of a molestation, of him by her. He grimaced. He wasn't proud of being conquered rather than conqueror.

King Swemmel's dining room, like his private audience chamber and the throne room, had an antechamber attached to it. The guards in the antechamber took Rathar's ceremonial sword from him. Then they patted him more intimately than Ysolt had, though he enjoyed their attentions rather less. Only after satisfying themselves that he carried nothing more lethal than his hands did they let him go on to the king.

In the dining room, he fell to his knees and then to his belly, knocking his forehead against the carpet. He sang Swemmel's praises, and his own love, awe, and loyalty for his sovereign. Some of the ritual phrases were as old as the Unkerlanter monarchy. Swemmel and his henchmen had devised most of them, though.

At last, the king said, "We give you leave to rise, and to sit at our table."

"Thank you, your Majesty. Powers above bless you and keep you, your Majesty." Rathar sat at the foot of the long table, Swemmel at the head. The king had a long, pale face, made longer by a receding hairline. His hair, going gray now, had begun dark; his eyes, of course, still were. Save for that, he looked more like an Algarvian than one of his own people.

But he was an Unkerlanter through and through. "Bring in the spirits!" he shouted to a servitor. Rathar had seen the man before, in bodyguard's uniform rather than waiter's. Once Swemmel and Marshal Rathar were served, the king raised his glass. "Death to Algarve!" he cried, and gulped down the potent stuff as if it were water.

"Death to Algarve," Rathar echoed—King Swemmel had chosen a toast he liked. He, too, had to empty his glass, and he did, though his gullet felt as if he'd swallowed a dragon while it was flaming. Impassively, the servitor poured both glasses full again.

"Death to traitors!" Swemmel shouted, and drained the second glass.

"Death to traitors!" Rathar agreed, and matched him. The dining room began to spin a little. When in command out in the field, Rathar couldn't afford to drink like an Unkerlanter peasant holed up in his hut for the winter. But, when summoned before his sovereign, he couldn't afford not to drink a toast against traitors—for King Swemmel saw traitors everywhere, and would surely see one in a marshal's uniform if he refused to condemn them.

As if to prove that very point, Swemmel muttered, "We are surrounded by traitors. Traitors everywhere." Two big glasses of potent spirits had put a hectic flush in his cheeks, but his eyes were wild and staring. "Everywhere," he repeated. To Rathar's relief, the king was looking up at the ceiling, not right at him.

Bowing his own head, the marshal said, "Thank you, your Majesty, for doing me the honor of inviting me here."

"Oh, aye," Swemmel said carelessly. He gestured to the servitor, who filled the glasses yet again. Rathar wondered what outrages the king might commit while drunk, and also whether he himself would be fit for duty in the morning. If an Algarvian mage were somehow keeping track of Swemmel's drinking bouts . . . Rathar shook his head. Mezentio's men could have worked far worse outrages than they had if that were so. The king, meanwhile, leaned toward the servitor and commanded, "Bring on the supper."

"Aye, your Majesty," the fellow replied, and went off to the kitchens.

Now King Swemmel did turn his bloodshot gaze full on Marshal Rathar. "Tomorrow or the next day, we shall have somewhat to say to the ministers from Lagoas and Kuusamo. They claim they are Algarve's foes, but leave to our kingdom the burden of fighting and dying."

"They *have* taken Sibiu back from the redheads," Rathar said, "and their dragons visit Algarve's towns by day and night."

Swemmel snapped his fingers. "This for the islands of Sibiu!" He snapped them again. "And this for dragonfliers! If our so-called allies would reckon themselves men before their mothers, let them come forth to fight on the mainland of Derlavai. 'Soon,' they say. 'Before long,' they say." He made his voice a piping, mocking falsetto to show what he thought of that.

"Well, all right, then, your Majesty," Rathar said. King Swemmel had a point. Had the Algarvians not chosen to grapple with Unkerlant to the death, they could have worked far more mischief in the east than they had. Were King Vitor of Lagoas and Kuusamo's Seven Princes grateful for the burden Unkerlant had so unwillingly assumed? So far as Rathar could see, only in the sense of being glad they hadn't had to shoulder it themselves.

The servitor came back from the kitchen with a large iron pot, the lid still on. He had cloths wrapped around the handles so he wouldn't burn his fingers. Setting the pot down on a trivet in the middle of the table, he bowed to the king. "Supper, your Majesty," he announced unnecessarily.

Or perhaps not so unnecessarily; Swemmel started as if he'd forgotten all about food. Once reminded, he nodded and said, "As a mark of our favor, you may serve Marshal Rathar first."

"As you say, Your Majesty." The servitor took the lid off the pot. A great cloud of savory steam rose from it.

"You do me too much honor, your Majesty," Rathar said, and not for politeness' sake alone. When the king sobered up to-morrow, would he remember what he'd done, remember and re-gret it? He might. *If I let Rathar eat before I did*, he might think, *my cursed marshal might decide he deserves first place in the kingdom all the time.* Other men, famous in their day, had van-ished when such thoughts occurred to King Swemmel.

But Swemmel seemed unconcerned now. As the servitor spooned meat from the pot, the king said, "We give you what you have earned, Marshal."

When the first whiff of that savory steam reached Rathar's redoubtable nose, he recoiled in something worse than mere horror. When Raniero went into the stewpot in Herborn, Rathar had smelled this precise odor of cooked flesh. He was sure of it. Swemmel wouldn't, couldn't, serve him . . . The servitor set the plate in front of him. Just as he was about to push it away and flee the table, heedless of what the king might think, the man murmured, "I hope the stewed pork pleases you, lord Marshal."

"Stewed . . . pork," Rathar said slowly. He looked down the length of the table to his sovereign.

Swemmel rarely laughed. He was laughing now, laughing till tears gleamed in his eyes and slid down his hollow cheeks. "Well, Marshal?" he said, dabbing at his face with a snowy linen napkin. "Well? Did you think we were serving you up a ragout of boiled traitor?" More laughter shook him. It hit him hard, as spirits smote a man who seldom drank.

"Your Majesty, I must say it crossed my mind," Rathar replied. Most courtiers would have denied the very idea. Rather had found the king could—sometimes—take more truth than most people thought.

Swemmel shook his head. "It may be that we shall eat of Mezentio's roasted heart, but we would not share that dish with any subject. It is *ours*." Was he still joking? Or did he mean every word of it? For the life of him, Rathar couldn't tell. Swemmel wagged a forefinger at him. "Before that day comes, though, we needs must drive the redheaded robbers from all our land, not merely from the south. How do you propose doing what we require?"

Rathar sighed with relief at dealing with a purely military matter. "I have some thoughts along those lines, Your Majesty," he replied, and took a bit of pork. He hoped it was pork, anyhow.

At the isolated hostel in the rustic Naantali district of south-eastern Kuusamo, Fernao felt like a pine in a forest of poplars. He was the only Lagoan mage—the only Lagoan at all—there. The rest of the theoretical sorcerers, all the secondary sorcer-ers, and all the servitors were Kuusamans: short, golden-skinned, black-haired, flat-featured, slant-eyed. As a tall, fair, straight-nosed, ponytailed redhead, he could hardly have stood out more.

No, that isn't quite true, he thought, and nodded to himself. *My eyes are set on a slant, too, even if they're green, not black.* Lagoans were of mostly Algarvic stock, descendants of the in-vaders who'd settled in the northwest of the large island off the Derlavaian mainland after the Kaunian Empire collapsed. But they'd intermarried with the folk they found there, and a fair-sized minority showed some Kuusaman features. Similarly, some few who lived under the Seven Princes, especially in lands near the Lagoan border, had the inches or the nose or the bright hair that spoke of foreign stock grafted onto the roots of their family tree.

Fernao waved to one of the serving women in the refectory. She came over to him and asked, "What is it you want?"

She spoke Kuusaman. Fernao answered in the same tongue: "An omelette of smoked salmon and eggs and cheese, and bread and honey, and a mug of tea, Linna." When he first came to Kuusamo, he'd known not a word of the local language. But he'd always had a good ear, and now he was getting close to fluent.

Linna nodded. "Aye, sir mage," she said. "I'll bring them to you as soon as they're done." She hurried off toward the kitchens.

"Thank you," Fernao called after her.

A hand fell on his shoulder. He looked up in surprise. "What are you thanking her for?" Ilmarinen demanded in coldly precise classical Kaunian.

"My breakfast," Fernao answered, also in the international language of magecraft and other scholarship.

"Is that all?" Ilmarinen said suspiciously. By his wrinkles and white, wispy little chin beard, the Kuusaman master mage carried twice Fernao's years, but he sounded like an angry young buck. He'd been chasing Linna ever since this hostel in the wilderness went up, and he'd been annoying doing it. Not long before, she'd finally let him catch her. He'd been much more annoying since.

With what patience Fernao could muster, he nodded. "As sure as I am of my own name. If you care to, you may sit down beside me and watch me eat it. And if you care to"—he paused, as if about to make a radical suggestion—"you may even get one for yourself."

"I think I'll do just that," Ilmarinen said, and slid into a chair.

"How are you this morning?" Fernao asked.

"Why, my usual sweet, charming self, of course," the older mage replied. Like most educated folk, Fernao had no trouble using classical Kaunian to communicate—at first, he'd used it all the time after coming to Kuusamo, since it was the only tongue he'd had in common with the locals. But, again like most educated folk, he spoke it with a certain stiffness. Not so Ilmarinen. He was so fluent in the ancient language, it might almost have been his birthspeech.

Fernao eyed him. "I must say, you did not seem particularly sweet and charming." Ilmarinen reveled in irony and crosstalk, but he hadn't seemed ironic, either. What he'd seemed like was a jealous lover of the most foolish and irksome sort.

Perhaps he even knew as much, for the smile he gave Fernao was more sheepish than otherwise. "But did I seem my usual self?" he asked.

"If you mean your usual self lately, aye," Fernao answered, not intending it as a compliment.

Before Ilmarinen could say anything, Linna came out again. She waved to the master mage, then walked over and ruffled his hair. Ilmarinen beamed. As long as she was happy with him, all seemed right with his world. Fernao wondered what would happen if—no, when—she tired of him. For the sake of the work on which so many mages were engaged, he hoped he wouldn't have to find out any time soon.

Ilmarinen asked for smoked salmon, too, and sliced onions to go with it. Linna's nose wrinkled. "Poo!" she said. "See if I kiss you."

Ilmarinen looked devastated—but not so devastated as to change his order. Fernao took that for a good sign. Sniffing, Linna headed back to the kitchens.

And then Fernao stopped worrying about Ilmarinen's infatuation, for Pekka walked into the refectory and he had to start worrying about his own. Like most Lagoan men, he'd always reckoned Kuusaman women on the small and scrawny side. By Lagoan standards, Pekka *was* on the small and scrawny side. Somehow, that mattered very little once Fernao had come to know her.

She sat down at the table with him and Ilmarinen. "I hope the two of you were talking about our next experiment," she said in classical Kaunian.

Since she was not only a woman in whom he was interested but also the theoretical sorcerer heading the project for which he'd come to Kuusamo, Fernao didn't want to lie to her. On the other hand, the prospect of telling her the truth didn't fill him with delight, either. It didn't bother Ilmarinen one bit. "Well, now that you mention it, no," he said breezily.

Pekka gave him a severe look. It rolled off him the way water rolled off greasy wool. She said, "What *were* you talking about?"

"Oh, I just wanted to let this Lagoan lecher know that, if I ever caught him sniffing around my Linna, I'd cut out his liver and eat it without salt," Ilmarinen replied.

He was on the small and scrawny side, too, to say nothing of being an old man. That didn't keep a small twinge of icy dread, like a detached bit of the savage winter outside, from sliding up Fernao's back. However small and scrawny and old Ilmarinen was, he was also, with Master Siuntio dead at Algarvian hands, the leading theoretical sorcerer of his generation, and a formidable practical mage as well. He wouldn't have to use a knife to make unfortunate things happen to Fernao's liver.

Fernao said, "For about the fourth time, I was not sniffing around her." When he brought out a phrase like that in classical Kaunian, he sounded both pompous and preposterous. Ilmarinen, now, Ilmarinen sounded menacing.

Pekka snorted. "I have never seen Fernao behave at all strangely around Linna," she said, "which is rather more than I can say for certain other people of my acquaintance." Linna came back with Fernao's omelette and Ilmarinen's smoked salmon and onions before the elderly theoretical sorcerer could make any more snide comments. He might well not have let that stop him; the serving girl didn't speak much classical Kaunian, and couldn't have followed whatever he said. But Pekka asked her for a plate of bacon and eggs and sent her off again.

Ilmarinen let out a cackle, the laugh of an old man who made trouble and had fun doing it. "Which women have you seen Fernao behaving strangely around, then?" he asked, and cackled again.

Without the least hesitation, Fernao kicked him in the ankle. And that wasn't the only small, dull thud from under the table. Pekka must have kicked him from the other side.

"Aii!" Ilmarinen said. That wasn't a cackle—more like a yelp. "Between the two of you, you can carry me out of here. I don't think I'll be able to walk."

"If you keep on being rude and obnoxious, someone will carry you out, sure enough: someone will carry you out feet first," Pekka said. Her voice was quite mild. As far as Fernao was concerned, that made her more intimidating, not less.

Ilmarinen attacked his food with single-minded determination. Unlike the other theoretical sorcerers, it wouldn't talk back—unless the onions did. He left an odorous trail behind as he got up and hurried out of the refectory.

"Both his ankles seem in good working order," Pekka remarked.

"Aye," Fernao said, and then, "Maybe I should have kicked him harder."

"I was thinking the same thing," Pekka said. "He *will* be difficult just for the sake of being difficult." Linna brought her the bacon and eggs; she dropped back into Kuusaman to say, "Thanks."

"You're welcome," the serving girl answered. She picked up Ilmarinen's plate. "He got out of here in a hurry, didn't he? Did you scare him away?"

Fernao understood every word of that, where he wouldn't have understood any of it when new to the land of the Seven Princes. He spoke in Kuusaman, too: "We did our best." That made Linna laugh as she went off, though he hadn't been joking.

Pekka also stuck to her own language, saying, "You're getting quite fluent. The only time we really need to use classical Kaunian these days is when we talk about the fine points of sorcery."

"Thank you." Fernao kept on using Kuusaman, not least because he plainly pleased Pekka by doing so. "You probably praise me too much, but thank you."

"Not at all," Pekka said seriously, which made Fernao glad he'd always had a good ear for languages. Then she dug into her breakfast, pausing only to tell him, "You should eat." She might have been speaking to a little boy, not to a fellow theoretical sorcerer.

She has a little boy, Fernao reminded himself; Pekka would sometimes talk about Uto. *She has a husband, too, a mage in his own right.* When Fernao was newly come to Kuusamo, Pekka had talked a lot about Leino, too. She didn't do that so much now. Fernao wondered why. Part of him hoped he knew the answer.

"Eat," Pekka said again, this time in peremptory tones. Aye, she might have been talking to her son.

"I'm sorry," Fernao answered, as contritely as if he were a boy. "I'm—how do you say, *going slowly without any particular reason?*" He used classical Kaunian where he lacked the Kuusaman word.

Pekka supplied it: "Dawdling." She took a big bite of bacon. "Don't dawdle. We have no time for it. There's no excuse for it. If we don't get to the bottom of this sorcery, if we don't get to the point where we can use it against the Algarvians, we'll be in a world of trouble no matter how the Derlavaian War ends up. Am I right or am I wrong?"

"Oh, you're right. Without a doubt, you're right." Fernao dutifully attacked his omelette. After a bit, though, he said, "It's only that . . ." When he paused again, it wasn't because he'd run out of words in Kuusaman.

"Only that what?" Pekka asked sharply. Fernao didn't answer. He looked down at his plate, then glanced back up to her. Despite her golden skin, she'd flushed. "Never mind," she said, and rose, and hurried away.

It's only that, if I dawdle, I can sit here and be with you. He would have said that, or something like it. She had to understand it even if he hadn't said it. And it had to be on her mind, too, or she would have joked about it.

Fernao sighed. He finished breakfast, then got to his feet and reached for his cane. He couldn't hurry away, not after a bursting egg almost killed him and did ruin his leg down in the land of the Ice People. And he and Pekka had to go on working side by side as if they felt nothing toward each other but professional respect. He sighed again. It wasn't easy, and got harder all the time.

Three

⟨∾⟩

Back before the war, Garivald had visited Tolk only a handful of times, though the market town lay less than a day's walk from Zossen, his home village. After King Swemmel's armies drove the Algarvians out of the western portion of the Duchy of Grelz, he'd left the band of irregulars he'd led before Unkerlanter regulars and inspectors could reward him for his fight against the redheads by making something unfortunate happen to him.

And so he'd gone back to Zossen, only to find the war there before him. The village, his wife, his son, his little daughter . . . all gone as if they'd never been. He'd trudged on to Tolk, farther west still, not least because he had no idea what else to do.

Tolk survived. The Algarvians and their Grelzer puppets hadn't made a stand there, as they must have at Zossen. Buildings were smashed. Only burnt-out rubble remained of a few whole blocks. But Tolk survived.

Sitting by the fire in a tavern there, Garivald turned to Obilot and said, "Powers above only know what we would have done if this place was gone, too."

Like him, she had a thick earthenware mug of spirits in front of her. She shrugged as she took a swallow from it. "Gone somewhere else, that's all. What difference does it make where we are? We haven't got anything left but each other."

Garivald still didn't know exactly what the Algarvians had done to her, and to whatever family she'd had, to make her flee to the irregulars. She'd fought Mezentio's men longer and harder than he had; she'd been in the band when Munderic, who'd led it before Garivald, rescued him before the redheads could take him to Herborn and boil him alive for making patriotic songs.

He said, "We might have starved before we got anywhere else." Late winter was the hard time, the empty time, of the year in peasant villages in Grelz, as it doubtless was in peasant villages all over Unkerlant.

Obilot shook her head. She had to bring up a hand to brush dark curls back from her face. She wasn't pretty, not in any conventional sense of the word: she was too thin, too fierce looking, for anything approaching beauty. But the energy that crackled through her made every other woman Garivald had known, including Annore who'd borne him two children, pallid in comparison. She said, "Two desperate characters with sticks in their hands don't starve."

"Well, maybe not," Garivald said, and drank from his own mug of spirits. In most winters, he'd have stayed drunk much of the time from harvest till planting. How else to while away the long winter with so much time in it and so little to fill that time? As an irregular, he'd found other ways. As a refugee, he was finding other ways still. But, when he put the mug down again, he said, "I don't feel like a desperate character."

"No?" Obilot's laugh held little mirth. "What else are you? What else is anybody in Grelz?" She lowered her voice: "What will you be if the inspectors catch up with you?"

"Dead," Garivald answered, and drained the mug. He waved it in the air to show the tapman he wanted it refilled. Obilot's mug was empty, too.

"Let's see some silver," the fellow said when he brought a jar of spirits over to their table.

Garivald dug a coin from his belt pouch and set it down on the scarred pine board. "Here. Fill us both up again."

The tapman scooped it up, looked at it, and made it disappear. He filled both mugs. But then he said, "If you haven't got the brains to be careful passing money with King Raniero's face—Raniero the traitor's face, I mean—you'll land in more trouble than popskull can ever get you out of. You're just lucky I know a jeweler who'll give me weight for weight—well, almost—in silver. He'll be able to melt it down and make earrings or something out of it."

Nobody at the next table could have heard a word he said. He went back behind the bar. Obilot asked, "How long have you been carrying that silver bit around?"

"How should I know?" Garivald shrugged. "Maybe since before King Swemmel's soldiers broke into Grelz. But maybe I got it yesterday, chopping firewood for that baker."

"If you did, he was probably glad to palm it off on you," Obilot said.

"I wouldn't be surprised," Garivald agreed. "But at least in a place like Tolk, I can find odd jobs to do and make a little money. In a peasant village, I *would* starve. Everybody hates strangers in a village. I ought to know. I did, back when people I hadn't seen before came into Zossen. For all I knew, they were inspectors or impressers sneaking around."

"It's not right," Obilot said savagely. "With your songs, you did as much as anybody to get the Algarvians out of Grelz. The redheads must've thought so, or they wouldn't have wanted to boil you. But what thanks do you get from your own side? Back in the woods, they were going to arrest you or kill you."

With another shrug, Garivald answered, "When have you seen a peasant win? Not with our own kings, not with the redheads, not ever." He didn't even sound bitter. What point, when he told simple truth?

A youngster who might have been the tapman's little brother or son brought in more wood and threw it on the fire. A couple of people in the tavern clapped their hands. The young man grinned, taken by surprise. The wood, well-seasoned pine, burned hot and bright.

"We've got the right table," Obilot said, and turned toward the flames. Their reflections danced in her eyes. Garivald was about to do the same when somebody new came in from outside.

"Close the door, curse you," someone inside said. "You're letting out the heat."

Garivald started to chime in, but the words never passed his lips. Instead, he turned his back on the door and leaned toward the fire, as Obilot had done. In a whisper even he had trouble even he had trouble hearing above the crackling flames, he said, "That's Tantris who just walked in."

"Tantris! What's he doing here?" Obilot's face went hard and feral. "He's supposed to be off in the woods seventy-five miles east of here. The only reason he'd come to Tolk . . ."

"Is because he knows what we look like," Garivald finished for her.

"He knows what *you* look like, the whoreson," Obilot said. "He's got to be after you. I don't count for anything, not to the likes of him."

She was bound to be right. When Garivald had slipped out of the woods with her and headed back toward Zossen without pursuit, he'd thought the Unkerlanters were willing to let him alone. That seemed a mistake, a bad mistake.

"I led fighters who didn't take orders straight from King Swemmel," he said. "I made songs people liked, songs that made people want to fight the redheads. This is how my own kingdom pays me back."

Mezentio's men had been ready to kill him. Now Swemmel's were, too. The knowledge tore at him, as if he'd set his foot in a trap. And maybe he had. He sipped spirits and watched Tantris out of the corner of his eye.

The soldier didn't want to be recognized for what he was; he wore a dark blue tunic of civilian cut rather than the rock-gray uniform tunic in which Garivald had always seen him in the woods. He glanced Garivald and Obilot's way, but gave no sign of knowing who they were. After a moment, Garivald realized the two of them were silhouetted against the flames in the fireplace. He stayed where he was. Tantris bought a beaker of ale and stood at the bar drinking it.

Obilot kept her voice very low. "Is it true," she said, "that now there are irregulars—Grelzer irregulars, I mean—fighting for the Algarvians in the lands our armies have taken back from them?"

"I've heard it, the same as you have," Garivald answered. "I don't know whether it's true . . . but I've heard it."

"Till that cursed Tantris walked thought the door, I wouldn't've believed it," Obilot said. "But now, do you know, I almost begin to understand." Considering how she felt about the redheads, that was no small statement.

"A good many peasants fled east when Mezentio's men had

to retreat," Garivald said. "I used to think they were the ones in bed with the Algarvians. I guess a lot of them were, but maybe not all." If he hadn't got in trouble with the redheads for his songs, his life in Zossen wouldn't have been too very different under them from what it had been before the war. That was a judgment on Algarve and Unkerlant both, he supposed.

Obilot turned her head ever so slightly toward Tantris. "What are we going to do about him?"

"Hope he goes away," Garivald answered. Tantris drank his ale. He bought a chunk of chewy bread and dipped it into the bowl of coarse salt the tapman kept on the bar. Bite by bite, the bread disappeared. He washed down each bite with another swig of ale. Garivald might have done the same. He had done the same, many times.

The tavern door opened again. This newcomer, unlike Tantris, did not try to disguise what he was: a military mage. Two troopers tramped in behind him. He strode up to the tapman and snapped, "Let me see your cashbox, fellow."

"Why should I?" the tapman asked. "Are you robbing me?"

"Why?" the mage echoed. "I'll tell you why. Treason to King Swemmel, that's why." He dropped a silver coin on the bar. It rang sweetly. "This is money of Raniero, the false king, the king of traitors. By the law of similarity, like calls to like. This foul coin calls to one in your box. Whoever harbors money of Raniero is a traitor to His Majesty."

Garivald's blood ran cold. The fellow behind the bar had to say no more than, *I got it from him*, and point, and he would find himself in more trouble than Tantris could give him. What the tapman did say was, "It's here, under the bar." He reached down. But what he came out with wasn't the cashbox, but a stout bludgeon he doubtless used to break up tavern brawls. He didn't break one up this time. With a shout, he brought the bludgeon down on the military mage's head.

With another shout, somebody else threw his mug at one of the Unkerlanter troopers behind the mage. It shattered against the back of the soldier's skull. He went down with a groan. Somebody shouted, "King Swemmel!" and punched the man who'd thrown the mug. Somebody else shouted, "Powers below eat King Swemmel!"—a shout nobody would have dared to raise before the Algarvian invasion—and kicked the fellow who'd yelled the king's name.

In the blink of an eye, the desperate struggle between the Grelzers who'd fought for Swemmel and those who hated him broke out anew in the tavern. The weapons weren't so fancy as those of the great war still wracking Unkerlant, but that made the battle no less ferocious. People kicked and punched and grappled and bit. Knives flashed in the firelight.

And Garivald and Obilot made their way through the chaos toward the door as best they could. He punched whoever got in his way, regardless of which side the fellow was on. "Let's see Tantris track us through *this*," he told Obilot, who'd just kicked a man where it did the most good. A savage grin on her face, she nodded.

A jar full of potent spirits flew into the fireplace and smashed. The spirits caught fire as they splashed out. Flames clung to an overturned chair close by. "Fire!" somebody shrieked. Then everybody was fleeing—everybody who could.

Garivald and Obilot weren't the only ones who ran not just out of the tavern but away from it as fast as they could. "We got away," she panted.

"This time," he answered, and ran harder.

The sun rose earlier and set later these days. Before long, the equinox would come to the Naantali district. In much of the world, that would mean spring, and so it would here—formally. Pekka was from Kajaani, which lay even farther south. She knew the snow and ice wouldn't start melting for quite a while after that.

If anything, the weather here was worse than in Kajaani, a port city that had the ocean to soften its climate. In most circumstances, Pekka would have complained about that. Not now. As she rode in the sleigh from the hostel to the blockhouse, she turned to Fernao and said, "I dread the spring thaw."

She'd spoken Kuusaman. The Lagoan mage nodded and answered in classical Kaunian: "I understand why—all this will

turn to mud, and we shall have a demon of a time moving
from where we stay to where we need to go to keep on with
our experiments."

"Exactly," Pekka said. "And we have to go on with the experiments." That blazed in her. Next to it, nothing else mattered.

The track to the hostel curved. As the horse rounded the
bend, the sleigh tilted a little. Under the fur robes that warded
them against the weather, Pekka slid toward Fernao. She was
very much aware of her body pressed against his for a moment,
and wished she hadn't been quite so aware of it.

It's harmless, she told herself, not for the first time. *Nothing
can come of it.* That wasn't quite the same thing, even if it
sounded as if it were.

After the sleigh straightened again, Pekka took an extra moment to move away from Fernao. The Lagoan mage raised an
eyebrow when she finally did. His eyes were shaped like hers,
but green, not dark brown. Was it the combination of strange
and familiar that drew her? Or was it just that she worked
closely with Fernao every day, while she'd seen Leino for one
brief leave since she came to the Naantali district and her husband went off to work on Habakkuk? Whatever it was, it disconcerted her.

She almost wished Fernao would do something overt. Then
she could tell him no, as forcefully as necessary, and they could
readjust as needed and go on. Of course, he'd saved her life two
or three times, from Algarvian sorcerous assault and from her
own botched spellcasting—and, this last time, he'd hurled
strong sorcery back against Mezentio's mages. *Do I really want
to tell him no?*

But Fernao hadn't done anything overt, and didn't seem
likely to. Ambiguity remained. Pekka laughed. *It might as well
be life,* she thought.

"What's funny?" Fernao asked.

"Nothing, really," she answered, at which he raised that eyebrow again. Ignoring it, she took her mittened hand out from
under the robes to point ahead. "We are almost there," she said
in classical Kaunian.

"So we are," Fernao agreed. He didn't expose any part of

himself but his eyes to the frigid air. "I wonder how the driver stands it up there, out in the open."

"We of Kuusamo do not let the cold trouble us quite so much as you do," Pekka said, which was true—but only to a degree.

When the sleigh stopped, as it did a couple of minutes later, Fernao had no choice but to come forth. The furs he wore were of Kuusaman make; he hadn't had anything in his own wardrobe to contend against winter in the Naantali district. That wasn't to say he hadn't known its like before. He re-marked, "The only difference between this place and the land of the Ice People is that the sun does come up for a little while here, even in the middle of winter."

"Er—aye," Pekka said. The idea that winter could get worse than it did here was horrifying all by itself.

As soon as she got inside the blockhouse, she started to sweat, and started shedding her outdoor clothes one layer at a time. Braziers and, soon, the press of bodies heated the cramped chamber in which she'd incant.

Ilmarinen and Piilis came into the blockhouse together. Il-marinen had always shared a sleigh with Master Siuntio, but Siuntio was dead, slain by murderous Algarvian magecraft. Now Ilmarinen rode with the younger theoretical sorcerer. Pekka didn't know when she would stop missing Siuntio, or if she ever would. Without him, this project would never have begun, would never had gained the backing of the Seven Princes.

Alkio and Raahe came in right behind Ilmarinen and Piilis. The married couple—both solid theoretical sorcerers—were about halfway between Pekka and Ilmarinen in age. *Solid,* Pekka thought. *Aye, they're very solid. So is Piilis. Nothing wrong with their work at all.* Were the three of them together a match for Siuntio? Pekka shook her head. She knew better. She wasn't a match for Siuntio as project leader, either. She also knew that. But she was what they had.

Secondary sorcerers hurried into the blockhouse, too. Some spells protected the animals at the heart of the experiment from freezing before they were needed. Others would transfer the spell Pekka and the other theoretical sorcerers had crafted to the animals when the time came. And with the secondary sorcerers came the protective mages. After two Algarvian attacks, Pekka knew how necessary they were.

But they didn't beat back Mezentio's mages the last time, she thought. *Fernao did that, Fernao and Ilmarinen and I. Three theoretical sorcerers who shouldn't be allowed to work magic like practical wizards.* She smiled, recognizing the ironic pride in her thoughts.

The blockhouse had been built with theoretical sorcerers and secondary sorcerers in mind. It hadn't been built to include the protective mages. When the weather got better, perhaps Pekka could prevail upon the Seven Princes to enlarge it. Meanwhile, people shoved and jostled and stepped on one another's feet and got in one another's way.

"Are we ready?" Pekka asked at last. But even her *at last* proved too soon; the mages were nowhere near ready. When she spoke again, it was in some exasperation: "Sooner or later, we shall have to go into the field. The Algarvians will not wait for us, and neither will the Gyongyosians."

Ilmarinen snapped his fingers. "That for the Gongs. They're honest foes, which means we can beat them without folderol, knock 'em back across the Bothnian Ocean one island at a time. As soon as the Algarvians started killing Kaunians to make their magecraft mightier, they put themselves beyond the pale."

Privately, Pekka agreed with him. Even so, she said, "Whichever way we aim the magic, we'll have to be able to do it in our time. The sooner we learn, the better."

Not even contrary Ilmarinen could quarrel with that. And Raahe said, "She is right. Let no one complain that we women are slow here." That made people laugh. More of the mages in the blockhouse were men than women, but only a few more. Kuusamans were emphatically aware of the differences between the sexes but, unlike Lagoans and most folk on the mainland of Derlavai, didn't think those differences applied to what each sex could do well.

When Pekka asked, "Are we ready?" again, she found that her colleagues were. "Before the Kaunians came, we of Kuusamo were here . . ." she said, and her fellow mages—all of them but Fernao—recited the ritual phrases, the phrases that moved them toward readiness for conjuration, along with her.

He has to feel very much alone, a foreigner, a stranger, whenever he listens to us, she thought. *I know I would if I were in Lagoas, say, and mages, just brusquely started to enchant without preparing first.*

But then such small thoughts slipped out of her mind, driven from it when she focused like a burning glass on what lay ahead. She took a deep breath to steady herself, let it out, and said, "I begin."

Every time she used the spell, it became sharper, more powerful. All the theoretical sorcerers tinkered with it between experiments. One couplet, one sorcerous pass, at a time, it grew closer to what it had to be. Had she seen this version a year before, it would have astounded her. She couldn't help wondering how much further they had to go.

If we come as far in the next year as we have in this past one, I'll be able to shatter the world like a dropped egg without even lifting a finger. She knew that was an exaggeration, but maybe it wasn't an enormous one. By the nature of things, spells that exploited the inverted unity she'd helped discover at the heart of the laws of similarity and contagion had the potential to release far more sorcerous energy than cantrips based on one or the other of the so-called Two Laws.

How close mortal mages could come to tapping that potential was one question. Another, more urgent question was how much attention she could give to such irrelevant quibbles before making a hash of the spell she was casting now and endangering herself and everybody in the blockhouse with her. She didn't like remembering Fernao had had to save her from the consequences of dropping a line in one of these spells.

Which is why practical mages make jokes about what happens when theoretical sorcerers go into the laboratory, Pekka thought. Too much of their kidding wasn't kidding at all, but sober truth.

But then even embarrassment and worry fell away as she lost herself in the intricacies of the spell she was casting. Getting the words precisely right; making sure the passes matched and reinforced them; feeling the power build as verse after verse, pass after pass, fell into place . . . It was almost like feeling pleasure build when she made love. And then she made *that* thought fall away, too—not without regret, but she did it.

Power built, and built, and built—and then, as she cried, "Let it be released!", it *was* released. She felt the secondary sorcerers take hold of what she'd brought into being, felt them hurl it forth to the banks of animal cages set far from the blockhouse, and felt it kindle there.

And then she needed no occult senses to feel it, for the ground shuddered beneath her feet. A great roar rumbled thought the air. She knew that, when she and the other mages went to examine the site, they would find another huge crater torn in the frozen ground. The Naantali district was starting to look like the moon as seen through a spyglass. Its wide stretches of worthless land were the main reasons experiments had moved here.

"Nicely done," Fernao said. "Very nicely done. When we measure the crater, we will be able to calculate the actual energy release and see how close it comes to what the sorcerous equations predicted. My guess is, the discrepancies will not be large. It had the right feel to it."

Pekka nodded—wearily, now that the spell was done. "I think you are right," she replied, also in classical Kaunian.

Ilmarinen said, "And, when we go out to the crater, we can see how much green grass and other out-of-season bits and pieces we find at the bottom of it."

Pekka grimaced. So did Fernao. The spells they were working with twisted time, among other things. The equations made that very clear. Ilmarinen, ever the radical, kept insisting the twist could be exploited for itself, not just for the energy it released. The unanimous opinion of the rest of the theoretical sorcerers was that the energy release came first.

As Pekka and Fernao rode out toward the crater, an exhausted little bird—a linnet—came fluttering down out of the sky and landed on their sleigh. When Pekka reached out for it, it flew off again, and was soon lost to sight. She stared at Fernao in no small consternation. She'd never seen a linnet in wintertime. They flew north for the winter, to escape the cold. Maybe this one hadn't escaped the cold. Maybe it hadn't escaped the sorcery, either.

And if it hadn't, what did that mean?

Hajjaj's carriage rolled up to the dragon farm outside Bishah, the capital of Zuwayza. When the carriage stopped, the Zuwayzi foreign minister descended to the sandy soil: a skinny man with dark brown skin and gray, almost white hair he'd earned by lasting close to seven decades—and also by guiding Zuwayza's relations with the other kingdoms of the world ever since his homeland regained its freedom from Unkerlant in the chaos following the Six Years' War.

General Ikhshid came bustling up to greet him. Ikhshid was paunchy, with bushy white eyebrows. He carried almost as many years as Hajjaj; he'd been a captain in the Unkerlanter army during the Six Years' War, one of the few men of Zuwayzi blood to gain officer's rank there.

Like Hajjaj, Ikhshid wore sandals and a broad-brimmed hat and nothing in between. In Zuwayza's fierce desert heat, clothes were nothing but a nuisance, however much Zuwayzi nudity scandalized other Derlavaians. Ikhshid had rank badges on his hat and marked with greasepaint on his upper arms.

He bowed to Hajjaj, wheezing a little as he straightened. "Good day, your Excellency," he said. "Always a pleasure to see you, believe me."

"You're too kind," Hajjaj murmured, returning the bow. "Believe me, the pleasure is mine." Aimed at a lot of men, Hajjaj would have meant that as no more than the usual pleasant hypocrisy. With Ikhshid, he meant it. He'd never been convinced Zuwayza's senior soldier was a great general, though Ikhshid was a good one. But Ikhshid, like Hajjaj himself, commanded the respect of every Zuwayzi clanfather. Hajjaj could think of no other officer of whom that was true.

"You do me too much credit, your Excellency," Ikhshid said.

"By no means, sir," Hajjaj protested. Zuwayzi forms of greeting and politeness, if uninterrupted, could go on for a long time.

Here, an interruption arrived in the person of Marquis Balastro, the Algarvian minister to Zuwayza. To Hajjaj's relief, Balastro was not nude, but wore the usual Algarvian tunic and kilt, with a hat of his own to keep the sun off his head. His bow, unlike Ikhshid's, was deep and flamboyant—Algarvians didn't do things by halves. "Good day to you, your Excellency," he said in his own language.

"And to you as well, your Excellency," Hajjaj replied in the same tongue. He'd been fluent in Algarvian for a long time: back before the Six Years' War (an era that seemed so distant and different, it might have been a thousand years ago), he'd spent his university days in Trapani, the Algarvian capital.

Balastro struck a pose. "Now, sir, you will see that Algarve stands by her allies in every way she can."

"I shall be glad to see it, very glad indeed," Hajjaj said.

That gave the Algarvian minister the chance to strike another pose, and he made the most of it, pointing to the sky and exclaiming, "Then look now at the dragons summoned to Zuwayza's aid!"

Hajjaj looked. So did Ikhshid. So did the writers from a couple of Zuwayzi news sheets summoned to the outskirts of the capital for the occasion. Sure enough, half a wing of dragons—thirty-two in all—painted in Algarve's gaudy green, red, and white spiraled down toward the dragon farm.

"They are indeed a pleasure to see, your Excellency," Hajjaj said, bowing once more. "Bishah shall be safer because of them. After the last raid, when the Unkerlanters pounded us from the air almost as they pleased, dragons to fly against those in Swemmel's rock-gray are most extremely welcome."

"I can see how they would be," Balastro agreed. "Till lately, Zuwayza has enjoyed all the advantages of the Derlavaian War, but only a few of the drawbacks: you won land from Swemmel, yet paid relatively little for it because he was more heavily involved against us."

That was imperfectly diplomatic, no matter how much truth it held. Hajjaj felt obliged to reply, "Do remember, your Excellency, that Unkerlant attacked my kingdom a year and a half before yours went to war against King Swemmel."

"Oh, no doubt," Balastro said. "But ours is the bigger fight with Unkerlant, even reckoning in the relative sizes of your kingdom and mine."

Another undiplomatic truth. When Hajjaj started to answer this time, a landing dragon's screech drowned out his words. Normally, that would have annoyed him. At the moment, it gave him the excuse he needed to say to Balastro, "Walk aside with me, your Excellency, that we might confer together in something a little closer to privacy."

Balastro bowed again. "With all my heart, sir. Nothing could please me more." That might well not have been true, but it was diplomatic.

When General Ikhshid started to follow the two of them away from the other dignitaries and the writers and the folk concerned with the mundane needs of dragons, Hajjaj sent him a quick, hooded glance. He and Ikhshid had served Zuwayza side by side for many years. The veteran officer stopped after a step and a half and began fiddling with a sandal strap.

Had Hajjaj and Balastro sought privacy among Algarvians, everyone close by would have swarmed after them: the redheads were powerfully curious, and also powerfully convinced they had the absolute right to know everything that went on around them. Hajjaj's countrymen showed more restraint. *They could hardly show less restraint than most Algarvians,* the Zuwayzi foreign minister thought.

"How now, your Excellency?" Balastro asked once he and Hajjaj had put a little distance between themselves and the other folk who'd come out to see the Algarvian dragons fly into the dragon farm.

"If you have a grievance with my kingdom, please come out with it," Hajjaj replied. "Your little hints and gives do nothing but make me nervous."

"All right, that's fair enough; I will," Balastro said. "Here's the grievance, in a nutshell: you expect Algarve to make you a perfect ally and come to your aid whenever you need something from her, and yet you refuse to return the favor."

"Zuwayza is a free and independent kingdom," Hajjaj said stiffly. "You sometimes seem to forget that."

"And you sometimes seem to remember it altogether too well," Marquis Balastro said. "I tell you frankly, your Excellency, those Kaunian exiles you harbor have sneaked back to Forthweg and done us a good deal of harm there."

"And I tell you frankly, I have trouble blaming them when I consider what you Algarvians have done to the Kaunians in Forthweg," Hajjaj answered.

"When you consider what Kaunians have done to Algarve down through the centuries, you might well say they have it coming," Balastro said.

Hajjaj shook his head. "No, your Excellency, I would never say that. Nor would King Shazli. I have made my views, and his, quite clear to you."

"So you have," Balastro agreed. "Now I am going to make something quite clear to you, and I am sure you will have no trouble making it quite clear to your king: if the Kaunians keep hurting us in Forthweg, they make it likelier that we lose the war against Unkerlant. If we lose the war against Unkerlant, you will also lose the war against Unkerlant. It is as simple as that. The more you want to deal with King Swemmel afterwards, the more you should look the other way when the blonds climb into their boats and sail east to Forthweg."

"We do not look the other way," Hajjaj insisted. "Our navy is far from large, but we have turned back or sunk several of their boats."

Balastro snorted. "Enough to show us a few: no more than that."

The trouble was, he was right. Hajjaj's sympathies, and those of his king, lay with the blonds who'd escaped from Algarvian occupation, and from the massacres the redheads inflicted on those blonds. As far as he was concerned, wars had no business being fought that way. Not even Swemmel of Unkerlant had fought that way till the Algarvians forced it on him. Waging war on the same side as the redheads made Hajjaj want to go sweat himself clean in the baths.

But when the choice was having Unkerlanters overrun Zuwayza . . . Hajjaj shook his head. When he and Ikhshid were young, an Unkerlanter governor had ruled in Bishah. If the Algarvians lost, if Zuwayza lost, that could happen again. Algarve, however monstrous its warmaking, didn't threaten Zuwayza's freedom. Unkerlant did, and always would.

Bitterly, Hajjaj said, "I wish we were an island in the Great Northern Sea, so we would not have to make choices such as these."

"Wish for the moon while you're at it," Balastro answered. "The world is as it is, not as you wish it were. But do you wonder that we hesitate to give you more help against Swemmel when we see how you repay us?"

"Knives have two edges," Hajjaj said. "If you want to keep us in the fight against Unkerlant, we need the tools and the beasts to go on fighting. If we go out of the war, how much likelier is it that Algarve will lose?"

Balastro looked as if he'd bitten down hard on a lemon. Hajjaj had turned his argument around on him. At last, the Algarvian minister said, "The marriage in which we're trapped may be loveless, but it is a marriage, and we'd both be hurt if we divorced. Whether we love you or not, your Excellency, we have sent you a present that costs us dear, for our own substance these days is not so large as we would wish, and we have, do believe me, no dragons to spare. We have nothing at all to spare."

Hajjaj bowed. "Is it so bad as that?"

"It is bad, and it does not get better," Balastro replied.

"That is not good news," the Zuwayzi foreign minister said.

"Did I tell you it would be?" Balastro said. "Now, sir, you may not love us, but you are wed to us no less than we are wed to you. Even if you do not think us as fresh and lovely as you did when you first went to bed with us, will you not give us a present for a present, to keep us from quarreling and throwing dishes at each other after supper?"

With some amusement, Hajjaj said, "You sound like an old

husband, sure enough. And what present would you have from us, as if I don't know?"

Balastro nodded. "Aye, that one, sure enough. No gauds, no jewels—just do as you say you've been doing all along. I am not even asking that you give over harboring Kaunians here. If you will harbor them, you will. But, your Excellency, harbor them *here*. If they want to go back to Forthweg, stop turning a blind eye to them. You *can* stop them, and I hope you will not do me the discourtesy of claiming otherwise."

"I shall take your words to King Shazli," Hajjaj said. Hating himself, hating what the war made him do for the sake of his kingdom, he added, "I shall take them to him with the recommendation that he follow your suggestion."

Balastro bowed. "I can ask no more." When Hajjaj recommended something to the king, whatever it was had a way of happening. Here, Hajjaj wished that were not so. Zuwayza's marriage to Algarve was indeed loveless. But, as the Algarvian minister had pointed out, it was indeed a marriage, too. Both sides would be worse off if it fell apart. And so, to keep it going, Zuwayza needed to give Algarve a present in return for the present she'd got. Almost, Hajjaj wished the Algarvian dragons had not come. Almost.

Sergeant Istvan and some of the Gyongyosian soldiers in his squad squatted in a muddy trench on the miserable little island called Becsehely, whiling away the time shooting dice. Istvan sent the bone cubes rolling across the flat board the big, tawny-bearded men used for a playing surface. When he saw a pair of ones staring at him, he cursed.

Szonyi laughed. "Only two stars in your sky there, Sergeant. I can beat that easy enough." He scooped up the dice and proved it—a throw of five wasn't anything much, but plenty to take care of a two. Szonyi gathered up all the coins on the board.

Still cursing his luck, Istvan leaned back and let the next trooper in the game take his place. Lajos hadn't been with him as long as Szonyi had. Istvan and Szonyi and Corporal Kun had been together since the fighting on Obuda, an island in the

Bothnian Ocean some distance west of Becsehely. They'd fought the Kuusamans there, then gone back to the Derlavaian mainland to battle the Unkerlanters in the Ilszung Mountains on the border between Gyongyos and Swemmel's kingdom and in the trackless forests of western Unkerlant. That was where Lajos had joined the squad. Now, with the stars not shining on the Gyongyosian cause in the fight against Kuusamo, they'd come back to island duty again.

Szonyi set a stake on the board. Lajos, young and eager, matched it. Szonyi threw first: a six. Lajos took the dice and threw another six. They each put down more coins, doubling the stake. Szonyi threw a nine.

Before Lajos picked up the dice, Corporal Kun nudged Szonyi and held out a silver coin in the palm of his hand—a side bet. "This that he'll beat Lajos by two or better."

"No, thanks." Istvan shook his head, and then had to brush curly, dark yellow hair out of his face. "Betting on the side is how you make your money. I've seen that."

Lajos threw an eight. Szonyi collected the twofold bets. Behind his gold-framed spectacles, Kun assumed an injured expression. "There," he said. "You see? You would have won."

"This time I would have, aye." Now Istvan nodded. "But anybody who takes a lot of side bets against you ends up without any money in his belt pouch, so go find yourself a new fish. You've hooked me too often already."

Szonyi won the next duel of dice, too. He said, "I don't make side bets against you, either, Kun. The sergeant's right—you win 'em often enough to make some people wonder whether you magic the dice."

"Oh, rubbish," Kun said, or perhaps something rather more pungent. Unlike most of the men in the squad, including Istvan, he wasn't a peasant or herder from a little mountain valley. Such sturdy soldiers gave the Gyongyosians reason to reckon themselves a warrior race. But Kun had been a mage's apprentice in Gyorvar, the capital, before taking service in Ekrekek Arpad's army. He knew little bits and pieces of sorcery himself. Enough to ensorcel dice? Istvan had sometimes wondered himself.

But he said, "Kun's luck's no better than anybody else's when he's got the dice in his own hand. I've noticed that. It's only when he's making side bets that he cleans up. I can't see how he'd put a spell on somebody else's dice but not on his own."

"Rubbish," Kun repeated—or, again, words to that effect. "I'll tell you what makes the difference: I know what I'm doing, and you back-country boys don't. There's no more magecraft in it than there is to cooking a goose."

"If there's no magecraft, we ought to be able to do it, too, once you tell us how—isn't that right?" Szonyi said. He and Kun often banged heads like mountain sheep.

Kun nodded now. "Aye, if you can remember a few simple things." He raised an eyebrow. By Gyongyosian standards, he was on the scrawny side; Szonyi came close to making two of him. But he had no fear, for he added, "For simple people, even simple things come hard."

Szonyi bristled. Istvan said, "Never mind the insults. If you can teach us, teach us. I wouldn't mind learning something to help me put a little extra silver in my belt pouch."

"All right, by the stars, I will, even if it'll cost me money," Kun said, and spent the next little while talking about how to figure odds while rolling dice.

By the time he got through, Istvan was frowning and scratching his head. "Are you sure that's not magecraft?" he asked.

"Anything somebody doesn't know how to do looks like magecraft to him," Kun said impatiently. "This isn't. It's nothing but a . . . fancy kind of arithmetic, I guess you'd call it."

"How can it be arithmetic?" Szonyi demanded—he was never content with anything Kun said. "Two and two is always four. With this, you're right some of the time and you're wrong some of the time. If you run out of silver and bet your tunic, you're liable to walk home naked."

"Over the long run, though, you won't." Kun's smile grew rather nasty. "And if you don't believe me, why won't you make side bets with me?"

Before Szonyi could answer, horns blared out an alarm from the high ground, such as it was, at the center of Becsehely.

"Scoop up that money, boys. Grab the dice," Istvan said. "Dowsers must've spotted another wave of Kuusaman dragons coming to pay us a call."

"Dowsing, now, dowsing is real magecraft," Kun said. "Sensing motion at a distance farther than you can see—how could you possibly do that without sorcery?"

Istvan nodded. "Well, that's true enough. I was a dowser's helper for a while, over on Obuda. They gave me the job for a punishment, because he had a heavy sack of rods to carry, but I ended up enjoying it—Borsos was an interesting fellow to talk to. Remember?—he showed up in the Unkerlanter woods, too."

"That's right." Szonyi also nodded. "He was trying to spy out something Swemmel's stinking goat-eaters were up to."

The horns cried out again. Booted feet thudded on wet ground as Gyongyosian soldiers who weren't already in trenches ran for shelter. "Take cover!" shouted Captain Frigyes, the company commander. "Take cover, and be ready to come up blazing if the Kuusamans bring boats up onto the beach."

"May the stars hold that idea out of their heads," Istvan said, and made a sign to avert the evil omen.

Becsehely was big enough to support a dragon farm. Wings thundering, Gyongyosian dragons painted in bold stripes of red and blue and black and yellow flew out to meet the enemies the dowsers had spotted. Kuusaman colors were sky blue and sea green, which made their dragons hard to see but easy to tell apart from the Gyongyosian beasts once noted.

"I wonder if this really will be the invasion," Kun remarked, making sure dirt didn't foul the business end, the blazing end, of his stick.

"They've pounded us before when we thought they would land, and they didn't," Istvan said. "Here's hoping they stay away again."

"Oh, aye, here's hoping." But Kun seemed unable to look on the bright side of things. "The trouble is, they've taken a lot of islands away from us, too. If they hadn't, our regiment would still be fighting the Unkerlanters in those woods that went on forever and ever."

"I'm not sorry to be out of the forest," Istvan admitted. "Of course, I'd've been happier if they'd sent us somewhere besides this miserable flat place. I miss having a horizon with mountain teeth in it."

"If the Kuusamans do come ashore . . ." Kun hesitated, plainly wondering how to go on. "If they do come ashore, I wonder if our officers will have to hold us to the oath we swore. The oath about . . . the strong sorcery, I mean."

"I know what you mean," Istvan said. Algarve and Unkerlant used the life energy from sacrificed people to power their sorcery. The Algarvians killed Kaunians they'd conquered; King Swemmel's sorcerers sacrificed those of their own folk they reckoned useless. Both those answers revolted the Gyongyosians. But they'd seen they might need such wizardry. With a shrug, Istvan continued: "We're a warrior race." Most of the company had volunteered to be sacrificed if the need ever arose. Istvan had, without thinking twice. Kun had, too, much more hesitantly.

"The stars already know," Szonyi said.

"They always know," Kun said. "But *I* don't."

That thin hiss in the air wasn't the stars telling Corporal Kun what would be. It was an egg falling, to burst in the sea just off the muddy, west-facing beach of Becsehely. Some dragonflier overhead had been too eager. But other bursts of sorcerous energy walked up the beach toward the trenches where Istvan and his comrades huddled. He hated taking a pounding from dragons more than any other part of war. He knew exactly why, too: he couldn't hit back. An egg falling out of the sky didn't care whether he belonged to a warrior race or not.

He looked up. Sure enough, the Kuusaman dragons were harder to see than those his countrymen flew. But, by the way eggs carpeted Becsehely, by the way Gyongyosian dragons tumbled out of the sky one after another, he had no trouble figuring out the Kuusamans outnumbered them. The Kuusamans had been the first to figure out how to transport dragons on board ship, and they'd got better and better at it since.

But they didn't have things all their own way here. The Gyongyosians had brought heavy sticks to Becsehely, sticks that could blaze through a behemoth's chainmail and through the behemoth, too—and sticks strong enough to blaze down a dragon no matter how high it flew.

Istvan whooped when a Kuusaman dragon faltered in midair. He whooped again when it started down toward the island. Nor was he the only one. "We nailed that son of a strumpet!" Szonyi shouted.

"He looks like he's coming straight toward us," Kun said, and people stopped whooping. Finishing a wounded, furious dragon with hand-held sticks was anything but a morning's pleasant sport.

This one landed on the muddy beach not a hundred yards in front of Istvan's trench. Its shrieks tore at his ears. Then, all at once, they stopped. Cautiously—a few eggs were still bursting—he stuck up his head to see what had happened. The dragon lay dead. The Kuusaman dragonflier was holding the stick he took into the air with him. He must have put a beam through the dragon's eye at close range.

Seeing Istvan, he threw the stick down on the beach and held his hands high. "I—to surrender!" he shouted in horrible Gyongyosian.

Istvan hadn't expected to capture a dragonflier, but he wouldn't complain. "Come on, get in this trench before your own people drop an egg on you," he called.

"I—to thank," the dragonflier said, and jumped down and ran over to Istvan. "You—no—to kill?" he asked anxiously as he slid into the trench.

In his boots, Istvan would have sounded anxious, too. But the Gyongyosian sergeant shook his head. "No. You Kuusamans, you've got captives from my kingdom, too. Once you start killing captives, where do you stop?"

Istvan had to repeat himself with simpler words to get the enemy dragonflier to follow that, but the fellow finally nodded. "Good," he said. "I—yours—to be." For a little while, Istvan wondered what was so good about being a captive, but only for a little while. The Kuusaman had come through the war alive. Istvan wondered if he would be able to say the same.

⚬〰⚬

Skrunda wasn't a big city. Jelgava held dozens, probably hundreds, of towns like it. As in so many of those towns, the people of Skrunda liked to think of it as bigger than it really was. News-sheet vendors hocked their wares as zealously as they did in Balvi, the capital, down in the southeast.

"Habakkuk explained!" one of them shouted, waving a sheet with great abandon. "Floating home of air pirates!"

Talsu couldn't remember the last time he'd bought a news sheet. They'd been full of lies ever since the Algarvians overran his kingdom. But he'd seen graffiti praising Habakkuk all over Skrunda. He'd also seen that the redheads didn't love them: they gathered work crews together to wash them off or paint over them. And so he dug into a trouser pocket and came up with a couple of coppers for the news-sheet vendor.

"Here you go, pal," the fellow said, and handed him the sheet he'd been waving.

"Thanks," Talsu answered. He kept his nose in the news sheet all the way back to the tailor's shop where he worked with his father.

That almost got him into trouble, for he noticed a couple of Algarvian constables just in time to get out of their way. He scowled after they swaggered past. Jelgava, like Valmiera to the south, was a Kaunian kingdom. Redheads in a land of blonds, kilts in a land of trousers, seemed shockingly out of place even though King Donalitu had fled to Lagoas and exile more than three years before, even though King Mezentio of Algarve had promptly named his younger brother Mainardo as King of Jelgava in Donalitu's place.

A whitewashed patch on a fence probably told where a graffito shouting HABAKKUK! had been painted. Talsu walked past it with a thoughtful grunt. He also nearly walked past the tailor's shop, and the rooms above it where he and his family lived.

His father was working on a tunic of Algarvian military cut in a fabric too heavy for Jelgava's weather when Talsu walked in. Traku frowned to see the news sheet—Talsu's father, in truth, spent a good deal of time frowning. "What sort of nonsense are the redheads spouting today?" he asked. He might make uniforms for the occupiers—especially, as now, for Al-

garvians sent west to fight in freezing Unkerlant—but he didn't
love them.

Neither did Talsu. He'd fought them before his kingdom collapsed, and he'd tried to fight them here in Skrunda, too. He'd
spent some months in a Jelgavan dungeon from trusting the
wrong people then. No, he had no reason to love Algarvians.

He set the news sheet on the counter. "I bought the miserable
thing because it said it would tell me what Habakkuk was."

"Ah." That interested Traku, too. He reached for the news
sheet. "And does it?"

"It *says* Habakkuk is an iceberg, or a swarm of icebergs,
fixed up with sorcery so they'll sail the ley lines like regular
ships and carry a whole great load of dragons while they're doing it," Talsu answered.

Traku skimmed through the article. "Aye, that's what it *says*,
all right," he remarked when he was through. "The next question is, do you believe it?"

"I don't know," Talsu answered. "We've had dragons from
Kuusamo or Lagoas or wherever they're from drop more eggs
on Skrunda lately than they did in the whole war up till now, so
they've got *something* new, I expect."

"Maybe." Traku nodded. "I'll give you that much, anyhow.
But giant chunks of ice with dragons on top of them? I doubt
it." He wadded up the news sheet and flung it in the trash can.
"My guess is, the redheads came up with this fancy nonsense
because they can't build real ships as fast as Lagoas and Kuusamo can, and they're making all the news sheets print it to
distract people."

"You're probably right," Talsu agreed. He'd got good at search-
ing out the truth buried in Algarvian lies. This story sounded more
like a lie than anything he could easily swallow. He went on: "I
saw one other thing in the news sheet—or rather, I didn't see it."

"What's that?" his father asked.

"No more boasting about how the redheads were going to
chase the Unkerlanters right out of that town down in the
south—Herborn, that's the name of the place," Talsu said.
"When the Algarvians stop bragging about something, it's because they haven't done it or they can't do it."

Traku's opinion of that needed only one word: "Good."

Talsu nodded. He pointed to the tunic his father was working on. "Do you need any help with that?"

"No, thanks," Traku answered. "I've done just about all the handwork it needs." He showed the stitches he'd applied himself. "After that, it's just a matter of laying out the rest of the thread and putting on the finishing touches. You can do some more work on that kilt over there, if you feel like you've just got to get some work in this very minute."

"All right, I'll do that, then." Talsu picked up the kilt, which at the moment was only a piece cut out from a bolt of heavy woolen fabric. As he did so, he remarked, "I never thought I'd have to worry about making one of these, not back before the war started I didn't."

"Who would have, in a Kaunian kingdom?" Traku said. "We wear trousers, the way decent people are supposed to." He paused to set thread along a seam he hadn't sewn. "I do hear that, down in Balvi, there were women wearing kilts even before the war, so they could show off their legs. Trollops, that's what I call 'em."

"Oh, aye, trollops is right," Talsu said, not without a certain interest. He went on. "You see a few Jelgavan women—even a few Jelgavan men—in Skrunda wearing kilts nowadays. But they just want to lick the Algarvians' boots."

"They want to lick 'em somewhere north of the boots," Traku said with a coarse laugh.

Talsu laughed, too, deliciously scandalized. Hearing the racket from downstairs, his sister Ausra called, "What's so funny?"

"Nothing," Talsu and Traku said in the same breath. The way they echoed each other set them both laughing again, harder than ever.

"What's so funny?" That wasn't Talsu's sister: it was his mother. And she came down into the tailor's shop to get an answer for her question.

"Nothing, Laitsina," Traku repeated, this time in more placating tones.

Laitsina looked from her husband to Talsu and back again. "Men," she said, a distinct sniff in her voice. "You sit around here telling each other filthy stories, and then you expect me to pretend I don't know you're doing it. You don't ask for much, do you?" With another sniff, she went back up the stairs.

"She was right," Talsu whispered.

"Well, of course she was," his father answered, also in a whisper. "But so what? Do you think she and Ausra—and now your wife, too, when Gailisa's up there with 'em and not working at her father's grocery—don't do the exact same thing when they figure we can't hear 'em?" Traku shook his head to show Talsu what he ought to think. "Not bloody likely, not when I've caught 'em a time or two."

"Have you?" Now Talsu was scandalized in a different way.

"Oh, aye," Traku said. "They can be as foul-mouthed as we ever are, only they don't want anybody knowing it. It's their secret, like."

Some of the things Gailisa had said made Talsu suspect his father had a point. He wasn't about to admit as much, though. He had far fewer illusions than when he'd gone into King Donalitu's army. He cherished those he'd managed to keep.

Traku went back to work. Once he'd laid out all the remaining thread on the tunic, he began to mutter to himself and to make quick passes over the garment. He and Talsu hardly thought of what they did as magic; it was just a trick of the tailor's trade. But magic it was, using the laws of similarity and contagion to make the unsewn thread conform to that which was sewn. The thread writhed and twisted, as if briefly coming to life. When the writhing stopped, the tunic was done.

Traku picked it up, tugged at the sorcerously made seams, and put on a pair of reading glasses so he could examine it closely. When he was done, he set it down and delivered his verdict: "Not bad, if I do say so myself."

"Of course not, Father," Talsu said. "You do the best work in town." He lowered his voice again to add, "Better than the cursed redheads deserve, too."

"It depends on how you look at things," Traku said. "I'm not doing this just for the Algarvians, you know. I'm doing it for my own sake, too. I don't think I could stand doing bad work on purpose, no matter who it's for."

"All right. I know what you mean." Talsu waved, yielding the point. "And it means one more Algarvian who's never coming back to Skrunda again."

"That, too," his father said.

The Algarvian in question, a captain, came into the tailor's shop that afternoon to pick up the tunic. After trying it on, he nodded. "It being good," he said in Jelgavan flavored with his kingdom's trilling accent. "Cloth being nice and thick." He dabbed at his forehead with a pocket handkerchief. "I sweating here. When I going down to frozen Unkerlant, I not sweating any more." He changed back into the thinner tunic he'd worn into the shop, set on the counter the price to which he and Traku had agreed, and carried away the garment he would need while fighting King Swemmel's men.

"I hope he sweats plenty, down in frozen Unkerlant," Talsu said after the redhead left.

"Oh, sure," Traku agreed, as if surprised Talsu would have bothered saying anything like that. "Sooner or later, either the Algarvians or the Unkerlanters will run out of men. Here's hoping it's the Algarvians." He scooped up the silver coins the redhead had left behind and put on his glasses again to examine them. "This Mainardo bugger the redheads call King of Jelgava's got a pointy nose."

"Aye, so he does," Talsu said. "From what I remember of the Algarvian coins I got before things fell apart, Mezentio's got a pointy nose, too." He shrugged. "They're brothers. No reason they shouldn't look alike."

"No reason at all," his father said. "No reason they shouldn't both be trouble, either. And they cursed well are, powers below eat 'em." He paused, got up off his stool, straightened, stretched, and twisted this way and that. Something in his back went *pop-pop-pop*, as if he'd cracked his knuckles. He sighed. "Ahh, that's better. I couldn't get the crick out of there no matter how hard I tried." He glanced over to Talsu. "How's that kilt coming?"

"I've done a couple of pleats by hand, and I've got the thread laid out," Talsu replied. "Now I'm going to put on the finishing touches." The charm he wanted, part Jelgavan, part the classical Kaunian that was Jelgavan's ancestor, part non-sense words was almost but not quite identical to the one his father had used with the tunic. Again, most of the kilt's stitch-ery shaped itself.

Traku examined the finished garment and patted his son on the back. "Nice job. I still think kilts are ugly as all get-out my-self, but the redhead who ordered this one'll get what he paid for—and a free trip to Unkerlant besides." Talsu's answering grin was every bit as nasty as his father's.

Out in the field, Marshal Rathar most often wore a common soldier's rock-gray tunic with the large stars of his rank on the collar tabs. That wouldn't do for a formal court function. At the orders of King Swemmel's protocol officer—who plainly out-ranked even a marshal in such matters—he put on his most gor-geous dress uniform before repairing to the throne room.

"You look splendid, lord Marshal," Major Merovec said loyally.

Rathar eyed his adjutant. "I doubt it, if you want to know the truth. What I look like is a gaudy popinjay." Unkerlanter military fancy dress, like that of the other kingdoms of Derlavai, was based on the regular uniforms of a bygone age, when officers needed to be recognizable at a distance and when cold-hearted snipers hadn't been able to put a beam through their heads from half a mile away. Rathar's uniform was scarlet and black, with ribbons and medals gleaming on his chest.

"Splendid," Merovec repeated. "His Majesty commanded it, so how could you look less than splendid?"

"Hmm." The marshal nodded. "When you put it that way, you've got a point."

Having satisfied both his adjutant and the fussy protocol offi-cer, Rathar made his way through a maze of palace corridors to the throne room at the heart of King Swemmel's residence. However magnificent the dress uniform he wore, though, he had to surrender his ceremonial sword to the guardsmen in the antechamber outside the throne room. He thought being with-out a blade detracted from the effect he was supposed to create, but his was not the opinion that counted. Swemmel's, as always, prevailed.

Inside the throne room, the king dominated. That had always been true in Unkerlant, and would probably stay true till the end of time. The great throne raised Swemmel—as it had raised his predecessors and would raise his successors—high above his subjects and drew all eyes to him. Set against the king's jewel- and pearl-encrusted robe and massy golden crown, Marshal Rathar's uniform might as well have been simple rock-gray. Nothing competed with Swemmel here.

Lesser courtiers nodded to the marshal as he walked past them up the aisle leading to the splendid throne. To them, he was a person of consequence. To Swemmel, Rathar was what the other courtiers were: an ornament, a decoration, a reflection of his own magnificence and glory.

The marshal prostrated himself before Swemmel, knocking his head against the carpet and crying out the king's praises as loudly as he could with his mouth an inch off that rug. "We suffer you to rise," King Swemmel said in his thin voice. "Take your place beside us. We are soon to receive the ministers from Kuusamo and Lagoas, as we have spoken of before, and would have you beside us that we might speak to them with greater efficiency."

"That is my pleasure, your Majesty, and my duty," Rathar replied, and stood to the right of the throne where Swemmel could easily seek his opinion. Whether Swemmel would want advice, or whether he would take it once he got it, were questions of a different sort.

A herald cried, "His Excellency, Count Gusmao, minister to Unkerlant from King Vitor of Lagoas! His Excellency, Lord Moisio, minister to Unkerlant from the Seven Princes of Kuusamo!"

As usual, Gusmao and Moisio walked up the aisle toward the throne together: a pair of oddly mismatched twins. Coming from the island their kingdoms had shared for so long gave them a similarity that transcended their complete lack of physical resemblance. Moisio was little and swarthy and flat-faced, with a few wisps of gray hair on his chin to do duty for a beard. But for Gusmao's neat ponytail and a few differences in the cut of his tunic and kilt, he could have been an Algarvian: he was tall and fair, with red hair and cat-green eyes. *Lagoans are of Algarvic stock, too,* Rathar reminded himself. *They're allies, not Algarvians.* Seeing Gusmao still made him nervous.

Both ministers bowed low to King Swemmel. Being their own sovereigns' direct representatives in Unkerlant, they didn't have to prostrate themselves. Swemmel nodded to each of them. "Through you, we greet your rulers," he said.

"Thank you, your Majesty." That was Lord Moisio—a Kuusaman title of annoying ambiguity. He spoke Unkerlanter understandably, but with the most peculiar accent Rathar had ever heard. "I appreciate your courtesy, as always." Was that sarcasm? With Moisio, you could never be sure.

Count Gusmao said, "King Vitor congratulates you, your Majesty, on the victories your brave soldiers have won against our common foe." His accent was different from Moisio's. It was also different from the way Algarvians spoke Unkerlanter, which helped Rathar feel easier around the redheaded Lagoan minister.

"We thank you," Swemmel said. That restraint astonished Rathar: restraint wasn't usually one of Swemmel's outstanding character traits. Then the king leaned forward on the throne and pointed a long, skinny finger at Count Gusmao. "We would thank you more were your soldiers fighting on the mainland of Derlavai, as ours are."

"Taking Sibiu back ought to count for a little something." Moisio spoke before Gusmao could. The Kuusaman minister courted lese majesty every time he opened his mouth. Swemmel had never executed a minister from another kingdom, not even the Algarvian minister after Mezentio beat him to the punch. There was always a first time, though.

Before the king could start roaring at Lord Moisio, Gusmao added, "And from Sibiu our dragons pound Valmiera and Algarve itself."

King Swemmel snapped his fingers, as he had with Rathar in discussing the islanders. "Sibiu is nothing but rocks and mud dropped into the sea. If it fell in Unkerlant, no one would notice. *We* fight the Algarvian murderers from the Narrow Sea in the frozen south to the Garelian Ocean in the steaming north. Have your overlords the courage to cross to Derlavai and close with the foe?"

He'd asked that question of the ministers from the two island kingdoms a year before. They'd talked about how many other wonderful things they were doing in the fight against Algarve. Rathar knew there was a good deal of truth in what they said. That didn't keep him, like a lot of Unkerlanters, from resenting them for the easy time they'd had of the war.

"We do close with the Algarvians," Gusmao said. "We close with them on the sea, we close with them on the air, we have driven them from Sibiu—"

"You do everything except the thing that truly matters," Swemmel said, and snapped his fingers again. "We know why you hang back, too: you hope to see the Algarvians maim us while we maim them, then come in and sweep up the leavings for yourselves. Is it not so, Marshal?" He nodded to Rathar.

Rathar wished he hadn't. He suspected Swemmel had a point. Whether the king had a point or not, though, he shouldn't have raised it with his allies. Rathar said, "His Majesty means we've carried the burden on the mainland of Derlavai by ourselves for a long time now. Help would be welcome."

"We mean what we said," Swemmel broke in, ruining Rathar's try for diplomacy.

"Shall we stop fighting the Gyongyosians out among the islands of the Bothnian Ocean, then?" Moisio asked. "That would let the Gongs concentrate on you, of course, but if it's what you want. . . ." He shrugged.

"Gyongyos is an ague," King Swemmel said. "Algarve is a plague. Do you understand the difference? Do you understand anything at all?"

The foreign minister will probably cut his throat, Rathar thought. But then, the king had always had even less use for the foreign minister's advice than he had for that from his chief soldier.

Count Gusmao said, "When we hit the Algarvians, you may be sure we shall hit them hard."

Swemmel yawned. "When you have something new to say, come before us again and let us hear it. Until then . . ." He made a gesture of dismissal.

"If you will not listen, your Majesty, how can you expect to hear anything new?" Lord Moisio asked.

Gasps rose from the Unkerlanter courtiers. One of those gasps rose from Marshal Rathar. He sometimes dared tell the king things others would have hidden from him. Never, not even in the days of the Twinkings War, had he dared be rude to Swemmel. The King of Unkerlant was conscious of his kingship, first, last, and always.

King Swemmel's eyes widened, then narrowed. Through those narrowed eyes, he stared down at the Kuusaman minister. "Do you seek to see how far you can try the immunity granted to a diplomat, sirrah?" the king inquired in a voice deadly cold. "We shall teach you the answer there, if you like, but you will not have joy of the learning."

"You are as good a foe to your friends as you are to your foes," Moisio answered. "Keep that up a while, and see how many friends you have at the end of it."

"Your Majesty—" Rathar began urgently. Whether Swemmel did or not, he understood that Unkerlant would have a much harder time beating Algarve and Gyongyos without help from the two island kingdoms.

"Be silent, Marshal," Swemmel snapped, and Rathar, ingrained to obedience, *was* silent. The king's head swung back to Moisio. "We grant immunity to no man, diplomat or otherwise, for insolence against our person."

" 'Insolence'? What insolence?" the Kuusaman said. "Count Gusmao told you a thing. You would not hear it. You refused to hear it. Where lies the insolence in that?"

More gasps rose from the Unkerlanters. This time, Marshal Rathar kept quiet. Every once in a while, someone taking a line like Moisio's could get through to Swemmel where flattery and court tricks failed. More often, of course, such attempts ended in disaster, which was why even Rathar used them only as a last resort.

Swemmel said, "I have heard such nonsense as he spouts

from both of you before. Why should I care to hear it again?" He wasn't shouting for his guards to take Lord Moisio away and do something dreadful to him. His failure to shout for them was as much as—more than—Rathar could have hoped for.

"'Why,' your Majesty?" Count Gusmao spoke for himself. "Because it is not nonsense. I told you the truth, and nothing but. When we hit the Algarvians, you may be sure we shall hit them hard."

"Aye, no doubt. And when will that be?" King Swemmel jeered.

Moisio did something then that Rathar thought would get him killed in the next instant: he stepped up onto the base of the throne and beckoned to Swemmel to lean down to him. To Rathar's astonishment, the king did—maybe Swemmel was too astonished to do anything else, too. And the Kuusaman minister, standing on tiptoe, whispered something into his ear.

"Really?" Swemmel, for once, sounded altogether human and not in the least royal.

"Really." Lord Moisio's voice was firm. Whatever he'd told the king, he believed it. Hearing the way he affirmed it, Rather believed it, too. The only problem was, he had no idea what Moisio had said. And, by Swemmel's conspiratorial smirk— one that Moisio shared—he wouldn't get to find out any time soon, either.

Four

◠◡◠◡◠

A blizzard howled outside the peasant hut in eastern Grelz that Colonel Sabrino had taken for his own. Sabrino wondered if it would be the last blizzard of the winter: it was heavy, wet snow, not the dry, powdery stuff that fell—or sometimes just blew sideways—when the weather was even colder. Whether it proved the last blizzard or not, it was too thick for the wing of dragons he commanded to fly. And so he sat in the hut in front of a roaring fire and poured down spirits to make time go by. The peasant who'd once lived here had probably passed the winter the same way.

"One thing, anyhow," Sabrino said, pronouncing each word with careful care.

"What's that, sir?" Captain Orosio sat on another stool not far away. He had a mug of spirits, too, and he'd also emptied it more than once.

"In weather like this, even the cursed Unkerlanters can't get their dragons off the ground," Sabrino said.

Orosio considered that with owlish intensity. Once it had penetrated, he nodded. "You're right, sir," he said, as if Sabrino had given him some hidden key to the true meaning of the world. "By the powers above, you're right."

"Of course I am," Sabrino said grandly. He drew himself straight on his stool, and almost fell off it. "I am a colonel of dragonfliers. Do I know these things, or do I not?"

"You're a colonel of dragonfliers. Of course you do." Orosio tilted back his mug and drained it. He reached for the jar that sat on the rammed-earth floor between Sabrino and him. The jar sloshed when he picked it up. Grunting in satisfaction, he poured himself a refill. After he drank, he turned—carefully—toward Sabrino. "How come you're still a colonel of dragonfliers?"

"What's that?" Sabrino asked.

"How come you're still just a colonel of dragonfliers, lord Count?" Orosio said again. "You've got the blue blood, and powers above know you fight your wing like a mad bastard. How come you're not a brigadier of dragonfliers, or maybe a lieutenant general of dragonfliers by now? Plenty of people who started behind you and weren't so good to begin with are ahead of you now. It doesn't seem fair to me."

"Ah." Sabrino reached out and patted Orosio on the shoulder. "You are a gentleman, my friend. Nothing less than a gentleman. But the war could go on till I was much older than I am now—which is quite old enough, believe you me it is—and I would die a colonel of dragonfliers. I suppose I ought to count myself lucky I wouldn't die a sergeant of dragonfliers."

"I don't understand, sir." Orosio sounded on the verge of tears because he didn't understand.

There had been times when Sabrino found himself on the verge of tears because he understood altogether too well. No more, though. He was—or he told himself he was—resigned to what had happened to his career. "Do you want to know why I'm not a brigadier of dragonfliers or even a lieutenant general of dragonfliers, Orosio? It's simple. Nothing simpler, in fact. I told King Mezentio to his face that he was making a mistake when he started sacrificing Kaunians for the sake of sorcery, and I turned out to be right. *That's* why I'm still a colonel of dragonfliers, and why I'll be one till my dying day." He emptied his own mug and poured it full again.

"Would you have had a better chance for promotion if you turned out to be wrong?" Orosio asked.

Sabrino shook his head. "No, not any chance at all," he said loudly—aye, he could feel the spirits, sure enough. "It didn't help that I turned out to be right, but it didn't matter much, either. You tell the king he's made a mistake and you've made a worse one, if you ever wanted to see rank higher than the one you owned."

"That's not fair. By the powers above, it's *not* fair," Captain Orosio said with drunken insistence of his own. "You're a free Algarvian. You've got as much right to tell him what's so as he's got to tell you."

"Oh, aye, I've got the right," Sabrino agreed. "I've got the right, but he's got the might." The jingling rhyme made him laugh—a telling measure of how drunk he was.

"Not fair," Orosio said again. "The way things are, we need every good soldier doing everything he can." He leaned over to pat Sabrino this time, and he too almost fell off his stool. "You're a good soldier, sir, but you're not coming close to doing everything you can."

"No? You think not?" Sabrino's laugh was loud and emphatic, too. "Right this minute, I'm doing everything I can just to sit up, same as you are."

"Who, me?" Orosio said. "I'm fine, just fine." To prove how fine he was, he burst into raucous song.

"That's lovely," Sabrino said, another telling measure of how low in the jar the level of spirits had got. He yawned enormously. "Let's go to bed."

"Aye, let's," Captain Orosio said, not that the hut boasted any real beds. Instead, it had benches against the wall, on which the Unkerlanter peasants who lived there had been wont to throw pillows and blankets and themselves.

Those pillows and blankets were long gone, as were the Unkerlanter peasants. Sabrino did not miss them. For one thing, the hut already boasted a generous oversupply of lice and bedbugs and fleas. For another, the dragonfliers were wearing the furs and leathers in which they rose high with their mounts. Those were warm enough to take the measure of even an Unkerlanter winter.

Sabrino lay down. So did Orosio. The wing commander heard Orosio start to snore. Then weariness and spirits rolled over him like an avalanche, and he heard nothing more for a long time.

When he woke up, he was lying on the floor by the bench. He had no recollection of falling off, but he must have done it. Orosio remained where he'd lain down. He was still snoring, too. The horrible noise made Sabrino wince.

Everything, just then, made Sabrino wince. The fire had died into embers, but even their faint red glow seemed too bright for his eyes. His head throbbed as if eggs were bursting inside it. "Powers above," he muttered. Talking hurt, too. He couldn't remember the last time he'd done such a thorough job of damaging himself with spirits.

He started to crawl toward the jar, then gathered himself, got to his feet, and walked over to it. He poured some spirits—not too much—into his mug and swallowed as if he were swallowing medicine. His outraged stomach tried to rebel, but he sternly refused to let it. After the first dreadful shock, the spirits started cutting into his hangover instead of making it worse.

Had he been an Unkerlanter peasant, he probably would have gone from hangover remedy straight into another drunk.

He was tempted to do that anyway, but shook his head, which also hurt. The blizzard might end. If the dragons hadn't frozen out there, he might have to fly. Flying hung over was painful; he'd done that a few times. Flying drunk . . . Flying drunk was asking to get killed. He might have felt like death, but he didn't feel like dying.

He shook Orosio. The squadron leader groaned, but then went back to snoring. Sabrino shook him again. Orosio opened one eye, which was redder than the embers in the hearth. "Go away," he croaked. His eyelids slid shut again.

"Duty," Sabrino said.

"Futter duty," Orosio answered. "I'm not fit for it, anyway. Can't you see I'm diseased? I need a healer."

"I know what you need." Sabrino poured some more spirits into a mug. It was the one from which he'd drunk, but he wasn't worrying about the niceties just then. And the gurgle and splash got Orosio's attention. The squadron leader opened both eyes. He sat up. When Sabrino held out the mug to him, he took it and gulped the spirits.

"Powers above, that's foul stuff," he said, and then, a moment later, "Let me have some more."

"No." Sabrino shook his head again, which made him wish it would fall off. "The idea is to cure you, not to start you down the slope again."

"Oh, I'm cured," Orosio said in hollow tones. "Into shoe leather, I think. I'm going to swear off spirits forever, or at least until the next time I feel like getting drunk again." He eyed the jar in Sabrino's hand. "A little more?"

"No," Sabrino repeated, and shoved the stopper into the jar again. He sat down beside Orosio: his legs didn't want to hold him up any more. "I didn't take any more for myself than I gave you—enough to take the edge off things, but that's all."

"You're a hard, cruel man, Colonel." Orosio grimaced. "I've got demons ringing bronze bells in my head."

"I know what you mean." With an old man's spraddle-legged shuffle, Sabrino walked to a window. He felt like a very old man just then. When he undid the leather lashings that held the shutter closed, he looked out on swirling white. "The snow hasn't let up."

"Good," Orosio said. "Maybe we'll be somewhere close to human before we have to fly again. Right now, I don't think the undertakers did much of a job embalming me."

"You embalmed yourself, same as I did," Sabrino answered. "I wonder how many men in the wing have gone and done the same."

"Nothing else *to* do in this miserable place," Orosio said. "Nothing to do on this whole front but drink and fly. If we can't fly, that only leaves one thing." He cast a longing eye at the jar of spirits.

"Don't remind me." Sabrino's laugh was half real amusement, half something darker, something grimmer. "When I'm drunk, I keep looking around for my wife to hit, the same as any Unkerlanter peasant would." He laughed again. "I wouldn't really hit Gismonda, mind you; she'd have the law on me in nothing flat. But if Fronesia were here . . ."

"But she's not *your* mistress any more," Orosio said. "Didn't you tell me she'd taken up with a major of footsoldiers?"

"A major, a colonel, something like that." Sabrino made a fist. "Well, my good fellow, what better reason to hit her than that?"

"Ah," Orosio said, again as if Sabrino had offered him a philosophical revelation.

Sabrino wasn't feeling philosophical. He was just feeling battered and abused. The last thing he needed was someone pounding on the door to the hut. He flinched at the racket. So did Orosio. The only way to make it stop was to open the door. When Sabrino did; he marveled at how young and clean-cut the crystallomancer looked. "Well?" he growled—softly.

The crystallomancer seemed oblivious to his fragile condition. He said, "Sir, we've got ten new dragons and ten new dragonfliers coming in as soon as the weather clears enough."

"*Do* we?" Sabrino said, and the youngster nodded. "Ten? Really?" Sabrino asked. The crystallomancer nodded again.

"That's about half the strength we've got here now," Orosio said.

"Aye, and it brings the wing up to something close to half-strength," Sabrino added. Though at the start of the war he'd never imagined it would be, that was something to celebrate. He went back into the hut, poured a mug full of spirits, and thrust it at the crystallomancer. "Here," he said. "Have a drink."

"I'm off to the Boulevard of Horsemen," Krasta said with as much gaiety as she could muster.

Colonel Lurcanio looked up from his paperwork, but not for long. "Try not to buy more than the carriage can carry back here," he told her: even for one of the Algarvian occupiers, he was notably cynical.

"I was hoping one of the lingerie shops might finally have something new," she said.

"Were you?" That got Lurcanio's notice, as Krasta had thought it would. If it hadn't, she would have been offended, and she would have let him know about it, too. He ran his eyes up and down her, as if imagining her in a new negligee, or perhaps being peeled out of a new negligee. "Here's hoping they do."

"If you come to my bedchamber tonight, maybe you'll find out," Krasta purred. "Maybe. If I decide to open the door and let you in." Giggling, she hurried out of his office. "Enjoy your papers," she called from the empty antechamber. No new adjutant had replaced Captain Gradasso, who was off somewhere in the barbarous wilds of Unkerlant.

Krasta's driver greeted the news that he was to take her into Priekule with something less than unrestrained enthusiasm. "Oh, very well, milady," he said. "It'll be a bit, though: I have to get the horses ready." When Krasta went out to the stables, she discovered, not for the first time, that getting the horses ready also involved getting his trusty flask ready.

But he still handled the carriage well enough. So long as that remained true, Krasta didn't care if he drank. He was a commoner, after all, and what were commoners but a pack of drunks?

The lingerie shop had the same wares it had displayed the last time she'd shopped there, a few weeks before—and on her visit before that, too. She'd sneered then. Today she bought a gown of filmy blue silk that would play up her eyes—as well as some other assets. She'd seen it before, aye, but Colonel Lurcanio wouldn't have.

She didn't even harass the shopgirl while making the purchase, which proved she had something on her mind. Carrying the parcel in her hand—the silk folded up into next to nothing—she hurried out of the shop. On the sidewalk, she paused and looked around. Everything looked as normal, and as dreary, as could be.

Shoes clicking on the slates, she hurried off the Boulevard of Horsemen and onto a side street. The blocks of flats there had a look of good breeding even wartime poverty and neglect couldn't mar. People who lived in them were people to be reckoned with. Krasta looked around again. She didn't see any of the people who'd been on the Boulevard when she left the lingerie shop. Satisfied, she ducked into one of the blocks of flats and went up to the third floor.

It'll be the one farthest from the stairs, she reminded herself. The hallway had carpeting thicker and softer than her mansion boasted. She knocked on the door.

Viscount Valnu opened it. "Well, come in, sweetheart," he said, smiling his bright, predatory, skeletally handsome smile. "No one followed you here, I hope?"

"I don't think so," Krasta said, before remembering that trusting him was liable to be even more dangerous than trusting Lurcanio. Hastily she added, "If I don't come back, I've left enough behind in writing to make sure you get what you deserve."

Smiling still, Valnu said, "I don't believe you." Alarm blazed through Krasta, for she was bluffing. Before she could say anything, before she could do anything, Valnu went on: "Before the war, though, you never would have had the wit to come up with the lie—so maybe it isn't a lie. Invasions are so educational, aren't they?"

"I don't know what on earth you're talking about," Krasta snapped.

Valnu laughed. "Well, that sounds more like you. But the question isn't what you don't know. The question is what you do know, and what you intend to do about it."

"I know . . ." Krasta paused and took a deep breath. "I know you're part of the underground, because if you weren't, Count Amatu wouldn't be dead."

"And so?" Valnu asked. "What do you propose to do about that? That Algarvian colonel's been in your bed ever since the redheads marched into Priekule. I don't care to have my name come up in pillow talk, you know."

The parcel Krasta was holding crinkled a little. That reminded her of what was inside the paper. Her cheeks heated. Even so, she said, "If you didn't care to have that happen, you shouldn't have tried molesting me at one party or another—at one party *and* another, I should say."

"Molesting you?" Valnu threw back his head and laughed. "My dear, you didn't seem molested. And who, if I may ask, was doing just what to whom?"

Krasta needed a moment to sort through that, too. Once she did, she put the parcel down on a table and walked right up to Valnu. "The last time we got caught," she said, putting her arms around him, "I was doing something like this." She kissed him.

He didn't respond for a moment. Then, his mouth still joined to hers, he started to laugh, and he kissed her back.

"That's better," she said after a while. "I was starting to wonder if those handsome Algarvian officers were the only ones who mattered to you any more."

"I already said you have a handsome Algarvian officer in your bed," Valnu replied. "Why shouldn't I have some in mine?" He was, as usual, altogether flagrant and altogether unabashed.

"Why?" Krasta said. "I'll show you why." She kissed him again, this time so hard that she tasted blood—hers or his she neither knew nor cared. Whatever his interest in Algarvian officers, she knew she'd excited him in the past. By the bulge in

his trousers, she was exciting him again, too. Now she
laughed in the middle of a kiss, laughed and ground her hips
against him.

"I asked you once, who was molesting whom?" Valnu panted.
His left hand cupped her right buttock; his right squeezed her left
breast.

"Oh, shut up," she told him, and rubbed him with her hand.

Deft and sure, his right hand undid the wooden toggles that
held her tunic closed. He bent to her and teased her nipples with
his tongue. Whatever his interest in Algarvian officers, he remembered how to excite her, too.

She fumbled with his belt. Once she got it unbuckled, she
yanked his trousers down. She fell to her knees in front of him.
But as she began, as one of his hands went to the back of her
head to guide her, he said, "The last time you put your mouth
there, you threw me out of your carriage when you found out a
pretty little shopgirl had done that before you."

"And so?" Krasta rocked forward and back a couple of times.
Valnu's breath sighed out of him. Krasta paused and said, "She
was just a commoner." She returned to what she'd been doing.
His fingers tangled in her hair. His hand urged her forward
again, urged her on. In spite of it, she paused again and looked
up at him. "I presume all your handsome Algarvians were of
noble blood?"

He gaped. Then he laughed. He laughed so hard, he lost the
most obvious evidence of his excitement. "There's no one like
you, is there?" he said.

"I should hope not," Krasta replied indignantly, and set about
repairing the damage. It didn't take long. She hadn't thought it
would.

After a bit, Valnu pulled away. "Shall we go back to the bedchamber?" he asked.

Krasta considered. "No," she said, and pulled him down onto
the floor with her.

She regretted that in short order: thrashing about on the carpet wasn't so comfortable as it would have been on a soft, resilient mattress. But that regret was only a small thing,
especially after Valnu poised himself above her, her thighs

clasping his lean flanks. He had stamina and to spare, and also had the courtesy to help her along with a finger so that she gasped and shuddered and stiffened at the same instant he drove himself deepest into her.

Afterwards, he didn't have the courtesy to keep all his weight on his elbows and knees. That mattered more on a hard floor than it would have in bed, too. "Let me up," Krasta said, and bit him on the shoulder to make sure she got the point across.

"So much for romance," Valnu said, but he did as she asked.

"Romance hasn't got anything to do with getting squashed." Krasta spoke with great conviction. She rubbed her backside. She hadn't noticed the carpet burn while she and Valnu were making love, but she did now.

He started putting on his clothes. As he did up the toggles on his tunic, he asked, "Whose side *are* you on, anyway?"

"Mine, of course," Krasta replied at once. Before she got dressed, she used the privy. As she returned, she asked a question of her own: "Did you expect anything else?"

"I never know what to expect with you, darling," Valnu said, running a comb through his hair. He cocked his head to one side, studying her. "I don't think anyone knows what to expect from you."

"Good," she said, which made him laugh again.

But then he sobered. "Not necessarily," he told her. "You ought to know, you've almost had the same sort of unfortunate accident poor Count Amatu did."

People in the underground have wanted to kill you, was what that meant. Krasta knew she had to keep up a bold front. "Just remember," she said, "that kind of accident wouldn't be unfortunate only for me." Without giving him a chance to answer, she picked up the paper-wrapped parcel and swept out of the flat.

Her driver hadn't drunk himself into a stupor. He touched the brim of his cap when she came up. "Home, milady, or on to more shops?" he asked.

"Home," Krasta said. He nodded and took her there without another word.

Colonel Lurcanio met her in the entrance hall. "I trust you had a successful campaign?" he asked, as if she'd gone to war rather than to the Boulevard of Horsemen.

How much did he know? Was he spying on her? Before, that would only have infuriated her. Now it might be deadly dangerous. As calmly as she could, she answered, "Aye," and held up the parcel as if it were spoils of war.

"Ah." Lurcanio's eyes lit up. "You will have to show me your plunder, then."

"Tonight," Krasta promised, doing her best to sound alluring. Lurcanio was a good lover. She'd first let him into her bed more from fear than for any other reason, but she'd come to want him, too. That wouldn't be so easy tonight, though, not after what had happened in the flat off Priekule's chief shopping boulevard. She sighed, and hoped he didn't notice. The more she wished things were simple, the more complicated they got.

After supper, she went up to her bedchamber and put on the negligee. Lurcanio knocked on her door not much later. When she opened it, he looked her up and down. "A successful campaign indeed," he said, and surprised her by picking her up and carrying her back to the bed.

He surprised her again when his attentions gave her a full share of pleasure, just as Valnu's had. Lazy in the afterglow, she leaned over and kissed him. If she was on her own side and no one else's, she'd won twice today.

Ealstan glared at Pybba. "You don't care," he said bitterly. "You've never cared. She's a Kaunian. As far as you're concerned, the powers below are welcome to her."

The pottery magnate glared back at Ealstan. "Aye, now that you mention it." Before Ealstan could hurl himself at him, Pybba went on: "But you're worth enough to me that I'd do something for her if I could. Only thing is, I can't."

"You haven't tried!" Ealstan exclaimed.

"What exactly do you think I can do?" Pybba asked. "If she's still in Forthweg at all, she's here in Eoforwic in the Kaunian district, right? Some of the guards there are Algarvians. The rest of the whoresons, the Forthwegians, are the ones who're just a step away from Plegmund's Brigade. They don't want to have anything to do with Kaunians except maybe to blaze 'em, and they don't want to have anything to do with me, either. I'm sorry, kid, but what does that leave?"

He didn't sound particularly sorry, and Ealstan knew he wasn't particularly sorry. But Ealstan also knew he had a point . . . or part of a point. "My father says you can always bribe an Algarvian if you go about it the right way."

"Go ahead and try," Pybba said. "Most of the time, your old man'd be right. But they've tightened up about the blonds. They need 'em too bad to want to turn any more of 'em loose." He shrugged. "It's a sign they're in trouble. If you think that breaks my heart, you're daft."

He had a point there, too. Ealstan didn't want to admit it, not when Pybba was talking about Vanai. "But—" he began.

"Shut up," Pybba said flatly. "I've listened for as long as I'm going to listen. Get your arse back to work. What you try by yourself, you try, that's all. But if anything goes wrong, you can bet I'll kill you before the stinking redheads get the chance to squeeze you. You know too bloody much."

"I don't know enough to do what I need to do," Ealstan said, though that wasn't what Pybba meant.

"You didn't know enough to keep from getting the hots for a blond girl," the pottery magnate told him, though that wasn't what he'd meant before, either. Pybba jerked a thumb at the door that led out of his inner office. "Go on. Get out of here. I haven't got the time to waste on you, and you haven't got the time to waste, with all the work piled on your desk."

If Ealstan said he was caught up on his work, Pybba would just give him more. He knew that. He had no choice but to leave. He slammed the door behind him. Pybba only laughed. Plenty of people slammed the door coming out of his office. It was usually a sign he'd got his way.

"Not this time," Ealstan muttered. A couple of people in the outer office glanced at him, but not with any enormous surprise. Plenty of people muttered to themselves coming out of Pybba's office, too.

To make things worse, one of the first items Ealstan had to enter in Pybba's ledgers was the payment the Algarvians had made for another large shipment of Style Seventeen sugar bowls. The potter magnate made plenty of money from the redheads—money he turned around and used against them. But would he do anything for Vanai? Ealstan shook his head. *What you try by yourself, you try, that's all.*

"Powers below eat you," Ealstan whispered. He clenched his fist till his nails bit into the palm of his hand. *I* will *try. And I will get her out, too.*

Mechanically, he worked through the day, as he'd worked through every day since coming home to find Vanai vanished. At last, quitting time came. He hurried out of Pybba's establishment and onto the streets of Eoforwic.

He didn't go straight home. He saw no point in going straight home. Without Vanai there, his flat was only a place to eat and sleep. He didn't want to spend time there, not any more. Spending time there reminded him of what he was missing, and that hurt too much to bear.

Instead, as he often did these days, he hurried to the edge of the Kaunian district. Prominently posted signs outside it declared that any Forthwegians caught inside the district would be blazed without warning. THUS WE THWART THE KAUNIANS' VILE SORCERIES, the signs proclaimed. THEY SEEK TO CONCEAL THEIR EVIL, BUT WE SHALL NOT LET THEM MASQUERADE AS DECENT PEOPLE.

As Forthwegians, was what that meant. Most of the guards patrolling the edge of the quarter were Forthwegians themselves; Pybba had been right about that. He'd also been right that they seemed enthusiastic about their work. Did that make them decent people? Ealstan couldn't see it.

One of the guards saw him. The fellow swung his stick Ealstan's way, not quite pointing it at him but ready to do just that. "You keep sniffing around here," the guard said. "I catch you again, you'll be sorry. You got that?"

"Aye," Ealstan said, and beat a retreat. He cursed and kicked at pebbles all the way back to his flat, wishing each one of them were the guard's face. How could he get into the Kaunian quarter to bring Vanai out when his own countrymen were so determined to keep her and all the other blonds in there till the Algarvians needed them?

Once he got home, he ate bread and olive oil and almonds and a chunk of smoked pork, washing them down with red wine. He hadn't bothered fixing himself anything fancier than that since the redheads had seized Vanai. He probably would have botched things anyhow. He'd never had to learn to cook for himself.

She's going to have a baby, he thought as he washed his few dishes. *Don't the Algarvians care?* Unfortunately, he knew the answer to that only too well.

He thought about pouring himself more wine, about drowning his worries in it. But then he shook his head, as if someone had suggested the idea to him out loud. As far as a lot of Kaunians were concerned, Forthwegians were a bunch of drunks. *I can't afford to get drunk now. If I'm drunk, I know I won't come up with any way to get my wife free.*

The only trouble with that was, even sober he couldn't find any way to get Vanai free. He'd tried and tried, and had no luck. He wandered out of the kitchen and into the front room. Like the bedroom, it had several cheap bookcases filled with secondhand books. Back before Vanai had come up with the spell that let her look like a Forthwegian, she'd had to stay in the flat all the time, with words on paper her only escape from boredom.

Ealstan's eye fell on the slim book called *You Too Can Be a Mage.* He scowled at it. "Miserable, useless thing," he said. Vanai had tried to use a charm in it to make herself look like a Forthwegian. The one time she cast that spell, all she'd accomplished was the opposite of what she'd intended: for a little while, she'd made Ealstan look like a Kaunian.

Fortunately, she'd figured out how to reverse that. But then she'd had to take apart the spell in *You Too Can Be a Mage,* see where the bumbling author must have mistranslated from classical Kaunian into Forthwegian, and reconstruct what the original Kaunian had been. That gave her a spell she could really use, not one that offered hope and then immediately betrayed it.

Ealstan had heard her use the spell dozens of times. With a couple of bits of yarn, he could have cast it himself. But so what? He already looked like a Forthwegian. Turning himself into one wouldn't do him any good.

He took *You Too Can Be a Mage* off the shelf and found the sorcery Vanai had modified. In its original, unchanged form, it would let him look like a Kaunian. For a moment, excitement blazed in him. That would get him into the Kaunian quarter. It would let him see Vanai. It would let him be with her.

But it wouldn't let him bring her out. That was what he needed, above all else. Going into the Kaunian district to keep her company was romantically splendid but altogether useless. All it would accomplish, in the long run—maybe in the not-so-long run—was getting both of them sent west.

"That won't do," he said, as if someone—someone inside himself, perhaps—had suggested it would. The idea wasn't for him to die looking like a Kaunian. The idea was for Vanai to live looking like a Forthwegian . . . or whatever else she had to look like to go on living. Ealstan nodded. He did clearly see what had to be done. He was the practical son of a practical father. Hestan would never have wasted time on a futile romantic gesture, either.

Fair enough, Ealstan thought. *I see what doesn't work. What does, though?* The Algarvians had set things up so that no Forthwegians could go into the Kaunian quarter and no Kaunians could pass out of it into the rest of Eoforwic—not unless they seized them and took them to the ley-line caravan depot. Their system wasn't slipshod, as it had been before. These days, they couldn't afford to waste Kaunians. With the war in Unkerlant not going well, they needed every blond they could catch and hold.

No Forthwegians inside. No Kaunians outside. Ealstan hurled *You Too Can Be a Mage* across the room. He slammed his fist down on the little table in front of the sofa on which he sat. Pain blazed up his arm. That left . . . nothing.

There has to be something. He shook his head. He wanted there to be something. That didn't mean it had to be. How many Kaunians had thought there had to be something? How many of those

Kaunians were dead now? Too cursed many. Ealstan knew that.

Wearily, he got to his feet and picked up *You Too Can Be a Mage*. The pages were almost ready to part company with the binding: this wasn't the first time he or Vanai had flung the book. With a curse, Ealstan put it back on the shelf.

"There has to be something." He said it aloud, even if he'd already figured out it wasn't true. The redheads had closed off every possibility involving Forthwegians and Kaunians, and what else was there? "Nothing. Not a stinking thing." He said that aloud, too, to remind himself not to be a fool. Then he went to bed.

When he woke up, he was smiling. At first, still half asleep, he didn't understand why. But as full awareness came, the smile only got broader. He knew what he had to do. A moment later, he paused and shook his head. He knew what he had to try. It might not work. If it didn't work, he was ruined. But if it did, he had a chance.

His breakfast was much the same as his supper had been, only with olives as a relish instead of almonds. He hurried downstairs, hurried out of the block of flats, hurried to the pottery works, hurried into Pybba's sanctum.

He'd been sure the pottery magnate would be there before him. And he'd been right. Pybba sat behind his desk, sorting through papers and muttering unhappily to himself. He looked up at Ealstan with no great liking. "What do you want?"

Before answering, Ealstan closed the door behind him. Pybba's eyebrows rose. They rose higher when Ealstan told him exactly what he wanted.

"You're out of your bloody mind, boy," the pottery magnate said when he was through.

"Probably," Ealstan agreed. "Can you get it for me? No— I'm sure you can. *Will* you get it for me?"

"I'd be crazy if I did," Pybba answered. Ealstan folded his arms across his chest and waited. Pybba said, "Anything goes wrong . . ." and sliced his thumb across his throat. Ealstan didn't move. Then Pybba said, "Odds are I'd be well rid of you anyhow," and Ealstan knew he had won.

Ukmerge had one park—or, at least, Skarnu hadn't been able to find more than one. In winter, with the weather cold and the grass dead and the trees bare-branched, not so many people came there. He could still walk through it, though, or sit down on one of the benches without drawing notice from the constables, if he came at noon. Even in the wintertime, some workers escaped from the nearby shoe manufactory to eat their dinners in the park.

The air stank of leather. In Ukmerge, the air stank of leather so much that Skarnu had almost stopped noticing it. Almost. He still found himself wrinkling his nose every now and again.

Most of the benches in the park faced a broad expanse of bare ground without trees, without even much in the way of dead grass. "Did something used to be here?" Skarnu asked the underground leader who called himself "Tytuvenai" after his hometown one noontime. "Something worth looking at, I mean?"

"Tytuvenai" nodded. "An arch from the days of the Kaunian Empire. The Algarvians put eggs under it and knocked it down, same as they did with the Column of Victory in Priekule, same as they've done all over Valmiera—all over Jelgava, too, if half what we hear from there is true."

"Powers below eat them," Skarnu growled. "They're trying to make us forget our Kaunianity."

"Aye, no doubt," "Tytuvenai" said. "They're trying to make themselves forget it, too—that we were civilized while they were just woodscrawlers. But that's not why I asked you to meet me here today."

"No, eh?" Skarnu tried to imagine what the arch had looked like. He had no trouble getting a general idea; he'd seen plenty of imperial monuments in Priekule and elsewhere. But he didn't know what this one had been for, what reliefs and statuary and inscriptions it had borne. He wouldn't be able to find out now, either. Nor would anyone else. That growl still in his voice, he said, "Maybe it should have been."

"Maybe." "Tytuvenai" didn't sound convinced. He explained why: "One of these days, when we have time, we'll worry about arches and columns and tombs. We don't have that kind of time now. We've got to worry about putting the Algarvians in tombs, and keeping them from putting any more of us into them. Isn't that more important than old marble and granite?"

"I suppose so," Skarnu said grudgingly. "It's more urgent, anyhow. Whether urgent is the same thing as important is something we can argue about another day."

"It's something we'd better argue about another day," "Tytuvenai" told him. "I called you here to ask if you were ready to get back to work."

"Ah," Skarnu said. That certainly was more urgent than marble. As his comrade had done, he got straight down to business: "Here in Ukmerge? What have you got in mind, planting eggs inside the shoe manufactories?"

"You laugh," "Tytuvenai" said, and he was smiling himself. "If you knew how many shoes this town's made for Mezentio's men, you'd laugh out of the other side of your mouth, believe you me you would. It'd be a shrewd blow against the Algarvians. If we can bring it off, it *will* be a shrewd blow against the Algarvians. But it isn't what we have in mind for you."

"What *do* you have in mind for me?" Skarnu knew he sounded relieved. The shoe manufactories, the whole town of Ukmerge, oppressed him almost as badly as they did Merkela. He would have loved to see the manufactories go up in smoke, but he didn't want to have anything to do with them himself.

"You'll know, better than most, how the Algarvians will bring Kaunians from Forthweg through Valmiera down to the coast of the Strait when they want to strike a sorcerous blow against Lagoas or Kuusamo," "Tytuvenai" said.

Skarnu's answering nod was grim. "Aye, I know about that. I'd better. I sabotaged one of those ley-line caravans before it could get where it was going, and a lot of those Kaunians escaped before the redheads got the chance to sacrifice them." He spoke with more than a little pride.

"Tytuvenai" nodded, too. "Aye, I'd heard that. And when you
find a Valmieran who's disappeared, a Valmieran who's got
'Night and Fog' scrawled on his doorway, he's off to be sacrificed, too. The Algarvians want it to seem like a mystery, but
that's what happens."

"Is it?" Skarnu said, and the other underground leader nodded again. Skarnu went on. "I didn't know that, but I'd be lying
if I said I was surprised. You still haven't told me what it's got
to do with me, though, or what you want me to do about it."

"I'm coming to that," "Tytuvenai" said. "Not so long ago, in
spite of everything we could do, the redheads got a couple of
caravanloads of Kaunians from Forthweg down to the coast,
out about as far east as they could go. It's pretty plain they were
aiming their sacrifice at Kuusamo, not Lagoas. And they made
the cursed sacrifice, and they stole the Kaunians' life energy,
and they used it to power their stinking sorcery, and . . . something went wrong."

"Good!" Skarnu exclaimed. "What happened? Did one of
their mages botch the spell, so that it came down on their own
heads? By the powers above, that'd be sweet—and fitting, too."

But now "Tytuvenai" shook his head. "That was our first
guess. It doesn't seem to be so, though, not from the way the
Algarvians have been running around down there by the sea
like so many ants whose anthill just got kicked. No, what it
looks like is, they made the sacrifice—made the murders—and
cast the spell, and everything went just the way it was supposed to . . . except that the Kuusamans somehow turned the
spell around and made it land on the redheads who'd cast it: either that, or they had a counterspell waiting that was even more
potent."

"How could they?" Skarnu asked. Then, one obvious—and
dreadful—possibility occurred to him. "Are they sacrificing
people for the sake of their life energy, too, the way the Unkerlanters are doing?"

"No." "Tytuvenai" spoke with great certainty. "They *aren't*
doing that, powers above be praised. If they were, we'd know
about it. The mages say they can feel those sacrifices, and they
haven't felt anything like that out of Kuusamo. But the Ku-

usamans threw back whatever Mezentio's men sent them, and
the Algarvians are jumping out of their kilts trying to figure out
how."

"Mmm, I can see why they would be," Skarnu said. "If
there's something out there that can master their magecraft,
that's got to be plenty to set them shivering and shaking."

"Now you're getting the idea," the other underground
leader said. "We're going to send you there, you and Palasta,
to see if you can't make them shiver and shake a little
harder."

"Palasta?" Skarnu knew he'd heard the name before, but
where? Then he remembered. "Oh. The little mage who hid my
trail when the Algarvians were after Merkela and Gedominu
and me in Erzvilkas."

"That's right," "Tytuvenai" said. "I know she looks like she'd
blow away in a strong breeze, but she's as good as we've got:
the best."

"All right," Skarnu said. "I won't be sorry to see the last of
Ukmerge, and I'd be a liar if I said anything different. And
Merkela will be even happier to get away from here than I am."

A bell rang in the nearby shoe manufactory. The workers
who'd been eating their dinners in the park hurried away. If
they weren't back before the bell rang again, they might lose
their positions. All at once, Skarnu and "Tytuvenai" seemed
conspicuous. Skarnu looked around nervously. He saw no constables, Algarvian or Valmieran. He relaxed—a little.

And then he noticed the expression "Tytuvenai" was wearing. The other man didn't say anything, but he didn't have to.
Skarnu did it for him: "You don't want Merkela to come along
with me."

"Well, now that you mention it, no," "Tytuvenai" admitted.
"I don't see what she can do to help you once you get down
there. And the redheads will be looking for a fellow traveling
with his wife and baby, not for somebody with a girl who could
be his almost-grown daughter or his kid sister. Everybody
would be better off if Merkela stayed behind."

"Everybody except her and me," Skarnu pointed out.

"Tytuvenai" shrugged. "This is still a war. Back before our

army fell apart, you went where you were ordered and you did what you were told, and you didn't think twice about any of it. Now you've got a new set of orders, my lord Marquis. Will you follow them, or won't you?"

"It's not the same," Skarnu said. In a certain sense, that was true. The formal structure of the Valmieran army no longer existed. Back in the days when he was a captain, his colonel had had authority to give him orders that they both recognized. "Tytuvenai" didn't. He could request. But he wasn't Skarnu's superior officer. He couldn't command, not unless Skarnu let him.

Despite that, the other man from the underground had weapons, had them and didn't hesitate to use them: "I'm not asking for myself, you know. This is for the sake of the kingdom. This is for the sake of the war."

"Curse you," Skarnu said wearily; he had no good argument against that. He pointed a finger at "Tytuvenai." "I'm going to bargain with you."

In the Valmieran army, that would have got him cashiered. "Tytuvenai" just nodded and said, "Go on."

"First, before I disappear, I'm going to go back to the flat and say good-bye," Skarnu said. He knew what "Tytuvenai" would say to that, and forestalled him: "I know better than to tell her where I'm going or what I'll be doing."

"All right," the other man said mildly. "But 'first' has 'second' on its trail. What else do you want?"

"Get Merkela and the baby out of Ukmerge," Skarnu answered. "She can't stand it here, and I can't say I blame her. Find her some place out in the country where she can stay. She's lived on a farm all her life. She's going crazy, cooped up in a flat. Do that and . . ." He sighed. "Do that and I'm your man."

"Agreed," "Tytuvenai" said at once. "There. You see how easy that was?"

"Futter you," Skarnu said. "Tytuvenai" laughed.

Except for having to climb out of his cot earlier than he would have liked, Bembo faced each new day in Gromheort with more zest that he would have imagined possible when he came west from Tricarico. As his unhappy leave back in Algarve had reminded him, he felt more at home here these days than he did in his own hometown.

Of course, constables back in Tricarico didn't get rich. Plenty of graft came their way, aye, but it was all petty graft: constables just weren't important enough to get any more. Things were different here in occupied Forthweg. Here, Algarvian constables often held the power of life and death over Forthwegians and Kaunians. Even with dour, brutal Oraste for a partner, Bembo had done amazingly well for himself.

He found himself grinning at Oraste as they queued up for rolls and olive oil and red wine for breakfast. "No, this isn't such a bad place after all," he said.

Oraste only grunted. He wasn't at his best before he'd had something to eat, and especially before he'd had something to drink. *He's not always at his best after he's had something to eat and something to drink, either,* Bembo thought, and his grin got wider.

"What's so fornicating funny?" Oraste demanded.

"Er—nothing." Bembo didn't want to quarrel with his partner. In a brawl, Oraste would tear him in two with no remorse and with no great effort.

"Better not be," Oraste said. He then clamped his jaw shut till he'd got his food and his wine. Bembo kept quiet, too, though he liked to talk. Intimidation cast almost as powerful a spell as magecraft. Only after Oraste had gulped down his wine and gone back for a second mug did he speak again: "That's more like it."

Bembo sipped from his own mug. He smacked his lips together, as if he were a connoisseur. "We can afford better, you know. Powers above, we can afford anything we want." He blinked. Back in Tricarico, he'd never imagined being able to say anything like that. But it was true.

Oraste grunted again. "Well, so what?" he answered. "I still say we should've turned in that Hestan item. He's trouble. He'll go on being trouble."

"Aye, no doubt," Bembo said. "But if we had turned him in, what would he have done? Paid off somebody else, that's what,

and you know it as well as I do. Go on—tell me I'm wrong."
Oraste let out one more grunt. Bembo wagged a finger at him.
"See? You can't do it. That's how the world works. And since
that's how the world works, I'd sooner see his money in my belt
pouch than anybody else's. The clowns who give us orders have
too much money already."

One of Oraste's eyebrows twitched—not much, but enough
for Bembo to notice. He glanced back over his shoulder. One of
the people who gave him orders, Sergeant Pesaro, was heading
his way. Fortunately, the fat sergeant couldn't have heard him;
he'd had the sense to keep his voice down. Had Pesaro ever
found out how much his two constables had squeezed out of
Hestan, he would have demanded a good-sized cut.

A large, meaty hand fell on Bembo's shoulder, another on
Oraste's. "I want to see you boys in my office as soon as you're
done with breakfast," Sergeant Pesaro said, and then went on
his way, his big belly wobbling as he walked.

Alarm and anger blazed through Bembo. "Oh, that son of a
whore!" he whispered fiercely. "That stinking son of a whore!
He knows, I bet. If that turd of a Hengist rang the bell on us,
he's going to be one dead Forthwegian."

But Oraste, whose temper was usually shorter than Bembo's,
shook his head. "I don't think he knows anything," he said—
not the first time he'd expressed such sentiments about Pesaro.
Now, though, he amplified them: "Look. He's picking on other
pairs, too."

"Probably going to shake down everybody." Bembo's voice
remained bitter, as if he'd never shaken down anybody. But if
Pesaro did have the goods on him, he knew he'd have to fork
over: getting your sergeant angry at you wasn't much different
from having the powers below eat you.

Along with the other constables, Bembo and Oraste trooped
into Pesaro's office. They crowded it to the point of overflow-
ing; it was none too big to begin with. Sitting behind his rickety
desk, Pesaro seemed almost trapped. "What's up, Sergeant?"
somebody asked—Bembo couldn't see who.

He had trouble seeing Pesaro, too. But the sergeant never
had any trouble making himself heard. He said, "I'll tell you

what's up. What's up is, they need more people to hold the lid on over in Eoforwic. There's a real live nasty Kaunian underground on the loose there, and Forthwegian rebels, and the Unkerlanters have been sending dragons over the place. And so you men are heading west. There's a ley-line caravan leaving from the depot here an hour before noon. You're all going to be on it."

"Eoforwic?" Half the constables in the crowded little office, Bembo among them, howled out the name of the Forthwegian capital in protest. But their hearts weren't in it—or at least Bembo's wasn't. He didn't much feel like packing up and going, but one Forthwegian town was likely to be much like another.

For any of the constables who didn't understand that, Sergeant Pesaro spelled it out: "Anybody who doesn't care for the idea can go put on a different uniform and get shipped a lot farther west than Eoforwic."

Protest was cut off as if sliced by a knife. Nobody wanted to go fight in Unkerlant. Soldiers coming through Gromheort cursed the constables and envied them their soft jobs. Bembo didn't envy the soldiers theirs, which were anything but soft.

Into the sudden silence, Sergeant Pesaro said, "That's better. You will be on Platform Three at the depot by an hour before noon. No excuses—not a chance. Anybody who misses the caravan *will* go straight to Unkerlant, and that's a promise. Don't bring anything more than you can carry, either. Questions?"

"Why did you pick *us*, Sergeant?" someone asked.

"Because you're so sweet," Pesaro growled. "Any more questions?" After that, there were none. Pesaro waved a hand. "Dismissed."

Bembo went back into the barracks and started loading a duffel bag. It got full long before he'd gone through everything around his cot. Cursing, he started editing his earthly goods. He needed three tries before finally deciding he could do no better. Even then, the canvas sack left him panting and sweating by the time he'd lugged it to the caravan depot.

"What have you got in there?" demanded the Algarvian who checked his name off a list.

"Your wife," Bembo snarled. He and the fellow with a clip-board cursed each other till, grunting with effort, he hauled the duffel bag onto the caravan car.

Oraste was already aboard. His sack held about a quarter as much as Bembo's. "Have you got everything you need?" he asked.

"No," Bembo said. He would have flung his bag against the wall of the car, but it was too heavy to fling. He eased it over there and flung himself into a seat. Oraste, who laughed at very little, laughed at him. Bembo petulantly glared at his partner till the ley-line caravan glided west out of Gromheort.

Before long, he was in country he'd never seen before. He took a while to realize it; the countryside didn't look much different from that around Gromheort. Fields with growing wheat and barley slid past his window. So did groves of olives and al-monds and citrus fruit. And so did villages full of whitewashed houses, some with red tile roofs, others—more and more as he got farther west—with roofs of thatch.

War had touched the countryside only lightly. Peasants went about their business as they had when King Penda ruled Forth-weg. As the ley-line cara-van passed through towns—it stopped three or four times to pick up more constables—the ruined buildings nobody had bothered to repair stood out much more noticeably, as they did in Gromheort. Once the caravan got into the territory Unkerlant had occupied before Algarve went to war with her, the wreckage got fresher and worse. King Swem-mel's men had fought hard every inch of the way.

Eoforwic surprised Bembo, who said, "I didn't think this miserable excuse for a kingdom had such a big city."

"It's still full of Forthwegians," Oraste replied with a shrug. "Them and Kaunians." He made as if to spit on the floor of the caravan car, but reluctantly thought better of it. When the car stopped at the depot, he shouldered his sack and hurried out. Bembo's duffel bag hadn't got any lighter while it lay there. Swearing, bent almost double under it, he followed his partner onto the platform.

Another cheerful fellow with a clipboard checked his name

off a list. Then the other Algarvian said, "We've got carriages waiting for you people, to take you to your barracks."

"Oh, powers above be praised!" Bembo said fervently. "I was afraid I'd have to walk." He carried his duffel bag with jauntier style, not least because he knew he wouldn't have to carry it far. They did things with class here in the capital.

That impression lasted till he got to the barracks, which were every bit as crowded and gloomy as the ones in Gromheort. He got an iron cot in the middle of a room full of constables—a room full, mostly, of strangers.

Someone called his name in a loud voice. "Here," he answered, and then, seeing the pips on the other constables' shoulder boards, "Here, Sergeant." He wondered what sort of a new boss he was getting.

"I'm Folicone," the sergeant said. He was younger and skinnier than Pesaro. Of course, even Bembo was skinnier than Pesaro, so that didn't say much. Folicone went on, "I'm going to partner you with Delminio here." He nodded toward a constable whose cot stood only a couple of spaces away from Bembo's.

"Pleased to meet you," Delminio said, and clasped wrists with Bembo. He wore bushy red side whiskers, and mustachios and chin beard waxed to spikes.

"Pleased to meet you, too," Bembo answered. But then he turned to Folicone and said, "Sergeant, Oraste and I, we've been partners a long time, you know what I mean?"

"And maybe you will be again, in a while," Sergeant Folicone said. "But I want you with somebody who knows the ropes here while you're breaking in."

That made too much sense for Bembo to argue with it. He nodded and said, "No offense," to Delminio.

"It's all right," Delminio answered. "Getting a new partner is a funny business. I know that." He eyed Bembo the same way Bembo was eyeing him. *What sort of partner will you be?* "You want to go into the Kaunian quarter with me?" Delminio asked. He hesitated. "You do know about the business with the Kaunians?"

"Oh, aye," Bembo said, and Delminio visibly relaxed. Bembo added, "I'm not what you'd call happy about it, but what can you do? It's wartime."

"Sounds like you've got some sense," Delminio said. Sergeant Folicone nodded. Bembo beamed. He'd made a good first impression. Delminio went on, "Just come with me. The quarter isn't far."

Bembo went past the same sorts of warning signs he would have seen in Gromheort. The Kaunian district here looked much the same as Gromheort's, too, though it was larger. He watched Kaunian women's backsides, as the blonds went around in trousers. So did Delminio. They noticed each other doing it, and they both grinned. "I think I can manage here," Bembo said. His new partner nodded. Bembo wondered if he could find a Kaunian wench for himself. It might not be too hard.

Up till the time when the redheads swept through the Kaunian quarter of Eoforwic, Vanai had been through only one roundup. And back then, she hadn't even known what the Algarvian constables were doing when they took Kaunians out of Oyngestun. They'd told soothing lies then: they'd said they were sending people west as laborers. Some of her fellow villagers had even gone with them of their own free will.

It wasn't like that any more. The surviving Kaunians knew the Algarvians wanted them for one thing and one thing only: their life energy. And so, when the redheads swarmed into the Kaunian district, the blonds did their best to hide.

The roundup, of course, came without warning. Anyone the hunters caught on the street was simply nabbed and grabbed and hauled away. But the captured Kaunians' cries of despair and the Algarvians' shouts of triumph warned others of the raid. Like any hunted animals, most of the Kaunians who weren't caught in the open had holes in which to hide.

Vanai was no exception. After she was captured and brought into the Kaunian district, she'd expected something like this to happen sooner or later—probably sooner. And so she'd gone exploring in the block of flats where the redheads had put her.

Waiting quietly in her flat for them to come get her and take her away . . . She shook her head. *By the powers above, I'm not going to make it easy for them,* she thought.

Exploring had been easier because so many of the flats stood empty. She didn't like to think about that. But it gave her a lot more choices than she would have had otherwise.

She'd found a good spot in a vacant ground-floor flat: a closet that had a lot more room than it seemed to, and one where a searcher peering in, even with a lamp, wouldn't be able to spy her. He would have to step all the way into the closet to notice it took an unexpected dogleg. Whoever'd made it that way might have had a hidey-hole in mind.

When the first terrified cries rang out, Vanai knew at once what they meant, what they had to mean. She wasted not an instant. She had to get downstairs and into her hiding place before constables started swarming through the building. If she didn't, she was ruined. The baby she carried made her awkward and slow, but she forced herself to hurry downstairs anyhow.

More Kaunians, many more, were going up than down. "You fool, it's death on the streets!" a man said as she pushed past him, moving against the tide.

He was bound to be right, of course. But Vanai wasn't heading for the streets, though she didn't say so. She burst out of the stairwell and went down the hallway toward that empty flat at a lumbering trot.

Just outside the open door, panic nearly froze her. *What if someone else has found this place, too? It won't hold two, and I won't have time to go looking anywhere else.*

Almost moaning in terror, she dashed back to the closet. No one cried out in fear even greater than hers, believing her to be one of the hunters rather than the hunted. And no one shouted for her to go away, either. She still had the place to herself.

"Powers above be praised," she gasped, making herself as comfortable as she could in the little hidden niche.

Only then did another bad thought strike her: if this hiding place was so splendid, why did this flat stand empty? The red-heads must have caught whoever had been living here before.

Would constables come casually walking in, check the closet, and take her away? She couldn't run, not any more. It was too late for that.

Footsteps in the hallway and loud Algarvian voices said she had indeed made her choice. Now she would have to live—or die—with it. "Miserable blonds," a man growled, his voice sounding as if it came from right outside the doorway to the flat in which she cowered. "Finding the lousy buggers is getting to be like pulling teeth."

"We've got to do it, though," another Algarvian answered. He might have been talking about any hard, not particularly pleasant job . . . till he went on, "The Forthwegians here won't miss them, anyhow."

"Well, of course they won't," the first constable said, as if his friend were belaboring the obvious. And then that first redhead's voice came from *inside* the flat: "Let's see what we've got here." Vanai shivered. She forced herself to stop—it might make a noise. She tried not even to breathe.

"Not bloody likely we'll flush anybody out of this place—Kaunians usually like to run upstairs, not hide down low." The second Algarvian spoke now as the voice of experience.

"I know, I know," his pal said. "We've got to go through the motions, though." A piece of furniture went over with a crash. The Algarvian grunted. "Nothing there. Let me check this closet here, and then we can go on upstairs, like you said."

He spoke his last few words just outside the closet where Vanai hid. The baby growing inside her chose that moment to kick. The unexpected motion within her made her want to jump. It made her want to scream. She did neither. She bit down hard on her lower lip and waited in dark, dusty silence.

Then she wanted to scream again; for the silence, while it remained dusty, was no longer so dark. That Algarvian had a lamp, which he used to illuminate as much of the closet as he could from the entrance to it. Just for a moment, light touched the tip of Vanai's right shoe. She started to jerk it back, but checked herself. Motion and sound could betray her, too.

"Anything?" the second Algarvian asked.

"Doesn't look like it," the first one answered. The hateful light receded. "Now we can go on upstairs and get down to business."

"Right," his friend said. "Here, I'll paint a cross on the front door to keep anybody else from wasting his time." The two sets of footsteps receded.

I'm safe, Vanai thought dizzily. *For a little while, I'm safe.* Now she could shake. Once she started, she discovered she had a hard time stopping.

And, just because she'd escaped the roundup for the time being didn't mean the other Kaunians in the block of flats were so lucky. She heard Algarvians hauling them downstairs, heard men cursing and begging, heard women shrieking in despair. Neither curses nor pleas nor shrieks had the slightest effect on the constables, except to annoy them. Then Vanai heard bludgeons striking flesh—which, if they didn't quiet the curses and pleas, did turn them to shrieks.

"Well, that's not a bad bag," one Algarvian said to another in the ground-floor hallway.

"Not too bad, anyhow," his companion agreed. "How close to quota are we?"

"How should I know?" the first man answered. "You think our officers tell me anything more than they tell you?"

"Fat chance," the second man said. "Screw 'em all."

They're just doing their job, Vanai thought again. *They don't much like the people who give them the work, but they do it. How can they? I don't understand. Could anyone understand?*

Silence returned. Vanai didn't dare move. They'd said they were done with this block of flats, but had all of them left? If she came out before they had, she was sure they would be happy enough to scoop her up. How would she know? When could she be sure? She shook her head. She couldn't be sure. When would she have to take a chance?

She wished she had some way to gauge things inside the closet. She feared her guesses weren't worth much. It already seemed as if she'd been trapped inside here forever.

She was about to come out and see if she could sneak upstairs when she heard new voices in the hallway. An Algarvian spoke in his own language: "Look at the crosses on the doorways, sir. They've already searched this building."

The fellow who answered did so with aristocratic scorn: "You are looking with your eyes. I look with more than that. I look with senses you haven't got. And I shall find what you've missed, too—you wait and see."

A mage, Vanai thought, with terror dulled only because she'd already been through so much other terror. She wasn't warded. She hadn't imagined she would need to be warded. If he started incanting—no, *when* he started incanting—she was ruined. *It's not fair.* That was probably true, but it would do her no good at all.

Out in the street—Vanai thought it was out in the street, anyhow—a shout rang out: the same word, repeated over and over. Hidden in the blind dogleg closet, she couldn't make out what the word was. Neither could the Algarvian mage. "How am I supposed to concentrate with this racket?" he snapped, his voice peevish.

"You don't need to concentrate, sir," the constable with him answered. "They're yelling that they've got their quota. They don't need any more blonds this time around."

"Oh," the mage said. "Is that so? Well, if I don't have to work, I'm bloody well not going to work. That's fair enough—better than fair enough, by the powers above." He began to whistle. His footsteps, along with those of the constable who'd come into the block of flats with him, faded in the distance as the two men left again.

Vanai didn't move for a long time. By then, she wasn't sure she *could* move. At last, a bladder that threatened to burst drove her to her feet.

She came out of the closet ever so cautiously. She came out of the flat even more cautiously. When she saw someone come up the stairs and into the block of flats, she almost jumped out of her skin. But it was only another Kaunian. He waved to her. "So I'm not the only one they missed here, eh?" he said, sounding more cheerful than he had any business doing. "Well, good."

He saw Vanai, who'd survived the roundup, and resolutely didn't see all the people who hadn't. She couldn't think like that.

When she went back up to her flat, she found that the Algarvians had turned it inside out. She wasn't upset; she'd expected nothing less. She had little that could be broken, and even less that she minded losing. Before long, she had the flat set to rights again.

And, before long, just as if the roundup hadn't happened, bells clanged in the Kaunian quarter, summoning the blonds who'd come through uncaught to get their food so they could stay strong and healthy till the Algarvians needed more of them. Vanai didn't go, in case it turned out to be another trap, another betrayal. The Algarvians who'd gone through the flat had been after her person, not the couple of small chunks of stale bread and dried fruit she'd secreted there. She didn't have a lot to eat, but she had some.

As she nibbled a dried apricot, she looked out the window and down onto the street below. Not many Kaunians could have escaped in this neighborhood, but she saw a fair number of people heading for the feeding stations the Algarvians had set up. She grimaced. *If they're that stupid, they deserve to be caught.* Then she grimaced again, this time at herself. *Why do they deserve to get caught for having empty stomachs?*

And then she spotted the Algarvian constable who came down the street chatting up every young woman who passed. She muttered the foulest curses she knew, and wished she knew worse ones. Even though she couldn't hear him, she could guess what he'd be saying. *Come with me, sweetheart. Give me what I want, and you won't go west*: the same sort of vicious bargain Major Spinello had struck with her back in Oyngestun. The redheads were great ones for deals like that. Vanai shrank back from the window, lest he see her. When she peeked out again, a few minutes later, he was gone. She let out a long, heartfelt sigh of relief.

Five

Night in the Strait of Valmiera: a nasty night, with rain and even a little sleet beating down. Wind-whipped waves slapped against the *Habakkuk*'s port side as she slid north along a ley line toward the Derlavaian mainland. Secure in the bowels of the great, sorcerously enhanced iceberg, Leino hardly noticed the motion.

When the Kuusaman mage remarked on that, Xavega raised a scornful, elegant eyebrow. "In a *proper* ley-line ship, we would not feel the waves at all," she said, using classical Kaunian as he had. "We would glide above the water, and not be subject to it." She didn't add, *You ignorant Kuusaman oaf,* but she might as well have.

Leino sighed and didn't answer. *Why did my fancy fix on someone who despises me and all my people?* he wondered. One of his own eyebrows quirked, in wry amusement. *Because I've been away from Pekka too long, that's why. And because Xavega packs her bile in such a nicely shaped container.*

Ramalho was every bit as Lagoan as Xavega, but he shook his head. "In a *proper* ley-line ship, those waves might capsize us or push us off the ley line and then sink us," he said. "Plenty of hulks on the bottom of the sea hereabouts, and not all of them from the days when ships went by sail."

Xavega glared at him. She didn't just disagree with Leino; she was ready to take on the whole world. "What do you know about it?" she demanded of Ramalho.

"Before the war, I was a ship's mage," he said calmly. "My father spent some time as a ship's mage, and so did his father before him. I might ask you the same question."

He might ask it, but Xavega didn't answer it. She just tossed her head, sending wavy, copper-colored locks flying back from her face, and went over to the tea kettle to pour herself a fresh cup. She slammed the kettle back onto its iron stand almost hard enough to shatter it.

"Rain is a worse nuisance for *Habakkuk* than for ordinary ships," Leino said, trying to find something the mages could talk about without quarreling. "We always have to work to keep the sea from melting us, but worrying about the air, too, makes the sorcery twice as complicated."

"Well, that is true enough," Ramalho said. Xavega just sniffed and sipped at her tea. She couldn't very well argue with what Leino had said, but she didn't care to agree with it, either. Ramalho went on: "If we sailed *Habakkuk* into Setubal harbor back in the days of the Six Years' War, all the mages in Lagoas would be going mad trying to figure out how we have done all this."

"Now, there is a picture," Leino said, rather liking it. "The same would have been true in Kuusamo a generation ago—or, for that matter, any time before the Derlavaian War started."

"A picture of nonsense," Xavega said. "A daft conceit." Ramalho had offered the conceit, but she sounded as if she blamed Leino for it.

With another sigh Leino said, "I hope the dragonfliers will be able to leave the ship in this weather." How would Xavega take exception to that?

"The storm will help shield them from the Algarvians," she said, which *was* disagreement, but of a relatively tepid sort. She continued, "Dowsers start tearing their hair when they have to find moving dragons in the midst of millions of moving raindrops."

"True," Leino said.

"Also less true than it would have been in the days of the Six Years' War, though," Ramalho said. "Our motion-selectivity spells are much better than they used to be."

Leino waited for Xavega to start squabbling about that, too. Instead, to his astonishment, she burst into tears. "No one ever lets me say anything without arguing!" she wailed, and fled the chamber in which they'd been sitting.

"What on earth—?" Leino said to Ramalho.

"I was hoping you might explain it to me," the Lagoan mage answered. "You are the married man, after all. Does that not mean you understand more of women than we bachelors do?"

"I understand my wife fairly well, I think," Leino said. "Understanding one woman, though, does not mean I understand all women, any more than understanding one man means I understand all men."

"Too bad," Ramalho said. "I was hoping it would be simpler than that." He shrugged and rolled his eyes. "Of course, asking anyone to understand Xavega is probably asking too much."

"Ah?" Leino said, his voice as neutral as he could make it. "I wondered if it was just me."

"Oh, no," Ramalho assured him. "She can be difficult. In fact, there are times when I wonder if she can be anything else. I knew her in Setubal, and she was the same way there."

"Was she?" Leino asked. Ramalho nodded solemnly. Leino said, "How interesting," and left the icy chamber.

Interesting, he jeered at himself as he walked down an equally icy corridor. *Is that really the word you want to use? The woman is trouble, nothing else but. Even if you got her into bed, she'd be nothing but trouble. She'd be more trouble then, most likely. The only reason you care about her is the way she looks.*

And isn't that reason enough? a different, rather deeper, part of his mind asked in return.

He shook his head, as if he were arguing with someone else and not with himself. *No, it isn't,* he insisted. *Pekka would laugh at you if she knew you were mooning over a bad-tempered Lagoan, just because she has long, shapely legs and fills out her tunic nicely.*

That deeper part of his mind didn't answer. Maybe that meant he'd convinced it. Somehow, he didn't think so. Those legs and the way Xavega filled out her tunic stayed with him no matter how bad-tempered she was. Aye, Pekka would laugh at him, but Pekka wasn't a man.

And a good thing, too, he thought. There, at least, both parts of his mind agreed completely.

He headed toward one of the chambers where the mages worked to keep *Habakkuk* going—as opposed to the chambers where they gathered when they weren't working. He wasn't due back on duty for another couple of hours, but he had the feeling they would welcome him if he came in early. Rain really did put a lot of extra strain on *Habakkuk*'s structural integrity, and he'd done a lot of work while the ship was building to find out how best to foil the raindrops.

He'd almost got there when the iceberg-turned-dragon-hauler jerked and shuddered under his feet, as if it had run into a wall. The next thing he knew, he was on his backside in the hallway and all the lights had gone out. Somewhere in the distance, an urgent bell began clanging.

"What in blazes—?" Leino exclaimed as he scrambled to his feet, his spiked shoes biting into the ice. He laughed at himself once upright again. He was a true mage, all right: even then, he'd spoken in classical Kaunian. All around him, though, men and women were crying out in Lagoan and Kuusaman. Pain filled some of those cries. He realized he was liable to be lucky to have come away with nothing worse than a bruised bottom.

He hadn't thought about why something as immense as *Habakkuk* might stagger in midocean. That also proved him a mage: a mage, not a sailor. Some of the outcries in the dark had words in them, too. When those words were in Kuusaman, he could follow them. Two he heard most often were, "Egg!" and, "Leviathan!"

"Powers above, I *am* an idiot!" he said—still in classical Kaunian. The dragons *Habakkuk* carried had done nothing but give Algarve grief ever since the strange craft first went into action when Lagoas and Kuusamo took Sibiu away from King Mezentio and restored King Burebistu to the rule over his own island kingdom. Of course the Algarvians would strike at the sorcerously enhanced iceberg if they got the chance—and an Algarvian leviathan-rider evidently had got it.

Now Leino knew he urgently needed to make his way to the chambers where his fellow wizards worked. But how? The darkness in the bowels of *Habakkuk* was absolute. He hadn't thought about how completely the strange vessel depended on magecraft to sustain it in every way till it was suddenly deprived of that magecraft.

Then, to his vast relief, a light—a hand-held lamp—pierced the gloom. A woman called out in classical Kaunian: "Mages—follow me! Damage-control parties are forming!"

"Here!" Leino shouted, first in Kuusaman and then in classical Kaunian. He pushed past sailors toward the lamp, using his elbows to force his way through them when nothing else worked. When he saw the sorcerer holding the light was Xavega, he didn't stop to admire her. He just asked, "What needs doing most?"

"Everything," she said at once, which was probably true but wasn't very helpful. Then she got more specific: "You have worked on protecting the ship from rain damage, is it not so?"

"Aye," Leino answered. "I wrote that spell, as a matter of fact."

"Good." Xavega stayed altogether businesslike, for which he was duly grateful. She gestured with her free hand. "Come with me."

She led him back to one of the work rooms. A Kuusaman mage there used a little of her power and skill to keep another lamp faintly lit. Two more mages sat with her: two Lagoan men, neither of whom Leino knew well. One of them had a cut on his cheek, but hardly seemed to know it. "Rain repair?" Leino asked.

Everyone nodded. Xavega left again, shouting for more mages. The other wizards in the chamber went back to their sorcery. Leino sat down and began to chant. The lamp was so dim, he could hardly see his colleagues. But his mind's eye reached up to the ice-and-sawdust surface of *Habakkuk*, reached up to the little bit of ice every raindrop melted. He was glad to the very core of his being that the iceberg-turned-ship remained on the ley line. He drew energy from it and used that energy to preserve and restore *Habakkuk*'s proper structure. He could feel the other mages doing the same thing, resisting the rain, refusing to let it harm the vessel that carried them.

Peripherally, he also sensed other mages doing more things to keep *Habakkuk* intact. Now that the first moments of surprise and dismay had passed, they found things weren't so very bad after all. Cheers rang out when the lights went back on all over the ship.

"Knocked a good-sized chunk out of the ice on our bottom," a sailor reported. "Smashed up some stuff, but nothing we can't live with."

"*Habakkuk*'s not so bad," another sailor said. "Any regular ship, and we'd be sunk. But ice floats no matter what."

Unless it melts, of course, Leino thought. The sailor hadn't worried about that. He took it for granted that such things wouldn't happen. Leino, who knew better, didn't. But *Habakkuk* did go on, and that was all that mattered.

Garivald threw more wood onto the fire in the hearth. He and Obilot both stood close to the flames, enjoying the warmth. He said, "We got lucky here."

Obilot shook her head. "This isn't our good luck. It's somebody else's bad luck. How many peasant huts are standing empty in Grelz these days? How many peasant huts are standing empty all over Unkerlant? Powers below eat the stinking Algarvians."

"Aye." Garivald would always say aye to that. But he went on, "Plenty of wrecked huts. Plenty of burnt huts. But not so many huts just standing empty like this one, I don't think. Nobody even plundered it."

"Powers below eat the Algarvians," Obilot repeated. But then she added, "And powers below eat King Swemmel's inspectors, too. If it weren't for them, you could go on with your life again. We could go on with our lives again."

"Maybe we can, now," he answered, and set a hand on her shoulder. "Nobody knows we're here. This place is in the middle of nowhere. After the thaw, we'll see what kind of planting we can do. Maybe we'll see if we can scare up some better tools, some livestock. Maybe. And we'll get used to wearing new names, so nobody'll find out who we used to be."

"Who we used to be." Obilot tasted the words. She nodded.

"I've been a couple of people by now. I'm ready to turn into somebody else."

"I never much wanted to be an irregular," Garivald said. "I just wanted to go ahead and live my life." He'd had a family. He didn't any more. He glanced at Obilot. Maybe she'd had one, too. Maybe the two of them would again.

She snorted. "What? Do you think what you want has something to do with what you get? If the war hasn't taught you what a cursed stupid idea that is, I don't know what would."

"Oh, hush," he said roughly—it wasn't so much that he thought she was wrong as that he just didn't want to hear about it. Then he kissed her: that was one way to keep her from telling him things he didn't want to hear. They ended up making love in front of the fire. Obilot didn't tell him anything he didn't want to hear then, either. Afterwards, they fell asleep. If anyone told Garivald anything he didn't want to hear in his dreams, he didn't remember it when he woke up.

What woke him was rain beating on the roof—and rain dripping through the roof and splatting down in little muddy puddles on the rammed-earth floor. The hut was amazingly sound for one that had stood abandoned for who could say how long before Garivald and Obilot found it, but that also meant nobody'd tended to the thatching for who-could-say-how-long.

Have to fix it when I get the chance, was Garivald's first, still sleepy thought. Then he sat up and spoke his second thought aloud: "Rain."

"Rain," Obilot echoed. She sounded blurry, too. But her gaze quickly grew sharp. "Rain. Not snow."

"That's right," Garivald said. "It really is spring. Before long, we're going to be knee-deep in mud. And then we'll have to try to get some crops in the ground. Either that or we starve, anyhow."

"We'd have starved already if we weren't eating the seed grain this fellow brought into his hut before whatever happened to him happened," Obilot said.

"I know." Garivald shrugged. "I thought of that, too. I didn't know what to do about it, though. I still don't. When you're hungry now, you worry about later later."

Obilot nodded. "You have to. Once the snow all melts, maybe we'll be able to find more grain buried somewhere not far from here. We did that in my village whenever we thought we could get away with it, to try to keep the inspectors from stealing quite so much."

"Aye. We did the same thing in Zossen," Garivald said. "I bet there's not a single village in Unkerlant where they don't. Of course, if the peasant who had this place hid his grain so the inspectors couldn't get their thieving hands on it, we won't have an easy time finding it, either." He walked over to the jug they were using as a chamber pot. "We'll have to try, though. You're right about that. If we don't find some more, we can't stay here. And the way things look, the way that cursed Tantris came after me, I'm a lot safer in the middle of nowhere than I am in a village or a town."

"I know." Skirting puddles, Obilot got breakfast ready: she poured crushed barley and water into a pot and hung it over the fire for porridge. Sometimes she would make unleavened bread instead. She'd found the jar in which the vanished peasant's wife had kept her yeast, but the yeast was dead and useless—not that barley bread ever rose much anyhow. Garivald had got sick of tasteless flatbread and equally tasteless porridge, but they kept him going.

"Maybe I can kill a squirrel or two," he said. "Not as good as pork, but a lot better than nothing. And I'll start making rabbit traps, too."

"Birdlime," Obilot suggested. "Now that it's really spring, the birds will be coming back from the north." Neither of them said anything about finding other people and getting chickens or pigs or other livestock from them. *Maybe one of these days,* Garivald thought once more, but no, he wasn't ready to try it any time soon.

As Obilot put more wood on the fire to boil up the porridge, another thought struck Garivald. "Maybe we could use sorcery to help us find the buried grain—if there's any buried grain to find," he said. "We've got grain here, and like calls to like. I'm no mage, but I know that."

Obilot raised a dark and dubious eyebrow. All she said was, "Remember Sadoc."

"I'm not likely to forget him," Garivald said with a shudder. A member of the band of irregulars he'd led, Sadoc was a peasant who'd fancied himself a wizard. And he'd succeeded in casting spells, too. The only thing he hadn't succeeded in doing was getting them to perform the way he intended. Each one seemed to go wrong more spectacularly than its predecessor.

"Well, then," Obilot said, as if she needed to say no more.

And perhaps she didn't. But Garivald said, "Sadoc liked big spells. This would just be a little one. And I can make songs, after all. That's an important part of casting a spell. It could work."

"It *could*." Obilot still didn't sound convinced. "It could burst like an egg, too, and scatter you all over the landscape the way an egg would."

"I'd be careful." Listening to himself, Garivald started to laugh. He sounded like a small boy trying to convince his mother he could do something she thought dangerous. He sounded a lot like his own son Syrivald, in fact. His laughter broke off as if cut by a knife. Syrivald was almost surely dead. So was his mother.

By the time the rain stopped, it had melted a lot of the snow. The sun came out from behind the clouds and went on with the job. The ground couldn't possibly hold all the water thus released. As it did during every spring thaw, it turned to porridge itself.

That didn't make Garivald unhappy. He said, "For the next few weeks, nothing is going to happen very fast, not till things dry out."

"Good," Obilot answered, and he nodded.

But, day by day, the barley and rye and the little bit of wheat inside the hut dwindled. Before long, it wasn't a question of having enough left to make a crop. It was a question of how much longer they would have enough to eat. The next time Garivald said, "Maybe I ought to try to make a spell," Obilot didn't remind him of Sadoc's disasters.

What she said instead was, "Well, be careful, by the powers above."

"I will," Garivald said, though any magecraft at all was for him a long leap into the unknown. *It will be all right*, he thought. *Why shouldn't it? I'm not trying to kill anybody or do anything big, the way Sadoc always did. It'll work.* He had trouble making himself believe it.

But Obilot, he discovered, hadn't quit trying to talk him out of it: "Have you ever, in all your born days, used magic to try to find things that were hidden under the ground?"

To what was surely her surprise—indeed, to his own, for he'd almost forgotten till she asked—he nodded. "Aye. Two springs ago, it was. Waddo—he was firstman in Zossen—and I had buried the village's crystal to keep the redheads from getting their hands on it. I dug it up because I was afraid he might betray me on account of it. I gave it to some irregulars operating in the woods not far from there. I hope they got some use out of it."

"*Did* you?" She nodded, too, more than half to herself. "All right, then. Maybe you do have *some* idea of what you're up to." She still didn't sound as if she thought he had much idea of what he was doing.

He wasn't altogether sure he did, either, but he knew he had to make the effort. He put some wheat, some barley, and some rye in a little clay pot, then tied a length of twine to the handles and swung it pendulum-fashion. Then, doing his best not to let Obilot fluster him by watching, he began to chant:

> "*Like calls to like—so magic's found.*
> *Let like show like, down under ground.*
> *Show me now the grain that's hidden.*
> *Do it now, as you are bidden . . .*"

On he went. He knew it wasn't an outrageously good song—he knew it was likely a long way from a good song—but he hoped it would serve. And it did serve, or he thought it did. The direction in which the pot of grain was swinging suddenly changed, and he'd done nothing to change it. Obilot let out a small, surprised exclamation. Garivald felt like doing the same thing. Instead, he moved from one side of the hut to the other. The arc in which the pot swung changed as he moved, so that it kept indicating the same direction.

Garivald went outside into the rain and chanted again. The

swinging pot led him away from the hut and off beyond a low swell of ground a furlong or so away. He nodded to himself. The fellow who'd lived here thought like a peasant, all right. He didn't want to make things easy for King Swemmel's inspectors.

As soon as Garivald started down the other side of the slope, the pot stopped swinging and pointed straight down. He hadn't found a spade in the hut. He dug in the mucky ground with the edge of an iron pan. If it hadn't been soaked and soft, he couldn't have made much progress. As things were . . .

As things were, the edge of the pan clanked off fired clay before he'd got down much more than a foot. He set down the pan and softly and wonderingly clapped his hands together. "I did it," he breathed, and breathed in raindrops. Then he dug as if he were digging himself a hole while the Algarvians tossed eggs at him. Grunting with effort, he pulled out the great jar, which weighed more nearly as much as he did. Pitch sealed the lid. He had to hope the seal had stayed good.

He dragged the jar back to the hut. Inside, he scraped away the pitch with a knife and levered up the stopper. "Ahh!" He and Obilot stared down at the golden wheat. "We won't go hungry," she said.

"We'll have something to plant," he added, and then, "This isn't likely to be the only hidden jar, either. Maybe I can find more the same way."

"Maybe you can," Obilot agreed. "Why not? You *can* work magic." She sounded awed.

"By the powers above, so I can." Garivald sounded awed, too. Awed or not, he hedged that, as any canny peasant would: "A little, anyhow." But a little had proved enough.

Colonel Spinello was not a happy man as he rode east toward division headquarters to confer with his fellow brigade commanders. The rain that pelted him and his driver did little to improve his spirits. Neither did the fact that even the local wagon, with its curved, boatlike bottom and high wheels, had trouble negotiating the bottomless river of mud badly miscalled a road.

At last, just outside the northern Unkerlanter town called

Waldsolms, cobblestones reappeared. The wagon wasn't really made to cope with them. It rattled and jounced abominably. Spinello didn't mind that so very much. "Civilization!" he exclaimed, and then, "Well, of sorts, anyhow. This *is* Unkerlant."

His driver seemed less impressed. "A few miles of this jerking and we'd both be pissing blood," he said. "Sir."

Like most towns in Unkerlant that had gone through the fire of war, Waldsolms had seen better days. Brigadier Tampaste, who commanded the division, made his headquarters in what had probably been a merchant's house; what had been the local governor's castle was no longer standing.

Tampaste was young for a brigadier, as Spinello was young for a colonel. No: they would have been young for their ranks before the war. Nowadays, a man could rise quickly . . . if he lived. Like Spinello's, Tampaste's wound badge and ribbon showed he'd been hit twice.

"You're the first one who's made it here," he told Spinello. "I've set out smoked fish and black bread and spirits. Don't be bashful."

"That's never been one of my vices, sir," Spinello answered, and helped himself. The smoked fish was tasty, but full of tiny bones. The spirits packed enough punch to make his hair stand on end. "Good," he wheezed through a charred throat. "Good, but strong. If we're truly short on cinnabar, we ought to feed the dragons this stuff, to make them flame farther."

"By what I hear, people *are* talking about doing something along those lines," Tampaste said, which took Spinello by surprise. "The drawback, of course, is that drunken dragons are even wilder and stupider than they would be otherwise, if such a thing is possible." He sipped his own spirits without flinching; Spinello wondered if he'd copper-plated his gullet. "How do you view the situation in front of us, Colonel?"

"Sir, I don't like it," Spinello said at once. "Swemmel's men are up to something, but I don't know what. I don't like it whenever they try to get cute with us; it means they've got something up their sleeves."

"Do you think we can throw in another spoiling attack and disrupt them?" Tampaste asked.

Spinello shook his head. "Not my brigade, anyway. We're in no shape for it, not after the attack on Pewsum failed."

"You handled your men well there, Colonel," Tampaste said. "No blame to you that the try didn't succeed. Just . . . too many Unkerlanters in the neighborhood. We've sung that song before."

"If we sing it again too often, we'll have too bloody many Unkerlanters in Algarve, sir," Spinello said.

Tampaste grimaced. "You shouldn't say such things."

"Why?" Spinello asked. "Because they're not true? Or because nobody wants to think about them even if they are true?"

The division commander plainly didn't want to answer that. At last, he said, "Because saying them makes them more likely to come true. A mage would tell you the same thing." Spinello thought that held an element of truth, but only an element. Too many things got said all over the world for any one of them to have much chance of swinging things one way or another. Before he could say as much, Tampaste changed the subject, asking, "Where in blazes are the rest of my brigade commanders?"

"Stuck in the mud, unless I miss my guess," Spinello replied. "Whatever the Unkerlanters are doing, they won't do it right away." He took another pull at his spirits, which made it easier for him to sneer at anything and everything Unkerlanter. "It's not as if they bothered paving their roads so they could move on them all year long."

Tampaste said, "Captives claim one of the reasons Swemmel didn't pave more of the roads was for fear we could move on them."

"I hadn't heard that," Spinello admitted. "If it's true, we must have taught them quite a lesson during the Six Years' War."

"Maybe now they're teaching us some things we'd rather not learn," the brigadier said, and then, before Spinello could call him on it. "And now who's speaking words of ill omen?" The gesture Tampaste used to turn aside the omen dated back to the days when the Algarvians skulked through the woods in the far south and the Kaunian Empire bestrode most of eastern

Derlavai. Spinello had seen it reproduced on classical Kaunian monuments, and on pottery in the museum at Trapani.

Two of his fellow brigade leaders did eventually show up. The meeting that followed wasn't worth having, not as far as Spinello was concerned. Both other colonels, like him, had seen more going on among the Unkerlanters opposite them than they would have liked. But both of them, also like him, claimed to lack the force to do anything about it. "Can you get us more men, sir?" one of them asked Tampaste.

The division commander unhappily shook his head. "I've got everything I can do to hold what strength I have," he answered. "The bigwigs keep trying to rob me and send men south. That's all they can think of. That's where the worst of the fighting has been, so they think it always will be."

"They're a pack of fools, in that case," Spinello burst out.

"As may be," Tampaste said dryly. "But they're a pack of fools with fancier rank badges than yours, Colonel, and fancier badges than mine, too. Any other comments?" After his depressing remarks, nobody said a thing. He nodded as if he didn't seem surprised. "Very well, gentlemen. Dismissed."

Spinello headed back toward his brigade, east of Pewsum, thinking dark thoughts. His mood did not improve when an Unkerlanter dragon dove at his wagon. He and the driver both leaped off into the mud. Had the enemy dragonflier timed his beast's burst of flame as well as he might have, that would have done them no good. As things were, the Unkerlanter waited too long, and the flame kicked up steam east of the wagon. He didn't come back for a second attack, but flew on, looking for another target.

Dripping and cold and filthy, Spinello scrambled back up into the wagon. "He didn't think we were important enough to bother finishing off," he said. "He went off to find something bigger and juicier."

His driver was every bit as wet and cold and dirty as he was. "Are you complaining, sir?" the fellow asked.

"Not complaining, exactly," Spinello admitted. "But my self-importance is tweaked. I want the Unkerlanters to think I'm *worth* killing, if you know what I mean."

"Aye, sir." The driver nodded. An Algarvian who didn't think himself the center of the world was hardly an Algarvian at all.

By the time Spinello got back to the tumbledown hut in the village of Gleina that he was using for his own headquarters, he was shivering and his teeth were chattering. The soldiers in the village made sympathetic noises. So did Jadwigai, the brigade's pretty little Kaunian mascot. "What can we do to make you feel better, Colonel?" she asked.

Come to bed with me. That'd do a proper job of warming me up. He thought it—he thought it very loudly—but he didn't say it. *What I do—or don't do—for my men.* The really annoying thing was, he didn't think he would have to force her to slip between the sheets with him. If he broached the idea, he thought she'd lie down beside him gladly enough. Vanai would never have opened her legs for him if he hadn't set her grandfather to building roads, but Jadwigai genuinely seemed to like him.

But the brigade came first. If finding out he'd bedded their pet would upset the men, he couldn't do it. *Powers below eat the brigade,* he thought, not for the first time. What came out through his clicking teeth, though, was, "Tell them to heat up the steam room for me, would you, sweetheart?"

"Of course." Jadwigai hurried away. She came back in a few minutes and took Spinello by the arm. "You get a fresh uniform and come along with me, Colonel. You'll be better for it."

"I'd follow you anywhere, darling," he said, but he made sure he kept his tone light. Jadwigai laughed. So did Spinello, though it wasn't easy.

Just as well for him that he did: his driver waited outside the steam room, too. They scurried in together, and shut the door behind them. "Ahh!" Spinello said, stripping off sodden tunic and kilt. The driver did the same.

Few Unkerlanters had their own bathing tubs. They didn't go in for public bathhouses, either, the way their Forthwegian cousins did. Instead, they sat around roaring fires and sweated themselves clean. A circle of benches surrounded the central fire in the hut that did duty for a steam room in Gleina. Spinello and his driver sat down side by side and baked.

"Ahh!" This time, the driver said it, though Spinello would have. Warmth flowed into him, banishing the chilly damp. Then he began dripping again, this time with sweat. That felt better still. He picked up a bucket and poured water onto the hot stones around the fire. A great cloud of steam rose. He sweated more than ever.

During the wintertime, the Unkerlanters would go out and roll in the snow after baking long enough. In warmer weather, they made do with a bucket of cold water. Spinello had always considered either of those more nearly death-defying than anything else. When he got warm, he wanted to *stay* warm. Here, though, he couldn't, or at least not indefinitely. He had to put on his uniform and hurry back to his own hut once he couldn't bear the steam heat any more. Running through the rain wasn't all that much different from getting splashed with a bucket of water. Spinello failed to see how it improved things.

But when Jadwigai asked him, "Isn't that better, Colonel?" he found himself nodding.

"So it is, my dear," he replied. "Of course, anything would be an improvement on the drowned puppy I was when I got back here."

She nodded. She herself was a puppy saved from drowning. Unlike a puppy, she had to know it. She gave no sign, though. Maybe she didn't want to think about it, for which Spinello could hardly blame her. Or maybe she never mentioned it for fear of giving ideas to the Algarvians who'd made a pet of her instead of flinging her into the river. Spinello could hardly blame her for that, either.

"What did Brigadier Tampaste say?" she asked, as if she were one of Spinello's regimental commanders.

He answered her as if she were one of his regimental commanders, too: "He said that, whatever the bloody Unkerlanters are up to, we've got to stop them with what we've got—no hope for reinforcements."

"Oh." Jadwigai considered that very much as an officer would have. "Can we?"

No. Spinello didn't care to admit that to her, or even to himself, so he leered and struck a pose. "My sweet, when an Algarvian sets himself between a beautiful girl and war's desolation, he can do anything," he said grandly.

Jadwigai blushed bright pink. *Well, well,* Spinello thought. *Isn't that interesting?*

When Talsu's mother came downstairs into the tailor's shop where he worked with his father, she caught him not working: he was eating almonds dusted with sugar crystals and washing them down with citrus-flavored wine. Since Traku was doing the same thing, Talsu hardly felt guilty.

Laitsina wagged her forefinger at both of them. Sadly, she said, "My husband and my son—just a couple of lazy bums."

"I am not." Talsu would have sounded more indignant if he hadn't tried talking with his mouth full.

"No?" his mother said. "Well, I'll give you the chance to prove it. I was going to walk over to the grocer's shop for some olive oil and some capers, but you can go if you're not too lazy to get there."

Talsu hopped down off his stool. "Sure," he said, and started for the door at something close to a run.

Traku chuckled. "I just know his heart's breaking, when you gave him an excuse to go see his wife before she gets back from work. He looks heartbroken, doesn't he?"

"Like in a stage melodrama," Laitsina answered. Talsu was already out on the street when she called after him: "Have you got any money?"

"Oh." He stopped, feeling foolish, and went through his pockets. Then, feeling more foolish still, he went back inside and took some silver from the cash box. He went on his way again, jingling the coins to prove he had them.

Spring was in the air in Skrunda. Jelgava was a northerly kingdom, and not cursed with harsh winters; but the bright sun, the brilliant blue sky, and the dry heat all looked ahead toward summer, not back at the rain and clouds that did duty hereabouts for blizzards. Birds trilled in the bushes and from rooftops. New leaves were on the trees.

And new graffiti were on the walls. DONALITU LIVES! cried the hastily painted scrawls. THE TRUE KING WILL RETURN!

King Donalitu had lived in Lagoan exile the past three and a half years. Back in the days when he'd ruled Jelgava, Talsu had taken him as much for granted as the weather, and feared his storms a good deal more. The Algarvians hadn't needed to introduce dungeons to Jelgava after he fled; they'd just taken over the very respectable ones he already had running.

No, Talsu hadn't thought that much of Donalitu while he reigned. But when the choice was between oppression from one's own countryman or from foreign occupiers, the exiled king didn't look so bad. A choice without oppression in it somewhere hardly seemed real to Talsu.

The grocer's shop was only a couple of blocks away. He must have seen six or eight scrawls in the little stretch. Whoever'd been putting up Donalitu's name had been diligent about it. *Good,* he thought.

He was grinning when he opened the door to the shop. Gailisa's father owned it, as his family had for three or four generations. Predictably, he was nowhere in sight, leaving her to do the work. She was putting jars on a shelf behind the counter when the bell over the door chimed to announced a customer. "Hello," she said without turning around. "What can I do for you today?"

"Well, you could give me a kiss," Talsu answered.

That made his wife whirl. Indignation vanished when she saw him. She hurried out from in back of the counter and gave him what he'd asked for. "There you are, sir—your order, personally delivered," she said, mischief in her gray-blue eyes. "Can I give you anything else?"

"Sure." Talsu squeezed her and let his hands wander a little. "But people would talk if they came in while you were doing that."

"I suppose so." Gailisa sounded disappointed, which in turn disappointed Talsu. Now he'd be counting the minutes till she got home, till they could go back into the bedchamber that had once been his alone, that was so much more cramped these days but so much happier, too. Gailisa went on: "Did you come in here with anything else on your mind?"

"Aye," he said virtuously. "Olive oil and capers."

"I can do that," she said.

While she was doing it, he asked, "Did you see the new scribbles on the walls when you were coming over here?" When she nodded, he went on. "For some reason, people don't much like the redheads. I wonder why." He looked down to the floor planks. The stain of his own blood there had been scrubbed at and had faded, but he could still make it out. An Algarvian soldier had stabbed him after he objected to the fellow's remarks to Gailisa. Nothing had happened to the redhead, of course. In Jelgava, the occupiers could do no wrong.

"Here you are," Gailisa said brightly, as if he were just another customer. He made a face at her. They both laughed. He set silver on the counter. She shoved the coins back at him, whispering, "What my father doesn't know won't hurt him." Sometimes she would do that. Sometimes she wouldn't. Talsu had never figured out how she made up her mind.

He kissed her again, then spoke regretfully: "I'd better get back to work." After one more kiss, out he went, large jar of olive oil in one hand, small jar of capers in the other. He nodded every time he passed one of the graffiti proclaiming King Donalitu's return. After Algarvian rule, he would indeed welcome the rightful king with open arms.

He'd just delivered the groceries to his mother and gone back downstairs to return to work when two Algarvians came into the shop. One of them pointed to him and asked, "You being Talsu son of Traku?"

"Aye, that's who I am." Talsu fought the impulse to mimic the way the redhead spoke Jelgavan.

Keeping a civil tongue in his head probably proved a good idea. He didn't think so at the time, for both Algarvians whipped short sticks from their belts and pointed them at him. "You coming with us," said the one who'd spoken before.

"What in blazes is this here all about?" Traku demanded.

The other Algarvian swung his stick toward Talsu's father, who had something of the look of a bruiser to him. "We are investigating treason against King Mainardo." He spoke Jelgavan almost perfectly. "If your son is innocent, he will be released."

Talsu had arranged the untimely demise of Kugu the silversmith, the man who'd betrayed him to King Mezentio's men. If the Algarvians knew about that, he was in a lot of trouble. If they didn't—and they'd never shown any sign of it—he thought he could hope to come home again. In any case, a needle was no argument against a stick. He set it down and slid off the stool. "I'll go with you," he said.

"Of course you coming with we," the first Algarvian said. All the redheads Talsu had ever met were arrogant whoresons. But then, he'd met only occupiers, a role bound to breed arrogance.

As he'd expected, Mezentio's men took him to Skrunda's constabulary station. Most of the people working there were the Jelgavans who'd patrolled the town before Algarve overran their kingdom. They kept doing the same job, but for new masters and with new purposes. Talsu wondered how they slept at night. By the look of them, they had no trouble. One, in fact, was all but dozing at his desk now.

But the redheads didn't turn Talsu over to his own countrymen, as they had the last time they captured him. Instead, they took him into a small, windowless chamber and closed the door behind them. He braced himself for a beating. He'd had several in the dungeon, all from fellow Jelgavans.

"What do you know about these new foul scrawls on the streets of Skrunda?" asked the Algarvian who spoke Jelgavan well.

"Nothing," Talsu answered. "I've seen them"—he couldn't very well deny that—"but that's all."

"Liar!" shouted the Algarvian who wasn't so fluent. He brought out that word with ease; he'd doubtless had practice.

Talsu shook his head. "No, sir. That's the truth." And so it was. He hoped its being the truth would do him some good.

"You were released from imprisonment on condition that you cooperate with us," the fluent Algarvian said. "But we have not seen much cooperation from you. Do you wonder that we do not trust you?"

"I can't tell you what I don't know," Talsu said. "All I do is mind my own business." *By the powers above, I wish you'd do the same,* he thought.

"Liar!" the other Algarvian shouted again. "We fixing you, you and your lyings."

The door to the chamber opened. Another Algarvian came in: not a torturer, as Talsu first feared, but a mage. That might be even worse. The redhead who spoke good Jelgavan said, "Because we do not trust you, we shall have to interrogate you with a sorcerer present."

"You lying, you paying," the second Algarvian added, slashing his thumb across his throat.

"I'm not lying," Talsu said, and then, to the first redhead, "Go on and ask your questions. I can't very well stop you." *No matter how much I wish I could.*

"What do you know of the new graffiti that falsely claim the fled King Donalitu will come back to Jelgava?" the Algarvian asked.

"Nothing except that I've seen them," Talsu repeated.

"Do you know who painted them?"

"No, sir," Talsu said.

"Can you guess who might have painted them?"

"No, sir. I have no idea."

His interrogator glanced over at the mage, who'd been muttering to himself during the questions and answers. The wizard spoke in Algarvian, punctuating his words with a fanciful shrug. The other redhead, the one who spoke Jelgavan badly, cried out in obvious disbelief. The mage shrugged again. Talsu's interrogator tried a different tack: "Are you shielded against magecraft?"

"No, sir," Talsu said.

"Have you ever had a shielding spell laid on you?"

"Not since I went into the army," Talsu answered. "I know they tried to protect soldiers as best they could."

The Algarvian waved that aside with an impatient gesture. "Do you know of anyone in Skrunda with reason to dislike Algarve?"

"Of course I do," Talsu exclaimed. "I don't much like your kingdom myself. Why should I, after your soldier stuck a knife in me and then walked free?"

More back-and-forth between the interrogator and the mage. Talsu knew he'd told nothing but the truth. Of course, the Algarvian hadn't asked the right questions. The interrogator said,

"Think what you will, but we are not unjust. You may go. Your answers set you free."

"Thanks," Talsu said, and found himself meaning it. This had indeed been easier than he'd expected. As he left the constabulary station, he couldn't help wondering how the mage's truth spell would have judged the Algarvian's claim of justice. He didn't know, but he had his own opinion.

Back in the days when Leudast was a common soldier or a sergeant, nobody in the villages the Unkerlanter army recaptured from the Algarvians ever paid any particular attention to him. Now that he was a lieutenant, he was discovering things were rather different. When the spring thaw started, his company was billeted in and around a village east of Herborn called Leiferde. He knew they would be billeted there for a while, too; hip-deep mud glued Unkerlanters and Algarvians alike in place for weeks each spring.

As company commander, he'd chosen a house in the village as his own temporary home. He would have done—he had done—exactly the same thing when commanding the company while still a sergeant. But when he'd done so while still a sergeant, the peasants on whom he'd been billeted had treated him like one of themselves.

That hadn't bothered him. He *was* a peasant, from a long line of peasants. The only difference between him and these Grelzer farmers was his accent, which announced he came from the northeast of Unkerlant, up near the border with Forthweg.

Having those little brass stars on his collar tabs, though, put things in a new light. The peasants in Leiferde bowed and scraped before him. As often as not, they called him *your Excellency*.

His own men figured out what was going on before he did. With a grin, Sergeant Kiun said, "Do you know what it is, sir?" When Leudast shook his head, Kiun's grin got wider than ever. "I'll tell you what it is. What it is is, they think you're a nobleman."

"A nobleman?" Leudast stared at his comrade. That idea had never entered his mind, not even for a moment. "You're bloody daft, is what you are."

"By the powers above, I'm not," Kiun retorted.

"*Look* at me," Leudast said. "Do I look like a nobleman to you? I need a shave. My tunic's filthy. There's dirt under my fingernails. There's dirt ground into my knuckles, too, so deep no steambath'll ever sweat it out. You think nobles have dirty hands?"

"There *is* a war on, in case you haven't noticed." Kiun shrugged. "You can let 'em know you're just a nobody, if that's what you want to do. I'll tell you something, though: you've got a lot better chance of getting the girl in that hut where you're staying to put out for you if she thinks she might have a baron's bastard than if you're just hoping she decides you're a handsome whoreson . . . sir."

Leudast raised an eyebrow. Now Kiun had his attention. "You think so?" he said. "Alize isn't bad, is she?"

"Well, *I* wouldn't throw her out of bed," Kiun said, "not that she's likely to end up in mine. But I haven't done too bad for myself. I may not be an officer, but I know what I want and I know how to get it. If you want, sir, everybody in the company'll talk you up for a blueblood. You've taken care of us. We can take care of you."

"You don't need to go that far." Leudast paused and scratched the side of his jaw. "But I don't suppose you have to go out of your way to tell people I know how to muck out a barn at least as well as they do, either." Kiun laughed, nodded, winked, and went on his way.

A nobleman? Me? Leudast still found the idea absurd. It was, in fact, absurd for several reasons, not least that Unkerlanter nobility wasn't what it had been back in the days before the Six Years' War. A lot of nobles had fallen fighting Algarve then. A lot more had sided with Kyot, Swemmel's brother, in the madness of the Twinkings War afterwards. Few who'd made that mistake remained among the living. And King Swemmel had gone right on getting rid of noblemen who met his displeasure all through his reign. The Algarvians had killed many more in this war. One reason the Unkerlanter army had so many officers without breeding was that there weren't nearly enough nobles to fill the required slots.

Then Leudast stopped thinking of absurdities and started thinking of Alize. She was a few years younger than he, which put her somewhere around twenty. She had bright eyes and very white teeth and a shape even the long, baggy tunics Unkerlanter women wore couldn't disguise. She'd given him plenty of pleasant smiles. If she wanted to give him more than smiles, he wouldn't mind at all.

For the time being, all he could do was think about it. He squelched through Leiferde and the surrounding fields, making sure his men were ready to fight in case the Algarvians attacked in spite of the mud—and making sure they were ready to go forward in case his own superiors gave the word. He hoped his own superiors would have the good sense to do no such thing, but years as a common soldier and a sergeant had taught him not to rely on his superiors' good sense.

When he got back to the house where he was billeted, he was all over mud. Alize's mother, a brisk, handsome woman called Bertrude, gave him a bucket of hot water from the kettle over the stove and a rag. "Here you are, your Excellency," she said. "This may not be so fine as you're used to, sir, but it should do the job."

She sounded more deferential than she had before. Had Kiun been telling tales? Leudast could hardly ask her. All he said was, "It will do fine," and cleaned himself off as best he could.

Bertude's husband, whose name was Akerin, rarely stirred from the bench where he was sitting. He had a jar of spirits beside him. Leudast had never seen him without a jar of spirits beside him. A lot of Unkerlanter peasants passed their winters that way. He'd done it himself.

Bertrude bustled over and poured Leudast a mug of spirits. "This will help warm you up, too, sir," she said.

"Well, so it will." Leudast drank. The spirits were potent, but no more so than he'd had back home. He pointed to a pot bubbling beside the hot-water kettle. "The stew smells good."

"I'm glad it suits you, your Excellency," Bertrude said, and dropped him a curtsy, as if she were a duchess herself. *Aye, Kiun's been running off at the mouth*, Leudast thought. The peasant woman went on, "Alize there put it together. She's a fine cook, Alize is, a fine cook—better than I was at the same age, I'm sure."

Alize was mending a tunic. Hearing her name, she looked up and smiled at Leudast. As an experiment, he bowed to her. Though her skin was as swarthy as his own, he saw her blush. "Why don't you let me have some?" he said.

Blushing still, she hurried to get a bowl and serve him. "I hope you like it, your Excellency," she said, her voice so soft Leudast had to bend toward her to hear.

She stood waiting nervously while he began to eat. He wondered what an Algarvian officer who didn't care for the stew might have done. Nothing good—he was sure of that. She had to fear his doing something just as dreadful. He smiled at her and said, "Very tasty."

Her own smile was the sun coming out from behind thick clouds. Her lips shaped silent words. *Powers above be praised.* She probably would have said the same thing after an Algarvian officer approved—or after one of King Swemmel's inspectors did. That thought shamed Leudast. Bedding Alize when she hardly dared say no struck him as unsporting.

Bertrude made a clucking noise and beckoned imperiously. Her husband came over to her. She spoke too quietly for Leudast to make out what she was saying. Whatever it was, though, she plainly intended to brook no disagreement. When Akerin started to say something, she poked him in the chest with her forefinger and talked through him. Only when he started nodding did she look satisfied. A lot of the time, Unkerlanter men slapped their women around. Not in this hut, though.

After a little while, Bertrude fell silent. Her husband cleared his throat a couple of times, and then spoke to Alize: "Your mother and I, we're going to go next door for a bit, see if we can get back that pot the neighbors borrowed from us. Likely we'll chat some, too."

"All right, Father," Alize said.

"You'll be all right by yourself with the lieutenant here," Bertrude added. "He can protect you better than we could, if you get right down to it. Come along, Akerin." She all but dragged her husband out of the hut.

Alize blushed again. Up till now, her mother and father had made a point of not leaving her alone with Leudast. Now they were making a point of going off. Leudast doubted Alize needed protecting. He thought Bertrude and Akerin were angling for a husband for her.

Of course, being an officer and being liable to get called away to fight as soon as the spring thaw ended, he could enjoy himself with her without worrying about details like weddings. She had to know the game her parents were playing. She probably knew he could do what he wanted without concern for consequences, too. More roughly than he'd intended, he said, "You don't have to do anything you don't want to do, Alize." Sure enough, his sense of shame was still working.

"Oh. That," she said. "I don't mind. I don't mind at all. If you want to know the truth, you're the first one who ever bothered saying anything like that." She made a wry face. "Mother would slap me silly if she heard me telling you such things. She'd want me to make you think I was still a maiden—and how likely is *that*, after everything that's happened the past few years?"

"I don't know," Leudast answered, though he had a pretty good idea.

"Well, then," Alize said, and pulled the tunic off over her head.

When Leudast saw her deep-breasted, sweetly curved form, his shame melted like the snow outside, only far faster and far more thoroughly. He reached for her. Her flesh was soft and warm under his hands. Her breath sighed out when he tilted her face up for a kiss.

He soon shed his own uniform tunic. Clinging to each other, he and Alize went over to the padded benches along the wall that made up most of the furniture of an Unkerlanter peasant house. When they lay down together, Leudast discovered that Alize would have had a hard time convincing him she was a maiden. She knew too much of men and what pleased them.

Because she did, he enjoyed himself more than he might have otherwise. He thought she did, too; if she didn't, she was artful about hiding it. After they finished, he took his weight on his elbows and knees, which made her nod in measured approval. Looking up at him, she said, "You'll be going away before long, won't you?"

"Probably," he answered. "I didn't come to Leiferde for this. It's more fun than fighting Algarvians, but it's not why the king gives me silver—when he bothers to give me silver, I mean."

That made Alize laugh. She nodded again, and then flipped back a lock of dark hair that had fallen in front of her face. She said, "Powers above keep you safe. Afterwards—if there is an afterwards—if you want to come back here and talk about things, that's all right. And if you don't . . ." Her shrug was delightful to behold.

Leudast caught her to him. They began again. He had no idea whether he'd want to come back to Leiferde if the war ever ended. He had no idea if it would ever end. *Powers above,* he thought, *I have no idea if her mother and father are going to walk in on us.* She wrapped her legs around him. For the moment, he didn't care about any of that, either.

Prince Juhainen steepled his fingers as he studied Pekka. "How soon will this sorcery be ready to use against the Algarvians?" he asked. His eyes flicked around her room in the hostel. He didn't seem much impressed. The Seven Princes of Kuusamo were neither so rich nor so ostentatious as the kings on the mainland of Derlavai, but such bare little chambers had to be alien to them.

She answered, "Your Highness, we've already used this sorcery against the Algarvians, when they trued to use their murderous magic against us."

"That isn't what I meant," Juhainen said. He was younger than Pekka; maybe that was why she had trouble taking him seriously. Or maybe it was just that she didn't reckon him a man to match his uncle, Prince Joroinen, whom he'd succeeded when the Algarvians' sorcerous attack on Yliharma slew Joroinen.

With some effort, Pekka kept her temper. "What did you mean, then, your Highness?" she asked.

"How soon will ordinary mages be able to use the spells your group of sorcerers has developed?" Juhainen did his best to make himself clear.

And that was a good question, a question worth asking. "As soon as we make the spells as strong and as safe as we can, we'll turn them over to the practical mages," Pekka promised.

"But when will that be?" Juhainen persisted. "How long will it take? Will it happen by the summertime? Will it be a year from now? Will it be five years from now? You will understand, I have an interest in knowing."

"Of course, your Highness," Pekka said. "But you will understand—or I hope you will understand—the question isn't easy to answer. The more we learn, the more we find we can learn. The more we do, the more we find we can do. I can't guess when that will stop, or if it ever will."

"Whether it does or not, you will understand that out beyond the Naantali district we are fighting a war," Prince Juhainen said. "We need the weapons you are readying here. If they aren't quite perfect . . . we need them anyhow, the sooner the better."

"We'll do what we can, your Highness," Pekka said.

"Please do. Time is shorter than you might think." Without waiting for an answer, the prince rose and strode out of Pekka's chamber. The door clicked shut behind him.

Well, well. How intriguing, she thought. Up till now, the Seven Princes had paid little direct attention to her project. Every now and then, they would ask questions. Every now and then, too, they would grumble about how much things cost. Other than that, they'd left her alone. Not any more. And what did that mean?

Only one answer occurred to her. *Before very long, we're going to need that sorcery, and need it badly.* As far as she could see, that could mean only one thing, too: before long, Kuusaman and Lagoan soldiers would be fighting on the Derlavaian mainland.

It wasn't anything that came as any great shock. Ships and leviathans and dragons weren't going to be enough to drive the Algarvians out of Valmiera and Jelgava, not without soldiers on the ground to go in and take those lands away from them. She sighed. There was so much left to learn about the relationship between the laws of similarity and contagion, and about the inverted unity lying at their heart.

After that sigh, though, came a smile. Ilmarinen was ready to experiment endlessly, to pursue his own theories about twisted time. Nothing likely to annoy him struck Pekka as altogether distressing.

By the time she got down to the refectory, Prince Juhainen had already left the hostel. He could escape whenever he chose. He didn't have to come here unless he wanted to. Pekka envied him. Oh, how she envied him!

As things were, she had to go on herding cats—at least that was what dealing with her fellow theoretical sorcerers often felt like. Raahe and Alkio sat in the refectory, drinking tea. They weren't so bad. Pekka waved to a serving girl and asked for some tea herself. Then she went over and sat down beside the married couple. As theorectical sorcerers went, they were pretty well civilized. Their being husband and wife probably had a good deal to do with that.

"What did his Highness want?" Raahe asked, setting down her cup. Juhainen had told Pekka nobody in the outside world knew where he was, but keeping secrets inside the hostel was impossible.

Pekka didn't try. "He wanted us to hurry toward turning our spells into something final."

"Ah." That was Alkio. More often than not, he let his wife do the talking. Now, though, he said, "They're wondering how soon they can put men on the mainland, unless I miss my guess."

"I thought the same thing," Pekka answered.

"What did you tell him?" Raahe asked.

"That we weren't quite ready yet, that we were still finding ways to make the spells stronger and safer," Pekka said. "I don't know if practical mages who used them could stand against the murderous magic the Algarvians hurl around."

"*We* did," Raahe said. "We didn't just stand against Mezentio's magic, either. We beat the Algarvians back, by the powers above."

"Aye, we did." Every word of that was true. But could practical mages match it if menaced by Mezentio's magecraft? *Could my husband defeat Algarvian wizards who were killing Kaunians to try to kill him?* Pekka didn't want to put it that way, even if that thought was uppermost in her mind. What she did say was, "We're not ordinary mages."

"I should hope not." Raahe glanced around to make sure nobody at the other tables was listening. She lowered her voice to a whisper. "If Ilmarinen were ordinary . . ." She rolled her eyes.

Before Pekka could get out more than the beginnings of a giggle, Alkio said, "The mages who attacked us probably weren't ordinary, either. The Algarvians knew we were doing something important. They'd have thrown their best at us."

"And we beat them," Raahe repeated.

That was also true. "I hadn't thought of it in those terms," Pekka admitted. But Alkio was likely to be right. Kuusaman and Lagoan mages fighting on the mainland might well not face magecraft of the same vicious intensity as that which had surmounted the Strait of Valmiera and struck at the Naantali district.

"Hadn't thought of what in which terms?" Ilmarinen demanded, hurrying toward the table where Pekka sat. "You've got to think of everything—either that, or you've got to have someone who will do it for you." By the way he preened as he sat down, he had someone in mind. Raahe rolled her eyes again.

Since Ilmarinen did commonly think in terms that occurred to no one else under the sun, Pekka couldn't even get annoyed at him—not for that, anyhow, though she knew he was bound to give her some other reason before long. She explained what the conversation had been about.

"Ah," Ilmarinen said when she was through. He nodded to Alkio. "Aye, that makes sense—which doesn't necessarily mean it's true. Their magic gets a large energy release any which way: killing is good for that, if you've got the stomach for it. Ours is different. Ours has to be done just right. If it isn't, you might as well not bother." His gaze swung toward Pekka. "And I hope you told Prince Juhainen as much."

"Not in those words, no, but I did say we weren't ready," Pekka replied.

"Good," Ilmarinen said. "Practical mages are a pack of thumb-fingered fools."

"They say the same thing about us," Pekka observed.

"Of course they do. So what?" Ilmarinen let out a wheezy chuckle. "Everything they say about us is a filthy lie, while everything we say about them is true."

Raahe nodded. Ilmarinen chuckled again. Pekka felt sorry for Raahe, who'd just proved she couldn't recognize irony if it walked up and bit her in the backside. Pekka said, "We do have to get ready pretty soon, to turn out magic even those thumb-fingered fools can use."

She waited. Would Ilmarinen understand she'd noticed his irony and respond in kind? Or would he singe her as he'd just singed Raahe, or perhaps roast her as he'd roasted so many others over the years? He dipped his head and answered, "You're right. The Algarvians have already arranged things so that *their* thumb-fingered fools can make the most of their magic."

"Powers below eat the Algarvians," Alkio said. "Do we want to imitate everything they do? Do we want to imitate anything they do?"

"We want to imitate everything they do that makes them like-lier to win the war," Pekka said, and then, before the other mages could tear her limb from rhetorical limb, "Everything we can imitate with a clean conscience. The kind of magecraft they use is one thing. The way they organize their mages is something else again. It's morally neutral, not wicked the way the wizardry is."

Alkio pondered that and nodded. Even the quarrelsome Il-marinen failed to find fault with it. Fernao came into the refec-tory just then. He carried his stick—he would always carry it—but he didn't put much weight on it. He'd made a lot of progress getting around since first arriving in Kuusamo. "What's wrong here?" he said in pretty good Kuusaman—he'd made a lot of progress with the language, too. "I see everybody nodding together, so something must be."

No one seemed quite sure how to take that, either. Pekka said, "Nothing too serious: only a visit from Prince Juhainen."

"Ah." Fernao nodded. "Let me guess. Is he trying to make us hurry?"

Ilmarinen gave him a suspicious look. "How do you know that?"

"It's what princes do," Fernao answered. He frowned in thought, but evidently couldn't come up with the words he needed in Kuusaman, for he switched to classical Kaunian to continue, "Princes do not bother to come when everything is fine. They come only to try to make changes. That is what they are for."

"That is what Juhainen did, sure enough." Pekka kept on speaking her own language. "I think it means we will invade the mainland soon."

.Ilmarinen raised an eyebrow. "Invade the mainland, eh?" He glanced over at Fernao. "Is that what they're calling it these days?"

For a moment, Pekka had no idea what he was talking about, even though he'd spoken Kuusaman, too. Then she also turned toward Fernao, and watched him turn red—with his fair Lagoan skin, the flush was easy to trace. Raahe and Alkio must also have figured out what Ilmarinen meant, for they were busy looking at the ceiling or out the window or anywhere but at her and Fernao.

Her own ears felt hot. "That will be quite enough of that," she told Ilmarinen in her frostiest tones. He laughed at her. She glared at him, which only made him laugh harder. Then she looked at Fernao again, and caught him looking at her. Their eyes jerked away at the contact, as if they'd been caught at something. *We haven't,* Pekka insisted to herself. *We really haven't.*

Six

Spring came early to Bishah and the surrounding hills. Hajjaj cherished it while it lasted, not least because it wouldn't last long. Zuwayza was the kingdom of summer. Soon, all too soon, the sun would bake everything yellow and brown. The foreign minister savored the brief, brave show of greenery and bright flowers as much for its impermanence as for its beauty.

"You Algarvians are spoiled," he remarked to Marquis Balastro at a gathering at the Algarvian ministry one evening. "You get to enjoy your gardens and woods through most of the year."

"Well, so we do, your Excellency," Balastro agreed. "Tell me, did you think we were spoiled when you went through your first winter at the University of Trapani?" His smile showed sharp teeth.

"Spoiled? No, your Excellency." Hajjaj shook his head. "How could you possibly spoil when you froze solid for a couple of months every year?"

Balastro threw back his head and laughed uproariously. "Oh, you are a funny fellow when you choose. I could wish you chose to be more often."

"I could wish I had more things to laugh about," Hajjaj replied, and Balastro's own mirth cut off as abruptly as if sliced by a knife. The war news from Unkerlant wasn't good, and not all of the Algarvian minister's verbal gymnastics could make it good. It wasn't dreadfully bad, not lately, not with the spring thaw miring Mezentio's men and Swemmel's alike, but it wasn't good. What little movement there was had the Unkerlanters pushing forward and the Algarvians falling back.

Over in one corner of the reception hall, a couple of stocky, swarthy men in Unkerlanter tunics were busily drinking themselves blind. If you asked them, they would insist they weren't Unkerlanters: they were Grelzers, from the free and independent (and Algarvian-backed) Kingdom of Grelz. Of course, with King Raniero horribly dead, their insistence mattered very little. The quondam Kingdom of Grelz mattered very little, too. Hajjaj sighed. Typical of the Algarvians to bring them up to Zuwayza and try to make something of them after the collapse and not before.

Doing his best to recover from the awkward moment, Marquis Balastro said, "I am glad our dragons have helped keep the Unkerlanter air pirates from troubling Bishah."

"They have done that, and I do thank you for it." Hajjaj bowed. The waistband of his kilt dug into his flesh as he moved. Nudity was far more comfortable. He went on: "Our own dragons, flying south into Unkerlant, have noted what looks to be something of a buildup of Unkerlanter soldiers in the northern regions of King Swemmel's realm."

"We have noted the same thing." Balastro didn't sound very concerned. "I assure you it is nothing we can't handle."

"I am glad to hear that," Hajjaj said, and hoped the Algarvian minister was right.

"We do keep an eye on things," Marquis Balastro said, as if Hajjaj had denied it. "We also do our best to keep enemy air pirates from ravaging Algarve itself."

"Aye, of course," Hajjaj said. *If you hadn't lost Sibiu, you'd have an easier time of it, too.* He didn't say that; it would have been most undiplomatic. But that didn't make it untrue.

Balastro bowed again; Algarvians were a punctiliously polite folk, even if they didn't spend so much time on it as Zuwayzin did. "King Mezentio has ordered me to express his thanks to King Shazli through you," he said.

"I shall be happy to do so." Hajjaj bowed in return. "Ahh . . . his thanks for what?"

"Why, for his help in keeping Kaunian bandits here and, more to the point, keeping them out of Forthweg, of course," Balastro answered.

"Oh." After a moment, Hajjaj nodded. "He is very welcome. I speak for myself at the moment, you understand. But I shall convey your sovereign's words to mine, and I am certain I speak in King Shazli's name here."

He also wished he weren't saying King Mezentio was welcome. As far as he was concerned, the Kaunians who'd managed to flee from Forthweg had every right in the world to try to hit back at the Algarvians. But when they hit back, they unquestionably hurt the Algarvians' war against Unkerlant. That, in turn, hurt Zuwayza. As foreign minister, Hajjaj found himself forced to condemn what he personally condoned.

Marquis Balastro smiled. "Believe me, your Excellency, I do understand your difficulty."

And he probably did. He was a civilized man, in the best traditions of civilization in eastern Derlavai. Had Hajjaj not admired those traditions, he never would have chosen to finish his education at the University of Trapani. That didn't keep him from wondering how such an eminently civilized man as Balastro could approve of the way his kingdom slaughtered Kaunians. He did, though—Hajjaj had no doubt of it.

His certainty oppressed him. He bowed his way away from Balastro and went over to the bar, where an Algarvian servitor who was almost surely also an Algarvian spy gave him a goblet of date wine. He was almost the only one in the room drinking the sweet, thick stuff. Even the Zuwayzi officers the Algarvian military attaché had invited to the reception preferred vintages pressed from grapes. Hajjaj enjoyed those, too, but the taste of date wine took him back to his youth. For a man with white hair, few things could work such magic.

Sipping the date wine, the Zuwayzi foreign minister looked around the hall. There stood Horthy, the Gyongyosian minister to Zuwayza, in earnest conversation with Iskakis, his Yaninan counterpart. They were both speaking classical Kaunian, a language that had never been used in either of their kingdoms but the only one they had in common. Hajjaj took another pull at his goblet, savoring the irony of that.

After a moment, Iskakis, a short, bald man with a mustache that looked like a black-winged moth perched between his nose and upper lip, sidled away from the large, leonine Horthy and started chatting up an Algarvian captain, one of the men on the military attaché's staff. The captain, a stalwart, handsome young man, beamed at the Yaninan. Iskakis was partial to stalwart, handsome young men. He was even more partial to boys.

His wife, meanwhile, was talking to Marquis Balastro. She was about half Iskakis' age, and extraordinarily beautiful. *Such a waste, that marriage,* Hajjaj thought, not for the first time. Balastro, now, Balastro had the sleek look of a cat who'd fallen into a pitcher of cream. What Hajjaj saw as a waste, he saw as an opportunity. However civilized Balastro was, no Algarvian born had ever reckoned philandering anything but a pleasant diversion—unless, of course, he found himself wearing horns rather than giving them.

Balastro wouldn't have to worry about that here. He stroked Iskakis' wife's cheek, an affectionate gesture that said he'd likely done other, more intimate stroking in private. Hajjaj wouldn't have been surprised. He'd watched the two of them at a reception at the Gyongyosian ministry the autumn before.

Here, though, Iskakis' wife twisted away. At first, Hajjaj thought that was playacting, and clever playacting to boot. Iskakis might prefer boys, but Yaninans had a prickly sense of honor. If Iskakis saw Balastro making free with the woman he thought of as his own, he would certainly call out the Algarvian minister. That their kingdoms were allies wouldn't matter a bit, either.

Then Hajjaj saw the fury distorting the Yaninan woman's delicately sculpted features. That wasn't playacting, not unless she belonged on the stage. He hurried over toward her and Balastro. Yanina and Algarve were both allied to Zuwayza, too. *The things I do for my kingdom,* he thought.

"Everything's fine, your Excellency," Balastro said with an easy smile.

"This man is a beast, your Excellency." Iskakis' wife spoke fair Algarvian, with a gurgling Yaninan accent that made Hajjaj pause to make sure he'd understood her correctly. But he had. Her glare left no room for doubt.

"She's just a trifle overwrought," Balastro said.

"He is a swine, a pig, a pork, a stinking, rutting boar," Iskakis' wife said without great precision but with great passion. Then she said a couple of things in Yaninan that Hajjaj didn't understand but that sounded both heartfelt and uncomplimentary.

Hajjaj said, "I gather the two of you have quarreled." Balastro nodded. Iskakis' wife dipped her head, which meant the same thing among Yaninans. Hajjaj went on, "You would be wiser not to show it. You would be wiser still not to show each other any kind of affection in public."

Balastro bowed. "As always, your Excellency, you are a font of wisdom."

Iskakis' wife snarled. "You do not need to worry about *that*." Could looks have killed, the Algarvian minister would have died. Iskakis' wife stalked away, arched nostrils flared, back ever so straight, hips working with fury.

With a sigh, Balastro said, "Well, it was fun while it lasted. Never a dull moment in bed, I'll tell you that."

"I believe you," Hajjaj said: Half the men in the room were eyeing that swiveling backside with one degree of longing or another. Iskakis, otherwise preoccupied, was not among them. *A good thing, too,* Hajjaj thought.

"Aye, in bed Tassi's splendid. Out of bed . . ." Balastro rolled his eyes. "A bursting egg for a temper and a razor for a tongue. I'm not all that surprised Iskakis would sooner stick it somewhere else." He glanced over toward the Yaninan minister and the officer with whom he was talking. He made a face. "Though not *there*, by the powers above."

"No accounting for taste," Hajjaj said, a profoundly unoriginal truth. Before too long, he took the opportunity to make his excuses and go back to his home in the hills above Bishah. Getting out of the clothes he'd worn and into the usual Zuwayzi outfit—sandals and, for outdoors, a hat—was, as usual, a great relief.

He was about to go down into the capital the next morning when someone knocked on the one door in the fortresslike outer wall to the sprawling compound that was as much clan center as dwellingplace. Tewfik, the ancient majordomo who presided over the residence, made his slow way out to see who was disturbing his master. He sent a younger, sprier servant hotfooting it back to Hajjaj. "Your Excellency, you've got to come see this for yourself," the servant said, and would say no more even when Hajjaj barked at him.

And so, grumbling under his breath, Hajjaj went out to the gateway. There he found Tewfik looking, for once, quite humanly astonished. And there he also found Tassi, the wife of Iskakis the Yaninan minister. Polite as a cat, she bowed to him. "Good day, your Excellency," she said. "I come to you, sir, seeking asylum from my husband, and from Marquis Balastro, and from everything and everyone outside Zuwayza."

"Do—do—do you?" Hajjaj knew he was stammering, but couldn't help it. He felt at least as astonished as Tewfik looked.

Tassi dipped her head, as she had at the reception: sure enough, a Yaninan nod. "I do. You see? I already begin to follow your customs." By that, she meant she stood before him wearing only sandals and a straw hat. Marquis Balastro occasionally aped Zuwayzi nudity. With Balastro, the effect was more ludicrous than anything else. With Tassi . . .

All at once, Hajjaj understood that the Algarvian words *nude* and *naked* were not perfect synonyms. His own people, who took their bare skin for granted, were nude. Tassi was naked, using her skin for her own purposes. Sensuality came off her in waves.

And she knew as much, too, and relished the confusion— among other things—she caused. "Take me in, your Excellency, protect me," she purred, "and I will do anything you like, anything at all. Take me in. I beg you." Gracefully, she dropped to both knees. It wasn't exactly, or solely, a begging gesture. It also promised something else. She bowed her head and waited.

"What will you do?" Tewfik hissed in Zuwayzi.

"Powers below eat me if I know," Hajjaj replied in the same tongue. He switched back to Algarvian: "Get up, milady. The least you can do is have breakfast here. Afterwards . . . Afterwards, we shall see." He was an old man, aye. Was he too old for such amusements? And if he wasn't, how much would domestic relations with Tassi hurt foreign relations with Yanina?

Fernao woke to the sound of dripping. He'd fallen asleep to the sound of dripping, too. He'd lived with it for the past several days. He would have to go right on living with it for a good many more days to come, no matter how much it made him want to go running to the jakes. All around the hostel in the Naantali district, the ice and snow were melting. They would take a while to finish the job, and the ground would stay soupy for a while afterwards: till the sun, which spent more and more time in the sky every day, finally dried up the accumulated moisture. As it did in Unkerlant and the land of the Ice People, spring announced itself in southeastern Kuusamo with a great thaw.

A malignant buzzing penetrated the drips. A mosquito landed on Fernao's arm, which lay outside the covers. The buzzing ceased. He slapped. The buzzing resumed. He cursed. That meant he'd missed the miserable thing.

Mosquitoes and gnats bred in puddles, of course. During the spring thaw, the Naantali district was all over puddles. For some time thereafter, it was all over mosquitoes and gnats, too. No wonder birds coming back from the north chose this time to mate and lay their eggs. They had plenty of food for themselves and for their youngsters, too. The only trouble was, they didn't, couldn't, come close to catching all the bugs. Plenty were left to torment people.

With a sigh, Fernao got out of bed and splashed cold water on his face. That wasn't torture, as it would have been during the winter. It still did help wake him up. He put on clean drawers and a fresh tunic, then pulled on his kilt, tucked in the tunic, and went downstairs to the refectory.

Ilmarinen already sat down there, eating smoked salmon and onions and drinking tea. "That looks good," Fernao said, sitting beside him and waving to a serving girl.

"It is," Ilmarinen agreed. "But it's mine. You can bloody well get your own."

"I did intend to," Fernao said mildly. The serving girl came up. Fernao pointed to Ilmarinen's plate. "I'll have what he's having." Seeing a wicked glint in the other theoretical sorcerer's eye, Fernao corrected himself: "Not his helping, but the same thing as he's having." Balked, Ilmarinen subsided.

The serving girl ignored the byplay. She just nodded and went off to the kitchen. Fernao patted himself on the back. He didn't win skirmishes with Ilmarinen all that often. Neither did anyone else.

Pekka walked into the refectory at the same time as Fernao's breakfast arrived. Seeing him, she smiled and waved and came on over. He spoke quietly to Ilmarinen: "Could you let the two of us be for once? Life's hard enough as is."

"I could," Ilmarinen said, but Fernao's relief was short-lived, for he added, "That doesn't necessarily mean I will."

Pekka sat down by Fernao. The serving girl—Fernao was just as glad it wasn't Linna—walked over and raised a questioning eyebrow. Pointing to Fernao, Pekka said, "I'll have what he's having."

Without so much as looking at Ilmarinen, Fernao shoved his plate and teacup over to Pekka. "Here," he said, deadpan, and nodded to the serving girl. "You can bring me more of the same."

"All right." Off she went again. The vagaries of mages fazed her not in the least.

"Something is going on here, and I don't know what," Pekka said darkly. She cast Ilmarinen a suspicious glance.

"I'm just sitting here," he told her. "Why are you picking on me? If something is going on and you don't understand it, you shouldn't complain, anyhow. You should experiment to find out what it is." His eyes flicked from her to Fernao and back again. "All sorts of interesting experiments you might try."

Fernao kicked him under the table. Pekka couldn't reach him to kick him, but looked as if she wanted to. Fernao had imagined some of those experiments. He didn't dare say so. He wished he hadn't given her his breakfast. Now he had nothing with which to busy himself.

Ilmarinen laughed, which only irked Fernao further—he knew he shouldn't have asked the Kuusaman mage to go easy. "Why are you getting upset?" Ilmarinen asked. "I can't be saying anything the two of you haven't thought of for yourselves."

"There is a difference between what I think and what I do." Fernao switched from Kuusaman to classical Kaunian for the sake of greater precision: "If there were not, I would be wringing your neck right now instead of quietly sitting here."

He'd hoped that might alarm Ilmarinen. Instead, it amused the elderly theoretical sorcerer, who laughed raucously. Fernao made himself stay in his chair, so that Ilmarinen never found out how close he did come to getting strangled. Ilmarinen finished his breakfast just as the serving girl brought Fernao more food. Getting to his feet, the master mage nodded to Fernao and Pekka in turn. "Well, I'm off," he said cheerily. "I'm sure the two of you have a lot to talk about, so you won't want me around anyhow." Away he went, whistling a tune that sounded bawdy.

At least Fernao did have something to do now, and he did it: he concentrated on his breakfast. He concentrated so fiercely, in fact, that when Pekka said something he didn't notice what it was, and hardly noticed she'd spoken at all. "I'm sorry," he said, looking up from his smoked salmon and blinking. "I'm afraid I missed that."

"I *said*, what are we going to do about Ilmarinen?" Pekka's voice was brittle. She was looking past Fernao's shoulder rather than at him.

"I don't know," he said. "The more I think about it, the better the idea of wringing his neck looks."

"We do need him for the work," Pekka said grudgingly. "Since it's hard to go out to the blockhouse and experiment with everything all over mud, I was hoping to use the quiet time to start standardizing our spells so practical mages can use them. That will make Prince Juhainen happy."

"So it will." Fernao sipped tea. He nodded, he hoped, judiciously. "It does need doing."

"So many things need doing, and we have so little time to do them," Pekka said. "Anything that distracts us from them is a nuisance. Anything at all." Now she did look straight into Fernao's eyes.

"Have I ever argued with that?" he asked. No matter what he'd been thinking, he'd always pulled his weight in the sorcerous research. He wasn't so brilliant as Ilmarinen, and knew he wasn't, but he didn't go around making people want to throttle him, either.

"No." Pekka shook her head. "You've always done everything I could have wanted, except . . . I mean . . ." Now she wouldn't look at him any more.

He finished his tea at a gulp, wishing it were something stronger. When he set down the mug, he said, "Come to my chamber with me." Pekka's eyebrows leaped upwards. As he had with Ilmarinen, he went back to classical Kaunian to explain exactly what he meant: "People have been gossiping about us for a long time now, even though we have given them nothing about which to gossip. If we make it seem as though something really has happened between us, perhaps they will take it for granted and leave us be so we can go on about our business."

"Perhaps," Pekka echoed, also in classical Kaunian. She sat beside him for half a minute or so, her face closed in thought. Then, abruptly, she nodded. "Worth a try." She got to her feet. So did Fernao. She slipped her hand into his. "It should look convincing," she murmured in a low, serious voice. He nodded and smiled and squeezed her hand a little. She squeezed back.

Mages and servers in the refectory eyed them as they walked toward the stairway hand in hand. *Either we'll stop the gossip about us*, Fernao thought, *or else we'll start a lot more.*

When they got to his chamber, he was glad he'd set the bed to rights and hadn't left anything but sorcerous tomes strewn about on the table and the stool and the chest of drawers that were the spare little room's only other furniture. "I don't want to disturb your work," Pekka said, and sat down on the bed while Fernao paused to bar the door.

"It wouldn't have mattered much," he answered as he sat beside her. "Now we just have to wait long enough so all the other people are sure they know what's going on in here."

"Aye." Pekka nodded. They sat close together, not touching

at all, not even looking at each other, for a couple of minutes. What happened next seemed likelier to have sprung from a three-hundred-year-old Valmieran comedy of manners than real life. Fernao slipped his arm around Pekka at exactly the same moment she leaned toward him. An instant after that, they weren't sitting on the bed any more. They were lying on it, clinging to each other as if they were lodestone and iron.

When at last their lips separated, Fernao whispered, "I've wanted to do this for so long." He trailed kisses across her cheek and down the side of her neck.

She shivered a little and sighed when he nibbled the lobe of her ear. She wasn't looking at him. She wasn't looking at anything; her eyes were shut tight. In a tiny voice, she said, "Please tell me you didn't have this in mind when you asked me to come up here with you."

"By the powers above, I didn't!" Fernao exclaimed, more truthfully than not. "It just—happened."

"It just—happened," Pekka echoed. Her eyes were still closed, but she nodded once more and reached for him. If anything, her kiss was even more desperate than his.

She shivered again when he unbuttoned her tunic, and once more when his mouth descended on her left breast. He teased her nipple with lips and tongue. She pressed his head to her. Then, panting and laughing, she reached under his kilt.

When all her clothes lay scattered on the floor, Fernao wondered how he could ever have thought her scrawny. She was what she was—a Kuusaman woman, made as Kuusamans were. And . . . Not much later, he stopped thinking at all, but leaned on one elbow above her for a moment while he guided himself in. She let out a low, breathy moan and clasped him with arms and legs. She still kept her eyes shut tight.

He had to fight not to explode in the first instant. Once he managed that, once he found a rhythm that suited them both, he thought for a while that he could go on forever. But Pekka's mounting excitement spurred him toward the end, too. She called out a name and gave a short, sharp cry of joy. Her nails scored his back. He gasped and shuddered and spent himself. Only afterwards did he notice the name she'd called wasn't his.

He stroked her cheek. With a little luck, she hadn't realized she'd cried her husband's name, there in the moment when all thought fled. But she had. She jerked away from his gentle hand and burst into tears. "Leave me alone!" she said. "What have I done?"

The answer to that was only too obvious. Fernao didn't point it out to her. He dressed quickly and hurried out of the chamber. Even though it was his, he fled it like an adulterer diving out a bedroom window when he heard footsteps on the stairs. He was halfway down the hall before he wondered what sort of rumors *that* would start.

Patrol. Somebody had to do it. Sidroc understood as much. The Unkerlanters had written the book on infiltration, written it and revised it several times. If you didn't go prowling forth and find out what they were up to and hold them at arm's length, you'd wake up one fine morning with them bellowing, "Urra!" from front, rear, and both flanks all at the same time.

But if you did go prowling forth, they were liable to kill you for your trouble. Patrols didn't always come back. Sometimes they just vanished as if they'd never been. Sidroc was painfully aware of that. He tried to tiptoe through the woods of the eastern Duchy of Grelz. Somebody had to go out on patrol, aye. He wished he weren't one of the somebodies.

He also wished he and his comrades from Plegmund's Brigade didn't have to rely on the guide who walked through the woods with them. Some Grelzer peasants hated King Swemmel and his inspectors and impressers worse than the Algarvians did. Others pretended to hate Swemmel so as to lure the redheads—and the Forthwegians who fought alongside them—to destruction. Finding out you'd trusted the wrong sort of guide was too apt to be the last discovery you ever made.

Sergeant Werferth spoke in Algarvian: "Where did you see these Unkerlanter soldiers?" Then he repeated the question in Forthwegian, which was at least related to the language spoken hereabouts.

"I see . . . by village," the guide said in bad Algarvian, and pointed west and a little north. "Two companies, maybeso three." He showed the numbers on his fingers to leave no room for error.

"Maybeso," Ceorl jeered. "Maybeso you're leading us into an ambush, eh?"

With a shrug, the guide answered, "You kill me then."

"Let him alone, Ceorl," Werferth said. "He's supposed to be on our side, remember?"

"He's supposed to be, aye," Sidroc said. "But *is* he?" Ceorl looked at him in surprise; they seldom agreed about anything. Sidroc went on, "I don't want him leading us down the primrose path, either, you know."

He'd spoken Forthwegian. Sure enough, the local could follow bits of the language, for he said, "No primroses." Then he said several other things in his own dialect of Unkerlanter. Sidroc got only fragments of that, but none of it sounded complimentary to King Swemmel. He kicked at the muddy pine needles underfoot. The guide would sound the same way no matter how he really felt about the King of Unkerlant.

"He knows this country better than we do," Werferth said. "It's his neck if the Unkerlanters catch him after he's helped us."

If he's the straight goods, Sidroc thought. *If he's not . . .* If the guide wasn't the straight goods, they could indeed avenge themselves upon him. That wasn't likely to do them much good, though.

Off in the distance, a wolf howled. Sidroc hoped it was a wolf, anyhow. So did the Algarvian lieutenant heading up the patrol. He said, "Do they really let those cursed things run loose in this part of the world?"

"Aye," the guide answered.

Sidroc wasn't altogether sure why anyone let the Algarvian lieutenant run loose in this part of the world. Sidroc hadn't seen his twentieth birthday yet, but he felt ten years older than the redhead. Even so, the Algarvian gave the orders, as if to proclaim that his folk were the conquerors, with the men of Plegmund's Brigade only along for the ride.

If they're the conquerors, how come they've spent most of the past year retreating? Sidroc wondered. *And what happens if they spend most of the next year retreating, too?* He didn't want to dwell on that. One of the reasons he'd signed up for Pleg-mund's Brigade was that the Algarvians had looked like world-beaters back in Forthweg. If the world was theirs, what better way to grab a chunk of it than fighting at their side?

He still couldn't imagine the world belonging to the Unker-lanters. They were too dowdy for that to seem possible.

Another wolf howled, this one in the direction where the guide said the Unkerlanters were based. "I don't like that," Sergeant Werferth muttered.

"Why not?" The Algarvian lieutenant sounded curious. A bright child might have sounded the same way. *We don't need a bright child leading our patrol,* Sidroc thought. *We need a nasty old veteran who knows what he's doing and how to go about it.* But the young Algarvian was what they had.

Patiently, Werferth said, "Because it sounds like signal and answer, sir. If it is signal and answer, we're liable to be walking into something we'd be better off missing."

"Ah," the lieutenant said, as if that hadn't occurred to him. He swept off his hat and bowed to Werferth, so maybe it hadn't. Sidroc sighed. If the lieutenant lived, he'd learn in a hurry. Fighting against the Unkerlanters, you had to. But if he didn't live, he was liable to drag the whole patrol down in ruin with him.

Very close by, a jay jeered. The guide froze. So did all the men from Plegmund's Brigade. That raucous cry made an even better signal than a wolf's howl. The Algarvian lieutenant took another couple of steps before realizing something might be wrong. He looked around wildly, his stick at the ready.

But then Sidroc spotted the bird, pinkish brown with a black tail, fluttering from one pine to another. As it flew, it screeched again. He breathed easier. "It's a real jay," he said.

"Nice to know something's real," Werferth said. Nobody argued with him.

The Algarvian lieutenant laughed and said, "If any Unker-lanters heard it, they probably started shivering, thinking it was us." Sidroc nodded. The lieutenant was likely to be right. Swemmel's men alarmed Sidroc, but he'd seen that Mezentio's men alarmed the Unkerlanters, too. That was fortunate, as far as he was concerned. Every so often, it kept the enemy from pressing an attack as hard as he might have.

"Forward," the young lieutenant said. Sidroc had heard the word too many times—mostly shouted, and emphasized by shrilling whistles—for it to spur him on as it had when he'd first joined Plegmund's Brigade. What was it but an invitation to get himself killed? Even the redhead seemed to realize as much, for he spoke quietly, as if to say the patrol needed to go on but shouldn't make a fuss about it.

Even though that jay had been real, Unkerlanters lurked among the trees. Sidroc could feel their presence even if he couldn't see or hear or smell them. The hair on his arms and at the back of his neck kept trying to prickle up. He was almost panting, as if he'd run a long way. But it wasn't exhaustion that had done it to him: it was nerves. He felt taut as a viol string about to snap.

Beside him, Ceorl started cursing under his breath: harsh, monotonous, vicious cursing, all in a tiny voice no one farther away than Sidroc could have heard. "You know they're there, too, eh?" Sidroc whispered. Ceorl looked astonished, as if he hadn't realized what he was doing. Maybe he hadn't. He nodded abruptly and went back to his oaths.

"Clearing," the guide said, first in his own language, then in Algarvian. The Unkerlanter word sounded like one that meant *market square* in Forthwegian, so Sidroc supposed he understood the fellow twice.

"Well, go on across it," the young lieutenant said. "We'll follow." That made good sense. Unkerlanter soldiers were far less likely to blaze a peasant than soldiers in the uniforms of their foes. Even so, the guide gave the redhead a look full of hate and fear as he started across the muddy open space. A couple of men at a time, the troopers from Plegmund's Brigade followed.

The guide had got about halfway to the trees on the far side of the clearing when he trod on a cunningly buried egg. Afterwards, Sidroc realized that was what must have happened. At the time, all he knew was the sudden roar and flash of light as the sorcerous energies trapped in the egg suddenly released themselves, all channeled upward to be as deadly as possible. The luckless guide didn't even have the chance to shriek. He simply ceased to be. One of his boots—probably not the one that had stepped on the egg—flew high into the air before thudding back to earth. That was the sole remaining sign he'd ever lived.

In automatic reflex, Sidroc started to throw himself flat. But he checked that reflex and stayed on his feet. He was liable to throw himself down on another egg, and to end as abruptly as the guide had done.

"Back!" the Algarvian lieutenant hissed, even more urgently than he'd ordered the advance not long before. He added, "Every Unkerlanter in the world is going to come see what happened here."

That was bound to be true, and made a powerful incentive to retreat in a hurry. Again, though, Sidroc didn't let himself be rushed. He tried to retrace his steps as exactly as he could. He hadn't stepped on an egg as he went west into the clearing. If he was careful, he wouldn't step on one going back east out of it.

He'd just slid behind a pale-barked birch when an Unkerlanter trooper in a rock-gray tunic stuck his head into the clearing. Sidroc whipped his stick up to his shoulder and blazed. The Unkerlanter toppled. Cries of alarm rang out from the woods on the other side of the open space.

"Nice blaze," Sergeant Werferth said. "They won't think we all ran for home with our tails between our legs."

He was right: the Unkerlanters didn't think that. Because they didn't, their egg-tossers started lobbing eggs into the forest to try to keep the patrol from making its way back to the encampment. Sidroc had endured far heavier bombardments in the fight in the Durrwangen bulge. Realizing that also made him realize this peppering shouldn't trouble him much—odds were, it would do him no harm.

Somehow, the comforting logic failed to comfort. Each bursting egg made him want to flee more than the one before. True, the fighting by Durrwangen had been far harsher. But Durrwangen had also been ten months before. Sidroc was ten months more battered, ten months more frazzled. He'd seen ten months' more disasters. He'd had ten months more to realize how easily disaster might visit him.

An egg burst, not far away. Someone started screaming. *One more down,* he thought. *One more who signed up in Forthweg for a lark, or maybe to stay out of gaol.* He looked back in time, trying once more to recall his own reasons for joining Plegmund's Brigade. With eggs bursting all around, with trees crashing down in front and behind, they didn't seem good enough.

"We did our duty," the young Algarvian officer said when they finally got back to the village from which they'd started. "We successfully developed the enemy's position. Now that we know where he is, our counterattacks stand a better chance of driving him back."

Sidroc didn't want to think about counterattacks. He'd lived through another day. He was content—he was delighted—to savor that.

Captain Frigyes prowled along the muddy beach of Becsehely. "Be ready, men," Istvan's company commander urged. "You must always be ready. No telling when the Kuusamans are liable to descend on us." He pointed to Istvan. "You wish to say something, Sergeant?"

"Aye, sir." Istvan nodded. "We've been hearing for months that the slanteyes would hit us, and they haven't done it yet. Why should we figure this time is any different?"

"Because I say so would be reason enough," Captain Frigyes answered, and Istvan winced. He'd meant no disrespect. But then Frigyes went on, "But there's more to it than that. Our mages have stolen emanations from their crystals. They're talking about Becsehely in ways they never have before. They're serious this time, no doubt of it."

"Ah." Istvan nodded again. "Thank you, sir."

"You're welcome." Frigyes pounded a fist into the palm of his other hand. "Are we going to lick those goat-eating whoresons when they try to take this island away from us?"

"Aye!" most of the men in the company roared. Istvan had to roar, too. So did Corporal Kun and Szonyi and a few other soldiers. Each of them bore an identical scar on his left hand: a remnant of the purification and penance Captain Tivadar, Frigyes' predecessor, had inflicted on them for inadvertently eating goat from a captured Unkerlanter stewpot. Tivadar was dead. Only the men who'd committed the sin—deadly, by Gyongyosian standards—knew of it these days. But a cry like Frigyes' still made Istvan sweat cold for fear he'd be discovered.

"We'll smash them like crocks! We'll beat them like drums!" That was Lajos. He hadn't been in Istvan's squad when they'd eaten from that accursed stewpot. He'd never fought the Kuusamans; they were just a name to him. He was young and brave and full of confidence. Life looked simple to him. Why not? He didn't know any better.

"We can beat them," Szonyi agreed. He'd been with Istvan a long time, ever since the fighting on Obuda, which lay a good deal farther west, in the Bothnian Ocean—and which, these days, belonged to Kuusamo once more. The difference between his *can* and Lajos' *will* was subtle, but it was all too real.

Kun didn't say anything. Behind the lenses of his gold-rimmed spectacles, his eyes were sober. Years of war had taught Szonyi some few reservations. Kun seemed to have been born with more than most Gyongyosians ever needed to acquire.

And what about me? Istvan wondered. Unlike Kun, he wasn't a city man. His home village, Kunhegyes, shared a mountain valley with a couple of other similar hamlets. Had it not been for the army, he might never have left that valley his whole life long unless he went raiding into a nearby one. His horizons now were wider than he'd ever imagined they could be. Sometimes he thought that marvelous. Rather more often, he wished it had never happened.

Not much horizon here. Even when he climbed out of the trench, all he could see was the low, flat, muddy island and the surrounding sea, which looked bare of ships. He found another question for Frigyes: "Captain, are they bringing more dragons to Becsehely to keep the slanteyes from pounding us the way they've done before?"

"We'll have plenty of dragons, Sergeant," the company commander replied, and strode on down the line.

Istvan beamed in considerable relief . . . until Corporal Kun spoke in a low voice: "You do realize he didn't answer your question, don't you?"

"He said—" Istvan broke off and thought about what Captain Frigyes *had* said. He kicked at the muddy ground. "You're right. He didn't. He might have been a father telling a little boy not to worry." The comparison angered him. He wasn't a little boy. He was a man. If he weren't a man, he wouldn't have been here with a stick slung on his back.

But Kun's voice held only calm appraisal: "He's a pretty good officer. He doesn't want people fretting about what they can't help."

"I wouldn't have, either, if you hadn't opened your mouth." Now Istvan was ready to be angry at Kun rather than Frigyes.

"One thing being a mage's apprentice taught me," Kun said: "what words mean and what they don't. I'd sooner find out the truth, whatever it is. And whatever it turns out to be, I expect I can look it in the eye. You can't say that about everyone."

"I suppose not," Istvan said. How would Kun take it if somebody pointed out the truth about his immodesty? Istvan didn't intend to do any such thing. Kun went on enough as things were.

And he had a gift for asking unpleasant questions. He found one now: "Suppose we look like we're going to lose Becsehely. Do you think our mages will start sacrificing us to build the sorcery they need to drive back the Kuusamans?"

"That's as the stars decide," Istvan answered. "Nothing I can do about it one way or the other. And you did volunteer, the same as I did, the same as most of the men in the company did."

"Oh, aye, I volunteered." Kun's eyes blazed from behind the lenses of his spectacles. "How could I do anything else, with everybody looking at me?"

"Aren't you the fellow who doesn't care what anybody else

thinks?" Istvan returned. He usually enjoyed turning the tables on Kun, not least because he couldn't very often. Today, though, the corporal didn't rise to the bait. He just scowled at Istvan and strode off, silent and gruff as if he'd come from a mountain valley himself.

For the next couple of days, everything on Becsehely stayed quiet. Gulls wheeled overhead. So did other, bigger, seabirds, some of them with a wingspan twice as wide as a man's outstretched arms. Those enormous birds spent most of their time in the air. Istvan had seen them on Obuda, too. When they did land, they often rolled and tumbled. Watching them crash to the ground—and watching them trying to get airborne again—was more entertaining than most of the things the Gyongyosian soldiers had to do on the island.

Alarm bells began clanging before dawn three days after Captain Frigyes delivered his warning. Troopers who weren't sleeping in their trenches ran for them. "This is no drill!" the company commander shouted moments after the clanging started. "The dowsers see enemy ships out over the horizon." He hesitated, then shouted one thing more: "Volunteers, remember your oath! You may be summoned."

Istvan wished Frigyes hadn't said that. How was he supposed to concentrate on staying alive against the Kuusamans if his own side was liable to kill him to drive back the invaders?

"Dragons!" That shout seemed to come from everywhere at once. Istvan hunkered down in his trench. Becsehely had been hit before. It had been hit hard, too. But Gyongyosian dragons flying off the little island had also struck back hard at the enemy. Not this time, or not for long. Kuusamo seemed to have gathered every dragon in the world and put all those beasts in the air above the island.

That was how it felt to Istvan, anyhow. The rain of eggs was the hardest he'd ever known. There were almost as many as if they'd been real raindrops, or so it seemed to him. The ground under him jerked and quivered, as if in torment. Dirt flew into the air and thudded down onto him and his squadmates—so much dirt, he feared being buried alive.

And the dragons swooped low, too, flaming whenever the

men who flew them found targets they judged worthwhile. Shrieks rose from the trenches, punctuating the roar of bursting eggs and the alarm bell's brazen clamor. Before long, Istvan smelled charred meat. He cursed. He knew what meat that was.

Then the bells redoubled their fury. "Boats offshore!" The cry reached Istvan as if from very far away. But he understood what it meant. It meant the Gyongyosian crystallomancers had had the right of it. This time, the Kuusamans were going to try to take Becsehely away from Gyongyos.

He stuck his head up out of the trench. He'd seen enemy boats approaching a Gyongyosian-held island before, back in the days when he was fighting on Obuda. It had meant trouble then. It meant trouble now, too. And he saw no Gyongyosian ships attacking the Kuusaman vessels from which those invasion boats came.

"It's up to us," he said. "If we don't throw the enemy back, nobody will."

"If we don't throw the enemy back, the mages will cut our throats and hope they can do it," Kun said. Istvan glared at him. But Kun hadn't spoken loud enough to demoralize any of the other soldiers, so Istvan did no more than glare.

The sea was full of boats. All of them seemed to be coming straight toward Istvan. The Kuusaman naval vessels started throwing eggs at the beaches of Becsehely. Istvan ducked down into the trench again. But he couldn't stay down there. If the Kuusamans got soldiers ashore, he was a dead man. That their eggs might easily kill him, too, was only a detail.

"Make them pay!" Captain Frigyes shouted, though his voice sounded small and lost amidst the endless roars of the bursting eggs. "By the stars, it'll cost them if they want to shift Gyongyosian warriors."

As soon as the incoming boats got close enough, Istvan started blazing at them. The Kuusamans blazed back, though the bobbing waves made most of their beams go wild. "We'll slaughter them," Szonyi said happily.

"I hope so," Istvan answered.

And the Gyongyosians did slaughter their foes, at least those who tried to come ashore in front of the trench where Istvan and his comrades crouched. A good many enemy soldiers never made it to the beach alive. None of the small, dark, slant-eyed men made it off the beach alive, not there.

But, even while Istvan's company beat back the Kuusamans, shouts of alarm rose elsewhere on Becsehely: "They've landed!" The soldiers' cheers turned to cries of alarm. If the Kuusamans had gained a foothold on the island, they would prove far harder to dislodge—by any ordinary means, that is.

No sooner had that thought crossed Istvan's mind than Captain Frigyes called, "Back toward the mages, my brave men. We are warriors—we can give all that warriors have to give. For Gyongyos and Ekrekek Arpad!"

"For Gyongyos and Ekrekek Arpad!" Istvan echoed. He followed Frigyes from the trenches without hesitation. If Gyongyos needed his life from him, Gyongyos would have it. And if fear made his legs feel as if they were made of gelatin and not flesh and solid bone . . . he would pretend it didn't.

"I told you this would happen," Kun said furiously. Istvan only shrugged. He'd thought it might happen, too. It bothered him less than it did the former mage's apprentice. Getting burnt to nothingness by a bursting egg before his life energy could serve his kingdom worried him more. Plainly, he would die on Becsehely one way or another. That being so, he wanted to choose the way.

But then even that choice was denied him, for a swarm of Kuusamans—a regiment's worth, at least—came rushing up from the south. They must have swept all before them there. "To surrender!" one of them shouted in bad Gyongyosian.

Istvan looked to Captain Frigyes. Had the company commander been ready to fight to the death, he would have fought, too. But Frigyes, though ready to die to aid Gyongyos, didn't care to perish to no purpose. He let his stick fall and raised his hands. And Istvan discovered he was not a bit sorry to do the same. A crazy grin spread across his face. That he'd been ready to die made living all the sweeter.

Pekka breathed a sigh of relief as she put a pad inside her drawers. Aye, she'd done something she wished, looking back on it, she hadn't. But she wouldn't have to face the consequences nine months from now.

A frown made a small vertical line appear between her eyebrows. It had nothing to do with the dull ache in her lower back, or even with the cramps that would follow. Try as she would, she couldn't make all of her wish she hadn't gone to bed with Fernao. Despite the tears and regrets afterwards, it had felt too good while it was going on.

It would have been just as good with Leino. It would have been even better with Leino. She nodded to herself while she finished dressing. That was probably true. But her husband, however much she missed him and wanted him, was far away, and had been for much too long. If she wanted Fernao, she had only to walk to his chamber and knock on the door.

She hadn't done it, not since that first time. And Fernao hadn't come knocking on her door, either. More than anything else, that made her believe he hadn't planned on seducing her when he invited her to his room. She shook her head as she walked to the door. It hadn't been a seduction, curse it. She couldn't claim it hadn't also been her fault, not even to herself. She'd wanted the Lagoan mage as much as he'd wanted her.

And he still wanted her. She knew as much. What she wanted . . . "is nobody's affair but my own," she murmured, stepping out into the hallway. She hadn't taken more than two steps toward the refectory before she stopped and kicked at the carpet. She wished she hadn't used the word *affair*, even if she didn't mean it like *that*.

When she got down to the refectory, she saw Fernao sitting at a table with Raahe and Alkio, animatedly talking shop. The table had four chairs around it. Alkio saw her and waved her to the empty one, which was by Fernao's. She didn't see that she had any choice but to go sit there. She would have before the two of them made love: that was certain.

"Good morning," Fernao said. Like her, he did his best to pretend in public that nothing too much out of the ordinary had happened.

"Good morning." Pekka made a particular kind of sour face.

"Fair morning, anyhow." Fernao looked baffled. So did Alkio. Raahe softly chuckled into her cup of tea. She understood that—but then, she was a woman, too.

Linna came bustling up. "What can I get you?" she asked. Her eyes traveled speculatively from Pekka to Fernao and back again.

"Tea," Pekka said, ignoring that glance. Going to Fernao's room hadn't stifled the gossip—no indeed. It just spawned more. "Oatmeal with berries and plenty of honey." She didn't feel like anything heavier. Linna nodded and went away.

Fernao returned to the conversation he'd been having with the husband-and-wife team of theoretical sorcerers: "I still say that instance we sensed yesterday felt . . . *odd* is the only word I can find for it."

Alkio shook his head. "I don't think so. It's just that we've got too used to feeling those murderous sacrifices. They don't jolt us the way they once did."

Nodding, Pekka said, "I know for a fact that that's true with me. And if it's not a judgment on us all, and on this whole sorry world, powers below eat me if I know what would be."

"A judgment? Aye, no doubt." Fernao nodded, too, and so did Raahe and Alkio. But, stubbornly, the Lagoan mage went on, "It didn't feel right, though, I tell you."

"Of course not," Alkio said. "If it *was* wrong, how could it *feel* right?"

Fernao exhaled through his nose in exasperation. "That is not what I meant," he said, switching from Kuusaman to classical Kaunian so he could get across exactly what he did mean. "I meant it did not feel like Algarvian magecraft, and it did not feel like Unkerlanter sorcery."

Alkio gestured dismissively. "Who else could it have been? No one but Mezentio's mages and Swemmel's uses those spells, and powers above be praised for that."

Before Fernao could answer—and, for that matter, before he could get any angrier, for he was already irked—Piilis came into the refectory. As he paused in the doorway, Pekka waved to him. He waved back and walked toward the table where she was sitting. She hooked a chair from another table with her ankle and scooted over to give Piilis room to join her colleagues and her.

Only after she'd done it did she realize she'd scooted closer to Fernao. Was that wise? *It's what I would have done before . . . what happened happened*, she told herself. Whether that answered her question was a question in and of itself.

"Thank you, Mistress Pekka," Piilis said. "I ran into one of the crystallomancers on my way over here, so I've got some news."

"Well, tell us," Pekka said. "If it weren't for the crystallomancers, we wouldn't know any of what was going on till it was already gone. It's not as if they send us news sheets every day."

"The miserable Gongs tried something new when we landed on that Bothnian island called Becsehely." Piilis pronounced the foreign name with care. "They were going to trot out the murderous magic the Algarvians use, but we overran them so fast, they didn't have the chance to kill many of their own soldiers, so the magic wasn't so big or so strong as it might have been, and Becsehely's ours."

"Ha!" Fernao said, and then, "Ha!" again. Piilis looked confused. He looked even more confused when Fernao wagged a finger at Alkio and declared, "I told you so."

"Well, so you did." Alkio clicked his tongue between his teeth. "The Gyongyosians are using this sorcery, too? That is not good at all."

"And killing their own soldiers to power it?" Pekka added. "That may be even worse than what the Algarvians and Unkerlanters do."

"Not to hear the Gongs talk about it," Piilis said. "By the reports we're getting from the captives we've taken, they won't slaughter anyone who didn't volunteer ahead of time—and a lot of men did. They think it's an honor to let themselves get killed for their kingdom. It makes the stars shine on them, or some such nonsense."

With profound unoriginality, Pekka said, "Gyongyosians are very strange people."

"They think the same of us," Fernao said, using classical Kaunian again. "All the other strong kingdoms share—more or less, and sometimes at several removes—the culture that springs from the Kaunian Empire. But the Gyongyosians have their own. When we bumped up against them a hundred and fifty years ago, they borrowed—"

"Stole," Alkio put in.

Fernao nodded, accepting the correction. "They stole some of our fancy magecraft, nailed it onto everything else they already had, and they went right on to make nuisances of themselves."

"More than nuisances," Alkio said, and all the other Kuusamans at the table spoke up to agree with him. He went on, "We've been squabbling with them over the islands in the Bothnian Ocean ever since. They want everything they can get their hands on, and a little more, besides."

"And what do they say about Kuusamans?" Fernao asked innocently.

"Who cares what Gongs say?" Alkio answered, proving he'd missed the point.

Pekka hadn't, but she had other things to worry about. "The next time we try to take an island the Gyongyosians hold, we may not be so lucky as we were at this Besce-whatever place," she said. "Prince Juhainen was right—all the more reason for us to get our own spells to the point where practical mages can use them."

All the more reason for us to get our own spells to the point when Leino can use them. Pekka wondered if her husband, wherever he was, was looking at other women, or even doing more than looking at them. Before she'd made love with Fernao, the idea would have horrified and infuriated her. It still horrified her, but in a way she almost hoped he was. Then, at least, they would both feel guilty when they finally got back together.

"Raahe and Alkio and I were talking about that before you got here," Fernao said.

He didn't sound as if he had any second thoughts about bedding her. *Why should he?* Pekka thought. *It's not as if he betrayed his wife . . . At least, I don't think it is.* She suddenly realized just how much she didn't know about the Lagoan mage's past and background. *What kind of fool was I, to go to bed with him?* One corner of her mouth quirked upward. The answer to that was only too plain: *a hot fool, a lickerish fool.*

Again, she made herself think about what she had to do, not about what she'd already done. "What in particular were you talking about?" she asked.

"Ways to simplify the spell while keeping the energy level high," Fernao replied. "Raahe has some good ideas, I think."

Piilis said, "I've been doing some calculations of my own along those lines." He took folded papers from his belt pouch and spread them out on the table—this just as Linna came out of the kitchen with his breakfast.

The serving girl gave him a severe look. "If you don't eat, sorcerous sir, you won't be strong enough to follow whatever it is you've written down there."

"Sorry." Piilis cleared some room in front of him. Linna set down his smoked salmon and eggs and went off. He promptly leaned over the plate of food so he could explain his line of thought. The other theoretical sorcerers leaned forward, too. The only heed Piilis gave the salmon and eggs was to keep from putting his elbow in the plate.

As Pekka and Fernao leaned toward his papers, their knees and thighs brushed under the table. Pekka was acutely aware of it. If Fernao was, he gave no sign. He didn't press himself against her to remind her of what they'd done. She nodded to herself. It wasn't as if she didn't know.

"Let me have a look at those," Raahe said, and turned Piilis' calculations so that she could read them—which meant they were upside down for Pekka. But when Pekka sighed and started to ease back in her seat, she brushed up against Fernao again. That kept her leaning forward. Then Raahe turned the leaves of paper back around once more, remarking, "That's not the approach I was taking, but you could be on to the same thing."

"No." Fernao sounded regretful, but very sure. He sounded so sure, in fact, that all four Kuusaman mages around the table bristled at him. But then he reached out and tapped a line about halfway down the second leaf of paper. "This whole expansion sequence is forbidden in this context. Mistress Raahe's approach will work. This . . ." He shrugged. "Following it will be like following a will-o'-the-wisp: you will never end up anywhere worth going, but only in the middle of a swamp."

Pekka took a longer look at the calculations. "You . . . may be right," she said.

"So you'll believe Fernao even when he leads you into a swamp, eh?" The voice from behind her made her start and whirl. There stood Ilmarinen, looking down on her with a sardonic grin. He shook his head. "How very strange. You wouldn't have said that even a little while ago."

Before you went to bed with him, was what he meant. Pekka glared. "See for yourself," she snapped.

"I was trying to." Ilmarinen didn't bother with his spectacles, but read at long range. After perhaps half a minute, he let out a soft grunt. "Sorry, Piilis. I don't think the Lagoan's the least bit cute, but he's right. You can't expand it that way."

For the life of her, Pekka didn't know whether to thank him or to brain him with a teapot. By the look on Fernao's face, he was even closer to swinging the teapot than she was.

"My, my," Colonel Sabrino murmured as his wing came spiraling down to land at the new dragon farm in southern Unkerlant to which they'd been ordered. "Isn't that fascinating?" He'd let the wind blow his words away, but now he activated his crystal and repeated himself for Captain Orosio: "Isn't that simply fascinating?"

"That's one word, Colonel," the squadron commander answered. "Maybe not the one I would've used, but one word. Who would've thought we'd end up flying alongside Yaninans again?"

They'd been together a long time. Sabrino nodded. "We haven't for a while now," he said. "Not since we were down in the land of the Ice People."

"I almost forgot the Yaninans were still in the war." Orosio's lip curled scornfully, as any Algarvian's might have done while he contemplated his kingdom's allies. His chuckle held scant mirth. "And don't you just bet all the cursed Yaninans wish they could forget they were still in the war, too?"

"Heh," Sabrino said—one syllable's worth of bitter laughter. He did his best to look on the bright side of things: "I've seen plenty of dragon farms I liked less."

Sure enough, this one was bigger than most of those from which his wing had been flying. It looked to have been here a while, too. Heavy sticks ringed it, sticks potent enough to blaze marauding Unkerlanter dragons out of the sky. The Yaninan dragonfliers lived in huts, not tents. *The only thing wrong with them is, they're Yaninans,* Sabrino thought. Had their dragons been painted green, red, and white instead of just white and red . . .

But Sabrino shook his head. Even that wasn't fair. Down on the austral continent, Colonel Broumidis' dragonfliers had fought just about as well as the men Sabrino himself led. Yaninan footsoldiers . . . Sabrino shook his head again, this time for a different reason. He didn't want to think about Yaninan footsoldiers. They'd proved less than Algarve would have wished in the land of the Ice People, and they'd proved even less than that here in Unkerlant. If they hadn't given way at exactly the wrong time, the great disaster at Sulingen might not have happened.

If there were enough Algarvians to go around, Sulingen wouldn't have happened, Sabrino thought. A lot of other things wouldn't have happened, either; he was certain of that. He was every bit as certain that there weren't enough Algarvians to go around, though. Had there been, his wing's true strength wouldn't have stood at less than half of the sixty-four dragons it carried on paper—and that after reinforcement.

His own mount beat its great, membranous wings a couple of times and settled to the ground. His teeth clicked together; he'd known gentler landings. But he'd also known worse ones—at least he hadn't bitten his tongue this time.

A Yaninan dragon handler, a swarthy little bandy-legged fellow with a big black mustache and bushy side whiskers, came hurrying up to the dragon and chained it to a stake so it couldn't fly off whenever the notion came into its tiny, savage mind. The Yaninan did the job as well as any Algarvian could have.

Sabrino had trouble taking him seriously, even so. His tights and his tunic with big, puffy sleeves were bad enough. The shoes with bobbling pom-pom ornaments—Sabrino had to look away, lest he burst out laughing and offend the little man.

As Sabrino descended from the dragon, a Yaninan officer strode up to greet him. The Yaninan had a crown and star on each shoulder strap, which made him a major. He saluted Sabrino and spoke in pretty good Algarvian: "Hello, Colonel. Welcome to Plankenfels." His wave encompassed the dragon farm. "And I have the honor to be Major Scoufas, at your service."

Sabrino returned the bow and gave his own name. "Happy to be able to help my kingdom's allies," he said politely.

Something sparked in Scoufas' dark, almost fathomless eyes. "You are gracious," he remarked. "If all Algarvians were like you, we would be happier in our alliance. Believe me, we already know we are your poor relations. Some of you want to remind us of it whenever you find the chance."

Sabrino had seen that for himself. He'd also seen that some Algarvians had good reason for treating Yaninans with something less than perfect courtesy and respect. He didn't say that; Scoufas wouldn't have appreciated it. What he did say was, "I am sorry about that, Major. Of course, your kingdom's other choice is Unkerlant. I'm sure King Swemmel's men would prove the picture of politeness."

Scoufas winced. "Savages," he muttered; Yanina feared Unkerlant, but did not love her. The dragonflier pulled himself together. "Your wing will be of great help in holding the river line there." He pointed west to show where the front lay.

"That's why we're here," Sabrino agreed. "And now that we are here, maybe you can give me a little more in the way of a briefing."

With a shrug—not an elaborate Algarvian shrug, but one in the Yaninan style, one that said things weren't all they might be, but nobody could do anything about it—Scoufas replied, "This is where the front was when the thaw pinned things in place. We are trying to keep it here. We have not enough men, not enough behemoths, not enough egg-tossers—but we are trying."

"Not enough dragons, either, I suppose." Sabrino fought to keep irony from his voice. Yaninans weren't the greatest warriors in Derlavai, but who came close to them when it got down to complaining?

"No, not enough dragons, either," Major Scoufas said gravely. He bowed to Sabrino. "Your coming will make a difference there, of course."

How big a difference? Sabrino wondered, returning the bow. But thinking about dragons naturally led him to his next question: "How are you fixed for cinnabar?"

Scoufas shrugged again. "Not very well. Such is life, these days. The Unkerlanters have plenty. Their dragons can flame farther than ours, thanks to all the quicksilver they give them. We fly better than they do, though, which takes away some of their advantage."

"All right." It wasn't all right—it wasn't even close to all right—but Sabrino couldn't do anything about it. "Let's get my dragons seen to, let's get my men settled, and then you'll show me the map."

"Everything shall be just as you say, of course," Scoufas replied with another bow.

The Yaninan dragon handlers did seem capable enough. They fed the newly come Algarvian dragons chunks of meat rubbed in ground brimstone, and they gave them some meat rubbed in cinnabar—about as much, or rather as little, as their Algarvian opposite numbers would have had available. The Yaninans had huts waiting and ready for Sabrino's dragonfliers. Sabrino could think of major generals who would be sleeping rougher than he was.

But when he got a look at the map, he forgot about everything else. "Powers above!" he burst out. "If they push hard—no, when they push hard—how in blazes do you propose to stop them?"

"I am not a major of footsoldiers," Scoufas said, which wasn't an answer. "We shall do everything in our power, I assure you," he added, which wasn't an answer, either. Then that rather nasty glint came back to his eyes. "Of course, you Algar-

vians have had a certain amount of trouble stopping the Unkerlanters, too."

Sabrino would have resented that more if it hadn't been true.
From the freezing Narrow Sea in the south to the warm Garelian Ocean in the north, the Algarvians were stretched too thin
against their bigger foe. This, though—what passed for the
Yaninan line looked like a wool tunic after an army of moths
had found it in a closet.

Scoufas added, "You Algarvians often say Yaninans can't
fight. Then you go to war with your great plenty of all the tools.
The Unkerlanters—they too have a great plenty of all the tools.
And what have we? Bodies. With bodies, Colonel, we do what
we can."

Sometimes what those bodies did was run away as fast as
they could go, sometimes even throwing away their sticks to
flee the faster. Sabrino knew that. Scoufas doubtless knew it,
too, even if he didn't feel like owning up to it. Like a lot of Yaninan officers, he had pride and to spare. And he needed it, for it
was about the only thing of which he had plenty.

"My men and I will do what we can for you, Major," Sabrino
said.

The Yaninan shrugged another pessimistic shrug. "If your
wing were not battered and used up, your superiors would
never have sent it here," he said. "We know we get your leavings." He waited for Sabrino to argue. Sabrino didn't. He
couldn't. That was also true. When he didn't, Scoufas raised
an elegantly arched eyebrow and asked, "Tell me, if you
would be so kind, what you did to get yourself sent among
Yaninans?"

"Do you want to know the truth?" Sabrino asked, and Scoufas dipped his head. Yaninans often did that instead of nodding; Sabrino had seen as much down in the land of the Ice
People. He went on, "I told King Mezentio he was wrong about
something, and I happened to be right."

"Ah," Scoufas said. "If you had done such a thing with King
Tsavellas, it might have proved a fatal error."

Who says it isn't? Sabrino thought. But he would not say that to a Yaninan. Instead, he said, "I've been a colonel a long time. I'll keep right on being a colonel for a long time to come." *Unless I get killed, of course.* He shrugged. *I have only my wife to provide for these days, now that Fronesia's squeezing money out of that footsoldier instead.*

"What did you, ah, say to your king to fall from his good graces?" Scoufas asked.

Sabrino didn't intend to answer that, but decided it couldn't make any difference. "I told him sacrificing Kaunians for the sake of strong sorcery would turn out to be a mistake, and it did."

"Well." Whatever Scoufas had expected, that plainly wasn't it. "You surprise me, Colonel. I thought all Algarvians killed Kaunians with a smile on their faces, I have not seen any who did not, at any rate, not till now."

"Life is full of surprises," Sabrino said, at which Scoufas dipped his head again.

Two days later, when Sabrino's wing flew their first mission alongside Scoufas' Yaninan dragonfliers, he got another surprise. It wasn't that the Yaninans performed well enough. He'd looked for that, remembering how well Colonel Broumidis' men had flown down on the austral continent. What really startled him was how weak the Unkerlanter forces opposite the Yaninans were. His wing came back from smashing up the enemy's outposts not only without losing a man but also without the feeling of having been in real danger.

"Maybe I should have said even more rude things to his Majesty," Sabrino told Captain Orosio once they got back to the dragon farm. "This isn't war—it's more like the rest cure they give consumptives."

"Swemmel's whoresons sure fight us a lot harder than they go after these buggers," Orosio agreed. "Till we got here, I didn't think the Unkerlanters *had* a second team. We've never seen it before, by the powers above."

"Of course," Sabrino said musingly, "it *is* all they need against the Yaninans."

"Oh, aye—no doubt about that." His squadron commander didn't bother hiding his scorn. "Powers above, if Swemmel had a third team, he could get away with using that, too. Hit Tsavellas' odds and sods with a real army and they'd break like a dropped pot."

"Aye, they would, wouldn't they?" Sabrino looked around, more than a little nervously. He wished Orosio hadn't put it quite that way.

Seven

Bembo swaggered through Eoforwic exactly as he'd swaggered through Gromheort farther east. Thanks to Delminio, his new partner, he'd already made the acquaintance of a good many taverns and eateries and bakeries where a hungry man could get what he needed to sustain himself through a long, hard, wearying shift on the beat. He was sustaining himself so much, he was thinking of letting out the belt that held up his kilt another notch.

He didn't enjoy going into the Kaunian quarter when his partner and he drew that duty, but he didn't shrink from it. And it had compensations patrolling the rest of Eoforwic didn't offer. As Delminio put it, "The blond women throw themselves at our feet or on their knees or however we want them." By the smug smile on his face, he'd had no trouble getting at least one exactly how he wanted her.

"Aye, no doubt about it," Bembo agreed. He'd had good luck with Kaunian women, too. As an Algarvian constable, one could hardly help having good luck with Kaunian women. "Hardly seems sporting, does it? They'll do anything, or a lot of 'em will, on account of they think we can keep 'em alive if we want to."

"Sporting?" Delminio shrugged. "Who cares about sporting? What I care about is getting my ashes hauled."

"Sounds right," Bembo said. Delminio didn't hate Kaunians the way Oraste, his old partner, had. But Delminio didn't hesitate in taking advantage of the blonds whenever he saw the chance, either. Since Bembo rarely hesitated himself when he saw that kind of chance, they got along fine.

After walking on for a few paces, Bembo said, "There are times I wish we hadn't started sending 'em west. I don't know what in blazes it's got us. The Unkerlanters are doing their own dirty work, and it pretty much cancels ours out."

With another shrug, Delminio said, "I don't worry about stuff like that. If it's good enough for King Mezentio, I figure it's good enough for me, too."

"You've got a sensible way of looking at things," Bembo said. That was plenty to make Delminio strut and preen as if he'd just been named a duke. Bembo wished he could take the whole Kaunian business so lightly. He could sometimes, as when he was getting a blond woman to go to bed with him. But he had more trouble shutting down his mind the rest of the time than Delminio seemed to.

A Kaunian woman came out of a block of flats. As soon as they saw her golden hair shining in the sun, Bembo and Delminio both swung their heads toward her, a motion as automatic as breathing to them. And then, when they noticed she was very pregnant, they both looked away again, too.

As for her, she looked through them as if they didn't exist. That was the common reaction among Kaunian women who didn't care to give themselves to the Algarvians. "Wonder if one of us stuck that baby in her," Delminio remarked.

"I doubt it," Bembo said, as the young woman waddled around a corner. "She doesn't look like she hates us enough for that." He fancied himself a connoisseur of such reactions.

"Mm, you're probably right," Delminio said. Either he agreed with Bembo or he didn't feel like arguing. *Odds are he thinks I'm right,* Bembo thought. *We Algarvians, we're an argumentative bunch.*

Bells began ringing, not just in the Kaunian quarter but all over Eoforwic. Blonds started running. Delminio started cursing. So did Bembo. "Stinking Unkerlanter dragonfliers," he snarled. "Over in Gromheort, we didn't have to worry about this much."

"Over in Gromheort, you were a lot farther east," Delminio pointed out. "Just thank the powers above that our dowsers are getting better at spotting Swemmel's dragons before the whoresons are right on top of us."

"Even if they weren't, I suppose we could always duck into a cellar with the Kaunians," Bembo said.

"Go ahead if you want to," Delminio said. "Me, I'd sooner take a chance on Unkerlanter eggs. Not long before you got here, a couple of constables went into a cellar full of blonds. They didn't come out again—not alive, I mean. And of course the cellar was empty by the time anybody found 'em. They weren't pretty," he added in meditative tones, "and we still don't know just who did for them."

"Oh." Bembo kicked at the slates of the sidewalk. "I hadn't heard about that."

"No, you wouldn't have," Delminio agreed. "They don't go out of their way to talk about it, if you know what I mean." The clanging of the bells grew more urgent. "But we ought to look for a cellar ourselves right about now, and that means one outside the Kaunian quarter."

"Oh," Bembo said again. "Right." He pointed to his partner. "Well, lead the way. You're the one who's supposed to know what's where in this town. If you don't know where the closest handy cellar is, what good are you?"

Neither of them ran from the Kaunian district. But neither of them dawdled, either. They ducked into a cellar already rapidly filling with Algarvian constables and soldiers and a few trusted Forthwegians just as the first eggs fell on Eoforwic. The floor beneath Bembo's feet shook. Lanterns swung on their mounting brackets. Shadows swooped and danced. Bembo tried not to think about what would happen if an Unkerlanter egg landed right on top of the cellar.

Savagely, someone said, "I hope we're paying the Unkerlanters back ten for one."

Someone else spoke in reassuring tones: "Of course we are."

Bembo wished he knew where that *of course* came from. Blind optimism, probably. Had the war been going altogether in Algarve's direction, the Unkerlanters wouldn't have been able to drop eggs on Eoforwic. Had the war been going alto-gether in Algarve's direction, Unkerlant would long since have been conquered.

And so Bembo decided there were worse things than hud-dling in a cellar while dragons painted rock-gray flew over-head. He could have been huddling in a trench, waiting for soldiers in rock-gray tunics to swarm over him. After a while, the dragons above Eoforwic would be gone. In a trench, the danger never went away.

"We ought to have more dragons and heavy sticks around Eoforwic," Delminio said. "This is an important place. Do we let the Unkerlanters knock chunks of it flat whenever they please?"

"If we put more dragons and heavy sticks back here, pal, we wouldn't have 'em at the front," a soldier said. "There's not enough to go around as is, in case you haven't noticed. Having Swemmel's whoresons tear a hole in the line is a bigger worry than anything else, believe you me it is." That echoed Bembo's thought too closely for comfort.

After what seemed like forever but couldn't have been much above half an hour, the eggs stopped falling on Eoforwic. Be-mbo could barely hear the bells announcing that the Unker-lanter raiders had flown back toward the west. All through the cellar, people sighed and stretched, getting ready to resume their interrupted lives. Somebody put it pretty well: "We got through another one."

"Now let's go see how many pieces need picking up," Be-mbo said to Delminio.

"There'll be some," Delminio predicted. "There always are." He did his best to sound like a jaded veteran. As far as Bembo was concerned, he succeeded. But then a soldier let out a snort. Delminio gave the fellow a dirty look, but the damage was done.

When they came out into the fresh air, it didn't seem so fresh any more. The stink of smoke made Bembo cough. Looking around, he saw several plumes rising into the sky. More bells jangled as crews hurried to try to cope with the fires. "Looks like they hit us a good lick," he remarked.

"They've done worse," Delminio said. But his bravado didn't last. With a sigh, he went on: "They are hitting us harder and more often than they were a year ago. We have to carry on. I don't know what else we can do."

At the edge of the Kaunian quarter, Algarvian constables eyed Bembo and Delminio's kilts and reddish hair, making sure of who and what they were before waving them on into the district. Bembo looked around in disgust. "Hardly seems like anything fell here."

"Swemmel's whoresons don't usually hit the Kaunians hard," Delminio answered. "They know the blonds give us trouble, and they know what we do with those blonds, too, so they don't see much point to dropping eggs on 'em."

"Stupid, if you ask me," Bembo said. "If the Unkerlanters know we're killing Kaunians to give 'em grief, they ought to do their best to kill 'em before we get the chance."

"Why don't you write a letter to Marshal Rathar?" Delminio said. Bembo made a horrible face at him. They both laughed.

Just as they were rounding a corner, another redheaded fellow in constabulary uniform hurried into a block of flats. "Boy, he didn't waste any time getting back here, did he?" Bembo said.

Delminio chuckled. "He's probably got himself a sweet little Kaunian tart stashed in there." His hands, expressive as any Algarvian's, shaped an hourglass in the air. "Has to make sure his darling is all right, don't you know."

"Makes sense," Bembo agreed. "You want to know what I think, though, what doesn't make sense is getting that stuck on any one blond girl. How long is she likely to last before they ship her west?"

"You know what your trouble is?" Delminio said. He waited for Bembo to shake his head, then continued, "Your trouble is, you've got your head on too straight. A lot of fellows, they screw a girl a few times and then they decide they have to be in love with her. You know what I mean?"

Bembo nodded. "Oh, sure. I've seen that. Powers above, back when I was a kid I'd do it myself. But it's especially stupid here."

"I won't tell you you're wrong," Delminio said. "Back before you got here, a couple of constables got caught tipping off their Kaunian girlfriends that roundups were coming, or else hiding them so they wouldn't get shipped out."

"Officers do that kind of stuff all the time," Bembo said.

"If these had been officers, they would've got away with it," Delminio said. "But they were just ordinary sods like you and me. The wenches went out on the next ley-line caravan west, and the bigwigs decided those constables had volunteered for the infantry, so they're somewhere off in Unkerlant, too—if they're still breathing they are, I mean."

Bembo grunted. "That's . . . probably worth knowing," he said at last. What went through his mind was, *You can enjoy yourself with these Kaunian gals, but don't—by the powers above, don't!—do anything stupid.* He didn't expect he would. His mother hadn't raised him to be a fool.

Delminio had been eyeing him. After a moment, his new partner nodded. "I said you had your head on straight."

"You'd best believe it," Bembo boasted, which made Delminio snort.

That pregnant Kaunian woman emerged from her cellar and made her way back to the block of flats next door to the one the Algarvian constable with the blond girlfriend had entered. Delminio pointed to her. "What do you suppose she's thinking right now?"

"When you get right down to it, that doesn't make much difference, does it?" Bembo pointed in the direction from which the Unkerlanter dragons had come, the direction in which so many Kaunians were going. Delminio thought it over. He didn't need to think long. After only a couple of heartbeats, he nodded.

"How are you this morning, milady?" Bauska asked.

"Sleepy," Krasta said around a yawn. "Very sleepy." She gave the yawn full rein. "Funny—I didn't get to bed all that late last night, or the night before, either." She yawned again. If she wanted to go back to bed, who would stop her?

But her maidservant, annoyingly, persisted: "How are you feeling today?"

Bauska's question had a certain eager avidity to it. No matter how tired Krasta felt, she noticed that. "I already told you," she snapped. "Why don't you go away and leave me alone?"

"Aye, milady. Shall I bring you some tea, to help you wake up?" the serving woman asked.

"No." Krasta shuddered. "The cup I had yesterday tasted most shockingly bad. I know there's a war, but the blenders will simply have to do better than that, or they shall hear from me."

"Aye, milady. Of course, milady." Bauska's nod was obsequiousness itself—or so Krasta thought, till her maidservant asked the next question: "When the baby comes, do you hope for a boy or a girl, milady?"

Krasta's jaw fell open. All at once, she wasn't sleepy any more. She'd just begun admitting that possibility to herself, and she still didn't care to think of it as more than a possibility. "How did you know?" she blurted.

"Milady, I handle your clothes," Bauska said patiently, as if to a foolish child. "Do you think I don't notice what happens— and what doesn't?"

"Oh." Krasta couldn't remember the last time she'd spoken to Bauska in such a small voice. She hated the feeling that Bauska had the advantage of her, but couldn't very well escape it.

Her maidservant went on, "Does Colonel Lurcanio know yet?"

"Of course not!" Krasta exclaimed. Bauska raised an eyebrow and said nothing. Krasta's face heated. She hated the idea that other people knew more about her life than she wanted them to or than she thought they did. But then, still unusually subdued, she changed her answer: "I don't think so."

Bauska's nod was businesslike. "I'm sure he'll look after you and the baby very well," she said, "as long as he's in Priekule." Krasta glared at her for that addition. Bauska's Captain Mosco had been very attentive to her—till he got sent to Unkerlant not long before her little bastard was born. From that day on, Bauska had never heard a word from him.

"I'm sure he will, too." Krasta did her best to sound sure. It wasn't so easy as she wished it were. Conceiving by her Algarvian lover would prove inconvenient any which way; she was already sure of that. What she wasn't altogether sure of, and what could prove worse than inconvenient, was whether she'd conceived by Lurcanio or by Viscount Valnu. She'd thoroughly enjoyed her infidelity, and hadn't worried in the least about consequences. But if she had a consequence growing somewhere behind her navel—she was vague about such details, although she supposed she wouldn't be able to stay vague much longer—that could end up complicating her life more than she wanted.

What *would* Lurcanio do if she bore a child who looked nothing like him, nothing like any Algarvian? It was a mild spring morning, but Krasta shivered anyhow. She didn't want to think about that.

To keep from thinking about it, she said, "I'm going down to breakfast." And, to keep Bauska from nattering at her any more, she chose a tunic and trousers without any help from her maidservant. Bauska seemed content to stand back and let Krasta do things for herself. *Of course she does, the lazy slut*, Krasta thought. *If I do the work, it means she doesn't have to.*

When she got down to the breakfast table, Lurcanio was already there. He sat sipping tea, nibbling on a roll he kept dipping in honey, and reading a news sheet written in Algarvian—Krasta couldn't make out a word of it. Punctilious as usual, he got to his feet and bowed. "How are you, my sweet?" he asked.

"Still sleepy," Krasta answered, yawning yet again. She sat down and accepted a cup of tea from the hovering servitor. Even if it didn't taste good to her, it would help her wake up.

"What else would you care for, milady?" the fellow asked.

"Something that will stick to my ribs," Krasta answered. Valmierans ate more heartily than Algarvians were in the habit of doing. "A ham and cheese and mushroom omelette, I think." She nodded. "Aye, that will do splendidly."

"Just as you say." Bowing, the servant took Krasta's request back to the kitchen.

"Is the news good?" she asked Lurcanio, pointing to the sheet she couldn't read.

"I've seen it better," he answered. "But, on the other hand, I've also seen it worse. These days, one takes what one can get."

Krasta could hardly disagree with that. She'd taken what she could get—and had got more than she'd bargained for. Thinking of Captain Mosco and his journey to Unkerlant—did he even remain alive these days, or had he given everything he could give for King Mezentio?—she asked, "How does the war against King Swemmel go?"

Lurcanio shrugged. "Largely quiet right now. The good news is that we aren't losing any ground. The bad is wondering why it's quiet and what the Unkerlanters are building up for."

"And what you're building up for yourselves—you Algarvians, I mean," Krasta said.

"Of course." Lurcanio seemed a little taken aback at the suggestion, but he nodded. Then he said, "Here comes your breakfast. How you Valmierans can eat such things day after day and not turn round as balls is beyond me, but you do seem to manage, I must admit." He dipped his roll in the honey and took a small, deliberate bite.

Krasta was not in the mood to be deliberate, especially since the tea hadn't tasted right despite more sugar than usual. *No matter what the dealer says, the blend is off,* she thought. *It's on account of the war. Everything is on account of the war.* Without the war, Lurcanio wouldn't have shared a breakfast table with her, that was certain. He wouldn't have shared a bed with her, either. And certain other consequences . . . might not have ensued.

Not caring to dwell on that, Krasta attacked the buttery omelette. She gobbled down three or four bites before she paused to listen to what her body was telling her. She gulped. Spit flooded into her mouth. The room seemed to spin.

"Are you all right, my dear?" Lurcanio asked. "You look a little green."

"I'm fine," Krasta said. More cautiously than she had before, she ate another couple of bites of egg and ham and cheese. That was a mistake. She knew it was a mistake as soon as she finished—which was a bit too late. She gulped again. This time, it didn't help. "Excuse me," she said in a muffled voice, and bolted from the table.

She got where she was going barely in time to keep from making the disaster worse. When she returned to the table, her mouth still burned and tasted nasty in spite of her having rinsed it again and again. She looked at the omelette and shuddered. She wouldn't have one again any time soon.

Colonel Lurcanio gave her another bow. "Are you all right?" he asked again, this time with more concern in his voice. Krasta managed a wan nod. Lurcanio waved to the servant. "Bring your lady some plain bread." The man hurried off to obey. Lurcanio's gaze swung back to Krasta. "I take it this *does* mean you will be having a child?"

"Aye," she said dully, and then, "You don't sound surprised."

"I'm not," he answered. "Not after I noted the way the veins stand out so much more than usual in your breasts the other night."

"Did you?" Krasta said—after letting out a small, indignant squeak. Everyone around her paid more attention than she did. *She* hadn't noticed any changes in her breasts, except that they were more tender than usual.

"I did indeed." Lurcanio raised an eyebrow. He waited for the servant to give Krasta the bread and depart, then said, "Tell me—is it mine?"

"Of course it is!" Krasta said indignantly, doing her best not to show the alarm that blazed through her. Taking a wary bite of bread helped. She gulped again as she swallowed, but the bread, unlike the omelette, seemed willing to stay down. "Whose else could it be?" she added, in tones suggesting the only possible answer was *no one*.

"That scrawny viscount we should have executed comes to mind." Lurcanio smiled at Krasta. She wished he hadn't; the curve of his lips reminded him how little luck she'd ever had trying to outmaneuver him.

"Nonsense!" she said. "I never did!" *I'm only off by one,* she thought. *That's hardly worth noticing.* True—under most circumstances. Here, though, the difference between *never* and *only once* might prove all too noticeable.

Lurcanio sipped his tea. It evidently tasted fine to him. He shrugged an elaborate, ever so Algarvian shrug and made a steeple of his fingertips. "I am a patient man," he said. "I am willing to give you the benefit of the doubt. For nine months, I am willing to give you the benefit of the doubt. After that, I will know, one way or the other. If the baby bears some passing resemblance to me, well and good. If not, milady, you will be sorry. I am not one who appreciates a cuckoo's egg being raised in his nest. Do I make myself clear?"

"Unpleasantly so," Krasta said. "Most unpleasantly so, in fact." She ate more bread. Sure enough, it sat quiet in her stomach. That made it easier for her to sound like her usual haughty self as she went on, "I assure you, I have told you the truth." *Some of it—I hope.* "If you are going to be boring about this business . . ."

Lurcanio threw back his head and laughed: guffawed, in fact. "Not at all, milady. By no means." To Krasta's amazement, he sounded as if he meant it. "I told you I would give you the benefit of the doubt, and so I shall. If I say even a word to you between now and the day, you may bring me up as sharply as you like."

"I'll remember that," Krasta said. "I'll hold you to it, too."

"Fair enough." Colonel Lurcanio nodded. "But you must also remember the rest of what I said, because I am going to hold you to that. And I think I shall give you one more thing to remember."

"Which is?" Krasta did her best to keep on sounding haughty. The alternative was sounding frightened, which would not do at all.

The Algarvian officer pointed at her, aiming his right forefinger as he might have aimed a stick. "Nothing is to happen to the child until such time as we are able to know what needs to be known. If anything should happen before that time, I shall make all the assumptions you least wish me to make, and I shall act on them. Is *that* plain, milady?"

Curse you, Lurcanio, Krasta thought. What he'd just forbidden would have been the most convenient arrangement all the way around—except that he'd just forbidden it. "Aye," she said coldly. "And will you let your wife know you've sired a brand new bastard?"

"I may," Lurcanio replied, "if it turns out I have. And now, if you will excuse me, I have work to do." He rose, bowed once more, and departed.

Krasta quietly cursed him again, this time for being so invulnerable, so impenetrable. A moment later, she started to giggle. *If only I'd been impenetrable myself. I wouldn't have anything to worry about then.* She wanted to call Lurcanio back so she could tell him the joke. Even as things stood, he would have laughed. She was sure of it. But she sat where she was and didn't say a word.

Kolthoum looked at Hajjaj and slowly shook her head. With a sigh, she said, "You really are going to have to do something about this impossible situation, you know."

"Of course I am," the Zuwayzi foreign minister agreed. "But I have no idea what. I am most open to suggestions."

He hoped his senior wife would have some. He and Kolthoum had been together for half a century. He told anyone who would listen that she was wiser than he. Few Zuwayzin seemed to want to hear that. As happened so often, the truth made people nervous. They dealt with him, so they wanted to think he had all the answers.

"As I see it," Kolthoum said, "you have four choices."

"Really?" Hajjaj said, his surprise altogether genuine. "Try as I would, I could find only three. Tell me, my dear, by all means tell me. Now you truly have my interest."

His wife laughed. Her body shook. She'd never been a famous beauty, and she'd put on flesh over the years. Hajjaj didn't care. He'd never cared. She understood him perfectly. He couldn't say that about anyone else in the world. She began to tick off points on her fingers: "First, you could send Tassi back to Minister Iskakis. That would make him stop screaming at everyone from King Shazli down to the Zuwayzin who walk past the Yaninan ministry."

"Well, so it would," Hajjaj said. "It would also probably be dangerous for Tassi. She didn't show up on my doorstep—she didn't show up naked on my doorstep—because she was madly in love with Iskakis. You know that as well as I do. She was just a bauble to him. And how will he use her, now that she's offended him by running off and showing the world a side he wanted hidden away?"

"Every word of that is true," Kolthoum said. "Which brings me to the next possibility—sending her to Marquis Balastro. He would take good care of her."

"For a while—till he got bored," Hajjaj said. Kolthoum laughed, though neither of them thought it was funny. "But he and Tassi have already quarreled. And if he flaunts her to infuriate Iskakis—and he will, being an Algarvian—he'll just make things between Algarve and Yanina worse than they are already. They're both supposed to be our allies, you know. I can't think of anything Yanina can do to hurt our kingdom, but I can think of plenty of things King Tsavellas might do to hurt Algarve."

"Would Tsavellas do them?" his senior wife asked. "In the war against Unkerlant, anything that hurts Algarve hurts Yanina, too."

"When Yaninans go after revenge, they're even worse than we are," Hajjaj said. "They don't care what happens to them as long as something worse happens to their foes."

"That does make things harder," Kolthoum admitted. "And you are right—Balastro wouldn't keep her. Next choice is to bestow her on some Zuwayzi noble, then, wouldn't you say?"

"I might do that. I've been trying to do that," Hajjaj replied. "But there are only so many nobles who might be interested in a foreign woman, and it's not obvious that Tassi would be interested in any of them. Which leaves, as far as I can see, nothing."

"No?" Kolthoum looked amused. "You could just keep her here, you know, for your own pleasure. She's young and pretty, and you haven't had a woman like that since you sent Lalla back to her clanfather."

"Do you know, I haven't thought about that in any serious way," Hajjaj said slowly. He looked down at his hands, at the dry, wrinkled skin and prominent veins. "And if my not having thought about it seriously doesn't prove I've got old, I don't know what would."

"You're not so old as all that," Kolthoum said.

Hajjaj smiled. "You're sweet to say so, my dear." The two of them hadn't bedded each other in something close to a year— but then, they needed less physical reminding of what they shared than they had when they were younger. He went on: "Things do still work . . . occasionally."

"Well, then," Kolthoum said, as if everything were all settled.

But Hajjaj shook his head. "It's not so simple, you know. Where I might see Tassi as my reward, she's more likely to see me as her punishment."

"No." His senior wife shook her head, too. "Not when she came here to your house and showed herself off to you without her clothes. I know what that means for people who aren't Zuwayzin."

Hajjaj grunted. The same thought had crossed his mind when he saw the young Yanina woman naked. Tassi hadn't done anything to discourage it, either; on the contrary. Were he younger himself, he supposed—no, he knew—he would have done more to explore her half-promises. As things were . . . As things were, he shook his head again and said, "I don't think I'm in urgent need of a pet, even one of the two-legged sort. Besides, I would feel as if I was taking advantage of her."

"As if you were," Kolthoum corrected.

"As if I was," Hajjaj repeated. "I don't think the condition would be contrary to fact, and so it doesn't need the subjunctive." He grinned at Kolthoum. Not even Qutuz, his secretary, quibbled with him over grammar.

She grinned back, unabashed, and stuck out her tongue at him as if she were a cheeky young girl herself. "You don't know whether the condition is contrary to fact or not, because you haven't bothered finding out," she said.

"True—I haven't," he said. "And doesn't that tell you something all by itself?"

"It tells me you are an old-fashioned gentleman," Kolthoum answered, "which is nothing I haven't known for a good many years. But, if you are going to make choices for this woman, don't you think you ought to know what she wants for herself?"

"Now I know why you let me win the grammatical arguments," Hajjaj said. Kolthoum made a small, questioning noise. He explained: "So I won't feel too disappointed when you win the ones that matter."

His senior wife hid her face in her hands. "My secret's out. What shall I do?" she asked, her voice muffled behind her palms.

Slipping an arm around her shoulder, Hajjaj said, "When we have this between us, why do I need a young woman, a stranger?"

"Why?" Kolthoum reached out and gently stroked him between the legs. "That's why."

"There. You see? I already have a shameless woman, too." Hajjaj kissed her. More than a little to his own surprise, he found himself rising to the occasion. He and Kolthoum made love slowly, lazily; somehow, the lack of urgency, the lack of fuss, added to his enjoyment—and, he hoped, hers—rather than taking away from it. Afterwards he said, "I didn't expect that to happen."

"Neither did I." Kolthoum wagged a forefinger in front of his nose. "But you're not going to use it as an excuse to keep from asking Tassi what she wants."

"Aye, my dear," Hajjaj answered. Under the circumstances, he could hardly say no.

Having made the promise, he had to keep it. A couple of days later, he asked Tewfik to bring Tassi into his study. The majordomo nodded. "Just as you say, your Excellency." His wrinkled, jowly face gave no hint of what he thought. He shuffled off and returned a few minutes later with Minister Iskakis' runaway wife.

"Good day, your Excellency," she said in her careful Algarvian, dipping her head to Hajjaj. She was still bare, and still seemed barer than any Zuwayzi would have—but then, she would also have seemed out of place in his house had she chosen to wear clothes.

"And a good day to you," Hajjaj replied in the same language. "Sit down. Make yourself comfortable. Would you care for tea and wine and cakes?" When she dipped her head in Yaninan-style agreement, Hajjaj nodded to Tewfik, who waited in the doorway. The majordomo left and returned with a silver tray bearing the essentials of Zuwayzi hospitality.

While Tassi and Hajjaj ate and drank, they stuck to small talk. He wondered if she knew the social rules of his kingdom. He had, from time to time, used them to annoy foreigners. Now she seemed as content with delay as he was.

But, at last, he could avoid things no longer. "Tell me," he said, "what am I to do with you?"

"Whatever suits your kingdom best, of course," Tassi answered. "That is the way of such things, is it not so?" She spoke with a curious bitter resignation.

Hajjaj shook his head. "Not necessarily. Not entirely. If I thought only about what suited my kingdom best, I would have sent you back to your husband at once. Do you doubt it, even for an instant?"

"No," she said in a small voice.

"All right, then," Hajjaj said. "We understand each other, at least so far. If you had your choice, what would you do?"

"Blaze my father when he made the match with Iskakis," Tassi replied without hesitation. "He could not have done worse if he tried for a hundred years."

"You cannot do anything about that now. Of the things you can do, what would you do?"

"I have no good answers for you," Tassi said, and Hajjaj nodded: he hadn't expected her to have any good answers. She went on, "If you are willing to let me stay here, I would like to do that. No one bothers me here. Until now, I have never been in a place where no one bothers me."

Well, Hajjaj thought with wry amusement, *this is hardly the time to ask if she wants to keep my bed warm. Not even Kolthoum could argue with me about that, not after what she just said.* Even so, his eyes traveled the length of her. Maybe it was the way her nipples and the hair between her legs stood out against her light skin that made her seem more naked than a Zuwayzi woman would have. That was the closest he'd come to an explanation that made sense, anyhow.

She mistook his silence for one of a rather different sort. Or perhaps it wasn't so different after all. As she had when she dropped to her knees in the doorway, she said, "I would do anything to be able to stay here, anything you might ask me."

That could mean only one thing. Hajjaj said, "If I took you up on that, you would not be able to say that no one here bothered you."

"I do not think it would be much of a bother," Tassi said.

And what is that supposed to mean? Hajjaj wondered. That she wouldn't mind doing whatever he wanted or that she didn't think he would want anything very often? He didn't ask the question. Not asking was better when he didn't really want to know the answer. Instead, he said, "You are welcome to stay here for as long as you like, but I do not think you can make this your true home. You are a young woman. One day, very likely, you will want to start a family of your own, and you will need to meet a man whose family is of a rank to match yours."

Tassi tossed her head so vigorously, her dark curls flew. Yaninans used that gesture when they meant *No*. She said, "Bloodlines are splendid—in a horse or a unicorn." A Zuwayzi would have spoken of camels. "But Iskakis has some of the best blood in Yanina, and how much joy did my marriage to him bring me?"

"Iskakis also has some . . . special tastes," Hajjaj pointed out, as delicately as he could.

"I know." She grimaced. "He tried them with me a few times. They hurt, if you must know. But even so, I did not much interest him that way."

Then he was a fool. But Hajjaj did not say that aloud. Tassi was too likely to judge he wanted pleasure from her body. And he knew he might, though taking it seemed more trouble than it was worth. "You may stay here—unbothered—for as long as you like," was what he did end up saying.

"Thank you," Tassi said softly.

"You are welcome," Hajjaj replied, "and you may take that however you like."

The ley-line ship slid to a halt. Since it wasn't moving any more, it settled down into the water instead of gliding above all but the worst of the waves. "Well, we're here," Istvan said, "wherever *here* is and whatever the Kuusamans are going to do with us now."

"They don't dare treat us too badly," Kun said. "Gyongyos has plenty of Kuusaman captives, and our people can take revenge on them."

"They haven't done anything too horrible yet," Szonyi said. "They've given us plenty of food, even if it is accursed fish all the time. If I eat any more fish, I'll grow fins."

Captain Frigyes said, "They are islanders. They eat fish themselves. They give us the same rations they give their own warriors. That is honorable." No matter how honorable it was, Istvan's company commander had been sunk in gloom ever since the Kuusamans captured him on Becsehely. He'd been ready to lay down his life to power the sorcery that would help drive the enemy off the island. He'd been ready, aye, but he hadn't got the chance—and Becsehely had fallen, as so many other islands in the Bothnian Ocean had fallen to Kuusamo.

"We did all we could, Captain," Istvan said, not for the first time. "The stars will still shine on us. We didn't do anything to make them want to withhold their light."

"We failed," Frigyes said. "We should have held Becsehely, and we failed."

"Too many Kuusaman ships," Kun said, reasonable and logical as usual. "Too many Kuusaman dragons. Too many Kuusaman soldiers. Once they got ashore, sir, how could we hope to hold the island?"

"With our life's blood," Frigyes answered. "But we had no chance to give it." He held his head in his hands, not bothering to hide his misery.

The iron door to the compartment housing the captives came open with a nasty squeal of hinges—even a lubber like Istvan could tell this ship had seen better years. A couple of Kuusaman troopers aimed sticks at the Gyongyosians. "To come out," one of them said, speaking Istvan's language very badly. "To go off this ship. To move—*now*." The last word held the snap of command.

One by one, Istvan and his countrymen got to their feet and filed out of the compartment and into the corridor beyond. The Kuusamans stepped back. If anyone thought of seizing a stick and raising a revolt, he never got the chance. Istvan didn't even think of it. He walked along the corridor and up the narrow iron stairway to the deck of the transport. It was the first time he'd seen the sky since going aboard the ship after Becsehely fell.

Then he saw the skyline—and started to laugh. A Kuusaman guard on deck swung his stick toward him. "Why you to laugh?" the little, slant-eyed fellow asked. By his tone, no captive had any business laughing.

Istvan didn't care. "Why? Because this is Obuda, that's why," he answered. He knew the shape of Mount Sorong—not much of a mountain by his standards, but still a peak of sorts—as well as he knew the shape of his own foot. "I fought here. I didn't expect to see the place again, I'll tell you that."

"You soldier here?" the guard said, and Istvan nodded. The guard shrugged. "Soldier no more. Now you to be captive here."

Kun said, "This harbor wasn't here when we were fighting on Obuda."

Istvan nodded. Since the island fell, the Kuusamans had run up an enormous number of piers—and all of them looked to have ships tied up at them. Gyongyos and Kuusamo had fought over Obuda not least because several ley lines converged there, making it important for one navy or the other to hold the place. The Kuusamans weren't just holding it these days—they'd taken it and made it their own.

"They couldn't have got this much work out of the Obudans," Istvan said as the guards marched him and his comrades toward the gangplank. "There weren't that many of them, and they're lazy buggers anyhow." He never had thought much of the islanders.

"They didn't even bother," Kun said positively. "Most of this port was hammered together by sorcery."

"How can you tell?" Istvan asked.

"Because all the piers and all the pilings are just alike," Kun answered. "That means they used the law of similarity a lot—it can't mean anything else." He scowled. "I wish *we* could afford to throw magecraft around like this. We'd stand a lot better chance in the fight, I'll tell you."

Under the sticks of the Kuusaman guards, the captives marched off the pier and onto the beach of Obuda. More Kuusamans waited for them there. One of the little men turned out to speak pretty good Gyongyosian. "I am Colonel Eino," he said. "I am the commandant of the captives' camp here. I want you to understand what that means. What that means is that, as far as you are concerned, I am the stars above. If anything good happens to you, it will happen because of me, and because of whatever you have done to please me. And if anything bad happens to you, it will also happen because of me, and because of whatever you have done to make me angry. Do not make me angry. You will be very sorry if you do."

"Blasphemous, goat-eating son of a whore," Istvan muttered. The captives around him—even Kun, that hard-boiled city man—nodded. Colonel Eino might know the Gyongyosian language, but he didn't know Gyongyosians.

Istvan's close comrades weren't the only ones to be appalled. More mutters rose from other soldiers captured on Becsehely— several hundred of them had filed off the transport. Some of them shouted instead of muttering.

Those shouts bothered Eino not at all. "I care nothing for what you think of me," he said. "I care only that you obey me. When the war is over—when we have won it—you will go back to Gyongyos again. Until then, you belong to Kuusamo. Remember that." He turned his back, ignoring the new shouts that rose from the captives.

The Kuusaman guards didn't speak so much Gyongyosian. Of course, they didn't need to, either. They shouted, "To march!"—and march the captives did.

"Somewhere not far from here, we beat these buggers back

from the beaches." Istvan heaved a sigh. "But they're like roaches, seems like. Stomp 'em once and they just come back again."

He'd expected to have to march all the way to the captives' camp, wherever on the island it turned out to be. He looked toward the forest that grew almost down to the beach. Parts of it were still battered from the fight his countrymen had put up before the Kuusamans finally seized Obuda. His own memories of that losing campaign were of hunger and fog and fear.

To his surprise, though, the guards marched his comrades and him only as far as what proved to be a ley-line caravan depot. "In! To go in!" the Kuusamans commanded. Into the caravan cars went the Gyongyosians.

Kun kept shaking his head, as he had at the harbor. "This is plainly the extension of the ley line the ship that brought us from Becsehely used," he said, though no such thing was plain to Istvan. "The Kuusamans use every bit of sorcerous energy they can. We don't. No wonder the war isn't going the way we wish it would."

"Silence, there," Captain Frigyes said sharply. "I'll hear no talk of defeatism. Have you got that, Corporal?"

"Aye, Captain," Kun answered, the only thing he could say— out loud, at any rate. To Istvan, he murmured, "No defeatism, is it? How does he think we got here? Have we invaded Obuda again?"

"We got caught, but that doesn't mean we've got to give up," Istvan said. His own attitude lay somewhere between Kun's and Frigyes'. Obviously, Gyongyos had lost the fight for Becsehely. and the whole war in the Bothnian Ocean was going Kuusamo's way. Even so . . . "If we let the slant-eyes think we'll do whatever they say, they'll end up owning us, do you know what I mean?"

Kun just grunted. Whether that meant he agreed or he didn't think the remark worth wasting words on, Istvan couldn't have said.

The ley line went through the forest, straight as the beam from a stick. It passed by a couple of little Obudan villages. The natives hardly looked up from their fields to watch it go past.

Before the Derlavaian kingdoms came to their islands, they'd lived a simple life. They hadn't known metalworking or much magecraft past exploiting obvious power points or how to tame the wild dragons that flew from one island to another and preyed on men and flocks alike. By now they'd grown so accustomed to the marvels of modern civilization, they took them for granted.

When at last the ley-line caravan stopped, it had climbed halfway up the slope of Mount Sorong. Istvan thought they were somewhere near the town of Sorong, the largest native settlement. He wondered how much of Sorong was left these days. Then he shrugged. The Obudans hadn't been strong enough to hold Gyongyos or Kuusamo away from their island. Whatever happened to them, they deserved it.

"Out! To go out!" shouted the guards on the caravan cars.

Out Istvan went. There straight ahead stood the captives' camp, behind a palisade with nails sticking out of the timbers like hedgehog spines, to make them all but impossible to climb. Istvan looked around and started to laugh again.

"What to be funny?" a guard demanded.

"This used to be my regiment's encampment," Istvan answered. The Kuusaman nodded to show he understood, then shrugged to show he wasn't much impressed. After a moment, Istvan wasn't much impressed, either. The Gyongyosians hadn't been strong enough to hold Kuusamo away from Obuda. Didn't that mean they deserved whatever happened to them?

That was a chilly thought with which to enter the captives' camp.

Some of the Gyongyosian barracks still stood. The guards took Istvan and his comrades to a newer, less weathered building. He turned out to have a better cot and more space as a captive of the Kuusamans than he'd had as a Gyongyosian soldier on Obuda. He didn't know what that said about the relative strength of the two warring kingdoms. Nothing good, probably, not from a Gyongyosian point of view.

"I wish to speak to Colonel Eino," Frigyes told a guard. The

Kuusaman went off to see if the camp commandant cared to speak with a captive captain.

To Istvan's surprise, Eino came to the barracks. "What do you want?" he asked. "Whatever it is, it had better be important."

"It is," Frigyes said. "I want your word of honor as an officer that you do not abuse us by feeding us the filthy, forbidden flesh of goats. We are in your power. I hope you are not so vile as to make us either starve or become ritually unclean."

Alarm blazed through Istvan. He glanced at Kun and Szonyi. They looked alarmed, too. The scar on his hand seemed to throb. His gaze swung back to Colonel Eino.

The camp commandant laughed. "Many of your people ask this. I give you my word, it does not happen." He laughed again, less pleasantly. "You may ask, what is a Kuusaman's word worth?" Off he went, leaving appalled silence behind him.

Colonel Spinello was bored. He'd been a great many things since the war took him to Unkerlant—wounded, hungry, freezing, terrified—but never bored, never till now. He yawned till his jaw creaked. He felt like ordering another attack on Pewsum, just to give his men—and himself—something to do.

No matter what he felt like, he refrained. He had no doubt whatever that his brigade was glad about the lull in the fighting. It didn't break his heart, either. He'd more than half expected King Swemmel's men to have laid on an attack against Waldsolms by now. Maybe the Unkerlanters were enjoying the lull, too.

If I want something to do, I ought to get Jadwigai into bed with me, he thought, not for the first time. Not for the first time, he turned the thought aside. Tampering with the brigade's luck would only be bad for his own. He even believed that, which made it easier for him to resist temptation—but not a great deal easier.

Then a shout rang out that sent him springing to his feet: "Field post! The field post's here!"

Spinello hurried out of the Unkerlanter hut where he'd been brooding. He hadn't even reached the unpaved street before turning into his usual jaunty self. "Come on, boys," he called to the other soldiers also hurrying toward the wagon that brought letters from home. "Time to find out how much your girlfriends are trying to squeeze out of you this time."

The men in the wagon started calling out names. Spinello's clerks took care of most of them, sorting the envelopes and packages by regiment and company so they could go on up to the front. Every so often, one of the clerks said, "He's wounded," or "He's dead," or, "He got transferred six months ago. Anybody who's looking for him here is out of luck."

"Here's one for Colonel Spinello," one of the field postmen called.

"That's me." Spinello happily reached for it.

Before giving it to him, the fellow in the wagon held it under his nose. "Perfumed!" he exclaimed, which made all the Algarvians in the muddy main street whoop and sigh and roll their eyes and pretend to swoon.

"Powers below eat every bloody one of you," Spinello said. "You're just jealous, and you bloody well know it."

None of the soldiers argued with him. They probably *were* jealous, but not in a bad way. Any officer in the Algarvian army who got a perfumed letter only saw his prestige rise—it made his men think he was good at some of the things that made life worth living.

"You going to read it to us, Colonel?" somebody called. A chorus of baying whoops followed that suggestion.

"Read your own letters—if you know how to read," Spinello replied with dignity. "I'm going to enjoy this one myself." It came from Fronesia; if the scent, the same one she used herself, hadn't been enough to tell him as much, her flowing script would have. He smiled. He'd had a splendid time with her back in Trapani, the sort of time that would have made his men whoop even more than they were already whooping if he'd chosen to tell them about it.

Before he tore the envelope open, he glanced up and saw Jadwigai peering out through one of the small windows in the peasant hut she used as her own. She rarely come out onto the street when Algarvians from outside the brigade could see her.

One more proof she knows what happens to most Kaunians,
Spinello thought, something that hadn't occurred to him before.

He took out the letter from his mistress, unfolded it, and began to read. The first part was all conventional enough. Fronesia missed him, she hoped he was safe, she hoped he got leave
soon so she could see him, she suggested several things she
might do to make his leave more entertaining if he got it. A couple of the things she suggested sounded entertaining enough to
make him want to head back toward Trapani whether he had
leave or not.

And then, three or four paragraphs into the letter, Fronesia
got down to business.

> *Someone has been ungenerous enough to slander or libel*
> *me to Colonel Sabrino, and he, in his ingratitude, has seen*
> *fit to cut off the allowance he used to give me. While I*
> *know I can rely on your kindness, I wonder if you might be*
> *sweet enough to send me just a little more than usual over*
> *the next couple of months, to help me wean myself away*
> *from Sabrino for ever and always. I promise you, dear,*
> *that I will show you just exactly how glad I am to have fi-*
> *nally fallen into the arms of a true man, not a cold-hearted*
> *calculator who holds the least little thing against me.*

Spinello read that several times. No matter how many times
he read it, it always added up to the same thing. "Why, you little tramp!" he said, half annoyed, half admiring. *Squeeze indeed,* he thought. Mistresses, of course, were and had to be
mercenary. They had custom on their side, but the law had
never heard of them. Fronesia, though, managed to turn greed
into something uncommonly like art.

To how many other officers was she sending similarly artful
letters? In peacetime, having multiple protectors was almost
impossibly difficult for a mistress. But the war made it easy.
What were the odds that two . . . friends would come into Trapani wanting to see a woman at the same time? Slim, no doubt
about it. A canny woman, or a grasping one, could do very well
for herself.

He had no proof, only the tone of the letter. In his own pre-war days, though, he'd studied the Kaunian classics, which left him uncommonly sensitive to tone. If Fronesia didn't have more than one protector, it wasn't solely because of love for him. He was sure, very sure, of that.

Instead of crumpling up the letter and tossing it into the mud, he took it back to his hut. He kept his head up and his stride brisk. He wouldn't let the men see that Fronesia had written anything to upset him.

When he got inside, though, he tossed the letter on the embers of the fire. Those were plenty to make it char and crackle and flare and burn. For a moment he smelled, or imagined he smelled, scorched perfume. Then the sharp odor of burning paper overwhelmed it, and then that too was lost in the usual smoky stink of the hearth.

He sat down at a folding table—Algarvian army issue; Unkerlanter peasant huts didn't boast such amenities—inked a pen, and began his reply. Halfway through the first paragraph, he set down the pen, shaking his head. If he wrote while angry, he would regret the letter as soon as he posted it. Fronesia didn't need to hear from him right away. If she didn't hear from him right away, she might worry a little. That wouldn't be so bad.

After a bit, the field-post wagon rattled off to deliver letters and packages to some other brigade. Half noticing the noise, Spinello nodded to himself. The military postmen were good, solid fellows; even footsoldiers respected them. They carried sticks when they got near the front, and they knew what to do with them, too.

Someone knocked on the door. Colonel Spinello started. He wished one of his regimental commanders would have picked a different time to bother him. He also sniffed a couple of times before going to the door. No, he couldn't smell the perfume from Fronesia's letter. That was something, anyhow.

But when he opened the door, no grimy, poorly shaved Algarvian officer stood there. Jadwigai did. "Oh," Spinello said in surprise. He managed a bow. "Come in, milady. What can I do for you?"

He intended to leave the door to the hut open, so the men in the brigade could see he was up to nothing nefarious with their mascot. Jadwigai, though, closed it after herself as she walked in. "Are you all right, Colonel?" she asked in that disconcertingly fluent Algarvian of hers.

"Why shouldn't I be?" Spinello asked in return, more surprised than ever.

"When the field post came, I saw you didn't like the letter you got," the Kaunian girl answered. "I was afraid it might be bad news from your family. This is a . . . very large war."

If it hadn't been a very large war, a Kaunian girl from Forthweg would never have found herself in the wilds of northern Unkerlant. But that wasn't what Jadwigai had meant. Touched, Spinello said, "No, no, it's nothing like that."

"Really?" She didn't sound as if she believed him. Maybe she'd heard other Algarvian officers making light of losses.

But, very firmly, Spinello said, "Really. My father and uncles are too old to fight. My brother and my cousins are all fine, so far as I know. So are my aunts and my sister, for that matter."

"All right," Jadwigai said—actually, the soldiers' expression she used had a literal meaning a lot more pungent than that. "I'm glad. Even so, though, you can't tell me that letter made you happy."

"No, it didn't," Spinello admitted. The Kaunian girl's face bore an *I-told-you-so* expression. Hoping to cure her of it, he went on, "If you really must know what the trouble is, my mistress back in Algarve is trying to squeeze more money out of me."

"Oh." She turned red. For a moment, he thought it was embarrassment. Then he realized it was outrage. "The nerve of her, doing something like that when you're out here where you're liable to get killed."

"That did cross my mind, aye," Spinello said. "Of course, from Fronesia's point of view my being out here only makes me a poor long-term investment."

Jadwigai said something inflammatory in Algarvian—she'd learned it from soldiers, sure enough. Then she said something even more inflammatory in classical Kaunian. It was the first time Spinello had heard her use her birthspeech.

He answered in classical Kaunian himself: "Letting such small things pierce one to the heart merely burdens the spirit to no purpose."

Jadwigai looked astonished. "I didn't think you knew my language, not when . . ." She didn't go on. She didn't need to go on. She had to know what happened at the camps the Algarvians politely termed *special*, sure enough.

Spinello grimaced. How was he supposed to respond to that? At last, after some thought, he said, "A kingdom will do what it thinks it has to do to win, to survive. Afterwards, maybe, it will look back and count the cost of what it did."

To his surprise, and more than a little to his relief, Jadwigai nodded. "Or, if it wins, it won't bother to count the cost at all." That jerked a nod from Spinello. The Kaunian girl went on, "It's the same for people, you know: you do what you have to do first, and then you count the cost later."

He nodded again. "Any soldier who's ever been blazed at, will say the same thing."

"Not just soldiers." Jadwigai stepped up to him and put her hands on his shoulders. She was, if anything, an inch or two taller than he. "You can have me if you want me, you know."

"And you'll count the cost later?" he asked.

Quite seriously, she nodded. "Of course. If there is a later."

Sleeping with you would improve my chances of having a later. Spinello had had no compunctions whatever about making Vanai bribe him with her body to keep her miserable grandfather alive. He hesitated now, and wondered why. The answer wasn't long in coming, not least because he'd seen so much more soldiering than he had when he was stationed in Oyngestun.

Gently, he kissed her. She stiffened in his arms. That had excited him with Vanai. Here, it just left him sad. He said, "I'm afraid you're not my pet—you're the brigade's pet." She stared at him, then started to cry. "Stop that!" he exclaimed, and he wasn't acting at all. "If the soldiers think I've done something to you that you didn't want, I'm a dead man."

Too late, he realized he'd just handed her a weapon. But she lidn't seem interested in using it. "Thank you," she said. "Oh, hank you."

"For what? For being a fool?" he said, and was relieved again when that made her laugh. She was still smiling when she eft the hut. *Later,* he thought, standing there all alone. *You count the cost later.*

Skarnu turned to Palasta. "If we go much farther, we fall off the edge of the world," he said.

The young mage smiled at him. She looked as if a strong breeze would blow her away. Here at the southeasternmost reach of Valmiera, there were plenty of strong breezes, most of them off the Strait of Valmiera that separated the Derlavaian mainland from the great island holding Lagoas and Kuusamo. The wind didn't stagger her, but it did blow her long blond hair into a mare's nest of tangles. Brushing a strand that escaped her flat knitted wool hat back from her eyes, she said, "Back in the days of the Kaunian Empire, they really thought they would."

"I suppose so, sis," he said, which made Palasta smile again. They'd decided to travel as brother and sister; he would have had to have started *very* young to claim her as a daughter. He wished she *were* his sister—he vastly preferred her to the one he really had. Palasta would never have given herself to the Algarvians, not for anything.

She said, "If we go to the top of that little hill there"—she pointed—"we might be able to see something interesting."

"Maybe," Skarnu said. Up to the top of the hill they went. The path was muddy; Skarnu almost slipped. Once they did get to the top, he shaded his eyes with the palm of his hand and peered south and east toward the beach where the Algarvians had murdered their Kaunian captives to assail the Kuusamans, and where something—no one on this side of the Strait of Valmiera seemed to know what—had gone wrong for the redheads. Even shading his eyes against the wan southern sun, he couldn't see as much as he would have liked. "I wish I had a spyglass," he muttered.

"Not safe," Palasta said, and he could hardly disagree.

Shaggy green fields, rich and lush, stretched down toward

the sea. A circle of tall, crudely shaped stones stood in one
those a few hundred yards away: a monument a thousand yea
older than the Kaunian Empire, maybe more. Lichen scrawl
red and yellow-green patterns up the sides of the stones.

Palasta pointed toward the monument. "That's a power poi
Even all those years ago, they knew about such things."

"Whoever *they* were," Skarnu said; that was another ridd
archaeological mages still labored to unravel. Some of *them*,
least, had not been of Kaunian stock. That much seemed plai
Even nowadays, a few folk here showed signs of blood mo
like that of the Kuusamans than of Valmiera's Kaunian majc
ity. Southeasterners had a way of staying on their land. Skarn
hadn't seen many before coming to this part of the kingdor
Dark hair, slanted eyes, and high cheekbones showed up oft
enough to disconcert him: they were certainly more comm
than he'd thought.

Between him and Palasta and the monument, a woman dro
a couple of goats toward a farmhouse. She was a Kaunian; h
yellow hair peeped out from under the white lace cap she wo
But that cap set her apart from most Valmierans. Every tiny di
trict here in the southeast had its own particular style, ea
striving to be more ornate than its neighbors. The goats were
a peculiar breed, too—shaggier than the ones he'd know
around Pavilosta, and with thicker, more twisted horns.

But he couldn't keep eyeing the local landscape forever, eve
if he wanted to. His eyes rose to the gray beach and the gra
green, rock-studded sea beyond, and to what had been the cam
where the Algarvians housed their Kaunian captives befo
killing them to capture their life energy.

Some of the fences that had surrounded the camp still stoo
Others were flat, or had been hurled some distance away by t
force of the magic that had come back from Kuusamo. As far
he could see at this distance, none of the buildings inside t
perimeter still stood, neither those that had housed the redhea
nor those where their victims had dwelt.

"What do you see?" he asked Palasta. The young mage wa
the one who'd needed to make this journey. Skarnu was alor
because he'd been fighting for a long time to keep Mezentio

men from massacring Kaunians from Forthweg, and because sending a girl on her own—even a girl who was also a mage—had risks the underground hadn't felt like facing.

"Power," she answered absently. "Great power."

"The kind the Algarvians get from killing?" Skarnu asked.

"Oh, that, too," Palasta said, though she sounded as if she needed to be reminded of it. "Aye, that, too. But something else, something brighter . . . cleaner." She frowned, groping for the word she wanted.

"Can you tell what it is?"

Palasta shook her head. "It's nothing I've run into before. I don't think it's anything anybody ever ran into before."

She seemed very certain. Skarnu studied not the camp where the Kaunians from Forthweg had been but Palasta. She couldn't have been more than sixteen. How could she know about what trained mages had run into over the years, over the centuries, over the millennia? (Those lichen-splashed standing stones made Skarnu think in longer stretches of time than he might have otherwise.) Carefully—he didn't want to offend her—he asked, "How can you be sure of that?"

"Suppose you've eaten beef and pork and mutton and chicken," Palasta said. "If someone serves you fresh oysters, will you be sure you've never had them before?"

"Aye." Skarnu nodded. "But I won't be sure no one's eaten them in all the history of the world."

"Ah. I see what you're saying." Palasta looked at him as if he were a bright pupil in primary school. Absurdly, that affectionate, forgiving glance made him proud, not angry. The young mage said, "I know what I know. What I know is based on what all the sorcerers before me have known, all the way back to the people who raised those stones, whoever they were." They were on her mind, too. She went on, "I can tell what's new and what isn't. Whatever did that"—she pointed to the ruined camp—"is something new."

"All right. And I see what you're saying, too." Now Skarnu believed her. She sounded as sure about what she knew and what she didn't as Sergeant Raunu ever had. As it had with the veteran underofficer, her conviction carried weight with

Skarnu. He asked, "Do you want to get closer, if we can? Do you think it would do any good?"

"I'd like to try it," Palasta answered. "I don't see any Algarvians around there right now, or sense any of their wizards, either. If we spot soldiers when we come up to the camp, we can always walk off in some other direction."

"Fair enough." Skarnu started down the slope that led to the camp.

Palasta stayed at his side. After a few steps, she said, "We may not need to do this, after all, now that I think about it. The answers I'm looking for are probably on the other side of the Strait of Valmiera. So if you want to go back . . ."

Skarnu kept walking. "Let's try it. We've come all this way"—*"Tytuvenai" yanked me away from my wife and son*—"to try to find out what happened here, and whether we can use it against the redheads, too. It would be a shame to stop half a mile short." *If we do stop half a mile short, I'll wring "Tytuvenai's" neck the next time I see him.*

"That makes good sense." Palasta sent him a speculative look. "You seem to have a very logical mind. Why didn't you ever think about becoming a mage?"

"I don't know," Skarnu answered. "I never did, that's all. I've never seen any signs I'd have the talent for it, either." As a marquis, of course, he'd never had to worry about making a living. Since his parents' untimely death, he'd never had to worry about anything till he took command of his company when war broke out. He'd done that as well as he could, and done a lot of other things since. Krasta, now—Krasta hadn't worried about anything but shops and lovers her whole life long. The corners of his mouth turned down as he thought about his sister's latest, Algarvian, lover.

"Talent does count," Palasta said, "but only so much."

"As may be," Skarnu said. "It's too late for me to worry about it now." Palasta looked at him as if he'd suddenly started speaking Unkerlanter. *Too late* meant little to her: a telling proof of how young she was. More roughly than he'd intended to, Skarnu continued, "Come on. Let's see how close we can get you."

Palasta didn't say anything as they walked on toward the ravaged camp. She didn't have to. Watching her face was fascinating. She either didn't know how to or else didn't bother with hiding anything she thought or felt. She seemed to grow more astonished, more interested, more excited with every step they took. She also grew more puzzled. "I don't know what they did," she said. "I don't know how they did it. But I don't think magecraft will ever be the same."

Skarnu wanted to laugh at her. She was much too young to speak with such self-assurance. But she was also too self-assured for him to dwell too much on her youth. She'd shown him she knew what she was talking about. What would she sense, what would she learn, if she could walk through the heart of the shattered camp?

He didn't get to find out. About a quarter of a mile short of the camp, an Algarvian soldier popped out of a hole in the ground so well hidden by bushes that Skarnu had no idea he was there till he emerged. "No going farther," he said in accented Valmieran. "Forbidden military area, by ordering of Grand Duke Ivone."

Ivone was the highest-ranking Algarvian in Valmiera. As a man of the underground, Skarnu knew that. Would he have known it if he were as ordinary as he wanted to seem? Maybe—but maybe not, too. He said. "My sister and me, we just want to go on down to the beach to hunt for crabs." He deliberately tried to sound none too bright.

The soldier shook his head. "Not here. Forbidden. You wanting crabs, you going back to town, finding wrong girlfriend." He guffawed at his own wit.

Try to bribe him? Skarnu wondered. He decided against it. More redheads were surely lurking around the camp. "Plenty of good crabs on this beach," he grumbled, for the Algarvian's benefit. "Lobsters, too." When the soldier shook his head again, Skarnu took Palasta's arm. "Come on, sis. We'll find 'em somewheres else."

"You leaving her with me, you go looking," the Algarvian suggested. That made Skarnu retreat in a hurry. The redhead had thrown out the notion in a casual way. Skarnu hustled

Palasta away from him before he decided she ought to be his because he was an occupier and he had a stick in his hands.

To Skarnu's relief, she waited till they'd got out of earshot of the guard to ask, "Can we sneak around to the camp some other way?"

"I doubt it," he answered regretfully. "They're bound to have more than one man keeping an eye on it. If they send us away from it once, that probably won't mean much to them. If they catch us trying to get there once they've told us no, that's liable to be a different story." He hesitated. "Unless you think you really have to get inside. If it's that important, I'll do my best to get you past the guards. You might have to use some of your magecraft, too."

"No," Palasta said after brief thought. "I've learned enough—and perhaps the biggest thing I've learned is how much I don't know." She spoke in riddles, but she sounded pleased doing it, so Skarnu supposed he should be pleased, too. And he was, for his own reasons: now he could go back to Merkela and little Gedominu.

Eight

Not for the first time, Marshal Rathar reflected on how glad he was to get out of Cottbus, to get away from the direct influence of King Swemmel. Away from the capital, he was his own man. Inside Cottbus, inside the palace, he might have been fitted for strings at the wrists and ankles, at the elbows and knees, for he knew himself to be nothing more than the king's puppet.

Even in getting away from Cottbus, though, Rathar followed Swemmel's will rather than his own. He would sooner have gone back to the Duchy of Grelz, to finish driving the Algarvians from it. But Swemmel was convinced Unkerlant had the battle in the south well enough in hand to entrust it to General Vatran. Vatran was a capable commander; he and Rathar had worked well together down in the south for a couple of years. Still, Rathar wanted to finish what he'd started.

As usual, King Swemmel cared nothing for what his subjects wanted. He'd sent Rathar up to the north, to a region where he hadn't laid his hand on the fighting. And he'd sent with him General Gurmun, who'd proved himself the best commander of behemoths Unkerlant had.

The two of them rode horses east toward Pewsum, a town the Unkerlanters had taken back from Algarve and then held in spite of counterattacks delivered with the redheads' usual skill and ingenuity. Looking around at the devastation through which he rode, Rathar said, "Nothing comes easy fighting Mezentio's men. It never has. By the time we drive them off a piece of ground, it's not worth having any more."

Gurmun pondered that. He was younger than Rathar—in his early forties—with hard, blunt features and cold, cold eyes. He'd risen through the ranks despite, or perhaps because of, King Swemmel's purges. He said, "They're tough, aye, but we can whip them. We've done it before; we'll do it again. And every time we do whip them, we leave them that much less to fight back with."

Ten months ago, his behemoths had stopped the Algarvians' last desperate push in the Durrwangen bulge, the push that might have torn the whole position open had it succeeded. Hundreds of the great beasts from both sides were left dead on the field. Unkerlant had been able to make good its losses. The Algarvian behemoth force hadn't been the same since the battles by Durrwangen.

Rathar said, "I just wonder how much of our kingdom will be standing by the time the war ends."

Gurmun shrugged. "As long as some of it's standing and there's nothing left of Algarve." That was also Swemmel's attitude. Rathar could hardly disagree with it.

In fact, he didn't disagree with it. But he did say, "The more we have left standing, the better."

"Well, of course," Gurmun said. "The better we keep our secrets, the more we'll be able to manage there. The redheads couldn't have been plainer about what they had in mind around Durrwangen if they'd hung up a sign—WE'RE GOING TO AT-TACK HERE. Stupid buggers." He spat in the muddy roadway.

His scorn made Marshal Rathar blink. To Rathar, the Algarvians were the touchstone of the military art. He'd spent the first couple of years of the war against them learning how they did what they did well enough to imitate it. Had he failed, Unkerlant would have gone under. That Gurmun could show contempt for the redheads proved he'd succeeded. It still disconcerted him, though.

Ropes dyed red warned soldiers and surviving locals away from a field by the side of the road. Rathar said, "One of these days, we'll have to clear out all the eggs we and the Algarvians have buried." The red ropes said that field was sown with Algarvian eggs. A crater not far from the road said some luckless fellow had discovered at least one of them the hard way.

Gurmun spat again. "It can wait. Right now, we haven't got the dowsers to spend clearing the buried eggs we've already passed. We've hardly got enough dowsers to clear the ones that are still in front of the redheads."

"I said, one of these days," Rathar answered. As far as Gurmun was concerned, the waste of having dowsers go up in bursts of sorcerous energy while clearing unimportant fields made that not worth doing. As long as they died doing something important, he didn't worry at all. A lot of the younger officers, the men who'd lived their entire adult lives during King Swemmel's reign, thought the same way. Since Swemmel thought that way, too, Rathar knew he shouldn't have been surprised, but every so often he still was.

"If we had more dowsers," Gurmun went on, "I wouldn't have to run peasants across fields ahead of my behemoths, the way I've done a couple-three times. That doesn't always work as well as you'd like—sometimes the Algarvian mages make their buried eggs sensitive to behemoths, not people." His horse walked on for a few paces before he added, very much as an afterthought, "And it's wasteful, too."

"So it is." Rathar had used such tactics himself; he didn't

know many Unkerlanter generals who hadn't. But he didn't take them for granted, the way Gurmun did. With a sigh, he went on, "I wonder if the kingdom will have any peasants at all left by the time this war finally ends."

"It doesn't matter if we only have a few, so long as Algarve hasn't got any," Gurmun said once more. Aye, those words might have come straight from King Swemmel's lips.

At the outskirts of Pewsum, a sentry stepped into the roadway, stick in hand, and snapped, "This is a forward area. Show me your pass."

General Gurmun undid the top couple of buttons on his rock-gray greatcoat, so that the general's stars on his collar tabs showed. "Are these pass enough?"

The sentry deflated like a pricked pig's bladder. He lorded it over those beneath him and groveled to those above. Such was life in Unkerlant. "Aye, sir," he muttered, and got out of the way in a hurry.

"Powers above help the next couple of common soldiers he lands on," Rathar remarked as he and Gurmun rode past. Gurmun laughed and nodded. He was on top almost all the time, so he found such things funny.

Inside Pewsum, Unkerlanter artisans and mages still labored to repair the ley-line caravan depot. Before pulling out, the Algarvians had done their ingenious best to make sure their foes would get as little use from the town as possible; and that best, as usual, proved quite good. "Stinking redheads," Gurmun growled. "That depot had better not slow us down, come the day. If it does, some of those worthless wizards will join these beauties here."

He pointed to a couple of corpses hanging from a gibbet in the market square. They'd been hanging for some time. By now, they were more bone than meat, and didn't stink too badly. Each was draped with a placard reading, COLLABORATOR. Soldiers and civilians walked past them without so much as a glance.

"They caught two," Gurmun said. "I wonder how many are still running loose."

"A good many, odds are," Rathar answered. "The inspectors

will root them out." General Gurmun nodded, as Rathar had been sure he would. Swemmel's inspectors were trained to sniff out treason whether it was there or not. When it really was . . .

A soldier was reading a news sheet, one prepared by the local army headquarters. He started to wad it up and throw it away. Gurmun called, "Here, fellow, let me have a look at that."

"Sure, pal," the trooper said agreeably. His rock-gray tunic had faded almost to white. A scar seamed his cheek, another his leg below the hem of the tunic. More than any of that, though, his eyes marked him as a veteran. They never stopped moving. Had the Algarvians flown dragons over Pewsum, he would have known exactly where to dive for cover.

Gurmun reined in to look at the news sheet. Rathar also stopped, and leaned toward him so he could see some of it, too. Gurmun read aloud: " 'In the north, the strong defense the brave soldiers of Unkerlant have shown under the glorious leadership of King Swemmel against the savage Algarvian invader has kept the enemy from making progress, and has tied down his forces so that he cannot move men to the south to hold off our victorious thrusts there.' "

"That's good," Rathar murmured. "That's very good."

General Gurmun nodded. "I've seen worse. Here, wait—there's more. 'Constant vigilance is vital in these hard defensive struggles. Although we often fight with the odds against us, our sacrifice ensures victory elsewhere. Always remember that a victory in the south is a victory for the whole kingdom.' "

"Someone should get a commendation for that," Marshal Rathar said. He called up the map in his head. "Headquarters should be—over there." He pointed. He and Gurmun rode in the direction he'd chosen. His gift for turning map into terrain didn't let him down.

At the headquarters—a battered building that had once been a greengrocer's—another officious sentry tried to stop Rathar and Gurmun. This time, Rathar was the one who flashed his collar tabs. At the sight of the big stars he wore, the sentry turned pale. He couldn't step away, as the one on the road had, but he did his best to disappear in plain sight.

Inside, Brigadier Sigulf saluted. "An honor to make your acquaintance, gentlemen," he said. "You've done great things for the kingdom."

"More needs doing," Gurmun said, his voice flat, almost hostile.

Sigulf looked alarmed, though he made a good game try at holding his face still. He was some years younger even than Gurmun. *Except for Vatran, all our generals are years and years younger than I am,* Rathar thought. The war had killed some of his contemporaries. King Swemmel had killed many more.

He took the news sheet from Gurmun and waved it. "This is a fine piece of work."

"Thanks, lord Marshal," Sigulf answered. "We've done our best to follow the directives we got from Cottbus. We've followed all the directives from Cottbus as closely as we could." That too was the Unkerlanter way.

"Good," Gurmun said. Like Sigulf, he was steeped in the idea that orders should always be followed exactly. Rathar sometimes wondered. One of the reasons the Algarvians got better results with fewer men was that their officers thought for themselves, and didn't feel paralyzed when they had no one above them telling them what to do. But that was how they were trained. Rathar wished his commanders were better at seizing the initiative, but that seemed beyond the mental horizon of most of them.

Sigulf went on, "We are making sure we move only at night. And our crystallomancers are sending more messages to regiments that aren't in place than to ones that are. It gets confusing sometimes, but we're doing our best."

"Those are important orders to follow." Rathar meant every word of it. "You can bet anything you care to name that the Algarvians are stealing as many of our emanations as they can. If your men are confused, think what it must be like for the redheads."

"Aye, sir," Brigadier Sigulf said earnestly. "I do think about that. I think about it all the time. If it weren't for confusing the redheads, all this would be more trouble than it was worth."

"Don't say that," General Gurmun growled. "Don't even

think it. You've been told what to do, and you'll bloody well do it. If you don't feel like doing it, there are plenty of penal companies that can always use one more stupid fool with a stick. Have you got that?"

"Aye, sir," Sigulf repeated, this time with a distinct quaver in his voice. He sent Marshal Rathar a look of appeal.

Rathar stared back stonily. Gurmun was an iron-arsed son of a whore, no doubt about it. But he got results. In war, that counted for more than anything else. "This is important, Brigadier," Rathar said. "If everything goes well, it may prove as important as Sulingen. Have you got *that?*" Wide-eyed, Sigulf nodded. So did Rathar. "Good. See that you do. Gurmun's right—you'd better not get in the way of this. Nothing and nobody will get in the way of this."

Garivald kicked at the dirt. He was worn and sweaty and filthy and more frustrated than he'd ever been in his entire life. "It's no good," he said. "It's just no cursed good."

"We've done a lot," Obilot said. She was every bit as tired and grimy as he was. "We can do more. Every day is longer than the one before. Planting time is always like this."

"No." Garivald shook his head. "I don't care how much we do with hoes and spades and such. We'll never get enough planted to bring in a crop we can live on—not all by ourselves, we won't. We've got to have a donkey or an ox to pull a plow."

"That means going into a village," Obilot said. "Going into a village means getting noticed. And getting noticed means trouble for you. It's liable to mean trouble for me, too. You're higher up on the inspectors' lists, aye, but who's to say I'm not on 'em with you? After all, I was fighting against the Algarvians without taking orders from any of King Swemmel's precious soldiers just the same as you were."

"Every word of that is true," Garivald said, "but none of it matters. If we're going to starve for sure, then we have to take our chances with the villagers and with the inspectors, powers below eat 'em all. They might recognize us, but they might not, too, and that's the gamble we're stuck with."

He waited for her to tell him he was wrong, and for her to tell him exactly how he was wrong. They'd had this argument several times before. Obilot had always stayed dead set against stirring from this hut in the middle of nowhere. Now . . .

Now, with a long sigh, she said, "Maybe we do have to try. I still wish we didn't. For one thing, we haven't got much money—not enough for an ox, sure as sure."

"We'll make some," Garivald said. "I was doing odd jobs in Tolk before Tantris, curse him, came sniffing around. Chopping wood, mucking out barns—there's always work people would sooner pay somebody else to do than do themselves. And you're a fine hand with a needle. I saw that in the woods, where you had next to nothing to work with. If you have decent cloth, proper thread . . ."

Obilot sighed again. "All that helps, aye. But do you know what will help even more?"

"Tell me." Now that Garivald had talked her around, or thought he had, he was more than willing to yield on as many of the little details as he could. Obilot wasn't pleasant to be around when she was brooding about losing an argument.

"Remembering the names we'll be using," she said. Garivald laughed, but it wasn't really funny. The less his own name was heard these days, the better off he would be. And the same was liable to be true for Obilot as well; without a doubt, she was right about that.

They took such silver as they had and headed for Linnich, the nearest surviving village. It was three or four hours away. Garivald discovered he'd lost the knack for marching. "Not like it was when we'd go out of the woods to pay a call on some village that got too friendly with the redheads," he remarked as he sat down on a stump to rest.

"No. Not even close." Obilot sat down beside him. She looked glad to take the weight off her feet, too. Suddenly, though, she snapped her fingers in alarm. "The redheads! We've still got some of false King Raniero's money. If we pass it . . ." She slashed a finger across her throat.

"Maybe—but maybe not, too," Garivald answered. "Some

people will still take it: some people figure silver is silver. Aye, we have to be careful; I know. I brought it along, but I've got it wrapped in a rag so it's not mixed in with Swemmel's money."

Obilot pursed her lips, then nodded. Garivald grinned. He seldom got the chance to feel he was one step ahead of her, and enjoyed it when he did.

Like almost every peasant village in the Duchy of Grelz that Garivald had seen—and he'd seen more villages than he'd imagined he would back in Zossen before the war—Linnich was battered. Neither the Unkerlanters nor the Algarvians had dug in there, or the village wouldn't have still stood. But craters showed where eggs had fallen, and ruins or sudden empty places like missing teeth in a jaw marked what had been houses.

A lot of the peasants were already in the fields; it was planting season for them, too. When Garivald walked up to a fellow guiding a plow behind an ox, the other peasant seemed glad enough to stop. He shook his head, though, when Garivald asked if anyone had a beast he might sell. "Don't know about that, stranger," he said. "Them as still has 'em left alive are mighty glad to be using 'em, you hear what I'm saying?"

"I hear," Garivald answered. *Stranger.* He would have used the word back in Zossen. Then, though, he wouldn't have known how being on the wrong end of it burned. He let coins jingle. "I can pay." He didn't say he couldn't pay enough. He wouldn't say anything like that till he had to.

"Like I say, money's not the only thing going on," the other peasant told him. Then he snapped his fingers, as if reminding himself of something. "Dagulf's got a mule, though. He's been hiring it out and drinking up the money he makes. Maybe he'd sell."

"Dagulf," Garivald echoed. It wasn't an unusual name, but . . . He pointed at the peasant from Linnich. "Is this Dagulf a short, skinny fellow with sort of a sour smile and with a scar on his face?"

"Aye." The local nodded. "You know him?"

"Never heard of him," Garivald said solemnly.

The other peasant stared, scratched his head, and at last decided it was a joke and laughed. Then he nodded. "So you know him, do you? He's some of the riffraff that's been coming through here ever since the war stirred things up." That he'd just, in effect, called Garivald and Obilot riffraff, too, never entered his mind. Garivald gave a mental shrug. He'd been called worse than that.

He said, "So Dagulf drinks up his money, does he? Would I find him in the tavern?"

"It's a good bet." The man from Linnich flicked his ox's back with a long springy branch and started it down the furrow. He'd done all the talking he intended to do.

"This Dagulf is from your village?" Obilot asked as she and Garivald started off toward Linnich itself.

"That's right. He's a friend of mine." Garivald checked himself. "He used to be a friend of mine, anyway."

Obilot thought about that, then nodded. "Do you want him to know you're still alive? Is it safe for him to know you're still alive?"

"Before the war, it would have been," Garivald answered. "Before the war, though, he wouldn't have spent all his time in the tavern." But he kept walking toward the village. For one thing, any Unkerlanter man was likely to spend a good deal of time in a tavern. For another . . .

"If he's from your village, he'll know what happened to your family, won't he?" Obilot said.

"Maybe." That thought had been uppermost in Garivald's mind, too. Almost apologetically, he went on, "I do want to find out, you know."

"Do you? Are you sure?" Obilot's voice was harsh, her eyes bleak and far away. "Sometimes you're better off not knowing. Believe me, you are."

That was as much as she ever said about what had happened to her before she joined Munderic's band of irregulars. "I want to find out," Garivald repeated. Obilot only shrugged, as if to say she'd done her best to warn him. By then, they were walking into Linnich. Eyes bright with suspicion, women looked up at them from their vegetable plots. Dogs barked. Garivald stooped and picked up a stone, ready to throw it in case any of the dogs did more than bark. None did. The whole scene achingly reminded him of Zossen; only the faces were different.

He had no trouble finding the tavern. It stood by the village square, and was one of the two biggest buildings in Linnich, the other being the smithy across the square from it. The drunk passed out a few feet from the entrance was another strong clue. Garivald could have seen men drunk into a stupor in Zossen, too.

"Do you want me to go in and try to get the mule?" Obilot asked once more. "That way, he wouldn't have to see your face."

Garivald shook his head. "No. It will be all right." Obilot looked at him, then shrugged and let him walk into the tavern ahead of her.

His eyes needed a moment to adjust to the gloom and to the smoky air—not all the smoke from the hearth went up the chimney. Four or five men and a couple of women looked up from their mugs to give him and Obilot a once-over. Sure enough, one of them was Dagulf.

Garivald walked up to him, hand outstretched. "You recall your old friend Fariulf, don't you?" He bore down heavily on the false name he was using; he didn't want his real one blurted out for everybody to hear.

Dagulf had never been a fool. His eyes narrowed now, but then he smiled and nodded. "Fariulf, by the powers above!" he exclaimed. "It's been awhile. I didn't know if you were alive or dead." He pointed to Obilot. "Who's your friend?"

She answered for herself: "I'm Bringane."

"Bringane," he repeated. Waving to the fellow behind the bar, he called, "Spirits for my friends here." The tapman nodded and waved back. Dagulf eyed Garivald. "I really thought you *were* dead. What do you want?"

As he sank down onto a stool by Dagulf, Garivald answered, "Somebody told me you've got a mule you hire out or that you might sell. I could use one."

"Could you?" Dagulf said. "Ever since I got out of Zossen, that mule's helped keep me alive. You have a plow?" He took it for granted that Garivald was working an abandoned farm somewhere.

"No, but I can slap something together," Garivald answered. "I've got enough iron to hammer something into a plowshare, or I could have the smith here do a better job for me. The woodwork is just woodwork; I can handle that. But I can't plant enough ground to get a decent crop without a mule or an ox."

"I might hire him to you," Dagulf said. "I won't sell him. I make more letting him out for a few days at a time."

He slid silver across the table to the taverner when the man brought mugs for Garivald and Obilot. "Thanks," Garivald said, and Obilot nodded. After sipping the fiery stuff, Garivald asked, "What *did* happen in Zossen?"

He phrased it no more directly than that, but Dagulf understood what he meant. "The redheads dug in, that's what. They had a few behemoths and maybe a company's worth of men, and they made a stand. I was lucky: I was out chopping wood when our heroes hit 'em." He sounded patriotic, not sarcastic—that was the safe way to sound. "I had the mule along to haul the wood back, but I got the blazes out of there instead. From what I hear, nothing's left of the old village."

"That's true. I've seen it." Garivald gulped his spirits and then slammed a fist down on the table. Obilot set a hand on his shoulder. He wanted to shake her off, but he didn't. Scowling at Dagulf, he said, "Curse it, I was hoping you knew more."

"Sorry, Gar—*Far*iulf," Dagulf said. "I don't think the news is good, though." Garivald scowled again, both at the slip and because he didn't think the news was good, either. Unperturbed, Dagulf went on, "Now, do you want to hire the mule or not?"

They haggled for a while. Garivald let Obilot take most of the burden. She was better at dickering than he was, anyhow. And his heart wasn't in the haggle. To have his hopes of learning what had happened to his wife and children raised, raised and then not fulfilled . . . it was very hard indeed. Obilot got a bargain with Dagulf. Garivald knew he should have been pleased, but all he wanted to do was drink himself blind.

"But that is not possible!" the Kuusaman mage said in classical Kaunian rather less fluent than Fernao's. Plainly, he wasn't so used to speaking the international language of sorcery and scholarship. A practical mage out in the provinces wouldn't have to use it very often. Gathering himself—and perhaps also gathering the vocabulary he needed—he went on, "It violates every known law of magecraft."

Six or eight other Kuusaman wizards in the class of twenty nodded in solemn agreement. Most of the rest looked as if they agreed, too, even if they were too polite to say so. A class full of Lagoan mages hearing similar things would have been an argument. A class full of Algarvian mages hearing similar things would have been a riot.

Fernao was glad, then—mostly glad, at any rate—to be teaching stolid Kuusamans. Smiling, he said, "Some of the laws now known are not the ones you learned when you were training." Since gray streaked the Kuusaman's hair, he might well have trained back before the Six Years' War.

He looked indignant nonetheless. "If what you say is true, why has none of this been published? It is too important to be kept a secret."

"No, sir." Fernao shook his head. "It is too important to be published. What would the Algarvians have done, had they got their hands on a couple of journal articles?"

To his astonishment, the Kuusaman got to his feet and bowed. "You are correct. I was mistaken. Please go on." He sat down again.

I would never have heard that from Lagoans, Fernao thought. *No one has heard that from Algarvians since the beginning of the world. They're always right. If you don't believe it, just ask them.*

He brought himself back to the business at hand. "Gentlemen, ladies"—not quite half the sorcerers in the class were women—"you do not need to learn much of the theory behind what you will be doing. In fact, if would be better if you did not, because what you do not know, you cannot tell the enemy if captured. You will need to know how to cast the spells as given to you, how to protect yourself from the things likeliest to go wrong, and how to teach these same things to classes of your own. You are the first cadre. Many more will come after you."

Some of the mages dutifully wrote that in their notebooks. The notebooks stayed in the lecture hall—a part of the hostel of whose existence Fernao had been ignorant till the classes began, and one that showed good planning on the Kuusamans' part. No one took anything in writing out of that hall.

"We shall try small demonstrations today," Fernao continued. "Even the smallest will show the large amounts of sorcerous energy that can be liberated by exploiting the inverse relationship between the laws of similarity and contagion."

He went through the chant and passes in the demonstration, working slowly and carefully to show the students how the spell operated and also to make sure he didn't slip up. Even with this toned-down spell, a mistake could be dangerous.

A glass beaker of water suddenly began to boil. A couple of the Kuusamans applauded. Fernao felt he ought to bow, as if he were a stage conjurer rather than a real wizard. Instead, he said, "As you see, I produced the desired result with much less effort than I would have had to use with more conventional sorcery. Now each of you will try it. Kaleva, please come forward."

As the woman rose and walked up behind the counter, Fernao set up the sorcerous materials she would need, and also put a fresh beaker of water on the stand for her. She went through the spell competently enough, and set the water boiling about as fast as he had. "Very good," she said. "However strange the theory, it *does* work."

She'd spoken Kuusaman. "So it does," Fernao agreed in the same tongue. She gave him a surprised look. "I know some of your speech," he said, "but this teaching needs me to be precise, so I use classical Kaunian—except for the spells themselves, of course. You did very well." Switching back to the classical tongue, he went on, "Next, please." He pointed to the man in the chair next to Kaleva's.

Everything went well till the seventh mage, another woman, turned the water to ice instead of boiling it. "What did I do wrong?" she asked anxiously.

"I think it was your pass in the second versicle," Fernao answered. "The motion needs to be across and then under, and I believe you went over with your left hand. Try again, please." The woman did, and succeeded. After all had gone through the demonstration, Fernao dismissed them and went looking for Pekka.

He found her in the refectory, eating a sandwich made of a round, chewy roll, smoked salmon, a sliced gherkin, and onions. She looked tired. She was teaching practical mages, too, as well as doing the administrative work for the project. She nodded to him as he came up. "Hello," she said. "You have something on your mind. I can see it."

"So I do." Fernao nodded. He looked around. The refectory was crowded with practical mages, a lot of whom he'd never seen before. "When you're done here, can we go someplace quiet and talk?"

Pekka hesitated. Fernao winced. She hadn't come knocking at his door after they'd made love that once. He hadn't knocked on hers, either, however much he'd wanted to. "About what?" she asked at last.

"Something important I don't want to talk about here," he answered, "but not *that*, in case you were wondering."

"All right. I trust you." But Pekka's voice held doubt—she still had to be wondering whether he'd planned to seduce her when he'd invited her to his chamber. She finished the odorous sandwich in a few bites, took a gulp of tea to wash it down, and stood. "Come to my chamber with me, then."

When they got there, Pekka sat down on the bed. Fernao would have liked to sit beside her, but didn't think she would like it if he did. He perched on the stool instead. Even as Pekka raised a questioning eyebrow, he asked, "Why are all the mages we're training Kuusamans? Why aren't there any Lagoans?"

"Ah." Pekka visibly relaxed. That *was* important, and it had nothing to do with their going to bed with each other. She ticked off points on her fingers. "Item—the spells are in Kuusaman. Until they get translated into classical Kaunian or Lagoan, my folk will have an advantage. Item—even if that weren't so, your Guild of Mages hasn't sent any sorcerers for

training. Item—the Algarvians would have an easier time planting a spy among Lagoans, because you are also an Algarvic
people. Shall I go on?"

Those were all good reasons. Fernao wished he could have
argued otherwise. He said, "You do understand why I'm worrying? If your mages all learn these spells and my countrymen
don't, who has the advantage if we quarrel after the war?"

"Aye, I see that," Pekka answered. "The first two points can
and should be addressed. I don't know how you can help looking like Algarvians, though." She winked at him.

He grinned; she hadn't done anything like that since they became lovers, and the only reason he could think of that she
hadn't was that she didn't want to encourage him. But the grin
didn't last. He said, "If we had more Lagoan mages here, the
problem of translating the spells would be smaller. Your people
have not seemed to want to let my countrymen join me,
though."

With candor that surprised him, she said, "We aren't very eager, no. You worry about what Kuusamo might do. Here, we
worry about what Lagoas might do."

"Why?" Fernao asked. "You're bigger than we are. Nothing
we can do will change that."

"Bigger, aye, but with this spell even a small kingdom will
be able to wreak havoc on its neighbors. And"—Pekka's nose
wrinkled—"Lagoans are Lagoans, after all. Who can guess
what you people will do next?"

"You're right, of course." Fernao slid down off the stool, took
two steps forward, gave her a quick kiss, and backed away
again while she was still letting out a startled squeak. He was
glad his leg had healed enough to let him move fairly fast; she
might have hit him had he lingered.

As things were, she shook her head and said, "Fernao," in
such a way that his name couldn't mean anything but, *I wish
you hadn't done that*.

He didn't wish he hadn't done it. He wished he'd done more:
"Pekka," he said, and got that into her name, too.

She shook her head. She'd heard what he meant, just as he'd

heard her. "It's no good," she said. "It's no good at all."

"That's not what you thought then," Fernao answered. He was in no doubt whatever about that.

Pekka didn't try to deny it. Instead, she said, "That makes it worse, not better. I was stupid. Now everybody's life is more complicated than it would have been."

"But—" Fernao struggled for words. He'd never tried dealing with a woman who'd enjoyed going to bed with him but still didn't want to do it again.

Pekka shook her head again. "No. It *was* good, but that isn't enough." She held up a hand before he could snort in disbelief or do anything else in like vein. "It *isn't*. For you, maybe, but, for one thing, you're a man, and—"

"Thank you so much," he said.

She talked right through him: "—and, for another, you're not a married man. Your life isn't *so* much more complicated than it was before. Mine is."

Fernao started to protest. But what complicated his life, at the moment, was Pekka's unwillingness to sleep with him again. Somehow, he didn't think that would impress her.

She sighed and said, "If I weren't happy with Leino, that would be something different. But I am. It's just that we were apart too long. Sometimes your body can make you stupid. I think it happens more easily with men, but it happens to women, too."

"I suppose so," Fernao said dully. He didn't much care to be reckoned no more than the object of her stupidity.

Pekka pointed a finger at him. "Maybe we ought to get more Lagoans to the hostel here, after all. I know how Lagoans think about my people. If you had those tall, round Lagoan women here, you wouldn't look twice at me."

But now Fernao shook his head. "I started wishing I could meet you back when I was reading your journal articles, before you Kuusamans stopped publishing all of a sudden. It isn't just that I think you're beautiful . . ." He hadn't quite intended to say that, which didn't mean it wasn't true.

Pekka looked down at the floor directly between her feet. In a very small voice, she said, "You're not making this any easier, you know."

"I'm sorry." Fernao shook his head. He wasn't sorry. He was about as far from sorry as he could be, and wanted to make things as hard as he could. Most of all, he wanted to bed her again, and again, and again, and let whatever happened afterwards take care of itself.

That must have been very plain. Pekka said, "I think you'd better go." She laughed—briefly. "In the romances, I'd throw yourself into your arms now, either because you were here and my husband wasn't or because you made me so passionate, I couldn't help myself. But life isn't always like the romances. You *did* make me passionate—I'd be lying if I said anything else. It's not enough, though, and I'm not going to let it be enough. I know where I belong."

He heard the finality in that. He wished he were so sure of such things. He didn't see that he could do anything but what she asked now. She looked relieved when he got up and started for the door. Relieved he was going? Or relieved he wasn't making her make hard choices? He wished he could believe the latter. Every fiber of him wanted to. Every nerve ending he had told him he'd be wrong if he did.

If only I hadn't been after anything but seducing her, he thought as his hand fell on the latch. But if there were two more dismal words than *if only* in Lagoan—or Kuusaman, or classical Kaunian, or any other language—he was cursed if he knew what they were.

A band stood on the deck of the *Habakkuk*, thumping away in the emphatic style the Kaunian kingdoms favored. To Leino, the Jelgavan royal hymn sounded like a lot of raucous noise. Not far away from him, Xavega twisted her face into a sneer. She looked pretty even while sneering, no mean feat. *I really have been away from Pekka too long,* Leino thought.

But looking at Xavega was more pleasant than looking at King Donalitu of Jelgava, whose presence aboard the *Habakkuk* occasioned the band. Donalitu was pudgy and graying. Neither his face nor his body seemed to match the splendid, dazzlingly bemedaled uniform he wore.

Xavega sneered at King Donalitu, too. Lagoas might be at war with Algarve, but that didn't mean Lagoans loved and admired folk of Kaunian blood, any more than they loved and admired Kuusamans. As far as Leino could see, Lagoans loved and admired nobody but other Lagoans, and often not too many of them.

He didn't love or particularly admire Xavega. *All I want to do is get it in,* he thought. She started to glance toward him. He looked away. He didn't want to see her sneer aimed at him. He knew it would be, but he didn't want to see it.

Captain Brunho, who commanded the *Habakkuk,* was also a Lagoan, which meant he towered more than half a head over Leino. He led King Donalitu up to the Kuusaman mage and spoke in classical Kaunian: "Your Majesty, I present to you Leino of Kajaani, one of the sorcerers who designed and created this ship here."

Leino bowed. "I am honored to meet you, your Majesty," he said. It was at least theoretically true.

The exiled King of Jelgava looked him over. By Donalitu's expression, what he saw didn't much impress him—he could have given Xavega lessons in sneering. He said, "So you will help me get my throne back? You will help drive the filthy, barbarous usurper from the high place that is not his?"

"Uh, I will do what I can, your Majesty," Leino said. Beside Donalitu, Captain Brunho turned a dull red: the color of hot iron. When Donalitu called Algarvians filthy barbarians, he also indirectly called Lagoans—his protectors, and another Algarvic people—filthy barbarians. He seemed unaware that might prove a problem. Odds were he'd been unaware of it ever since going into exile. Leino had no intention of being the one to enlighten him.

Donalitu said, "What good is this big icy boat? I hope I shall not catch cold here."

Now Leino suspected *he* was turning a dull red. By all appearances, no one had ever taught Donalitu anything resembling manners. Maybe kings didn't need them, though Leino had his doubts about that. Keeping a careful grip on his temper, he replied, "*Habakkuk* can carry many more dragons than any ordinary ship, your Majesty. This ship is also harder to damage than any of the ordinary sort."

"But it will melt," Donalitu exclaimed.

Patiently, Leino said, "Not if we have mages refreshing the ice—and we do." Maybe no one had ever taught King Donalitu to think, either.

Donalitu turned to Captain Brunho and said, "I shall be glad to go back aboard a proper ship, a natural ship, when this inspection is done."

"Aye, your Majesty." Brunho's face and voice were wooden.

Leino held his face straight, too, though it wasn't easy. Donalitu assumed an iron ship was a natural ship. What kind of sense did that make, when ice floated and iron sank? He almost said as much, but somehow managed to keep his mouth shut.

Captain Brunho led the King of Jelgava off to inspect the dragonfliers and their mounts. *With any luck at all, a dragon will bite off his head,* Leino thought. *That would do his kingdom some good.* As soon as King Donalitu was out of earshot, or perhaps rather sooner, Xavega said something in Lagoan. The mages who spoke her language snickered. Not wanting to be left out, Leino asked, "What was that?" in classical Kaunian.

"I said, 'What a horrid, stupid little man,'" she replied in the same tongue. In her loathing of Donalitu, she was willing to treat Leino as an equal. It was the first time she'd done that since the Algarvian leviathan-rider planted an egg on the *Habakkuk.* Plainly, she needed something drastic.

After what seemed like forever, King Donalitu left the iceberg–turned–dragon-hauler. He went down a rope ladder into a little patrol boat that took him back to the ley-line cruiser—*the iron ship, the natural ship,* Leino thought with amusement—in which he'd come out to visit *Habakkuk.* The cruiser sped away.

Leino waved after it. "Good-bye!" he called in classical Kaunian. "With any luck, we shall never see you again. Good-bye!"

"May it be so!" Xavega said. She beamed—she actually beamed—at Leino. His hopes, or something close to his hopes, rose. Common sense quashed that. Xavega's smile wasn't likely to show how much she liked him. It would show how much she despised Donalitu of Jelgava.

Captain Brunho came up behind them. "That will be enough of that," he said. "That will be more than enough of that, in fact."

"He insulted you, he insulted the ship, he insulted all of us, he is a moron," Xavega snarled. "Are we supposed to put our lips on his posterior?"

"He is a king. He is an ally. He deserves respect," Brunho said formally.

"Powers below eat him," Xavega said. "Even Leino here could tell he is more like a leg of mutton than a proper man."

A leg of mutton? Leino wondered. Maybe it was a Lagoan insult, translated literally. Maybe it just meant Xavega's command of classical Kaunian wasn't quite so good as she thought it was. Whatever it was, Leino felt he had to say something, and did: "The land of the Seven Princes would be ashamed to have him as one of the Seven."

"You are welcome to your opinion," Brunho said. "You are not welcome to express it on my ship, not where others can hear it, not where it can affect the morale of my crew."

"You would not have a ship—you would not have *this* ship— if it were not for us mages," Xavega pointed out.

"That is true. But I do have it now."

Maybe such relentless precision made Brunho a good captain. For his sake, for *Habakkuk*'s sake, Leino hoped so. Nevertheless, he observed, "Bringing King Donalitu aboard will do more to hurt morale than I could if I talked for a month."

Xavega laughed and clapped her hands and nodded. Captain Brunho stared down at Leino out of cold green eyes. "This was done at the command of my sovereign, King Vitor. I prefer his opinion to yours." He swung that disapproving stare toward Xavega. "King Vitor is your sovereign, too, in case you have forgotten."

"I remember perfectly well," she snapped. "But if he aproves of that Donalitu creature, he has less in the way of taste han I would have thought." She flounced off. Leino watched er do it. He watched carefully.

Captain Brunho was made of stern stuff—he kept his attenion on Leino. "You mages are an insubordinate lot," he said.

"Thank you," Leino answered. Whatever Brunho had been xpecting by way of a reply, that wasn't it. He spun on his eel—carefully, so as not to fall on the icy deck of the *Habakkuk*—and stalked away.

Before long, Leino went below to serve a shift fighting *Habakkuk*'s unfortunate tendency to melt. That tendency was nore in evidence than ever lately, as the ship cruised the ley ines in warmer, more northerly waters. Without constant attenion from mages, *Habakkuk* would have ceased to be. *We aren't oo insubordinate to keep you from swimming, Captain Brunho,* Leino thought.

Xavega was also part of this anti-melting shift. The mageraft, by now, was routine, though it hadn't been when Leino elped develop it down in the land of the Ice People. The sorerers didn't need to give it all their attention; they could gossip vhile they worked.

"A pity we have Donalitu for an ally," Xavega said. "He vould make a much better enemy."

"He does think the world of himself, does he not?" Ramalho aid, shaking his head. The Lagoan mage continued, "He thinks he world spins around him, too."

"If you told him that back in Jelgava, you would have ended p in one of his dungeons faster than you could blink," Essi renarked. Her hands never faltered in the passes she needed to upport the spell.

"All the more reason for throwing him into one of those duneons himself." Xavega stopped reviling Donalitu in classical Kaunian long enough to chant her portion of the spell that kept *Habakkuk* solid—also in classical Kaunian.

"He is a useful tool against Algarve," Ramalho said. "His ountrymen dote on him."

"Which only goes to prove Jelgavans are not so smart as they vould have other people believe," Leino said.

The other mages chuckled. Xavega said, "No one who ha Donalitu for a king could be very smart. And if our preciou Captain Brunho cannot see that, may the powers below ea him." To Leino's surprise, she nodded his way. "You could se it, whether Brunho could or not. Thank you for trying to ge him to be sensible."

"Er—you are welcome," Leino answered in some surprise She'd actually talked to him in friendly fashion. He couldn't re member the last time she'd done that. For a moment, he couldn't imagine why she'd done it. But that didn't take long to figure out. He'd agreed with her about Donalitu, and he'd said as much to Captain Brunho's face. What could be more calcu lated to endear him to her than agreement? Nothing he coul think of offhand.

As if to confirm that calculation, Xavega went on, "I had no realized you were such a sensible man." The look she gave him was frankly appraising.

"I do my best to hide it," Leino said, which made her laugh out loud. *If I'm so sensible, why do I want to flip up her kilt* But there was more than one kind of sense, and he knew it Bedding a good-looking woman needed no fancy justifications It was its own best argument.

He performed his share of the maintenance spell with casual competence. His eyes kept sliding Xavega's way. Hers kep meeting his, and she wasn't looking at him as if she wanted to go wash her hands afterwards any more, either. *Was it reall that easy?* he wondered. *Did I just have to make her think thought she was right, to make her forget I'm a Kuusaman?* He wasn't used to people who responded so simply.

Do I really want anything to do with somebody who respond so simply? If Pekka were here . . . If Pekka were there, Xaveg wouldn't have done anything but amuse him. He was sure o that. But Pekka was far away, and had been for quite a while Every time Leino looked at Xavega, and every time he caugh her looking at him, he was reminded of just how long he'd bee away from his wife.

Xavega was never one to beat around the bush. When th

shift ended, she waited for Leino in the corridor. "I was wrong about you," she announced.

"Oh?" His heart pounded. "How?"

"I never thought Kuusaman men could be so . . . interesting," she said.

Sure enough, I agreed with her, Leino marveled *That was all I needed to do.* It was probably all he should have done, too. Part of him knew it, anyhow. But that wasn't the part that said, "Now that we have spent all this time keeping *Habakkuk* solid, will you come to my cabin and see how much ice we can melt?"

She couldn't very well misunderstand that. If she didn't care for it, she'd slap him across the icy hallway. Instead, she said, "Aye," and set her hand in his. *I'll be sorry for this later,* Leino thought. But that would be later. Now . . . Now he hurried toward the cabin, Xavega at his side.

"Leave?" The Algarvian lieutenant stared at Sidroc. "You want leave?"

"Aye, sir," Sidroc answered stolidly. Speaking the redheads' language, he had to be stolid; he wasn't all that fluent. "I have had none since I came to Unkerlant more than a year and a half ago."

"Have any of your comrades had leave?" his company commander asked, and Sidroc had to shake his head. The Algarvian went on, "There are two ways to stop fighting here in the west. You can be wounded. Then you stop long enough for them to repair you. Or you can die. But if they could call you back from that, believe me, they would. Now go back go your squad and stop troubling me with foolish notions. Have you got that?"

"Aye, sir," Sidroc repeated. Back to his squad he went.

Ceorl was stirring the stewpot. He looked up. "Well?"

"Two ways to get leave," Sidroc reported. "You can get wounded, or you can get killed. Otherwise, forget it."

"Told you so," Sergeant Werferth said. "They're going to use us up. That's what we're here for. I'd hate it even worse if they didn't treat their own soldiers the same way."

"Wonderful." Speaking Forthwegian, Sidroc had no trouble sounding as sarcastic as he pleased. "I want to go home for a while, curse it. I'd come back."

"Of course you would," Werferth said. "It's not like anybody except our own kin loves us back there—and even some of them don't."

"Futter 'em all," Ceorl said, giving the pot another stir.

"Futter 'em all is right," Sidroc muttered. The trouble was, Werferth was also right. Most Forthwegians had no great use for either the Algarvians or the men from Forthweg who'd taken service in Plegmund's Brigade. "Ungrateful whoresons. If it weren't for the redheads, we'd still be stuck with all those stinking Kaunians back in our own kingdom."

"Well, that's the truth." Ceorl always sounded surprised when he agreed with Sidroc. He tasted the stew and nodded. "It's as good as it'll get, not that that's saying much."

Sidroc dug out his mess kit. Ceorl filled the tin tray with carrots and turnips and onions and bits of meat. "What is this stuff?" Sidroc asked, prodding one of those bits with his spoon. "Unicorn? Horsemeat?"

"No, it's mutton," Ceorl said. Sidroc laughed in his face. The ruffian grinned back, unabashed. "Well, close, anyhow. It's goat."

After tasting and chewing—after chewing for quite a while—Sidroc nodded. "All right, I'll believe that. It must have been in the pot a good long time. It's not too gamy, and it's all the way down to tough."

Werferth methodically emptied his mess kit. "Next to some of the stuff we've eaten, this is downright good. Remember that behemoth that had gone over?" He wrinkled his nose in disgust.

"Which one?" Sidroc asked. His own tin was almost empty, too. "It's not like we've only done it once."

Werferth laughed. So did Ceorl. After a moment, so did Sidroc. Werferth said, "Ah, the happy stories we'll have to tell our grandchildren."

That made Ceorl laugh harder than ever—harder than the joke deserved, as far as Sidroc was concerned. He asked, "What's so funny?"

"Grandchildren," Ceorl answered. "Who's dumb enough to think we'll live long enough to have kids, let alone grandchildren?"

"Oh." That brought Sidroc back to earth—to the muddy earth of Unkerlant—with a bump. It wasn't that Ceorl was wrong. Ceorl was too likely to be right. Sidroc turned to Werferth. "See, Sergeant, there's another reason I need leave. I should have told the lieutenant. How am I going to meet a girl in this miserable country?"

"Drag one down on the floor and have a couple of your pals hold her," Werferth said. "It's not like we haven't done that before, either."

"Curse it, that's not what I meant, and you know it," Sidroc said. "Even if we do father brats on these Unkerlanter women, we'll never find out about it. I want to meet a nice girl, settle down—if I live, I mean."

"If you don't, you won't have to worry about it, that's bloody sure." Ceorl laughed again, nastily, showing off bad teeth.

And Sergeant Werferth let out the grunt he used to show his patience had run short. "Powers above, Sidroc, you come home from the war, what in blazes makes you think a nice girl'd want anything to do with you?"

This time, Ceorl practically wet himself, he thought that was so funny. Sidroc started to scowl at Werferth, then carefully made his face blank instead. *You'll pay for that, Sergeant, powers below eat you—and they will. Aye, you'll pay. It'll look just like an accident, or like the Unkerlanters got you. Plenty of chances to make that happen.*

He went off to a little stream not far away to clean out his mess kit. By the time he got back, his face wasn't even blank any more. He looked like his usual self instead. If he seethed inside, nobody needed to know it. In fact, Werferth needed not to know it, or Sidroc wouldn't get his chance. Werferth hadn't lived long enough for gray to streak his beard by being careless.

"Behemoths!" The cry made everybody in Plegmund's Brigade who heard it grab for his stick. Sidroc was no slower than any of his comrades. He might want to make something unfortunate happen to Sergeant Werferth, but he didn't want the

Unkerlanters to make anything unfortunate happen to him.

Here came the thump of the great beasts' feet against the ground, the rattle and clank of their chainmail. Panic seized him—the noise came from the east, from the direction he'd thought safe. If Swemmel's soldiers had managed to bring behemoths into the rear of Plegmund's Brigade . . . *If they've done that, we're all dead men right now, and I won't have to worry about killing Werferth because they'll take care of it for me—and they'll get me while they're at it.*

Then somebody let out another shout, this one holding nothing but relief: "They're *our* behemoths, powers above be praised!"

Sure enough, the behemoths that tramped into the clearing had Algarvians atop them. The redheads looked as nervous about encountering the men of Plegmund's Brigade as the Forthwegians did at their unexpected appearance. "You boys look too much like Unkerlanters for your own good," one of them called.

"Your behemoths look too much like Unkerlanter beasts for *your* own good," a trooper retorted.

Sidroc nodded, but then hesitated—that proved true only at first glance. It wasn't only that Algarvian behemoth armor differed from what the Unkerlanters used. But the behemoths themselves seemed different. After a moment, he figured out how and why. "They're young beasts," he blurted.

An Algarvian on one of those behemoths heard him and nodded. "If the world were a perfect place, we'd leave 'em on the farm for another year—maybe for another two years," he said. "But the world's not perfect. Ready or not, they're got to go into the fight."

Thinking back on all the behemoths Algarve had left dead on the field on both sides of the Durrwangen bulge, Sidroc nodded. True, the Unkerlanters had also lost a lot of behemoths there. But Unkerlant seemed to have plenty left. The same didn't hold true for Algarve.

"Er—where *is* the fight?" Sidroc's company commander asked. He should have been left on the farm a while longer, too, but here he was.

"Didn't they tell you?" asked a fellow on behemothback, and the young lieutenant shook his head. So did the behemoth crewman, who went on, "We're supposed to make sure Swemmel's buggers don't cross over the river line. What do they call that river? The Fliss?"

"No, the Fluss," the Algarvian lieutenant said. "But the Unkerlanters already have a bridgehead on this side."

Now the men on the behemoths cursed. "Nobody bothered telling us that," one of them said. "It's a demon of a lot harder to dig them out of a bridgehead than it is to keep them from getting one in the first place."

That was only too true. Sidroc wondered if the Algarvians would call off the attack on realizing they were walking into a saw blade. No such luck; Mezentio's men didn't seem to think that way. Sidroc's company commander said, "We'll do our duty, of course."

"Let's go do it, then, or try." The behemoth crewman looked up to the heavens as if he were a Gyongyosian. "They don't let us know the bridgehead's already in place? Powers above, sometimes you'd think they really want us to get killed."

"Forward!" said the lieutenant with Plegmund's Brigade. He didn't blow his whistle, which proved he had some measure of sense.

Forward Sidroc went. He'd probed Unkerlanter bridgeheads before. Going after one of them was like grabbing a porcupine. But then Ceorl said, "We'll better drive 'em back over the river if we can. If we don't, they'll flood men through and swarm all over us. They've done it before, the whoresons."

Sidroc wished he could have disagreed. Unfortunately, the ruffian was right. Sidroc eyed a spot on the back of Sergeant Werferth's tunic. *Right about there*, he thought. *Aye, right about there, especially if they drive us back. It'll look like one of their beams.*

The Unkerlanters were indeed on the eastern side of the Fluss, and there in greater numbers than even the men of Plegmund's Brigade had thought. They had behemoths on this side of the Fluss, too, behemoths that promptly got into a brawl with their Algarvian counterparts and made the Algarvian beasts useless for spearheading any further advance.

"We have to do it ourselves," Sidroc said bitterly. "Isn't that how it always works? Whenever they find a tough job, who do they hand it to? Us, that's who."

"They'd sooner spend us than their own men," Werferth said, as he had before. Sidroc came close to forgiving him for that—close, but not close enough.

Before long, the Unkerlanters proved to have enough behemoths on this side of the river not only to keep the Algarvian behemoths in play but also to mount attacks of their own. They lumbered forward to toss eggs at Sidroc and his comrades at a range from which the Forthwegians couldn't reply. Sidroc went to earth, digging himself in behind a fallen tree. The other men of Plegmund's Brigade were quick to do the same.

On came the Unkerlanter behemoths, footsoldiers trotting along behind. "Those men on foot should be up farther," Sergeant Werferth said from close by Sidroc, as if the Unkerlanters were his troops. "We're going to make them pay."

Sidroc intended to make them pay. He waited quietly in his hole till an incautious behemoth drew too close. Then he flung one of the little pottery-encased sorcerous eggs the Algarvians had been issuing lately. As he'd hoped, it landed right under the behemoth, rolling beneath the animal's armored skirt before bursting. Mad with pain and fear, the behemoth rampaged back the way it had come, trampling a luckless footsoldier who stood in its path.

Other Unkerlanter footsoldiers started blazing at Sidroc when he stayed up too long to admire his handiwork. Werferth knocked him down. "Back in your hole, sonny boy," the veteran said. "We'll need you next time around."

"Right," Sidroc said. "Thanks, Sergeant." Only after the words were out of his mouth did he remember how angry at Werferth he was supposed to be. He shrugged. He didn't *have* to do anything about it now. If he decided he still wanted to later, he could take care of it. He'd have more chances. He was sure of that.

❧

Lieutenant Leudast sprang to one side, away from the wounded behemoth that now ran wild, far out of its crew's control. Trailing blood, the behemoth thundered west, back toward the Fluss River. It would keep spreading chaos through the Unkerlanter bridgehead till its injuries made it fall over or till someone finally killed it.

"Steady, men!" Leudast called. "Keep up the advance. We can do it."

In spite of his words, the Unkerlanter counterattack faltered. The Algarvians and their Forthwegian flunkies weren't going to be able to smash in the bridgehead and drive his countrymen back over the river. That much seemed clear. The enemy lacked both men and behemoths for the job. But no breakthrough was coming here, either, not until more Unkerlanter men and beasts and egg-tossers made it over the Fluss.

Little by little, both sides realized they wouldn't accomplish much, and the fighting tapered off. What point to risking your neck when getting killed wouldn't get you victory? *What point to risking your neck even when getting killed* will *get you victory?* Leudast wondered. He shook his head. That was a subversive thought for a soldier to have.

Sergeant Kiun said, "I don't like fighting those fornicating Forthwegians for beans. For one thing, they always fight hard."

"They're volunteers," Leudast answered. "They aren't conscripts, the way the redheads are." He didn't mention how impressers went through Unkerlanter villages herding young men into Swemmel's army. He didn't need to mention it. He'd joined the army that way. So, very likely, had Kiun, and so, very likely, had most of the men they led.

"Other thing is," Kiun went on, "they look more like us and they dress more like us than the Algarvians do. That means you're liable not to figure out who they are till too late."

"That's so," Leudast said. "It's not as bad as with the Grelzers, but it's so."

"Grelzers." Kiun rolled his eyes. "May we see the last of the stinking traitors, and soon."

Leudast nodded. He hadn't had anything in particular against the folk of the Duchy of Grelz before entering it. All he'd known about them was that they had what was, in his ear, a funny accent. Capturing Raniero, the redhead who'd called himself their king, had won him wealth and rank, no matter what it had done to Raniero himself after King Swemmel paraded him through Herborn.

But fighting Grelzers ... At the beginning of the war through the Duchy, some of the men who wore the dark green tunics of what called itself the Kingdom of Grelz had been half-hearted about fighting their Unkerlanter brethren. A good many had thrown down their sticks and surrendered the first chance they got.

That didn't happen any more. With most of Grelz in King Swemmel's hands these days, the Grelzers who kept on fighting against him were the ones who'd joined the late, not much lamented Raniero because they hated the King of Unkerlant with a deep and abiding passion, not because they'd been looking for advantage from the Algarvians. Few of the ones who wore dark green these days bothered trying to surrender. Few of the ones who did yield went back to captives' camps.

With a sly grin, Kiun said, "Bet you almost wouldn't've minded getting chased back over the Fluss, Lieutenant."

"You can't say things like that," Leudast answered, which didn't mean the underofficer was wrong.

"I just thought you'd like to get back to Leiferde and your lady friend there," Kiun said, his smile disarming now. "I've got a lady friend back there myself, matter of fact."

"Have you?" Leudast said, and Kiun nodded. "I didn't think you meant anything you shouldn't have," Leudast continued, "but you never can tell who may be listening."

Kiun's grimace said he understood exactly what Leudast meant. King Swemmel saw traitors everywhere. That he saw so many had helped create a good many here in the Duchy of Grelz. It had probably helped create a good many elsewhere in Unkerlant, too. But any Swemmel could reach suffered for it: a potent argument against treason.

Captain Recared, the regimental commander, came up to Leudast. "I think things here have settled down for a while," he said.

"Aye, sir." Leudast nodded. "Just one more little fight." *One more little fight I'm lucky I lived through. How many didn't this time? How many have I got left?*

"We've held the bridgehead," Recared went on, and Leudast nodded again. His superior said, "That's what really matters. Sooner or later, we'll break out and give the Algarvians another good kick in the teeth."

"We've given them a lot of kicks, the past year and a half," Leudast said. "Feels good to be the foot and not the backside."

Recared laughed. He'd seemed impossibly young when he first took command of the regiment where Leudast commanded a company. His features were still youthful—he couldn't have been much above twenty years old—but he'd been through a lot since then, just as all Unkerlanter soldiers had. *All of us who are still breathing, anyhow,* Leudast thought.

"You saw how they threw a few behemoths at us and tried to make them count for a lot," Recared said. "That's what they're reduced to these days. They're still dangerous—I expect they'll always be dangerous—but we can beat them."

They're still dangerous—but we can beat them. Almost three years before, Leudast had been near the border between Unkerlanter and Algarvian-occupied Forthweg. He and his comrades had been on the point of attacking the Algarvians, but the redheads struck first. After that, Leudast had done nothing but retreat for a long time, till Mezentio's men finally stalled in the snow of an Unkerlanter winter just outside Cottbus.

He'd done more retreating the following summer, down in the south, and missed some of the fight in Sulingen because he'd been down with a leg wound that still pained him now and again. But he'd come a long way east since then. *They're still dangerous—but we can beat them.* It would have seemed absurd in the days when the Algarvians swept all before them. Now it was simply truth.

"Do you know what I wish, sir?" Leudast asked.

"Probably," Recared answered. "You wish you were back on the other side of the Fluss, finding some way or other to be alone with that girl you met there. Am I right, or am I wrong?" He chuckled. He knew he was right.

And Leudast could only nod once more. "If I live through the rest of the war, I think I'll come back here."

"Who knows whether you'll think the same way then?" Recared said. "A girl goes to bed with you a few times, you decide you're in love." That was cynical enough to have come from an Algarvian's throat. Before Leudast could say anything or even shake his head, the regimental commander changed the subject: "Do you know, Lieutenant, we've been promised a new field kitchen, and it never did show up."

"Sir?" Leudast said blankly; this was the first he'd heard about a field kitchen. It was news to him that the Unkerlanter army boasted such things. In the field, even the Algarvians mostly cooked catch as catch can.

But Captain Recared nodded. "I've sent complaints west by crystallomancer, but you know what that's worth. They might as well be written on the air. I really need someone to look into it. Why don't you commandeer a horse or a mule or a unicorn and go raise a stink?"

"Me, sir?" Leudast squeaked. "I'm just a—"

"You're a lieutenant," Recared said. "And you're not just *a* lieutenant. Marshal Rathar personally promoted you, and everybody knows why. You'll have my written authorization, too. I'll make sure you take it with you." He smiled a small, thoughtful smile. "The cursed thing is supposed to be somewhere not too far from a wide spot in the road called Leiferde. I expect you'll be able to track it down in those parts, eh?"

Leudast stared at him. Recared looked back. No, he wasn't so young and innocent as he had been. "Thank you, sir," Leudast said.

"For what?" Recared answered. "You came back with that field kitchen and I'll thank you. With it or without it, be back here in three days."

"Aye, sir." Leudast saluted. Leiferde was about a day away. That would leave him a day—or whatever was left of a day after he chased after a field kitchen (*was* there one somewhere near Alize's village?)—to do what he pleased. And he knew exactly what he pleased. "Let me round up a mount . . ." He wasn't much of a rider, but he would manage. After all, he had an incentive.

"You do that." Recared sounded professionally brisk. "While you're doing it, I'll prepare your orders."

Leudast took charge of a horse that had been pulling a wagon now down with a broken axle. Getting riding gear took rather longer than scaring up the animal. He felt very high off the ground when he rode back to Recared.

"Here you are," Recared said. "Now you're official. Go find that field kitchen—and whatever else you happen to find around Leiferde." That was as close as he came to admitting he knew Leudast might have anything else in mind.

Saluting again, Leudast rode off. He wanted to boot the horse up to a gallop, to get to Alize's village as fast as he could. Only the accurate suspicion that he would fall off on his head long before he got to Leiferde kept him at a more sedate pace.

Unkerlanter artisans had thrown a couple of quick bridges of precut lengths of timber across the Fluss. Military constables stood at the eastern end of the one Leudast approached. They inspected the order Recared had given him, then nodded and stood aside. "Pass on, Lieutenant," one of them said, and grudged him a salute. "You *are* authorized." He sounded as if he'd turned back plenty who weren't. He probably had.

More artisans were bringing up the timbers for another bridge. Leudast waved to them as he headed west past their wagons. He neared Leiferde early the next morning, after sleeping rolled in his cloak by the side of the road. Before going into the village, he went to the supply dump in search of the possibly mythical field kitchen.

To his amazement, he found a sergeant who knew what he was talking about. "Aye, Lieutenant, your regimental commander's been bending everybody's ear about the cursed thing," the fellow said. "We're bloody short of draft animals, is the trouble. You can haul it away with your horse there right now, if you want to."

"I've got some other business on this side of the Fluss I need to take care of first," Leudast said. "I'll be back for it tomorrow morning."

"Suits me," the supply sergeant said. "It'll be ready and waiting."

It suited Leudast, too. He mounted the horse and rode into Leiferde. Most of the peasants ignored him: what was one more soldier, after so many? He found Alize weeding the vegetable plot by her father's house. She let out a squeal of delight and sprang to her feet. "What are you *doing* here?" she asked.

He grinned. "I was in the neighborhood, so I just thought I'd drop by."

Nine

Some people had always turned their backs on Talsu when he walked through the streets of Skrunda. They were the folk who thought no one could come back from a dungeon without giving himself to the Algarvians. Now that he'd come out of the constabulary building without visible damage, more people turned their backs on him. They thought no one could do that without telling the redheads what they wanted to hear.

Most of the time, Talsu was able to ignore such snubs. But when they came from young men who had been his friends before he was seized, they tore at him, no matter how much he tried not to show it. He sometimes wanted to scream at them. *Mezentio's men grabbed me because I was trying to fight back!* echoed through his mind. *What have you done since the Algarvians occupied Jelgava? Not a cursed thing, that's what.*

Holding in his fury led to a bad temper and a sour stomach. "It'll all get sorted out when King Donalitu comes back," Gailisa said one evening, trying to soothe him after he'd snarled at everyone in his family.

"Will it?" Talsu asked bitterly.

"Of course it will," she answered in the quiet of the cramped little bedchamber they shared. "That's why he'll come back— to sort things out, I mean."

She had a touching faith in the king. Once upon a time, Talsu might have had a similar faith in Donalitu. He tried to remember when he'd lost it. Before he went into the army: he was sure of that. "If he does come back, he'll probably throw me in the dungeon for being too friendly with the redheads."

That exercise in cynicism got him an appalled look from his wife. "He wouldn't do such a thing!" she exclaimed. "He'd never do such a thing! The only reason you ever got in trouble was because you wanted to do something to the Algarvians."

"Well, let's hope you're right about that." Talsu didn't think she was, but he didn't feel like arguing with her, either. He had other things on his mind. The other things ended up making him happy and then sleepy. The bed wasn't really big enough for the two of them, but they were young enough not to mind sometimes waking up all tangled together.

They were tangled together when they woke up that night. It was still dark: that was the first thing Talsu noticed. It was, in fact, pitch black. For a moment, Talsu couldn't imagine why he'd awakened. Then he heard the bells clanging out an alarm.

"Fire somewhere?" Gailisa asked.

Talsu listened, then shook his head. "I don't think so—they're ringing all over town. That means dragonfliers overhead."

"Aye, you're probably right." Gailisa untangled her legs from his and got out of bed. "We'd better go downstairs."

They'd huddled behind the counter in the tailor's shop during other visits from Kuusaman and Lagoan dragons. As Talsu got up, too, he said, "I wish we had a cellar here, the way your father does."

"Do you want to try to get over there?" she asked.

He shook his head. "Getting caught in the open when eggs start falling is the last thing you want to do. I saw what happens then in the army—and the first time the dragons came over

Skrunda, during the promenade in the square." He swatted Gailisa lightly on the backside. "Come on. Let's get moving."

"I was," she said. Talsu chuckled. He hadn't had to swat her. He'd just liked doing it.

He would have pounded on his mother and father's door, and on his sister's, to get them moving, but they all met in the hallway—Traku had been coming down the hall to make sure he and Gailisa were awake. After some confusion, they hurried downstairs. They huddled between the counter and the wall just as the first eggs started bursting all over Skrunda.

"Here's hoping they come down on the Algarvians' heads," Talsu said.

"Powers above, make it so!" his mother said. But Laitsina added, "Here's hoping not too many come down on ordinary people like us."

"They do aim as well as they can," Talsu said. That was true. But dragonfliers, high in the air and aboard bad-tempered beasts that tried to do what *they* wanted, not what the fliers wanted, couldn't aim any too well. That was also true, but Talsu didn't mention it. It was one more thing he didn't care to think about.

An egg burst down the street, close enough to make the floor shake under Talsu. The front window in the tailor's shop rattled in its frame, but didn't break.

"They're coming over more often than they used to," Talsu's sister said.

"Ausra's right," Laitsina said as another egg burst, this one a little farther away. "They're sending more dragons each time, too."

"It's these Habakkuk things, unless I miss my guess," Talsu said. "They can carry a lot of dragons."

"The Algarvians don't like 'em, that's for sure," Traku agreed. "They spend a lot of space in the news sheets screaming about 'em."

"Anything the Algarvians scream about can't be all bad." Talsu spoke with great conviction. No one in his family disagreed. Not many Jelgavans in Skrunda would have disagreed—only those few who'd ended up in bed with the redheads.

"I hope they have a couple of squads of soldiers right where he arch from the Kaunian Empire used to be," Traku said. 'And I hope an egg comes down right on those buggers."

"That would be good," Talsu agreed. "That would be very good." He'd watched when the Algarvian mages toppled that arch. The redheads hadn't cared for what it said about their ancestors. They probably didn't care for what a lot of modern Jelgavans had to say about the descendants of their ancestors, either.

"At least we get a little warning when the Lagoans and Kusamans come over now," Gailisa said, as the shop shook again.

"They've got dowsers here now, I suppose," Talsu said. "They aren't doing it for us, though. They're doing it for themselves."

Before she could answer, several eggs landed close together, and all of them close to the tailor's shop. The window blew n. Fragments of glass clattered off the front of the counter. More fragments clattered off the wall behind it. "Who's going o pay for that?" Traku growled. "I am, that's who. Curse 'em ll."

All things considered, Talsu thought they were fairly lucky. Had those eggs burst a little closer, the shards of glass might nave sliced right through the counter—and through the people behind it, too. He didn't say that. His father hadn't seen real war face-to-face, and didn't know everything it could do. As far s Talsu was concerned, Traku didn't know how lucky he was.

And then an egg did burst close by, close enough to slam the counter back against the people huddling behind it. Everyone shrieked. It didn't quite go over onto them, and it didn't quite crush them against the wall, but it came much too close to doing both. Talsu felt not the least shame in yelling along with the rest of his family. For a dreadful moment, he thought that yell would be the last cry that ever passed his lips.

When he realized he would live a little longer, he said, 'We're going to have to remodel the shop."

"Right this minute, son, that's the least of my worries," Traku said.

Gailisa pointed to the wall above the counter. "What's that funny light?"

Talsu looked up, too. It should have been dark; Skrunda left lights out at night to make it harder for Lagoan and Kuusaman dragons to find the town. *Not hard enough*, Talsu thought. But that orange, flickering glow was easy enough to recognize once you got over not expecting to see it there. "Fire!" he said.

It got brighter fearfully fast, too. "It's close," Gailisa said, and then, "We can't stay here."

"You're right." Talsu scrambled to his feet. Eggs were still falling, but that didn't matter. The eggs might miss. If he and his family stayed where they were, they would burn. He hauled Gailisa up, too, then reached for his sister. "We've got to get out while we still can."

"But—" his mother wailed.

"He's right, Laitsina," Traku said. "Come on. As long as we get out in one piece, we can worry about everything else later." He got up, and after a moment his wife did, too.

By then, Talsu was already at the front door. It didn't want to open; the blasts of sorcerous energy left it jammed in the frame. But the window beside it was bare of glass. Talsu helped Gailisa through the emptiness there. Ausra went through by herself. Laitsina started to balk. Traku slapped her on the behind, hard. She squawked and scrambled out into the street.

Talsu gaped. He'd never imagined his father hitting his mother. "Go out there, son, or I'll give you the same," Traku growled. "You're the one who said we've got to get out, and you're right."

"Aye, Father," Talsu said, as he might have to a sergeant giving him orders in combat. Out through the glassless frame he went. His father followed.

The shop across the street was burning. So was the one two doors down—and, even as Traku watched, the shop next door caught fire. "Where are the water brigades?" a neighbor asked.

"Probably busy somewhere else," Talsu said. "This can't be the only blaze burning." Water brigades were splendid for fighting the occasional fire that broke out during peacetime. If half a dozen, or a dozen, or two dozen, fires broke out all at once, they were going to be hopelessly overmatched.

"But my shop will burn if the water brigades don't come," the neighbor said.

"Our shop will burn, too," Laitsina said. She was clutching Traku's hand very hard. She wasn't angry about what he'd done to get her moving. If she wasn't, Talsu supposed he didn't have any business being angry, either.

"Sweetheart, there's nothing we can do about it," Traku said. "Not one fornicating thing." An egg bursting a couple of streets away punctuated his words. Shaking his head, he went on, "We're alive. That's all that matters right now."

Gailisa said, "Here's hoping the Algarvians here in Skrunda caught it as hard as we have."

"Aye, by the powers above," Talsu said.

A woman who lived a few doors away said, "It's a terrible thing when the people you want to win the war are dropping eggs on your head."

Everyone nodded. Talsu had been thinking the same thing. He hadn't dared say it, though. If he said anything too harsh about the redheads and it got back to them, what might happen to him? He could go back to the dungeon, and he knew it.

He made himself think about what was going on here and now, not what might happen later. "We'd better get moving, before the fire catches us," he said.

No one argued with him. He rather wished someone had. He also wished he could have gone back into the shop, gone back upstairs for . . . what? Everything that truly counted was here in the street with him. Only then did he notice his feet hurt, and that he was barefoot. He wondered how much glass he'd stepped in, and how badly cut his feet were. He shrugged. He could worry about that later, too.

Gailisa gasped and clutched at his arm. The corpse the fire-light showed wasn't pretty. Blood—it looked black—puddled in the gutter by the body. Talsu said, "We're lucky," and meant it.

Traku looked back over his shoulder. "There goes the shop," he said quietly. Laitsina started to cry. Talsu felt like crying, too. He'd thought he would grow old himself as a tailor in that shop. But he still counted himself lucky, for he still had a chance to grow old.

Half the time, Vanai hoped Unkerlanter dragons would smash the Kaunian district in Eoforwic to rubble. That way, the Algarvians wouldn't get the chance to use her life energy for their own needs. But then she would shake her head and wrap her arms around her swollen belly. Not just her life was involved here—she would have her baby soon. And she fiercely wanted the baby to live. What happened to her didn't seem nearly so important as what happened to it.

The Algarvians hadn't staged another roundup in her part of the Kaunian quarter, though they'd swept through other parts of it. Whenever cries and screams rose elsewhere in the district, Vanai felt a horrid sense of relief—it was happening, aye, but not to her. Afterwards, she always hated herself for that relief, but she could never stifle it at the time.

She looked out the window of her flat, then shrank back again. A couple of Algarvian constables strolled along the street. They twirled their bludgeons as they passed. If they didn't own the world, they weren't about to admit it. She muttered a curse under her breath, even though she'd already seen that curses wouldn't bite on Algarvians. That hardly surprised her. They cursed themselves, doing what they did to the Kaunians . . . didn't they?

One of the redheads was uncommonly plump. Vanai took a long look at him, though she was careful enough not to get close enough to the glass to let him have a good look at her. She nodded. She'd seen him before, back in Oyngestun. She and her grandfather had almost been sent west, but he'd spoken up on their behalf, and two others had gone instead.

Now he was here. What did that mean? Nothing good—she was sure of it. Were any Kaunians at all left alive in and around Gromheort? Maybe the Algarvians didn't need constables there anymore. Vanai didn't want to think that was true, but it made an unpleasant amount of sense.

Along with his partner, the plump constable strolled around the corner and disappeared. Vanai let out a sigh of relief, though she didn't know why. How was she in less danger now than she had been while the constables remained in sight? In no way she could see. But she did feel better, regardless of whether she had any rational reason to do so.

"My grandfather would not approve of such irrationality," she said. More and more these days, she'd fallen into the habit of talking aloud to the baby. She seldom had anyone else to talk to. Not many Kaunians were left in this block of flats, not after the latest roundup.

I suppose seeing that constable made my grandfather come into my mind, Vanai thought. Normally, Brivibas didn't enter her thoughts very often. When he did, she usually tried to force him out of them again. He would have disapproved of much more than a momentary lapse of irrationality. Her hands went to her belly once more. Having a child by a Forthwegian would have topped his list. She was sure of that. Brivibas would have thundered on and on about diluting Kaunianity.

"But don't you see, my grandfather?" Vanai said, as if he stood beside her. "The Algarvians have done more to dilute Kaunianity in Forthweg than the Forthwegians could have done if they'd made half our maidens marry their young men."

Her grandfather would have said something stuffy about that being beside the point. She didn't think it was. Back before the war—that magical phrase—perhaps one in ten of King Penda's subjects had been of Kaunian blood. How many Kaunians would be left alive by the time the war ended? Any at all? Even if there were some scattered handful, would they have any weight in Forthweg—assuming a Kingdom of Forthweg ever existed again? Penda had had to notice a tenth of his subjects. Would he have to notice a thirtieth, or a fiftieth, or whatever remnant of blonds was left?

Vanai laughed bitterly. Not being noticed by King Penda—if Penda ever came back from exile—was, at the moment, the least of her worries, and of the Forthwegian Kaunians' worries, too. Surviving till he returned—if he returned—took pride of place there.

The baby kicked inside her, strongly enough to make her hand move on her belly. She nodded to herself. The baby kicked hard these days. Once or twice, it had kicked in just the wrong place and made one of her legs go weak beneath her for a moment. She counted herself lucky that she hadn't fallen.

Patting her swollen stomach, she said, "And you ought to count yourself lucky that I didn't fall, too." The baby rewarded her with another kick and a wriggle. It wasn't listening to her. She sighed. No one did, these days. The only person who'd ever really listened to her, as long as she could remember, was Ealstan.

Tears welled up in her eyes. She'd known terror after the Algarvians captured her. She'd expected that. What she hadn't expected was the most crushing loneliness she'd ever known. She'd got used to having someone with whom she could talk, someone to whom she really mattered, someone to whom she wasn't just a research assistant or a convenience (or, occasionally, an inconvenience).

She hadn't realized how important, how marvelous that was, till she didn't have it any more. She wiped the tears on her sleeve. Before she got pregnant, they would have embarrassed her. Now she almost took them for granted. They came more easily these days. She didn't know why that was so, but she knew that it was so.

Even back in the days of the Kaunian Empire, people had noticed the same thing. A couple of quotations from the days of the Empire flashed through her mind. Her mouth twisted. That she knew such things was her grandfather's doing. And what had it got her? A flat in the Kaunian district, a wait till the Algarvians caught her and took her away.

For that matter, what had Brivibas' erudition got him? First, the attentions of Major Spinello, who'd had plenty of attentions to give Vanai, too, curse him. And last, a makeshift noose in an Algarvian gaol cell after he got recognized in spite of his sorcerous disguise as a Forthwegian.

"So much for scholarship," she said, though she did wonder how her grandfather had been recognized. Had the magic worn off, as hers had done? She found that hard to believe: Brivibas was nothing if not careful and precise. Had someone known his voice in spite of the way he looked? That seemed more plausible. But who could have?

Major Spinello might have. Vanai shuddered. Spinello had

gone off to the west to fight the Unkerlanters. She hoped he was dead, horribly dead. But even if he wasn't, he was there, in the west, not in Gromheort. Who else? That plump constable? Would he have had any special reason to remember and recognize Brivibas? Vanai could only shrug. How could she know what had happened in Oyngestun after she left with Ealstan?

The baby wiggled and twisted inside her. The sensation was like none she'd ever known. She wondered how she could put it into words for someone who hadn't known it. After a moment, she shook her head. She didn't think there were any such words.

"Oh, stop," she said, when the baby seemed to be trying to learn to dance inside a space that didn't have room for fancy steps. "If it weren't for you, I'd be back at my own flat, not here."

She was sure the baby made the masking spell she'd devised fade away faster than it would have otherwise. She wondered how long the spell would hold if she tried it now, with the baby so much bigger. She'd probably have to renew it every half hour, maybe even more.

"I could," she said. "I would. But . . ." Anyone who looked like a Forthwegian caught inside the Kaunian quarter would be blazed, no questions asked. "If it weren't for that, I really could," Vanai repeated. She had the dark brown strand of yarn and the yellow one. She even had a Forthwegian-style woman's tunic. She'd found it going through a now-empty flat in the building. She sometimes wore it when the weather got warm. She'd always despised those baggy tunics, but they were a lot more comfortable for a pregnant woman than any trousers.

Here came that Algarvian constable and his partner, back along the street. They were both talking and gesturing animatedly, as Algarvians did. The plump constable laughed at something the other one said. *How can you do that? How can you laugh?* Vanai wondered. *You must know what goes on here. How can you not care?*

Bells began to clang then, not just in the Kaunian quarter but all over Eoforwic. The two Algarvian constables stopped laughing. The plump one shouted a phrase Vanai didn't understand—one she judged unlikely ever to have appeared in polite literature—and shook his fist at the sky. Then he and his partner stopped strolling along and started hurrying away from the Kaunian quarter.

Blonds on the street started hurrying, too: hurrying toward those blocks of flats that had cellars. From the gossip at the feeding stations the Algarvians maintained, Vanai had heard that her own people had killed a couple of constables rash enough to go down into a cellar with them. She didn't know if that was true—it sounded almost too good to be true—but she hoped so.

There wasn't quite the desperate dash and scramble there would have been a few months before. For one thing, the redheads' dowsing techniques had improved, which gave people a little more time to take shelter. And, for another, Unkerlanter dragons over Eoforwic were no longer a horrid surprise. They'd come often enough by now to let folk know what to expect.

One of the things to expect was disaster, if you had the misfortune to be on the upper story of a building that a bursting egg leveled. Vanai started for the door, intending to go downstairs into a cellar herself. As pregnant as she was, she couldn't go anywhere very fast, and so was grateful for the extra warning time the Algarvian dowsers gave. *Not that they're doing it for the likes of me,* she thought.

With a hand on the latch, though, she checked herself. She'd seen those constables leave the Kaunian quarter. She suspected the pair she'd seen hadn't been the only ones getting out, either. How likely was it that the guards around the edge of the district were all staying at their posts? Not very, unless she missed her guess.

Which meant . . . "Which means that, if I'm lucky, if they're in cellars, if an Unkerlanter egg doesn't tear me to pieces, this is the best chance I'll ever have to get out of the quarter," Vanai breathed.

Once the idea came to her, she didn't hesitate for a moment. She grabbed the long, Forthwegian-style tunic, then checked her pockets to make sure she had the brown yarn and the yellow. It was death to look like a Forthwegian inside the Kaunian quarter. It was also death to look like a Kaunian out of it. But if no one saw her appearance change from the one to the other . . . *I have to try,* she thought. *What have I got to lose?*

She left the block of flats and came out onto the street just as the first eggs began bursting in Eoforwic. Looking up, she saw rock-gray dragons wheeling in the blue sky. "Get into a cellar, you cursed fool!" somebody shouted to her.

But Vanai had no intention of getting into a cellar, and didn't think herself at all foolish. At the awkward waddle that was the fastest gait she had, she hurried toward the edge of the Kaunian quarter, only a few blocks away. More and more eggs fell, some of them quite close. She moaned with fear, but kept going.

Someone else behind her shouted something. She looked over her shoulder and moaned again—an Algarvian constable, a plumpish one. But he wasn't close, and he might not have been shouting at her. She still had a chance.

She ducked into a doorway, tore off her Kaunian clothes, and threw on the Forthwegian tunic. Then she raced through the spell that let her look Forthwegian, too. She stepped out onto the sidewalk and trotted—a lumbering trot, but a trot nonetheless—toward safety (barring eggs, of course) now only half a block away.

Another shout rang out behind her—another shout, and the thud of boots on flagstones. However much she didn't want to, she turned her head. A stick in his hand, that Algarvian constable came thundering after her.

Ealstan felt as if he'd been running for a hundred miles. His heart sledged in his chest. He'd been wrong before, so often that hope was almost dead. He didn't think he could stand to be wrong again. *But I have to try,* he thought, and kept running as hard as he could.

He rounded a corner . . . and saw no one ahead of him. Panting, he cursed loudly—in Algarvian. Then somebody ducked out of a doorway and hurried toward the edge of the Kaunian district. Ealstan cursed again, louder and more furiously—but still in Algarvian. He'd been running after a blond woman, and this was a Forthwegian. If she hadn't been so very pregnant, she would have looked a lot like his sister, Conberge . . . He started running as if he'd never run before.

He let out another great shout—"Vanai!"—as he thudded toward her. She glanced back over her shoulder and came to a stop, every inch of her sagging, her face full of hopeless despair. "Vanai!" he yelled again, and then, "Thelberge!" and then, most important of all, "Darling!"

She stared. She swayed. For a moment, he thought she would faint. An egg burst only a block or so away. Ealstan hardly noticed it. He didn't think Vanai noticed it at all. "Ealstan?" she whispered as he dashed up and swept her into his arms. "I don't believe it," she went on, though the words were muffled because he was doing his best to smother her with kisses.

"It's true, by the powers above," he said in the brief moments when he wasn't otherwise occupied.

"But you're an Algarvian," she said. "I mean, you look like an Algarvian. How can you be—?"

"*You Too Can Be a Mage*," Ealstan said solemnly. "I'm an Algarvian the same way you're a Forthwegian." He took her by the elbow and steered her in the direction she was already going. "Come on. Let's get you out of the quarter here. As soon as we've done that, we can worry about everything else."

If he ran into any guards at the edge of the quarter, Ealstan intended to talk his way past them. The constabulary uniform he was wearing, which Pybba had got him despite grumblings, would give him a long head start toward that. But there was no need. Like any men of sense, the guards had sought shelter from the Unkerlanter eggs. So had everybody else; but for the two of them, the streets were empty.

"Out!" he said triumphantly as they passed into the part of Eoforwic where Forthwegians could go and Kaunians—at least Kaunians who looked like Kaunians—couldn't.

"Out," Vanai echoed. She raised an eyebrow in an expression unmistakably hers, no matter how much the magic made her look like Conberge. "I could have done this myself, you know."

"I know, sweetheart," Ealstan said. "Now I know. But I didn't know before I started coming into the quarter looking for you." His chuckle was grim. "Any Algarvian constables who saw me—any real Algarvian constables, I mean—must have figured I had a Kaunian girlfriend." He squeezed her hand. How fine the touch of her flesh felt! "And they were right, but not the way they thought."

Eggs burst only a couple of blocks away. Ealstan waved to the Unkerlanter dragons still circling overhead, still looking for targets in Eoforwic. The longer they stayed up there, the better his chances of getting back to his flat with Vanai.

He poked his head into the lobby of a block of flats just outside the Kaunian quarter. As he'd hoped, it was empty. Everyone there had run for a cellar. He pulled Vanai inside and stripped off his constable's uniform. After pulling out a proper Forthwegian tunic from a pouch on his belt, he stuffed the Algarvian-style tunic and kilt and hat into the pouch. "Pybba may need them again," he told Vanai.

"Pybba!" she said. "But Pybba's got no use for Kaunians. I don't know how many times you've told me that."

"No, but he hasn't got any use for Algarvians, either," Ealstan answered. "And he has got some use for me, and so I managed to persuade him to get me this." He hugged his wife. "I know what's important, by the powers above."

From another, smaller, pouch he took a length of coppery yarn and one of dark brown. He went through the spell he'd devised to shift him back from looking like an Algarvian to his usual self. Vanai clapped her hands together, which told him he'd succeeded. She said, "You patterned that charm after the one I made."

"Well, of course I did," he answered. "I know what works—and having a model helps when I compose in classical Kaunian."

"You did splendidly," Vanai said, which warmed him all over. "You must have done splendidly twice, in fact, or you wouldn't have been able to look like an Algarvian in the first place."

He kissed her. Even as he did, though, something else struck him. "You'd better renew your spell, too, while you've got the chance. No telling how long you'll keep looking Forthwegian. We need to be back to the flat before you go back to looking like your regular self."

"You're right," she said, and did just that. Her looks didn't change, but she would keep on looking a lot like his sister for a while longer. Long enough? *Maybe I'll have her renew it again before we get home, if I see a chance,* Ealstan told himself. Vanai's thoughts were running along a different ley line: "I'll have to get a new bottle of hair dye. No point to dyeing it—no way, either—when I was caught there."

Ealstan shook his head. "No, you won't. There's still plenty left at home. I didn't throw it away—I thought you'd be back." *I hoped you'd be back* was closer to the truth, but he said it the way he wanted to.

Vanai kissed him for it. That made it worthwhile, and more than worthwhile. She took his hand. "Come on. Let's go."

Eggs were still bursting all over Eoforwic. Ealstan said, "Now that I've got you back, I want the Unkerlanters to go away and leave us alone. Before, all I wanted them to do was knock Eoforwic topsy-turvy."

"So did I," Vanai said as they went out onto the street once more. She grinned at him. "I wanted to get back to the flat by myself and be there waiting when you walked in. You spoiled my surprise." The grin disappeared. "You almost frightened me to death, too."

"I'm sorry," Ealstan said. "I'm so sorry. But looking like one of the redheads was the only way I could find to get into the Kaunian district." He drew himself up. "It worked, too."

Vanai couldn't argue with that, and she didn't try. The Unkerlanter dragons did fly away. After the eggs stopped falling, people started coming back out onto the streets. No one looked twice at Ealstan and Vanai; the only thing in the least out of the ordinary about them was her pregnancy.

They stopped in a tavern for a glass of wine to celebrate, though they didn't say why they were celebrating. When Vanai asked if she could use the pot, the fellow behind the bar just nodded and pointed to the right door. "My wife was always running back and forth when she was expecting, too," he said.

"Thank you." Vanai closed the door behind her. When she came out, she nodded to Ealstan. The spell would last a while longer.

It lasted long enough for them to climb the stairs to the flat. Ealstan made Vanai hold the splintery bannister with one hand and his own hand with the other. "I'm not made of glass, you know," she said tartly.

"We've come this far," he said. "I don't want anything—*anything*—to go wrong now. Is that all right?" Vanai made a face at him, but she didn't say anything more, so he supposed he'd won his point.

He opened the door to the flat. He stood aside to let Vanai go in ahead of him. He closed the door. He barred it. He turned back to Vanai. "I love you," he said.

They held each other for a long time. Then Vanai said, "Thank you," and squeezed him harder than ever. "There were . . . times when I didn't think I would ever see you again."

Ealstan knew what that had to mean. Vanai trembled against him. He felt like trembling, too. He stroked her hair. "You're safe here," he said.

"Don't be silly," she answered. "I'm a Kaunian. I'm not safe anywhere. How are you going to bring a midwife here when the baby comes? I'm liable to start looking like what I am right in the middle of labor."

He hadn't thought of that. "Somehow or other, we'll manage," he said.

"We'll manage without a midwife, is what we'll do," Vanai said.

"I suppose so." Ealstan kept his reservations to himself. If anything looked as if it was going wrong, he vowed he would get a midwife and think about everything else later. He had a good deal of silver. He could bribe her, enough to keep her quiet for a little while, and then move before she brought the redheads down on Vanai and him and the baby.

Vanai said, "We can worry about that when the time comes." She smiled at him. "I know what you're thinking now."

That wasn't thought. That was automatic bodily response to holding the woman he loved in his arms. "Should you, so close to your time?" he asked.

"Once won't hurt," she answered. "And if you think I haven't missed you, too, you'd better think again." She pulled the tunic off over her head.

Her body startled him. Because she'd been locked away in the Kaunian quarter, he hadn't been able to watch it change day by day. He hadn't realized just how much her belly bulged. And . . . "Is your navel supposed to stick out like that?" Ealstan reach out a gentle, cautious finger to touch it.

"I don't know," Vanai answered. "All I know is that it does." When Ealstan pulled off his own tunic and drawers, she laughed. "I'm not the only one sticking out, either."

"I know I'm supposed to," Ealstan said, an odd mix of dignity and eagerness in his voice. He led her back to the bedchamber.

Because of her bulging belly, they fumbled a bit before finding a way that suited them both. She lay on her back, a pillow under her bottom. He poised himself on his knees between her legs. "Oh," she said softly as he went into her.

"I love you," he said, which meant about the same thing. Slowly and carefully, he began to move. The posture made it easy for him to tease her with a fingertip at the same time. His pleasure built. By her sighs, Vanai's did, too. Then, all at once, he laughed in surprise and lost his rhythm. Vanai made a noise wordless but indignant. "I'm sorry," he told her. "Your magic just wore off. I didn't expect it to."

"Oh," she said, this time thoughtfully. "All right." They resumed.

Not much later, it was a great deal better than all right. When Vanai gasped and quivered, her belly went tight and hard for a little while.

Ealstan laughed again when her flesh rippled from the inside out. "I can really see the baby move now," he said.

"I can really feel it," Vanai said. "We made things crowded in there for a little while."

"It will be all right. Everything will be all right." For the first time since coming home to an empty flat, Ealstan dared believe that, too.

"How are you feeling this morning, my sweet?" Colonel Lurcanio asked at the breakfast table.

Krasta found his solicitude cloying. *He's worried because he thinks it's his brat in there*, she thought. She thought it was Lurcanio's, too, but she knew she had reason to be uncertain, where the Algarvian officer had only a nasty, suspicious mind making him doubt. But she had to answer him. Straight-out defiance didn't work; she'd found that out a good many times, always to her dismay. "I'm . . . fairly well," she said.

"Good," Lurcanio said briskly. "Food staying down better?" His manner declared that he'd been through this business a good many times, and was somewhere between amused and annoyed at having to go through it again.

"So far," Krasta said. "So far today, anyhow." Her voice turned petulant as she went on, "I don't know why they call it morning sickness. It can happen any time, and it's always disgusting when it does." Her stomach quivered nervously at the mere thought of being sick again.

Colonel Lurcanio laughed. *Of course he's laughing*, Krasta thought. *He's a man. He never has to worry about things like this. The only thing he's got to do with babies is having fun while they start.* Oblivious—or at least indifferent—to what was going through her mind, Lurcanio said, "I'm afraid I must tell you good-bye for some little while. I have business to attend to down in the south."

"Oh?" That made Krasta forget her belly, at least for a while. She hoped she didn't sound too alarmed. One of the reasons Lurcanio had left Priekule for the south was to go after her brother. The Algarvians called the Valmierans who fought against them bandits. Krasta had thought of them the same way till she found out Skarnu was among them.

"Aye. Trouble brewing down there." Lurcanio didn't sound happy. For once, he didn't sound as if he were trying to pry information out of her, either. His long face seeming even longer than usual, he continued, "Something nasty is going on across the Strait of Valmiera—the Lagoans and Kuusamans are gathering ships and men in their north-facing ports."

Even Krasta, unschooled in every military art, saw what that meant. "An invasion!" she exclaimed.

"Maybe," Lurcanio said. "On the other hand, maybe not, too. It may just be a bluff, to make us shift men around. I happen to know Kuusamo is also fitting out a big fleet in Kihlanki—"

"In where?" Krasta broke in.

"In Kihlanki," he repeated. "It's their easternmost port, so that's surely bound against Gyongyos. Can the islanders do two big things at once? I doubt it."

"If . . . if they do invade, can you beat them?" Krasta asked. Most of what she'd done since the Algarvians marched into Priekule, she'd done on the assumption that they would win the war. If that assumption turned out to be wrong . . .

But Lurcanio just smiled and said, "That's why I'm going down there, my dear: to help make sure we do exactly that. I promise you, they shall have a very hard time of it indeed if they try to cross the Strait and land in Valmiera."

He got up from the table, kissed her, and reached down to fondle her breasts through the silk of her pyjama tunic. She yelped. She couldn't help herself. "Be careful," she said. "They're sore. They're always sore these days."

"I'm sorry," Lurcanio said. She judged he meant it. He was always sorry when he hurt her without intending to. Those occasional other times . . . He'd burned those into her memory forever.

Off he went, as if he owned the mansion. He'd been here close to four years; Krasta had grown very used to having him around. She'd grown fond of him, too, most of the time. Of itself, her hand flattened on her belly. If she hadn't grown fond of him, she . . . might not have been carrying a child there. Of course, she might have been, too. She sipped at a mug of apple cider. As she set the mug down, she glowered at it. Apple cider didn't come close to matching tea as a way to start the morning. But tea refused to taste the way it was supposed to these days. As long as it tasted nasty to her, she had to stay away from it.

Shouting for Bauska, she went upstairs to change. The maid-servant hurried into her bedchamber. "How may I help you, mi-lady?" she asked.

Something in her tone of voice rubbed Krasta the wrong way. It had been there ever since Bauska found out she was pregnant. It was as if, without words, the serving woman was saying, *I had a baby by a redhead, and now you're doing the same thing. How are we different, then?* But Krasta couldn't punish her for a tone of voice. She said, "Help me find something to wear. I'm going into Priekule."

"Aye, milady," Bauska said—and, sensibly, no more than that.

Every time Krasta did go into Priekule, the city looked sadder and shabbier than it had the time before. Maybe that was because her prewar memories—her standard of comparison—receded ever further into the past and seemed ever rosier. But maybe, too, it was because Priekule, after going on four years of Algarvian occupation, *did* grow sadder and shabbier every day. The redheads took whatever they wanted, whatever they needed. Whatever chanced to be left after that—if anything chanced to be left—they grudgingly let the Valmierans keep.

Even the Boulevard of Horsemen wasn't what it had been. Priekule's chief avenue of splendid shops still showed more wealth than the rest of the city, but it had also fallen further from what it was. Some shops had been shuttered for years. Others were still selling goods from long ago, unable to get more. And others—the ones that did the best business—catered to the Algarvians and to the Valmierans, male and female, who had adhered to their cause.

Redheaded soldiers on leave strolled the Boulevard of Horsemen, staring at the clothes and jewelry and furniture on display, and staring in a different way at the Valmieran women who'd come to the Boulevard to shop. Once upon a time, Krasta had come to the Boulevard of Horsemen to display herself as well as to see what was new and expensive and chic. Now she wished the men in kilts would take no notice of her.

Whenever one of them tried to do more than look, she said, "Colonel Lurcanio is my protector." Not all of them spoke

Valmieran, but they did understand the rank and—mostly—kept their hands to themselves afterwards.

But one of them spoke to her in classical Kaunian: "If he is an occupation soldier, he is not a real man. Do you want a real man?"

Her own classical Kaunian was sketchy, but she got the gist of that. And she managed to say, "He is a real colonel," in the old language. The Algarvian looked disgusted, but he went away.

After that, she discovered she had little trouble telling redheads on occupation duty in Priekule from those who'd come to the city for surcease from the grinding war in the west. The latter were younger, rougher-looking, and wore tunics and kilts whose light brown was sometimes faded almost to white. The soldiers actually garrisoned in the city wore smarter uniforms and were better fed, but they put her in mind of dogs set next to wolves.

And then, from behind her, someone called, "Hello, sweetheart!" in a voice purely Valmieran. She turned. Sure enough, there was Viscount Valnu hurrying toward her. He squeezed her and kissed her on the cheek. "You look good enough to eat," he said.

"Promises, promises," she answered, which made him laugh. But she had trouble caring about badinage today. More wearily and more angrily than she'd thought she would be, she added, "Half the Algarvian army seems to think the same thing."

"Well, I do understand why, I do indeed." Valnu's eyes sparkled.

"If you wear your kilt any shorter, some of the redheads will think the same thing about you," Krasta said, acid in her voice.

"Oh, some of them do," Valnu replied blithely. "And some of them think I make a proper ally, and some of them want to beat me senseless for presuming to wear their clothes. Life is never dull."

"No." Krasta, for once in her life, rather wished it were. She took him by the arm. "Buy me a brandy, will you?"

"I'm putty—or something—in your hands." Valnu pointed in the direction from which they'd both come. "The tavern back here isn't too bad. It's only a block or so." Krasta nodded; she remembered walking past it. As Valnu steered her toward the place, he asked, "Is it really true? Have you got a loaf in the oven?"

With a yawn, Krasta said, "Aye." She hated being sleepy all the time.

He gave her an arch grin. "Is papa anyone I know?"

"You may know him very well," she answered.

"Really?" he said, and Krasta nodded again. One of his pale eyebrows rose. "Well, well. Isn't that interesting? Shall we elope? Or shall I be angry at you because I may *not* know papa as well as all that?"

"As if you had any business being angry about what I did or didn't do," Krasta said as Valnu held the door to the tavern open for her. He laughed. She didn't think it was so funny. Lurcanio was convinced such things were his business. If the baby turned out to look like Valnu, he was liable to make himself very difficult. No, worse—he wasn't just liable to; he'd already said he would.

The brandy didn't taste right, any more than tea had lately. Krasta drank it anyway, and drank it fast. She needed not to think about Lurcanio for a little while. That was what she needed, but she didn't get it. Valnu said, "I hear your . . . friend has gone down to the seashore for a while."

"What if he has?" Krasta said. The brandy was hitting her hard, maybe because she hadn't drunk any for a while, maybe just because she was pregnant.

When Valnu leaned toward her across the little table they shared, the smile stayed on his face for the benefit of the fellow behind the bar, but his voice came low and urgent: "You silly little twat, are the Kuusamans and the Lagoans going to land down there? Does Lurcanio think they are?"

"He thinks so, aye, but he isn't sure. He's going to talk with some of the Algarvians there," Krasta answered. Only afterwards did she realize she should have been insulted.

Valnu grunted. "That's a little more than I knew before, but not so much as I would have liked." His shrug was almost as ornate as a redhead's. He gulped his ale, then got to his feet. "I must dash. Always delighted to see you. And the *other* news you gave me was fascinating, too; it truly was." He left some coins on the tabletop and hurried out.

"Another brandy, milady?" the tapman asked.

"No." Krasta got up and left, too.

Out on the Boulevard of Horsemen, a band played a stirring march—Valmieran-style music, not Algarvian. And up the Boulevard came the first blond soldiers in Valmieran uniform Krasta had seen since the surrender. She stared, as a lot of other people were staring. But then she realized it wasn't *quite* Valmieran uniform: each soldier wore a red, green, and white patch sewn onto the left sleeve of his tunic, to show he served not King Gainibu but King Mezentio of Algarve.

Only a couple of companies of the soldiers marched down the Boulevard of Horsemen, but they were enough. Krasta hurried back into the tavern and poured down another brandy, and then another after that. The spirits didn't come close to taking away the taste of what she'd seen.

"A roundup?" Bembo sent Delminio a reproachful look. "Do we have to?"

His new partner nodded. "Aye, we have to. You'll have done them before, won't you, back in whatever no-account town you served in before you got sent here?"

"Gromheort." Bembo didn't know why he bothered supplying the name. Delminio wouldn't care. "I've done 'em, but I never liked 'em. Any way I can get out of it? My old sergeant would sometimes excuse one of the fellows in my squad. Evodio just wasn't any use for that business—didn't have the stomach for it. Even when Pesaro made him do it, he'd drink himself blind afterwards."

"Your sergeant must have been a softy," Delminio said, which made Bembo snort in disbelief. But the other constable went on, "Here, you get a choice. You can do what you're told, or you can put on a footsoldier's uniform and head for Unkerlant."

"You just talked me into it," Bembo said.

"I thought I would." Delminio tapped his fingernail on the refectory tabletop. "We have had a few fellows who went off to fight King Swemmel's whoresons. Strange birds—stupid birds, if you ask me. We haven't had many, and none at all I can think of the past year or so."

"I believe that." Bembo shivered, though it was warm inside the refectory. Things in Unkerlant hadn't been going Algarve's way the past year or so. *Fine choice,* he thought. *I can stifle my conscience and do as I'm told, or go off and get myself killed.* But he'd already made his choice, and told Delminio as much. He hardly knew why he was fussing about a conscience distinctly vestigial. *It's nothing I haven't done before.*

Before going into the Kaunian quarter, he and Delminio and the other constables drew army-issue sticks. Bembo waved to Oraste. His old partner from Gromheort waved back. "Going hunting," he said. Rounding up Kaunians bothered him not at all.

Some of the guards outside the quarter were Forthwegians. "We should send them in for the roundup," Bembo said. "They hate the blonds more than we do."

But Delminio shook his head. "It looks like it's a good idea, but it just doesn't work. Some of the Kaunians would use their stupid little spell and get away."

Bembo grunted. "I suppose so. It's a good thing they haven't got a spell to let 'em look like Algarvians."

His partner's hand writhed in a very old sign for turning away evil omens. "Bite your tongue. Powers above, wouldn't that be all we needed?"

A pompous constabulary captain strode out in front of the men he'd led to the district. He made exactly the sort of speech Bembo had known he would make, full of the greater glory of Algarve and a lot of other things every man there had surely heard too many times before. Then he said, "We have to meet our quota. Nothing and nobody will keep us from meeting our quota. Now let's go do it."

The constables tramped into the Kaunian quarter. As Bembo strode past the officer, he saw him looking about ready to burst a blood vessel. "What's his trouble?" he asked Delminio. "Did he think we were going to burst into cheers?"

"Probably," Delminio answered. "Have you ever known a

captain who wasn't a cursed fool?" Bembo stared at him in astonished delight. He didn't make such a bad partner after all.

Cries of alarm and the sound of running feet ahead warned that the Kaunians knew the roundup was under way. Bembo scowled. "Now we're going to have to dig the buggers out of their hiding places," he grumbled. "There are times when this job looks a lot too much like work." It did, however, look a great deal better than going off to fight in Unkerlant.

Not all the Kaunians were hiding, not yet. Something came hurtling down from the sill of an upper-story window in a block of flats. It landed on the head of a constables three ranks in front of Bembo. The noise was that of a brickbat smacking a calabash. The constable went down as if blazed—perhaps more surely than if he'd been blazed. He thrashed briefly, then lay still. Blood poured out of him, pooling among the cobblestones. His bowels let go; Bembo wrinkled his nose at the sudden stink. Flies began gathering almost at once.

The constables shouted and pointed. Bembo didn't know why they bothered. None of them had any better idea than he did from which window the missile—by the shards, he judged it a flowerpot full of dirt—had come.

"Every blond in that building!" the captain screamed. "I want every blond in that building out here, and I want all those whoresons out here in nothing flat. Capture squads, forward!" His whistle shrilled as if he were ordering footsoldiers into battle against the Unkerlanters.

Bembo and Delminio weren't in a capture squad. They were in a holding squad, to make sure none of the Kaunians escaped once captured. They waited in the street for their comrades to start bringing out blonds. They waited in the very middle of the street, and kept looking nervously up toward the buildings on either side of it.

"Kaunian bastards have their nerve," Delminio said angrily.

Shrieks and screams rang out inside the block of flats. Before long, Kaunians started stumbling out of the building. The men were all bruised and bloody. The women were bruised and bloody, too, and some of them came down the steps without trousers. "Revenge," Bembo said.

Delminio nodded. "Makes me wish I was in a capture squad," he said. Bembo answered that with a shrug. Rape had never been his favorite sport.

A Kaunian spat on the dead Algarvian constable's corpse. All that got him was another beating from the constables in the holding squad. Bembo swung his bludgeon with as much zeal as anyone else. "We can't kill the bastard—that'd waste his life energy," he said. "But we can sure as blazes make him wish he was dead."

"All right, on with the rest of the business," the captain said, when the last constables came out of the building. "They'll pay. Oh, how they'll pay."

"Only one trouble with that," Bembo said. Delminio raised an eyebrow. Bembo explained: "If the blonds know we're going to do for them, why shouldn't they try and boot us in the balls before they go west?"

His partner made a sour face. "That's a nasty thought. You're full of them today, aren't you? Here's hoping the Kaunians don't have it, too."

"Kaunians, come forth!" the captain shouted in front of the next block of flats. Bembo wondered why he bothered. Predictably, no blonds came forth. He just gave them another few seconds to conceal themselves before the capture squads swarmed in. The extra time didn't seem to matter much, though. Soon, more battered Kaunians came out. The Algarvians would take their vengeance through the whole quarter.

As the holding squads took charge of the blonds the capture squads prised out of their flats, the captain kept a tally on a leaf of paper stuck in a clipboard. Bembo knew what that was all about. "Quota," he said. "Not much point to this business if we don't make quota, is there?"

Privately, he wondered if there was any point to it regardless of whether they made quota or not. For every Kaunian Algarve got rid of to fuel its magecraft, what would the Unkerlanters do? Kill one of their own, or two of their own, or three, or four. Maybe King Mezentio hadn't realized how very much in earnest about the war King Swemmel was. If he didn't realize it by now, he was a fool. And if he did realize it by now . . .

maybe he was a fool anyhow, for biting off more war than he could chew.

No, I can't say anything like that. I shouldn't even think anything like that. But Bembo couldn't help it. He wasn't blind. He wasn't deaf. No matter what sergeants thought, he wasn't stupid. If something hovered there in front of his nose and yelled at him at the top of its lungs, he couldn't very well not notice it.

A lot of people he knew didn't seem to think that way, though.

Delminio said, "I still wish we'd been on a capture squad. Some of these Kaunian wenches look pretty tasty, or they would have before our boys started roughing them up. Wouldn't mind tearing off a piece, not even a little I wouldn't."

"If you want a broad that bad, pick one who suits you and throw her down on the cobblestones," Bembo said. "Nobody's going to do anything but cheer you on and line up behind you, not today." He looked back toward the crumpled body of the Algarvian constable. Poor whoreson hadn't known what hit him, anyhow. One second walking along, the next dead. There were worse ways to go.

Into the next block of flats charged the men from the capture squads. As before, they beat all the Kaunian men and most of the women before sending them out. As before, they had their sport with some of the women, too. Delminio said, "They keep on like that, they'll be too cursed tired to finish the job."

"They'd better not be," the constabulary captain said. "They can do whatever they want—as long as they make quota. If they don't make quota, they answer to me. There are still plenty of Kaunians in here, for us to harvest what we need."

Quota. Harvest. Those were nice, bloodless words. They had very little to do with the bruised and bleeding and raped blonds huddled under the sticks of the holding squads. They let the captain do his job without thinking much about what he was doing. *They'd let you do the same, if you didn't keep poking and prodding at things,* Bembo told himself. *It's only Kaunians, after all.*

But the noises they made—not the words he could hardly understand, having forgotten the classical Kaunian he'd had beaten into him at school, but the wordless sounds of pain and sorrow and despair—were the same as those so many Algarvians might have made. Bembo violently shook his head. What was he doing, thinking of Algarvians in such straits? What was the war about, if not making sure Algarvians never found themselves in such straits?

One block of flats after another, the capture squads seized Kaunians and sent them down to the street. At last, the captain blew his whistle. "Quota!" he shouted. "Now let's get 'em to the caravan depot for transport."

Transport. Another bloodless word. *Let's send them off to be killed.* That was what the word meant. That was what the captain meant. But he didn't have to say it, so he didn't have to think it. Bembo shook his head. *You're thinking too much yourself again.*

Some of the Kaunians were too badly battered to have an easy time walking. The constables' solution to that was to beat them some more. They set other blonds to carrying the ones that didn't spur into motion.

"See?" a constable said as they left the Kaunian quarter. "You're out. Aren't you glad? Aren't you happy?"

Forthwegians on the streets jeered the Kaunians on their way to the ley-line caravan depot. By the way some of the Kaunians flinched, that hurt more than the beatings they'd taken from the Algarvians. Bembo didn't understand that, but saw it was so.

As some desperate Kaunian had hurled the flowerpot down on the constables, so somebody—a woman—hurled one word in Algarvian at them from an upper story: "Shame!"

Delminio laughed. So did the captain leading the constables. Bembo only shrugged. The flowerpot had done some damage. What could a word do?

As always, shoving too many Kaunians into not enough caravan cars was hard work. As always, the constables did what needed doing, and barred the doors from the outside when they finished. The windows were already shuttered.

To Bembo's surprise, the caravan glided off toward the east, the direction of Algarve and the Kaunian kingdoms beyond. "Haven't seen that in a while," he said. "What's going on?"

"I hear the fellows with the thick spectacles are worried about Valmiera," Delminio answered. "If Lagoas and Kuusamo try invading, we'll throw 'em right back into the Strait, by the powers above."

"Aye," Bembo said, and then, "We'd bloody well better."

Skarnu liked the farm the Valmieran underground leaders had found for Merkela and little Gedominu—and now for himself. It wasn't so big as the one outside Pavilosta where she'd lived, but the land was richer. He chuckled when that thought crossed his mind. Before the war, he wouldn't have been able to tell good farmland from bad.

He thought Merkela would laugh, too, when he told her that. But she didn't. She said, "That's something you should have known." She had Gedominu on her hip. She always did when she needed to do chores, and the farm always had chores to do. The baby didn't slow her down a bit. She got more work done with him than Skarnu did without him.

"You're probably right," Skarnu said. "No, you're certainly right. But I didn't. I didn't know a lot of things back then." He reached out and stroked her cheek. "I didn't know what mattered to me. That's most important."

She flushed. She never seemed to know how to take endearments. Maybe she hadn't got many while married to old Gedominu. That hadn't stopped her from loving him, or from naming their baby after him. Before she could say anything in return, her eyes swung away from Skarnu and toward the road that ran by the little farmhouse. "Someone's coming."

Not many people came down that road; the farmhouse was a long way from the nearest village, let alone Ramygala, the nearest real town. Skarnu looked, too. Anyone who did come this way was liable to mean trouble. But then he grinned and exclaimed, "That's Raunu!"

"You're right." Merkela waved to the veteran sergeant. "I'm always glad to see him come up my road."

As Raunu waved back, Skarnu raised an eyebrow. "Should I be jealous?" he asked. As soon as the words were out of his mouth, he wished he had them back: the answer might be *aye*. True, Raunu was old enough to have fought in the Six Years' War. But her first husband had fought in the Six Years' War, too, so would she mind?

To Skarnu's relief, she laughed at him instead of getting angry. "I ought to say you should, just to see you fuss."

Skarnu made a face at her, and she laughed again. Then he hurried forward to clasp Raunu's hand. "Good to see you," he said. "What's up? Or did you come for a social call?"

Raunu's snort showed how likely that was. "Captain, I like you fine, and your lady, too"—he nodded to Merkela, whose answering smile was almost warm enough to make Skarnu fuss—"but this is business. Something's brewing in the south, and you're one of the fellows who's been busy down there."

Alertness surged through Skarnu. "You'd better tell me about it." He pointed back toward the little farmhouse. "Will you come in and drink some ale while you talk?"

"Thank you kindly. I'd be glad to." As Raunu passed Merkela, he paused to eye little Gedominu. "He's grown a lot since the last time I saw him. They've got a way of doing that, babies do."

"Forgive the ale," Merkela said as she poured. "It's bought; I didn't brew it myself."

Raunu sipped and shrugged. "I've had plenty worse. Don't fret yourself."

After drinking from his own mug, Skarnu said, "The south."

"Aye, the south," Raunu agreed. "The redheads are as nervous down there as a cat trying to watch four mouseholes at once. They've been sending all kinds of bigwigs to the seashore to try and figure out what's going on." He coughed. "Colonel Lurcanio's down there right now, for instance."

"Is he?" Skarnu gulped the mug dry. His sister's lover had come too close to capturing him back near Pavilosta. Merkela handed him the bottle. He poured the mug full again. "Are they down there for the obvious reason? Are the Lagoans and Valmierans finally going to cross the Strait of Valmiera?"

He'd never asked that question before. He'd always been

professionally incurious about it. What he didn't know, nobody could rip from him if things went wrong. But Raunu wouldn't have come here talking about the south if such a thing were impossible.

"By all the signs, Mezentio's men think they are," Raunu answered. "They're hauling in Kaunians from Forthweg again, and you know what that means."

"Murder," Skarnu said. His old sergeant nodded. "Nasty magecraft," he added, and Raunu nodded again. "Powers below eat the Algarvians," he finished. This time, both Raunu and Merkela nodded.

"That's about the size of it," Raunu said. "We've wrecked some of the ley-line caravans, but some of them have got through." He scowled. "Even if we'd wrecked 'em all, there's nothing really stopping the redheads from grabbing as many Valmierans as they need and doing them in. Only reason they don't do that more, I think, is to keep from spooking us. But if they've got a chance to throw an invasion back into the sea, I figure they'd worry about that first and everything else later."

"You're right." Merkela's voice held no doubt. "It's just like them, the—" She cursed as foully and fluently as a veteran underofficer.

"*Are* the Lagoans and Kuusamans going to invade?" Skarnu demanded. "Do we know one way or the other?"

Raunu shook his head. "They won't say aye and they won't say no. Cursed foreigners don't trust us."

"There are times when they have reason not to," Merkela said. "We have traitors in the underground. What we know, the Algarvians have a chance of learning."

"Count Amatu," Skarnu said. Raunu had looked unhappy at Merkela's comment, but he couldn't argue with that.

And, as if being reminded of Amatu reminded him of something else, he said, "The redheads have started recruiting Valmierans to fight for 'em, too. They've got maybe a regiment's worth. Some of them paraded through Priekule a few days ago, wearing Algarvian flags on the sleeves of Valmieran uniforms."

Merkela's curses this time made the ones she'd used before

sound like endearments. Skarnu said, "They must be scraping the bottom of their own barrel." Again, he did his best to stay professional. That way, the idea that his own countrymen would go to war for their conquerors was just a piece of information to be analyzed, not something to disgust and sicken him. Try as he would, detachment didn't come easy. He asked the next question: "What has all this got to do with me?"

"You know what's going on down in the south," Raunu repeated. "Some people want you to look around and tell them what you think."

"If they think that will help, I can do it," Skarnu said. "Do they want me to travel by myself, or with Palasta again?"

Merkela made a noise down deep in her throat. "Should *I* be jealous?" she asked.

Raunu looked blank. Skarnu laughed and shook his head. "She's a girl," he said. "I like women, thanks." That satisfied Merkela. It did more than satisfy her, in fact; by her smile, it pleased her. Pleased with himself for satisfying her and telling the truth at the same time, Skarnu turned to Raunu. "When and where do I meet her?"

"She'll be in the second car of the ley-line caravan coming through Ramygala at noon tomorrow," Raunu answered. "The caravan will take you down to the Strait of Valmiera. Here's money for your fare and food and such, and for the return trip." He pulled a small leather sack from his pocket and gave it to Skarnu. It clinked.

After another mug of ale, Raunu went on his way with the air of a man who had further important business to attend to. He probably did. Merkela nursed little Gedominu till he fell asleep. Then she turned to Skarnu in a marked manner. "If you're going off again," she said, "will you give me something to remember you by?"

"What have you got in mind?" he asked, and did as much as he could then and in the night to attend to that. When he left early in the morning to walk to Ramygala, he was yawning. Even had he been drawn to Palasta, he wouldn't have been able to do much about it for a while.

The ley-line caravan was late. When it finally got to town,

the young mage was in the car where Raunu had said she would be. She smiled as he sat down beside her. "How are you, sis?" he asked.

"Just fine, thanks," she said. "Couldn't be better. It'll be good to get down to the seaside and say hello to Mother." Skarnu nodded, even though Mother was fictitious. *I wish you were my sister*, went through his mind, as it had on the trip to the southeast he'd made with Palasta. *I'd rather have you than Krasta.* But, whatever he wished, he had no more luck choosing his relatives than did anyone from King Gainibu on down.

Because the caravan car filled up fast, they spent the trip south talking about the family they didn't have and the plans they hadn't made. Skarnu kept looking at the men and women around them. No telling who might be in King Mezentio's pay. If Valmierans could fight with Algarve's banner sewn to their sleeves, Skarnu's countrymen were capable of any enormity.

"Alsvanga!" the conductor called when the ley-line caravan came to a stop at the depot by the sea. "All out for Alsvanga!"

Along with Palasta, Skarnu got out. In peacetime, he could have taken a ferry across the Strait of Valmiera to Lagoas, for the ley line continued even if the land petered out. These days, there were no ferries. Lean, sharklike little Algarvian patrol boats filled the harbor. "How can the Lagoans even think of getting an army across the Strait in the face of all this?" Skarnu asked in a low voice.

"I don't know," Palasta answered, also quietly. "Maybe it has something to do with . . . what I felt the last time we went traveling." She was young, but she was sensible, too sensible to speak much about where they'd gone and what they'd done.

And she was wise to be so sensible, too, for Alsvanga was full of Algarvians—not just sailors but also soldiers. Some of the soldiers were older men in neat uniforms: typical occupation troops. But Skarnu saw a few who were plainly combat veterans. Their eyes were hard and watchful, as his were. They didn't care so much about how they dressed. A good many of them wore wound badges, sometimes with the ribbons that said they'd been hurt more than once.

"They're ready," Skarnu murmured. "They're as ready as they can be." By then, he and Palasta had left the town of Alsvanga and were walking along a country road. She led the way. She had more senses to guide her toward what needed discovering than Skarnu did.

But she didn't know everything there was to know. "Where are the Algarvians coming up with their men?" she asked.

"Only one place they can be pulling 'em from, and that's Unkerlant," Skarnu replied with a certain somber satisfaction. "And that won't do them any good—no, no good at all—when the fighting picks up there. And it will. I'm sure it will."

"Powers below eat the redheads," Palasta whispered fiercely. She paused, gathered in thought, and pointed. "There. The camp where they're holding the Kaunians from Forthweg is beyond that stand of beeches."

But Skarnu, for once, hadn't needed her sorcery to tell him that. The wind had swung. He could smell the nasty stink of unwashed humanity and human misery. "They'll have mages around here too somewhere, won't they?" he asked. Palasta nodded. So did Skarnu, grimly. "Aye, they're ready, all right," he said. "If Lagoas and Kuusamo are going to cross the Strait here, I don't see how they can hope to land." He kicked at the dirt. "Curse it."

Ten

❦

Now that so many practical mages came to the wilds of the Naantali district to train, more copies of Kuusaman news sheets also arrived. When Pekka walked into the refectory of a morning, she found Fernao working his way through one. "You're reading it without a lexicon," she said, and softly clapped her hands together to applaud him.

"I've always been good at languages," he replied. "Where is this place called Kihlanki? Somewhere in your east, isn't it?"

"As far east as you can go and stay in Kuusamo," Pekka said as she sat down beside him. She wasn't so nervous about being with him as she had been after they ended up in bed, though she did sometimes wonder whether that lack of nerves was a good sign or not. "Why?"

He waved the news sheet. "Because unless I'm reading this wrong, it says that your navy has gone and launched a big fleet into the Bothnian Ocean from there, bound for the islands Gyongyos still holds."

"Let me see," Pekka said. Fernao handed her the sheet. Their fingers brushed for a moment. Fernao noticed it; his breath caught. Pekka noticed it, too, and did her best to pretend she hadn't. She quickly read through the article Fernao had been talking about. "You read it rightly. That's what it says."

"If any Lagoan news sheet published a story like that, King Vitor's men would close it down the next day—maybe the same day," Fernao said. "It tells the enemy what you're going to do."

Pekka shrugged. "We don't like to close down news sheets unless we have a truly important reason. I've seen things like that before. We would rather be open and tell ourselves the truth than have someone say we may not."

"Even if it hurts your kingdom?" Fernao asked.

"Even if it hurts some in the short run," Pekka said. "In the long run, we think it's better."

Fernao scratched his head. "You Kuusamans are peculiar people." He smiled a lopsided—and oddly attractive—smile. "Maybe that's why I'm so fond of you." He set his hand on hers.

Something close to panic swept over her, as if he'd made much more overt, much cruder advances. What caused part of the panic was that alarm wasn't the only reason her heart beat faster. Even so, she took her hand away. "That's over," she said. "It has to be over."

"Why?" he asked, in much the same tones her son Uto might have used with an endless series of *Why?*s when he was four years old.

She felt like answering, *Because*, which had the virtue of stopping that whole ley-line caravan of questions. In fact she did say, "Because," but went on, "I have a family, and I want to go on having a family. Once"—she shrugged—"anything can happen once. If something like that happened again and again, though, what would I have to go home to?"

"Me," Fernao answered.

He meant it. She could see as much. That made it worse, not better. "It's impossible," she said. "It has to be." She grimaced; that left her open to another, *Why?*

Instead of using it, Fernao just shook his head. "It doesn't have to be that way," he said. "You've decided you want it to be that way, which isn't the same thing at all. If you think I'm going to quit trying to get you to change your mind, you're wrong."

He told her that in fluent, idiomatic Kuusaman. A few months before, he would have had to use classical Kaunian to get his meaning across. Pekka wished he still did; that would have accented the differences between them. She said, "If you go on this way now, you'll make me angry. That won't do you any good."

Fernao studied her face, plainly trying to decide if she meant it. She did her best to look stern, partly to convince him, partly to convince herself. Most of her recognized the need for that. Part of her, though, kept saying things like, *Of course you can enjoy yourself here, and then break it off when the war's over or when Leino comes home or when you and Fernao get assigned to two different places.*

A serving woman came up and asked her what she wanted. She ordered smoked salmon and eggs, glad for the distraction. *How am I going to make Fernao believe I don't want to go to bed with him again when I have trouble making myself believe it?* she wondered. She called after the serving woman: "Oh, and a pot of tea, too." The woman nodded. Pekka hoped the tea would help her think straight. She hoped something would.

By Fernao's expression, he knew she was fighting a war with herself. He wasn't of two minds; he knew exactly what he wanted. In a way, that was flattering. In another way, it just made life more difficult.

Before Fernao could find anything to say, a serving girl came up to the table they were sharing. "Mistress Pekka?" she asked.

"Aye?" Lost in her own thoughts, Pekka needed a moment to realize it wasn't the woman who'd taken her breakfast order. "What is it, Linna?" she asked. She needed another moment to realize that, whatever it was, it wasn't good. Linna was pale and biting her lip. "What's wrong?"

Fernao was a jump ahead of her: "Is it something to do with Ilmarinen?"

Looking paler than ever, Linna nodded. "Is he—?" Pekka broke off the question without finishing it. Ilmarinen wasn't a young man, and Linna was a young, pretty woman. If he'd tried to do something too strenuous, he might have died happy, but that could only be horror for the person in whose company he was at the time.

But Linna said, "I don't know where he is. I went to his chamber this morning, and I found two envelopes. This one was addressed to me." She pulled out an envelope and took a note from it. "It says, 'If I come back, we'll celebrate. If I don't, there's a little something in my will to remember me by. Have fun with it. I had fun with you.' " She folded the leaf of paper, and then produced another envelope. "This one has your name on it, Mistress Pekka."

"So it does." Pekka took the envelope with a certain reluctance. She glanced over at Fernao. "Do I want to find out what's in it?"

"I think you'd better." He was all business now, not mooning over her at all.

Pekka sighed. "I think I'd better, too. But do I want to?" She opened the envelope and pulled out the leaf of paper inside. Fernao and Linna both bent toward her to see what Ilmarinen had written. *I still think I'm right*, the note said, *and I think I can prove it. I'm going to try, anyhow*. The rest of the page was covered with closely written calculations.

"Right about what?" Linna asked. "What's he talking about?"

Of course the calculations made no sense to her. Pekka said, "I'm not quite sure myself. I'll have to look at this. Thank you for bringing it to me. It's something I need to see." *And something you don't,* she added by implication.

Linna took the hint. "All right," she said. "Please let me know what you find out, though. I'm worried about him." She went off, looking back over her shoulder.

When the other serving woman brought breakfast a moment later, Pekka hardly noticed. She and Fernao had their heads together, both of them bent over the note Linna had brought. Their index fingers traced Ilmarinen's calculations line by line. Pekka's finger moved a little faster than Fernao's. When she got to the bottom of the paper, she exclaimed, "He can't do that!"

Fernao grunted. He didn't say anything till he'd got to the bottom, too. Then he replied, "No, but he thinks he can. He may even be right, but I don't think so." He switched to classical Kaunian for precision's sake: "See this indeterminacy two-thirds of the way down?" He pointed. "He treats it as if its value were defined, but it is not. If he acts on that basis, I believe the spell will fail."

Pekka studied. She nodded. "Thank you," she said. "I missed that when I hurried through. I think you're right. I'm not sure, but I think so. But if the spell does fail, *how* will it fail?"

Some spells that didn't work just didn't work: the world went on as if nothing had happened. Others . . . Fernao summed up the others in one classical Kaunian word: "Energetically."

She feared he was right. They both got to their feet. "Your breakfast, Mistress Pekka!" the serving woman said. Pekka ignored her, but hurried out of the refectory, out of the hostel, with Fernao. He limped and leaned on his stick, but still moved fast enough to suit her.

When they went to the stable for a carriage, they discovered one was already gone. "Are you heading out to the blockhouse with Master Ilmarinen?" their driver asked. "He left a while ago."

"Did he?" Pekka said tonelessly. "Well, then, maybe you'd better hurry, hadn't you?" The fellow barely had time to nod before she scrambled into the passenger compartment with Fernao. She looked at the Lagoan mage. "If it does fail energetically, it occurs to me that we might get there just in time to be caught in the energy release."

"Aye, that occurred to me, too," Fernao agreed. "We have to try, though, don't we?" He waited for her to nod, then went on, "There's a worse possibility, too, you know: he might succeed."

"In going back through time? In changing things?" Pekka shook her head. "I don't believe that. Powers above, I don't want to believe it. And if he does it no matter what I believe . . ." She shuddered.

Fernao took her hand. She let him; she was glad of the contact. "If he can meddle, others will be able to do it, too," he said. "And we won't have a past to call our own any more."

Pekka leaned out the carriage. "Faster!" she told the driver. Obligingly, he got the horses up to a trot.

"Are you sure you want to do that?" Fernao said. "If we're late—"

"We have to try," Pekka said, though every instinct in her shouted for turning around and going the other way. If Ilmarinen failed . . . energetically, Leino would lose his wife and Uto would grow up not remembering much of his mother. Pekka clutched at Fernao's hand. Suddenly, absurdly, she wanted him very much. No chance of that, not now. *I know I might die at any moment. That's what it is.*

The carriage stopped. Pekka and Fernao piled out. She ran for the blockhouse. He followed at the best pace he could manage. In spite of the stick, his long legs made him not much slower than she.

When Pekka threw open the door, her worst fear was finding the place empty. That would mean Ilmarinen had done what he'd set out to do, and that would mean disaster. But there stood the elderly mage, still incanting. "Stop!" Pekka shouted. He hadn't come to the indeterminacy, but he couldn't be far away.

He smiled and shook his head and kept on with what he was doing. Fernao wasted no time talking. He simply tackled Ilmarinen and knocked him down. Ilmarinen shouted in fury, but Fernao, bad leg and all, was much bigger and younger and stronger than he. Pekka quickly chanted a counterspell to neutralize the sorcerous potential Ilmarinen's magecraft had built up.

"You idiots!" Ilmarinen cried, and then several choicer epithets.

"No," Fernao and Pekka said together. She went on, "Your calculations have an error in them. Fernao found it, and I'm sure he's right." Ilmarinen kept right on cursing. Pekka didn't care. She still had a future—and the world, despite Ilmarinen's best efforts, still had a past.

King Donalitu of Jelgava paced along *Habakkuk*'s icy deck once more. Leino made a wish. Wishes had very little to do with magecraft; the Kuusaman sorcerer knew as much. He made this one anyhow.

And, whether by the powers above or just dumb luck, it came true. As Donalitu was pompously declaiming, "And so we approach once more the land from which I was unjustly driven almost four long years ago—" his feet went out from under him and he landed, hard, on the royal backside.

Leino had all he could do not to clap his hands in glee, as Uto would have done. Like everyone else aboard *Habakkuk*, Donalitu wore shoes with cleats or spikes to keep such mishaps from occurring. Maybe he hadn't paid attention when people had explained how to walk in them. He didn't seem much in the habit of paying attention to anything.

Beside Leino, Xavega did clap her hands. But even she tried to pretend she hadn't done it afterwards. She grinned at Leino. He smiled back. If it hadn't been for Donalitu, they never would have ended up in bed together. If it hadn't been for Donalitu, she still would have looked down her nose at him—not hard, when she was taller than he was.

He wasn't about to arrange a dissolution from Pekka to spend the rest of his days with Xavega. She remained bad-tempered, arrogant, difficult, prejudiced. He could see all that clearly enough. But when she stripped off her clothes and lay down beside him, there was never a dull moment. He hadn't been sleeping well aboard *Habakkuk*. He did now.

Assisted by Captain Brunho, Donalitu got to his feet and managed to stay upright. He started to go on with his remarks, but didn't get the chance. One after another, screeching with fury, dragons flapped their way into the air and flew off toward the west. Not even a king so manifestly foolish as Donalitu was foolish enough to try to outshout a dragon.

Leino looked around and then back over his shoulder. Every ley line leading west toward the Jelgavan mainland was full of ships. Some of them flew Lagoas' crimson and gold banners. Quite a few more, though, showed the sky blue and sea green of Kuusamo. Xavega might not think much of either his home-land or his countrymen, but Kuusamo was stronger than her kingdom.

Since she thought well enough of him to open her legs, her other opinions distressed him less than they had. He knew that was wrong, but had trouble doing anything about it.

He didn't want to think about her other opinions just now, anyway. He said, "I hope the ruse worked. When the fleet sailed from Kihlanki, we made it very plain we were sailing against Gyongyos—so plain, the Algarvians couldn't help but find out about it. All the ships flew Kuusaman flags then, till we were out of sight of land."

"Everything seems fine so far," Xavega said. "We are close enough to the Jelgavan coast to send out our dragons, and the Algarvians have not troubled us with dragons of their own, or with ships of their own, or with leviathans. It looks as if our surprise is complete."

"It will not stay complete for long," Leino said. "Having dragons drop eggs on you and flame your soldiers will probably draw your notice."

"Aye, I suppose so," Xavega said. Leino hid a sigh. He'd tried to be playful with his classical Kaunian—the only lan-guage they had in common, since he'd never needed to learn Lagoan and Xavega showed less than no interest in everything Kuusaman except him. Had she even noticed? He shook his head. She hadn't.

So what are you doing with her? he wondered. But the answer to that was as obvious as it was trite: *I'm screwing her till we annoy the people in the cubicles on either side of ours.* He'd been surprised at how much a man in his mid-thirties could do—pleasantly surprised. Very pleasantly.

"We have to smash them," Xavega said. "If we do not smash them, the landing on the Jelgavan coast will fail. And it must not fail."

"It had better not, anyhow," Leino agreed. "And so the war comes back to eastern Derlavai. I wonder if the Jelgavans will thank us for it."

"Of course not," Xavega said—she was no more fond of Jelgavans as a people than of Kuusamans as a people. But then she asked a perfectly reasonable question: "Does King Donalitu seem grateful?"

"No. As far as King Donalitu is concerned, he is doing us a favor by allowing us to convey him back to Jelgava on *Habakkuk.*"

That made Xavega laugh, though Leino hadn't been joking. He looked toward the west. More dragons were flying in that direction, not only from *Habakkuk* but also from other ice-ships in her class and from the smaller, more conventional (which, to his way of thinking, also meant old-fashioned) dragon-haulers Kuusamo had devised to fight the war against Gyongyos in the wide reaches of the Bothnian Ocean. Again, some of the dragons were painted red and gold, but more were Kuusamo's sky blue and sea green.

Along with the ships that carried dragons were a great many more that bore soldiers, and others with behemoths and horses and unicorns and egg-tossers and all the other supplies an army needed to fight on land these days. Xavega said, "This is a far mightier armada than the one the Algarvians used to take Sibiu."

"So it is," Leino said. "But the Algarvians were sneaky in a different way, for their ships did not use the ley lines at all: they were just sailing ships, like those of ancient days. They got into the Sibian ports before the defenders even realized they were there."

Xavega cared nothing for such details. "This fleet is might-ier," she said again, which was indeed true. "Lagoas is mightier than Algarve." Taken by itself, that struck Leino as much less obviously true.

Coughing a couple of times, he said, "Kuusamo has also had a certain amount to do with this fleet"—that certain amount be-ing about two parts in three.

"Well, aye, a certain amount," Xavega allowed reluctantly. By her tone, that certain amount might have been about one part in ten.

A shout rose from *Habakkuk*'s tall watchtower: "Land ho!" Down on the deck, Leino couldn't see the Derlavaian mainland, not yet. Before long, though, he would. *Habakkuk* and the other dragon-haulers would want to stay as close to the mainland as they could, to let the beasts aboard them fly as far into Jelgava as they could. Before too long, the Kuusaman and Lagoan drag-ons would fly from farms on Jelgavan soil, but Kuusaman and Lagoan footsoldiers would first have to take that soil away from the Algarvians.

Xavega said, "Still no trouble from King Mezentio's men. They are all looking across the Strait of Valmiera, thinking we would try to strike against them there. But we fooled them by sailing out of that eastern port." She didn't remember the name.

Leino nodded. "We seem to have fooled them. The better our job of that, the smaller the price we shall have to pay." He pointed. "Look—some of the ships are sending their landing boats toward the shore."

Sure enough, men were scrambling down nets and rope lad-ders from the ley-line transports to the smaller craft that would take them up onto the beaches of southeastern Jelgava. Be-cause a good many ley lines ran toward those beaches, the smaller craft also had sorcerers aboard to take advantage of the world's energy grid. In earlier invasions by sea, some Ku-usamans had had to try to reach Gyongyosian-held islands from their transports in rowboats and little sailboats. Logistics here had improved.

"They are not going to be able to make behemoths, or even

unicorns, climb down ladders," Xavega said. "How do they propose to get them into the battle?"

"I do not know," Leino answered with a shrug. "I have not tried to find out, either, I must admit. Keeping *Habakkuk* going has been plenty to occupy me for now. If I thought they did not have a way, I would worry. But I expect they do. If I transfer to the land campaign, I suppose I will have to worry about that kind of thing."

He looked west again. Now he could see the mainland of Jelgava. He'd been here on holiday with Pekka, but that was at the resorts of the far north. Whatever this was, a holiday it was not. *I hope it's not a holiday for the Algarvians, either. It had better not be, or we're all in trouble.*

He didn't just see the mainland. He saw smoke rising from whatever Algarvian fortresses or barracks or other installations the dragons could find. And he also saw fountains of water rising from the sea not far in front of the foremost ships of the invasion fleet. He cursed softly in Kuusaman: cursing in classical Kaunian never satisfied him. *The dragons haven't wrecked all their egg-tossers. Too bad.*

An egg landed on one of the small craft taking soldiers toward the shore. After Leino blinked away the flash of light from the burst of sorcerous energy, he stared at the spot, hoping to spy survivors clinging to bits of wreckage. But he saw only empty sea there, empty sea and other landing boats hurrying toward the shore.

Xavega had chanced to be looking in the same direction. "Brave men," she said quietly.

"Aye." But Leino wondered. Then he shrugged. Whether they'd been brave or terrified, what difference did it make? The egg hadn't cared. And what they were now, irretrievably, was sunk. A moment later, another egg struck a boat. That vessel too, vanished as if it had never been.

And, a moment later, alarm bells aboard *Habakkuk* clanged. A dowser shouted, "Enemy dragons!" and pointed toward the west.

For a long moment, Leino didn't spot them: he was looking

high in the sky, where the Lagoan and Kuusaman beasts had flown. When his gaze fell closer to the sea, he spied the dragons—two of them, a leader and his wingman—driving straight toward the fleet just above the wavetops. Each of them flamed a light craft full of soldiers. Then they pressed on toward the bigger ships of the fleet itself.

Every heavy stick aboard those bigger ships started blazing at the Algarvian dragonfliers. None struck home, though. The dragons flamed a few men on the deck of a ley-line cruiser not far from *Habakkuk*. That done, they dodged their way back toward the Jelgavan mainland.

"I hope they get home safe," Xavega said. "I do not care if they are the foe. They have great courage."

Algarvic peoples—Lagoans as well as Algarvians—were prone to such chivalrous notions. Leino didn't argue with Xavega, but he didn't agree with her, either. As far as he was concerned, a particularly brave enemy was an enemy who particularly needed killing.

The Algarvian dragons did escape the massed blazing power of the whole allied fleet. But they were the only two enemy dragons Leino saw that whole day long. And, even as they escaped, the first small craft let their soldiers out on the beaches of Jelgava. Now the Algarvians had a new fight on their hands.

Talsu was discovering that life in a tent was less different from life in his home than he'd expected. He was warm enough. He had a roof over his head. True, it was a cloth roof, but with spring edging toward summer that mattered very little in Skrunda. If he was still under canvas when rain came with fall and winter, that would be a different story. He'd worry about it then, though—he couldn't change it now. After the eggs from Kuusaman and Lagoan dragons burned him and his family out of their house, he was glad they were all alive and in one piece.

Worst about sharing the tent on the edge of town—one of many—with his father and mother and sister was that he and Gailisa had so little privacy. His parents were considerate enough to go out walking every now and then, and he and his wife did the same for them (both pairs taking Ausra along as needed), but still. . . .

He also went out walking and into town for other reasons than privacy these days. For most of four years, ever since the Jelgavan army collapsed and King Donalitu fled to Lagoas, he'd taken Algarvian occupation for granted. It wasn't that he liked the redheads—he despised them. But he hadn't seen anything that would get them out of his kingdom. In certain minimal ways—accepting coins with King Mainardo's beaky profile on them, in making clothes for Algarvian officers, in not using his every waking moment thinking up ways to dismay or kill them—he'd acquiesced in their presence in Skrunda.

Everything was different now. After days of uneasy silence, Skrunda's news sheets had to catch up with rumor and admit what could no longer be denied: the islanders had landed on the Derlavaian mainland. They'd landed, in fact, not far from Balvi—the capital of Jelgava lay close to the beaches where they'd come ashore.

After fetching a news sheet back to the tent, Talsu waved it in his father's face. "Just listen to this."

"Well, I will, if you ever read it to me," Traku answered.

"All right." Talsu stopped waving the sheet and started reading from it: " 'King Mainardo, the rightful ruler of the Kingdom of Jelgava, expresses his complete confidence that his forces and those of his valiant Algarvian allies will succeed in repelling the vicious invasion by the air pirates whose raids have already caused the Jelgavan people so much hardship.' "

"He'd be pissing in his pants if he wore pants instead of Algarvian kilts." Traku had heard enough news-sheet stories to have little trouble extracting accurate meaning from deliberately inaccurate words. He screwed up his face and made as if to spit. "I'm sure Mainardo loses hours and hours of sleep worrying about the Jelgavan people. Aren't you?" He spoke in a low voice; canvas walls were thinner than those of brick and wood.

"Aye, worrying about how to do more and worse to us than he has up till now," Talsu said, also quietly. "But wait—there's more. 'Jelgavan forces and their bold Algarvian comrades have inflicted heavy losses on the enemy and are making gains in several areas. Fierce fighting continues all along the line. The invaders' hopes for a speedy triumph are doomed to disappointment.' You know what that's really saying, don't you?"

"Of course I do." His father looked irate. "Think I'm stupid or something? It means the redheads tried to boot 'em back into the ocean and they cursed well couldn't do it. Or d'you think I'm wrong?"

"Not me." Talsu shook his head. "That's what I think it means, too. And here's the best part of all: 'An impostor claiming to be the abdicated fugitive King Donalitu has been reported to be in the grasp of the invaders. This effort to incite the contented populace of Jelgava will surely meet the failure it deserves.'"

"So the real king's back, eh?" Traku said.

"Can't very well mean anything else, can it?" Talsu returned.

"No." Traku's tough, rather battered features wore a thoughtful expression. "Those fellows who were scrawling street signs about the king coming back knew what they were talking about, didn't they?"

"Seems that way, doesn't it?" Talsu said. "I wish I knew who in blazes they were. I'd join 'em in a minute, and you'd best believe that's true." There, his voice dropped to a whisper.

And, of course, whether the anti-Algarvian underground would want anything to do with him was a different question. He knew it. He'd gone into a dungeon, and then he'd come out again. The assumption had to be that anybody who came out of a dungeon cooperated with the redheads. And so Talsu had, at least by giving them names. That the names were of people at least as likely to collaborate with them as to struggle against them might not matter. He knew as much, though it pained him. His hand went to the scar on his flank, the scar from an Algarvian soldier's knife. That had pained him, too, and a great deal more.

Outside, some called in fair but Algarvian-accented Jelgavan: "Is this being where I am finding Traku the tailor?"

"Aye," Traku and Talsu said together. Talsu didn't know what was going through his father's mind. As for him, he quickly had to send his thoughts down different ley lines. The redheads might be in trouble in Jelgava, but they hadn't been heaved out of Skrunda—and Skrunda, unlike Balvi, lay a long way from the invasion. Here, the Algarvians still ruled the roost. As the redhead—a captain, by his rank badges—ducked into the tent, Talsu cautiously asked, "What can we do for you today, sir?"

"You are still getting cloth? I am needing a new kilt," the officer answered. His eye fell on the news sheet, which Talsu had set on a blanket. He pointed to it. "You are reading this?" Talsu stood mute. So did his father. Admitting it might land them in trouble. Denying it might be too obvious a lie. The Algarvian's laugh was bitter. "What are you saying when my back is turning?"

Talsu saw even less way to answer that than the other question, and so he didn't. Traku must have been thinking along with him, for all he said was, "Aye, I can get cloth—the bank didn't burn, so I've still got some money. What sort of kilt will you need, sir? Lightweight, or something heavier?" *Are you staying here, or have they sent you to Unkerlant?*

"Lightweight," the redhead said. "I am to be staying and fighting in Jelgava. I am to be staying until they are capturing me or until they are killing me. The officers over me are so ordering, and I am obeying. And the powers below are eating everything here."

"Lightweight," Talsu echoed. He'd borrowed a tape measure from another tailor who remained in in his own shop. "If you'll let me take your measurements . . ."

The Algarvian laughed. It was not a happy laugh. Talsu had laughed that same kind of laugh sitting around a fire with other soldiers while he was in the army. It said, *Here we are, and we may as well laugh, because nothing else is going to help, either.* Having laughed, the captain said, "I am seeing your troubles. You are not knowing if I am trying to trap you."

Again, Talsu stood mute. So did his father. The Algarvian was right, but admitting as much was dangerous. Talsu stepped forward with the tape measure.

"I am telling you this," the Algarvian said. "You are not having to say anything. Algarve in Jelgava is . . ." He used a word in his own language. Talsu didn't know what it meant, but the officer's gestures were expressive enough for him to get the idea: *ruined* was the politest term he could think of. Idly, he wondered if Algarvians would be able to talk at all with their hands tied. "How are we fighting here?" the redhead asked. "All our good men, all our good behemoths and dragons— where are they being? Here? No, Unkerlant!" He used that word again, with vast scorn.

"If that's what you think, why fight?" Talsu asked. "Why not just give up?"

"No, no, no, no." The Algarvian wagged a forefinger under Talsu's nose. "No doing that. I am being a soldier. Fighting is what I am doing. And who is knowing?" He shrugged an elaborate Algarvian shrug. "Maybe Kuusamo and Lagoas will be making mistakes. We can be doing that—so can they be doing it. If they are making mistakes, we may be winning yet. And so"—another shrug—"I am fighting still."

He sounded like a soldier, sure enough. Talsu hadn't gone into the fight against Algarve with any great hope or expectation of victory, but he'd kept at it till his superiors surrendered. On a personal level, he didn't suppose he could blame the redhead for doing the same. On a level slightly different from the personal . . .

Talsu shook his head. If he started thinking that way, he'd stab the officer instead of measuring him for a kilt. Were the fighting right outside of Skrunda, he would have thought about that. As things were, nobody was going to kick the Algarvians out of this part of Jelgava any time soon. And so, with a small sigh, he advanced with the tape measure, not with a knife.

Traku drummed a fingernail on the three-legged stool that was the sole bit of real furniture in the tent. After Talsu finished measuring the Algarvian, his father said, "What with things being the way they are right now"—his wave encompassed the canvas walls and the blankets on bare ground—"I think maybe you'd better pay up front." He named his price.

The Algarvian raised an eyebrow. Talsu expected him to

aise a fuss—Mezentio's men, to a Jelgavan, were some of the ussiest people ever born. But, instead of turning red and throwng a tantrum, or even haggling, the captain dug into his belt pouch and set silver on the stool. "Here," he said, and started to valk out. As he reached for the tent flap, he looked back over is shoulder. "Two days' time?"

"Three," Talsu said.

"Three," the redhead agreed. "I am seeing you in three days' ime, then." He ducked out of the tent and strode away.

Once he was gone, Talsu and his father stared at each other. "Did you hear that?" Talsu breathed. "Did you *hear* that? By he powers above, there's a redhead who doesn't think Algarve :an hang on in Jelgava!"

"King Donalitu's back," Traku said. "We're going to be free again."

"Aye," Talsu said, but then, quite suddenly, "No. We're going o have our own king back again. It's not exactly the same thing." His father made a questioning noise. Talsu explained: "When the edheads arrested me and threw me in the dungeon, the fellow who interrogated me wasn't an Algarvian. He was a Jelgavan, loing the same job for King Mainardo as he'd done for King Donalitu. And if King Donalitu's giving orders in Balvi again, what do you want to bet that same son of a whore will go right on loing his job in the dungeon, except with different prisoners?"

Traku grunted. "Gaolers are all bastards, no matter who they work for."

"Oh, aye." Talsu nodded. "But you have to be a *particular* kind of bastard to do your job without caring who you work for." He hesitated, then added, "And you have to be a particular kind of bastard to want your dungeons full of people—if you happen to be a king, I mean."

Traku looked around, as if fearing people were leaning up outside the tent with hands cupped to their ears. Even in the lays before the war, such words incautiously spoken could cause a man to disappear for months, for years, sometimes forever. "If it's a choice between our bastard and the Algarvians' bastard, I'll take ours," he said at last.

"Oh, aye," Talsu said again, and then sighed. "That's the

choice we've got, sure enough. I wish we had another one, but
don't know what it would be. Most kings are whoresons, noth
ing else but."

They got supper that evening from kettles full of slop no
much better than he'd eaten in his army days. After the
brought their bowls back to the tent, Gailisa said, "Somebod
who came into the grocery shop today said that Mainardo wa
going to run away from Balvi and back to Algarve. That woul
be wonderful."

"Even the redheads don't think they can go on holding ou
kingdom down," Traku said, and recounted the Algarvian cap
tain's words earlier in the day.

Talsu bent down to spit a bit of gristle onto the ground. The
he said, "The redheads may not think they can hold Jelgava, bu
they've got to keep trying."

"Why?" his wife asked. "Why don't they just go away an
leave us alone?"

"I wish they would," his sister added.

"So do I, Ausra," Talsu said. "But if they go away, the Lagoan
and Kuusamans—and I suppose our own army, if we have a
army again—will follow them right on into Algarve. And s
they've got to fight here, to hang on to their own kingdom."

"We'll just have to help throw them out, then," Ausra said
not quite so quietly as Talsu would have liked. He didn't answe
that. He'd tried to help throw out the redheads, and what had i
got him? Time in the dungeon and an undeserved name as :
collaborator. Of course, his timing had been bad.

If I saw the chance, would I fight the Algarvians again? h
wondered. He gnawed on another piece of gristly meat. Tha
helped hide the fierce smile on his face. *Of course I would. I
only I could kill them all.*

Ilmarinen looked at Fernao as if he hated him. He probably did
"You miserable pup," Ilmarinen said. "I was after experimenta
proof."

Fernao shrugged. "You wouldn't have got it. Even you've
admitted you ignored that indeterminacy. All you would have

done was take out a big piece of the landscape, and you have to admit that, too."

"I don't have to do any such thing, and I'm not about to, either," Ilmarinen retorted. "It might have worked fine. We'll never know now—thanks to you."

They *could* find out. Ilmarinen could go off and repeat his experiment. Fernao kept his mouth shut. If he suggested any such thing, the Kuusaman mage was altogether too likely to take him up on it. He could think of nothing he wanted less. To keep Ilmarinen from coming up with the same notion, he changed the subject: "Our armies are pushing farther into Jelgava. So far, the Algarvians haven't started killing people to try to stop them."

"So far," Ilmarinen echoed. He leaned across the refectory table. "But I have friends in interesting places. One of them said the redheads—the other redheads, I mean: not your lot—moved a lot of Kaunians from Forthweg down to the edge of the Strait of Valmiera, because they thought the blow would fall there. How long will it take to drag those poor whoresons to Jelgava, or else to start hauling Jelgavans off the street?"

"Not long," Fernao said.

Ilmarinen grunted. "There—you see? You're not as foolish as you look. And I was trying to go back and change all that—change everything that's happened since this war started—and you and Pekka had the nerve to try to stop me? You ought to be ashamed of yourselves." His eyebrow rose. "You ought to be ashamed of yourselves for all kinds of reasons, but that's the one I've got in mind right now."

"I don't know what you're talking about," Fernao replied, and Ilmarinen laughed raucously. Ignoring him, the Lagoan mage switched to classical Kaunian: "And suppose—just suppose, mind—that you were right about what you tried to do. Suppose the sorcery does have a true timelike component. I do not think it does, but suppose as much for the sake of argument."

"I have supposed as much," Ilmarinen said in the same language. "That is why I tried to do what I did. And if I had succeeded, the world would be a different place, and a better place,

right now. Because of Pekka, that wouldn't make you so happy
I know, but it's still true." He spoke the language of scholarship
as fluently and idiomatically as he used Kuusaman.

"Different? Aye. Better?" Fernao shrugged. "Perhaps yo
would have changed things to your heart's desire. But wha
would the next person who meddled in the past have done
What about the fellow after *him*? How long before we had n
true past at all, only an endless war of changes? If the Kaunia
Empire had beaten the Algarvians at the Battle of Gambolo
would it have fallen? If Sibiu had beaten Lagoas in our sea war
two hundred and fifty years ago, the Sibs would have got mor
from Siaulia and the islands in the Great Northern Sea tha
they did, and we less. And so on, with every kingdom trying t
set its lost cause to rights. Do you see?"

He spoke classical Kaunian like most scholars and mages
well enough, but without real liveliness. But that didn't matte
so much here. All he wanted to do was get his point across. An
he did. Ilmarinen didn't answer right away. "You've given this
good deal of thought, haven't you?" he said at last.

"Aye," Fernao answered. "Pekka and I had little else to do
while going out to the blockhouse but think and worry. The
other thing we worried about was how much energy your spel
would release if it went wrong."

"Nothing you could have done about that—except jumping
on me and stopping me the way you did, I mean," Ilmarine
said. He added, "I saw the carriage you came in. You should
have spent your time screwing—the driver wouldn't have
known. If you were going to die, at least you would have died
happy."

Fernao got to his feet. "You are impossible," he said. "Fortunately, the spell you tried is also impossible." He wanted to
warn Ilmarinen not to try it again, but refrained once more. He
wished he could have strutted away with his nose in the air. His
permanent limp and the stick he used prevented that. He did the
best he could, given his physical limitations. It was good
enough to make Ilmarinen laugh at his retreating back.

And he got his nose high enough in the air to keep him from
paying much attention to where he was going. He almost ran

over Pekka before he realized she was there. "What did I do to you?" she asked.

"You?" he replied. "Nothing, sweetheart." Her expression warned him not to say such things. It always had, ever since he'd fled his own bedchamber after they'd made love. But this time, he was able to go on. "Ilmarinen, on the other hand . . ."

Pekka's face cleared. She was always ready to be annoyed at the elderly theoretical sorcerer, even if he was her own countryman. "What now?" she asked.

"Oh, nothing new," Fernao said. "But he still thinks he's right in spite of the evidence, and—" He broke off again.

"And what?" Pekka asked. When Fernao didn't answer right away, she drew her own—accurate—conclusion. "He's teasing you about what we did, is he?" Fernao nodded. Pekka wagged a finger at him. "You see? Going to bed didn't stop the gossip. It didn't slow it down. It didn't solve anything."

"But it was wonderful," Fernao said.

That didn't solve anything, either; it just brought the annoyed look back to Pekka's face. "It made things more complicated," she said. "We don't need things to be more complicated right now. The most important thing we can do is work on this magecraft. Anything that gets in the way—anything at all—we have to push aside."

She didn't deny that they'd had a good time in bed. She'd never denied it. But she did keep on behaving as if it hadn't happened. That might not have been calculated to drive Fernao out of his mind, but it certainly had that effect.

"What are we going to do?" he said.

"When I get the chance, I'm going back to my husband and my son," Pekka answered. "As for you, I hope you find a wonderful Lagoan woman—or even a wonderful Kuusaman woman, if you find your tastes running that way."

"I already have," Fernao told her.

"One without encumbrances," Pekka told him. When she saw he didn't understand the word in Kuusaman, she translated it into classical Kaunian. He could have done without such thoughtfulness. She added, "And I'm not feeling any too wonderful right now, either."

Fernao looked around. By some accident, nobody was star-ing at them as they stood just outside the refectory. That wouldn't last long, though. It couldn't, by the very nature of things. While he had the chance, Fernao kicked at the boards of the floor—after carefully positioning his stick so he didn't fall on his face. "What's the use?" he muttered. "What's the cursed use?"

"You see?" Pekka set a hand on his arm. It was a sympa-thetic gesture, not an affectionate one—or not an affectionate one of the sort he craved. "It complicated your life, too, even without encumbrances." Now she used the Kuusaman word without explanation.

"It wouldn't have, if . . ." he said.

"If I'd decided to keep doing what we did once," Pekka said, and he nodded. She shook her head. "The complications would just have taken longer to get here and been worse when they fi-nally did. I'm sorry, Fernao; by the powers above, I'm very sorry. But I can't imagine anything that would make me change my mind now."

"All right," he said. But it wasn't all right, nor anywhere close. He limped off toward his room. Pekka didn't come after him or try to call him back. He hadn't really expected her to. He'd hoped—but expectation had the encumbrance of truth, while hope lived its own life, wild and free.

Once he got back to his chamber, he wondered why he'd come. All he had here was the chance to be alone with his mis-ery. He sat down on the bed, then wished he hadn't. Sitting there made him think of those frantic few minutes when he'd got everything he wanted . . . only to discover that, once he'd got it, he couldn't keep it. That felt worse than not getting it, for now he could look back on what he'd had, know it was real, and know—or at least be certain enough for all practical pur-poses—it wouldn't happen again.

Muttering something pungent under his breath, he got up and left his room. He did, at least, know where he was going: to the crystallomancers' chamber, where the mages and their crystals kept the hostel in the Naantali district connected to the outside world throughout the year. As spring gave way to summer, getting here was easy enough, but that didn't hold in fall or early spring or through the seemingly endless winter blizzards.

"I want a crystal for private communication with my Grandmaster," he told the Kuusaman mage in charge of the chamber.

"Of course," she said. It hadn't always been *of course*; he'd had to make a nuisance of himself to gain the privilege. Only by pointedly asking whether Lagoas was truly an equal ally to Kuusamo had he prevailed. The chief crystallomancer took him to a crystal in the corner. The couple of Kuusamans closest to that crystal moved away so they couldn't listen to him. "Here you are," the chief said. "Do remember that the Algarvians are always trying to spy on our emanations."

"I will," Fernao said. Looking discontented, the Kuusaman mage went back to her desk. Fernao murmured the charm that would link this crystal to the one in Grandmaster Pinhiero's office back in Setubal. As the crystal activated, light flared inside it. A moment later, Pinhiero's image filled the glass globe.

"Who's that?" the Grandmaster said, peering into his own crystal. Then he recognized Fernao. "Ah, it's you. What do you want? What sort of trouble are you in?"

So far as Fernao knew, Pinhiero hadn't heard about his entanglement with Pekka. Fernao hadn't told him, anyway, which might not have been the same thing. Pinhiero could learn things from all sorts of unlikely places. Fernao said, "When will the first contingent of Lagoan mages come here for training? We really need our own wizards familiar with the new magecraft now that we're fighting on the Derlavaian mainland." Speaking his own tongue with Pinhiero felt odd after using classical Kaunian and Kuusaman for so long.

"They'll be leaving Setubal day after tomorrow," Pinhiero said, scratching at one end of his graying, sandy mustache. "The demon of getting them ready, of course, was making sure none of them would start whispering in Mezentio's ear. Would you believe it, we found one mage the Algarvians planted on us twenty-five years ago? He'd had a past made up that was perfect till you looked really hard, and he speaks Lagoan better than I do."

"I'm glad you found him," Fernao said. "Now—can you find someone to take over for me here? I think I've done about as much in Kuusamo as I can do."

Pinhiero shook his head. "In a word, no. In two words, definitely no. I don't care if your affair with that Kuusaman mage didn't work out the way you hoped. This is more important than you, my boy. This is for the Guild and the kingdom. You stay right where you are."

Fernao scowled. He might have known Pinhiero had a peephole of some sort into the gossip here. "Aye, Grandmaster," he said, and broke the etheric connection with no more of a goodbye than that.

King Swemmel glared out of the crystal at Marshal Rathar. Rathar stolidly stared back; he much preferred dealing with the King of Unkerlant at a distance to trying to deal with him face-to-face. "We are not amused, and we are not pleased," Swemmel said in his harsh, high-pitched voice.

"I'm sorry to hear that, your Majesty," Rathar replied. That, on the whole, was true; when Swemmel felt aggrieved, he was even more hair-raisingly erratic than in his calmer moods.

"They mocked us," the king snarled. "They mocked us most unforgivably—Count Gusmao and in especial Lord Moisio. Were they not ministers of kingdoms also at war against Algarve"—he couldn't bring himself to say, *friendly kingdoms*—"their heads should answer for it. We do not tolerate insolence."

Rathar wondered when anyone had last dared be insolent to Swemmel. Not for a good many years; the marshal was sure of that. But the ministers from Lagoas and Kuusamo had the advantage of not being Unkerlanter subjects. Swemmel risked real wrath if he abused them. Of course, even that might not stop him if he reckoned himself provoked enough.

"They have the gall to say, 'I told you so,' to us. To *us*!" Swemmel snapped, still fuming.

Gusmao and Moisio *had* told Swemmel what was going to

happen. And they'd told him the truth. He hadn't seemed much
interested in hearing it at the time—he'd actively resisted believing it at the time—but it had turned out to be true. And . . .
"Your Majesty, now that the Lagoans and the Kuusamans finally are on the Derlavaian mainland, that can only help us,"
Rathar said. "The redheads can't concentrate all their strength
against Unkerlant alone."

"That is so." Swemmel sounded unhappy about admitting
even that much. But Rathar had distracted him. "Aye, that *is* so.
And we shall make the Algarvians pay." He stabbed a finger out
at Rathar; even though it was only an image in the crystal, the
marshal had all he could do not to flinch. "Do you suppose that,
if they capture the Algarvian pretender in Jelgava, they shall
use him as we used the Algarvian pretender in Grelz?"

"I . . . don't know, your Majesty." Rathar tried to imagine the
Kuusamans boiling King Mainardo alive. The picture refused
to form in his mind. But he couldn't very well tell his sovereign
that.

"Well, never mind." Swemmel waved a hand. "You carry on
with what you have been ordered. And mind you, Marshal—we
expect to see results." His image vanished. The crystal flared,
then went back to being an inert glass globe.

As often happened after a conversation with the king, Rathar
needed to shake himself to return to the real world. The commandant's headquarters in Pewsum weren't so very much, not
as the real world went. Rathar got up, stretched, and walked out
onto the street. No one followed him. No one dared disturb his
privacy. Who would disturb the most powerful man in Unkerlant save Swemmel alone?

After a little while, General Gurmun dared. Gurmun, from
everything Rathar had seen, had as much daring as any officer
needed, and a little more besides. "What news from the king?"
he asked.

Marshal Rathar eyed him. Gurmun also had as much ambition
as any officer needed, and a little more besides. One of the posts
to which an ambitious Unkerlanter general might aspire was the
one Rathar held. Even so, the question was reasonable. Picking
his words with care, Rathar replied, "His Majesty is irked at the

Kuusaman and Lagoan ministers for not being as polite as they might have when talking about their invasion of Jelgava."

"He's got a right to be irked, too, if anybody wants to know what I think," Gurmun answered. "We've been carrying the load against Algarve all by ourselves the past three years. And now the islanders are crowing like roosters because they've taken on a little? Powers below eat 'em, *I* say."

That held some truth. It certainly matched Swemmel's view of things. Rathar said, "They haven't been idle, not altogether." Gurmun snorted. The marshal went on: "And, as I told his Majesty, the more the redheads have to put into fighting Lagoas and Kuusamo, the less they'll have left to use against us."

"Well, that's true enough." Gurmun nodded vigorously. "It should have happened last year, or maybe even the year before, but it is true now. We'll make Mezentio's men pay, too."

"I expect we will," Rathar agreed. "Our edge has always been in manpower and behemoths and dragons. Now it will be a bigger edge, and I intend to take advantage of it." He pointed to General Gurmun. "You're going to help me do it, too."

Gurmun showed his teeth in a wolf's smile. "That's just what I've got in mind, lord Marshal. I'm really looking forward to it."

"We're all looking forward to it, General," Rathar replied. "We've been looking forward to it for a long time. If all goes well, we get to show the Algarvians what good scholars we've been these past three years."

"Did the king say anything about the timing of what we've got laid on?" Gurmun asked.

"Not a word." More than a little relieved at that, Rathar shook his head. "We're still two weeks away, more or less. That's always provided the redheads don't do something we didn't expect."

"They're not bloody likely to attack us first, not with everything they've got on their plate," Gurmun exclaimed.

"I should hope not." But then Rathar shook his head again. "No—I should hope so. If they want to waste their substance, they're welcome to do it as far as I'm concerned. But that isn't what I meant."

"What did you mean, then, sir?" General Gurmun sounded

suspicious. He didn't care for Rathar's seeing things he couldn't.

Here, Rathar wasn't sure what he was seeing, or whether he was seeing anything at all. He answered, "It's just that . . . you never can tell with the redheads. They might pull some new sorcery out from under their kilts, they might not try to stand their ground, they might have ready lines farther east. . . ."

"No sign of it from the dragons," Gurmun said. "No sign of it from the mages. No real sign they even know what's building against them here in the north. As far as we can tell, they're still worried most about the Duchy of Grelz."

"Aye, as far as we can tell," Rathar agreed. "I just hope we can tell far enough." His chuckle held no mirth. Back in the days of the Twinkings War, he'd always had a good notion of what Kyot's forces were likely to do. Like him, they were Unkerlanters; he'd understood how they thought. "Anybody who's sure he understands what the Algarvians are up to deserves to get his head handed to him, and he probably will."

"They aren't as smart as they think they are, and we aren't as stupid as they think we are," Gurmun said. "We've used that against them a few times."

Rathar nodded. Pretending to do something foolish in the hope the Algarvians would pounce on it and thus fall into a later trap they *hadn't* foreseen, had worked well fairly often, in fact. Mezentio's men were proud of their own cleverness. If they saw the ignorant Unkerlanters acting stupid, they felt duty bound to punish them—and ended up punishing themselves in the process. And, in their arrogance, they had trouble realizing what they'd done wrong.

"Are your behemoths in place?" the marshal asked.

Gurmun's blunt-featured head bobbed up and down. "I'm right on schedule, lord Marshal. If we weren't moving only at night, if we weren't keeping quiet with our crystals, we'd be farther along still. Not being able to send a message ahead to let people prepare for the beasts slows us down."

"I know," Rathar said. "But all the emanations we've been able to intercept from the redheads show they don't know what's coming. That's just how I want things to stay. The surprise will make up for everything."

"I hope you're right, sir." Gurmun's eyes flashed. *If you're wrong, King Swemmel will hear about it. I'll make sure he hears about it.*

Rathar almost let his smile show on his face. One thing he'd seen was that Swemmel didn't think he aimed at usurpation. He was content to be marshal; the idea of being king horrified him. Did Gurmun feel the same way? Rathar had his doubts. And, if he had doubts, Swemmel surely had deep, dark suspicions. *I may not be so easy to topple as you think, General.*

A wagon in no way out of the ordinary pulled up. The driver asked, "Ready to go on up to the front?" Rathar nodded and climbed in, Gurmun right behind him. Lots of wagons went up to the front. Both Rathar and Gurmun wore uniform tunics ordinary but for their rank badges; not even a dragonflier at treetop height would judge them anything but common soldiers. *Of course, even common soldiers get attacked,* Rathar thought. He shrugged. Life didn't come without risks. If Gurmun worried, he didn't show it. Rathar had never had any reason to doubt his courage.

The wagon rattled east out of Pewsum. The trees—the ones still standing after the fighting in winter and spring—were in full leaf. Men and behemoths sheltered under the cover of those leaves. So long as day stayed in the sky, they didn't move. Men and behemoths sheltered under trees and in barns and huts and under mats that looked like grass for many miles back of the line of battle. When night came, they moved forward from one place of concealment to the next.

"This is all very good," Rathar said to the colonel commanding a brigade at the front line. "The redheads still don't seem to realize just how much we've built things up here."

"They will." Anticipation was naked and hungry in General Gurmun's voice. "Before very long, by the powers above, we'll show them."

Worry in his voice, the colonel said, "The brigade opposite me has a good commander. Spinello, his name is. He's always active. You never can tell what he'll do next."

"Are you worried about a spoiling attack?" Rathar asked.

Gurmun's laugh was hungry, too. "It'd be a sorry-looking attack after it tried biting down on everything we've got in the neighborhood."

"Oh, we'd beat the bastards back—I'm not worried about that," the colonel said. "I'm more afraid he'll try raiding along my front and learn from the captives he takes that we're a lot stronger than he thinks right now."

Marshal Rathar nodded. That was a sensible worry to have. A lot of Unkerlanter officers wouldn't have fretted about such things. This fellow was someone to watch. Rathar said, "The best way to keep anything like that from happening is to make sure only the regiments the redheads already know about are in the forwardmost positions. That way, they won't take captives from any units they'd expect to find somewhere else."

"Aye, Marshal. I'll see to it," the colonel said earnestly.

"Good." Rathar glanced over to Gurmun, and wasn't unduly surprised to find Gurmun eyeing him. He spoke one more word: "Soon." The commander of behemoths nodded.

Muttering under his breath, Hajjaj buttoned his Algarvian-style tunic. Just putting on the garment made sweat pour from him. At this season of the year in Bishah, the sun stood as close to straight overhead as made no difference. He would have been hot nude but for sandals and a hat. Muffled in tunic and kilt, he felt as if he were stifling. "The things I do for Zuwayza," he said.

Qutuz—who, being but a secretary, could remain comfortably unclothed—came in and announced, "The Algarvian minister is here to see you, your Excellency."

"Send him in," Hajjaj answered.

"Shall I bring tea and wine and cakes?" Qutuz asked.

Hajjaj had used his kingdom's rules of hospitality to delay discussion with Marquis Balastro a good many times. Today, though, he shook his head. "No, by the powers above," he said. "The sooner I am out of this cloth bake oven, the happier I shall be."

"As you say." Qutuz sounded as if he disapproved. Technically speaking, the secretary was right to disapprove. Hajjaj didn't care about technicalities. As foreign minister, he could ignore them if he so chose—and, every so often, he did so choose. Not quite shaking his head, Qutuz went out to bring the Algarvian minister into Hajjaj's office.

By the way Marquis Balastro strode in, it might have been three years before. Algarve might have been invincible, unstoppable, leaping from one triumph to another in the east of Derlavai and about to embark on the campaign that would surely bring Unkerlant to heel. Balastro's stride hadn't changed in those three years. The world? The world had.

After polite bows and handclasps and professions of mutual esteem, Balastro plopped himself down on the carpet and made himself at home with a mound of cushions. He adapted to Zuwayzi customs more readily than most foreigners. This once, Hajjaj wouldn't have minded his coming to call without his clothes, even if that meant having to stare at his pale skin and his circumcision.

Balastro was no fool. He noted the absence of the ritual food and drink, and drew the proper conclusion from it: "You must be suffocating in your clothes."

"I am," Hajjaj admitted.

"Well, let's get down to business, then, Your Excellency," Balastro said. "What's on your mind?"

"His Majesty, King Shazli, asked me to invite you here to get Algarve's view of the present situation in light of recent developments," Hajjaj replied. The language was fine and diplomatic. Nevertheless, it couldn't completely hide the real meaning underneath the fine words. *The king wants to know just how much trouble you think you're in.*

Balastro understood that, too. His grin also flashed as jauntily as if Algarve remained on top of the world. "We are not beaten," he said stoutly. "I repeat it: we are *not*. We are fighting hard in Jelgava; the enemy has not gone far from the beaches where he landed, and he will have a demon of a time doing it. And in Unkerlant, here it is summer, and still Swemmel's soldiers stay silent. We have taught them what assailing Algarve costs."

"Fair enough," Hajjaj said. It was a more optimistic assessment than he would have made, but Balastro's job was to be optimistic, and he did it well. Hajjaj's job was to expose optimism with no visible means of support. He raised an eyebrow. "Suppose you're wrong, Your Excellency."

"All right. Suppose I'm wrong." When Balastro smiled, his teeth seemed much too sharp to belong in his handsome, fleshy face. "In that case, you get to treat with Swemmel of Unkerlant, and I wish you joy of it."

Hajjaj winced. The Algarvian minister had chosen a good moment to be undiplomatic. Negotiating with Swemmel was the last thing Hajjaj or any other sensible Zuwayzi wanted to do. *You will do as I tell you*, was the only style of negotiation the King of Unkerlant understood. With a sigh, Hajjaj said, "I shall hope you are right, then." Hoping and believing were two different things, however much Hajjaj wished them one and inseparable.

This time Balastro's smile looked less frightening. He said, "Believe me, we are in this fight for as long as it takes."

"I am glad to hear it," Hajjaj replied. *I hope it's true.* "I do also want to bring to your attention once more the evidence our soldiers and sorcerers have gathered of an Unkerlanter buildup of some size here in the north. Details, I am sure, will have been passed from General Ikhshid's office to your soldiers, but I would be remiss if I did not mention it myself."

"Fair enough." Balastro sounded almost amiable now—indulgent might have been a better word. "You've mentioned it. I'm sure our attaché here knows about it, as you say, and he will have passed on to Trapani whatever he thinks important."

And if he decides it isn't important, no one in your capital will hear about it, Hajjaj thought. That was what being the junior partner in an alliance meant. Algarve could make Zuwayza dance to her tune. The reverse did not hold true. Like a child tugging at an adult's arm, Zuwayza had to work hard to get Algarve to pay attention when she spoke.

Hajjaj did his best to tug: "Ikhshid and his staff reckon this a matter of some urgency, one you should take seriously."

"I'll pass that on to our attaché, too," Balastro said—aye, he might have been humoring a child.

I could point out how many times Algarve has already been wrong about Unkerlant. But Hajjaj kept his mouth shut. Balastro had already made it plain he wouldn't listen to much more. And Zuwayza had been wrong about Unkerlant, too. *If we'd been right, we would have stayed neutral when the war between the two behemoths started.*

And then, suddenly, Balastro's glass-green eyes sparkled. "And how are your own foreign relations these days, Your Excellency?"

"My—?" For a moment, Hajjaj didn't know what the Algarvian minister meant. Then he did, and rather wished he hadn't. "Minister Iskakis' wife prefers to remain in seclusion at my home for the time being," he said stiffly.

"I hope she's not too secluded to keep you from enjoying yourself." Balastro leered a very Algarvian leer. "Never a dull moment there, not between the sheets, but watch out when she loses her temper—and she will."

"I wouldn't know, not yet," Hajjaj said. Balastro rolled his eyes, as if to say Hajjaj was obviously mad, if harmlessly so. Hajjaj wasn't so sure Balastro was harmlessly mad. He went on, "You know, your learning such things about Tassi may have done more to hurt your kingdom's ties with Yanina than several misfortunes on the battlefield could have."

"Nonsense," Balastro said. "King Tsavellas isn't going to run off and embrace King Swemmel just because his minister here would sooner sheathe his lance in a handsome guardsman than in his own wife."

"Not for that, no," Hajjaj agreed. "But you, your Excellency, were altogether too public about where *your* lance found a sheath. Yaninans have long memories for that sort of slight, and they will avenge themselves, now and again, even when they would be wiser not to."

Balastro shook his head. "Nonsense," he repeated.

"I tell you, your Excellency, it is not," Hajjaj said earnestly.

"I understand them in this regard. They are very much like Zuwayzin there."

"Ha!" Balastro said. "I'm not going to lose any sleep over this, and you can believe me that King Mezentio isn't going to lose any sleep over it, either. I would advise *you* to lose a little sleep, though, your Excellency—enough to find out how tasty the treat is. What have you got to lose? Even if you're right, Iskakis will blame me, not you."

Hajjaj scratched his head. How strange to have his senior wife and the Algarvian minister telling him the same thing. And it wasn't that he wasn't tempted, either, or that Tassi had shown herself obviously unwilling. *What is it, then?* he wondered. Back in the days of the Kaunian Empire, some philosophers had advocated fighting temptation just because it *was* temptation. That had never made much sense to Hajjaj, and he couldn't see that it had done the ancient Kaunians much good, either.

Well? he asked himself, and gave the best answer he could: "I think it would be more trouble than it's worth."

"I'm sorry for you." Balastro got to his feet and bowed. "And I also think we've covered everything on account of which you summoned me. Good day, your Excellency. Always a pleasure." He swept out of Hajjaj's office with much less ceremony than the occasion called for.

In mild weather, Hajjaj might have been offended. As things were, he felt so glad to get out of his tunic and kilt that any other emotions ran a distant second. As soon as he was comfortably nude once more, he hurried to King Shazli's audience chamber. Shazli was talking about taxes with the treasury minister; Hajjaj waited till that troubled-looking official departed.

"Well?" Shazli asked after Hajjaj had bowed before him. "What does the Algarvian say?"

"What you would expect, your Majesty—no more, no less," Hajjaj replied. "He makes light of the enemy landings in Jelgava, says Algarve will triumph in spite of them, and predicts victory against Unkerlant, too."

"That would be nice." For a relatively young man, King Shazli could be dry when he chose. "The hope of victory against Unkerlant was what brought us into the war."

"I know," the foreign minister replied, in tones that could only mean, *Don't remind me.*

"Did he say why he thinks his kingdom will beat the Unkerlanters?" the king asked. "Or was it the usual promises with nothing behind them?"

"He offered the quiet front as proof King Swemmel has come to the end of Unkerlant's strength," Hajjaj said.

"Did you tell him what we have learned?" Shazli asked.

"Of course, your Majesty." The question came close to offending Hajjaj. But Balastro's attitude had annoyed him, too. "He thanked me most politely. After all, though, we're only naked savages, so what could we possibly know?"

"The Algarvians are very clever. Their chief failing is how well they know it," Shazli remarked. Hajjaj dipped his head in delight; he would have been pleased to claim the epigram for his own. The king continued, "I have also had another letter from Minister Iskakis, with him threatening to swell up like a skink if this Tassi woman isn't delivered to him forthwith."

"She does not wish it," Hajjaj said. "Something bad—something very bad—would happen to her if she were delivered to Iskakis. And you know of Balastro's role in this."

"Aye." King Shazli sighed. "The worst thing I can say about my foe is that he makes my friends look good." That was another fair epigram—and a searing verdict against the whole world.

Eleven

When Colonel Spinello went east to Waldsolms to report his brigade's condition to Brigadier Tampaste, who commanded his division, he was not a happy man. "Sir," he said, "I've got my men dug in east of Pewsum like so many moles. And if I had three times as many of them, and five times as many behemoths, and ten times as many dragons to back them up, I might be able to hang on when the Unkerlanters come down on me. I *might*, sir. I wouldn't guarantee it."

Tampaste couldn't have been much more than Spinello's age himself. "Do you know what, Colonel?" he said. "Over the past few days, our scouts and mages have concluded the Unkerlanters may be planning an attack here in the north after all."

Spinello rolled his eyes. "About fornicating time . . . sir. We've been worrying about it for weeks."

"All we are is the folk on the spot," Tampaste answered. "If that doesn't prove we can't possibly know what we're talking about, I don't know what would."

"How big an attack do they think is coming?" Spinello asked.

"They don't know," Tampaste said, and Spinello rolled his eyes again. The brigadier went on, "Swemmel's boys have been doing their best to mask whatever it is they're up to, so we're having a hard time telling."

"If it weren't something bigger than we'd like, they wouldn't be trying to hide it." Spinello hoped Tampaste would tell him he was wrong, he was worrying too much. Instead, the brigadier solemnly nodded. Spinello said, "I don't suppose there's any hope of reinforcements?"

At that, Tampaste threw back his head and laughed as if at the best joke in the world. "Tell me another one, Colonel," he said. "The odds would have been bad before the cursed islanders invaded Jelgava. Now? Well, my dear fellow, what can I say?" He spread his hands.

That said all that needed saying, or almost all, anyhow. Spinello asked, "How *are* things back in the east?"

"They've been on the ground in Jelgava for more than two weeks now. We haven't thrown them into the sea," Tampaste replied. "I've heard they're moving on Balvi, the capital. That's not official—all the reports from Trapani say the fighting is still by the beaches. But I've got a brother in Jelgava."

"Oh." Spinello whistled tunelessly. "Things can't be going any too well if they think they've got to lie to us."

"You have a nasty, suspicious mind," Tampaste said. "I would have more to say about it if the same thought hadn't occurred to me." He nodded to Spinello. "Go back and set your men digging again. The more holes they have, the better their chances are. Good luck, Colonel. Powers above go with you."

Spinello didn't know what sort of dismissal he'd expected. Whatever it was, it was nothing so abrupt as that. He rose, saluted, and went out onto the dusty streets of Waldsolms. Here in the town, the streets were paved. Once the buildings stopped, though, the cobblestones did, too, and the wind blew hard across the endless plains. He climbed into his carriage. "Back to Gleina," he told the driver.

The village between Waldsolms and Pewsum didn't pretend to be anything it wasn't. None of its streets had ever been paved. Spinello doubted any of them ever would be. A sergeant tramping along one of those dirt tracks called, "What's the word, Colonel?"

"They're going to hit us," Spinello answered. "Don't know how hard, don't know how soon, but they're going to hit us. If I had to guess, I'd say they won't wait long and they won't give us a little tap. Take it for what you think it's worth."

He could have said a lot of other things, but they would have amounted to more pungent versions of what he had said, so he didn't see the point. He hopped down from the carriage. His wounded leg protested. He tried to ignore it, though he limped a little going to the hut that did duty for brigade headquarters.

Inside the hut sat a jar of raw Unkerlanter spirits that did duty for the fine brandy Spinello would have preferred. As he lifted it, he asked himself, *Do you think the Unkerlanters will hit us before you can sober up?* When the answer to that turned out to be no, he poured a mug's worth out of the jar and started the serious business of getting drunk.

He hadn't got too far when somebody knocked on the door. Muttering a curse, he set down the mug and threw the door open. "Well?" he growled.

Jadwigai flinched. "I—I'm sorry, Colonel," the Kaunian girl stammered, turning red. "I'll come another time." She turned to go—more likely, to flee.

All at once, Spinello was ashamed of himself. "No, come

back. Please, come in," he said. "I'm sorry. There are plenty of people I don't want to see, but you're not any of them."

Still wary, Jadwigai asked, "Are you sure?" When Spinello vigorously—just how vigorously proved he had some spirits in him—nodded, she said, "All right," and walked past him into the hut. "I just wanted to ask how your meeting with Brigadier Tampaste went."

"It went so well, I'm getting drunk to celebrate." Spinello took another swig from the mug. "Want some?" Without waiting for an answer to match his own. "I'm glad you're here, sweetheart. I can tell you more of the truth than I can my own men. Isn't that funny?"

"I don't know." The brigade's mascot took a small sip. She made a face, but then sipped again. "What is the truth?"

"The truth," Spinello said grandly—aye, he'd poured down some spirits, all right—"is that we're in trouble. They're going to try to smash us flat, and they have a pretty bloody good chance of doing it." He emptied the mug and then filled it again.

"Oh." Jadwigai took a longer pull from her own mug of spirits. She looked west, sighed, and drank again. When she spoke once more, it was to herself, and in the classical Kaunian that was her birthspeech: "Well, I bought myself a little extra time."

Spinello eyed her profile, the way her pale lashes fluttered, the pulse in the hollow of her throat. *She thinks the luck is gone,* went through him. *So do I. And if it is . . .* He used classical Kaunian, too: "Will you do something for me?"

"What?" she asked, but her eyes said she already knew before he asked the next question.

He did ask it, but, for some reason, in Algarvian: "Will you sleep with me? I won't touch you if you say no—by the powers above, I *won't*—but I want you, and I don't think we've got much time."

Jadwigai set the mug down on a stool. "Aye," she whispered. "You could force me. We both know all about that. Since you don't, since you haven't—why not?"

It wasn't much of a recommendation, but Spinello decided he would take it—and Jadwigai. Altogether sober, he might not have. He might have thought that, no matter what he said, she couldn't very well tell him no, not unless she wanted to go from pampered mascot to cursed Kaunian in the blink of an eye. With spirits coursing through him, with Jadwigai unbuttoning her Algarvian-issue tunic, such thoughts never once entered his mind.

When she was naked, she lay down on the Algarvian-issue cot he used in lieu of the benches lining the walls of the hut. He shed his own uniform in a hurry. "I'll do my best to make you enjoy it, too," he promised.

Rather to his surprise, his best turned out to be good enough. He'd never managed to kindle Vanai. Of course, she'd despised him, which was half the fun of bedding her. The only time she'd shown any warmth was the last time, when he told her he'd been sent to Unkerlant—and that, without a doubt, was because it *was* the last time.

Jadwigai might have feared him, but she didn't hate him. Maybe that made the difference. "You see?" he said, grinning at her after she let out a gasp that sounded distinctly startled.

She nodded. "Aye. I do see." Sure enough, she seemed astonished.

"My turn now." Spinello mounted her. He'd wondered if he would find her a maiden, as he had Vanai, but no. What had happened there in western Forthweg before she became the brigade's pet? Maybe—no, certainly—such questions were better left unasked. Considering how much pleasure she gave him, Spinello didn't want to ask any questions just then.

Afterwards, she said, "You were gentle. You were kind. You have been, all along. All the soldiers here have been kind to me. And yet . . ."

"What?" Spinello asked lazily. He felt too pleased with the world, too pleased with himself, to worry about any question Jadwigai might put.

Or so he thought, till she said, "How can you be like this with me and . . . the other way with so many Kaunians?"

Spinello shrugged. "It's war. It's revenge. It's just one of those things." He could afford to answer like that. His people built the special camps. They didn't have to dwell in them.

Jadwigai might have had something sharp to say about that. She'd never been shy, and letting him have her might have made her think she could be frank—and she'd been drinking, too. But, before she could reply, thunder rolled in from the west. Only it wasn't thunder. It was countless eggs, all bursting at once.

"Oh, by the powers above!" Spinello exclaimed, and sprang from the cot. He dressed with frantic haste. Jadwigai clothed herself almost as fast as he did. Even so, he hadn't finished buttoning his tunic before eggs started bursting in and all around Gleina, too.

"It's the attack, the one we've been waiting for," Jadwigai said.

"It certainly is." Spinello didn't think he'd ever heard so many eggs burst all at the same time—it might have been a continuous wall of noise, and it went on and on. He'd never imagined he would hear worse than what he'd known in Sulingen, but this fit the bill.

Someone pounded on the door to the hut, shouting, "Colonel Spinello! Colonel Spinello, sir!"

"I'm here." Spinello opened the door. The crystallomancer outside looked as if he'd just taken a punch in the jaw: he was wobbling, glassy-eyed. "Are you all right? What's going on?"

"Sir, there are at least three breakthroughs on our brigade's front, and I'm getting shouts for help from the north and south," the mage answered.

"Tell 'em no," Spinello said. "We've got nothing to give."

"I know that, sir," the crystallomancer said. "One of the mages . . . one of 'em got killed while I was talking with him, sir. The energy, it's . . . hard for a man to take." That no doubt explained his punch-drunk state.

More eggs burst, all over Gleina. Spinello smelled smoke and heard flames crackling. A metal fragment of eggshell buried itself in the doorframe a few inches from his head. He hardly even flinched. "We've got to fight back as hard as we can," he said. "If the Unkerlanters break through our lines, the powers below will eat our whole army in the north."

The crystallomancer nodded, but just then a man on a unicorn splashed with green and brown paint galloped through the village shouting, "Behemoths! Unkerlanter behemoths! There's millions of 'em, and they're all heading this way!"

Spinello peered west. The cloud of dust there wouldn't hold millions of behemoths, but it would hold dozens or hundreds. And it wasn't the only such cloud he saw. "We aren't going to hold Gleina," he said, and then, "I wonder if we can hold Waldsolms." One more thought flashed through his mind: *I wonder if we can hold anywhere.* He looked back over his shoulder at Jadwigai. "You ready to move fast, sweetheart?" She nodded, her eyes enormous but less afraid than they had been before Spinello first lowered his mouth to her pink-tipped breasts. "Good," he told her. "Now we have to see if we can stay ahead of Swemmel's little chums till we're able to throw them back. If we ever are. Come on." More dragons painted in Unkerlanter rock-gray flew low over Gleina as they fled the burning village.

News-sheet vendors cried their wares as Ealstan came home from Pybba's pottery works. "Heavy fighting in northern Unkerlant!" they shouted. "Algarvians inflict heavy losses on Swemmel's savages in fierce defensive battles!"

Ealstan fumbled in his belt pouch and came up with a couple of coppers for a sheet. The redheads had occupied Forthweg for close to five years now. He'd learned to read between the lines of their lies to get some notion of the truth hiding behind them. When they talked about "fierce defensive battles," that meant the Unkerlanters were hitting them hard. He was always willing—no, eager—to read about anybody hitting the Algarvians hard.

With his nose in the news sheet, he almost walked past his block of flats. He almost broke his neck going upstairs, because he kept trying to read and climb steps at the same time. He almost walked too far down the hall and gave the coded knock on the door to the wrong flat. And he still had the news sheet in front of his face when Vanai opened the right door.

She looked indignant when he finally lowered the sheet. Kissing her didn't mollify her much. But when he said, "I think the redheads are really in trouble this time," she was suddenly all smiles.

"Tell me," she urged. "Tell me right now."

"They're talking about defensive battles," Ealstan said. "Whenever they talk about defensive battles, that means they're taking a pounding. And they're talking about fighting in Sommerda, and Sommerda was a long way behind their line not so long ago. They think people are too stupid to look at a map to find out where these places are, but they're wrong."

"We can look at a map." Vanai went and pulled an atlas from a bookshelf. "You got this for me when I had to hide here all the time." She made a face and corrected herself: "The last time I had to hide here all the time, I mean." She didn't leave the flat these days. Her sorcerous disguise still worked, but for shorter and shorter—and ever less predictable—stretches of time.

Ealstan flipped the atlas open to a map of Derlavai. He started to laugh. "I didn't realize it was *this* old."

"I did," Vanai told him. "It dates from back before the Six Years' War." No kingdom of Forthweg showed on the map; Algarve ruled the eastern half of the land, with Unkerlant holding the west. She went on, "This map doesn't show where Sommerda is. Go to the one of Unkerlant."

"All right." Ealstan turned pages till he found it. When he did, he whistled in surprise. "Even I hadn't realized it was *that* far east of the Cottbus River. Powers above, the Algarvians *are* in trouble if the Unkerlanters have come that far this fast."

"Good." Vanai wrapped her arms around her enormous belly. Surely the baby couldn't wait more than another few days. "I hope they take back all their own kingdom. Then I hope they come into Forthweg and take it away from the Algarvians, too. I hope they do it fast. It's the only way I can think of to have even a few Kaunians left alive here."

Ealstan nodded. He couldn't deny that. He had his own worries about the Unkerlanters. If they overran Forthweg, would King Penda ever return? Or would King Swemmel try to rule the kingdom as his father had in the distant days when the atlas was printed? That mattered a great deal to him. But he had to admit that Vanai's concern was more urgent.

Kaunian-lover. In Forthweg, even before the Algarvians overran it, that had been a name with which to tar a man. Ealstan didn't care. He reached out and touched Vanai's hand.

She looked up, startled; she'd been studying the map hard. But she'd been thinking along with him, too, as she often did. She said, "I wonder if the Kaunians who are left will have to go on disguising themselves—ourselves—as Forthwegians. That would be the end of Kaunianity in Forthweg."

"I know," Ealstan said quietly. He didn't know what to do about it. He didn't think anyone could do anything about it. He also didn't think he could say that to Vanai. What he did say was, "Turn to the map of Jelgava. I want to see where the fighting's moved there."

"All right." Vanai turned pages with what looked like relief.

"The news sheet says there's fighting in Salacgriva, and says that's an oceanfront town," Ealstan said. He and Vanai bent over the map, their heads close together. "Why, those lying whoresons!" he exclaimed. "Salacgriva is more than halfway from the sea to Balvi."

"They *are* in trouble," Vanai said softly. "I've dreamt for so long that they would be, and now they finally are. But will anything still be standing by the time they're finally beaten?"

That was another question with no good answer. Instead of trying to answer it, Ealstan kissed her. She smiled at him, which made him think he'd done about as well as he could do.

When he went off to work the next morning, the news-sheet vendors were yelling about the terrible price the Unkerlanters had paid for overrunning Sommerda. Ealstan smiled and walked on without buying a sheet. He could figure out what that meant: Sommerda had fallen. The news sheets were putting the best face they could on it, but they couldn't deny the brute fact.

Pybba waited for Ealstan when he walked into the pottery. "Do you sleep in your kilns?" Ealstan asked him. As far as he could tell, Pybba was always there. He talked about having a home, but that seemed talk and nothing else.

"Only when I'm in my cups. Get it—my cups?" Pybba laughed uproariously. "Now that you're finally here, you lazy good-for-nothing, come on into my office. We've got things to talk about, you and I." He pointed with a stubby finger, much scarred from old burns, toward the door to his sanctum.

With that door slammed shut behind them, Ealstan spoke first: "Mezentio's bastards really are taking it on the chin now."

"Aye, they are," Pybba agreed. "That's one of the things I want to talk to you about: won't be long, if things keep going the way they are, before we'll be able to rise up against the redheads, throw 'em out of Eoforwic, maybe throw 'em out of the whole of Forthweg, too."

Excitement blazed through Ealstan. "That would be wonderful," he breathed. "And about time, too."

Voice dry, the pottery magnate answered, "It does help to have the Algarvians distracted, you know. But we've got to rise up before the Unkerlanters do all the work for us, or else we'll never get our own kingdom back again."

Ealstan nodded. How not, when the same thought had gone through his mind the night before? "What can I do to help?" he breathed.

"Well, you've already done this and that," Pybba allowed. "That little spell you came up with to let you look like an Algarvian and get your wife out of the Kaunian quarter—we've used that a couple of times, and it's worked."

"Good," Ealstan said.

"The redheads are looking for Kaunians who look like Forthwegians," Pybba said. "They aren't looking for Forthwegians who look like them. One of their special constables, a whoreson who had to be part bloodhound by the way he sniffed out everything we did, isn't among those present any more thanks to that little spell, and we don't miss him one bloody bit, either."

"Good," Ealstan said again, this time with savage gusto.

"Aye, not so bad." Pybba raised a shaggy eyebrow. "I almost forgive you for taking up with a Kaunian girl."

"That's nice." Ealstan raised an eyebrow, too. "And I almost forgive you for just almost forgiving me."

He'd hoped to anger Pybba. Instead, he made him laugh. "If you were as pure as you think you are . . ." the pottery magnate began, but then he checked himself. "Maybe you are, by the powers above. When you come down to it, that's a scary thought. Go on, get back to work." His voice rose to a familiar bellow. "You think I pay you for sitting around doing nothing?"

Ealstan always had plenty of work to do, even when dealing with Pybba's legitimate business. When he added on the rest, he wondered how he ever slept at night. But he didn't stay late, as he had so often in the dark days when Vanai was a captive in the Kaunian quarter. With her so close to her time, and with no one but him she could trust, he wanted to be there as much as he could. If Pybba didn't like it, he would have thrown his job in the pottery magnate's face. But Pybba hadn't said a word.

On the way home, Ealstan walked through the park where he'd gone with Vanai just after she worked out the spell that let her look like a Forthwegian. He'd named her Thelberge there, when he'd run into Ethelhelm the drummer and singer, whose books he'd once kept. *Poor Ethelhelm*, he thought. *Poor, cursed Ethelhelm*. A man of half-Kaunian blood, the musician had been putty in the Algarvians' hands. He'd liked his riches too well, and had got much too involved with the redheads, though he'd finally used the sorcery to escape their clutches.

I wonder why I thought of him. Maybe it was just going through the park. Maybe it was the musicians playing on the grass—although Ethelhelm wouldn't have had much to do with the trumpeters or the viol player. The drummer, now, the drummer wasn't bad.

The drummer, in fact, was good enough to make Ealstan pause and listen for a little while and toss some silver into the bowl the band had set in front of them. A nondescript, stocky fellow, the drummer could have made much more money playing in clubs or even in theaters. He sounded . . . He sounded like someone doing an excellent impression of Ethelhelm.

After a bit, the drummer's eyes met Ealstan's. That wasn't surprising; only eight or ten people were standing around listening. What was surprising was that the drummer's eyebrows rose slightly, as if he recognized Ealstan. If he did, he had the advantage, for Ealstan was sure he'd never set eyes on the fellow before.

He'd almost got back to the block of flats when he stopped so suddenly, the woman behind him bumped into him and let out a

torrent of shrill complaint. He apologized, but too absentmind-
edly to suit her.

Up in the flat, though, he said, "I'm sure that was Ethelhelm,
sorcerously disguised to look all Forthwegian. He can hide the
way he looks, but he can't hide the way he plays the drums.
And he knew who I was—I'm sure of that, too."

"For his sake, I hope you're wrong," Vanai said. "You told
him as much yourself: if he wants to stay safe, he has to stay
away from music. If you recognized who he was, someone else
will, too, and then the Algarvians will have him."

"I know. That would be too bad." Ealstan had had his quarrels with Ethelhelm—he'd had quarrels with most of his em-
ployers—but he wouldn't have wished falling into Algarvian
captivity on anyone, especially on anyone of even partly Kaunian blood.

Looking back on it, Vanai had trouble defining exactly when
she went into labor. Her womb had been squeezing now and
again throughout the last couple of months of her pregnancy.
She thought that was normal, but had no one she could ask.
Over the couple of days after Ealstan saw, or thought he saw,
Ethelhelm, the squeezes grew stronger and came more often.

Are these labor pains? she wondered as she walked around
the flat. They didn't keep her from walking, or from doing anything she needed to do. And they didn't hurt. How could they be
pains if they didn't hurt?

She lay down beside Ealstan, wriggled till she found the least
uncomfortable position—finding a comfortable one, with her
belly so enormous, was impossible these days—and fell asleep.
When she woke, right around dawn, it was to the sound of a
snap. She also discovered she needed to use the pot, but she
couldn't stop herself before she got there, and dribbled on the
floor.

"What is it?" Ealstan asked sleepily.

"I think . . . my bag of waters just broke," Vanai answered.
She hoped that was what it was. If it wasn't that, it was something worse.

"Does that mean this is it—I mean, that you'll have the baby pretty soon?" The mattress creaked as Ealstan sat up in bed.

"I don't know," Vanai said irritably. The truth was, she didn't know much more about it than he did. But it was happening to her, not to him. It hardly seemed fair. He'd been there at the beginning. Why shouldn't he be there at the end, too? She went on, "I think—oof!"

"What's the matter?" Ealstan could hear that something was.

"Now I know . . . why they're called . . . labor pains." Vanai got the words out in small bunches. This time, when her womb clenched, she really felt it. Maybe the water in there had shielded her from the worst of the squeezes. Nothing was shielding her any more. She'd been looking forward to having the baby. Now, all at once, she wasn't so sure.

"Pybba won't get his accounts cast today," Ealstan said. "I expect he'll figure out why I'm not there."

"I expect so," Vanai agreed—once the pang eased, she could speak freely. She also seemed to have stopped dribbling. She got up off the pot and waddled back to bed. She hadn't been there long before her womb clamped down again. She grunted. This one was stronger than the last.

"Can I get you anything?" Ealstan asked anxiously.

Vanai shook her head. "I'm going to do this till I'm done," she said. "I can tell. It's real now." She wanted to laugh at herself—she made it sound as if she were going into battle. But the laughter wouldn't come. This *was* a battle, and some women didn't come back from it. She wished she hadn't thought of that.

To keep from thinking, she got out of bed and started walking. It wasn't so easy now, not with the pangs coming every few minutes. When the third or fourth one caught her in the middle of a step, she almost fell. *That would not be a good thing to do, not now*, she told herself. She stood there, waiting for the labor pain to end and her belly to ease back from rock hardness. That seemed to take a very long time. She was gasping by the time it finally happened. Moving slowly and with great care, she walked back to the bed and lay down.

"Are you all right?" Ealstan looked faintly green. But he stayed by the bed and clutched her hand, and she didn't suppose he could do much more than that.

"I'm as well as I can be," Vanai answered. "I don't think I'll do any more walking, though, thank you all the same."

Before very long, her womb squeezed in on itself again. The baby didn't like that, and kicked and wiggled as if in indignation. Because there was very little room in there and the walls of the womb were tight, that hurt, too, where it usually hadn't before. Vanai hissed, which made Ealstan jump.

When the tension eased, she said, "This is all supposed to happen, I think." Both of them had read as much as they could about what happened when a baby was born, but the Forthwegian books on the subject told less than Vanai would have liked. Back in Oyngestun, her grandfather had had classical Kaunian gynecological texts in his library, but they might as well have been a mile beyond the moon for all the good they did her now.

And the Kaunians of imperial times had known a lot less about medicine than modern folk did—even the Forthwegians whom the descendants of those Kaunians reckoned barbarians. A lot of what was in Brivibas' texts was probably wrong.

Ealstan suddenly said, "You look like yourself again, not like a Forthwegian."

Vanai started to laugh again, only to break off in the middle when another pang hit. She started to say something in spite of the labor pain, only to discover she couldn't. What her body was doing took charge now, and her mind had to wait till her body gave it leave to work once more. In the time between pains, she said, "That's the least of my worries." Sweat ran down her face; her hair, newly re-dyed black, felt wet and matted. She might have been running for hours. People called giving birth *labor* for a reason, too.

And it went on and on. The pangs came closer together, and each one seemed a little stronger, a little more painful, than the one just before. After what felt like forever, Vanai asked, "What time is it?"

"Midmorning," Ealstan answered.

She almost shouted that he had to be lying to her, that it had to be midafternoon at the very least. But when she looked at the light through the windows, she realized he was right. In a small voice, she asked, "Would you get me a little wine?"

He frowned. "Should you have it?"

"I don't know," she answered. "I don't *think* I'll puke it up if I drink it, and my mouth is dry as the Zuwayzi desert right now."

"All right." Ealstan brought it to her. He also brought in a wide-mouthed basin in case she proved mistaken. But the sweet red wine went down smoothly and stayed down, and she felt better for it. Her mouth no longer seemed caked with dust.

Another eternity that might have been an hour or two dragged by. Ealstan stayed by the side of the bed, squeezing her hand, running a cool, damp cloth over her forehead and neck every so often, occasionally holding up the winecup so she could take another sip. She was glad to have him there, gladder than she would have been to have a midwife, even if a midwife knew more.

And then, all at once, she wasn't. "You—you—you *man*, you!" she said furiously, in between two pangs that hardly left her room to breathe, let alone talk. "If it weren't for you and your lousy prick, I wouldn't be in this mess now."

Ealstan looked stricken. After a moment, though, his face cleared. "One of the books said that when you started calling me names, it was a sign the baby would come soon," he told her.

Vanai called him more names then, all the names she could think of, in both Forthwegian and classical Kaunian. She hated to stop when the next labor pang took her, but had very little choice; just breathing through it was quite hard enough. But she resumed when it finally ebbed.

After a few more pangs, she felt the urge to use the pot again, as if her bowels badly needed to move. When she said so—her sudden storm of anger against Ealstan had passed away as fast as it blew up—he answered, "That means you're ready to push the baby out."

That wasn't what it felt like. It felt as if she were straining to pass a stool the size of a football. She'd heard that a couple of times, from women talking back in Oyngestun before the war. She hadn't imagined it could be true—how could having a baby be so crude? Now she found out for herself.

But, no matter how hard she bore down, the baby didn't

seem to want to move. "I'm trying to shit a boulder," she panted as Ealstan ran that cloth across her face. "I'm trying to, but it's stuck."

"Keep trying," he said. "It's what you're supposed to do."

She had very little choice. Her body kept straining to force out the baby. It would have kept on doing that whether she wanted it to or not. The most she could do was concentrate, take a deep breath, and try to help it along. She pushed with all her might—and this time felt movement. That made her push harder than ever. She let out a noise half squeal, half groan, and all effort.

"Oh, by the powers above," Ealstan said softly. "Here comes the head." He let out a startled squawk. "No—here comes the baby."

Once Vanai had pushed out the head, everything else was easy. That was the hard part, both figuratively and literally. Shoulders, torso, and legs followed in short order. So did the afterbirth. Ealstan made gulping noises. "You'll have to throw away these sheets," Vanai said, before asking the question she should have asked first: "Is it a boy or a girl?"

"A girl," Ealstan answered. "Here—I'm tying the cord with one hank of dark brown yarn and one of yellow. Now I'm cutting it. Now . . ." He held up the baby. She started to cry, and quickly went from purple to pink.

"Give her to me," Vanai said. "Give me Saxburh." That was the girl's name—the Forthwegian girl's name—they'd picked. Vanai also thought of her as Silelai—her own mother's name. If things in Forthweg ever improved for Kaunians, perhaps the baby could use that name, too.

Ealstan handed her to her mother as if he had in his hands an egg that might burst at any moment. Saxburh had a little hair, incredibly fine. What there was of it was dark. Her eyes were dark blue, but that meant nothing: all babies' eyes were that color at first. Whether her skin would prove fair or swarthy, whether she'd be lean like a Kaunian or blocky like a Forthwegian—who could say? Too soon for such guesses.

"Here," Vanai said, and set the baby on her breast. Saxburh knew what to do; she began sucking right away. That made

Vanai's womb contract painfully. She let out a hiss and began to realize how worn she was. She felt as if she'd been run over by a wagon full of logs.

And then Ealstan had the nerve to say, "Move a little." But when, after a groan, she did, he swept off the fouled bedclothes and gave her a pair of drawers and a cloth pad of the sort she wore when her courses came. She set Saxburh down for a moment so she could put them on. The baby's high, thin wail made Vanai pick her up again in a hurry.

As Saxburh went back to nursing, Vanai asked Ealstan, "Could you get me something to eat, please? I feel like I haven't had anything in years."

"Of course." He hurried away and came back with bread and sausage and olives and cheese and two big mugs full of wine. As Vanai fell to like a famished wolf, he raised his mug high. "To our baby!"

"To our baby!" Vanai echoed with her mouth full. After she swallowed, she took a long pull at her own mug. She wanted to bathe. She wanted to sleep for a year. For the time being, she was content to lie there with Saxburh and try to rest.

Major Scoufas looked up from his mug of ale at Colonel Sabrino. "Well, your Excellency, now I know you are truly in bad odor at King Mezentio's court," the Yaninan dragonflier said.

Sabrino's mug held spirits, not ale. He hadn't got very far down it, though, not yet. "I told you that the day my wing got here," he replied. "Why do you say you know it now?"

"Because if your superiors cared for you at all, they would have sent you north to try to stem the Unkerlanter tide there," Scoufas replied. "But no—they have left you here to keep us Yaninans company. And I happen to know they are sending everything they can possibly spare to the north."

That called for a long pull at the mug of spirits. Sabrino wished he could have contradicted Scoufas. Unfortunately, the Yaninan was right. Sabrino said all he could say: "I am a soldier. I can only go where my orders take me. I can only do what my superiors tell me."

"I understand that, and the answer does you honor," Major Scoufas said. "But is it not true that something very like a catastrophe is taking shape for Algarve in the north?" He spoke with a certain avid interest. If Algarve went down to defeat against Unkerlant, Sabrino didn't see how Yanina could avoid also going down to defeat. That didn't stop some Yaninans from enjoying Algarve's misfortune. Having tasted defeat so often themselves, they enjoyed seeing the once-invincible Algarvians learn what the dish tasted like.

"Disaster?" Sabrino shrugged. "I don't think it's so bad as that, Major. Sooner or later—probably sooner—Swemmel's men will run out of soldiers, and we'll mend the front, the way we've done here in the Duchy of Grelz."

He realized, too late, he should have called it the Kingdom of Grelz. Scoufas raised a dark, elegantly arched eyebrow to show he realized the same thing. Using the Unkerlanter name for the region showed how much ground the Algarvians had lost in the past year.

And he realized he was liable to be talking through his hat when he claimed things would soon get better in the north. The Algarvian army defending that long and vital stretch of front seemed simply to have disappeared. Algarvian reports from the north grew more tight-lipped day by day. Swemmel's men, by contrast, declared victory after victory and claimed the recapture of town after town. If those claims were lies, the Algarvians might have done a better job of denying them.

Scoufas said, "If you were truly a lucky man, Colonel, or a well-favored one, you might have been sent off to Jelgava and escaped from Unkerlant altogether."

That held some truth, too, but rather less. Not many Algarvian formations were leaving Unkerlant to fight in the east. Mezentio didn't have enough men in Unkerlant to hold back Swemmel's soldiers as things were. The east would just have to take care of itself.

And if it doesn't? Sabrino wondered. *If it can't?* He finished the spirits at a gulp. *Then we're in even more trouble than we were before.*

He eyed Major Scoufas. "You may not like Algarvians all

that well, but I suggest you remember one thing: before the Unkerlanters get into Algarve—if we're so unlucky as to have that happen—they have to go through Yanina."

Like most Yaninans, Scoufas had an expressive face. The emotion he expressed wasn't delight, nor anything close to it. Sabrino smiled. Maybe Scoufas thought he was allowed to snipe at Algarvians but they couldn't say anything about his kingdom. That wasn't how things worked, no matter what he thought.

Before either wing commander made the occasion more unpleasant, a Yaninan crystallomancer burst into the peasant hut where they were drinking and spoke rapidly in his own language. Yaninan always put Sabrino in mind of wine pouring out of a jug, glug glug glug. But he didn't speak it, and had to ask, "What's he saying?"

"The Unkerlanters seem to be stirring down here after all," Scoufas replied. "They're trying to cross the Trusetal River and set up a bridgehead on the east side."

"Can't have that." Sabrino sprang to his feet. "If they get a company over today, it'll be a brigade tomorrow, complete with behemoths."

Scoufas dipped his head in the Yaninan equivalent of a nod. "Aye, that is so," he said. "We may not love each other, but there is nothing like a common foe to point out where our interests lie."

"True enough," Sabrino said. "Shall we go pay a call on the common foe and try to make him extinct rather than common?"

"Extinct?" Scoufas frowned; he needed a moment to understand the wordplay, which robbed Sabrino of half his pleasure in it. But then the Yaninan smiled. "Oh, I see. Aye, indeed it would be well if the Unkerlanters were extinct." They both hurried out of the hut, shouting for their men.

The Yaninan dragon handler with the big black mustache had taken it upon himself to minister to Sabrino's dragon. He was as good as any Algarvian could have been. His name was Tsaldaris. He had no breeding to speak of; had he come from a notable family, he would have been flying dragons, not handling them. He spoke Algarvian after a fashion: enough to talk about dragons, at least. As Sabrino mounted the screeching, bad-tempered beast, Tsaldaris said, "Careful. Cinnabar—*pfui!*" He made a disgusted noise and held thumb and forefinger close together to show he'd had little to give the dragon.

"Any hope of getting more any time soon?" Sabrino asked, fastening his harness so the dragon couldn't pitch him off no matter how much it wanted to.

Tsaldaris tossed his head, as Yaninans did when they meant no. "Supply got unicorn's prick up arse," he said, which, Sabrino feared, summed things up altogether too well.

Sabrino waved to Major Scoufas. Scoufas waved back. Sabrino looked to his own men. They were ready. He'd known they would be. And so were the Yaninans. They made perfectly good dragon-fliers. Their trouble was, they had not enough dragons and not enough men trained to fly them, especially when facing a foe who came in such great numbers as the Unkerlanters did.

At Sabrino's nod, Tsaldaris loosed the chain that held his dragon to its stake. Screaming fury at the world, the dragon leaped into the air with a great thunder of wings. Algarvian dragons painted in varying patterns of green and white and red rose with it. So did their Yaninan counterparts, those beasts painted simply red and white. Some carried eggs slung beneath them; others would protect those dragons and do what damage they could with their flames. Sabrino cursed the dearth of cinnabar. "The land of the Ice People," he muttered. "The Mamming Hills." Plenty of cinnabar both places. The Algarvians would never get to use any of it, not any more.

Flying west, though, always made him feel better. When he was flying west, he was going on the attack. He'd had too much of the Unkerlanters' coming to him. He was, he'd always been, a man who wanted to make things happen, not one who sat back and waited for them to happen to him.

He didn't need long to spot the Unkerlanter bridgehead. Eggs were bursting all around the edges of it. Most of them looked to be Unkerlanter eggs—King Swemmel's soldiers had far more tossers than did the Yaninans facing them, too. And . . . Sabrino started cursing again, this time in good earnest. The Unkerlanters had thrown a plank bridge across the

Trusetal River—their artisans were clever at such things—and
were sending behemoths across to the eastern bank.

Sabrino had two crystals with him—one to link him to his
own squadron leaders; the other, with somewhat different emanations, to Major Scoufas. He spoke into both of them at the
same time: "Those behemoths are our target. If we can slay
them and wreck that bridge, the footsoldiers on the ground
ought to be able to close out the rest of the Unkerlanters this
side of the river."

Had they been Algarvian soldiers, he would have been sure
of it. With Yaninans, one could only hope. However good their
dragonfliers were, their footsoldiers had singularly failed to
cover themselves with glory. No, plurally, for the Yaninans had
failed again and again. But Sabrino couldn't say that, no matter
how true it was, for fear of offending Major Scoufas, who was
as touchy as any Yaninan.

The dragons carrying eggs dove on the bridge. The Unkerlanters had heavy sticks mounted nearby to protect it, of course.
One dragon—an Algarvian beast—went straight into the Trusetal. Sabrino cursed yet again: one more comrade he would
never see again. But eggs burst in large numbers, in the river
and on both banks. Then one struck the bridge, square in the
center. The burst of sorcerous energy pitched two behemoths
into the water and set the bridge afire. Sabrino whooped.

Whooping still, he gave new orders: "Now we attack the behemoths on the east bank of the Trusetal."

"Cover us, if you would be so kind," Major Scoufas said.
"My men and I will show you what your allies can do."

Although Sabrino had been about to order his own dragonfliers to swoop down on the Unkerlanter behemoths, he was
willing to salve Scoufas' pride, and so he answered, "Let it be
as you say."

"My thanks," the Yaninan told him, and gave his own orders
in his own language. Sabrino understood not a word of them,
but what they were was hardly in doubt. And, almost as if diving on targets in a practice field, the Yaninans carried out the attack. The behemoths below scattered, as targets would not and
could not, but that mattered little, for what was a behemoth's

speed when measured against a dragon's? If Scoufas and his men had to get a little closer to flame the behemoths than they would have needed to do with more cinnabar in them, what difference did that make?

But, just as Sabrino began to gloat in good earnest, Captain Orosio's face appeared in the crystal that kept the wing commander in touch with his fellow Algarvians. "Enemy dragons!" the squadron leader shouted. "A whole great swarm of them, coming out of the west!"

They were painted rock-gray, of course, and Sabrino hadn't seen them against the clouds. *I'm getting old,* he thought. If he wanted to get much older, he would have to fight hard now. "Melee!" he ordered. "If we break up their formation, we have the edge." The Unkerlanters did fine as long as they acted in accordance with someone else's plan. If they had to think for themselves, to decide quickly, they had trouble.

A wild melee it was, too, once the Algarvians got in amongst the Unkerlanters. Dragons spun crazily through the sky. Sabrino tried to flame one of Swemmel's sparrowhawks—that was the name the Algarvians gave the Unkerlanters' best dragonfliers— but couldn't come close enough to do it. When an Unkerlanter dragon got on his tail, he had to fly like a man possessed to keep from getting flamed himself. But he managed to blaze the enemy dragonflier with his stick—a lucky blaze, but he was glad to take it—and the rock-gray beast went wild, attacking every dragon around it. Since the Unkerlanters had far more dragons in the air than he did, that helped his side more than theirs.

It didn't do enough to help the Yaninan dragonfliers down below, though. The Unkerlanters had enough dragons to assail the Algarvians and Yaninans at the same time. Major Scoufas' image appeared in Sabrino's crystal. "We have to pull out!" he shouted.

"We haven't got rid of the bridgehead," Sabrino said, blazing at another Unkerlanter dragonflier and missing.

"If we stay, we still will not be rid of the bridgehead—and the Unkerlanters will be rid of us," Scoufas replied.

Sabrino cursed as he pondered. Had he not judged Scoufas right about the first part of that, he would have ignored the second; men and dragons fought to be used up at need. As things were . . . "Aye," he said bitterly, and began the tricky business of getting his wing free. They'd hurt the Unkerlanters, but Swemmel still had men—and, worse, behemoths—on this bank of the Trusetal.

All things considered, Garivald was pleased with the crop he and Obilot had managed to plant. They'd started late, with the mule they'd hired from Dagulf. But, looking over the soft green of growing barley and rye, he thought they should end up with plenty to get them through the winter.

"Not so bad," he told her after a long day of weeding.

"No, not so bad," she agreed. "The farther we are from anybody else, the better, too." She dipped a horn spoon into the porridge of barley and leeks they were eating for supper.

Garivald grunted. "That's true enough, by the powers above. I didn't think I'd end up a hermit, but you never know, do you?"

"No." Obilot's eyes went far away. Back to whatever she'd had before the Algarvians swarmed into the Duchy of Grelz? Maybe. Garivald had never had the nerve to ask such questions, and she'd never said what drove her into the irregulars. All she said now was, "You never know."

Sooner or later, they would have to go back into Linnich. The farm had no salt lick; they could trade herbs and vegetables from the garden plot for salt, and for tools, and maybe for some chickens or ducks, too. When spring came again, they would need a draught animal for the plowing. Garivald was in no hurry. Not even the thought of seeing Dagulf cheered him. His friend reminded him of all he'd lost when Zossen vanished off the face of the earth.

And he wasn't sure he could trust Dagulf, not any more. They hadn't seen each other for a couple of years. A lot had happened in that time. A lot could have happened, too. The only way to find out would be the hard way.

Filled with such gloomy thoughts, Garivald was glad to lie down on the benches against the wall of the hut he and Obilot had taken for their own and go to sleep. As usual, a day in the fields made him sleep as if he were stuffed into a rest crate till the next morning.

When he woke, he ate more barley porridge and went out to the fields to begin all over again. He might not do exactly the same thing day after day, but he always had plenty to do. No one who lived on a farm ever complained of too little to do, not between planting time and harvest.

He'd just thrown a rock at a rabbit—and, to his disgust, missed, for it would have gone into the pot had he hit it—when three men came up the path leading to Linnich. They were the first men he'd seen on the path since he and Obilot found this farm. Now that spring had come, it was hardly a path at all, being much overgrown. Whoever had used this place before he came hadn't had much use for company, either.

Those three men saw him, too. One of them waved. Without thinking, Garivald waved back. He cursed himself for a fool afterwards, but it probably wouldn't have mattered one way or the other. Two of the men carried sticks slung on their back; the third had his in his hand. If they were bandits, Garivald was in trouble. If they served King Swemmel, he was liable to be in more trouble still.

"Hail!" called the one who'd waved. "Are you Fariulf?"

"Aye, that's me," Garivald answered with something approaching relief. If they were using his false name, they didn't want him for the crime of fighting the Algarvians without doing it under King Swemmel's auspices. He hadn't done much as Fariulf to get into trouble. "What do you want?" he added as the men came forward.

Obilot was watching from the garden. He wondered if she would get a stick from inside the farmhouse and start blazing. But he stood between her and the three oncoming men, who'd got very close by then.

"Are you hale?" asked the fellow who was doing the talking. He answered his own question: "Aye, I can see you are. Come along with us."

"Come along with you where?" Garivald asked.

"Someplace you should have been long before this: King

Swemmel's army," replied the—the impresser, Garivald realized he had to be. "You think you can sit out the war here in the middle of nowhere? That's not how things work, pal. Come along quiet-like and nothing bad'll happen to you till the cursed Algarvians have their chance at your worthless hide." By then, all three aimed their sticks at him.

Considering what they could have done to him, considering what they surely would have done to him had they known his real name, going into the Unkerlanter army didn't strike Garivald as such a bad bargain. All he said was, "Let me tell my woman good-bye." He pointed back toward Obilot.

He expected them to refuse; impressers had an evil name. Maybe they were relieved he didn't put up more of a fuss, for the man who talked for them replied, "Go ahead, but make it snappy."

"I will." Garivald beckoned Obilot forward. She came with obvious reluctance, but she came. Her face was hard and closed, showing nothing to the impressers but nothing to him, either. He made the best of things he could: "Bringane, they're taking me into the army."

"How will I get the crop in without you?" she cried. But her voice, like his, held a note of relief. This wasn't good, but it could have been worse. In the army, at least, he'd have a chance to fight back.

With a certain rough sympathy, the impresser said, "Things are hard all over the kingdom, lady."

"Why are you making them harder for Fariulf and me?" Obilot demanded.

"Because we need men if we're going to whip the Algarvians," the impresser replied. "Now let's get going. We haven't got all day."

Garivald squeezed Obilot. He kissed her. He said, "I'll come back." She nodded. He hoped she believed him. He tried to believe himself. The impressers snickered. He wondered how often they'd heard the same promises. Then he wondered how often those promises came true. Having done that, he wished he hadn't.

The impressers led him away. He shook his head at Obilot as

he went, warning her not to try to blaze them. One against three—even two against three—wasn't good odds. Her shoulders went up and down in a sigh, but she finally nodded.

By the time he got into Linnich, Garivald wondered if he shouldn't have let Obilot try to stop the impressers. He was hungry and tired, and wanted nothing so much as to go back to the farm, forget about the world, and have the world forget about him, too.

Most of the people on the streets in Linnich were women and old men. He wondered who'd told the impressers he was out there on that farm away from the village. If he ever found out, if he ever got his hands on that person . . . He hoped it wasn't Dagulf. That would be a terrible thing to think of a man who had been his friend. But he knew he would wonder for a long time to come.

More impressers stood in the market square, along with the men they'd rounded up. He didn't see Dagulf there, which raised his suspicions. Some of the men who would be going into King Swemmel's army were hardly men at all, but youths. Others had gray hair and gray stubble on their cheeks. Only a couple were, like Garivald, somewhere in the prime of life.

"Let's get moving," an impresser said. *He* was in the prime of life; Garivald resentfully wondered why he wasn't out there trying to blaze Algarvians instead of rounding up his own countrymen. The impresser went on, "We've got a long way to go to the closest ley-line caravan depot."

Where *was* the closest ley-line caravan depot? Garivald didn't know. Ley lines weren't so dense in this stretch of the Duchy of Grelz. He didn't think there was one within half a day's walk of Linnich, though. That gave him a certain amount of hope. With a little luck, he might slip away during the night. He'd had plenty of practice slipping away in his days as an irregular.

But if he knew tricks, the impressers knew tricks, too. Sure enough, they had to halt by the side of the road for the night. They proved to have light leg irons in their packs, and fastened their recruits together before doling out black bread and sausage to them. Garivald sighed. That was the sort of efficiency King Swemmel surely approved of.

Garivald never found out the name of the town with the caravan depot. He was formally taken into the army—as Fariulf son of Syrivald—inside the depot, before boarding the caravan. A bored-looking clerk asked, "Do you take oath to defend the Kingdom of Unkerlant and King Swemmel from all foes, as directed by those set over you?"

"Aye," Garivald answered, as everyone else surely did. What would Swemmel's men do to someone who refused to swear that oath? Garivald knew he didn't want to find out.

Riding the ley-line caravan was something new and exciting. He'd sabotaged them, but he'd never ridden in one before. By the way some of the other new recruits exclaimed, he wasn't the only one aboard a caravan car for the first time. How the countryside whizzed past as the caravan glided northwest! That was the first thought that struck his mind. The second was how devastated the countryside looked. It had all been fought over at least twice, parts of it more often than that. As he went through one wrecked village after another, he began to realize just how vast the war against Algarve really was.

More recruits—again, mostly boys and older men—boarded at each stop, till they filled his caravan car and, presumably, the others. Food was more black bread; drink was water. He'd never tried to sleep sitting up on a hard bench. He didn't think he could. When he got tired enough, though, he did.

He stayed on the caravan for two and a half days, rising from that seat only to ease himself in a privy that stank and soon began to overflow. By the time the caravan stopped somewhere far outside the Duchy of Grelz, ever so much farther from home than Garivald had ever gone before, he could barely hobble from the car.

No one waiting for him seemed to care. He got a rock-gray tunic and socks and a knapsack and a pair of stout boots. He got a stick. When the sergeant who issued it to him asked if he knew how to use it, he just said, "Aye." The sergeant made a mark on a leaf of paper and sent him to the right. Those who said no went to the left.

A mage came before the group of tired, confused men on the right and began chanting spells over them. Someone asked what they were for. "They'll ward you against Algarvian wizardry—some of it, anyway," a watching soldier answered. Garivald thought of Sadoc the irregular and hoped this mage knew his business better than Sadoc had.

Once the magic was done, the new soldiers got back onto a caravan car. This one had a bad privy, too. After another day and a half, the ley-line caravan stopped again. As Garivald got out, he asked, "Is this where we train?"

"Train?" Somebody already on the ground laughed. "We haven't got time to waste on training you. We gave you a stick, right? If you live long enough, you'll get trained, by the powers above." And with no more fanfare than that, Garivald trudged off to battle against the Algarvians.

Sidroc couldn't remember the last time he'd been on a quiet stretch of front. There were Unkerlanters west of him: he knew that. But Plegmund's Brigade, for once, wasn't in the midst of desperate fighting at every hour of the day and night. Patrols went out with some reasonable expectation that they wouldn't come back chopped to pieces or fail to come back at all.

"Enjoy while it lasts," Sergeant Werferth said to anyone and everyone who would listen. "Before long, the Algarvians are going to ship us north. That's where they're in trouble, so that's where we'll go."

"Not fair," Sidroc said. "They've been loafing in the north for the past two years. Let them worry about Swemmel's whoresons, and leave us alone."

"Life isn't fair, sonny." Werferth looked around to make sure no redheads were in earshot, then went on, "Besides, they may really need us. From what I hear, the powers below have got their teeth into that whole Algarvian army up there."

"That's not good," Sidroc said slowly.

"Did I say it was?" Werferth answered. "Of course, there's another reason they might send us up there, too. If they run into much more trouble, the fight'll be heading back toward Forthweg. They might figure we'd fight harder trying to keep Swemmel's bastards out of our own kingdom."

"They might be right." Sidroc had seen enough of the war in

Unkerlant to know what both sides did to villages they overran. He winced at the idea of that happening inside Forthweg. It mostly hadn't when the redheads conquered his kingdom; the Forthwegians had been overwhelmed too fast.

"My arse," Ceorl said. The ruffian had been scraping mud from his boots with a knife. Looking up, he went on, "Far as I'm concerned, the powers below are welcome to Forthweg, and so are the Unkerlanters. I joined Plegmund's Brigade to get the demon out of there. I don't give a flying futter if I never see the stinking place again as long as I live."

Plenty of people up in Forthweg would probably be glad never to see Ceorl again, either. Sidroc didn't say that. It held true for him as well. It held true for a lot of the men in Plegmund's Brigade.

Sergeant Werferth, Sidroc judged, was one of the few for whom it might not hold true. Werferth hadn't joined the Brigade because everyone hated him. He'd joined because he liked being a soldier, and this gave him the chance to keep doing what he liked and what he was good at.

Before Sidroc could say anything along those lines, a runner came trotting up and spoke in Algarvian, which meant Brigade business: "Brigadier Polinesso orders everybody who's not on patrol to report to the village of Ossiach at midafternoon. He's got something special to say."

"Must be special," Sidroc said. "He's never done anything like this before."

"Do you know what it is?" Ceorl asked the runner, who shook his head. Ceorl cursed the fellow as he went off to spread the word elsewhere.

"Something special," Werferth repeated in musing tones. "I wonder what it could be. You don't suppose the war's over, do you?"

Sidroc and Ceorl both laughed. "Fat chance," Sidroc said. Werferth looked rueful. After a moment, he laughed, too. Sidroc didn't think the war would ever end.

Ossiach wasn't far away. The rough-looking, bearded men of the Brigade filled the market square to the bursting point. If any

Unkerlanters remained in the village, they prudently stayed out of sight.

Brigadier Polinesso climbed up onto a crate so the soldiers he commanded could see him. "We have a special new regiment alongside of us on the left, men," he said. "You need to know this, so you will not take them for the enemy. They will wear the flag of Algarve on their left tunic sleeves. We expect them to fight like tigers—like tigers, do you hear?"

"Aye, Brigadier," the assembled men of the Brigade chorused.

"Good. Very good. You are dismissed," Polinesso said.

Sidroc scratched his head all the way back to his squad's encampment. "What in blazes was he talking about? Who's coming in next to us? We know about the Algarvians. We know about the Yaninans."

"I'd like to kill the Yaninans, the way they run," Ceorl said.

"They had some regiments of Sibians," Werferth said, "but I think the Sibs went into Sulingen and never came out. Besides, Mezentio's lost Sibiu, so he won't get any more regiments there."

"Black Zuwayzin?" Sidroc suggested.

Ceorl howled laughter. "I'd like to see those naked whoresons down here, especially in the wintertime. They'd freeze their balls off, and that's no joke."

"Besides," Werferth added, "they don't wear tunics. How can they put flags on the sleeves of tunics they aren't wearing?"

"All right, not Zuwayzin," Sidroc said. "But who, then?"

"They'd better not be Yaninans," Werferth said. "Ceorl's right about that. I don't want them on our flank, not with the itchy feet they've got. If they bug out, they leave us naked as a Zuwayzi for the Unkerlanters."

"Polinesso wouldn't say the Yaninans fight like tigers." Sidroc scratched his head again. "Powers above, he *wouldn't*. The redheads haven't got any use for Yaninans, either."

Werferth and Ceorl both grunted, but neither one argued, from which Sidroc concluded they thought he was right. Werferth said, "Maybe they're Grelzers."

"Since when are Grelzers special in Grelz?" Sidroc asked, and again got no good answer.

He found the truth two days later, coming in from another blessedly uneventful patrol. He paused to fill his water bottle in a stream not far from where his squad was camped. When he looked up, another soldier was filling a bottle on the other side of the stream. In careful Algarvian, the other fellow said, "You are from Plegmund's Brigade, is it not so? We were told we would have Plegmund's Brigade on our right hand."

"Aye, I'm from Plegmund's Brigade." Sidroc gave his own name, and added, "Who in blazes are *you*?"

The other man's uniform was dark green, almost the color of those the Grelzers who fought on Algarve's side wore. But this fellow was no Grelzer: he was tall and slim and blond and wore trousers and short tunic with, sure enough, the Algarvian flag sewn to the left sleeve. *He's a Kaunian,* Sidroc thought dazedly. *He's got to be a Kaunian. But* that's *not what the redheads use Kaunians for . . .*

"I am Brusku," the stranger said, which both did and did not sound like a Kaunian name—the ending was different from the *s* Forthwegian Kaunians used. Then he went on, "I am a soldier in the Phalanx of Valmiera."

"Ahh." Sidroc slowly nodded. Now things grew clearer. The Algarvians didn't massacre blonds from Valmiera and Jelgava, maybe for fear of touching off revolts in the east. But they were getting some use from them, anyway. Sidroc nodded again in a more friendly way than he'd thought he would show to any Kaunian. "Welcome to Unkerlant. You can't go home again either, can you?"

Brusku's pale stare suddenly sharpened. "No," he said after a moment. "So it is the same for you, is it? I did what I wanted to do. It is enough."

Sidroc had done what he wanted to do, too. Was it enough? Whether it was or not, he was stuck with it. He said, "Come back to my camp with me." He pointed north. "You can meet my pals."

"All right." Brusku splashed across the stream, which was no more than ankle deep. As Sidroc led the way, he thought about how strange it was to be fighting alongside a Kaunian. A few years before, though, he would have thought it strange to be fighting alongside Algarvians, too.

"Greetings," Ceorl called when he walked up to the fire. The ruffian pointed behind him. "Who in blazes is that?"

"His name's Brusku," Sidroc answered—in Algarvian, so Brusku could follow. "He's from the Phalanx of Valmiera— that's the outfit Brigadier Polinesso said was going in on our left."

He wondered if Ceorl would make a crack about Kaunians escaping from Algarvian camps. That wouldn't do anybody any good. Maybe the Valmieran Kaunians didn't know what happened to their blond brethren from Forthweg. Maybe they knew and tried not to think about it. By the way the ruffian's lips pursed, he thought about it. But then, visibly, he thought better of it. He said, "Let's kill some Unkerlanters," and let it go at that.

"Aye," Brusku said. "That is what we came for."

Sergeant Werferth passed the Valmieran his flask. "Here. Try this."

Brusku drank. He coughed a couple of times. "Unicorn piss and fire," he said. "Is that what you Forthwegians drink?"

"We drink wine and plum brandy when we're home," Werferth answered. "Down here, we drink anything we can get our hands on. I think the Unkerlanters brewed this stuff out of turnips."

Brusku looked at the flask as if he wanted to throw it away. Instead, he took another pull and handed it back to Werferth. Then he said, "I had better go, or my sergeant will come down on me." He nodded to Sidroc and headed off in the direction from which he'd come.

Once he was gone, Ceorl spat into the fire. "Fighting side by side with Kaunians? I've thought of a lot of strange things, but never any like that."

"I'll tell you something, though," Sidroc said: "I'd rather have them on my left hand than a pack of jumpy Yaninans." He watched Ceorl weigh that. The ruffian didn't take long to nod.

Werferth said, "A good thing you boys didn't talk about what happens to Forthwegian Kaunians. I'm going to tell everybody to keep quiet about that."

"What happens when the Phalanx of Valmiera—what in blazes is a phalanx, anyway?—finds out about it?" Sidroc asked. "Sooner or later, they will. They're bound to."

"Good question," Werferth said. "We'll probably see before too long, like you say. And when we do . . . You know what it's like when an egg bursts almost close enough for the sorcerous energy to kill you?" He waited. Sidroc nodded. Everybody who'd been in battle for a while knew what that was like. Werferth went on, "When they find out, it'll be like that, only more so."

Sidroc thought it over. How would he feel if the Algarvians started slaying Forthwegians to make their magic stronger? He could think of some Forthwegians he wouldn't miss, starting with Ealstan and Hestan. Still . . . "Aye, you're likely right."

Twelve

Istvan proved less unhappy as a captive on Obuda than he'd expected to. He lived in a barracks no worse than the one where he'd lived while a Gyongyosian soldier on that same island. He was a good deal more comfortable than he'd been in the forests of western Unkerlant or in the trenches on the island of Becsehely. The food his Kuusaman captors fed him and his comrades wasn't especially good, but it wasn't especially bad either, and there was plenty of it. He had no work harder than chopping firewood under the watchful eyes of the Kuusaman guards. It could have been far worse.

When he said as much in line for breakfast one morning, Kun nodded and replied, "Aye, I thought they'd send us off to the mines or some such. This—it's as if they've made Obuda into a crate, and they'll keep stowing captives here till it fills up."

"Nothing to do but sit around and get fat," Istvan agreed

"I've been a soldier for a long time. I don't much mind being an old soldier for a while, if you know what I mean."

"I'm with you," Szonyi said from behind him. "Nobody's trying to blaze me or drop an egg on my head. Anyone who thinks I'm sorry about that is plumb daft."

"Well, the two of you get no arguments from me," Kun said. Watery island sunshine glinted off the gold frames of his spectacles. "I've never been what you'd call eager to have people trying to kill me. I leave all that up to you fierce country lads."

If he hadn't fought bravely every time he had to, he would have condemned himself out of his own mouth there. Even as things were, Istvan spoke a little stiffly: "We *are* a warrior race."

Corporal Kun said nothing to that but, "Aye, Sergeant." Istvan couldn't possibly call him to account for two unexceptionable words. But then Kun looked around, the sun sparkling off his spectacles once more. His glance took in the captives' camp, the palisade around it, the brisk, alert Kuusaman guards on the palisade, and the bedraggled Gyongyosians moving forward one at a time to be fed.

Ears burning, Istvan said, "Well, we *are*."

"Aye, Sergeant," Kun repeated, which finished the job of demoralizing Istvan. The one-time mage's apprentice made as if he didn't even know what he'd done. *He fights,* Istvan thought. *He just doesn't fight fair.* He didn't say that out loud. It would have made Kun unbearably smug.

An Obudan—a medium-sized, dark-haired man with light reddish-brown skin—slapped oatmeal mush into Istvan's mess tin. "Here you is," he said in bad Gyongyosian. Gyongyos had held Obuda, been driven off by the Kuusamans, retaken the island, and then been driven off again. The locals had had their chances to learn the languages of both occupiers.

"Thanks." Istvan turned away and started spooning up the mush. His own people flavored oatmeal with butter and salt. The Kuusamans put in sugar and spices and raisins instead. It wasn't what he was used to, but it wasn't too bad.

When he'd finished, he took his tin over to a basin of water to wash it. He was sloshing it around in the basin when another captive came up beside him. He blinked. "Hello, Major Borsos," he said. "I didn't know the stars-accursed slanteyes had got you, too."

He'd fetched and carried for Borsos back in the days when Gyongyos still held Obuda. He'd seen the mage again in the vast forests of Unkerlant. Borsos had had trouble remembering him then, and plainly had trouble remembering him now. After a moment, he said, "Ah, hello, Sergeant. Aye, I'm among the unlucky, too. Gyongyos hasn't had much luck lately."

"Couldn't you use your magecraft to do . . . something?" Istvan's voice trailed away. Here on an island now far away from any that Gyongyos held, what could even a true mage do?

And Borsos hissed, "Shut up, by the stars. The Kuusamans don't know what I am, and I don't want them finding out, either, or they'll send me somewhere worse than this."

"Oh." Till then, Istvan hadn't noticed Borsos wasn't wearing his sorcerer's badges along with his emblems of rank. As in most armies, Gyongyosian mages held officer's rank not so much by virtue of their blood as to give them the privilege of telling common soldiers what to do. Real aristocratic officers—most of them—would look down their noses at Borsos, but they probably wouldn't tell the Kuusamans what he was. In fact . . . "It might be nice, having a real wizard in here on our side."

"I'm hardly even that," Borsos said. "I'm just a dowser. You ought to remember, if you hauled my gear around for me."

"Better than nothing," Istvan said. *Better than Kun*, he thought. Kun had been an apprentice before going into Ekrekek Arpad's army. Borsos, at least, was fully trained in one specialty of magic.

From behind Istvan, someone asked, "Is this man bothering you, sir?" Istvan turned. There stood Captain Frigyes, as stiff and erect and formal as if still in command of soldiers in the field. He might have been even more stiff and erect and formal here in the captives' camp, to try to hold his men together.

Borsos said, "No, Captain. We've known each other for a while."

Frigyes still looked dubious. Leaning toward him, Istvan spoke in a low voice: "He's a mage, sir."

"Is he?" Frigyes answered, also quietly. He eyed Borsos' collar tabs. Unlike Istvan, he didn't need an explanation from Borsos. "You don't want the enemy to know your skill, eh?"

He didn't bother calling Borsos *sir* any more. Officers—real officers—didn't take seriously mages' claims to rank. Borsos didn't get angry; a good many mages didn't take those claims seriously, either. The dowser replied, "That's about the size of it, Captain."

"All right." Frigyes nodded briskly. "I can understand that. And it might be useful for us to have a sorcerer here. Who knows? Maybe we can find a way to hit back at the Kuusamans yet."

"Maybe." But Borsos didn't sound as if he believed it. "They have strong wards up around the camp, though. They're the enemy, Captain, but they're not fools. If they were fools, they wouldn't be moving forward."

They wouldn't be beating us, was what he surely meant, but no Gyongyosian soldier—not even a mage in military uniform—would come right out and say that. The traditions of a warrior race died hard.

"Wards can do only so much," Captain Frigyes said, and led Major Borsos aside. He spoke to the mage too softly for Istvan to make out what they were saying. Istvan didn't even bother resenting it. That was how officers were; as best he could tell, the stars had made them that way.

The cry of horror Borsos let out a moment later wasn't too soft to hear. It made Istvan jump, and he wasn't the only one. "No!" Borsos said a moment later, and wagged a finger under Captain Frigyes' nose as if he were a real major and not just an officer by courtesy. That was enough to put Frigyes' back up; he stalked off like an offended cat.

"What on earth?" Istvan said. He wasn't really asking Borsos what Frigyes had proposed; it was more an exclamation of astonishment.

"By the sweet, pure, and holy light of the stars, Sergeant, you don't want to know." Borsos' face was pale as milk. A back-country man—a herder, say, from the valley from which Istvan sprang—might have looked that way after seeing a ghost. Borsos didn't strike Istvan as a man likely to see a ghost, or to panic if he did. But the dowser went off in the direction opposite the one Frigyes had taken. He staggered once, plainly a man shaken to the core.

"What on earth?" Istvan said again.

Again, he got an answer, this time from Kun: "Can't you figure it out for yourself, Sergeant?"

Istvan whirled. The sorcerer's apprentice and corporal was right behind him, dirty mess tin in hand. "If I could figure it out, would I be going, 'What on earth?' " Istvan asked in some irritation. "And I know bloody well that you didn't hear as much of it as I did, so what makes you so fornicating smart?"

"Your friend there is a mage of sorts, aye?" Kun said. He waited for Istvan to nod, then went on, "What was Captain Frigyes doing with us when all the Kuusamans in the world jumped on our company?"

"Huh?" The jump there was too wide for Istvan to follow him across it. "What *are* you talking about?"

Patiently, Kun guided him across: "Our company commander was good and ready to sacrifice us all, to let the mages make the magic that would have thrown the slant-eyes off Becsehely, remember? But they captured us before he got us to wherever the wizards were. And so . . ." He waited.

He needed to wait a while; Istvan had trouble with the jump even with a guide. At last, though, Istvan's mouth fell open. "You think he was talking with Borsos about making that same kind of sorcery here!" Once the words were out of his mouth, they made a horrid kind of sense. He wished they hadn't.

And Kun nodded. "That's just what I think. Captain Frigyes wants to go on fighting the war. How else can he do it?"

"*Could* Borsos make that kind of magic here?" Istvan asked. "He's a dowser, mostly. Does he even know enough to cast that kind of spell?"

"Ask him," Kun answered. "I can't tell you."

With a shudder, Istvan shook his head. "I don't think I want to know."

Kun clicked his tongue between his teeth in sharp disapproval. "You should always want to know. Knowledge is bad, but ignorance is worse."

"Is that a fact?" Istvan said, and Kun nodded as if it most assuredly were. Istvan put his hands on his hips. "If knowing is such a great thing, how come we both wish the mages had never figured out how to use the magic they get from killing people? Answer me that, O sage of the age."

"It's not the same," Kun said stiffly. "The only reason our mages turned toward that spell was that the Unkerlanters used it against us. We have to be able to fight back."

Istvan shook his head again. "You're not really answering me. You're just pushing it back one step. Don't you wish the Unkerlanters hadn't worked out how to use that spell, then? You can't be real happy about it, or you wouldn't have been so very thrilled to volunteer to help power the sorcery."

Now Kun winced. "Volunteer to have my throat cut, you mean. No, may the stars turn their light from me if I was happy about that. And I suppose you've made your point. Huzzah for ignorance!" He held his hands in front of his face, as if playing a fanfare on a trumpet.

I got him to admit I was right, Istvan thought proudly. The pride was in proportion to how seldom that happened. But then he wondered what Captain Frigyes would do, and what he could make Major Borsos do. He didn't know, and wished he did. As soon as the wish crossed his mind, he realized Kun wasn't entirely wrong. He thought about admitting as much, but in the end did no such thing. He gained such triumphs too seldom not to want to savor them to the fullest.

Leudast had got used to life in the bridgehead on the eastern bank of the Fluss. The Algarvians kept pounding away, trying to drive the Unkerlanters back over the river and seal off the bridgehead. They kept throwing in attacks every so often, too, going at the Unkerlanter regiments on the east side of the

Fluss as if the whole war depended on wiping them out.

After Swemmel's men had beaten back one such assault, a trooper in Leudast's company said, "Isn't this the worst fighting you've ever seen in all your days, Lieutenant?"

The fellow couldn't have been above seventeen. Unkerlanter soldiers in the field didn't get to shave very often, but his cheeks remained smooth and beardless even when he was nowhere near a razor. Leudast wanted to laugh in his face. Instead, he just shook his head. "Sonny, I was wounded down in Sulingen. They fixed me up in time to let me fight in the Durrwangen bulge. After those scraps, anything the redheads have done to us here is like a walk in the meadow with a pretty girl." He thought of Alize, back in the village of Leiferde.

Sergeant Kiun shook his head. "Oh, it's not so easy as *that*, sir," he said. "More like a walk through the meadow with an *ugly* girl, if you want to know what I think."

"Who wants to know what you think?" Leudast returned. They grinned at each other. Why not? Between the two of them, they'd captured the Algarvian noble who'd called himself King of Grelz. Just as Leudast wasn't quite an ordinary lieutenant, so Kiun wasn't an ordinary sergeant.

The young soldier was unimpressed. "You're making fun of me!" he said, and his voice broke in the middle of the sentence, going from the baritone he would have as a grown man to the squeaky treble he was just escaping.

"Well, what if we are, Gilan?" Leudast asked. "You said something silly. If you don't expect people to make fun of you after you say something silly, you're making a big mistake."

"But I didn't know it was silly," Gilan protested.

"That makes it more silly, not less," Leudast said. Had he been that naive when King Swemmel's impressers pulled him into the army? If he had, how in blazes had his sergeants and officers put up with him? He thought of Sergeant Magnulf, who'd died in the first year of the war with Algarve. They'd shared a hole in some village they were trying to defend. Had he looked out of the hole when the egg burst in front of it, he would be dead now and Magnulf might still be alive. It had happened the other way round. He knew neither rhyme nor reason for it.

As if the mere thought of eggs were enough to conjure them up, they started bursting not far from the trench in which he and Kiun and Gilan stood. They weren't quite close enough to make the soldiers throw themselves flat, but they weren't much farther off than that. "Powers below eat the redheads," Kiun said. "I thought they were supposed to be moving everything north to fight our push there."

"Lots of odds and sods in the men they're throwing at us," Leudast said. "Those Forthwegian whoresons are almost as bad as Grelzers—you can't tell they're the enemy till too late. And now these blond Kaunian buggers."

"They fight hard," Kiun said.

"Aye." Leudast nodded. "There were a few Kaunians not so far from my village. I grew up pretty close to the border with Forthweg, you know. They're just . . . people who don't look like us. What I don't get is how come they'll fight for the Algarvians when the redheads kill 'em to make their magic."

"These aren't Kaunians from Forthweg," Kiun said. "They're from way the demon off in the east somewhere. I hardly even know the names of the kingdoms on the other side of the world."

"They're Valmierans," Leudast said. Before Kiun could put in a jab, he held up his hand. "Only reason I know is because Captain Recared told me. He knows all that stuff. But still, they're blonds, and so are the Kaunians from Forthweg. So why would they help Mezentio's bastards?"

"Have to take some prisoners, squeeze it out of 'em," Kiun said.

"I suppose so," Leudast allowed.

Unkerlanter egg-tossers started answering the Algarvians. They still didn't respond as fast as the redheads, but they were there in numbers in the bridgehead. Nothing the Algarvians or the foreigners fighting for them had done had stopped Unkerlant from bringing egg-tossers and behemoths forward, which was not the least of the reasons they still held the foothold on this side of the Fluss.

Dragons flew by, dragons painted rock-gray. "They'll drop their loads on the Algarvians' heads, too," Leudast said. "Serves the redheads right—this is what they used to do to us all the time."

Before long, the Algarvian egg-tossers fell silent. "That's more like it," Kiun said. "Maybe they'll learn not to try that any more."

"Here's hoping," Leudast said. "That's one lesson I wish they'd learned already, as a matter of fact." Kiun chuckled and nodded, for all the world as if Leudast were joking. They'd both been in the front lines a long time. If you didn't joke, you'd go mad sooner or later—unless the redheads killed you, which was rather more likely.

Here, though, the Algarvians really did seem to learn a lesson. Things stayed very quiet for the next couple of days. They were so quiet, in fact, that Leudast almost lost the feeling of being stuck in a bridgehead.

He remarked on that the next time he saw Captain Recared, adding, "If we hit them hard enough to make them stay this quiet, maybe we can break out of this cramped little place and start pushing them back again."

Recared shook his head. "Not yet, Lieutenant. I'd like to just as much as you would, but not yet. We'll have to see how things go up in the north before we find out what we can do here. All the spares we have, and all the reserves, are going into that push. If it goes well, then we can try pushing here, too. Or that's my guess, anyhow—ask Marshal Rathar if you want a better notion."

"Oh, of course, sir." Leudast laughed. Unlike most junior lieutenants, he'd met the marshal, and Rathar might, if reminded, remember who he was. None of that meant he could go asking questions of Rathar. None of it meant Rathar was anywhere within a thousand miles of the River Fluss at the moment, either.

Recared laughed, too, and said, "You've got attitude, Leudast."

"Do I?" Leudast shrugged. "I don't know anything about that. All I know is, I'm still here, and that makes me luckier than a lot of people." Poor Magnulf crossed his mind again. He asked, "How *are* things going up in the north, sir?"

"Better than we expected. As well as we hoped," Recared answered. Leudast blinked; he hadn't really looked for a reply quite so optimistic. The regimental commander went on, "That whole Algarvian army up there is getting smashed to pieces. With any luck at all, we *will* be able to start moving here pretty soon—but not just yet."

"I'm in no hurry, sir, not as long as the redheads and the whoresons who fight for them leave us alone, the way they have lately." Leudast snapped his fingers. "That reminds me— Kiun and I were talking about the Kaunians who fight on Algarve's side. Has anybody figured out why they're daft enough to do it?"

"We've caught a few," Recared said. "We haven't found any answers that tell us a whole lot. Best guess so far is, they're about like the buggers in Plegmund's Brigade: ne'er-do-wells and men down on their luck and a few just looking for a fight and taking one anywhere they can find it."

Leudast grunted. "Bunch of cursed fools, if anybody wants to know what I think. You'd have to be, wouldn't you, to fight for somebody who was doing that to your own people?"

"Well, I think so," Captain Recared said. Then he changed the subject, and then, sooner than Leudast had expected, he left. Leudast scratched his head for a while, wondering if he'd somehow offended the regimental commander. He ran the conversation over in his mind. He couldn't see how.

And then, as he was drifting toward sleep that night, he did. After all, King Swemmel was killing powers above only knew how many Unkerlanters to fuel the sorcery that thwarted the Algarvians' murderous magic and helped beat the redheads and their allies out of Unkerlant. Even though he was doing that, Leudast didn't hesitate to fight for him. Neither did countless other Unkerlanters.

Maybe the Valmieran Kaunians felt the same way. *If they do, they're wrong,* Leudast thought, and dozed off.

After black bread and sausage the next morning, he led

Kiun's squad out on a patrol through the woods. He could have stayed back in camp and let the sergeant take charge of the patrol himself; a lot of officers would have. But he'd been on plenty of patrols himself. If he went on this one, he thought—he hoped—he gave everyone a little better chance of coming back in one piece.

A jay screamed. A woodpecker drummed on the trunk of a birch. A flock of waxwings flew from one wild plum tree to another. No one who'd ever heard them could mistake their soft metallic *zree! zree!* for the call of any other bird. "All seems pretty quiet," Kiun said. "No sign the redheads are trying to sneak in and make trouble."

"You sound disappointed," Leudast said.

"Not me." Kiun shook his head. "Surprised, maybe, but not disappointed. I haven't seen the Algarvians back on their heels like this for a long time." He shook his head again. "I don't think I've ever seen the Algarvians back on their heels like this. Doesn't seem natural, you know what I mean?"

"I think so." Leudast nodded. "They're not doing anything themselves. They're waiting for us to do something. They never used to do that. We used to wait for them, especially in the summertime. It's not the same fight it was a couple of years ago." *A good thing, too,* he thought. *If the Algarvians were still kicking us around like that, we'd have long since lost the war.*

Kiun started to answer, then silently toppled, his stick falling from hands that would no longer hold it. He didn't even twitch; he was dead before he hit the ground. A patch of leaves near his feet started smoldering.

"Sniper!" Leudast called, and dove for cover. "Sniper up a tree!" he added—the trajectory of the beam that had slain Kiun proved as much.

If the whoreson stayed quiet, how were they supposed to find him? He'd got Kiun through the head. Kiun had been about *there*, and the patch of plants on the ground that had caught fire was about *there*, so the enemy had to be over in *that* direction. "There!" Leudast pointed northeast. "One of those trees there. Work carefully, boys—he'll be looking for us."

The Unkerlanters slid from tree to bush to rock, trying to show themselves as little as possible. And the sniper evidently knew what he was about, for he sat tight in whatever tree he'd chosen for himself. If the Unkerlanters didn't spot him, he was free to get away, free to wait for the next unlucky soldier to come within range of his stick. But then a trooper shouted, "There he is!" and pointed to a big, leafy oak—a tree so big and leafy, the mere sight of it had made Leudast suspicious.

Once seen, the sniper didn't last long. He wounded one more man—not badly—before tumbling, dead, out of the tree. He was a trouser-wearing Kaunian with an Algarvian banner sewn to the sleeve of his tunic. Leudast kicked the body. "One more down," he said, and the patrol moved on.

Colonel Spinello stumbled south and east, trying to pick his way through a marsh east of Sommerda. He was weary and filthy and unshaven. He hoped he wouldn't meet any Unkerlanter soldiers, for he wasn't at all sure whether his stick held enough sorcerous energy to blaze. At that, he reckoned himself better off than most of the soldiers in the regiment he'd commanded. He remained alive and able to go on retreating. Most of them were either dead or captive.

He missed a step and went into muck up to his knees. Before he could sink any deeper, Jadwigai, who remained on firm ground, grabbed him and helped him get back to decent footing himself.

"Thank you, sweetheart," he said, and gave her a kiss. She was every bit as worn and dirty as he, but still contrived to look good to him. It wasn't just that she didn't grow whiskers to add to a raffish appearance. She'd been so pretty starting out, grime and exhaustion only gave her beauty more sharply sculpted edges.

"You're welcome." She pointed toward a clump of man-high bushes a couple of hundred yards ahead. "If we can get there, we'll have a pretty good hiding place for the night."

"Aye, I think you're right." Spinello's bones creaked when he started moving, but move he did. Unkerlanters were bound to be prowling in this swamp. If they caught up with him, he'd never make it out the other side to reconnect himself to the Algarvian army. He wondered if any Algarvian army remained in northern Unkerlant to be reconnected to. He couldn't prove it not at the moment, not by the way Mezentio's forces had collapsed under the hammer blow the Unkerlanters dealt them.

He went into muddy water again before reaching the bushes. This time, he pulled himself out without help from Jadwigai. The water was also stagnant and smelly. The last time he'd risked a fire, he'd used a lighted twig to get a leech off his leg. Mosquitoes hovered in buzzing, thrumming clouds.

As he and Jadwigai had hoped, the bushes marked slightly higher ground. He stretched out, almost ready to fall asleep right there where he lay. Jadwigai sat down beside him. Maybe she was still full of luck—he was still breathing, after all. Or maybe he'd broken the regiment's luck, and the whole northern army's as well, when he first brought her to his bed.

"Or maybe that's nonsense," he muttered.

"What?" Jadwigai asked.

"Nothing," he told her. "Or I think it's nothing, anyway." He rolled onto his side and leaned on one elbow, studying her. "Ask you something?"

"Go ahead," she said.

"Why are you still here with me? You might do better to let the Unkerlanters catch up with you. Especially . . ." Spinello's voice trailed away. *Especially since we're killing Kaunians, and they're not* didn't strike him as the most politic thing to say, no matter how true it was. He sometimes wondered why she hadn't cut his throat while he lay sleeping. Asking her that didn't seem politic, either. *Last thing I need is to put ideas in her head if she hasn't got 'em already.*

Jadwigai shook her head. "I'd just be a body to them, I think. They don't care about Kaunians. We always made jokes about them in my village—it wasn't that far from the border with Unkerlant."

She might well have been right. Both sides here in the west fought the war without restraint. Algarvian soldiers did as they pleased with Unkerlanter women in villages they'd overrun. The Unkerlanters sometimes killed Algarvians they captured in lingering, painful ways and left their bodies where their comrades could find them.

"Besides," Jadwigai went on, "I know you'll keep me safe when we find the rest of the army."

"I'll do my best." Spinello wondered how good that best would be. A colonel normally would have no trouble getting whatever he wanted for his mistress. But times weren't normal, and most mistresses weren't Kaunians. More urgent worries reared their head at the moment. "What have we got left to eat?"

"Bread. Hard and stale, but bread," Jadwigai answered. "And spirits. If we mix the spirits with swamp water, we can drink the swamp water, too." She was right again. Spinello shuddered all the same. The swamp water tasted as nasty as it smelled, and that remained true regardless of whether it would give him a flux of the bowels.

The bread wasn't just hard; it could have done duty for a brick. Spinello and Jadwigai shared. "If I had bad teeth, I'd starve," he said.

Before Jadwigai could answer, eggs burst off in the distance. "What's happening to the army?" she asked. "Have you got any idea?"

"In detail? No," Spinello said. "In general? Aye. They threw more at us than we could stand up against, and they broke us. I was afraid they were going to do that, but they've done more than I thought they could. They used columns of behemoths to smash through our lines, then turned in so they'd either surround us or make us fall back . . . and they did it over and over and over. I didn't know they had that many behemoths—or dragons, either. I don't think anybody in Algarve knew what all Swemmel had before this fight started."

"You might have done better if you had known," Jadwigai remarked.

"Aye, that's so." Spinello admitted what he could hardly deny. "But it's too late to dwell on it now. Now we have to hope we can stay alive"—when he said *we*, he meant not only himself and Jadwigai, but every Algarvian in the north of Unkerlant—"and somehow stop the enemy."

More eggs burst. "Do you think we can?" Jadwigai asked.

"Sooner or later, we have to," Spinello replied. "They'll run out of men and beasts and supplies. If we have anything at all left by then, we'll stop them. But when? Where?" He shrugged an elaborate Algarvian shrug. The answer was important, but he couldn't do much to influence it, not as a harried fugitive he couldn't. He took off his hat and laid it under his head for a pillow.

Jadwigai lay down beside him in the bushes. They'd made love a few times during the grinding retreat, but they were both too weary now. Spinello reached out to pat her hand. Then he dove headlong into oblivion.

He woke a little before dawn. Jadwigai still slept. With care and worry gone from her face, she looked improbably young. Spinello shook his head. She was as tough as she was pretty. She'd done as well as she could for herself in a situation as near impossible as made no difference. She'd done far better than most of the rest of the Kaunians from Forthweg. And if she stayed with him now, that was bound to be hard self-interest.

He shook her awake, ready to clap a hand to her mouth if she made more noise than she should. She'd done that once or twice. Not now, though. Reason came into her eyes almost at once. "Let's get going," Spinello said quietly.

"Aye." Jadwigai nodded. "Maybe you can blaze some of these marsh birds."

"Maybe." But Spinello remembered a coot he'd killed. It hadn't been worth eating once dead. Of course, when you got hungry enough . . .

The sun was still low in the southeast when they came on a couple of squads' worth of soldiers. For a moment, Spinello thought himself a dead man. Then he realized they were Algarvians, stragglers like himself. No, not stragglers: just defeated men in full retreat. They even had a crystallomancer with them. "We're supposed to have a strongpoint in Volkach," the fellow said. "If we can get there, maybe we'll get back to the real war." Under his breath, he added something like, "If there's any real var left up here." But he didn't say it loud enough to make pinello ask him to repeat it.

As they fought their way through the swamp, one of the roopers asked, "Where'd you pick up the twist, Colonel?" He ounded curious and a little jealous, as he might have had pinello carried a knapsack full of smoked pheasant and fine vine.

Unlike a knapsack, Jadwigai could speak for herself. "I'm ot a twist, you—" What she called him proved she'd learned oldierly Algarvian. "I was—I *am*—the luck of the Alberese Regiment."

"Oh!" To Spinello's surprise, the soldier bowed to her as if to n Algarvian duchess. "I've heard about you. A lot of folks up ere have heard about you."

"Aye, that's right." Another soldier nodded. He turned to pinello. "Anybody gives you a hard time about her, Colonel, ou just yell. There's plenty of people won't let anything hap-en to her."

"That's good to hear," Spinello said.

He sounded less happy when they came out of the swamp nd up onto solid ground. The vast plains of northern Unkerlant vere ideal ground for behemoths. Back in the early days of the var, that had all been to Algarve's advantage. Now, when the Jnkerlanters could put three, four, five beasts in the field for very Algarvian animal, moving across the plains made sweat rickle from his armpits and down the small of his back.

Swemmel's men had been through here, on their way farther ast. Bloated, stinking corpses, may of them still wearing kilts, ay here and there. But no Unkerlanters were in sight now. "Get our bearings on this Volkach place," Spinello told the crystal-omancer. "Is it still holding?"

After squatting over his crystal, the mage nodded. "About ten niles, they tell me," he said. "We can do it."

"We have to do it," Spinello said, and the other worn, beaten, lirty Algarvians nodded. Actually, there was one alternative. If hey didn't get to Volkach, they would die. For that matter, if he Unkerlanters had a tight perimeter around the town, they vere in trouble.

But they stumbled into Volkach late that afternoon, though nervous pickets almost blazed them for enemy soldiers. They'd had to hide a couple of times while Unkerlanter columns went by. Swemmel's men, though, were after bigger game than a few handfuls of holdouts, and kept right on hurrying east. Back when the war was new, Algarvian soldiers had stormed west the same way.

The officer in charge in the Unkerlanter town was a major. He commanded most of a regiment of soldiers, a few egg tossers, and half a dozen behemoths—not enough to do anything with, but too much for the Unkerlanters to gobble down at a gulp. It was the biggest Algarvian force Spinello had found in one place in a couple of weeks. The major seemed relieved to see him there, and cared not at all that a Kaunian girl sat beside him.

"What will we do, sir?" the fellow asked, as if Spinello had any answers. "What *can* we do? We can't hold on here much longer—Volkach isn't anything but a shield that lets our men farther east retreat. And everything in the north is ruined. Everything, I tell you!"

"I know." After all Spinello had been through since the Unkerlanter blow fell, he thought he knew better than the major did, but what point to saying so? "Sooner or later, we're bound to stop them." He hoped he wasn't whistling in the dark. He wanted a bath and food and clean clothes.

Before he could ask for any of them, the major said, "If only the islanders hadn't invaded Jelgava. We'd get the reinforcements we need then."

"Maybe," Spinello said, and then, in spite of everything, he fell asleep where he sat.

Leino saluted Captain Brunho and spoke in classical Kaunian: "Sir, I request your leave to transfer from *Habakkuk* to the forces now on the ground in Jelgava."

Brunho studied him: a tall, somber Lagoan staring down at a stubby little Kuusaman. "May I ask why?" he said, also in the old language—the only tongue the two of them had in common.

"Of course, sir." Leino had to stay polite. If he affronted the captain, he wouldn't get what he wanted. "I want to have the chance to give the Algarvians what they deserve. We have largely won the war at sea, and my duties on *Habakkuk* these days have more to do with maintenance than anything else. This ship is not new any more. It is proved. It no longer needs me. The land war does."

"You want to do something you have not done before," Brunho said.

Though Leino couldn't tell whether the captain approved of his lust for novelty, he nodded. "Aye, sir." And it was true. But it wasn't the whole reason. The other side of the coin was that he wanted to get away from Xavega. Volunteering to go forward into battle would let him break clean without hurting her and without making her angry. However much he enjoyed his time in bed with her, he couldn't spend all his time with her in bed, and he still found her annoying when they weren't in bed. She also intimidated him enough that he didn't want to come right out and tell her so.

Brunho stroked his chin. "You are not the first mage aboard *Habakkuk* to make this request."

"You see, sir?" Leino said. "We have the chance to strike directly at Algarve now. I am not surprised I am not the only one who wants to take it."

"If we lose too many mages from *Habakkuk*, our ship here will abruptly cease to be a ship," Captain Brunho said. "An iceberg in the warm waters off the coast of Jelgava would not last long."

"You have plenty to keep *Habakkuk* safe, and the margin for security is large." Leino knew that was true; he'd made the staffing arrangements for sorcerers himself. "And I repeat, maintaining the ship is now routine. For most of the tasks involved, you do not need mages of the highest rank. The fight on the mainland, though . . ."

"These are almost the same arguments the other mage used against me," Brunho said with a wintry smile. "Since I had a difficult time disagreeing then, I am not surprised at having a difficult time disagreeing now. Your request for transfer is ap-

proved." He reached into his desk. "I have some forms for you
to fill out."

"I thought you might," Leino said dryly. The forms were
printed in both Kuusaman and Lagoan. Like any cooperative
project, *Habakkuk* produced twice as much paperwork as it
would have had one kingdom undertaken it. With a sigh, the
Kuusaman mage inked a pen and set to work. *Escaping from
Xavega* appeared nowhere on any leaf of paper, no matter how
large it loomed in his mind.

When Leino finally finished the forms, he pushed them
across the desk at Captain Brunho. The Lagoan officer just accepted them; for all the sense he could make of them, they
might have been written in demotic Gyongyosian. "I thank you
for your services," he said in the one tongue he and Leino did
share. "Gather your effects and report to the starboard bow. I already have a boat scheduled to take the other mage ashore. You
may share it."

"Thank you, sir," Leino said. After saluting—by Captain
Brunho's upraised eyebrow, he might have done it better—he
hurried away.

His effects, as Brunho called them, fit into a duffel bag. It
was a heavy bag, because a lot of those effects were sorcerous
tomes. Walking with the bag over his right shoulder and with a
list to the left, he made his way to the starboard bow.

To his surprise, he found Xavega there, the sea breeze blowing her coppery hair out behind her and also blowing at her kilt
so she had to use one hand to hold it down. He hadn't intended
to say good-bye, just to go. Better that way, he'd judged. Now
he had no choice.

Or so he thought, till Xavega said, "Farewell, Leino. I am
leaving *Habakkuk*."

Leino gaped. Then he started to laugh. "So you're the other
mage!" he exclaimed. Xavega looked blank, and he realized
he'd been startled into Kuusaman. He translated his words into
classical Kaunian.

"The other mage?" Xavega still looked puzzled.

"I am leaving *Habakkuk*, too." Leino set down his duffel on
Habakkuk's ice-and-sawdust deck. "We have just been sailing

here. It is all routine. I wanted the chance to fight the Algarvians on the mainland."

Xavega threw her arms around him and kissed him. A nearby Lagoan sailor whistled enviously. Squeezed against Xavega's firm, soft warmth, Leino couldn't imagine why he'd wanted to leave her. He knew he would remember as soon as he no longer felt her breasts pressing against him, but that would be later. Now . . . Now he wanted to go back to his cabin with her.

No time for that. They got into the boat, and sailors lowered it down to the sea. Another mage, a Lagoan, stood at the stern to seize the sorcerous energy in the ley line and propel the boat toward the distant shore. Xavega said, "When I volunteered to go to the mainland, I did not think I would see you again."

"Why not?" Leino asked. He hadn't expected to see her, either, but he didn't care to come right out and say so.

"Well . . ." Xavega hesitated, but then spoke with her usual frankness: "You are a Kuusaman, after all." *Her usual frankness and her usual ignorance*, Leino thought as she went on, "I did not know if you would be eager to see the fighting up close."

"My dear, we do not revel in war the way Algarvic folk do," Leino replied with a sigh. "That does not mean we cannot fight well. We are fighting Gyongyos by ourselves, as near as makes no difference, and two out of every three soldiers from the island in Jelgava are Kuusamans."

Xavega made a sour face. She had to know Leino was telling the truth. No one, not even the most ardent Lagoan patriot, could deny that. Liking it was another matter. At last, she said, "It is not my fault that your kingdom is bigger than mine."

"I never said it was your fault. But you must not think that we Kuusamans cannot fight, or that we are afraid to fight." Leino raised an eyebrow of his own, perhaps imitating Captain Brunho. "Your King Vitor did not think we were afraid to fight. When he went to war against Algarve, he was afraid we would go to war . . . against Lagoas."

He remembered some of the hotheads at a party at his brother-in-law's wanting to do just that. Mezentio's men wouldn't have attacked Yliharma then—not in this war, anyhow. But an Algarve bestriding Derlavai would surely have looked across the Strait of Valmiera before long, regardless of whether the kingdom dominant there was a nominal ally.

The boat skimmed up to the edge of the beach. The mage said something in Lagoan, then condescended to translate it into classical Kaunian for Leino: "All out."

Out Leino went, into calf-deep water. He was glad he didn't get his duffel wet. Xavega splashed down beside him. The boat slid away toward *Habakkuk*. As so many soldiers had before, the two mages squelched up onto the Jelgavan sands. Few signs of the fight were left close by the sea, though a handful of sticks, some with Kuusaman hats tied to them, others with Lagoan headgear, had been thrust into the sand to mark soldiers' final resting places.

A Kuusaman soldier came up to Leino and Xavega and said, "You are the mages we were told to expect?"

"No, just a couple of tourists, a little early in the season," Leino answered. The trooper grinned. Xavega squawked. That was when Leino realized he'd spoken his own language. He translated for her. She rolled her eyes. Out of bed, she didn't believe in foolishness.

"Just over that rise is a ley-line caravan depot where you can go forward, up toward the front," the soldier said.

Again, Leino turned his words into classical Kaunian. After he'd done that, he asked the fellow, "How close to Balvi will the caravan take us?"

"About fifteen miles. That's where the front is," the soldier answered. "King Donalitu is practically pissing himself on account of he can't get back into his precious palace." He set a hand on his chest. "Breaks my heart, it does."

"I'll bet," Leino said, which made the other Kuusaman laugh out loud. When he translated for Xavega, she laughed, too. Leino did a little laughing himself. He wasn't angry, or wasn't too angry, at Donalitu. Without the bad-tempered Jelgavan monarch, he wouldn't have found himself in Xavega's arms.

And you wouldn't have left Habakkuk *to get away from her,* he told himself. *See how well that worked.*

He and Xavega trudged along with the Kuusaman soldier till

they got to the depot, which was canvas over bare timbers. A sergeant there checked their names off on a list. Leino threw down his duffel bag with a groan of relief after climbing into a car. Xavega's didn't seem to bother her. She sat down beside him, showing a lot of leg and not bothering to fuss with her kilt to show less.

A few soldiers boarded the ley-line caravan, and a couple of men, one Kuusaman, the other Lagoan, with the green sashes of healers. Then the caravan, still not very full, began to glide west, away from the sea and toward the fighting. The country rose rapidly; much of the interior of Jelgava was a high plateau, none too well watered and very hot—especially by Kuusaman standards. Few mountains towered above the plateau. It was as if, having got that high, the land refused to do much more.

Before long, Leino saw fresh signs of war: craters from bursting eggs scarring fields; a grove of apricots ravaged by more eggs and half burned; the carcass of a dragon, with buzzards all over it; a group of men working to get the armor off a dead behemoth. The behemoth was Kuusaman, the armor the ceramic-and-steel composite Leino's own sorcery had helped create. It was stronger against beams than regular chainmail, but hadn't saved this particular beast. He hoped the crewmen had managed to escape.

The caravan car glided past trenches, and past hastily dug graves—red-brown lines on green. Still . . . Leino turned to Xavega and spoke in classical Kaunian: "The Algarvians have not put up the hardest of fights."

"No. The Lagoans have rolled over them." She coughed a couple of times, then grudgingly added, "And the Kuusamans as well." It was more like the Kuusamans and the Lagoans as well, but Leino didn't bother correcting her.

They also glided past dragon farms and fields full of grazing behemoths and unicorns and horses and rows of egg-tossers and piles of eggs ready to fling and endless files of tents, some Lagoan brown, others—more—Kuusaman green: all the appurtenances of modern war.

And, when they arrived at the sorcerers' encampment, they found another Kuusaman sergeant. This one used classical

Kaunian so well Leino wondered what he'd done before becoming a soldier: "Ah, the pair from *Habakkuk.* I have you assigned to the same tent."

Xavega smiled and nodded. The smile was full of promise, so much promise that Leino nodded, too. *So much for your good intentions,* he thought. *Well, you'll enjoy yourself . . . till the quarrels start again.* He sighed. *Odds are, it won't be long.*

Marshal Rathar's headquarters had moved east, out of Pewsum. Had he stayed there, the front in northern Unkerlant would have left him behind, as the sea leaves bathers behind when the tide goes out. Now he directed the attack against Algarve from a village just west of Sommerda, a village whose name he hadn't bothered to learn. As things stood, he didn't think he would ever know it.

He turned to General Gurmun and said, "You know, we're going to have to move again soon."

"Looks that way," Gurmun agreed. "The troopers are getting ahead of us, sure enough. By the time we're through, this Algarvian army will be gone from the board. Powers below eat all the redheads. I won't miss 'em a fornicating bit."

"Neither will I." As it had a way of doing, Rathar's gaze fell on the map pinned to a table undoubtedly stolen from a fancier hut than this one. He shook his head in slow wonder. "It's going just the way we drew it up back in Cottbus. If anything, we're ahead of the timeline we drew up back in Cottbus. Who would have imagined that would happen against the Algarvians?"

Dispassionate as if he had clockwork in his belly, Gurmun answered, "We broke the buggers last year in the Durrwangen bulge. Now it's just a matter of kicking down the door and charging through."

Rationally speaking, Rathar supposed he was right. Still, he said, "This is the fourth summer of the war against them. It's the first time they haven't tried an attack of their own. Do you wonder that I'm happy at how things are going?"

"No, lord Marshal," Gurmun said. "You can be happy. Just don't be surprised." He sounded like what he was: an officer tough, competent, and altogether confident. Unkerlant hadn't had many officers like that when the war against Algarve started. She still didn't have enough, but one Gurmun made up for a lot.

"How are the behemoths holding up?" Rathar asked.

"Losses are within the range we expected," Gurmun answered. "The farms in the west are sending enough fresh beasts forward. The redheads' dragons never could fly that far, not even when things looked worst for us. And the Gongs never have put a whole lot of dragons in the air against us. I wouldn't want to try flying over the Elsung Mountains, either."

"Something to that," Rathar agreed.

"A week—maybe even less—and we'll be swarming over the Forthwegian border," Gurmun said. "What was the Forthwegian border, I mean."

Marshal Rathar started to call him a mad optimist. Then he took another look at the map, and at what the Algarvians could put between his behemoths and the old Forthwegian frontier. "You may be right," he said.

"You bet I'm right," Gurmun declared.

"Getting more footsoldiers on horseback helps, too," Rathar said. "Even though they fight on foot, moving 'em mounted helps 'em keep up with the behemoths. The redheads used that trick, too, whenever they could scrape up the mounts."

"Powers below eat the redheads," Gurmun said again. "The powers below *are* eating the redheads, and we're serving them up. The first couple of years of this fight, they taught us lessons. Now we're better than our schoolmasters."

Rathar doubted that. The Algarvians still had more flexible arrangements than the soldiers of his own kingdom. They coordinated better among footsoldiers and behemoths and dragons. Each of their regiments or squadrons had more crystals than its Unkerlanter counterpart, which made them more responsive to trouble. An Algarvian regiment was probably worth close to two Unkerlanter units.

But if King Swemmel's soldiers threw three or four or five regiments at each Algarvian formation . . . Here in the north, the Unkerlanters had thrown a lot more than that at each Algarvian regiment at the spearpoint of the attack. And the redheads, however fiercely they'd fought, couldn't stand up against such an overwhelming weight of numbers. This time, they'd really and truly broken.

"Our way of putting out a fire is throwing bodies on it till it smothers," Rathar said. "Sorry, Gurmun, but I don't think that's the most efficient way to do things."

"It works," Gurmun said. "It's worked."

"So it does," Rathar agreed. Again, if it hadn't worked, Unkerlant would have lost the war. But the price the kingdom was paying . . . Every ruined, empty village he rode through as his countrymen fought their way east tore at him. How would Unkerlant rebuild once the fighting finally ended? Where would the peasants to fill those villages come from? He had no idea.

Before he could say as much—not that General Gurmun would have worried about such a thing; his mind focused solely on using his beloved behemoths against the Algarvians—the sound of many marching feet came to his ear. His head swung toward it: toward the eastern side of the village, the side closest to the fighting. Gurmun's head swung the same way. A grin spread over his blunt-featured face as he said, "How much do you want to bet those are captives?"

"I'd sooner keep my silver, thanks," Rathar answered.

Gurmun's grin got wider. "Let's go have a look at the whoresons." Without waiting for a reply, he hurried out of the peasant hut. Rathar followed a little more slowly. He'd seen captive Algarvians before.

Still, being reminded what these attacks were doing to the enemy wouldn't hurt. And the column of captives coming through the village represented more than a regiment's worth of men. The guards in their rock-gray tunics wore grins a lot like Gurmun's. Some of the Algarvians were grinning, too: the nervous grins of men glad to be alive and unsure how much longer they would stay that way. More of them looked glum. They might be alive, but they didn't want to be in Unkerlanter hands. Their light brown tunics and kilts were shabbier than Algarvian uniforms had been when the war was new. It wasn't just that they were filthy and worn; the cloth itself was thinner and cheaper and flimsier than what they'd used then.

Despite everything, a few redheads strode along as if they owned the world. They towered over their captors, as Algarvians usually did tower over Unkerlanters, and gave the impression that the guards were actually escorts, taking them someplace where more Unkerlanters would serve them. Rathar admired Algarvian arrogance and despised it at the same time. Regardless of their true situation, Mezentio's men still reckoned themselves the masters of Derlavai. Some of them almost made even their foes believe it.

Rathar held up a hand. When the Marshal of Unkerlant gave even an informal order, his mean leaped to obey. "Column halt!" the guards screamed, some in their own language, others in fragments of Algarvian.

"Who here speaks Unkerlanter?" Rathar asked. He had a little Algarvian himself, but only a little, and knew no classical Kaunian, the language that tied together educated men of all kingdoms in the east of Derlavai and on the island Kuusamo and Lagoas shared.

A redhead stepped toward him: one of the ones who'd kept his spirit in spite of captivity. "I being in your kingdom three years," he said, trilling his words in a way no Unkerlanter would. "I learning your speech, some. What you wanting?"

"Your head on a plate," Gurmun growled.

But Rathar waved him to silence. "What do you think of things now that we have beaten Algarve in the summer as well as the winter?"

The redhead's shrug was a masterpiece of its kind. "I being in your kingdom three years," he repeated. "No Unkerlanters in Algarve. No Unkerlanters ever in Algarve. Sooner or later, we winning war."

Gurmun wasn't the only one who growled then. So did all the guards who heard the Algarvian. Rathar waved for quiet again. He got it, but he suspected the captive would have a hard time once out of his sight. "How can you say that," he demanded, "when we've driven your countrymen out of most of what they held here in the north in just a few weeks?"

With another shrug, the Algarvian replied, "We having secret sorceries. We using them soon. Turning Unkerlant upsydown,

insyout. You seeing." He sounded like a man who knew exactly
what he was talking about.

And Unkerlant had already known too much horror from Algarvian sorceries. Some of the guards muttered among themselves. A couple made signs the peasants used to turn aside evil
omens. And now, instead of growling, Gurmun barked: "What
kind of sorceries?"

"Not knowing." The captive shrugged yet again. "If likes of
me knowing"— he had a corporal's pips on his shoulder
boards—"not being secret, eh?"

"I think you're lying," Gurmun said in a deadly voice.

"Thinking how you liking." The Algarvian's voice made it
plain he didn't care what an Unkerlanter, even an Unkerlanter
general, thought. "King Mezentio saying these things so. I believing he."

Marshal Rathar gestured once more, waving the captives on.
The guards screamed at them. They got moving. Before long,
the arrogant redhead was lost in the throng. *Not soon enough,
though,* Rathar thought.

"Do you believe the son of a whore?" Gurmun asked, sounding unwontedly nervous.

"I believe he believes himself," Rathar answered. "Whether
Mezentio is telling lies . . . That's a different question."

"It's not the first we've heard of these secret sorceries." Aye,
Gurmun was unhappy. "A lot of the captives we've taken lately
go on about them. Where there's smoke, there's liable to be
fire."

"Where there are Algarvians, there's liable to be trouble,"
Rathar said, and his general of behemoths nodded vigorously.
He went on, "Reports have gone back to Cottbus, though, and
King Swemmel doesn't seem to worried about this."

"Good," Gurmun said.

Although Marshal Rathar nodded, he wondered whether it
was good. True, Swemmel saw plots behind ever chair and under
every rug. If he didn't think these worrisome reports true, it was
a good sign he judged them an Algarvian bluff. That was fine—if
he proved right. Every once in a while, though, his instinct let
him down badly, as when he'd judged that the Algarvians

wouldn't expect an Unkerlanter attack three years before. Maybe the redheads hadn't expected such an attack, but if not, it was only because they'd been so far along with plans for their own, which had gone in first. No mistake now could cost as much as that one had—or so Rathar devoutly hoped—but he didn't want to have to deal with the king's mistakes under any circumstances.

A crystallomancer burst out of the hut next to the one in which Rathar made his headquarters. "Lord Marshal!" the young man shouted. "We've got men inside Forthweg, sir!"

"Told you so." General Gurmun went from anxious to smug in a heartbeat.

"This is even faster than you thought it would happen," Rathar said, and Gurmun nodded. The marshal went on: "We have to move east, we truly do. We're getting too far behind the line again." Gurmun nodded once more. Rathar laughed. "Plenty of worse problems to have, by the powers above." Gurmun chuckled, too. To the men in charge of an advancing army, life looked good.

Talsu set silver on the grocery counter. Since Gailisa's father was in the shop, she put the money in the cash box before sliding the jar of green olives in a brine flavored with garlic and fennel across the counter. He spoke in a low voice, so her father wouldn't hear: "With luck, we won't have to look at Mainardo's pointy-nosed Algarvian face too much longer."

"That would be good," she agreed, also quietly. Then she raised her voice to tell her father, "I'm going home with Talsu now, Papa."

"All right," he answered. "I'll shut the place up myself. You don't need to worry about that." He'd stopped trying to persuade her and Talsu to spend their nights there instead of in the tent on the outskirts of Skrunda.

Gailisa took Talsu's hand as she emerged from behind the counter. They walked out of the grocer's shop and into the warm twilight of a Jelgavan summer evening. A couple of news-sheet vendors were still waving leaves of paper and shouting their news: "Invaders thrown back before Balvi! King Mainardo's heroic Algarvian allies triumph in savage fighting!"

When one of the vendors waved his sheet at Talsu, he shook his head and kept walking. To Gailisa, he said, "The redheads keep right on telling lies."

"I know." She nodded. "You'll never believe what I heard from one of the women who came into the shop today, though."

"Will I want to believe it, though?" Talsu asked. When Gailisa nodded again, he said, "Then tell me!"

"Well, what she said was . . ." Gailisa paused, either for dramatic effect or just to take a breath. "What she said was, either Mainardo's already run away from Balvi or he's just about to. He doesn't want to end up like what's-his-name, his cousin, did over there in Unkerlant."

"Boiled alive, you mean," Talsu said. The news sheets had screamed of Unkerlanter barbarism when that happened. His wife nodded once more. He scratched his head. That was a rumor he wanted to believe. But no matter what he wanted, he saw certain basic difficulties. "How did this woman here in Skrunda know what was going on with the Algarvians way over in Balvi?"

"I don't know," Gailisa answered. "I'm telling you what she told me, that's all. I hope it's true, don't you?"

"Of course I do," Talsu said with a nod of his own. "The only thing better would be having the Lagoans or the Kuusamans catch him and give him to King Donalitu. He'd envy his cousin by the time Donalitu was through with him."

"He would, wouldn't he?" Gailisa smiled, but then shook her head. "The things I'm imagining, the things I'm hoping for—even thinking about them would have made me sick a few years ago."

"It's the war." Talsu had seen things and done things and had things happen to him that he never would have imagined before the war, either. One of the things that had happened to him was only too obvious right now. Pointing to the ruins past which he and Gailisa were walking, he said, "Aye, it's the cursed war. We used to live here."

Gailisa squeezed his hand. "Your father will find a way to rebuild. He would have already if it were an ordinary fire and not eggs from the sky. We can't go on living in a tent too much longer." She sounded more hopeful than sure of that, but Talsu didn't argue with her. He thought the same thing.

He started to say so, but then exclaimed in surprise instead. Someone had been hurrying up the sidewalk toward them. Now, despite the deepening dark, Talsu recognized him. "Father!" he said. "What are you doing here? It's close to curfew time, and you know how jumpy the redheads are."

"Powers above be praised," Traku said, panting a little. "I found you before you got in. I just hope they haven't followed me."

"What are you talking about?" Talsu asked, though he had a horrid fear he knew.

Traku said, "Someone—never mind who—came by today and warned me the Algarvians were going to come after everybody they'd ever caught before. I don't know why. Maybe lock 'em up again, maybe do something worse. But for all I know, they've got somebody—probably a Jelgavan, too, curse the bugger—watching the tent waiting for you to get there so they can drop on you."

"Something worse," Talsu repeated. People whispered about what the Algarvians did to people of Kaunian blood off in the west. If they were in trouble in Jelgava, what would keep them from doing the same thing here? Nothing he could think of. He said, "No, I can't go home, not with that waiting. I have to disappear."

"I think you're right," his father said. Gailisa nodded.

"Will *you* be all right if I don't come home tonight?" Talsu asked Traku.

"We'll find out," Traku answered with a shrug. "If it's not quite all right, I'll make my getaway, too."

Traku knew it was liable not to be that easy. He didn't say anything for fear of alarming Gailisa. He clasped Traku's hand, then clutched his wife to him. He kissed her for a long time. When at last he had to let her go, he said, "I'll come back. If I made it back from the dungeon, I can make it back from this."

He knew that was liable not to be so easy, too. Again, he kept quiet. Gailisa said, "Don't tell us where you're going. If we don't know, the redheads can't tear it out of us."

"Good luck, son," Traku said gruffly. He held out a small cloth sack. It was heavy in Talsu's hand, and clinked softly. Traku went on, "Get going now. Maybe that'll buy you a little luck. Hope so, anyhow."

With a wordless nod, Talsu started up a side street. When he looked back, he couldn't see his father and Gailisa any more. He stuffed the sack of coins into a pocket. He didn't know how long it would last, but having it was ever so much better than going into exile with no more than a couple of coppers.

He wished Gailisa hadn't been carrying the olives. They would have given him a snack, if nothing else.

In the old days, Skrunda, like most towns, had had a wall around it. No more. Hardly any of the wall remained; once Jelgava became a united kingdom, builders started making the most of all that ready-cut stone. Why not, when the town was unlikely to have to stand siege? These days, Skrunda had long since outgrown the old walled-in area, anyhow.

As Talsu got to the outskirts, then, he wasn't in town one minute and out in the countryside the next. He kept passing houses, but less and less often, with more and more open space between them. Presently, he started going past little almond orchards and groves of fragrant lemons and oranges.

At first, all he wanted to do was put distance between himself and Skrunda. The longer the Algarvians had to chase him and the farther into the country they had to go, the better. "If they want to catch me, they'd better work for it," he muttered. An eagle owl let out a couple of deep hoots, as if agreeing with him.

But once he was well away, he started wondering where he should go and what he could do. Head for Dobele, the next town farther west? What would he do when he got there? The redheads knew he was a tailor, so looking for work with a needle would be asking to get caught. Could he work as a day laborer? He supposed so, but the idea roused no enthusiasm in him.

What I really want to do is fight the Algarvians, not run from them, he thought. *If I had a stick in my hands, I wouldn't be running now.* All he'd ever wanted to do was fight Mezentio's men. Trying had landed him in the dungeon. Trying again might land him in something worse. He didn't care. That was what he wanted, more than anything else in the world.

And so, instead of staying on the road and making for Do-bele, he turned down a little path that led up toward low, rolling hills south of the two towns. He didn't know whether bandits lurked in them; what he did know was that, were he a bandit, he would have lurked up there.

He didn't get to them that night, but fell asleep in bushes by the side of the track. That was uncomfortable, but not too bad on a summer's night in Jelgava. He wouldn't have cared to try it in some southern kingdom.

When he came to a farm the next morning, he asked the farmer, "If I give you a day's work, will you give me a couple of days' food?" The farmer just stood in the yard, tossing feed to his hens. His eyes measured Talsu. After the silence stretched for a while, Talsu said, "Or, if you want, you can turn me in to the redheads. They'd thank you." He hadn't wanted to roll the dice so soon, but seemed to have little choice.

And it worked. The farmer said, "Well, I'll find something for you to do." He went into the house and came out with barley bread and hard white crumbly cheese and some olives much like the ones Talsu had bought at the grocery and a flask of wine sharpened with citrus juices. Talsu ate and drank. Then he chopped wood till his palms blistered, and pulled weeds in the vegetable garden after that. The farmer and his wife gave him bread and ham and olive oil and more wine for lunch, and a stew of mutton and grain and almonds and apricots for supper. He slept on straw in the barn.

The following morning, the farmer brought him a couple of loaves of bread, a small flask full of a paste of garlic and olives and oil, and a large flask full of wine. He even gave him a knapsack that had seen better days in which to carry the food. Talsu came to attention and saluted as he might have to an officer.

He wasn't altogether astonished when the farmer returned the salute. The fellow said, "If you go six or eight miles south, you'll come to a track that heads southwest into some of the steeper country. It's the one with a milepost from the old Kaunian days just in front of it. Follow it, if you care to."

"Why?" Talsu asked. The farmer just shrugged. After a moment, Talsu shrugged, too. He slung the knapsack over one shoulder and started south. His hands hurt. His joints ached and his muscles were stiff and sore; he wasn't used to the work the farmer had set him. After a while, though, walking along under the warm sun eased the kinks.

There was the milestone, its gray-streaked marble much weathered but the inscription still legible. And he could make sense of that classical Kaunian inscription, thanks to Kugu the silversmith. He'd had other, less pleasant, things for which to thank Kugu, and he'd had his revenge. He turned right and walked down the track the farmer had mentioned.

Sure enough, the country did get rougher. Anyone with a stick on one of those bluffs could have potted him before he knew where danger lurked. But the fellow with a stick—Algarvian military issue; Talsu recognized it at once—stepped out from behind a tree. "You may have made a mistake, coming along this track," he said. *A fatal mistake,* he meant.

"Not if you're fighting Mezentio's buggers. A farmer"—Talsu described the man and his farm as well as he could—"sent me on this way. I was in the army till we quit. I know what to do."

"Do you?" The bandit—or 'was diehard a better name?—rubbed his poorly shaved chin. He lowered the stick, but not by very much. "Come along with me. We'll see what we find out." Talsu gladly came.

Thirteen

◌⟊⟋◌

Krasta stood naked by the side of the bed, staring down at herself. "I still don't look like I'm pregnant," she said, sounding as if she was trying to convince herself.

Colonel Lurcanio, lying naked in the bed, lazy and cheerful after making love, nodded. "Not, not very much," he answered agreeably.

"What do you mean, not very much?" Krasta demanded, her indignation quick to kindle even toward her dangerous Algarvian lover. "My belly doesn't bulge at all."

"Well, so it doesn't." Lurcanio reached out and set the palm of his hand on that still-flat belly. Krasta expected it to slide lower, down between her legs. Instead, Lurcanio went on, "But your breasts are larger than they were—not that I mind, you understand." Rather than reaching down from her belly, he reached up to caress her.

She hissed. "Be careful. They're more tender than they used to be, too." She couldn't help admitting that. It was both blessing and curse. When his hands weren't gentle, or sometimes simply when she moved too fast, they would hurt. But they also gave her more pleasure when he did a proper job of caressing them than they ever had before she quickened.

"Sorry, my dear." Lurcanio continued in almost clinical tones: "And your nipples are larger and darker than they were."

"Are they?" Krasta looked down at herself again. "I hadn't noticed that."

"I'm not surprised, or not very," Lurcanio said. "Men are liable to pay more attention to that sort of thing than women do."

"I should hope so." Krasta sat down beside him—carefully, so her tender breasts wouldn't bounce. "As far as I'm concerned, they're just . . . there." A sudden thought took her by surprise. "But I suppose they'll matter to me if I decide to nurse the baby myself."

"Aye, I'm sure they would." Lurcanio raised an eyebrow. "And would you do such a thing, or would you hire a wet nurse?"

"*I* don't know," Krasta said with an impatient toss of the head. She promptly regretted it, for it jerked the upper part of her body, too. She hissed again, and brought a protective hand up to her breasts. "They're just . . . there," she repeated.

"Like Algarvians in Valmiera," Lurcanio said.

She nodded. "Aye, like Algarvians in Valmiera." Only after she'd repeated that, too, did she pause to wonder about it. "What an odd way to put things."

"Not so odd. We have been here four years. *I* have been *here* four years," Lurcanio said. "Considering some of the places I might have gone instead, I have no complaints. You may rest assured that that is the truth. But I do not know how much longer I can stay here."

"What do you mean?" Krasta had always hated change. These days, Lurcanio in her bed and Algarvians on the streets of Priekule were what she was used to.

He stroked her again. That was all he was likely to do. He wasn't a young man any more, and wouldn't want her more than once of a night. Voice detached and ironic as usual, he answered, "Unlike some people I could name, I am usually in the habit of meaning what I say, and neither more nor less than that."

"But . . ." Krasta frowned, trying hard to think despite finding the exercise unfamiliar. "Where would you go? What would you do?"

"Unkerlant or Jelgava, most likely," he replied. "I would fight for my king and my kingdom. That is one of the things a soldier may be called upon to do from time to time, you know."

"But what would *I* do?" Krasta exclaimed. When she did think, she usually thought about herself first.

Colonel Lurcanio laughed. "I presume that, were I to depart this mansion tomorrow, the very next day you would start trying as hard to convince Viscount Valnu that your baby is his as you've spent the last few weeks trying to convince me it is mine."

"It *is* yours," Krasta insisted with much more certainty than she felt. All along, though, she'd done her best to make herself believe the baby was Lurcanio's. And if the Algarvian officer should disappear, would she have to start believing the child was Valnu's? She glared at Lurcanio. "You're a horrid man, too, you know."

"Thank you," Lurcanio said, which only annoyed her more. He laughed, but the amusement wouldn't stay on his face. When it faded, he looked a long way indeed from young. "I have not got my orders yet, you understand, but I fear they may not be far away."

Krasta didn't feel so happy, either. Seeing her lover look not so young reminded her she wasn't quite so young, either. So did the weariness that came with carrying a child. Fighting back a yawn, she said, "If you Algarvians need all your officers and soldiers in those other kingdoms far away, how will you hold on to Valmiera?"

She thought about the soldiers she'd seen marching up the Boulevard of Horsemen, the blond soldiers in Valmieran uniform with Algarvian flags on their sleeves. Did the redheads think they could use men like that to hold down the kingdom? If they were right, what did that say about Valmiera? What did lying naked here beside an Algarvian say about her? It was all very confusing.

Lurcanio patted her. He liked to touch her even when he didn't feel like doing—or couldn't do—anything more. "That is a good question, my sweet," he said. "When King Mezentio figures out a good answer for it, I hope he will let me know. Until then . . ." He got out of bed and started getting into his clothes. When he was dressed, he bowed to her. "I shall see you in the morning." He seldom spent nights in her bedchamber.

Krasta turned out the lamp without bothering to put on pyjamas. A month into summer, the night was fine and warm—nothing like the long, frigid, miserable hours of darkness the winter before. And she'd had it easier than most, because of the Algarvians in the mansion with her. She didn't dwell on that for long; she just slid under the linen sheets and fell asleep.

A couple of hours later, distant rumblings woke her—those and flashes of light on the horizon. *Thunder?* she wondered muzzily. *But the day was bright and clear.* Then her wits began to work, and she remembered the sorry world in which she lived. "Oh," she said out loud, around a yawn. "The islanders are dropping eggs on us again."

She took it for granted. Why not? It had happened before, a good many times. It would doubtless happen again, too. She sighed and went back to sleep.

When she came down to breakfast the next morning, she found Colonel Lurcanio in a foul temper. "How are we supposed to go about fighting a proper war if they keep dropping eggs on our heads?" he demanded.

"They have dragons," Krasta said, spreading butter and Jelgavan marmalade on toast. "Don't you have dragons, too?"

"Of course we have dragons, too," Lurcanio answered irritably. He was going to be difficult. Krasta could feel it. And she was right. More irritably still, Lurcanio went on, "We have dragons fighting to keep the Lagoans and Kuusamans on Sibiu from dropping eggs on Algarve herself. We have dragons, some dragons, fighting the islanders down in Jelgava. And we have dragons in the west, in Unkerlant and Forthweg, fighting Swemmel's men."

"Unkerlant *and* Forthweg?" Krasta asked. "I hadn't heard that before."

"And you have not heard it now, either. Forget I said it," Lurcanio told her. He passed a hand across his face. It was still early morning, but he looked weary. After a moment, he looked up at Krasta again. "Where was I? Ah, aye. With all those dragons flying over the rest of Derlavai, how many do you think Algarve has left to put in the air above Priekule?"

"Not enough—that's plain," Krasta said. "And so eggs land on Valmierans. You people should have thought this out better before you got into such a big war, if you want to know what I think."

Lurcanio stared at her out of red-rimmed eyes. He started to laugh. Krasta started to get angry. Then her Algarvian lover said, "Out of the mouths of babes." He got up, walked around the table, and kissed her. "You are right, my sweet. We probably should have thought this out better. But it is rather too late to worry about that now, would you not agree?"

"Lurcanio . . ." she said as he went back to his seat.

He looked her way in some surprise. She hardly ever called him by name. "What is it?" he asked, his voice more serious than usual, the mocking note so often in it now entirely gone.

"You're going to lose the war, aren't you?" The words came forth in a rush, blurted out before Krasta had the chance to think about whether she really wanted to ask that question.

"Eat your breakfast," Colonel Lurcanio told her, as if she were a child asking something whose answer had to be too hard for it to understand. But then he shook his head, a gesture aimed more at himself than at Krasta. "Things are not easy these days," he said slowly. "I do not know when they will be easy again. I do not know if they will ever be easy again. But I tell you this: if Algarve goes down, we shall go down fighting. Do you doubt it, even for a moment?"

"No." Krasta shivered, though the day already promised considerable heat.

"We shall go down fighting," Lurcanio repeated, as if she hadn't spoken. "We shall put sticks in the hands of the veterans left alive from the Six Years' War, and in the hands of fourteen-year-old boys still sore from their circumcisions. For if we lose this war as we lost the last one, what shall be left for Algarve?"

For once in all the time they'd spent together, Krasta wanted to go around the table and comfort him. But she didn't. She just sat where she was. She wished the baby inside her would let her drink brandy, even so early in the day. But the mere thought made her belly clench.

Lurcanio shrugged and smiled, as if deliberately pushing worry to one side. "Well," he said, "the evil time has not yet come for us. And, while it may come, it also may not. I intend to do what I can to enjoy myself in the meanwhile."

No, the evil time hasn't come for the Algarvians yet, Krasta thought. *What about for the Kaunians of Forthweg? What about for Kaunians all over Derlavai?*

She couldn't ask Lurcanio that question. That she couldn't ask it of him was probably the most important reason she hadn't got up and gone around the breakfast table to him. She was, in an odd way and with certain gaps, truly fond of him. But he was an Algarvian, and she had yellow hair. Walls would always stand between them, whether he fully realized it or not.

He rose and bowed to her. "And now I needs must go do what needs doing, to hold the evil time at bay as best I can. If you will excuse me"—one of his eyebrows twitched—"or even if you will not . . ." He bowed again and left.

He sits at a desk, but he fights for Algarve, just as much as if he had a stick in his hand. Krasta had known that for four years, but knowing it and having it hit home were two different things.

He's worth even more than an ordinary soldier, because he can do things no ordinary soldier can do.

And you . . . may have his baby inside you. No matter what Lurcanio would do to her if she bore a blond, Krasta hoped with all her heart the child was Valnu's.

After the impressers hauled Garivald into King Swemmel's army, he hadn't got much in the way of training. He hadn't got any training, as a matter of fact. They'd given him a uniform and a stick and told him to obey the officers and underofficers set over him if he knew what was good for him. Then they'd taken him to the front in northern Unkerlant, stuck him in a squad there, and thrown him at the Algarvians. He still had trouble recalling that his name was supposed to be Fariulf.

And now, less than a month after he'd followed a behemoth over and through the Algarvian trenches when the assault began, he found himself a corporal, and a corporal in a foreign kingdom at that, for his regiment had pushed into Forthweg a couple of days earlier. Forthwegian peasant villages didn't look much different from their Unkerlanter equivalents, except that the locals painted their houses in brighter colors and that the men wore beards.

No, another difference: there *were* a lot of men in the villages. That took some getting used to. "When the redheads came through, these Forthwegians knuckled under," one of Garivald's squadmates said. "They didn't fight back, not like we did."

And so more of them are left alive, Garivald thought. He kept that notion buried down deep; getting a name for the subversive kind of grousing might have proved fatally inefficient. What he did say was, "The redheads put up a tougher fight down in the south than they're doing up here."

"That's 'cause half the Grelzers are traitors," another trooper said, which wasn't quite true but came too close to truth for comfort. The fellow went on, "Besides, what do you know about it, Corporal? Even if you did get promoted, you're a new fish."

Garivald started to answer that. He'd seen plenty of fighting down in Grelz, even if not formally as one of King Swemmel's soldiers. His irregulars—Munderic's, till he took over the band—had harassed the Algarvians and their Grelzer puppets . . . and even a few Forthwegians, the ruffians in the outfit called Plegmund's Brigade.

But, in the end, Garivald kept his mouth shut and let the question go with just a shrug. He didn't want people knowing Corporal Fariulf was really Garivald, the fellow who'd led irregulars and written songs and done other things to draw the unfriendly notice of people in Cottbus. King Swemmel and those who followed him trust no one who'd fought the redheads on his own. After all, such people might turn and fight him one day, too.

Dragons streaked by overhead, flying east. They were all painted the rock-gray of Garivald's tunic. "Haven't seen many Algarvian dragons lately," he remarked. That seemed a safe enough way to change the subject.

"Don't miss those bastards, either, not even slightly." Two soldiers said it at the same time, in almost identical words. Garivald hadn't had to worry about Algarvian dragons down in Grelz. Mezentio's men hadn't had so many that they bothered using them against irregulars. Almost every beast they put in the air flew against King Swemmel's main army.

But now Garivald was part of that main army. If the Algarvians put dragons in the air here in the north, they would be flying them at his comrades and him. But if the Algarvians put dragons in the air here in the north, swarms of Unkerlanter dragons would try to knock them down. Garivald had never seen so many dragons in his whole life. He'd never imagined that so many dragons could be gathered together and fed and flown over one stretch of the front.

"Halt! Who comes?" a sentry called as someone approached their campfire. The answer came back in Forthwegian. Some Unkerlanters, especially those from the northeast, could make sense of the related language, but it was just tantalizing noise to a Grelzer like Garivald. The sentry was a northern man. When he said, "Come ahead, then," in his dialect of Unkerlanter, the Forthwegian must have been able to follow him, for he approached the fire.

Except, as he got close, he proved *not* to be a Forthwegian. Oh, he had dark hair and a dark beard, as Forthwegian men did, but he was tall and slim and had blue eyes and a short, straight nose, nothing like the beaks belonging to Forthwegians and their Unkerlanter cousins. And, instead of a sensible knee-length tunic, he wore a short tunic and trousers, garments Garivald had heard of but, till now, had never seen.

"Corporal?" he asked Garivald: that was a word nearly identical in Forthwegian and Unkerlanter. When Garivald nodded, the local bowed low before him, as if he were at least a colonel rather than a junior underofficer. He said something that might have been *Thank you* or might as easily not have been. Then he jabbed a thumb at his own chest and said, "I—Kaunian."

"Kaunian?" Garivald said. "I thought Kaunians were blond." He didn't think a whole lot of Kaunians were left alive in Forthweg, either, but saying that didn't strike him as the best way to make this fellow his friend. As things turned out, it wouldn't have mattered, for the local plainly didn't understand his dialect. In some exasperation, Garivald called out to the sentry: "Come back here and translate for me, Rivalin."

"Aye, Corporal," Rivalin said. "I'll do my best."

"That's all you can do," Garivald agreed. "Ask him why his hair isn't yellow if he's one of these Kaunian buggers."

Rivalin spoke in his own dialect, exaggerating some of the sounds and slurring others till Garivald could scarcely make out what he was saying. The Kaunians seemed to get it, though, and answered quickly. Too quickly: He and Rivalin had to go back and forth a couple of times before the sentry turned to Garivald again. "Corporal, he says he is a blond, only he dyed his hair for some kind of a magical disguise he had that made him look like a Forthwegian so the redheads wouldn't grab him."

"Oh." Garivald started to nod, then checked himself. "Wait a minute. If he had this magical disguise, why did he need to dye his hair? Wouldn't the magic take care of that for him?"

More back-and-forth between Rivalin and the Kaunian. At last, Rivalin returned to a brand of Unkerlanter Garivald could readily understand: "Corporal, I *think* he's saying he did it on account of his hair would turn yellow again if it got cut while he had the spell on, but I'm not quite sure."

"Oh," Garivald repeated. "All right, now ask him why he decided to quit his disguise and start wearing those silly clothes."

When Rivalin translated that, the Kaunian spoke with considerable heat—so much heat that the Unkerlanter sentry had to ask him to slow down several times. When the torrent of words finally ebbed, Rivalin answered, "I don't think he's got a whole lot of use for Forthwegians."

"Powers above," one of the troopers behind Garivald said, "I haven't got a whole lot of use for Forthwegians, either." Garivald shrugged. Except for the men of Plegmund's Brigade, these were the first Forthwegians he'd ever seen.

The Kaunian spoke again. "He says he wears those clothes on account of those clothes are what Kaunians wear," Rivalin reported. Garivald shrugged again. Forthweg was a lot warmer than the Duchy of Grelz. Why anybody would want to wear trousers up here . . . Even the Algarvians weren't so foolish. And then, through Rivalin, the Kaunian said, "He wants to know how to join up with us, Corporal. He wants to start killing Algarvians. Says it's his turn now."

"I can't do anything about that. You know I can't," Garivald said, and Rivalin nodded. Garivald went on, "Take him to Lieutenant Andelot. Maybe he'll figure out what to do with him—and he'll be out of our hair."

"Right." Rivalin grinned at him. "You haven't been a corporal very long, Fariulf, but you know eggs is eggs." He led the Kaunian away.

"I should hope I know eggs is eggs," Garivald said. "I know we need a new sentry, too." He named another man and sent him out to take Rivalin's place.

When Rivalin came back, he looked astonished. "I think they're going to recruit that whoreson," he said.

"Why not?" Garivald said. "He wants to blaze some redheads. If he gets a couple before they get him, that's a bargain for us. And even if he doesn't, they blaze him instead of an Unkerlanter. That's a bargain, too."

Rivalin eyed him. "You sure the impressers just scooped you off your farm?"

"Too right I am," Garivald answered. "I wish I were back there now, getting my crop in." He paused. "Part of me wishes that, anyway. The rest . . . Well, it's not like I don't owe the Algarvians anything."

Heads solemnly went up and down. A lot of the newer soldiers in Swemmel's army came from lands regained from the redheads. They'd seen how the Algarvians ruled the countryside they held. A lot of them had kinsfolk missing or dead, the way Garivald did. And a lot of them fought as if the war were a personal struggle against Algarve. In some fights, not a great many captives got taken.

More behemoths came up during the night. Before dawn the next morning, they rumbled forward, tearing a hole in the Algarvian line through which footsoldiers swarmed. Garivald had done that again and again. He almost got the feeling he—or rather, the Unkerlanter army—could do it any time.

Almost. He'd already seen that Mezentio's men, even when outnumbered and outflanked, fought hard for every foot of ground. And they didn't fight with sticks and behemoths alone. He'd heard about the magic that shook the ground and tore fissures and sent lambent purple flames shooting up from it. Now his squad met that magecraft at first hand.

Men screamed when the earth opened and then closed on them. Men whom the flames caught had no chance to scream and simply ceased to be. One burst of flame not only charred a behemoth but also touched off the eggs it carried, spreading ruin through the footsoldiers closest to it.

But then the magic ebbed, almost as swiftly as it had sprung up. Lieutenant Andelot happened to be crouched by Garivald as it faded. The officer said, "That's our mages, sacrificing our people to beat down their wizardry."

"Is there any other way to beat it?" Garivald asked.

"If there is, we haven't found it yet," Andelot answered. "Life energy gives mages a lot of force to work with."

Life energy: a bloodless way to say *killing people*. Garivald found exactly what it meant that afternoon, when he and the

survivors from his squad pushed past the sacrifice the Algarvian mages had made to try to stop them: row upon row of
blond men and women, all blazed through the head. "No wonder that Kaunian wanted to join up," Garivald said. "If the Algarvians had done this to us, I'd want to kill every Algarvian
ever born."

"No wonder at all," Rivalin said. Like Garivald's, his eyes
kept coming back to the dead blonds in sick fascination.

But then Garivald reflected that Mezentio's men hadn't lined
up Unkerlanters row on row and sacrificed them. Their own
mages had done that. He wished he hadn't thought of it in such
terms. *They only do it because the Algarvians are killing these
blonds.* That was true, but eased his mind only so much. They
were doing it, and *why* counted little. Sooner or later, a day of
reckoning would have to come. . . . Wouldn't it?

Whenever Bembo went out on the streets of Eoforwic these
days, he found himself looking west. That was the direction
rain came from, not that rain was likely in the Forthwegian capital in the middle of summer. But, despite heat and bright blue
skies and dazzling sun, a storm was brewing in the west, and he
knew it.

The Algarvian constable noticed he wasn't the only one
glancing that way. With a distinct effort of will, he turned his
gaze away from the west and onto his partner. "It's on your
nerves, too, eh, Delminio?" he said.

"Aye," Delminio answered, not needing to ask what *it* was.
"Who would've thought things could just fall apart like that?"

"Not me," Bembo said. "And tell me, what difference will it
make to the cursed Unkerlanters, powers below eat 'em, if I'm
toting a long stick like a soldier and not the regular short one?
This miserable thing is heavy." He could always find something
to complain about, even though he'd carried an army-issue
stick going into the Kaunian quarter.

Despite the long stick slung on his own back, Delminio had
no trouble shrugging an elaborate Algarvian shrug. "No, it
probably wouldn't make much difference to Swemmel's bastards, if they ever get here," he allowed.

"Powers above grant that they don't," Bembo said. "Powers above grant that the army stops 'em somewhere, anywhere." He'd never imagined sounding plaintive and worried about the Algarvian army, but that was how he felt.

Delminio went on as if he hadn't spoken, repeating, "It won't matter much to the Unkerlanters, no. But suppose these Forthwegian whoresons here in town start feeling frisky. Wouldn't you rather be toting something that'll knock 'em over from more than a hundred feet away?"

"Urk," Bembo said, and meant it most sincerely. "D'you think it'll come to that?"

"Who knows?" Delminio shrugged again. "But I'll tell you this: there's an awful lot of Forthwegians walking around with their peckers up because they know we're hurting. Or do you think I'm wrong?"

He sounded as if he hoped Bembo would tell him he was just imagining things. Bembo wished he could do that, but he couldn't. Before, the Forthwegians on the streets had scrambled out of the way when they saw constables coming. They might not have loved them (*Who ever loves a constable?* Bembo wondered, not wasting a chance for self-pity), but they feared them, which would do.

Now . . . If they weren't laughing behind the constables' backs, Bembo would have been astonished. Some of them had the nerve to laugh in the constables' faces. Bembo wouldn't have minded teaching them a lesson, but he didn't. Orders were not to do anything that might touch off a riot. The Algarvians had enough to worry about in Forthweg these days without adding the Forthwegians to the mix.

Delminio's grunt might have meant he thought Bembo's silence proved his point. Since Bembo thought the same thing, he didn't push his partner. The stinking Unkerlanters were getting close to the Twegen River, the stream that flowed north to the sea right past the western edge of Eoforwic.

"Do they think they'll have a happy time if Swemmel's whoresons take this place away from us?" Bembo asked no one in particular. "Not likely."

"No, not likely at all," Delminio agreed. "Other question is do they care? And that's not likely, either. Most of 'em don't think about Unkerlanters one way or the other, except that Swemmel's men are giving us a hard time. They think King Penda will come back if they throw us out, and they'll all be happy again."

"Don't hold your breath," Bembo said. "Wasn't Swemmel about ready to boil somebody alive because whoever it was wouldn't hand Penda over to him?"

"Tsavellas of Yanina had him," Delminio said.

Bembo snapped his fingers. "That's right. Thanks. I'd forgotten who it was. When I was back in Tricarico, reading about all this stuff in the west in the news sheets, it didn't seem to matter so much."

"Only goes to show, you can't tell ahead of time," Delminio said, and Bembo nodded. He hadn't thought much about Forthweg at all, not in the days before the war started. He'd never imagined he would have the bad luck to get stuck in this miserable kingdom for years.

A Forthwegian with a gray-streaked black beard reaching halfway down his chest came out of his shop and shouted at the constables in bad Algarvian: "When you catch villains who theft from me? How I make living, they theft my trunks?"

"Well, however you make a living, it won't be as an elephant," Bembo answered. Delminio snickered.

The shopkeeper, who sold luggage, didn't speak Algarvian well enough to get the joke. "Elephant? What you talk about, elephant?" he said. "Powers below eat elephant. Go catch thefts. What you good for? All you Algarvians, you nothing but crazy peoples."

Bembo swept off his plumed hat and bowed, as if at a compliment. "Thank you," he said. Delminio snickered again. The shopkeeper said something in sonorous, guttural Forthwegian. Whatever it was, Bembo didn't think it was praise. The fellow turned around and stumped back into his shop.

"If the bugger who stole from him starts selling those trunks, maybe we'll nab him," Delminio said. "If he doesn't, how can we get our hands on him?"

"And why should we care?" Bembo added. "You think I want to work hard for somebody who calls me names? If he'd dropped a little silver, now, that'd be a different story."

"Sure enough," Delminio agreed. "Far as I'm concerned, the powers below are welcome to all these Forthwegians. I wouldn't shed a tear if we started shipping them west along with the blonds."

"Trouble with that is, it'd really spark off an uprising," Bembo said.

After pondering for a couple of paces, Delminio nodded. "Aye, you're probably right." He took another step. "Of course, the uprising's liable to come anyway. If it does, these buggers ought to be fair game, you ask me."

"You talk like Oraste," Bembo said.

"Who?" Delminio waggled a finger. "Oh, your old partner. He seems like a pretty good man to have at your back."

"He is." Bembo let it rest there. Along with being a good man to have at one's back, Oraste believed the way to settle problems was to settle the people who made them—by choice, permanently.

The shift was long and slow and dull. Another argument with a Forthwegian right at the end made it even longer. Delminio was furious, and didn't even try to hide it. He was all for arresting the local, who was unhappy because somebody'd flung a rock through a window he'd just replaced. Bembo didn't want to arrest him. He wanted him to shut up and go away. Then his partner and he could go back to the barracks and relax.

"If we drop on him, we have to drag him over to the gaol and fill out all the cursed forms," he said. "That always takes hours, and we're already late getting back, and I'm hungry." He patted his belly. To him, that argument, like the belly in question, carried considerable weight.

In the end, it carried weight for Delminio, too. He contented himself with taking hold of his stick and starting to swing it toward the Forthwegian. That stopped the argument in the middle of the ley line: the Forthwegian turned pale and led. "We ought to ship *him* west," Delminio said. "Nobody'd miss him a bit."

"Powers below eat him," Bembo said. "Let's go home and see if there's anything left in the refectory. Those other greedy buggers better not eat everything in sight." He was almost hungry enough to hurry back to the barracks to make up for lost time—almost, but not quite.

He and Delminio were still three or four blocks away, and squabbling good-naturedly over what the evening's entree would be, when a great roar ahead staggered them both. The ground shook under Bembo's feet. Windows shattered without rocks pitched through them.

Bembo listened for the bells that warned of Unkerlanter dragons, but didn't hear them. He had trouble hearing much of anything. "They somehow snuck one through, the bastards," he shouted, and even had trouble hearing his own voice.

Delminio's words came to Bembo as if from very far away: "Was that the barracks?" Bembo's eyes opened wide. He hadn't thought of that. He and Delminio started to run.

When they rounded the last corner, Bembo skidded to a stop. Broken glass and pebbles skritched under his boots. The whole front of the barracks was gone. Not far from him, a big chunk of stone had come down on someone—a Forthwegian, by his tunic. The result wasn't pretty.

"This must have been an enormous egg." Delminio had to shout it two or three times before Bembo's battered ears caught it.

He nodded. "Too big for a dragon to carry, you'd think." He had to do some shouting of his own to get his partner to understand. "And I still don't hear any warning bells." Someone came staggering out of the barracks: an Algarvian, badly burned and bleeding. How anyone could have lived through that blast of sorcerous energy was beyond Bembo, but he ran toward the other constable to give him what help he could.

Before he reached his countryman, the fellow clapped both hands to his chest and toppled. He might almost have been

blazed. Then a beam burned the ground by Bembo's feet, and
he realized the other Algarvian *had* been blazed.

He wasn't a soldier. He'd never been a soldier. He had no in
terest in becoming a soldier. He had a great deal of interest i
never becoming a soldier. All of which, when someone starte
blazing at him, meant exactly nothing. He dove for cover as i
he'd been fighting in the west against the Unkerlanters fo
years.

"Get down!" he shouted to Delminio, who still stood ther
staring as if he hadn't the slightest idea what was going or
Maybe Delminio didn't. A moment later, Bembo's partne
clutched at his shoulder and went down, so he'd got his lessor
Bembo hoped it wouldn't prove too expensive.

Other shouts started piercing the ringing in Bembo's ears
They weren't in his language, but in raucous Forthwegian. H
couldn't understand a word of them. No, that wasn't true afte
all. One word he understood very well: Penda.

Stupid buggers have gone and risen up, sure as blazes, h
thought, peering out from behind the smoking rubble in back o
which he sprawled. *They'll pay for that. Oh, how they'll pay.*

Someone in a half-shattered building across the street fron
the barracks moved. Bembo didn't know exactly what the mo
tion was or just who'd made it. Whoever it was, though, wa
bound to be a Forthwegian, which meant—which suddenl
meant—an enemy. Bembo raised his stick to his shoulder an
blazed. He heard a shriek. He heard it very clearly, and shoute
in fierce triumph. All at once, he was delighted he had that long
heavy army-issue stick.

"You want us, you'll have to pay for us!" he yelled. A bean
seared the air inches above his head. He smelled thunder an
lightning. Exultation trickled out of him as he realized th
Forthwegian rebels were liable to be willing to do just that.

Saxburh wailed in her cradle. Vanai hurried to pick up th
baby and put her on her breast. That was what Saxbur
wanted. Her cries ceased. She sucked and gulped contentedly
Vanai stroked her fine, soft hair. It was dark, as Ealstan's was
but the baby's skin was too fair, too pale, for a full-blooded

Forthwegian's. Sure enough, Saxburh showed both sides of her family.

Eggs burst, not far away. The windows rattled. They hadn't shattered yet; powers above only knew why. Vanai felt like shrieking, too, but who would comfort her if she did? No one she could think of. Not even Ealstan could do that.

Vanai cursed softly, desperately. Was Ealstan here, staying close by her side while she took care of their daughter? She shook her head. "He had to go fight," she told Saxburh. "He had to try to kick the redheads out of Eoforwic. He thought that was more important."

Her daughter stared up at her out of eyes darkening from blue toward brown. The baby had just learned how to smile. She tried to smile and nurse at the same time. Milk dribbled down her chin.

"He's a fool," Vanai went on in classical Kaunian, dabbing at Saxburh's face with a rag. "He's nothing but a fool. He thinks the Algarvians will go away just like that." She snapped her fingers. The sound startled the baby, who jerked her head—and tried to take Vanai's breast with it. Vanai yelped. That made Saxburh look back toward her, again without letting go. Her moving that way hurt less.

After a little while, Saxburh grunted and made a mess in her drawers. Vanai changed them, cleaned the baby off and rubbed olive oil on her bottom, and then nursed her some more. Saxburh's eyes sagged shut. Vanai slid the nipple out of her mouth, hoisted the baby to her shoulder, and got a sleepy belch out of her. A couple of minutes later, she set Saxburh back in the cradle and closed the toggles on her tunic.

She went to the kitchen and poured herself a cup of wine. Nursing always left her thirsty. As she drank, she looked out the window. She wasn't afraid anyone on the street would recognize her as a Kaunian. For one thing, the Forthwegians held this part of Eoforwic. And, for another, her masking spell worked as well as it always had, now that she wasn't pregnant any more. She looked like a Forthwegian, and she would for hours yet.

Dark brown bloodstains marred the gray slates of the sidewalk. Vanai couldn't tell which ones came from Algarvians and which from Forthwegians. No Algarvians were left alive hereabouts, not now.

Smoke's sharp scent filled the air. So did the nastier deadmeat stench from unburied bodies. Looking west, Vanai saw fresh smoke rising from a dozen fires inside Eoforwic and even more smoke, huge black columns of it, on the far side of the Twegen River. The Unkerlanters were closing in on Eoforwic, moving so fast that not even the news sheets, which had to give forth with Algarvian lies, could cover up the magnitude of the disaster that had befallen Mezentio's men here in the north.

Vanai's mouth twisted. If the Unkerlanters hadn't come so far so fast, the Forthwegian underground wouldn't have risen up. Vanai didn't much care whether Forthwegians or Unkerlanters gave orders in these parts—anyone but Algarvians suited her fine.

But Ealstan cared. Though he differed from most of his countrymen in his views about Kaunians, Ealstan was a Forthwegian patriot. He wanted King Penda back. He wanted the Forthwegians to free their own kingdom, or as much of it as they could. And he was willing—no, he was horribly eager—to risk his life to help bring that about.

"He's an idiot," Vanai whispered—she didn't want to disturb Saxburh. But she meant it all the way down to the depths of her soul. The baby was real. The baby was there. Set against Saxburh's reality, what did the kingdom of Forthweg matter? Nothing, not so far as Vanai could see. But Ealstan thought differently.

Men are stupid, went through Vanai's mind, not for the first time. She'd done everything she could to keep Ealstan here in the flat. Nothing had worked: not argument, not pleading, not tears. *Pybba told him there was going to be a fight, and after that he might as well have been deaf and blind.* Vanai had no trouble at all hating the pottery magnate.

More eggs burst, all in one sector of the city north of the flat. Vanai cursed again, in classical Kaunian and in Forthwegian. The Algarvians had far more egg-tossers than Pybba's ragtag and bobtail. True, Mezentio's men needed everything they could scrape together against the Unkerlanters, but they also couldn't afford to lose Eoforwic. They were fighting back hard.

Footsteps in the hallway. Vanai's heart beat faster. She didn't have to fear Algarvian constables, not for a while. That thudding heart meant hope. And, at the coded knock, she jumped in the air and squeaked for joy.

Carrying a stick with the Algarvian green-red-and-white shield enameled on near the touch-hole, Ealstan strode into the flat. His tunic was filthy. So was he. He wore an armband, also grimy now, that said FREE FORTHWEG—as close as the irregulars came to having real uniforms. "Home for a little while," he said around a yawn. "Then I have to go back."

Despite the dismay stabbing through her at that, and despite his not having bathed for days, Vanai threw her arms around him and kissed him. Then she said, "There's hot water on the stove. I can pour some in a basin. If you want to clean up while I get you something to eat . . ."

"Aye," Ealstan said, and yawned again. He pulled off his tunic, his shoes and socks, and his drawers, and stood there in the kitchen careless of his nakedness. Vanai just smiled and hurried to get the hot water. A few years before, she would have been shocked. What her grandfather would have said . . . *I don't care what my grandfather would have said,* she thought firmly. *This is my husband.*

She gave him bread and oil and cheese and olives and onions: all sorts of food that would keep. She wished they had a rest crate for meat and other perishables. They could have afforded one, but they'd never got around to buying it. Now they had to do without. Ealstan sat down, still naked. He wolfed down everything in sight and looked around for more.

"When did you eat last?" Vanai demanded.

"Yesterday?" he said vaguely. "Aye, yesterday, I think. It's been busy out there." He shook his head; a few drops of water sprayed out from his hair and his beard. "We're doing what we have to do—so far, anyway. How's the baby?"

"She's fine," Vanai said, which drew a grin from Ealstan. She got up and filled his mug with wine once more. A moment later, it was empty again. Vanai went on, "She really is starting to smile."

"That's good. That's very good," Ealstan said. "Here's hoping we're able to give her something to smile about." As if to underscore his words, more eggs burst. He grimaced. "Powers below eat the Algarvians. They don't care if they knock Eoforwic flat, as long as they get rid of us."

"Will the Unkerlanters help us?" Vanai asked.

"Who knows what the Unkerlanters will do?" Ealstan said. "Who cares what they'll do? This is *our* kingdom, curse it. It doesn't belong to Swemmel any more than it belongs to Mezentio."

"Which is all very well," Vanai said, "but will Swemmel pay any attention if you tell him that?"

"I doubt it." Ealstan spoke with a bitter cynicism Vanai had heard from other Forthwegians talking about their kingdom's unhappy history. "When have our neighbors ever paid any attention to us?"

Vanai got up, walked around the table, stood beside Ealstan, and set her hands on his bare shoulders. "I'll pay attention to you, if you wouldn't sooner fall asleep."

He laughed as he looked up at her, but hesitated even so. "Will you be all right if we do?"

"I think so," she answered. "It should be long enough— and I've missed you, too, you know." She kissed him. That might have been a cue in a farce: Saxburh started to cry. Instead of getting angry, Ealstan laughed again. Vanai hurried off to tend the baby. Saxburh turned out to be both wet and hungry. She also turned out to be wide awake and full of smiles.

"Maybe I will just fall asleep," Ealstan said after a while.

"Whatever you like." Vanai knew she would be up a couple of times in the night. Saxburh hadn't quite got the idea of sleeping through it yet. In a way, having the baby in the flat was an advantage; it left her so tired, the din of fighting outside seldom disturbed her rest.

After a couple of hours, Saxburh went back to sleep again.

Vanai set her in the cradle. Ealstan, to her surprise, was still awake. "I must be important to you," she said as she got undressed.

"You think you're joking," he said.

"No." Vanai shook her head. "I don't. I know what being tired means, too."

Ealstan soon proved he wasn't *too* tired. Vanai straddled him, carefully lowering herself onto him. It hurt. She wasn't surprised that it did, not after a baby had gone through there. It hurt almost as much as her first time had. She did her best not to let Ealstan see that. She took no pleasure from it. No, that wasn't true. She took no sensual pleasure, but she did enjoy pleasing Ealstan. He moved slowly and carefully, doing his best not to hurt her, even when he groaned and clutched her backside and spent himself.

She leaned down and kissed him. "Go to sleep now, sweetheart. Nothing's going to happen till the morning." Saxburh would, inevitably, wake up between now and then, but Ealstan couldn't do anything about that.

When the baby did wake up, Ealstan didn't even hear her cries; he kept on breathing deeply, not quite snoring, in the bed beside Vanai. His breathing didn't change when she slid out of bed. She shook her head in bemusement. Back in the days when he'd gone to work and she'd had to stay in the flat for fear of being seized as a Kaunian, he'd often risen without waking her. Now the shoe was on the other foot.

Occasional flashes of light came through the shutters as Vanai changed Saxburh's wet linen and put the baby to her breast: bursts of sorcerous energy, along with the fires those bursts could start. Those flashes meant men shrieking and buildings crashing to ruin, but they looked and sounded like nothing so much as a thunderstorm without the drumming rain.

Saxburh nursed. She burped. She went back to sleep without much fuss. Vanai laid her in the cradle, then lay down beside Ealstan. All sorts of questions filled her mind. Would this uprising do Forthweg any good? If it did, would Ealstan come through safe? The second mattered more to her than the first. If anything happened to Ealstan, she didn't care what happened to Forthweg.

And then she fell asleep herself. No matter how worried about Ealstan she was, she couldn't hold her eyes open another moment.

When she woke, it was beginning to get light outside. She found herself alone in bed. She hurried out to the kitchen. Ealstan had left a note behind. *I hope I see you again soon,* he'd written in classical Kaunian. *Whatever happens, I shall love you as long as I live.* She stared at that. Tears filled her eyes.

Saxburh chose that moment to wake up with a yowl. Vanai scooped her out of the cradle and sat down to give her her breakfast. As the baby began to nurse, they were both crying.

Ealstan wondered whether he'd been wise to go home during the lull in the fighting. He loved Vanai, and wanted to see her as much as he could. His new little daughter entranced him. But seeing them, while it reminded him of why he was fighting, also reminded him of how much he had to lose. He didn't need that reminder, not if he was going to lay his life on the line against the redheads.

Leofsig did it, he thought. That brought his fury up to the proper pitch. If it hadn't been for the Algarvians, his cousin Sidroc never would have quarreled either with him or with his brother. Ealstan hoped Sidroc was dead these days. If he wasn't, he was still fighting in Plegmund's Brigade on the Algarvian side. Recruiting broadsheets for Plegmund's Brigade remained on some walls, though the Forthwegian rebels who held most of Eoforwic had whitewashed the greater number of them.

Ealstan picked his way through rubble up to the barricade of brickwork and boulders and benches behind which the rebels sheltered. A fellow named Beortwulf, who'd been a sergeant in the Forthwegian army and served as a captain here, nodded to him. "Pretty quiet right now. The redheads have been busy further west." He pointed across the Twegen before continuing, "To them, we're an afterthought. They're really sweating about Swemmel's men."

"Afterthought, eh?" Ealstan bared his teeth in a fierce grin. "Let's seem 'em try moving men through Eoforwic and call us an afterthought."

"Something to that," Beortwulf agreed. "Far as I'm concerned, the powers below can eat Algarve and Unkerlant both."

"Aye." Ealstan nodded. "It'd make things a lot easier for Forthweg, that's certain."

Before Beortwulf could answer, a runner called Ealstan's name. When he admitted to being in the neighborhood, the fellow said, "Come on with me. The big boss wants to have a chat with you."

"Oh, he does, does he?" Ealstan said. "Suppose I don't feel like talking to him?" But he followed the man deeper into Eoforwic, to find out what Pybba had in mind. Whatever it was, the Algarvians wouldn't like it.

Pybba still worked out of the pottery, and ran the rebellion from there as he'd run the underground before seizing the chance to strike at Mezentio's men. The Algarvians still hadn't figured out who their chief tormentor was. Had they done so, eggs would surely have smashed Pybba's establishment to potsherds.

"What now?" Ealstan asked when he came into Pybba's sanctum. "Do you want me to cast accounts for you?"

"I'd ask you to if I didn't have something better for you to do," the pottery magnate replied with a laugh. He turned to the two Forthwegians already in the room with him and said, "Here's the clever lad who figured out how to make us look like Algarvians when we need to."

Both the other Forthwegians were in their mid-to late thirties: *old men,* Ealstan thought uncharitably. Then he took a second look at them and realized either one could tear him to pieces without breaking a sweat. He prudently kept his unkind thought to himself. Pybba's pals were looking him over, too. One of them said, "I suppose he'll have to come along, then. He looks like he might be able to cut it."

"He's already got himself an Algarvian stick," the other noted, approval in his voice.

Ealstan refused to let himself be baited. He also refused to show undue curiosity, no matter what he felt. He just nodded to Pybba and said, "Tell me what you need me to do."

Pybba nodded, too. So did the other two, unnamed, Forthwegians. The one who'd spoken first said, "Kid sounds like he's got his head on straight. He may do."

"He's got gall," Pybba said, high praise from him. He turned back to Ealstan. "The redheads are still hanging on to the royal palace and the ley-line caravan depot and one ley-line route through Eoforwic. That lets 'em ship some men west, and it lets 'em give us a hard time. If their military governor all of a sudden came down with a slight case of loss of life . . ."

"Ah." Ealstan nodded again, doing his best to stay dispassionate. "You'll have the right kind of Algarvian uniforms to let us get away with a masquerade?"

"Kid's no dummy, sure enough," one of the—assassins?—said to his comrade. The fellow suddenly switched to unaccented Algarvian: "You understand me, kid? Can you talk like this, too?"

"I understand," Ealstan answered in the same language. "If I talk much, I give us away. I do not talk well."

"Could be worse," the other Forthwegian said. "All right, you'll be junior to us. We'll do the talking. At least you'll know what's going on. How long does your fancy spell hold?"

"Six or eight hours," Ealstan said.

That seemed to please both of the men in the office with Pybba and him, and the pottery magnate as well. "Plenty of time," Pybba said. "You can get into your new clothes just before sunup and sneak into Algarvian territory, do what you want to do, and then lie up somewhere till you can get back to our lines."

"Why lie up?" Ealstan asked. "Why not hustle back to our lines?"

"Ha! You don't think of everything after all," one of the rough men said. "We hustle back looking like redheads, our fornicating pals'll fornicating blaze us before we can tell 'em who we are."

"Don't worry about that," Ealstan said. "I can turn us back as easy as I can make us look like Algarvians." Everyone else beamed; maybe he hadn't mentioned that part of the sorcery to Pybba before.

Before sunrise the next morning, Ealstan put on an Algarvian sergeant's uniform, while his comrades—he still didn't know their names—donned the clothes of a captain and a major. Ealstan had to fiddle with his cantrip a little to shift it from first person to third so it would work on the other two men. He cast it twice in quick succession, and the other two men took on the appearance of the enemy. Then he used the original version on himself. A grunt from one of the others told him it had worked; he couldn't sense it on himself, any more than Vanai could tell that she looked like a Forthwegian after casting her own disguising spell.

"Good thing we saw you do that," a Forthwegian fighter said, "or we'd kill you on the spot." One of his pals nodded.

Ealstan was content to follow the older men's lead as they sneaked out of the Forthwegian positions and toward the corridor through Eoforwic the Algarvians still held. As soon as they were on a street where redheads might see them, the two Forthwegians in officers' clothing became Algarvians themselves, with what seemed a deeper magic than the one with which Ealstan had disguised them. It wasn't just that they spoke the language. They imitated the strut and swagger that distinguished Mezentio's men, imitated those things so well that it did not seem an imitation, but rather something real.

Ealstan had to work hard to imitate them. His own swagger seemed painfully artificial to him, but none of the real Algarvians pointed his way and shouted, "Impostor!" After a bit, he noticed that a lot of underofficers and troopers—not all of them, but a good many—were less flamboyant than their officers. Once he'd seen that, he stopped worrying so much about having to overact.

What amazed him as he pressed on toward the royal palace was how ordinary the Algarvians acted among themselves. He'd seen them up to now only as occupiers, harassing his fellow Forthwegians and doing worse than harassing the Kaunians of Forthweg. Now, though, even more than when he'd sneaked into the Kaunian quarter looking for Vanai, he might have been an Algarvian among Algarvians, which gave him a whole different perspective.

Among themselves, they were just people, going on about their business and laughing and joking as he might have done with his friends. *No one is ever the villain in his own story,* Ealstan reminded himself. It was a far cry from what he usually thought of the Algarvians, and far from the most comfortable notion he'd ever had.

If he hurried after the other two, he didn't have to think. Redheaded guards in short tunics and kilts ringed the palace from which King Penda had once ruled Forthweg. The palace had suffered worse indignities than Algarvian guards, too. The Forthwegians had made a stand there when Unkerlant stabbed Ealstan's kingdom in the back, and the Unkerlanters in their turn had tried and failed to keep the Algarvians from capturing it. Many of the towers famous throughout the kingdom had fallen in one fight or another. But the Algarvian banner still flew from a tall flagstaff in front of the palace, and an Algarvian military governor still ruled Forthweg for King Mezentio from inside it.

One after another, the guards stiffened to attention as Ealstan's comrades and he went past them. No one barked a challenge. If they looked like Algarvians, they were assumed to be Algarvians. Ealstan had to fight down the urge to snicker. *That* might have given the game away.

"We have a situation report for the governor from the west," said the Forthwegian who looked like an Algarvian major. He kept saying that, again and again; it was plenty to get him and his companion who was dressed like a captain and Ealstan with them whisked through the palace and toward the governor, their target. The speed with which it got them whisked through the palace again told Ealstan what the redheads truly reckoned important. The Forthwegian uprising in Eoforwic was a nuisance to Algarve; the endless grinding war against Unkerlant really mattered.

Ealstan had expected to see some of the magnificent trappings of the Forthwegian monarchy on display in the palace.

He didn't. Before long, he realized he'd been naive. What the Unkerlanters hadn't stolen, the Algarvians surely had.

He was halfway through the throne room, in fact, before he recognized it for what it was. The throne remained, but only as a chair; all the gold leaf had been stripped off. He hadn't even time to feel outrage. Before it could start to grow, he was pressing on toward the governor's office, which had been the king's.

Although the governor—a fat man with a duke's silver dragon perched on the left breast of his uniform tunic—was talking with some other, lesser, official, he sent the man away at once, declaring, "The front comes first." Ealstan understood him very clearly. When the other redhead went out, Ealstan shut the door behind him. The governor went on, "What is the latest, gentlemen? *Will* we be able to keep Swemmel's men from crossing the Twegen and aiding these stinking Forthwegians?"

The two men dressed as officers led him toward a map. He paid no attention whatever to Ealstan. Why should a governor notice a sergeant? Ealstan unslung his stick. He had all the time in the world to blaze the Algarvian duke in the back of the head. The man crumpled without a sound.

"Good work," the Forthwegian dressed as a major said. "Let's get out of here." Out they went, locking the door behind them. "His Grace is preparing a response for us," the counterfeit major told the fellow who'd been conferring with the governor. "He'll need a little while." The genuine redhead nodded.

Ealstan and his comrades were out of the palace and in the back room of an abandoned house two blocks away when the hue and cry began. By then, he'd already turned the other two men who looked like Algarvians back into Forthwegians, and they'd pulled ordinary Forthwegian tunics from their packs and put them on. He gave himself his proper appearance, too. Leaving their sticks behind was a nuisance, but couldn't be helped.

They went out onto the street once more without the slightest trace of fear. Ealstan felt like cutting capers. Mezentio's men were looking for three of their own kind. They paid no attention to lowly unarmed Forthwegians, just as the governor had paid no attention to a lowly sergeant. Ealstan grinned and clapped his hands together once, liking the comparison very much.

For once, even Marquis Balastro's bravado failed him when Hajjaj called on him at the Algarvian ministry in Bishah. The Zuwayzi foreign minister took that as a bad sign. Doing his best to conceal his worry, he said, "You are gracious for agreeing to see me on such short notice, your Excellency."

"You are gracious for wanting to see me at all, your Excellency," Balastro returned. "I am glad you do not find Algarve a sinking ship, to be abandoned as soon as possible."

As a matter of fact, Hajjaj did reckon Algarve a sinking ship. Abandoning it was another matter. Abandoning Algarve meant casting Zuwayza on King Swemmel's mercy, and Swemmel hardly knew the meaning of the word.

"I am sorry to find our officers were right about the building Unkerlanter offensive in the north," Hajjaj said, "and even sorrier you have not had better fortune repelling it."

"So am I," Balastro said bleakly.

"Do you think you will be able to hold on the line of the Twegen?" Hajjaj asked.

"For a while," the Algarvian minister replied. "Perhaps for a long while." Hajjaj wondered if that was bravado returning. But Balastro went on, "After all, Swemmel lets us do him a favor if he stops there."

"A favor?" Hajjaj scratched his head. Having to wear clothes on a blisteringly hot day like this, he felt like scratching everywhere at once, but refrained. "I'm sorry, your Excellency, but I don't follow that."

"We did the Forthwegians a favor. We got rid of their Kaunians for them, and precious few of them miss the blonds even a little bit," Balastro said. "Now we're getting rid of a whole great whacking lot of Forthwegians who enjoy rising up and causing trouble. If we kill them, they can't very well rise up and cause trouble for the Unkerlanters, now can they?"

"Oh," Hajjaj said. "I see what you mean. Do you really think King Swemmel is that devious?"

"When it comes to getting rid of people who might cause him trouble one fine day, nobody's better than Swemmel." Marquis Balastro spoke with great conviction.

And he was probably right, too. Turning the subject away from Forthweg and toward something more immediately important to him, Hajjaj said, "You will understand that King Shazli has a certain amount of concern because the front has shifted so far to the east."

That was a diplomatic way to say, *King Shazli is scared green because there aren't any Algarvian soldiers anywhere close enough to help us hold back the Unkerlanters, and we can't do it by ourselves. We already tried, and we lost.* To Hajjaj's relief, the Algarvian minister understood it as such. Balastro said, "We will send you more dragons, your Excellency. We will send you as many behemoths as we can spare. We will send as many soldiers and mages as we can spare, too."

"Thank you for your generosity," Hajjaj said. "You might have done better to send us all these things earlier, you know."

"Maybe." Balastro sounded bland. "But King Mezentio has not forgotten you, and that is something you must always remember."

Hajjaj nodded. Now he understood. The more worried Algarve was that Zuwayza might drop out of the war, the more the redheads would do to keep her in it. The more enemies Unkerlant had to fight, the better off Algarve was. In a way, that was reassuring. In another way, as the Zuwayzi foreign minister had said, it was liable to be too little, too late. Hajjaj rose and bowed. "I shall take your reassurances back to the palace. His Majesty will be glad to have them."

When he got back to the palace, though, he went to General Ikhshid before calling on the king. Ikhshid's fleshy face was unhappy. "So they'll send us more dragons and behemoths, will they?" he said, one white eyebrow rising. "They'd better do it fast, if they're going to do it." He didn't sound convinced. He didn't sound cheerful, either.

"Fast?" Hajjaj raised an eyebrow, too. "Do you know some thing I don't?"

"Maybe," Ikhshid answered, "but it's nothing that'd surpris you very much, I'd bet. The Unkerlanters are starting to brin more and more soldiers up against our lines in the south."

That didn't surprise Hajjaj. It did alarm him. "Can we be: them back?" he asked anxiously.

"We'll do the best we can with what we've got and whateve the Algarvians give us," General Ikhshid said. "You hit any thing hard enough, though, and it'll break. If the Unkerlanter put enough men in the fight, we're in trouble. We saw that for and a half years ago."

"Do you think they can?" Hajjaj asked.

"Depends on how they're doing against Algarve and Gy ongyos." Ikhshid's jowls wobbled as he frowned. "Odds ar better now that they can than they were six weeks ago. They'v gone a long way east, and the redheads don't seem able to sto them anywhere." Hajjaj explained Balastro's theory of why th Unkerlanters had paused on the Twegen. It made Ikhshid n more cheerful. He said, "I wish that made less sense than does."

"My thought exactly," Hajjaj said. "Have you told the kin what you just told me?"

General Ikhshid shook his head. "Not yet."

"I have to see him now," Hajjaj said. "I'll give him the broa outline, if that's all right with you, and you can fill in the detail later."

"Fine. Fine." Now Ikhshid nodded. "He'll likely take it bette from you than he would from me."

Hajjaj thought the general overestimated his powers of per suasion, but headed off to see Shazli nonetheless. The kir served him tea and wine and cakes, and didn't take the roya privilege of cutting short the small talk that accompanied th refreshments. Having played many such games himself, Hajj: judged that Shazli knew the news would be bad and didn much want to hear it.

At last, though, with a sigh, King Shazli said, "I'm comfor

ably certain this is no mere social call, your Excellency, although I am always glad of your company."

"No one ever pays a king a mere social call, save perhaps another king," Hajjaj said, and quickly summarized what he'd learned from Balastro and Ikhshid.

King Shazli sighed when he finished. "We knew this day was coming when the Unkerlanters began driving the Algarvians back this summer." Before Hajjaj could speak, Shazli held up a pale-palmed hand. "We knew this day might come when the Algarvians failed before Cottbus, and we knew it probably would come when they failed in Sulingen. Now we have to deal with it as best we can."

Hajjaj gave the king a seated bow. "Just so, your Majesty. As long as you keep that view of the world, Zuwayza is in good hands."

"Provided the Unkerlanters don't end up parading through Bishah," Shazli said. "Well, if worse comes to worst, your Excellency, I rely on you to keep that dark day from dawning."

"I'll do my best," Hajjaj promised, though he thought the king relied on him for altogether too much.

After his busy and gloomy morning, after a nap in the heat of noontime, Hajjaj left Bishah and went up into the hills to pass the rest of the day at home. "I didn't expect you back so soon, young fellow," Tewfik said when Hajjaj alighted from his carriage.

"Life is full of surprises," Hajjaj said, doing his best to forget how many of them were unpleasant. "Would you be so kind as to have a servant"—he would never have offended the majordomo by saying *another servant*—"bring some date wine to the library for me?"

"Of course, your Excellency," Tewfik replied; Hajjaj would have been astonished had he said anything else.

Once inside the library, Hajjaj pulled out a book of poetry by a Kaunian named Mikulicius, who'd lived in what the historians called Late Imperial times. Mikulicius had watched things fall apart all around him, and written about what he'd seen. With his kingdom's Algarvian allies in headlong retreat, with the Unkerlanters massing against Zuwayza, the bitter verses seemed perfectly timely even if they were more than a thousand years old.

The door opened. *The servant with the wine,* Hajjaj thought. Without glancing up from the book, he said, "Just set the tray down, if you please."

"Aye, your Excellency."

That answer did make him look up, in surprise. It came in throatily accented Algarvian, not the Zuwayzi he'd expected. There with the tray and the wine jug and the cup stood Tassi. She wore no more than she had when she'd first knocked on the door to Hajjaj's home. He looked her up and down; he could hardly help doing that. He switched to Algarvian— sharp Algarvian—himself to ask, "Who sent you here?" Minister Iskakis' very estranged wife hadn't learned much Zuwayzi yet.

"Why, Master Tewfik did," she answered, her eyes perhaps too convincingly innocent. "He said you needed some wine."

"Did he?" Hajjaj said. Tassi dipped her head, as Yaninans often did instead of nodding. "And did he say I needed anything else?"

"No." Now she tossed her head, a gesture that gave birth to enchanting motions of other parts of her body. *Curse it, she does look naked to me, not nude.* Hajjaj had to think in Algarvian to have that make any sense to him; his own tongue lacked the distinction between the words. Tassi went on, "He did say you seemed unhappy."

"Did he say why?" Hajjaj asked.

Tassi tossed her head again. "Why does not matter," she replied, which went dead against a lifetime of experience for Hajjaj. She took a deep breath. Hajjaj admired that, too. She said, "I have been unhappy, too. I know what it is like. I know it is bad. I understand."

Do you? he wondered. *Does being unhappy because your husband likes boys more than he likes you let you understand a man who is unhappy because he sees his kingdom in mortal danger?* Analytical as always, Hajjaj found the idea unlikely, but couldn't quite dismiss it out of hand.

Tassi had not an analytical bone in her body. She got down on the carpet beside Hajjaj. "What *are* you doing?" he demanded, though he knew, and knew he could do what she obviously had in mind.

"Making you happy for a little while," she answered. "Your senior wife said I should just do this, and not pay any attention to your grumblings."

"Kolthoum said that, did she?" Hajjaj asked. Tassi dipped her head again. Her hair—she'd perfumed it—brushed over his chest and belly. "And Tewfik sent you?" he said. She didn't bother responding to that; she'd already answered it once. Hajjaj took off his reading glasses and wagged a finger at her. "I sense a plot."

Tassi didn't respond to that, either—not with words, at least. But she didn't need words to be very distracting. Hajjaj supposed he could have picked her up bodily and thrown her out of the library. But that would have been undignified, and a man would suffer almost anything before losing his dignity. *Not,* he thought as his arms went round her, *that I'm suffering too much.*

Fourteen

Every news sheet, every rumor, that came to the farm in southern Valmiera brought Merkela ferocious joy. "They're losing," she gloated. "They're running. They'd running like whipped, bleeding dogs with their tails between their legs." Then, suddenly, her grim delight faded. "Gedominu!" she exclaimed. "What did you just put in your mouth?"

The baby had started crawling not long before. That meant she and Skarnu had to keep a closer eye on him than ever. She reached down, grabbed him, and stuck a finger in his mouth. She got something out of there, then wiped her hand on her trousers. "What was it this time?" Skarnu asked with clinical curiosity.

"Just a dust bunny, powers above be praised," Merkela answered. She glared at Gedominu with mock fury. "At least you didn't swallow that dead cockroach a couple of days ago." Gedominu laughed. He thought it was funny—though he squealed in outrage when his mother took the bug away from him. Merkela set him down once more. He started to crawl backwards, but then decided to go ahead instead.

Adventures with Gedominu notwithstanding, Skarnu hadn't forgotten what Merkela was saying. Every news sheet, every rumor, that came to the farm brought him nothing but frustration. "Aye, they're losing," he said. "Aye, they're running. They're running in the west. They're running in Jelgava. But what are they doing here? Not bloody much, powers below eat them."

"That's not true," Merkela said.

And, in fact, it wasn't true, or it wasn't strictly true. The Algarvians occupying Valmiera had sent a lot of men west to fight the Unkerlanters, and a few north to fight the Lagoans and Kuusamans in Jelgava. Their grip on the countryside had loosened. Skarnu worried much less than he had before about an Algarvian patrol swooping down on the farm here.

But the redheads still held the southern coast strongly against invasion from across the Strait of Valmiera. They still held the kingdom's towns—with no small aid from the Valmieran constabulary and from the many traitors they'd recruited to do their dirty work for them. True, the underground could strike more readily than it had. Still, its strikes remained pinpricks, and everywhere else, or so it seemed, Mezentio's men were taking hammer blows.

"I want to *smash* the Algarvians," Skarnu said. "I want to smash them till they can't get up again. Our army fell to pieces. I was there. I watched it happen. We never knew what hit us. We need revenge for that now if we're ever going to be able to hold our heads up once this war finally ends."

"Ends?" Merkela stared at him as if she'd never heard the word before. She pursed her lips. "Do you know, I never thought about the war ending. Never once. Either the Algavians would have us down, or we'd have them down. Having them down is what I look forward to. . . . Gedominu!" She grabbed their son. This time, she got whatever was in his hand before he could stick it in his mouth.

"I look forward to having them down, too," Skarnu said. "But I also look forward to knocking them down. It won't be the same if a pack of foreigners does it all for us."

"I don't care how it happens," Merkela said. "I just want it to happen."

"I want to have something to do with it," Skarnu said stubbornly. "I want to march into Priekule at the head of an army and go back to my mansion and clean out my sister and every sign the Algarvians were ever there. I want to do that myself, with my countrymen. I don't want a bunch of foreigners telling me, 'All right, little boy, it's safe to go home now.' "

"Priekule. Mansion." Merkela spoke the words as if they were foreign to her. And so they were, even if they were in Valmieran. Skarnu had discovered that the capital and what went on there didn't seem real to a lot of Valmierans from the countryside. As for the other . . . Merkela murmured, "Most of the time, I forget what blood you bear."

Before the war, being a marquis had mattered more to him than almost anything else. Now he said, "Our son bears my blood, and he bears yours, too. And when the war is over, I intend to wed you and set you up in that mansion . . . unless you decide you'd sooner dwell somewhere else. In that case, wherever it is, I'll live there with you."

She shook her head. "It's like something out of a fairy tale. Nobles don't come to farms and want to marry peasant girls, not in real life they don't."

"No, they don't get that lucky," Skarnu said, which brought a smile to her face. He went on, "Having the Algarvians swallow up the whole kingdom isn't something out of a fairy tale, either. It's out of a nightmare."

Merkela nodded. Before she could say anything, someone knocked on the door. At a good many times over the past couple of years, that would have brought panic to Skarnu. No more. Merkela walked to the door and opened it. "Raunu!" she exclaimed, real pleasure in her voice. "Come in. Let me pour you a mug of ale."

"Don't mind if I do," Skarnu's veteran sergeant said. "Don't mind if you do, either." He looked down at Gedominu, who had drool on his chin—he was cutting a tooth. "He's just about big enough to march."

"Seems that way," Skarnu agreed. Merkela came back with not one but three mugs of ale on a wooden tray, and a pitcher from which to refill them, too. Skarnu eyed Raunu. "But you didn't come here to tell me what a big boy I've got, not unless I miss my guess."

"No." Raunu took a pull at his ale, then nodded to Merkela. "Now this is your own brewing—I can taste it."

"Aye." She looked pleased, but not for long. "Skarnu's right. You wouldn't be here if you didn't need him to do something. A while ago, you would have needed us both to do something. That's not so simple any more." Her glance toward Gedominu was fond, but also wistful. She missed the days when she could easily go forth against the redheads, too.

"Well, I'm always glad to come here," Raunu said, "but you're right—it's got to do with business." He nodded to Skarnu. "We've had some practice wrecking the redheads' ley-line caravans, you and me—and you to, milady," he added, as if Merkela were already a marchioness. "But you've got other things on your mind for a spell." She nodded. Her eye kept going back to Gedominu.

"Where?" Skarnu asked. "What needs doing?"

"Up in the north," Raunu answered. "They'll be moving a good many caravans before long, using the ley lines through that rugged country to get soldiers to Jelgava by the shortest way. It'd be nice if some of 'em didn't get there."

"It would be nice if a lot of them didn't get there," Skarnu said, and both Raunu and Merkela muttered agreement. He added, "Fitting if we give them a hard time up in the north, too." That puzzled his lover and the sergeant. He didn't try to explain, but still thought he was right. Four years earlier, Mezentio's men had moved footsoldiers and, more important still, masses of behemoths through country Valmiera had thought too rough for such maneuvers. The Valmierans, full occupied with another Algarvian attack down in the south, hadn't noticed the stroke till it had already slipped between their ribs and into their heart. Revenge, even a small measure of revenge, would be sweet.

"You'll come, then?" Raunu asked. He meant it seriously; the underground wasn't like the army, even if most of its members had been soldiers.

"Of course I will," Skarnu answered.

As he'd gone down to the southern seacoast, so he rode the ley-line caravan from the little town of Ramygala up to the wooded hills and gullies of northern Valmiera. He felt like a stranger there, half a foreigner, wary of opening his mouth: the local dialect was a long way from the brand of Valmieran he spoke. "Don't worry about it," Raunu told him when he worried out loud. "The cursed Algarvians can't tell the difference between how they talk here and the right way."

"No, the Algarvians can't," Skarnu agreed, "but there are bound to be traitors here. There are traitors everywhere." If he'd seen one thing in occupied Valmiera, that was it.

"Some of them have had accidents," was all Raunu said to that. "The rest of the whoresons . . . they're thoughtful, you might say." Skarnu hoped he was right.

Right or wrong, they both had work to do. The locals had got them papers showing they were foresters, and other papers—which they were not to display—that gave them enough jargon to pass as the real article unless questioned by someone who really knew what he was talking about. With luck, that wouldn't happen. The papers gave them the excuse they needed for going out into the woods.

As Skarnu tramped those hills and valleys, as he eyed the narrow, winding roads—in the stretches of the landscape where there were any roads at all—he grew to admire more and more what the Algarvians had accomplished by making a thrust through such terrain. "No matter how much you hate them, you can't ignore them," he told Raunu.

"No. They're too dangerous for that—like any other snakes,"
Raunu said. Skarnu laughed and nodded, though the veteran
underofficer hadn't been joking.

In all that contorted country, the only straight lines were the
ley lines. The world's energy grid ran where it would. Once
mages learned to exploit the ley lines, men had to hack down
trees if caravans were to glide where they needed to go. And so
many long, narrow stretches of cleared ground marked the ley
lines' paths through the woods. Algarvian patrols marched
along the ley lines, too. The redheads were no fools; they knew
the underground would try to disrupt their movements.

But knowing and being able to do anything about it were
able to prove two different things. Here as elsewhere in
Valmiera, as elsewhere throughout the east of Derlavai, Mezentio's men were stretched too thin to do everything that wanted
doing. They couldn't patrol all the ley lines all the time, or even
most of them most of the time.

"I think this seems a likely spot," Skarnu said at last. "The
ley-line caravan will be just coming over that rise"—he
pointed—"and won't have the time to stop even if the conductor should notice anything wrong about the line. What say
you?"

Raunu considered briefly. "Aye, it suits me."

"Good enough, then. See how simple it is?" Skarnu suspected—indeed, he was sure—Raunu could have found the
spot as readily as he had. But he was here. He took a crystal
from his trouser pocket, activated it, and spoke briefly, using
code phrases to give the bearings of the stretch of ley line
they'd chosen while not calling it that. Then he and Raunu
left in a hurry. He didn't know the redheads had overheard
him, but had to act as if they were tracking every emanation
around.

"Pity we can't be here when they do the job," Raunu remarked.

"Aye." Skarnu nodded. Somewhere not far away, a team of
his countrymen had assuredly heard what he'd said. He didn't
know where; what he didn't know, Mezentio's men couldn't
pry from him. "But knowing we helped, knowing we told them
where to bury the egg—that counts for something, too."

"Reminds us we're still in the war, like," Raunu said.

"That's it," Skarnu agreed. "That's just it. In fact, when you knocked on my door, I was complaining to Merkela that the Algarvians were going to the powers below everywhere but in Valmiera. It's still true, more or less, but we've helped make it not quite so true."

"Sooner or later, the redheads'll get what's coming to 'em," Raunu said.

"I don't just want them to get it," Skarnu said. "I want to be the one who gives it to them, and now I am—at least a little."

Back when the Unkerlanter attack on Algarve in the north was new, Major Scoufas had called it a catastrophe and Colonel Sabrino had told the Yaninan dragonflier he didn't think it was quite so bad as that. Since then, King Swemmel's men had pushed the Algarvians out of the north of Unkerlant. They'd pushed them out of western Forthweg and had fought their way to the line of the Twegen River, the river that ran by Eoforwic. If that wasn't a catastrophe, Sabrino didn't know what would be.

But catastrophe or no, the wing of dragonfliers he commanded remained here in the south. He had even gone so far as to send a written petition to King Mezentio, begging his sovereign to send him into the urgent fighting. Mezentio hadn't told him no. Mezentio hadn't deigned to reply at all. More than anything else, that told him in how bad an odor with the king he really was.

Major Scoufas had stopped twitting him about it. Yaninans were politer, or at least more formal, people than his own countrymen. The officers in his wing hadn't stopped grumbling about their fate.

At last, Sabrino took aside Captain Orosio, who'd been with him longer than anyone. He said, "If you want to transfer, I won't stand in your way. I don't blame you for wanting to go where the action is. I want to go up north myself, but nobody will listen to me. Nobody will listen to you, either, as long as you serve under me. But if you don't, I have the feeling you'll get what you want."

To his surprise, Orosio shook his head. "No, thank you, sir," he said. "I don't know anyone who wants to leave the wing, sir. That'd just be another slap at you. We want the wing to get what it deserves, and we want to give the Unkerlanters what they deserve."

Touched, Sabrino set his hand on Orosio's shoulder. "One thing Algarvians are, by the powers above, is loyal to their friends."

The squadron commander nodded. "Well, of course, sir," he said, though in the world at large it was anything but *of course*. "And the king bloody well ought to be loyal to you, too. You gave him the best advice you knew how, and not only that, you were right, too."

"And much good it did me," Sabrino said. "I told that to Scoufas: You can get in every bit as much trouble with a king for being right as you can for being wrong. Maybe even more trouble."

"Scoufas." Orosio looked around before continuing. The two of them stood off to one side of the dragon farm; from the beginning, this hadn't been the sort of conversation for which they wanted eavesdroppers. Satisfied no Yaninans were in earshot, Orosio went on: "I wish we were by ourselves and not tied to Tsavellas' people. It's like being married to a dead woman."

"I know," Sabrino answered, "but I don't know what to do about it. If we were here by ourselves, we'd be here *by ourselves*, if you know what I mean: no Algarvian footsoldiers for miles around. Out here in the west, we're stretched too thin. We've got to use whatever allies we can scrape up."

"Yaninans." Captain Orosio rolled his eyes. "Forthwegians. Powers above, do I hear right? Is there really a Kaunian regiment somewhere down here?"

"I've heard that, too," Sabrino answered. "Kaunians from Valmiera, I think."

"Those people are crazy," Orosio declared.

Since Sabrino thought he was right, he didn't argue. In fact, he waved Orosio to silence: A Yaninan was trotting toward them. In accented Algarvian, the fellow called, "Colonel Sabrino to tent of crystallomancers."

"I'm coming." Sabrino hurried after the fellow. He wondered what had gone wrong now. He also had to do his best not to laugh at the way the pompoms on the Yaninan's shoes bounced up and down. Algarvians always had a hard time taking their Yaninan neighbors seriously.

All but a couple of the crystallomancers inside the tent were Yaninans. For some reason or other, Sabrino had trouble getting Algarvian replacements. He had to admit the little swarthy men did know their business. Their specialists—which also included dragonfliers—were pretty good. Their army as a whole . . .

He sat down at the crystal to which a Yaninan waved him. "Sabrino here."

An Algarvian face looked back at him. "Hello, Colonel. I am Major Ardalico. I want to let you know that I am establishing a special camp a couple of miles to the rear of your position."

"A special camp?" Sabrino repeated tonelessly.

"That's right." Ardalico's voice was bland. Even the Algarvians who slaughtered Kaunians from Forthweg for the sake of their life energy weren't comfortable about saying that straight out. *Special camp* was their favorite euphemism.

"Why are you setting up a special camp back there?" Sabrino asked.

Major Ardalico's image in the crystal gave him a large, hearty, false smile. "Because I've been ordered to, sir."

"Thank you so much," Sabrino said, and the major's smile got larger and falser. "Now be so good as to tell me *why* you were ordered to put that camp there."

"Sir, I wouldn't care to speculate about that." Ardalico was smooth. He was so smooth, he was downright greasy. Colonel Sabrino hated him on sight.

"Powers below eat you, you miserable little turd," Sabrino ground out. "You're going to tell me the truth, or I'll get my dragons in the air and knock that camp down around your ears. And if you don't think I'll do it, you can bloody well think again."

He'd succeeded in knocking the smug, self-satisfied smirk off Ardalico's handsome face. "You wouldn't dare," blurted the officer in charge of the special camp.

"Sonny boy, you just go ahead and try me," Sabrino said. "I'm already under a cloud in Trapani. What can King Mezentio do to me? Send me to the west to fight the Unkerlanters? I've been here since you were in diapers. Now are you going to talk to me, or do I pay you a visit on dragonback?"

He wasn't bluffing. Some few of his own men might balk, but the Yaninans would surely follow him. For one thing, it would infuriate Algarve. For another, the idea of sacrificing Kaunians appalled them. They weren't really hard enough to fight in a war like this, but what choice did they have when they found themselves sandwiched between Mezentio and Swemmel?

Major Ardalico licked his lips. He wasn't stupid, except in the particular way that had let him become an officer heading up a special camp in the first place. He had to realize Sabrino meant what he said. But he tried one last delaying tactic: "What was it you wanted to know?"

"Why are you running up that bloody murder manufactory of yours?" Sabrino demanded. Ardalico winced; thinking of it as a special camp probably helped him sleep at night. Sabrino didn't care. He had his own worries. Most of them—the ones that weren't centered in Trapani—lay due west of him. He went on, "Are you putting it up because it looks like the Unkerlanters are going to mount an attack in these parts, and we need some way to stop them?"

"I shouldn't be speaking of this by crystal," Ardalico said unhappily. Sabrino drummed his fingers on the tabletop. The motion drew Ardalico's eyes: Sabrino could see as much from his image. More unhappily still, the young major said, "Aye, there is some fear of that."

Although Sabrino heard the words, he didn't want to believe them. "How?" he whispered. "With everything they're doing up in the north, where can they find the men and the beasts to strike another blow against us down here, too?"

"It's a big kingdom, Unkerlant is," Ardalico answered, which meant he didn't know how Swemmel's men were doing what they were doing, either. The Algarvians hadn't believed Unkerlant would be able to fight back so strongly when they first launched their attack against Swemmel's kingdom. Here more than three years later, Sabrino's countrymen still had trouble believing it, which doubtless went a long way towards explaining why the tide of war flowed against them.

"If they do attack, can we stop them?" Sabrino asked: the one question besides which none of the others mattered.

Major Ardalico said, "Having a special camp in the neighborhood will give us a better chance."

Sabrino's laugh held knives of bitterness. "Oh, aye, all the Kaunians we've killed so far have done just what we wanted. That's why we marched into Cottbus week before last, isn't it?" He had the satisfaction of watching Ardalico's image wince. Instead of shouting, he went on in a small, quiet, deadly voice: "You stupid clot, don't you see the Unkerlanters will kill as many of their own as they need to to block whatever you do?"

"If the camp weren't here, Colonel, the Unkerlanters would still kill their own," Ardalico replied. "And then where would you be?"

That held enough truth to make Sabrino wince in turn. Even so, he said, "If we hadn't started it, Major, they wouldn't have." Every interrogation record he'd seen confirmed that. The Unkerlanters hadn't imagined using large-scale murder for the sake of life energy as a weapon of war, not till the Algarvians showed them the way. But they hadn't stepped back from learning, either.

"Which may be true and which may not, sir, but which has nothing to do with what will happen—not with what may happen, mind you, but with what *will* happen—if King Swemmel's buggers do hit this section of our line," Ardalico said.

"I suppose that's true," Sabrino admitted. "As you know, we're rather short of footsoldiers hereabouts. Shall I try to see if I can bring in a few companies from the Phalanx of Valmiera to protect your special camp?"

For a moment, he thought Ardalico would nod. But the

younger officer only gave him the look any junior officer gives his senior when the latter has just told a joke that is anything but funny. "Good day, sir," Ardalico said, and broke the etheric connection. Light flared in the crystal before which Sabrino sat. When it faded, the crystal was for all practical purposes inert once more.

With a grunt, Sabrino got to his feet and left the crystallomancers' tent. He strode over to the nearby tent in which Major Scoufas made his headquarters. The Yaninan looked up from the papers on his folding table. "Good day, sir," he said. "I hope you will forgive me for saying so, but you do not look like a happy man."

"I'm not." Like any Algarvian, Sabrino had spent a fair amount of time sneering at Yaninans. But he wouldn't have traded Major Scoufas for a company of Ardalicos.

"Will this help?" Scoufas produced a jar of the local spirits and a couple of mugs. "Not much for flavor, but it numbs the brain."

"I could use some numbing, thanks." But Sabrino went on before he'd had anything to drink: "They're putting in a special camp in this sector. You know about special camps?"

"I know of them, aye." The Yaninan dragonflier's dark eyes were particularly unfathomable. "A filthy business." He waited to see how Sabrino would respond. When Sabrino nodded, Scoufas continued, "And not a good sign, if one is coming into being here." Sabrino nodded again. The two officers proceeded to get very drunk.

Ilmarinen came up to Sabrino in the hallway and poked him in the chest with a bony forefinger. When the elderly theoretical sorcerer didn't say anything and did keep poking, Fernao poked back. For a moment, they might have been fencing with fingers. Since Fernao was much younger and had a longer reach, he got the better of the duel. Ilmarinen said, "You deserve it, you cursed Lagoan."

"What have I done now?" Fernao was only too sure Ilmarinen would come up with something scandalous.

And the Kuusaman mage did: "You turned out to be right, you miserable, unprincipled son of a whore."

"Oh?" That wasn't an admission Fernao heard from Ilmarinen every day. "Right about what?"

"About expanding that one series," Ilmarinen answered. "You really can't do it the way I tried. I'm not saying my notion is impossible, mind you, but my spell wouldn't have worked. If you want my thanks for stopping me, you can have 'em."

Fernao shrugged. "I'm glad the energy release didn't happen. That spell would have released . . . a lot of energy." He hadn't tried to calculate how much. Now, in an offhand way, he did. "You know, if we wanted to, we could try to turn it into a weapon, too."

"Aye, I suppose we could." Ilmarinen shrugged. "I'd sooner try to turn it into a spell that does what I want it to do." He was incorrigible. He reveled in being incorrigible. Now he waited for Fernao to pitch a fit.

The best way to frustrate him was not to do what he wanted. With a shrug of his own, Fernao said, "With everything else going on, you probably won't have time to work on it. If you aren't busy here, something is badly wrong."

Ilmarinen grunted. "You only think you're joking." Fernao shook his head. He didn't think he was joking at all. Catching him with his defenses down, Ilmarinen poked him again. As he yelped, the Kuusaman mage added, "One of these days, I may even forgive you."

"For being right?" Fernao asked.

"For being right," Ilmarinen agreed. With a last poke—he had a sharp fingernail, too—he went past Fernao and down the hall.

"If you want to thank somebody, thank Linna," Fernao called after him. "She was the one who let Pekka and me know where you'd gone."

"I've already thanked her," Ilmarinen said over his shoulder. "Believe me, it was much more fun than thanking you ever could be." He turned a corner and disappeared. Fernao stared after him, then shook his head and started to laugh.

Trying to get the last word against Ilmarinen was a losing battle.

Laughing still, Fernao went back to his own chamber and looked without much warmth on the report he was drafting for Grandmaster Pinhiero. The first Lagoan mages had finally come to the research station in the barren Naantali district. They weren't doing so well as either Fernao or Pinhiero had hoped. Language problems were part of the reason: they were less fluent in Kuusaman than they needed to be. And, even more than Kuusaman mages, they had trouble accepting that One Law lay under the Two with which they'd long been familiar.

Fernao cast about for a way to say that without making his countrymen sound like imbeciles. *Morons, perhaps, but not imbeciles,* he thought. He'd just inked his pen when someone knocked on the door. He suspected it would be Ilmarinen, coming back for the word after the last word.

He put the pen down even so. Listening to Ilmarinen's impudence was bound to prove more entertaining than explaining to the head of the Lagoan Guild of Mages why some of the sorcerers he'd sent weren't measuring up. But when he opened the door, Ilmarinen wasn't standing in the hallway. Pekka was. "Oh," Fernao said in surprise, and then, recalling himself, "Come in." He stepped aside.

"Thank you." Pekka's voice wasn't quite steady. The small quaver in it alarmed Fernao more than a scream from another woman might have. She sat down on the stool he'd been using to draft his report—sank down onto it, really.

"What's wrong?" he asked as he sat down on the bed. Something obviously was. One possibility sprang to mind right away: "You told me you weren't with child. Were you wrong?"

"What?" Pekka's eyes widened. To his vast relief, she shook her head. "No, it's not that, powers above be praised. I'm just . . . upset, that's all."

"Why?" he said, and then, before he could stop himself, "Why come to me?"

Pekka chose to answer the second question first: "Because whatever else we are, we're friends." He nodded, though his lips tightened. Because that was true, their not being lovers any more hurt all the worse. Pekka went on, "I just got a letter from Leino. He's left *Habakkuk* so he can join in the fighting in Jelgava."

"Has he?" Fernao said. Now Pekka nodded, miserably. Fernao made himself say what needed saying: "I hope he stays safe." Did he mean it? Part of him did, anyhow, the larger part, the part not centered on his crotch.

"You know the spells the Algarvians use," Pekka said. "They've never used them against ships. They use them on land whenever they can scrape together enough Kaunians to kill. I'm frightened for him. I wish he hadn't done it."

"He should be all right." Fernao want to take her in his arms to comfort her. Did part of her want that, too? Was that why she'd come here? He wished it were, but he didn't believe it. He also wished he were better at fooling himself. With a sigh, he went on, "If the news sheets are right, Mezentio's men aren't putting up much of a fight in Jelgava, so you shouldn't have anything to worry about."

"I don't trust the Algarvians," Pekka said, which made good, hard sense. "They can't just go on retreating through Jelgava. If they do too much more retreating, they lose the war."

That also made sense. The same thought had crossed Fernao's mind. If it had crossed the minds of the people who wrote news sheets, they did their best not to let it show. Their best was quite good; the news sheets had a tone of giddy euphoria that sometimes made Fernao want to gag.

Leaning on his stick, he heaved himself to his feet once more and limped over to set a hand on her shoulder. She didn't flinch, but she didn't turn toward him, either. He sighed again. He didn't see a wish coming true. "He'll be fine," he repeated.

Pekka rose, too. "Thank you, Fernao," she said. "You *are* a good friend. I shouldn't have troubled you with this."

You're right—you shouldn't have, went through his mind. But, again, that wasn't altogether true. Aloud, he said, "It's all right. We *are* friends . . . whatever else we are, as you said." Becoming lovers was destructive of friendships. He knew that. He was glad it hadn't—quite—happened here.

"Do you ever want to go and fight the Algarvians yourself?" Pekka asked. Comparing him to her husband? Then she went on, "Sometimes I have all I can do, just staying here and working on this sorcery. It doesn't seem enough."

Fernao lifted his cane into the air. For a moment, he stood on two legs, one good, one bad. The cane was the point of the exercise. Pekka realized as much. As her eyes followed its motion, she turned red. Fernao said, "They already have as much of me as I care to give them, thank you very much."

"Oh," Pekka said softly. "I was foolish. I'm sorry."

He shrugged, which made his bad arm and shoulder twinge, but only for a moment. "Don't worry about it," he said, and then, almost as romantic as an Algarvian, "If Mezentio's men hadn't ruined me for anything strenuous, Grandmaster Pinhiero probably wouldn't have sent me here, and then I wouldn't have been lucky enough to meet you."

Pekka blushed once more. Not looking at him, she said, "You're being difficult again, Fernao."

"Am I?" He thought about shrugging again, and promptly thought better of it. "Well, maybe I am."

"I'd better go," she said quickly, and, as quickly, did. Fernao listened to her fading footsteps in the hall. If she hadn't gone quickly, what would she have done? Thrown herself into his arms after all? Or found the nearest blunt instrument and hit him with it because he'd chosen to be difficult again?

How much would you give to know the answer to that? he wondered, but he didn't have to keep wondering very long. *Everything I have. Everything I could conjure up or borrow or steal.*

He limped over to the desk, and to the report he'd been drafting for Pinhiero. With a grimace, he pushed it away. How was he supposed to pay attention to it when he had really important things on his mind? If Pinhiero had to wait a day or two longer for his answers, the world wouldn't end, especially since he wouldn't like them when he got them.

Another knock on the door. Fernao jumped. Inside him, his heart jumped, too. Was that Pekka coming back? At a sort of shambling trot, he hurried across the chamber and opened the door. "Oh," he said dully. It wasn't Pekka. It was, in fact, one of the Lagoan mages who'd come to the Naantali district to learn the new sorcery. After so long using Kuusaman and classical Kaunian, he had to make a conscious decision to speak his own language: "Come in, Viana."

"Thank you," she answered. She was perhaps a year or two older than he, nicely shaped but on the plain side, earnest, hardworking. "I hope I'm not disturbing you."

"Not at all," he answered, limping back to the desk to flip the papers so she couldn't read them. "What can I do for you? Sit down. Make yourself at home."

"Thank you," Viana said again. "I wanted to ask you some questions about what we were doing here and how we would use the sorcery in the field."

"Go ahead," Fernao said. Viana did, one question after another. Some of them were things she already should have known, but none was downright foolish. Mechanically, he answered them all.

After what seemed like forever and was in fact something above an hour, she said, "I've taken up enough of our time. Things are much clearer now. I appreciate your patience." She got to her feet.

So did Fernao, using good leg, good arm, and cane to return to vertical. "It's all right," he said. After that session, he looked forward to getting back to work on the report for Grandmaster Pinhiero. It would have to be more interesting. With a last polite nod, Viana left.

And Fernao did start writing again. Halfway down the second leaf of paper after he did, his pen abruptly stopped scritching. He looked out the window and scratched his head. *I wonder if Viana came here trying to find out something that didn't have anything to do with those spells.* She must have known—mustn't she?—the answers to a good many of the questions she'd asked. *Was she trying to find out if I were interested in her?*

Well, if she was, she had her answer. Fernao had gone on and on about magecraft without the slightest concern for anything else. He supposed he could repair that the next time they met.

He supposed he could, but he didn't really intend to, because the truth was, he wasn't interested.

He muttered a low-voiced curse, then started to laugh. Life would have been so much simpler if he were.

Summer on Obuda meant long, misty days—it never got very hot—and mild, misty nights. Istvan remembered that from his days on the island as a Gyongyosian warrior. He was, he supposed, still a Gyongyosian warrior in some technical sense, but he thought of himself as a captive of the Kuusamans much more often.

Not everyone in the large captives' camp on Obuda shared that view. As far as Captain Frigyes was concerned, for instance, the war remained a going concern. Frigyes was ready to sacrifice himself and all the other captives to loose potent magecraft against the Kuusamans, just as he'd been ready to sacrifice the men under his command back on Becsehely.

"He's daft, you know," Kun said one morning as he and Istvan squatted over stinking latrine trenches. "Even if our sorcerous energy knocks this island out of the Bothnian Ocean and up onto the peaks of the Ilszung Mountains, it won't change how the war turns out by even a copper's worth."

"You know that." Istvan grunted. "I know that." He grunted again. Kuusaman guards strode the palisade not far away. Having to take care of his needs without privacy had left him badly constipated for a while. He didn't even notice any more. "The captain doesn't know it, or else he doesn't care." He tore off a handful of grass.

"Aye, well, no doubt you're right." Kun grabbed some grass, too. Fortunately, it grew very fast. "But I care. I don't much fancy having my throat cut for nothing."

Since Istvan didn't, either, he just threw the grass down into the trench, got to his feet, and set his clothes to rights. "What are we going to do, then?" he asked. "We can't very well go and tell the Kuusaman guards. That would get our throats cut, too, and not for nothing—when our friends found out."

"My dear boy," Kun said, as if he were Istvan's father rather than his comrade. "My dear boy, if we ever had to do such a thing, we would also have to make sure our friends never, ever, found out." That was so obvious, Istvan felt like a fool for not having seen it himself. In the nastier ways of the world if not in years, Kun *was* a good deal older than he.

They queued up for breakfast. They queued up for everything in the captives' camp: The Kuusamans regimented them even more thoroughly than the Gyongyosian army had done, which was saying a good deal. A few of the cooks were Kuusamans; more were Obudans—the occupiers put the natives to work for them. One of the Obudans, a medium-sized, medium-brown man—larger and darker than a Kuusaman—wore a dragon's tooth on a leather thong around his neck. As Istvan, mess tin in hand, came up to him, the Gyongyosian pointed to the fang and said, "You might have bought that from me, once upon a time." A lot of Obudan men were eager to get their hands on dragon's teeth, thinking they reflected well on their virility.

The cook fingered the heavy tooth. "Maybe I did," he replied. No reason he shouldn't understand Gyongyosian; Istvan's kingdom had had a couple of spells of ruling Obuda before the Kuusamans finally seized the island. Plunging his ladle into the kettle of fish-and-barley stew—heavy on the barley, light on the fish—he gave Istvan a bigger helping than usual.

"You lucky son of a goat," said Kun, who hadn't got any more than the usual. Istvan only smiled and shrugged. He knew some things about getting along with people that his sour-tempered friend had never figured out.

Once they finished eating, they washed their mess tins in big tubs of water set out for the purpose. Istvan's spoon clanked in his tray. He had another spoon hidden under the mattress of his cot, the handle scraped down to make a knife blade of sorts. He'd never mentioned that to Kun, or to anyone else, but you never could tell when a weapon might come in handy. As he carried the mess kit back to his bunk for the daily inspection, he stole a glance at Kun. Maybe Kun had a ground-down spoon knife stashed away somewhere, too. That hadn't occurred to Istvan till now.

A Kuusaman lieutenant strode through the barracks as the Gyongyosian captives stood at attention by their cots. A sergeant would have done a better, more thorough job. So thought Istvan, at any rate, and never once stopped to wonder if his own underofficer's rank had anything to do with his opinion.

Once the Kuusaman was satisfied, Frigyes pointed to Istvan and the men who'd served in his squad. "Wood-chopping detail," he said, as if Istvan didn't know what he was supposed to be doing. "This is something that needs to be done properly. Without enough wood, we don't eat hot food."

"Aye, Captain," Istvan said resignedly. Still, he understood what Frigyes meant. Some of the work the Kuusamans gave their captives was designed to keep them busy, nothing more. Fortunately, they didn't seem to mind the captives' going through the motions on that sort of job. But firewood, as Frigyes had said, was serious.

It was, in fact, serious in several ways. The Kuusaman corporal who issued the captives their axes kept careful count of just how many he was issuing—no chance of stealing an axe and stowing it under a mattress. If the number turned in at the end of the day didn't match the number given out at the start, there would be trouble.

Kun grumbled at chopping wood. Kun grumbled at a good many things, but he was particularly vain about his hands, which, for a soldier's, were soft and fine. "How am I supposed to cast a proper spell with them all rough and bruised and battered?" he complained.

"You couldn't cast much of a spell any which way," Szonyi said. "You were only a mage's apprentice, not a mage yourself." Kun gave him a look full of loathing and swung his axe as if he would have liked to bring it down on Szonyi's neck.

To Istvan, chopping wood was just a job. He'd been doing it since he was a boy. Back in his home valley, chopping wood meant staying warm through the harsh winter as well as having hot food in your belly.

He was raising his axe to split another chunk of beech when

the gates to the captives' camp, not too far away, swung open. "More poor buggers coming in," Szonyi predicted.

"Aye, no doubt." Istvan lowered the axe without chopping; he was willing to pause for a little while to see some new faces.

And new faces he saw—newer than he'd expected. "Who are *those* fellows?" Szonyi's deep voice cracked in surprise. "They sure aren't Gyongyosians."

The Kuusaman guards led in four men who towered over them, as Gyongyosians would have, but who, as Szonyi said, plainly did not come from Istvan's kingdom. The newcomers were slimmer of build than most Gyongyosians, and their hair was coppery, not tawny. They wore Kuusaman military clothing, which did not fit them well at all.

"I know who they have to be," Kun said. "They're Algarvians."

"Stars above, I think you're right." Istvan stared at the redheads, the only real allies his kingdom had. "But what are they doing out here in the middle of the Bothnian Ocean? Algarve is . . . way over on the other side of the world somewhere." What he knew of geography would have filled the heads of perhaps two pins—even though, thanks to his army service, he'd seen much more of the world than he'd ever expected (or wanted) while growing up in the little village of Kunhegyes.

"Let's ask them when we get off our shift," Szonyi said.

Kun smiled a sour smile. "And what language will you ask them in?" he inquired.

Szonyi had only one answer for that, which was no answer at all. A typical Gyongyosian peasant, he spoke only his own language. Sheepishly, he said, "I don't suppose they know Gyongyosian."

"About as much as you know of Algarvian, probably." Aye, Kun enjoyed making Szonyi look like a fool.

The new captives, naturally, noticed everybody staring at them. They waved to the Gyongyosians and bowed from the waist as if they were visiting nobles. "Show-offs," Szonyi muttered.

Then one of the Algarvians, waving again, called out, "Hello, friends! How are you?" in almost unaccented Gyongyosian.

"So they don't speak our language, eh?" Istvan said. Just as Kun enjoyed making Szonyi look like a fool, Istvan enjoyed turning the tables on clever Kun. He got fewer chances than he would have liked, but made the most of the ones he did find.

Kun, as usual, looked furious at getting caught in a mistake. Doing his best to discover how such a disaster might have happened, he asked the Algarvian, "Where did you learn to speak Gyongyosian?"

"My father was on the staff of the minister to Gyongyos years ago," the redheaded man answered, "and I was born in Gyorvar. So you could say I learned your language in your capital."

That was more than Istvan could say himself. His own upcountry accent sometimes made him feel self-conscious when he spoke to officers or others who had a more elegant turn of phrase—sometimes even to Kun, who sprang from Gyorvar. But Istvan knew what he wanted to find out: "Why are you here, so far from Algarve?" Asking the question that way let him disguise his own geographical shortcomings, too.

With a wave to his comrades, the Algarvian said, "We crewed two leviathans that were bringing . . . oh, one thing and another from Algarve to Gyongyos. We would have brought other things back from Gyongyos to Algarve: the kinds of things you have more of than we do, and that we could use in the war."

Istvan started to ask what sorts of things those were, but decided not to. Some of the Kuusaman guards were bound to speak his language, and he didn't want to give them the chance to learn anything interesting. Instead, he said, "And something went wrong, did it?"

"You might say so," the redheaded man replied. "Aye, you just might say so. Some Kuusaman dragons were flying east to drop eggs on some island or other that belongs to you, and they saw our leviathans and dropped their eggs—or enough of their eggs—on them instead. They hurt the animals too badly to let them go on. After that, it was either surrender or try to swim home by ourselves." He shrugged. "We surrendered."

Istvan tried to imagine guiding a leviathan—no, a couple of leviathans—from Algarve all the way to Gyongyos. From one side of the world to the other. He couldn't very well tell the foreigners that they should have fought to the death, not when he'd wound up in a captives' camp, too.

Eyeing the barracks and the yard with something less than delight, the Algarvian asked, "What do you people do for fun around here?"

"What do we do for fun?" Istvan returned. "Why, we chop wood. We dig latrines. When we're very lucky and we haven't got anything else to do, we sit around and watch the trees out beyond the stockade grow."

The Algarvian had a marvelously expressive face. Hearing Istvan's reply, he looked as if he'd just heard his father and mother had died. "And what do you do for excitement?" he inquired.

"If you want excitement, you can try to escape," Istvan answered. "Maybe you can get out of the camp. Then maybe you can steal a ship. Then maybe you wouldn't have to swim home."

"I am always glad to meet a funny man," the redhead said. Istvan started to puff out his chest, till the Algarvian added, "Too bad I am not so glad to meet you." His smile took away most of the sting; it might have taken away all of it had Kun not sniggered. Istvan gave him a dirty look, which only made him snigger again, louder this time.

Even when he'd commanded a company as a sergeant, Leudast hadn't been allowed to attend officers' conferences. He was still commanding a company, but, thanks to luck and Marshal Rathar, he was a lieutenant these days. That entitled him to know what would happen before it happened to him.

Here, he and Captain Recared and a couple of dozen officers commanding units much larger than their ranks properly entitled them to lead sat in a barn that still stank of cow and listened to a colonel who was probably doing a lieutenant general's job explaining the details of what the Unkerlanter army would try next in the south. "And so," the colonel was saying, "if we succeed, if all goes as planned, we shall finally drive the cursed Algarvians from the soil of the Duchy of Grelz, exactly as our glorious comrades in arms have driven them out of northern Unkerlant. High time, I say—high time indeed."

A low-voiced rumble rose from the officers: "Aye." Leudast joined it, but had other things on his mind. *So they've driven the redheads out of the north altogether, have they? That means my home village belongs to Unkerlant again.* The thought would have cheered him more had he not paused to wonder if any of it was still standing. It would have been fought over at least twice, and, for all he knew, more often than that.

"Have you any questions?" the colonel asked. A couple of majors did, and even a brash captain. Leudast kept his mouth shut. He was without a doubt the most junior officer in the barn, and didn't want to remind anyone else that he was there at all. The colonel efficiently disposed of the queries; unlike a good many commanders Leudast had known, he actually had some notion of what he was talking about. He finished, "We've wanted to pay those whoresons back for years. Now we put them in a sack and then pound the sack to pieces."

Somebody said, "We'll find all sorts of strange things in the sack, too."

"So we will," the colonel agreed. "Algarvians, Yaninans, Forthwegians, even blonds from out of the far east." He shrugged. "So what? It only shows the redheads are scraping up everything they can to try to hold us back. But it won't work. Glory to King Swemmel! Glory to Unkerlant!"

"Glory to Swemmel! Glory to Unkerlant!" the officers chorused. The meeting broke up.

Leudast and Captain Recared walked back to their position together. Leudast pointed. "Look at all the egg-tossers we've got waiting for the redheads."

"Egg-tossers and behemoths and dragons and men," Recared said. "The river is running our way now. They'll try to dam it up—they always fight hard—but we should have our way with them."

"Aye." Leudast nodded. "They threw everything they had at the Durrwangen bulge last year. They haven't done any throwing since. They've been catching instead."

Recared nodded, too. "That's right. And they'll catch it good and proper come tomorrow morning."

And Leudast and Recared passed a stockade. Guards stood stolidly around the perimeter. The stink of long-unwashed bodies wafted over the wall. "Is that what they're doing with the soldiers they court-martial these days?" Leudast asked. "I thought they just put them in punishment battalions and threw them at the redheads first."

"They do," Recared answered. "Those aren't soldiers in there. Come on." He walked faster, plainly wanting to get away from the stockade as soon as he could.

"They aren't soldiers?" Leudast said. "Then who . . . ? Oh." He walked faster, too. "I wish we didn't have to do that." How had the wretches behind the stockade ended up where they were? By being desperate criminals? Maybe. By being in the wrong place at the wrong time? That struck Leudast as much more likely. He said no more. Those who complained about such things might end up behind a stockade themselves.

When he got back to his own encampment, he feigned cheeriness, whether he really felt it or not. "We've got a good plan and plenty of what we need to make it work," he told his company. Every word of that was true, too. If it wasn't the whole truth, the soldiers didn't need to know it. "Tomorrow morning, we're going to make the Algarvians sorry they ever set foot in Unkerlant."

His men cheered. Sergeant Hagen, who'd replaced Kiun, said, "We'll do better than that. We'll make the cursed Algarvians sorry they were ever born—isn't that right, Lieutenant?" Hagen was very young, and had a youngster's terrifying enthusiasm.

"That's just right," Leudast said. "You ought to get whatever sleep you can tonight, because all the eggs we're going to fling will wake you up early."

The eggs they were going to fling would wake some of his men up early. Others had found a knack for sleeping through anything. Leudast envied them, wishing he had the same knack himself.

As company commander, he didn't get much sleep. He stayed up late, making sure everything in the company was as ready as it could be. And he had a soldier shake him awake half an hour before the eggs were due to fly so he could be ready to lead the men eastward.

Hissing and whistling noises in the air announced eggs flying toward the enemy. A few moments later, the eastern horizon lit up, as with sunrise a couple of hours early. Leudast thrust his whistle into his mouth and blew a long, piercing blast. It was fun—as much fun as he'd had with toys while a boy—and he suddenly understood why officers enjoyed the privilege of carrying them. "Forward!" he shouted. "For King Swemmel and for Unkerlant!"

Other company commanders' whistles were shrilling, too, and so was Captain Recared's. "Urra!" the men yelled. "Urra! Swemmel! Urra!" They swarmed toward the Algarvian lines. Part of that was eagerness to close with the hated foe. Part of it was knowing that hard-eyed impressers with sticks would follow the advance and mercilessly blaze anyone who wasn't moving forward fast enough to suit them. Those impressers sometimes met mysterious fatal accidents of their own, but they did help inspire most of the soldiers.

Eggs burst among the advancing Unkerlanters, too—King Mezentio's men hadn't been caught altogether by surprise, and the pasting they were taking hadn't put all their egg-tossers out of action. Shrieks mingled with the cries of, "Urra!" But what the Algarvians gave was only a pittance, a nuisance, compared to what they were taking. Some of Leudast's men, newly swept into the army, shrieked from terror rather than from pain, but he knew better. He'd been on the receiving end of far, far worse than this.

Pulses of light began flickering in the night ahead—Algarvian sticks, their beams probing for his countrymen. No, the redheads hadn't been completely fooled, and they hadn't been completely silenced, either. Leudast cursed under his breath. *Why don't they start killing the poor sods they've rounded up?* he thought. *We could use the help.*

He was ashamed of himself a moment later. Algarvian foot-soldiers must have felt the same way when their mages first started slaughtering Kaunians back in the dark, fearful days when Cottbus looked as if it would surely fall. If they were wrong to wish for such a thing, how was he right, especially when his kingdom's sorcerers slaughtered his own countrymen for their effects?

How am I right? It's my neck, that's how. Some of the enemy's beams zipped past him, fearfully close, before the ground ahead shook and violet flames burst up from it. Some of his men whooped with glee as the sorcery struck the foe. Maybe they were naive enough not to know how their mages did what they did. Maybe—more likely—they wanted to live themselves, and didn't care.

"Forward!" Leudast yelled. "Hit 'em hard while they're groggy!" The Algarvians wouldn't stay groggy long. Three years and more of fighting them had made him all too sure of that. They didn't have enough men or beasts to hold back the Unkerlanters or drive them as they once had, but the troopers they had left were as deadly dangerous as ever.

And the redheads still had Kaunians left to kill. Leudast had hoped the Unkerlanter bombardment would have slain a lot of the blonds without giving the Algarvians the chance to seize their life energy and turn it into sorcerous energy. No such luck. The dreadfully disruptive and destructive sorcery the Unkerlanter wizards raised now quieted much sooner than it should have, as Mezentio's mages used, and used up, the Kaunians to counteract it.

Could be worse, Leudast thought. *In the old days, we'd've been fighting like mad bastards to counter their conjuring, not the other way round.*

A column of Unkerlanter behemoths thundered forward. The egg-tossers and heavy sticks the armored beasts bore on their backs battered down surviving Algarvian strongpoints. And once it got moving east, that column kept moving. The only thing that could reliably stop a behemoth was another behemoth. The Algarvians had been short of behemoths ever since losing so many in the enormous battles of the Durrwangen bulge, and most of the animals they did have were in the north, trying to hold the Unkerlanters there.

"Come on, men!" Leudast shouted, almost stumbling over a kilted corpse. "They can't hold us! We're breaking them! Their crust is tough, but once we're past it, what have they got left? Nothing!" He blew the whistle again, exulting in the squeal.

He exulted in what he saw, too, as the sky grew light and true dawn approached. Watching Algarvians run was something Unkerlanter soldiers didn't get to do often enough. The redheads almost always fought till they couldn't fight any more. Not here. Hit with overwhelming force, Mezentio's men fled for their lives. It didn't help much; the fleeing footsoldiers fell one after another.

Leudast was in the middle of yelling, "Forward!" yet again when an Algarvian who didn't run—some stubborn whoresons always stood their ground—blazed him in the leg. The word went from a command to an anguished howl. He fell heavily, clutching at his right thigh.

"Lieutenant's down!" Sergeant Hagen shouted. Leudast heard the words as if from very far away. He'd heard such cries countless times before, but he'd gone through three years of war and been wounded only once—till now.

How bad was it? He made himself yank up his tunic and look. The beam had gone right through his leg, outside the thighbone. Such wounds often cauterized themselves. This one hadn't. He was bleeding, but not too badly. He had a wound bandage. Unkerlant didn't issue such things; he'd taken it off a dead Algarvian. Covering both sides of the wound was awkward, but he managed.

He'd just got the bandage into place when a couple of troopers hauled him upright. He screamed again; the way they manhandled him hurt as much as getting blazed had in the first place. "Sorry, sir," one of them said. "We'll get you back to the healers."

"All right." Leudast tasted blood; he must have bitten his tongue or lower lip. The men were glad to help him. Why not? It took them away from danger, too. And, he realized, in dull, pain-filled astonishment, he was getting his own second holiday from the war. But the price of the ticket was very high. He bit down on another scream, and then on another still. Before long, he wasn't biting down on them any more.

Pekka hadn't needed long to realize she disliked Viana. The more she knew her, the more she disliked her, too. It wasn't that the Lagoan sorceress was particularly annoying, or that she lacked the wit to understand the spells she'd come to the Naantali district to learn. For a little while, Pekka had trouble figuring out what it was.

For a little while, but not for long. Viana was tall and straight and high-breasted, with a narrow waist and long, elegant legs the short kilts she wore showed to best advantage. Standing beside her, Pekka felt twelve years old and half-sprouted all over again. Having stood beside Viana once, Pekka made it a point of never doing it again.

She's a Lagoan. Lagoan women are bigger and rounder than Kuusamans. After Pekka told herself that a couple of times, she suddenly quit. It wasn't the answer to the problem. It *was* the problem.

It wouldn't have been, if Viana hadn't cast sheep's eyes at Fernao every chance she got—and she made sure she got plenty of them. Just watching her, just listening to her, made Pekka want to retch.

You're jealous, Pekka thought. *He's not your man—you made a point of telling him he's not your man—and you're jealous. You told him to find a Lagoan girl. Here's one practically throwing herself at his feet, and you want to kill her. You don't just want to kill her. You want to kill her slowly, an inch at a time, and take days and days to get it over with.*

She stared at herself in the mirror above the sink in her room. Jealousy was the green-eyed monster, but her eyes remained brown. "No, Viana's eyes are green," Pekka hissed.

She stepped away from the mirror. No, she whirled away

from the mirror so she wouldn't have to look at herself or think about the color of Viana's eyes. *Am I going out of my mind?*

In a way, it would have been easier had Fernao fallen head over heels for his countrywoman. Then Pekka would have known how things were, and she could have gone on with her own life. But, as far as she could see, Fernao was much less interested in Viana than Viana was in him. Which meant . . .

"Which means trouble," Pekka said aloud. Which meant Fernao was still interested in her. If that wasn't trouble, she didn't know what was.

Going to him to let him know how upset she was at Leino's jointing the war on the Derlavaian mainland had been a mistake. She saw that now. If she revealed her most intimate feelings about her husband to another man, with whom was she being more intimate? The answer to that was depressingly obvious. The reason for it was pretty obvious, too: Leino was far away, while Fernao was here.

"I was only *really* intimate with him once," Pekka said. As long as she could keep on saying that . . . *As long as I can keep on saying that, what?* she wondered. *As long as I can keep saying that, I'm going to be sick-jealous of Viana whenever I see her or even think of her.*

And what if I were really intimate with Fernao more than once? She didn't see Leino's face in her mind when she asked herself that. She saw Uto's. Thinking about her son made Pekka raise a hand to her cheek, as if someone had slapped her in the face.

After that, Pekka couldn't make herself stay in her chamber another instant. For that matter, she couldn't make herself stay in the hostel any more. Instead of going into the refectory to gab with her colleagues, she fled the place as if it were full of demons. And so it was, but the demons were her own.

Outside, things felt easier somehow. The day was mild, not warm: the Naantali district got warmer in summer than her southern seacoast home town of Kajaani, but not a lot warmer. White clouds drifted slowly from west to east across a watery blue sky. Grass and shrubs remained green, but they would start turning yellow in only a couple of months. Before long, winter would reclaim this land and hold it for a long, long time. A lapwing flew by, peeping. Before long, it would fly north. It could flee. She was stuck here.

The lapwing's motion made her notice other motion in the sky, far, far higher. Something up there circled lazily, right at the edge of visibility. *A hawk?* she wondered, and shook her head. It was bigger than a hawk, and higher than a hawk, too. A dragon.

But what was a dragon doing up there? How long had dragons circled over Naantali? She didn't remember seeing one before. Had the Seven Princes taken to warding the hostel and the blockhouse and the land in between? It wasn't the worst idea in the world. If they had, though, why hadn't they told her about it? This was *her* project. She was supposed to know about such things.

She watched the dragon. It continued to wheel, far too high up for her to tell anything about it except what it was. Then something fell away from it. Pekka let out a gasp of horror, fearing the dragonflier had somehow fallen off. But the dragon didn't change course, as it would have if suddenly deprived of intelligent control. It kept right on circling, as the the speck tumbled down to earth.

Pekka had a while to watch that speck fall, to watch it grow larger, to wonder what it was. She didn't wonder long. If it wasn't a dragonflier, it almost had to be an egg. But if it was an egg, either something had gone dreadfully wrong up there or. . . . *Or the Algarvians have managed to sneak a dragon south from Valmiera, the way we pound their kingdom.* The thought formed, blizzard-cold, in her mind.

One egg, though? The dragon had flown a long, long way. It couldn't possibly have carried more than one. What were the odds the fellow flying it could hit anything worth hitting with a single egg? Good enough to risk a dragon and a highly trained man? Pekka couldn't see how.

Unless . . . She had to keep her eye on the plummeting egg now; had she glanced away, she would have lost it. It looked as if it would fall some little distance behind the hostel—but then, at the last instant, the direction in which it fell suddenly shifted, bringing it back toward the building.

Magecraft! flashed through her mind just before the egg
burst. She knew of no spell that could catch a quickly falling
object like an egg and swing it back toward its target, but she
didn't know everything there was to know, either. The Algarvians had talented mages of their own. If they'd concentrated
on this kind of magic, they might be as far ahead with it as her
group was with its special spells.

Even as she realized that, the egg released its sorcerous energy with a great roar and a flash of light just behind the hostel.
Although she'd wandered a couple of hundred yards away before she saw the dragon, the noise was terrific, a hammer-blow
against the ears. Part of the hostel sagged down toward the
back, like a tired old man sagging into a sofa. Smoke began to
rise.

"No!" Pekka screamed, and dashed back to the battered
building. As she ran, she looked up into the sky. She couldn't
spot the dragon at first. Then she did. It wasn't circling any
more. It was flying off toward the north, as if the man aboard it
knew he'd done what he was supposed to do. And so, no doubt,
he did.

Pekka cursed him with all her heart. She doubted the curse
would bite; her own countrymen were warded against such, and
the Algarvians were bound to be, too. She cursed anyhow.

People started spilling out of the hostel, some bleeding, some
limping, some helping others who had trouble moving on their
own. There was Ilmarinen, with blood running down his face
from a cut cheek—and with the plate of smoked salmon from
which he'd been eating still in his hand. He waved to her, calling, "They managed to sneak one in on us, the stinking
whoresons." Was he angry, or did he admire the Algarvians'
professional skill? Pekka couldn't tell.

She waved back and said, "Aye." She was glad to see Ilmarinen not badly hurt, but he wasn't the one who'd made her
come tearing back the way she had. "Where's Fernao?" she
cried.

In the midst of death and destruction, Ilmarinen laughed at
her. But the laughter cut off. "He's in there somewhere," he an-

swered, "one way or another." He took the last bite of salmon off the plate and ate it.

More smoke poured from the hostel and more of it slid toward ruin. More people came staggering out, too, mages and servants and cooks all mixed together. Pekka's heart leaped when she saw a tall, redheaded man with a ponytail—but it wasn't Fernao, only one of the Lagoan mages who'd come here to learn the sorceries he'd helped shape.

Fernao had rescued her when the Algarvians assailed the blockhouse. Could she do anything less for him? She started into the hostel. A couple of men caught her and held her back. "Don't go inside, Mistress Pekka," one of them said. "The whole thing is liable to fall down."

"I don't care." She kicked out at them. "Let me go!"

"No, mistress," the man replied. "We need you safe. Plenty of other people to go in there and get out the hurt and the dead. You're staying right here." Between them, he and his friend were much stronger than she.

She struggled anyhow, and had to bite her tongue to keep from cursing them as savagely as she had the Algarvian dragonflier. And then, all at once, she went limp in their restraining arms. There was Fernao, staggering out through the door Ilmarinen had used. He'd lost his stick and made heavy going without it, but didn't seem badly hurt.

"Pekka! Where's Pekka?" he shouted in his accented but now fluent Kuusaman.

"Here I am," Pekka called. When she said, "Let me go," this time, the men who had hold of her did. She hurried over to Fernao. "Are you all right?" she demanded.

"Not too bad," he answered. "How in blazes did the Algarvians manage to do this to us?" His face went thoroughly grim. "If one of the Lagoan mages I brought in turns out to be a spy, you can do whatever you please with me. I'd deserve it."

"No," she said. "It had nothing to do with you or any of the other Lagoans." She explained how she knew.

"Guiding falling eggs by sorcery?" Fernao said when she was through. "I wouldn't want to try that. But I won't argue with you—you saw it, and I didn't. I'm just glad you're all right."

"I'm glad *you're* all right," Pekka said. They clung to each other. Now that she knew he was hale, Pekka's wits started working again. "I've seen Ilmarinen. Now we have to find out if the rest of the theoretical sorcerers are safe."

"There's Piilis." Fernao pointed. "And who's he dragging out? . . . Oh, powers above, it's Viana."

The Lagoan sorceress' neck bent at an unnatural angle. She was plainly dead. Piilis let her rest on the grass and hurried in after someone else before Pekka could tell him to stop. She stared at Viana's corpse, which looked skyward with blank eyes. In an odd way, her jealousy of the Lagoan might have saved her life. Shame filled her. She began to cry.

Fifteen

A t some point in his life, Sidroc had surely heard the phrase *Misery loves company*. If he had, the exact meaning of that phrase had escaped him till he found himself not far from the town of Mandelsloh, in the extreme east of Unkerlant, surrounded by King Swemmel's soldiers.

He didn't know how many men who fought for King Mezentio were surrounded with him, but he did know the number wasn't small. And he knew that the miserable men in the Mandelsloh pocket came from just about every kingdom that had followed Algarve into war against Unkerlant. Had he not known, the men sitting and lying around the fire with him would have done a good enough job of teaching the lesson.

Even in the chaotic, desperate fighting that marked the Algarvian response to the Unkerlanters' latest blow here in the south, he hadn't lost touch with Sergeant Werferth or Ceorl, though he wouldn't have particularly missed the ruffian had something happened to him. A young, exhausted Algarvian lieutenant sprawled on the ground close by them. He'd been attached to Plegmund's Brigade, but not to Sidroc's company of Forthwegians in Algarvian service.

A couple of Grelzers in dark green tunics by now had beards that would have let them pass for Forthwegians—except that Sidroc understood very little of what they said. One of them was roasting some meat: probably a chunk of dead unicorn, but possibly dead behemoth. Not far from them, a blond from the Phalanx of Valmieran lay snoring. A Yaninan in leggings and the funny shoes the soldiers of his kingdom wore changed the bandage on a minor wound.

Unkerlanter dragons flew by overhead. They ruled the skies these days. They didn't bother dropping an egg on the campfire: they were after bigger targets. Before long, eggs burst half a mile or so away. Sidroc didn't even stir. If a burst wasn't close enough to put him in danger of his life, he didn't intend to worry about it. Even if it was that close, he wouldn't worry about it much. Next to what would happen if Swemmel's soldiers got their hands on him alive, dying didn't look so bad.

"Where do we go from here?" he said—in Algarvian, the one language all the weary, frightened, battered soldiers nearby might understand.

Sure enough, the Yaninan answered in the same tongue: "East."

"Plenty of Unkerlanters east of us, too," Werferth said fatalistically.

That lieutenant sat up. "But our comrades are there to the east." He was worn and filthy, not at all the proper, dapper Algarvian officer. "We have to break through. If we don't break through, we're all dead."

"And if we do break through, we are still all dead." That was one of the Grelzers, the one who wasn't roasting meat. "It will take a little longer, that is all." His Algarvian was so heavily accented, Sidroc had a hard time understanding him. But, once Sidroc did make sense of the words, he had a demon of a time disagreeing with them.

The Yaninan finished fiddling with his bandage. He pointed to the Grelzers. "You not have to go east," he said, also haltingly. "You take off tunics, you just peasants."

They both shook their heads. "I will not live under King Swemmel," said the one who'd spoken before. "He kills his whole kingdom."

When the other Grelzer took his meat off the fire, Ceorl pointed to it and said, "You want to share that?" As usual, he had his eye on the main chance. The Grelzer plainly wanted nothing of the sort. He glared at Ceorl as a dog with a bone might glare at another dog who'd looked at it. But, unlike a dog, he thought before he fought, and reluctantly nodded. He started cutting up the gobbet so everyone could get a couple of bites from it.

Sidroc wolfed down his portion. He had some bread in his pack, but he didn't take it out. What he showed, he would have to share. If he went hungry now, he might be able to eat more a little later. Meanwhile, the Yaninan shook the Kaunian from Valmiera awake so he could get his little portion.

"Thank you," the blond said around a yawn. He'd been asleep when the other trapped soldiers talked about what to do next, but he had the same idea: "We had better get moving." The accent he gave to Algarvian was even stranger than that of the Grelzers. But he still thought straight, for he went on, "The longer the Unkerlanters have to tighten the noose around us, the more trouble we will be in."

Ceorl said, "I'm sick to death of marching."

"If you stay here, you'll get your death whether you're sick or not," Sidroc said. Ceorl glared at him. They still didn't like each other. Had they not had worse worries, they might have fought.

With a groan, the Algarvian lieutenant heaved himself to his feet. "He's right," he said. "We've got no good chances, but moving fast is our best one."

Sidroc groaned, too, as he made himself stand. He wanted to sleep, with luck for about a week. But he wasn't ready to sleep forever, not yet, and so he trudged off with the rest.

Everything inside the Mandelsloh pocket painted a picture of the disintegration of the army trapped there. Unkerlanter drag-ons had caught a column of supply wagons out in the open and smashed it to bits. The wagons lay burnt and scattered like sav-aged toys; the animals that had drawn them were bloated and starting to stink.

A battery of Algarvian egg-tossers had suffered a similar fate. The engines made to fling death at the Unkerlanters wound up on the receiving end of what they were supposed to dish out. Their tumbled and broken disarray argued that this fight would not be won, not by the Algarvians.

And a ley-line caravan had taken an egg and now blocked the line it was intended to travel. Soldiers struggled to move it aside so other caravans might pass. *How much good will that do?* Sidroc wondered. *They still can't get through the ring Swemmel's buggers have around us.*

The lieutenant leading the motley little group of which Sidroc was a part must have had the same thought. He didn't let them get close enough to the wrecked caravan to be ordered to help shift it. They just went on their way, one band among many without much hope but without much choice, either. With only one choice, in fact: Break out or die.

More dragons appeared overhead. Sidroc promptly dove into the crater a bursting egg had left behind. His comrades took cover, too. He waited for more eggs to fall, for the earth to shake at their bursts, for the screams of wounded men to start. Nothing of the sort happened. After a moment, the blond from the Phalanx of Valmiera said, "Those are Algar-vian dragons."

Algarvian dragons *had* flown over the Mandelsloh pocket before, but not very often. When they did, they sometimes dropped food or medicines for the soldiers. Sidroc looked up to the sky with sudden hope. The thought of getting his hands on a food package made his belly growl and his mouth water.

But no food parcels plummeted down. In a way, they were only cruel hoaxes, since the dragons couldn't possibly bring in enough even to come close to supplying all the men trapped around Mandelsloh. Every little bit helped someone, though.

Instead of food packets, leaves of paper fluttered in the air, slowly dancing toward the ground. Sidroc grunted. "What sort of lies are they telling us?" he asked nobody in particular. The Unkerlanters sometimes dropped leaflets urging their foes to surrender and promising them good treatments if they did. The leaflets would have been much more persuasive had those foes not known what had happened to Raniero of Grelz.

Sidroc didn't even have to climb out of his hole to get his hands on a leaflet. Two of them swirled down into the crater; one hit him in the shoulder. He grabbed it and turned it right side up.

Soldiers of Algarve, help is on the way! it read. *A strong counterattack from the east has been launched to regain contact with you and reestablish the front in this area. We expect your rescuers to fight their way through the forces of the barbarous foe and join you within two days' time. You are urged to break out toward the east to aid this movement and to insure that it is crowned with success no matter what the result of the attack from the rescuing units.*

He read it through twice. He spoke Algarvian better than he read it. But there still didn't seem any room for doubt. "They're going to try," he said as he came out of the crater. "They're going to try, but they don't think they can do it."

"That's what it sounds like to me, too," Sergeant Werferth said. The Algarvian lieutenant nodded. *He* read Algarvian perfectly well. And he also had no trouble reading between the lines.

The Kaunian from Valmieran was holding a leaflet, too. "This attack of theirs will make the Unkerlanters turn away from us," he said in his odd accent. "This will give us a better chance."

He was probably right. He was, in fact, almost certainly right. But his being right didn't turn the better chance into a good one. Nevertheless . . . Sidroc started tramping east. "We'd better get moving," he said. "We want to break out while they're still trying to break in."

No one argued with him. The other soldiers emerged from their holes and slogged east, too. They weren't any sort of formal unit, just a double handful of men thrown together by chaos. They clung to one another now, though, as if they'd fought shoulder to shoulder for years.

Until, that is, they tramped past the wreckage of what the Algarvians called a special camp. Eggs had hurled the neat rows of sacrificed corpses this way and that. Several days in the sun had turned them black and bloated and stinking. But they were all unquestionably blond.

Sidroc stared at the Kaunian from the Phalanx of Valmiera. What was he thinking? What *could* he be thinking? Had Sidroc been the Algarvian lieutenant, he wouldn't have waited around to find out. He would have run for his life.

The blond looked at the stick he carried. Sidroc thought about running for his life even though he wasn't the Algarvian lieutenant. Slowly, the Valmieran said, "Algarve gave me this stick to fight Unkerlant. Fighting Unkerlant is the most important thing."

Everybody relaxed. Sidroc realized he hadn't been the only anxious trooper. He glanced over at the Valmieran. His private opinion was that the fellow was a little bit crazy. But then, if he weren't a little bit crazy himself, why the demon had he signed up for Plegmund's Brigade?

Crazy or not, he'd read that leaflet right. However hard the Algarvians farther east were trying to break into the Mandelsloh pocket, the Unkerlanters were holding them away. That meant his comrades and he had to break out, to make their own way toward the men fighting to link up with them. It meant the army in the pocket had to leave most of their weapons behind. It meant, in the end, that Sidroc had to throw away his stick and his uniform and swim fifty yards across a freezing river.

But there were Algarvians on the other side of it. They hauled him out of the water and gave him spirits and dry clothes—a short tunic and kilt, but that couldn't be helped. And they did the same for the blond from the Phalanx of Valmiera. Exhausted, shivering, half drunk—the spirits went straight to his head—Sidroc stuck out a hand. The Kaunian clasped it.

Ealstan didn't need long to discover that raising a revolt against the Algarvians in Eoforwic was not so simple as sorcerously disguising himself as a redhead and going off to assassinate somebody. Maybe his comrades and he had hurt the Algarvians with that murder. He hoped so. But Mezentio's men had found somebody else to put in the dead man's slot, and they went right on about the business of grinding the rebellion into the dust.

Reporting to Pybba one morning, Ealstan pointed west across the Twegen and angrily demanded, "What in blazes are the Unkerlanters waiting for? We're tying up powers above only know how many brigades of Algarvians for them. Why don't they cross the river and help us?"

Since the uprising started, Pybba looked to have aged ten years. His voice was grim as he answered, "There's no good reason. I can think of a couple of bad reasons, if you want 'em."

"Go ahead," Ealstan said.

"All right. First thing that springs to mind is that they're letting the Algarvians solve their Forthwegian problem for 'em. A Forthwegian who'd fight the redheads'd fight Swemmel's buggers, too, so they may reckon a lot of us are better off dead."

Ealstan grunted. That made entirely too much sense. He said, "The same way we let the Algarvians solve our Kaunian problem for us, eh?"

"Aye, just like that," Pybba answered, before realizing exactly what Ealstan had said. When he did, he glared. "Funny fellow. Ha, ha."

"I wasn't joking," Ealstan said. "How is it different?"

"Shut up," the pottery magnate said in a flat, hard voice. "Just shut up. I don't have time to argue with you. If you want to be a Kaunian-lover once we don't have the stinking Algarvians on our hands, fine, go right ahead. For now, though, you'd cursed well better keep in mind which is more important."

In that moment, Ealstan hated him: hated him with a hatred all the more bitter because Pybba was his own countryman and they would never, ever see eye-to-eye on this. Ealstan had to take a deep breath to keep from telling the pottery magnate exactly what he thought of him. By the look on Pybba's face, he thought the same thing of Ealstan.

"Tell me what you need from me," Ealstan said at last. "I'll go do it, and then we won't have to have anything to do with each other for a while."

"A bargain," Pybba said at once. "You're a stubborn whoreson. You're almost as stubborn as I am, I think—the only difference is, you're a fool."

Ealstan, of course, reckoned Pybba the fool. "Never mind," he said. "You got in a last insult. Huzzah for you. Now give me my orders, so I can go do them."

"Right." Pybba pointed toward the center of the city. "We've got a force building in a park, getting ready to cut the Algarvians' corridor to the palace and to the ley-line terminal. Go make sure they're ready to move. Tell 'em the attack is still on. The fellow in charge there already knows what time."

"Fine. Shall I join it?"

"If you want to." Pybba spoke with relentless indifference. A moment later, though, he checked himself and shook his head. "No, you know too cursed much. Can't have the redheads nabbing you and tearing it out of you."

"Right," Ealstan said tightly. He turned on his heel and strode—almost stomped—out of Pybba's office and out of the pottery works that was now the headquarters for the rebellion. As he left, he laughed a little. One thing the uprising had done: it had cost the Algarvians their source of Style Seventeen sugar bowls. They would have to use something else instead of hold their little eggs.

Eoforwic looked like what it was, a city torn by war. Smoke thickened the air. Ealstan hardly noticed; he'd got very used to it. Eggs burst not far away. He'd got used to that, too. And he'd got used to glassless windows, to buildings with chunks bitten out of them, and to charred beams sticking up like leafless branches from the wreckage. The Forthwegian capital hadn't suffered too badly when the Unkerlanters seized it, or when the Algarvians took it away from King Swemmel's men. It was making up for lost time.

He found the park without much trouble. Finding the man in

charge of the attack took more work, but he finally did. The fellow nodded brusquely. "Aye, I know what we're supposed to do," he said. "We'll bloody well do it, too. You can go back and tell Pybba he doesn't need to hold my hand. I'm not a baby."

"Keep your tunic on." Ealstan hid a smile. He had that same reaction to the pottery magnate, usually a couple of times an hour. He knew he was here more to get him out of Pybba's hair than for any other reason. He didn't care. Right this minute, he couldn't think of anything he wanted more than to be out of Pybba's hair.

When he didn't say anything more, the local commander nodded again, as if he'd passed a test. "All right, kid. We'll feed the powers below plenty of dead Algarvians. Don't you worry about a thing."

That *kid* made Ealstan bristle, but he didn't show it. When you showed things like that, people just laughed. "Right," he said again, and walked away, almost as fast as he'd walked away from Pybba.

The park didn't look like a place where an attack was building. The Forthwegian fighters didn't gather out in the open. That would have shown them to redheads on dragons overhead or with spyglasses up in tall buildings, and would have invited massacre. Instead they crouched under trees and in the buildings around the park, waiting for the order to go forward. They all wore armbands that said FREE FORTHWEG, so the Algarvians couldn't claim they were fighting out of uniform and blaze them on the spot if they caught them.

As Ealstan was going by, one of the Forthwegian fighters under the oaks called his name. He stopped in surprise. He didn't recognize the other man. But then, after a moment, he did. It was the fellow who'd been playing drums in another park—the fellow who played so much like the famous Ethelhelm. Now that Ealstan heard him speak, he sounded like Ethelhelm, too.

"Hello," Ealstan said. "The face is familiar"—which wasn't quite true—"but I can't place your name." He didn't know which name Ethelhelm was using. If Ethelhelm had even a dram of brains, it wouldn't be his own.

And, sure enough, the musician said, "You can call me Guthfrith."

"Good to see you again," Ealstan told him. "Getting your revenge on the Algarvians, are you, Guthfrith?"

"It's about time, wouldn't you say?" Ethelhelm answered.

"Probably long past time," Ealstan said, and the Kaunian half-breed nodded. Ealstan went on, "What have you been doing with yourself lately?"

"Odd jobs, mostly," said Ethelhelm—*no, I should think of him as Guthfrith,* went through Ealstan's mind. "Did you recognize me, there in that other park? I saw you, and I thought you might have."

"I thought I did," Ealstan replied, "but I wasn't sure. You didn't look just the way I thought I recalled you"—*you were sorcerously disguised*—"but your hands hadn't changed at all."

Ethelhelm—no, Guthfrith—looked down at the hands in question as if they'd betrayed him. And so, in a way, they had. Even now, they looked more as if they should be poised over drums than holding a stick. With a chuckle, he said, "Not everyone has ears as good as yours. I'm not sorry, either. I'd be in trouble if more people did."

"You would have been in trouble," Ealstan said. "Not any more. Now you're getting your own back."

"No." Guthfrith shook his head. "The thieving redheads have taken away everything I had. I can't get it back. The most I can get is a piece of revenge. I wasn't very brave before. Now . . ." He shrugged. "I try to do better."

"That's all anyone can do," Ealstan said.

"Took me a long time to figure it out," Guthfrith said. "How's your lady? What was her name? Thelberge?"

"That's right." Ealstan nodded. "She's fine, thanks. We've got a little girl."

"Do you?" Guthfrith said, and Ealstan nodded again. Then Guthfrith reminded Ealstan he was also Ethelhelm, for he went on, "You used to go with a blond woman before that, didn't you? Do you know what happened to her?"

"Uh—no." Ealstan's ears heated in dull embarrassment, but he was not about to tell the musician that Vanai *was* Thelberge. He wished he hadn't had to tell Pybba about his family arrangements. The more people he told, the more Vanai found herself in danger, for there was no guarantee that the Forthwegians would succeed in ousting the Algarvians from Eoforwic. And if Mezentio's men won this fight, they would surely take the most savage vengeance they could.

"No, eh?" Guthfrith's voice was toneless as he added, "Too bad."

Ealstan wanted to explain everything to him. He wanted to, but he didn't. Aye, the fellow who had been Ethelhelm was a half breed, but he'd got much too cozy with the Algarvians, and stayed that way much too long. If they ever captured him now, he was liable to feed them a genuine, full-blooded Kaunian to save his own neck.

He looked at Ealstan with something like loathing, though they'd been friendly while Ealstan was casting his accounts for him. Ealstan looked at him in much the same way. Neither of them, plainly, would ever trust the other again. When Ealstan said, "I've got to go," he knew he sounded relieved, and Guthfrith looked the same way.

"Take care of yourself. Take care of your little girl, too." By the way Guthfrith sounded, Ealstan was welcome to walk in front of a ley-line caravan.

"You take care, too." Ealstan sounded as if he wished the same for Guthfrith. He hurried off toward Pybba's headquarters, and didn't look back once. Whatever warmth he'd known for the man who'd been one of the most popular musicians in Forthweg, was dead now.

He needed a while to get back to the pottery magnate's place. Algarvian dragons appeared overhead and dropped load after load of eggs on Eoforwic, forcing Ealstan into a cellar. No Unkerlanter dragons flew east from over the Twegen to challenge the beasts painted in green, red, and white. The enemy could simply do as he pleased, and he pleased to knock down big chunks of the Forthwegian capital. He doubtless assumed anyone still inside the city opposed him. Had he been wrong in that assumption, the destruction he wrought helped make him right.

"Took you long enough," Pybba growled when Ealstan finally did get back. "I didn't send you out to buy a month's worth of groceries, you know."

"You may have noticed the Algarvians were dropping eggs again," Ealstan said. "I didn't want to get killed on my way back, so I ducked into some shelter till they quit."

Pybba waved that aside, as if of no account. Maybe, to him, it wasn't. "Will the attack go through on time?" he demanded.

Ealstan nodded. "Aye. The fellow in charge of it told me to tell you he didn't need any reminders."

"That's my job, reminding," Pybba said. His job, as far as Ealstan could see, was doing everything nobody else was doing and half the jobs other people were supposed to be doing. Without him, the uprising probably never would have happened. With him, it was going better than Ealstan had thought it would. Was it going well enough? Ealstan had his doubts, and did his best to pretend he didn't.

Leino had been in Balvi, or rather, through Balvi, once before, on holiday with Pekka. Then the capital of Jelgava had impressed him as a place where the blond locals did their best to separate outsiders from any cash they might have as quickly and enjoyably as possible.

Now . . . Now, with the Algarvian garrison that had occupied Balvi for four years fled to the more rugged interior of Jelgava, the city was one enormous carnival. Jelgavans had never had a reputation for revelry—if anyone did, it was their Algarvian occupiers—but they were doing their best to make one. Thumping Kaunian-style bands blared on every corner. People danced in the streets. Most of them seemed drunk. And anyone in Kuusaman or Lagoan uniform could hardly take a step without getting kissed or having a mug full of something cold and wet and potent thrust into his hand.

Even though Leino walked through Balvi hand in hand with

Xavega, Jelgavan women kept coming up and throwing their arms around him. Jelgavan men kept doing the same thing with Xavega, who seemed to enjoy it much less. When one of the blond men let his hands wander more freely on her person than he might have, she slapped him and shouted curses in classical Kaunian. By his silly grin, he didn't understand her and wouldn't have cared if he had.

Looking around at the way most of the Kuusaman and Lagoan soldiers were responding to this welcome, Leino spoke in classical Kaunian, too: "They seem to be having a good time."

"Of course they do—they are men," Xavega answered tartly in the same tongue. "And, nine months from now, a good many half-Jelgavan babies will be born. I do not care to have any of them be mine."

"All right," Leino said, reflecting that any Jelgavan man who tried to drag Xavega into a dark corner—not that every couple was bothering to look for a dark corner, not in the midst of this joyous madness—would surely get his head broken for his trouble, or else have something worse happen to him.

And then he and Xavega rounded a corner, and he discovered that not all the madness was joyous. There hanging upside down from lampposts were the bodies of several Algarvians and the Jelgavans who had helped them run the kingdom under puppet king Mainardo. The crowd kept finding new horrid indignities to heap on the corpses; everyone cheered at each fresh mutilation. Leino was glad he didn't speak Jelgavan: he couldn't understand the suggestions that came from the onlookers.

He glanced toward Xavega. What they were seeing didn't seem to bother her. She caught his eye and said, "They had it coming."

"Maybe," he answered, wondering if anyone could ever have . . . that coming to him. Or to her: he pointed. "That one, I think, used to be a woman."

"I daresay she deserved it, too," Xavega snapped. Leino shrugged; he didn't know one way or the other. He wondered if the people who'd hung the woman up there with those men had known, or cared.

And then a fierce howl rose from the Jelgavans, for a wagon bearing a blond man with his hands tied in front of him came slowly up the street through the crowd. Leino needed no Jelgavan to understand the roars of hatred from the people. The captive in the wagon shouted something that sounded defiant. More roars answered him. The crowd surged toward the wagon. The fellow with his hands tied had guards, but they didn't do much—didn't, in fact, do anything—to protect him. The mob snatched him out of the wagon and beat him and kicked him as they dragged him to the nearest wall. Some of them had sticks. They blazed him. He fell. With another harsh, baying cry—half wolfish, half orgasmic—they swarmed over his body.

"When they find some more rope, he will go up on a lamppost, too," Leino said. Classical Kaunian seemed too cold, too dispassionate, for such a discussion, but it remained the only tongue he had in common with Xavega.

"Good riddance to him," she said. "These people knew him. They knew what he should have got, and they gave it to him."

"I suppose so," Leino said, and then, after a moment, "I wonder how many in that mob have things of their own to hide, and how many names that Jelgavan did not get to name because they killed him so fast."

Xavega gave him a startled look. "I had not thought of that," she said. But then she shrugged. "If they do not get the names from him, they will surely get them from someone else. A lot of these Jelgavans collaborated with the Algarvians."

That was also likely—indeed, almost certain—to be true. "Some of the same ones will probably end up collaborating with us," Leino said. The thought saddened him. He wondered why. He'd never labored under the delusion that war was an especially clean business.

A couple of blocks farther on, a fat Jelgavan rushed out of his tavern to press mugs of wine in Leino and Xavega's hands. Quite impartially, he kissed them both on the cheek and shouted out something in which Leino heard a word that sounded a lot like the classical Kaunian term for *freedom*. Then he bowed and went back into his place, only to emerge again a moment later to give wine to a couple of Kuusaman soldiers. By the way they staggered, they'd already had a good deal.

Xavega let out a scornful sniff. "If the Algarvians knew what things were like here, they could run us out of Balvi with about a regiment and a half of men."

"Maybe." Leino raised an eyebrow. "Would you have said the same thing if you had seen a couple of drunken Lagoan soldiers?"

"Our men have too much discipline for . . ." But Xavega's voice trailed away. Not even she could bring out that claim with a straight face. Too much evidence to the contrary was not just visible but blatantly obvious. Leino laughed. She contented herself with giving him a sour look. That only made him laugh more.

More shouts of savage glee came from up a side street. *They've caught another collaborator,* Leino thought with something between joy and alarm. Watching a man, even an enemy, die as that one Jelgavan had done was nothing to face with equanimity.

But these collaborators—there were about a dozen of them—were not going to their end, only to their humiliation. They were women who must have had Algarvian lovers. They'd been stripped to the waist and had red paint smeared in their hair. People shouted curses at them and pelted them with eggs and overripe summer fruit, but no one aimed a stick their way.

"Little whores," Xavega said.

"Most of them are taller than I am," Leino said.

Xavega snorted again. "You know what I meant," she said, and this time he had to nod.

They passed an empty square half overgrown with rank grass, not something Leino would have expected to see in the middle of a large, crowded city like Balvi. At the edge of the square sprouted a small brickwork of memorial tablets, all of them obviously new. Leino tried his classical Kaunian on a few of the locals: "Excuse me, but whom do these tablets remember?"

On his third try, he found a man who could answer him in the old language. "Not 'whom,' man from another kingdom, but 'what,' " the fellow said, his accent odd in Leino's ears but understandable. "Once an assembly hall from the days of the Kaunian Empire stood here. But the Algarvian barbarians, may the powers below eat them, destroyed it. We could not mourn it as we should have while false King Mainardo ruled here. Now that he is gone, we show we remember."

"Thank you," Leino said. He'd heard about Algarvian wrecking in the Kaunian kingdoms, but this was the first he'd seen of it himself.

"I thank you, man from another kingdom," the Jelgavan replied. In classical Kaunian, the usual word for *foreigner* also meant *barbarian*—that was the word the man had applied to the Algarvians. He found a politer substitute for Leino. After bowing, he added, "I thank you for setting us free and for giving us back our own true and rightful king."

"Er—you are welcome," Leino said, and got away in a hurry. From everything he'd seen of King Donalitu aboard *Habakkuk*, the Jelgavans were welcome to him.

Here and there in Balvi, signs in the Algarvians' slithering script remained; no doubt they told garrison troops and soldiers on leave from the horrors of the west how to get about in the city. Even as that thought crossed Leino's mind, he noticed a couple of Jelgavans busily tearing down one of those signs.

A Lagoan soldier wearing the silver gorget that marked a military constable held up his hand. He spoke in his own language. Xavega angrily answered. He shrugged and said something else. She answered even more angrily.

"What does he want?" Leino asked: he had next to no Lagoan of his own, just as Xavega had never bothered learning Kuusaman.

In classical Kaunian, she replied, "He says all mages are to report to a center they have set up near the palace. He says we cannot enjoy ourselves here even for a day, but that we have to report at once so we can return to duty once more."

"It makes sense," Leino said. Xavega kept right on grumbling; whether it made sense or not, she didn't like it.

Perhaps noting as much, the military constable came up and spoke in Lagoan. Then, to Leino's surprise, he added a few words in Kuusaman: "Come with me. I take you there."

"You don't have to do that," Leino said.

This time, the Lagoan surprised him by laughing. "I think maybe I do have to do that. You come with me." Leino shrugged and nodded. Xavega looked ready to bite nails in half once the military constable put that into Lagoan, but she nodded, too.

At the center, a bored-looking Kuusaman clerk checked their names off a duty roster. In his own language, he said, "The two of you haven't had the special training, isn't that right?"

"Aye, that's so," Leino answered. He translated for Xavega, who looked miffed at not hearing Lagoan or at least classical Kaunian. She grudgingly nodded again.

"All right." The clerk went right on speaking Kuusaman, and made a couple of more check marks. "I'll assign you to the training center north of here. Shall I billet the two of you together?"

"What's he saying?" Xavega asked. Leino translated again. She nodded once more and told the clerk, "Aye, put us together," in classical Kaunian. He evidently followed that language even if he chose not to speak it, for he made more checks still.

Leino had left *Habakkuk* to find a painless way to break things off with Xavega. He still didn't know exactly why she'd left—to get at the Algarvians, he supposed. And she'd seen having him around as one more comfort she'd grown used to.

And you—you really hate the idea of going to bed with her, Leino thought. He didn't care for most of Xavega's opinions or for large chunks of her rather bad-tempered character, but when they lay down together . . .

If I had any gumption, I would say, "No, put us apart." He said not a word. He let the clerk finish the paperwork. The fellow pointed to a bench. "Wait there. Before long, a carriage or a wagon will take you to the ley-line caravan depot for your trip to the center. Things are a little crazy now." Leino went over and sat down. Xavega perched beside him. With an inward sigh, he slipped his arm around her waist and drew her close. For once most obliging, she snuggled up against him.

"Are you almost ready?" Colonel Lurcanio called up to Krasta from the foot of the stairs. "This is a reception at the royal palace, remember. King Gainibu will probably behead you if you are late."

Krasta looked at herself in the bedchamber mirror. She tugged at the waistband of her trousers. Her pregnancy still didn't show, not quite, but she knew she was heavier than usual. Her trousers should have been snug, but not *this* snug. But they would have to do.

"I'm coming," she said. She and Lurcanio hadn't been invited to the palace for some months. She didn't want to offend King Gainibu by being late, even if she didn't worry about the headsman's axe. As she grabbed a handbag, she wondered if she was fretting over nothing. Probably. Odds were, Gainibu would be too drunk to care, or even to notice, who arrived when. He'd stayed drunk most of the time since the Algarvians occupied Priekule.

By the way Lurcanio's eyes lit up, she knew the trousers weren't too snug the wrong way. And she also knew that she had rather more on top than she'd had before Lurcanio (or, curse it, was it Valnu?) put a baby in her. With men, that never went to waste.

Lurcanio handed her up into his carriage. His driver—another redhead, of course—picked his way through evening twilight and then through darkness toward the palace. No lights showed. Lagoan and Kuusaman dragons flew over the capital of Valmiera all too often these days. If patrolling Algarvians or the Valmieran constables who served them saw lights, they would sometimes start blazing without warning.

After getting lost a couple of times and grumbling in his incomprehensible language, the driver finally found the palace. Lights gleamed inside, with dark curtains making sure no stray beams leaked out.

"Colonel the Count Lurcanio!" a flunky bawled out. "His companion, the Marchioness Krasta!" On Lurcanio's arm, Krasta strode into the reception hall.

She'd gone into that reception hall on Lurcanio's arm a good many times. At first, everything seemed the same as usual: Algarvian officers with their good-looking Valmieran companions, along with the Valmieran nobles who inclined toward

Algarve and their ladies. King Gainibu stood in a receiving line with Grand Duke Ivone, the redhead who really ran Valmiera these days.

But something in the hall was different tonight. Krasta sensed it at once, though she needed a little while to realize just what it was. Far fewer Valmieran nobles had come than would have been true a couple of years before: only those who'd most closely tied their fate to the occupiers. Krasta hadn't paid a great deal of attention to the news sheets—she never did—but she knew the war news for Algarve wasn't good.

The fair-weather friends are flying, she thought. She almost said it aloud, but caught herself in time. Lurcanio would not have taken it kindly; his temper had a way of slipping when some Algarvian position in Unkerlant or Jelgava did some slipping of its own.

Krasta got her second surprise when she and Lurcanio greeted the King of Valmiera in the receiving line. As usual, Gainibu had a glass in his hand. But it held only wine, not the stronger spirits he'd preferred since yielding to the redheads.

"Good evening, Colonel," Gainibu said when Lurcanio made his polite bow. Krasta dropped a curtsy. "And a good evening to you, Marchioness," the king added. His voice and his eyes seemed clearer than they had for years. As Lurcanio started to go on, Gainibu remarked, "There are a few things I should like to discuss with you tonight, Colonel."

"Of course, your Majesty," Lurcanio said, cat-courteous as usual. But he couldn't quite keep the faintest hint of astonishment—or was it alarm?—from his voice. And he couldn't keep from glancing over to Grand Duke Ivone. Ivone's smile looked as if it were held in place with carpet tacks.

"This may be an interesting reception after all," Krasta said as they made their way toward the tables piled high with food and drink.

"So it may." Lurcanio sounded anything but happy at the prospect. "What in blazes is wrong with Gainibu?"

"He seemed better than he has in a long time," Krasta said.

"That is what I meant," Lurcanio snarled. He took a glass of something potent and knocked it back at a gulp. Krasta chose a mug of ale for herself. She had less of an urge to drink herself blind at these affairs than she'd had before she found herself expecting a baby. She couldn't decide whether that was good or not.

On a raised platform in one corner of the reception hall sat several musicians softly playing. They were Valmierans themselves, but played soft, delicate, tinkling, Algarvian-style music rather than the more emphatic rhythms and more raucous instruments—bagpipes and thumping drums—of their own kingdom. Krasta had got used to hearing the occupiers' music in the royal palace. Now, for some reason, she noticed it again.

Colonel Lurcanio didn't need long to notice it, either. "They must have got drunk up there," he growled, pointing to the men (and one woman) on the low platform. "Either that or they are making a hash of things on purpose just to annoy us."

"Why would they do that?" Krasta asked.

"It is called kicking a man when you think he is down," her Algarvian lover answered. His eyes glittered; his smile seemed more carnivorous than usual. "You had better be right, or you will be very sorry."

But Krasta hardly heard those last few words. *Kicking a man when you think he is down.* Much suddenly became clear: things she was seeing here, and things she had seen elsewhere. The Valmierans thought their occupiers were in trouble, and so they could afford to show insolence.

Some of them thought that way, anyhow. But a big, swag-bellied man with a provincial accent came up to Colonel Lurcanio and boomed, "Ho! Congratulations on your armies' bold, brave defensive stand along the Twegen River." By his tone, the Algarvians were still cocks o' the walk.

Lurcanio bowed. "For which I thank you, your Excellency."

Krasta had never heard of the Twegen River. She'd never heard of a lot of the western places that found themselves written into the chronicles of the war with letters of blood. She stared down into her mug of ale, wishing she felt like drinking more, while Lurcanio and the Valmieran noble from the back of beyond talked endlessly about the fighting and how it was going. After a while, she yawned and found a chair and sat down. Carrying a baby gave her an excuse for showing she was tired and bored.

The Valmieran baron or whatever he was talked loud enough to let the whole reception hall know his opinions—*as if anyone cares,* Krasta thought acidly. Still booming like a courting grouse, he went on, "Surely the Unkerlanter hosts will break themselves on the rock of your might."

"May it be so," Lurcanio answered with another bow. "And now, if you will excuse me—" He hurried off to get himself another drink.

By the time he got back, the Valmieran had gone off to boom in someone else's ear. Lurcanio poured down the drink even so. "What *was* he going on about?" Krasta asked.

"Something about which he knows much less than he thinks he does." A certain amused malice in his voice, Lurcanio went on, "There are, I suspect, a great many things about which he knows much less than he thinks he does."

Even though Krasta still hadn't emptied her first mug of ale, that made her giggle. She might have said the same sort of thing herself. Then she quickly got to her feet and curtsied once more: King Gainibu was coming toward her and Lurcanio. The king's walk had more purpose and less wobble in it than she'd seen for years.

Lurcanio noted the same thing, as he'd noted Gainibu's unusual steadiness in the receiving line. His bow was politeness personified, but hard suspicion ruled his voice as he murmured, "Your Majesty."

"Good evening, Colonel . . . and milady, of course," Gainibu said. But after that, he might have forgotten Krasta was there. It irked her less than it would have from a lesser personage; the king was the king, and did as he pleased. Swinging his attention back to Lurcanio, he continued, "I told you earlier in the evening that we should have somewhat to discuss."

"So you did, your Majesty," the Algarvian replied. "By all means, say on."

"I shall. You need not worry about that." King Gainibu's wave somehow encompassed not only the reception hall but the whole kingdom of Valmiera. "At some point or other, probably sooner rather than later, you will have to evacuate this land to fight elsewhere."

"It could be," Lurcanio said. "It is, on the other hand, anything but certain."

"Don't bandy words with me." Gainibu's voice was sharp, peremptory—the voice of a king. "You are already moving men out of Valmiera, moving them through Priekule, to fight in the west and the north. Before long, parts of the kingdom will be all but bare of Algarvians."

"We shall hold what we need, your Majesty." Lurcanio, for his part, spoke with studied self-assurance. "If you think we shall let ourselves be dispossessed of the main cities and the roads and ley lines between them, I must say I believe you to be mistaken."

"This may come to a test," Gainibu said. *They're bargaining,* Krasta realized in sudden surprise. The Algarvians hadn't had to bargain in Valmiera for some time.

She looked around for Viscount Valnu, but didn't see him. She shrugged. Even if she had, he probably would have been in the company of one Algarvian officer or another, and she really didn't want to see him like that. Her free hand went to her belly for a moment. All at once, she hoped Valnu had sired her child. He'd had the first chance, after all. And a Valmieran father might prove much more . . . convenient than she'd thought only a few weeks before.

She'd missed a little of what the king and Lurcanio were saying. "—would regret it," came from Lurcanio's mouth.

"Both sides would regret it," Gainibu answered. "Do you doubt that? And so, my proposal: if there are no outrages—and you know the sort I mean—you will find your withdrawal easier than it would prove otherwise. If not . . ." He shrugged. "It will not be withdrawal, but a running fight."

"Words. Rhetoric." But Lurcanio sounded uneasy. "How can you hope to make your promises good?"

"I have ways," the king said. "Remember what Algarve managed after the Six Years' War despite being beaten and occupied. We can do the same, especially as you will be busy elsewhere. I told Ivone as much. He said you were the man for the details. Good evening, Colonel." He nodded and walked off.

"What sort of details?" Krasta asked. "What exactly was he talking about?"

"The sort of details, my sweet, that are all too likely to put me in charge of combat troops once more, however tedious that may prove," Lurcanio answered. Careless of who might be watching, he closed his hand on her breast. "I shall have to make the most of things while I can."

Hajjaj woke to the sound of distant thunder. That was his first thought. His second thought was that the first was idiotic—thunder in Bishah might have been more likely than snow there at that season (or at any season), but it wasn't a great deal more likely.

Beside him on the low bed, Tassi stirred and muttered. After a particularly loud roar, she stiffened and sat up and said something or other in Yaninan. Hajjaj spoke in Algarvian, the only language they had in common: "The Unkerlanters have sent dragons against Bishah again. Their eggs should not burst close to here, not when we're up in the hills."

"Oh," she said, now fully awake. "I thought it was a storm." She snuggled against him. He enjoyed the touch of her soft, bare skin. He would have enjoyed it more had sweat not sprung out wherever their bodies touched. Zuwayzi summer nights were not really made for lovers who craved clasping each other close.

"In winter, it might have been a storm," Hajjaj replied. "At this season . . . I hope our dragonfliers and the Algarvians do a proper job of punishing the raiders."

"May it be so," Tassi said, and then, "As long as we are awake, would you like to . . . ?"

Hajjaj chuckled. "Ask me again in a couple of days and I'll gladly say aye. You pay me the compliment of treating me as if I were younger than I am. It *is* flattering; far be it from me to deny that. But I know what this old carcass can do and what is beyond its powers these days."

"Do you?" Tassi said, mischief in her voice. She slithered

down toward the foot of the bed. "Maybe I can surprise you."

Maybe she could have, too. She'd pleasantly surprised Hajjaj once or twice before. Kolthoum had been right, as usual; Tassi made a splendid amusement. But she hadn't even begun when someone tapped on the bedchamber door. She let out a startled squeak. Hajjaj was a little startled, too; he always slept lightly, and his retainers knew better than to bother him in the night without urgent need. "What is it?" he called out in Zuwayzi.

"Your Excellency, you are wanted at the crystallomancer's." Tewfik's voice came from the other side of the door. "It is General Ikhshid."

Despite the summer heat, ice ran up Hajjaj's back. "I'll come, of course," he said, and got out of bed.

"What's wrong?" Tassi asked in Algarvian, not following the quick conversation between the two Zuwayzin.

"I don't know," Hajjaj answered in the same tongue, though he feared he did. "But I had better go and find out."

"I'm sorry to disturb you, lad," Tewfik said as Hajjaj stepped out into the dimly lit hallway. The wrinkled old majordomo's laugh had a leer in it. "I hope I didn't interrupt anything."

"No," Hajjaj said, and let it go at that. "You can go back to bed now yourself, Tewfik. I'll take care of whatever needs doing."

But Tewfik shook his head. "I'm up. I'll stay up. You may need more from me before the morning comes."

How much did he know? How much did he guess? Hajjaj had no time to find out. Whatever his majordomo knew, Tewfik would keep it to himself. Hajjaj did know that. He hurried down the hall toward the chamber where the crystallomancers kept this isolated clanfather's house in touch with the wider world.

Sure enough, General Ikhshid's image stared out at him as he sat down in front of one of the crystals there. As soon as Ikhshid saw him, the Zuwayzi officer began to speak: "Well, your Excellency, the whoresons have dropped the other boot."

"The Unkerlanters?" Even now, Hajjaj could hope he was wrong.

But Ikhshid nodded grimly. "I'm afraid so. This isn't just another raid on Bishah. They're pounding us all along the front—pounding us hard, I mean. They aren't playing games any more, your Excellency. They've got a demon of a lot of men and behemoths and dragons and egg-tossers."

"Are we holding?" The Zuwayzi foreign minister asked the question he had to ask, and asked it with more than a little dread.

"For now—mostly," Ikhshid said. "That's by the reports I have right this minute, mind you. I don't have reports from the whole line yet, and that worries me. Some of our brigades may not be reporting because they aren't there to report any more. And if they aren't . . ." His bushy white eyebrows came down and together in a frown.

"If they aren't, Swemmel's soldiers are liable to be pouring through the gaps," Hajjaj said. "That's what you mean, isn't it?"

Most unhappily, General Ikhshid nodded. "Aye. And if they are, powers above only know how we're going to stop them."

"We gave them a good fight when they attacked us almost five years ago," Hajjaj said. That was true. Also true was that the Unkerlanters had prevailed in the end.

And Ikhshid said, "What worries me most, your Excellency, is that they're a lot better than they were back then. We haven't changed all that much, but they've had three years of lessons from the Algarvians. You don't get any better schoolmasters than Mezentio's men."

That didn't sound good. *No, it doesn't sound good at all,* Hajjaj thought gloomily. He asked, "Have you told King Shazli yet?"

"I don't mind so much waking you up," Ikhshid said. "I thought I'd let his Majesty sleep till morning—if the Unkerlanter eggs will."

"Wake him. He is the sovereign, and he needs to know," Hajjaj said. "Don't tell him you've told me first. Tell him you're about to let me know, and that he doesn't have to. I'm going to head down into the city right now."

"All right. I'll do it just as you say." Ikhshid nodded to someone Hajjaj couldn't see—presumably his crystallomancer, for the crystal flared with light and then went inert as the etheric connection was broken.

Hajjaj went out into the hall. He wasn't surprised to find Tewfik waiting. "I'm going to need a driver right away, I'm afraid," he said.

The majordomo nodded. "I've already got him out of bed. He's harnessing up the carriage."

"Thank you, Tewfik," Hajjaj said. "You are a wonder." The ancient retainer nodded, accepting the praise as no less than his due.

By the time Hajjaj got down into Bishah, the Unkerlanter dragons had flown off to the south. A bit of smoke hung in the air. The moon was down, or Hajjaj judged he would have seen dark columns rising into the sky. Eggs had fallen close to the royal palace, but not on it. A few minutes after Hajjaj got to the foreign ministry, Qutuz came in.

"Did General Ikhshid have a crystallomancer get hold of you, too?" Hajjaj asked his secretary.

Qutuz shook his head. "No, your Excellency. The attack seemed bigger than usual, so I thought I should be here in case something was going on. I gather it is?"

"You might say so," Hajjaj answered. "The Unkerlanters have struck the lines down by our southern border, and they've struck hard."

"Are we holding?" Qutuz asked anxiously.

"We were when I spoke to Ikhshid," Hajjaj said. "I hope we still are."

General Ikhshid himself strode into Hajjaj's offices a little past sunrise. As he had on the crystal, he wasted no time: "They've broken through in several places. I've ordered our men back to the next line of positions farther north. I *hope* we can hold them there."

"You hope so?" Hajjaj said, and Ikhshid nodded. Like a man picking at a sore, Hajjaj elaborated: "You may hope so, but you don't think so, do you?"

"No," Ikhshid said bluntly. "We may slow 'em up there, but I don't see how we can stop 'em. The next line north of *that* is on our old frontier. That's a lot deeper, because we spent years building it up between the Six Years' War and the last time Swemmel's buggers hit us."

"Can we stop the Unkerlanters there, then?" Hajjaj asked.

"I hope so," Ikhshid answered, in much the same tones he'd used the last time he said that.

Hajjaj ground his teeth. That wasn't what he'd wanted to hear, nor anything close to it. He hadn't thought he would ever wish Ikhshid weren't quite so honest. "What should the kingdom do if the soldiers can't hold along that line?" he asked.

"Make peace as fast as we can, and get the best terms King Swemmel will give us." Again, General Ikhshid spoke without the least hesitation. "If the Unkerlanters break through at the old frontier, powers below eat me if I know how we can stop them—or even slow them down very much—this side of Bishah."

"It's summer," Hajjaj said, looking for hope wherever he might find it. "Won't the desert work for us?"

"Some," Ikhshid said. "Some—maybe. What you have to understand, though, and what I don't think you do, is that the Unkerlanters are a *lot* better at what they're doing than they were the last time they struck us a blow. We're some better ourselves: Thanks to the Algarvians, we've got more behemoths and dragons than we did then. But curse me if I know whether it'll be enough."

No sooner were the words out of his mouth than a young captain hurried past Qutuz and saluted. "Sir," the junior officer said to Ikhshid, "I'm sorry to have to report an enemy breakthrough at Sab Abar."

Ikhshid cursed wearily. Odds were he hadn't slept all night. He said, "That's not good. Sab Abar is in the second defensive line, not the first. If they've got through there already . . . That's not good at all."

"How could they have reached the second line so fast?" Hajjaj asked. "How could they have broken through it so fast?"

"They probably got there about as fast as we did," Ikhshid said unhappily. "It's not a neat, pretty fight when both sides are moving fast, especially if the whoresons on the other side have got their peckers up. And the stinking Unkerlanters *do*, powers below eat 'em. They think they can lick anybody right now, and when you think like that, you're halfway to being right."

Qutuz asked the next question before Hajjaj could: "If they've broken through at this Sab Abar place, can we hold the second line, even for a little while?"

"I don't know. I'll have to see." General Ikhshid sounded harried. "We'll do everything we can, but who knows how much that will be?" He bowed to Hajjaj. "If you'll excuse me, Your Excellency, I'd better head back. In fact, unless I miss my guess, I'll be going down south before too long. As I say, we have to do what we can." With another bow, he tramped away, the young captain in his wake.

"What are we going to do, your Excellency?" Qutuz asked.

"The best we can," Hajjaj answered. "I have nothing better to tell you, any more than Ikhshid had anything better to tell me. What I have to do now, I think, is let King Shazli know we have . . . difficulties."

He didn't know what Shazli could do. He didn't know what anyone could do. It was up to Zuwayza's soldiers now. If they did what he hoped, the Unkerlanters still had their work cut out for them. If they didn't . . . If they didn't, Zuwayza might not need a foreign minister much longer, only an Unkerlanter governor ruling from Bishah, as one had back before the Six Years' War.

One of the nice things about serving as an Algarvian constable, even an Algarvian constable in occupied Forthweg, was that Bembo hadn't had to go to war. It was always other poor sods who'd had to travel west and fight the Unkerlanters. They'd hated him for his immunity, too. He'd known they hated him, and he'd laughed at them on account of it.

Now that laughter came home to roost. The war had come home, too, or at least come to Eoforwic, which he had to call home these days. For one thing, the Forthwegians in the city kept on fighting as if they were soldiers. And, for another, Swemmel's men sat right across the Twegen from Eoforwic. If they ever swarmed across the river . . .

Bembo clutched his stick a little tighter. These days, he always carried an army-issue weapon, not the shorter one he'd used as a constable. For all practical purposes, he wasn't a constable any more. All the Algarvians still in Eoforwic came under military command nowadays.

Ever so cautiously, he peered out from behind a battered building. He ducked back again in a hurry. "Seems all right," he said. "No Forthwegian fighters in sight, anyhow."

Oraste grunted. "It's the buggers who aren't in sight you've got to watch out for," Bembo's old partner said. He and Bembo and half a dozen real soldiers had been thrown together as a squad. "You never see the one who blazes you."

"Or if you do, he's the *last* thing you see," a trooper added cheerfully.

"Heh," Bembo said. If that was a joke, he didn't find it funny. If it wasn't a joke, he didn't want to think about it.

Running feet behind him made him whirl, the business end of his stick swinging toward what might be a target. The Algarvians held—and held down—this section of Eoforwic, but their Forthwegian foes kept sneaking fighters into it and making trouble. Bembo had no desire to find himself included in some casualty report no one would ever read.

But the fellow heading his way was a tall redhead in short tunic and kilt: an Algarvian constable like himself. Relaxing a little—relaxing too much was also liable to land you in one of those reports—he asked, "What's up?"

"Nothing good," the newcomer answered. "You know how a bunch of our important officers have come down with a sudden case of loss of life?" He waited for Bembo and the men with him to nod, then went on, "Well, the brass—the ones who're still left alive, I mean—think they've figured out what's gone wrong."

"Tell, tell!" That wasn't just Bembo. Several of his comrades spoke up, too. Disliking the men in command was one thing. Wanting to see all of them dead was something else again—at least, Bembo supposed it was.

With the self-importance of a man who knows he has important news, the other constable said, "Well, what happened is— or the big blazes think what happened is—the fornicating Forthwegians have worked out a spell that makes them look like us. What could be better for assassins?"

"Like the cursed Kaunians looking like Forthwegians, by the powers above!" Bembo exclaimed.

"Aye, it sounds wonderful," Oraste said. "Now all we need is a spell that makes *us* look like Kaunians, so we can go off and cut our own throats and save the Forthwegians and the Unkerlanters the trouble."

"That isn't much of a joke," one of the soldiers said, echoing Bembo's thought.

"Who says I was joking?" Oraste's face and voice were cold as winter in the south of Unkerlant.

The soldier glared back at him. That was enough to intimidate most Algarvian constables pressed into combat duty. It would have been plenty to intimidate Bembo, who knew perfectly well that he was softer than the men who went to real war. But Oraste glared right back—anyone who reckoned himself the harder man would have to prove it by beating him. And the soldier looked away first. Bembo was impressed.

He was also worried. "How in blazes are we supposed to know the whoresons with us are proper Algarvian whoresons and not disguised Forthwegian whoresons just waiting to cut our throats?" he asked the fellow who'd brought the bad news.

"They're still working on that," the other constable answered. "Some of the Forthwegians don't trim their beards enough before they go into disguise, so they end up looking fuzzier than we usually do. And some of them have that foul accent of theirs when they try and speak Algarvian. But some of 'em . . . We wouldn't have so many dead men if they were all easy to spot. If you don't know the fellows around you, keep an eye on 'em." He sketched a salute and hurried off to spread the news further.

"Well, *that's* jolly," Bembo said. "Can't trust the Forthwegians, can't trust the Kaunians"—*and didn't we do that to ourselves?* he thought—"and now we can't trust each other, either."

"Probably just what the stinking rebels want—us blazing us, I mean," one of the soldiers said. Bembo wished he could have argued with that, but it seemed pretty self-evidently true.

He would have said so, but the Algarvians chose that moment to start tossing eggs at the Forthwegians just in front of his companions and him. He'd found out in a hurry that a certain number of such eggs were liable to fall short of where they were aimed. He threw himself into a hole some earlier burst had made and hoped none would land on him.

"I hate this!" he shouted to anybody who would listen. But how likely was it that anybody would? And even if somebody would, how likely was it that he could hear one man's cry of protest through the endless roar of bursting eggs?

As soon as that roar let up, someone shouted, "Forward!" Bembo scrambled to his feet and went forward with the rest of the soldiers and constables. He was no hero. He'd never been a hero. But he couldn't bear to have his comrades reckon him a coward.

Would you rather have them reckon you a dead man? he asked himself as he advanced. The answer was evidently aye, because he kept going. Sometimes saving face counted for as much as saving his neck.

The houses and blocks of flats ahead had been battered before. They were more battered now, with smoke and dust rising from them in great clouds. Broken glass glittered in the streets and on the slates of the sidewalks. It could slice right through a boot. Bembo noticed it as he ran, but it was the least of his worries. That thunderstorm of eggs hadn't got rid of all the Forthwegian fighters up there: someone was blazing at the Algarvians from a building ahead.

Bembo threw himself flat behind what had been a chimney before it came crashing down in ruin. He was used to going after people who tried to get away from him, not after men who stood their ground and blazed back. No one cared what he was used to. He stuck up his head and waited to see where the Forthwegian's beam came from. When he did spot it, he blazed, and was rewarded with a howl of pain.

More eggs started bursting ahead. Bembo hunkered down again. Every block of Eoforwic the Algarvians took from the rebels had to get pounded flat before they could be sure of holding on to it.

"Forward!" That hateful shout again. Forward Bembo went, cursing under his breath.

From a doorway twice its natural size, somebody stepped out and flung what looked like a cheap sugar bowl. The Forthwegian fell an instant later, blazed by three beams. But then the bowl landed among the oncoming Algarvians, and the burst of sorcerous energy trapped inside flung pottery fragments in all directions.

Something bit Bembo's leg. He yelped and looked down at himself. Blood trickled along his calf, but the leg still bore his weight. He ran on toward a doorway. When he dashed into the meager shelter it gave, he discovered he shared that shelter with Oraste. "I'm wounded!" he cried dramatically.

His old partner glanced down at the cut on his leg. "Go home to mama when this is done," Oraste said. "She can kiss it and make it better."

"Well! I like that!" Bembo struck a heroic pose—carefully, so as not to expose any of his precious person to lurking foes. "Here I am, injured in service to my kingdom, and what do I get? Mockery! Scorn!"

"About what you deserve," Oraste said. "I've seen people get hurt worse if they scratch themselves while they've got a hangnail."

"Powers below eat you!" Bembo cried. "I'm going to put in for a wound badge when we come off duty."

"You'll probably get one, too. From what I've seen, the only way you can keep from getting a wound badge is if you get killed—and then they probably give the bastard to your next of kin." Oraste's cynicism knew no bounds.

Before Bembo could let out another indignant squawk, somebody up ahead yelled, "Forward!" again. Oraste left the shelter of the doorway without the least hesitation. Bembo had to follow him. On he ran, puffing, marveling that the fear of looking bad in front of his comrades once more proved stronger than the fear of death.

A Forthwegian's head appeared in a second-story window. Bembo blazed at the Forthwegian, who toppled. Bembo ran on. He had no idea whether the man he'd just blazed was a fighter or an innocent bystander. He didn't care, either. The fellow had shown up in the wrong place at the wrong time. He had to pay for that. If the penalty was death, too bad. *Better his than mine or one of my pals'*, Bembo thought.

More Forthwegians were holed up in a furniture shop not far ahead. No chance they were innocent bystanders: they blazed at the oncoming soldiers and constables. Bembo wasted no time ducking for cover. He wasn't ashamed to do it, for he was far from the only one doing it.

Then several eggs crashed down around the furniture shop, and one right on it. "Surrender!" an Algarvian yelled to the Forthwegians still inside. "You can't win!" He switched to Forthwegian so rudimentary, even Bembo could follow it: "Coming out! Hands high!"

"You no to kill we?" one of the Forthwegians called back in equally bad Algarvian.

"Not if you give up right now," the soldier answered. "Make it snappy—this is your last chance."

To Bembo's surprise, half a dozen Forthwegians did come out of the wrecked shop, their faces glum, their hands up over their heads. When more eggs burst not far away, they all flinched. Not one of them tried to take shelter, though. They must have been sure the Algarvians would blaze them if they did. And they were, without a doubt, right.

"You constables!" one of the Algarvians soldiers said to Bembo and Oraste. "You know what to do with captives. Take these buggers away."

"Right." Bembo grunted as he got to his feet. That *was* something he knew how to do. *And, while I'm away from the lines, I'll see how I go about asking for that wound badge, too.*

Sixteen

Leudast had served in the Unkerlanter army for a long time. He'd been fighting in the Elsung Mountains in what was then King Swemmel's desultory border war with Gyongyos when the Derlavaian War first broke out between Algarve and most of her neighbors. He'd been part of the Unkerlanter force that gobbled up western Forthweg while the redheads were smashing most of King Penda's army. And he'd spent a demon of a lot of time fighting the Algarvians himself.

Two leg wounds weren't so very much to show for all that. He'd started out a common soldier, with no hope of rising higher, and here he was, a lieutenant.

In all those years in the army, he'd never been particularly eager to go into a fight. In fact, he'd always been happiest during the brief spells of quiet he'd found. And here he was now, forced to stay quiet as he recovered from this second wound well behind the fighting front.

He hated it. He hated every minute he had to lie on his back. He hated every minute the healers used to poke and prod at his blazed leg, and hated the wise things they muttered back and forth in a language that hardly seemed to be Unkerlanter at all.

"When will you let me go?" he demanded. "When will you let me get back to my men? When will you let me get back to the fighting?"

Am I really saying that? But he was. Now, at last, after so much terror, he could begin to smell victory against the Algarvians. They still fought bravely. They still fought cleverly— more cleverly than his own countrymen, most of the time. But there weren't enough of them to hold back the rising Unkerlanter tide no matter how bravely and cleverly they fought. And, having gone through all the black days when the Algarvians seemed sure to overwhelm Unkerlant, Leudast wanted to be there to help beat them. How much he wanted that amazed him.

But the healers shook their heads. "You will not be ready for some weeks, Lieutenant," one of them said, and they went on to their next patient.

Alone in his cot, Leudast quietly laughed to himself. The last time he'd been wounded, down in Sulingen, his treatment had been a lot rougher than this. As soon as he could hobble around, they'd put a fresh stick in his hands and thrown him back into the fight.

Of course, he'd been only a sergeant then. Even the Unkerlanter army took better care of its officers than of its other ranks. And Sulingen had been as dreadful a struggle as any the war had seen. They'd needed every body they could find. But even so . . .

He asked the healers again the next day when he could go back to the fight. They gave him another evasive answer. "Count your time here as a leave of sorts, Lieutenant," one of them said.

"I don't want this sort of leave," Leudast said, whereupon all the healers looked at him as if he were daft. "If I get leave, I want it to be with my sweetheart." They nodded then, but they still didn't take him seriously. *I've got strings to pull,* he thought. *I'm not quite an ordinary lieutenant, even if they think I am. Time to remind them otherwise.* "Please get me pen and paper. I want to write to Marshal Rathar and request an immediate return to duty."

Now the healers looked at him as if he might be dangerous. Cautiously, one of them asked, "How do you know Marshal Rathar?"

"He commissioned me after I captured false King Raniero of Grelz," Leudast replied. *Take that.*

The healers didn't seem to know how to take it. They put their heads together and muttered among themselves. At last, one of them said, "You really are not fit to return to duty yet, you know. That leg will not support you."

"Well, all right," said Leudast, who could not disagree with what was obviously true. "But it doesn't seem to me like you people are doing much to get me back to duty. You're just letting me lay here."

"You do need to rest and recuperate, you know, Lieutenant," the healer said.

"If I got any more rested, I'd be bored to death," Leudast returned. "You're a bunch of mages. Isn't there anything you can do to send me back faster?"

They put their heads together again. Leudast hadn't really expected anything else. They seemed unable to do anything without consulting among themselves. The one who served as

their spokesman said, "You mean, use more sorcerous energy
to expedite your recovery?" He sounded faintly scandalized.

Leudast didn't care how he sounded. "That's just what I
mean," he said. "You're healers, aren't you? What the demon
good are you if you won't do any real healing?"

They all looked indignant. He wanted to laugh. They thought
that would impress him. After all the time he'd spent in the
field, nothing this side of a stick aimed at his face impressed
him. The fellow who did their talking said, "I hope you realize
we have only so much sorcerous energy to expend."

"Aye, I've noticed that." Leudast sounded as sardonic as he
could. "Common soldiers get next to nothing, officers get as little as you think you can get away with giving. Fetch me that paper. I *do* need to write to Marshal Rathar."

He knew he was being unfair. The healers were desperately
overworked men. But he'd told a good-sized chunk of truth,
too. A man who wasn't important or well-connected—often the
same thing—or whose wound wasn't either as easy as possible
to treat or in some way interesting got short shrift.

Once upon a time, Leudast had been a man without connec-
tions. He wasn't any more, though, and he intended to keep hitting the healers over the head with such importance as he had
till they did what he wanted.

They knew it, too. Glaring, their spokesman said, "You wish
us to give you preferential treatment." He might have been a
Gyongyosian accusing Leudast of wanting him to eat goat.

"That's right," Leudast said cheerfully. "You do it all the
time. I want you to do it for me."

They put their heads together yet again. When they separated, the man who did the talking said, "You realize this may
cause you some considerable pain?"

Leudast shrugged. The healers blinked. They didn't know
what to think of a man whom pain didn't horrify, which only
went to prove they'd never been up to the front. He said, "How
much pain do you think you'll get once I tell the marshal you
wouldn't treat me even after I asked you to?"

They winced. Leudast didn't think he'd prove able to do

much to them, but they didn't have to know that. Plainly, they didn't feel like taking chances. In their shoes, Leudast wouldn't have felt like taking any, either. "Let us review your case," said the one who spoke for them. "If we find some sorcerous therapy that might help you, we shall apply it tomorrow."

"I hope you do," Leudast said, which seemed to him wiser than, *You'd cursed well better*.

Then he had another day of waiting flat on his back. He would sooner have been in a trench waiting to start an attack, which proved how bored he was. *Either that or it does prove I've lost my mind*, he thought.

The next morning, the healers appeared with a wheeled chair and a couple of muscular attendants who manhandled Leudast into it. Other wounded soldiers stared curiously at him as they took him off. The healers had a tent of their own, well away from the wounded they attended. It was almost alarmingly quiet in there.

"What are you going to do to me?" Leudast asked, wondering if browbeating them had been such a good idea after all.

Before any of them answered, their attendants hauled Leudast out of the wheeled chair and propped him up on a table. Then the mages draped his leg—all of it except the area of the wound—with gauze made from a glistening fabric he had never seen before.

"What are you going to do?" he asked again.

"Treat your leg—or rather, the wounded portion of it, and no other—thus the insulating cloth," a healer told him, which left him no wiser. Then the fellow condescended to explain: "We are going to age the flesh that has been blazed, so that, being a month older than the rest of you, it will also have already healed."

"That's wonderful!" Leudast exclaimed. "I didn't know you could do such things."

"You will not enjoy it so much while it is happening," the healer replied. "Also, once the month has passed, you would be very wise to have the sorcery reversed. I will give you a letter authorizing the reversal. Hold on to it and do not forget to have the second sorcery done."

"All right," Leudast said. "But why?"

The look the healer gave him was anything but cheery. "Because if you fail to have it done, if you should forget, that flesh will die a month before the rest of you—and I promise you, it will make your last month alive much less pleasant than it would have been otherwise."

Leudast thought about that. He gulped. "Oh," he said in a small voice.

"We begin," the healer declared. He and his colleagues started to chant. Burning heat coursed through Leudast's wound. He gasped and tried to jerk away. The attendants grabbed him, making sure he couldn't move. "This is what you asked for," the healer told him. "This is what you get."

And you'll enjoy every moment of giving it to me, won't you? Leudast thought. But he refused to give the healer the satisfaction of knowing he understood that. In a voice as steady as he could make it, he said, "Get on with it, then." The healer eyed him and nodded in reluctant approval.

Before long, Leudast was panting and trying not to curse or scream. The healers hadn't told him he would feel all the pain of a month's worth of healing, distilled down into the few minutes the sorcery took. He clenched his fists. The smaller hurts of nails digging into palms and of biting down hard on the inside of his lower lip helped distract—a little—from the torment in his leg.

Then, suddenly, that torment eased. Leudast let out a long, astonished sigh of relief. The healer said, "You were brave. We do few such procedures where the patient does not cry out."

"I believe it." Leudast sounded shaky, even to himself. But the gnawing pain in his leg *had* eased. That was what he'd wanted. "Can I put my weight on it?"

"You may," the healer replied, precise as a schoolmaster. "I hope you can—that was why we performed the sorcery."

"Well, let's find out." Leudast swung down off the table. One of the attendants who'd hauled him up onto it reached out to steady him. He waved the man away. The leg wasn't perfect, but it would do. He could use it. He nodded to the healers. "Thanks. I'm ready to go back into the line."

"We shall fill out the necessary papers," one of them said. Another very carefully peeled the shining cloth from Leudast's leg. The healer who was doing the talking went on, "Make sure you have this sorcery reversed in a month's time. As I said, if you forget, your last month will be nothing but torment to you."

"I understand," Leudast said, and he did. The mere idea of knowing a month ahead of time that he would be dead . . . He shuddered. Even war against the Algarvians seemed clean next to that. And he was suddenly more eager than ever to get back to the field. If he died in battle, at least it would be over fast— he hoped.

Merkela glared at Skarnu and at the underground fighter who called himself "Tytuvenai" after the town where he was based. She said, "I don't think you ought to be talking with the Algarvians. I think you ought to be blazing them."

"Oh, we'll do some of that even yet," "Tytuvenai" said lightly. He winked at Skarnu. "Eh, 'Pavilosta'?"

"Aye, no doubt," Skarnu answered. He glanced over to Merkela. "Like it or not, we have to talk with them now."

"Give me one good reason," she snapped.

"They hold the towns. They hold the roads. If they want to, they can start slaughtering Valmierans the same way they've been slaughtering the Kaunians from Forthweg," Skarnu said. "They can do it any time they please."

Merkela winced. Reluctantly, she nodded. "There is that."

"Aye, there is," "Tytuvenai" agreed. "If we want to have a kingdom left when this cursed war finally ends, we have to walk a little softer than we might like right now. And so . . ." He nudged Skarnu. "We'd better get moving."

"Right," Skarnu said without any great enthusiasm. Whether he recognized the need or not, he wasn't thrilled at the idea of talking with the Algarvians, either. But he kissed Merkela and went out to the horses "Tytuvenai" had waiting outside the farmhouse. As he mounted and rode off, he grumbled, "Why don't the people up in the north handle this themselves?"

"They do," "Tytuvenai" answered. "But we have to do our part, too." As usual, he was cheerfully cynical: "You can't expect those fellows up there to count on their fingers and get the same answer twice running." Skarnu laughed, though he was sure the northern Valmierans said the same thing about him and "Tytuvenai" and the other irregulars here in the south.

He and his comrade rode for about three hours. Skarnu's backside started to hurt; he wasn't used to so much equestrianism. By the way "Tytuvenai" started grunting every so often, Skarnu suspected he was feeling it, too.

After a while, "Tytuvenai" grunted again, this time in relief. "We're supposed to meet the redheads in that apple orchard ahead. I've got a flag of truce in the saddlebag here. Demon of a thing to have to use with the Algarvians, isn't it?"

"It's war," Skarnu answered with a shrug. "There's nothing dishonorable about it." But he was trying to convince himself as much as "Tytuvenai."

They tied their horses to a couple of the apple trees. Skarnu didn't fancy going into the orchard armed with nothing more than a white flag on a little pole. *If the Algarvians grab us, they'll be sorry,* he thought. *They've got to know they'll be sorry . . . don't they?*

A tall man in his later middle years stepped out from between a couple of trees. He, too, carried a flag of truce. "Good day, gentlemen," he said in fluent if accented Valmieran, and gave the two irregulars a courteous bow. "I have the honor to be Colonel Lurcanio, administrator of Priekule under Grand Duke Ivone. And you are . . . ?"

"Tytuvenai," "Tytuvenai" said.

"Pavilosta," Skarnu said. He eyed Lurcanio. Till now, he'd had only one brief look at the redhead who was his sister's lover. He hoped Lurcanio wouldn't recall the name of the hamlet he used as a sobriquet.

No such luck. Lurcanio's cat-green eyes kindled. He bowed again, this time to Skarnu alone. "So pleased to meet you at last. We have . . . an acquaintance in common."

"I know," Skarnu said, and said no more.

"You may be interested to learn she is expecting a child," Lurcanio remarked.

"Is she?" Skarnu said tonelessly. But that wasn't quite

enough. And so, loathing Krasta, he asked the question he had to ask: "Yours?"

To his surprise, the Algarvian didn't smirk and nod. Indeed, the fellow's voice was cautious as he answered, "So I have been given to understand."

What was that supposed to mean? Before Skarnu could ask—before he could even decide whether he ought to ask—"Tytuvenai" said, "Let's get down to business, shall we?"

"An excellent suggestion," Lurcanio said. "You would be wise to bear in mind that we are still strong enough to punish acts of madness aimed against us."

"We would reckon some of your punishments acts of madness, you know," Skarnu said.

"No doubt. One day, perhaps, we can discuss the role perspective plays in human affairs." Lurcanio was a cool customer. Skarnu wondered what Krasta saw in him. The Algarvian resumed: "We have other business before us at present, however."

"So we do," "Tytuvenai" said. "Such as making us believe we shouldn't do more to hold up the ley-line caravans you're using to ship your soldiers out of here."

"Go ahead." Lurcanio gave him a smile half charming, half coldly vicious. "The people of Valmiera will not be happy with the choice you make, but go ahead. Do as you feel you must, and we shall do as we feel we must."

"A lot of the people of Valmiera will be happy with anything that gets you people out of our kingdom," Skarnu said. "Anything at all. And you know why. 'Night and Fog.'" That was what the Algarvians or their henchmen scrawled on buildings whose occupants had vanished for good—usually into the camps where the redheads kept Kaunians they killed.

"The people most intimately concerned with our vengeance will not be happy," Lurcanio said. "On that you may rest assured."

"Why, you—" "Tytuvenai" began.

"Wait," Skarnu said. The other irregular looked at him in some surprise. Skarnu seldom spoke like a nobleman giving a servant an order; that tone more often appeared in Krasta's mouth. Here, though, he made an exception—and "Tytuvenai" *did* fall silent.

"You own some glimmering of sense," Colonel Lurcanio said.

"I wonder if you do," Skarnu answered. "Tell me, do you really think Algarve still has any hope of winning the war?"

"With King Mezentio's leadership, with our strong sorceries, one never knows," Lurcanio said.

Skarnu laughed in his face. He waited for Lurcanio to get offended, but the Algarvian just waited to see what he would say next. What he said was, "Do you think Algarve has any *realistic* chance of winning the war?"

Lurcanio shrugged one of the elaborate shrugs in which his countrymen delighted. After a few heartbeats, Skarnu realized that was as far as the redhead would go. He didn't suppose he could blame Lurcanio—for that, anyhow. He hadn't wanted to talk, or even think, about Valmiera's troubles back in the days before Algarvian behemoths and dragons leveled his kingdom's hopes.

"You might want to bear one thing in mind," Skarnu said. "If you do lose this war, your enemies will remember everything you did while you held their kingdoms down. How large a price do you want to pay after your armies can't fight any more?"

For once, Colonel Lurcanio had no quick answer, no snappy comeback. He eyed Skarnu with no liking, but with wary respect nonetheless. "There is enough between your ears for sparks to strike, is there not?" he remarked. "Your sister is prettier than you, but her head is empty."

With a shrug of his own—he didn't want to show Lurcanio he agreed with him—Skarnu said, "That's also something to talk about some other time. But if you start killing Valmierans for the sport of it, think what will happen when Valmieran soldiers march into Algarve."

Lurcanio raised an eyebrow. "And if our best chance to keep Valmieran soldiers from ever marching into Algarve lies in killing all the Valmieran civilians we can lay our hands on?"

This time, "Tytuvenai" spoke before Skarnu could: "If you

try something like that, Algarvian, you'd better be sure you do win. Can you do that? Trying and losing anyhow will be worse than not trying at all."

But Colonel Lurcanio shook his head. "By the powers above, nothing would be worse than not trying at all." He and the two Valmierans eyed one another in perfect mutual incomprehension.

"We will not attack ley-line caravans taking your soldiers out of Valmiera if you don't take our civilians out with you and if you don't start killing them for your magecraft," Skarnu said. "If you do, everything is fair game. And we reckon any caravan bringing your soldiers *into* Valmiera is fair game, too."

"That is not right. That is not just," Lurcanio said. "Many—most, even—of the men we bring here do not come to fight. They come for leave from the fight they have been making in the west."

"They're still soldiers," Skarnu said. "If you give them sticks, what will they do? Start to dance?"

He surprised a laugh out of the Algarvian colonel. "There may perhaps be something to that," Lurcanio said. "I speak for myself when I say so, however, not for Grand Duke Ivone. You were an officer. You will understand the need for following orders."

Skarnu started to nod. "Tytuvenai" broke in, saying, "Some orders are wicked. No one should follow those. Anyone who follows an order to murder people deserves whatever happens to him."

"Anyone who lets his kingdom lose a war it might win deserves whatever happens to him," Lurcanio answered. They glared at one another once more, at a fresh impasse. Lurcanio said. "Can we agree to anything?" he asked.

"Leave our civilians alone, and we'll let your caravans leave in peace," Skarnu said.

"We had that bargain before, or so I thought," Lurcanio said. "So King Gainibu hinted, at any rate."

Maybe he thought the king's name would fill the Valmierans with overwhelming awe. And maybe it would have . . . before the war. Skarnu said, "These past four years, we've been on our own. We haven't paid much attention to his Majesty—and that's the fault of you Algarvians. Why should we start over now?"

He hadn't seen Colonel Lurcanio taken aback till then. "Why? Because he is your sovereign, of course," the redhead—actually, he'd gone quite gray—replied.

"He's welcome to reign," "Tytuvenai" said. "Why should he rule? What has he done for us lately?"

Lurcanio wagged a finger at him, a very Algarvian gesture. "If we should ever leave this kingdom, you will find that he still intends to rule, mark my words. May you have joy of it." He paused. "I think we have said everything that wants saying." He paused again, then nodded to Skarnu. "Have you any message for your sister?"

"I have no sister," Skarnu said stonily. "No point even telling her you saw me."

"You take this business altogether too seriously," Lurcanio said. Skarnu did not reply. The Algarvian shrugged. "It shall be as you wish, of course." He turned and strode away.

Skarnu started to call something after him, but didn't. What point to it? What was Lurcanio but an enemy? He might be—Skarnu thought he was—an honest enemy, but an enemy he remained. Skarnu turned to "Tytuvenai." He nodded once. "Let's go," he said.

After a long, deep, restful night's sleep, Colonel Spinello yawned, stretched, and finally opened his eyes. The mattress was large and soft; the house not far outside of Eoforwic had, he thought, belonged to a Kaunian before Kaunians in Forthweg fell on hard times. It was ever so much more comfortable than lying down on bare dirt, which he'd done far too often while escaping the disaster that had overtaken the Algarvian armies in northern Unkerlant.

"Not so bad, eh, sweetheart?" he said.

When Jadwigai didn't answer, Spinello rolled over toward her. She wasn't lying in bed beside him, either. He shrugged. No law said she couldn't get up before him, though he wouldn't have minded pinning her to that soft, resilient mattress just then: why not start the day with pleasure, when it was all too likely to end in death or some other disaster?

Spinello pulled on his tunic and kilt and ambled out into the kitchen to see what Jadwigai had put together for breakfast, or what he could. Some Algarvians—the ones who'd never gone west to fight in Unkerlant—complained about how miserable things were in Forthweg. Spinello and the others who'd been driven out of Swemmel's kingdom only laughed—they knew better.

"Jadwigai?" Spinello called when he didn't see her. She didn't answer. He shrugged again, and went to get himself some food. Bread and olive oil and wine wasn't his favorite breakfast, but it beat the blazes out of bugs and nasty, sour berries and swamp water.

A leaf of paper lay on top of what was left of the loaf of black bread. Spinello picked it up. He hadn't seen Jadwigai's script before, but this couldn't belong to anyone else. His own name was written on one side of the paper. He turned it over to the other.

> *By the time you read this,* Jadwigai had written in classical Kaunian, *I will be gone. I do thank you for saving me in the fight and flight through Unkerlant. I know you did not do it all for my sake, but also for your own. Even so, you did it, and I am grateful.*
>
> *But I also know what happens to Kaunians in Algarvian hands. I know it could happen to me if you get hurt or get tired of me. I have learned that Kaunians, these days, have little trouble looking like Forthwegians. I would rather do that than live the way I have been living. Even if Unkerlant conquers Forthweg, I would rather do that.*
>
> *I do not wish you ill, not in your own person. I do not wish ill on any of the men of the Albarese Regiment who still live. They could have killed me or kept me to give their bodies relief until I died, and they did not. But I do not want Algarve to win this war. I find I cannot forget after all that I am a Kaunian. Farewell.*

She'd scrawled her name under the note.

Spinello plucked at his chin beard (he'd neatened up after returning to civilized company). Jadwigai had been naive to leave the leaf of paper. If he wanted to, he could give it to a mage to use the law of contagion to track her through it. *Should I do that?* He stroked his chin again. She wouldn't be happy, or anything close to it.

Of course, he'd enjoyed bedding Vanai precisely because she hadn't been happy about it. But things would be different with Jadwigai. He'd be breaking a bond of trust if he hauled her back. He'd never had one with Vanai, only a bargain: her body in exchange for keeping her grandfather from getting worked to death on a road gang. Jadwigai could have killed him or betrayed him to the Unkerlanters more times than he could count.

And so . . . He was, in his own way, an honest man. There were live ashes in the hearth. He got a little fire going and tossed the note into it. The paper charred, blackened, and burst into flames. He ate his bread and oil, and washed them down with not one mug of wine but two.

When he walked outside, the sentry in front of the house stiffened to attention. Spinello's resolution wavered a little, perhaps under the influence of wine. "Have you seen Jadwigai?" he asked.

"Your wench? No, sir. I would've remembered." The Algarvian soldier's eyes lit up, as any man's would when he thought of Jadwigai. "I thought she was in there with you." *You lucky whoreson.* He didn't need to say it. Again, Spinello could read it in his eyes.

"No." Spinello let it go at that. Jadwigai would know when sentries went off duty and when they came on. If she'd timed her disappearance to just before the last fellow went off, he wouldn't wonder that she hadn't returned and his replacement wouldn't know she was gone. The only risk would have been waking Spinello when she got out of bed. And if she had wakened him, she would have just had to put up with him one more day before trying again.

"Is something wrong, sir?" Like any Algarvian, the sentry had a nose for scandal.

"No, not a thing." Spinello lied without hesitation. "She went off somewhere without telling me, that's all."

"That's liable not to be healthy, the way things are around here these days," the sentry remarked.

"I don't know what you're talking about," Spinello said

dryly. The sentry chuckled. Spinello went on, "Next to Unkerlant, this is a fornicating walk in the fornicating park." The sentry laughed again. He wore the ribbon for a frozen-meat medal, the decoration King Mezentio had given out by the tens of thousands to the men who'd come through the first winter's fighting in Unkerlant. Spinello had one, too.

Smoke rose from Eoforwic, where the Forthwegians still battled desperately to drive back the Algarvian armies. The Unkerlanters across the Twegen still stayed quiet, though Spinello could see distant smoke in the south, where Swemmel's men had forced a bridgehead over the river. They weren't trying to break out of it yet, but the Algarvians hadn't been able to crush it, either. When Spinello let himself think about that, he worried.

But he had plenty of other things to worry about, too. The sentry spelled out one of them: "Are we going back into Eoforwic today, sir? I wouldn't mind a holiday, and that's a fact."

With a chuckle, Spinello said, "I wouldn't, either, old man. Neither would Algarve, come to that. When the Forthwegians and Unkerlanters and islanders decide to give us one, though—that's another question. So aye, we'll be going back into town."

"I thought you were going to tell me that." The corners of the sentry's mouth turned down; like so many Algarvians, he wore his heart on his sleeve. "I'd just as soon sit this one out, if it's all the same to you."

"I'm going in," Spinello said. "I could use the company." He and the sentry grinned at each other. They were both going in, and they both knew it. They both hoped they would both come out again when the day was done.

Spinello found himself in charge of a force he would have laughed at if he were throwing it against the Unkerlanters. A lot of the soldiers he led had sat out most of the war on occupation duty in Valmiera. They were both older and fatter than they might have been. Some of them held their sticks as if not quite sure what to do with them. But they went forward when he told them to go, and he didn't suppose he could ask for more than that.

He was none too thrilled about going forward himself. He'd fought block by block, house by house, in Sulingen till he took a beam through the chest. He'd been lucky, in an odd, painful way: that was early enough in the fight there to let a dragon take him out of the city. Had he stayed unhurt till the end, he wouldn't have come out of Sulingen alive.

Eoforwic hadn't been knocked about quite so badly as Sulingen, not yet. Most blocks of flats still stood, though window frames gaped bare like the eye sockets of countless skulls. Spinello wasn't so sure he wouldn't rather have seen rubble. Anyone could be watching from those upper stories. They made perfect sniper's nests.

He couldn't read the Forthwegian warning whitewashed on walls here and there, but he knew about what it said: *anyone blazes from a building, the building gets wrecked, and we won't bother clearing out the people who live there first.* That kind of warning hadn't stopped the sniping, but had slowed it down. Ordinary Forthwegians didn't want to be driven from their homes, or killed in them, any more than anyone else did.

He wondered how many people in those flats weren't Forthwegians at all, but sorcerously disguised Kaunians. He wondered if Jadwigai had been foolish enough to go into the city, or if she'd had the sense to flee out into the countryside where she was less likely to get killed.

And then he remembered that that constable back in Gromheort had told him Vanai was supposed to have come to Eoforwic. He laughed to himself. He wouldn't recognize her if he saw her—he was sure of that. If she looked like a Kaunian, his countrymen would long since have seized her. And if she didn't, he wouldn't know her from any other dumpy Forthwegian girl.

Even a dumpy Forthwegian girl is better than a cold, empty bed, he thought. But then girls, Forthwegian or Kaunian, dumpy or elegantly lean, slipped out of his mind. Ahead lay enough rubble to satisfy even the most ambitiously destructive wrecker of all time.

"Fan out, men," he called. "There'll be rebels in there, sure as we're all missing foreskins." He watched the troopers take cover and slowly shook his head. No, most of them hadn't

spent the past three years honing themselves against the Unkerlanters. Even against the Forthwegians, more would fall than
might be true with better soldiers.

As he ducked behind a tumbledown wall himself, a beam
charred wood a couple of feet above his head. Part of a broad-
sheet still clung to the brickwork: a bearded Forthwegian stran-
gling a dragon painted in Algarvian colors. Spinello snorted.
Nothing subtle there. Nothing very interesting, either. Even the
Unkerlanters turned out better broadsheets.

Eggs started bursting on the rubble. Now Spinello nodded.
Unlike footsoldiers, the men who handled egg-tossers had to
know what they were doing. And the Unkerlanters, as they had
for some weeks, just kept sitting quietly on the far side of the
Twegen River. Spinello thought that was funny. He suspected
the Forthwegians weren't laughing.

"Forward!" he called, and blew his shiny new officer's whistle. He'd lost the old one in an Unkerlanter swamp.

Forward his men went. They weren't so young or so dashing
as the soldiers he'd led in Unkerlant, but they cleared the surviving Forthwegians from the wreckage and lost only a couple
of men doing it. Crouched in amongst the reconquered rubble,
Spinello felt proud of them till a question crossed his mind:
now that we've got it, what the demon good is it?

He shrugged a fancy Algarvian shrug. If soldiers spent all
their time worrying about things like that, how would they fight
their wars?

Talsu peered down at the road leading toward Skrunda from behind a rock most of the way up a low hill. Another irregular
shared the cover of the boulder with him. "By the powers
above, it's good to have King Donalitu back in Jelgava, back in
Balvi, again," the other fellow said.

"It's good to have the Algarvians getting kicked out of Jelgava." Talsu didn't quite agree with his comrade, but didn't
want to cause a quarrel, either.

"It's the same thing, near enough," the other man said. He
was older than Talsu, and leaner, with a scar seaming his left
cheek. He looked like a murderer. From what he'd said, he'd

been a dyer before the war. The skin of his hands still bore strange mottling.

"Not quite." Talsu couldn't let that go unchallenged.

"What's the difference, then?"

"Well . . . when I was in the dungeon, the fellow who squeezed me wasn't an Algarvian. He was as Jelgavan as we are. He'd worked for the king before he worked for the redheads, and I'll bet he goes back to working for the king once the redheads run away or get beaten. Some of our troubles'll go with 'em— some, but not all. People like that interrogator will still be here."

"You can't help people like that," the other Jelgavan said.

"Why not?" Talsu asked.

"Because they're part of the way things work," his comrade said. "You can't get rid of them, any more than you can get rid of the pits in olives."

"You can do that," Talsu said. "It just takes work."

He started to add something to that, but the other irregular gave him a shot in the ribs with an elbow and pointed west, toward Skrunda. Talsu's head swung that way. A column of Algarvian soldiers—a couple of regiments' worth—was coming east along the road, along with three or four behemoths and a motley collection of wagons.

"They're still moving men forward to fight the Lagoans and Kuusamans," Talsu said.

"They're trying to," his companion answered. "Our job is to make sure they don't have an easy time of it."

How many men were hidden here and there along these hills? Talsu didn't know. How had the irregulars' leaders heard the redheads would move soldiers along this road? He didn't know that, either, though he could make guesses he thought good. Some Jelgavans sold out their fellows to the Algarvians. Why shouldn't others sell out the redheads to their countrymen?

Maybe some of the Algarvians there were the ones who'd seized him when he went with Kugu the silversmith for what he'd thought would be his introduction to the underground but turned into his introduction to the dungeon. Talsu knew that was wildly unlikely, but hoped it was true just the same. *Do you really need that kind of help to want vengeance?* he wondered.

A moment later, he shook his head. *No, I don't need it, but it would be nice.*

Somewhere on a hilltop not far away, the irregulars had an egg-tosser or two. Talsu didn't see the first egg fly through the air, but he did watch it burst just in front of the Algarvian column. The next egg, better aimed, landed among the redheads. The burst of sorcerous energy flung men and pieces of men high into the air.

"Let's see how they like *that*, by the powers above!" the Jelgavan next to Talsu said with a fierce whoop of glee.

The Algarvians, of course, liked it not at all. Talsu had been away from real war for close to four years. He'd forgotten how quickly trained men could react—and he wondered if soldiers from the Jelgavan army could ever have reacted so quickly. Mezentio's men spread out even before the third egg hit. Then they swarmed up the hills on either side of the road, blazing as they came.

Talsu stuck his head out from behind his side of the boulder for a quick blaze at the enemy. A beam zipped past his own head, close enough for him to feel the heat and smell the lightning in the air. He ducked back into cover in a hurry.

Over on the other side of the boulder, the dyer was cursing. "Some of the bastards blaze while the rest run," he complained. "How are we supposed to blaze at them?"

"You weren't in the army during the war, were you?" Talsu said with a dry chuckle, which startled a nod from the other Jelgavan. "That's just one of the chances you take in this business."

Another quick blaze from Talsu. The Algarvian at whom he aimed went down, but he didn't know whether he'd hit the man: like the redhead, he dove for the dirt, too, whenever somebody started blazing at him. He turned to his comrade, intending to tell him something on the order of, *That's how it's done.*

Whatever he'd been about to say, he didn't. The other irregular sprawled bonelessly in the dust, blazed through the head. Blood pooled beneath his body. He was still twitching a little, but Talsu had seen enough men killed to know another one.

He snapped off another blaze. But the Algarvians were coming hard and fast. Before long, they'd be on his flank if he didn't fall back. Keeping the boulder between himself and most of them, he scurried back over the crest of the hill. He wasn't the only one in full retreat, either. He didn't think the irregulars' leaders had expected Mezentio's men to hit back so fiercely. He wasn't particularly surprised himself. The Algarvians had always been aggressive, even back in the days of the Kaunian Empire.

Talsu threw himself down behind a bush and watched the crestline. *Aye, I still remember a trick or two,* he thought with somber pride. *Now if one of those cursed redheads forgets . . .*

And one of Mezentio's men did. He charged over the top of the hill. He couldn't have done a better job of exposing himself if he'd tried for a week. *Not a smart thing to do,* Talsu thought, and blazed him. The redhead wore a look of absurd surprise as he crumpled.

But not all of Mezentio's men were fools. The Algarvians couldn't have done nearly so much harm if they had been fools. Many more of them came over the rise with proper care. Talsu fell back again, and then again. He saw more of his comrades who weren't so lucky.

He got away into the deeper hills where the irregulars had been sheltering for a long time. The Algarvians didn't pursue so hard as they might have. Some of the raiders were jubilant about that. "They know better than to stick their noses in here too far," one of them said. "If they tried it, they'd be sorry."

Although Talsu didn't argue with those bold spirits, he didn't think they were right, either. The redheads had been on their way east to fight the Kuusamans and Lagoans. Once they'd broken up this harassing attack, wouldn't they get back to their chief business as fast as they could? If they had any sense, they would. And anyone who looked at things with an ounce of sense would see the same thing.

Maybe the irregulars didn't have a whole lot of sense. Maybe they'd been so starved for victories for so long, anything looked bigger than it really was. Maybe . . . *Maybe all sorts of things,* Talsu thought, laughing at himself. Whatever the truth was, he couldn't do anything about it.

Later that evening, the Algarvians did something about it, or tried to. They sent a few dragons over the hills. A few eggs came hissing down out of the sky. A couple of them burst near the irregulars' camps. None of them did any harm. That raised the Jelgavans' spirits, too.

"Hardly even worth being afraid of the stinking Algarvians any more," somebody said. Somebody else nodded. Several men clapped their hands. *Maybe they're right,* Talsu thought hopefully.

A couple of nights later, the Algarvians showed they still deserved fear.

The night was very black, one of those late-summer nights when the air was so warm, so clear, so still, the stars in the sky hardly twinkled. On sentry-go, Talsu kept staring up at them.

Somewhere between midnight and dawn, not long before a replacement was supposed to come and he was supposed to go back to camp, he felt something wrong. For the first moment or two, he didn't know what it was. *Earthquake?* he wondered. Jelgava got them from time to time, though Skrunda's neighborhood hadn't been hit hard in his lifetime.

When the ground quivered beneath his feet, he thought at first he was right. But the shaking didn't build, as an earthquake did; it just went on for a while. Looking back in the direction of the camp, he saw purple flashes, as if lightning were striking close by. But where would lightning come from, out of as clear a sky as he'd ever seen?

Fear ran through him in the wake of that thought. Replacement or no replacement, he hurried off toward the camp. By the time he got there, everything was over. If it were an earthquake, it had struck the irregulars alone. Their fires were thrown higgledy-piggledy; a couple of small shrubs burned close by.

There were rents in the ground from which smoke still rose. At first, when Talsu smelled burnt meat, he thought the odor was left over from cooking earlier in the evening. Then he realized what it was really coming from, and his stomach did a slow lurch. That was burnt meat, all right, but some of the burnt meat still shrieked and begged to die.

That could have been me, he thought numbly. *If I hadn't been out standing sentry, that could have been me.*

"Powers below eat the Algarvians!" someone not far away shouted. "Powers above curse their sorcery!"

Talsu's stomach lurched again. He knew what kind of sorcery Mezentio's men used. People had been whispering about it for a couple of years, maybe longer. But . . . "How are they getting Kaunians from Forthweg into Jelgava?" he said, as much to himself as to anyone else. "They have trouble moving their own soldiers around this kingdom."

Bitter laughter answered him. "Who says it has to be Kaunians from Forthweg? If they need bodies bad enough, they can start pulling people out of Skrunda or any other town and bloody well killing them."

That hadn't occurred to Talsu. Take people out of his home town, line them up, and kill them to tap their life energy? Take, say, his wife, his father, his mother, his sister?

"No," he said, again largely to himself.

"Why not?" the other surviving irregular said. "They're Algarvians. They hate all Kaunic peoples as much as we hate them. If they can't get Kaunians from Forthweg here, you think they won't grab Jelgavans?"

However much Talsu wished he thought that, he didn't, not down where it mattered. "We might not have a kingdom left by the time they're through with us," he exclaimed.

"That's why we've got to keep fighting the bastards," the other irregular said. "Whatever they do to us, may it come back on their heads ten times over."

"A hundred times over," Talsu said. He couldn't get the picture of Algarvians seizing his family out of his mind no matter how hard he tried, and he tried as he'd never tried before in all his days.

Vanai had known fear a good many times in the course of the Derlavaian War. Anyone in Forthweg who hadn't known fear surely had something wrong with him. This, though, this was terror. And terror, she discovered, was a very different beast from mere fear.

"I saw him," she told Saxburh in classical Kaunian. She held out her hand in the posture of one taking an oath. "By the powers above, I *did* see him."

Her daughter thought it was funny, and laughed the pure, clean laugh of a happy baby. To Vanai, it was no laughing matter. She knew Spinello's stride when she saw it, even if the Algarvian officer had acquired a slight limp since going off to fight in Unkerlant. And if that wasn't he leading soldiers up the street past her block of flats, her eyes were useless.

He wouldn't recognize her, not when she looked like a Forthwegian these days. *Thelberge,* she thought, shivering. *I can be Thelberge and he'll never know me.* Of course, he might not care, either. He might blaze her any which way. After all, the rebels in Eoforwic were for the most part Forthwegians.

He might blaze me, but he'll never bed me again, she thought fiercely. *Never, by the powers above!*

Logically, bedding her might be—was almost bound to be—the last thing Spinello had in mind at the moment. Logic had nothing to do with anything, though, when she remembered the Algarvian coming again and again to her grandfather's house in Oyngestun and taking her to bed instead of taking Brivibas into a labor gang. He'd known she despised him. He hadn't cared— or maybe he had, for sometimes she thought her resentment only excited him more.

I want to kill him, she thought. *I want to kill him with my own hands. Maybe then I'll feel clean again.* There were a good many stories from before the days when the First Kaunian Kingdom grew into the Kaunian Empire about ravished women avenging themselves on the men who'd abused them. Brivibas had taught her those tales with scorn in his voice: they were legends, maybe even myths, and not sober history. But teach them to her he had; legends or not, they were part of the underpinnings of Kaunianity.

What made things harder was that she couldn't talk to Ealstan about this. He knew nothing of Spinello, and Vanai wanted to keep it that way. And so, whenever he did manage to come home, filthy and exhausted, she forced the Algarvian to the back of her mind. But she couldn't force him out of it, any more than she could have pretended a bad tooth didn't really ache.

Once, after Ealstan kissed her good-bye and patted her on the backside and went out to try to cause the redheads more trouble, a really horrible thought ran through her mind: *What if he and Spinello come up against each other? Spinello has all the might of Algarve behind him. What if he . . . ?*

Vanai violently shook her head. She *wouldn't* think of that— so she told herself. And so, of course, the thought kept coming back again and again, each time more dreadful than the one before. She cursed as foully as she knew how. *If only I hadn't picked the wrong time to look out the window!*

But she had to go into the kitchen, and when she went into the kitchen she couldn't very well help looking out the window. Seeing Algarvian soldiers prowling through this part of Eoforwic would have been enough of a jolt even without recognizing Spinello. The Forthwegian rebels had securely held it only days before. Little by little, the redheads were pounding the uprising to bits.

Across the Twegen River, the Unkerlanters sat and waited. Vanai had never thought much about them one way or the other. Now she hated them. Had they come to the Forthwegians' aid, Eoforwic wouldn't have an Algarvian left in it. Ealstan was surely right—Swemmel's men were letting the redheads solve their Forthwegian problem for them.

. When Vanai went into the kitchen again, she found she had problems of her own: problems in the larder. Last time she'd ventured out, she'd got as much food as she could carry back. Now she would have to do it again.

She went over to the cradle and looked down at Saxburh. The baby smiled to see her, smiled and laughed. Vanai smiled, too, but she had to work at it. She didn't like the idea of taking Saxburh out with her when she sallied forth to get food, but she liked leaving her behind even less. Saxburh might cry every minute till she got back. Or, worse, she might not be able to come back. Taking the baby out was dangerous, but so was leaving her behind. There were no safe places, no safe choices, in Eoforwic these days.

Vanai scooped the baby out of the cradle. "Come along, you little nuisance," she said. Saxburh thought that was very funny. Vanai, unfortunately, didn't. If she had to carry Saxburh, that was so much less food she could bring back. Before setting out, she renewed the masking spell on herself and cast it on her daughter. On Saxburh, she could see it take effect; the baby looked plumper and a little darker. On her ventures out of the house, Vanai had seen a handful of Kaunians bold enough to look like themselves. She admired their courage without wanting to imitate it.

Carrying Saxburh downstairs was easy. Carrying her and a lot of groceries back up to the flat would be a lot more work. *I'll worry about that once I get the food*, Vanai thought. She'd managed before. She expected she would be able to do it again.

She paused inside the lobby near the door to make sure everything was quiet before venturing out. Algarvian soldiers wouldn't know her for a Kaunian now, but they or their Forthwegian counterparts were liable to blaze anyone who appeared unexpectedly.

No redheads were in sight when she stepped out onto the street, only a couple of Forthwegians—people who looked like Forthwegians, anyhow, just as she did. One, a woman, smiled toward Saxburh. The other, a fighter as unkempt and grimy as Ealstan was these days, paid neither Vanai nor the baby any attention after a quick glance to make sure she wasn't an Algarvian. Satisfied as to that, he tramped on down the middle of the street, a stick in his hands and ready to blaze.

No matter how Forthwegian Vanai looked, she couldn't match that display of self-assurance. She stayed close to the walls as she hurried toward the market square where she'd gone so often before Mezentio's men seized her and flung her into the Kaunian quarter. People still bought and sold things there, but it was a smaller, more furtive place than it had been.

Getting there wasn't quite so simple as it had been, either. She had to skirt or climb over piles of rubble that had been houses and shops and blocks of flats. That would have been easier without carrying Saxburh, too. Coming back with food, again, would be even more delightful. *You do what you have to do*, Vanai thought. *You do it, and then you think about how you did it. One thing at a time, that's all.*

Worried-looking Forthwegians scurried around the market

square, getting what they could and cursing the prices they had to pay. The people who sold, most of them, were as hard-faced as the Forthwegian fighter Vanai had seen. Several of them had guards with sticks at their backs to make sure they got paid for their goods.

Vanai winced when she heard the prices they were asking. "That's twice as much for flour as I paid the last time I was here," she complained.

With a shrug, the man from whom she was buying said, "That's on account of I used to have twice as much to sell. If you don't want to pay it, sweetheart, somebody else will."

He was doubtless right about that. Vanai paid. She did have plenty of silver. She paid for cheese and beans and almonds and peas, too. Nothing exciting there, only stuff that would keep and could go into easy stews and porridges. She wasn't worrying about fancy meals these days, only about holding starvation at bay.

Saxburh started to cry when Vanai was about halfway back to her block of flats. Vanai didn't know whether the baby was hungry or wet or just sick of being toted around like—quite literally—one more sack of beans. She didn't care, either. She couldn't do anything with Saxburh till she got back to the flat, not unless she wanted to put all the food down. And that was about the last thing she wanted to do. In a city at war, getting back out of sight was far and away the smartest course.

She soon found out just how true that was. Something—noting motion in the sky, perhaps—made her look up in spite of the constant struggle to keep her feet. She gasped in horror. Flying straight toward her, hardly higher than the housetops, were half a dozen dragons, all of them painted in gaudy, crazy patterns of red, green, and white—Algarvian beasts. They carried eggs slung under their bellies.

Vanai shrank back against a wall, not that that would have done the slightest bit of good had they decided to flame her or drop those eggs close by. But they swept on past, so low that their wings kicked dust up from the ground into her eyes. Without a free hand to rub at them, she blinked frantically.

A moment later, eggs burst in the market square. The noise smote her ears. Saxburh's wails grew louder. She heard screams behind her, too. "I can't do anything, sweetheart," Vanai said, jiggling the baby up and down in the crook of her elbow. "I'm just glad we went out early."

Saxburh wasn't glad, and didn't care who knew it. Vanai couldn't do anything about that without slowing down, and she wasn't about to slow down for anything or anybody, Saxburh included. Getting home was the most important thing she could do. She'd already had that thought. It was especially true now. And she did it, wailing baby or no wailing baby.

Getting the door to the block of flats open without putting anything down proved another adventure, and getting up the stairs another one still. But she did what needed doing, and she was able to set some of her bundles on the floor in the hallway in front of her flat so she could use a key to open the door. That done, she hustled groceries inside and closed and barred the door behind her.

By then, Saxburh wasn't just red in the face; she was a nasty, blotchy purple. "I know," Vanai said soothingly. "I know. Nobody was paying enough attention to you. Now I can." She cuddled the baby and nursed her. Saxburh settled down and quickly went to sleep. Vanai wished somebody could calm *her* down as easily as that.

She put the grain and nuts and vegetables and cheese in the kitchen cupboards. Then she turned the tap. Only a trickle of water came out. She said something in classical Kaunian that surely would have shocked Brivibas, then something even more incendiary in Forthwegian. Up till now, she'd always been able to rely on the water. If she couldn't . . .

Cursing again, she put a pot under the tap to catch as much water as it would give. Where could she get more? The fancier parts of Eoforwic had a good many fountains. This grimy district? No. She would have to get some from somewhere. You could live a lot longer without food than without water.

The trickle stopped. Vanai stared in dismay. Maybe people would repair the mains, and the water would come back on again soon. Maybe they wouldn't, and it wouldn't. However things turned out, she had to do her best. *If I can,* she thought. *If I can.*

Marshal Rathar could look east across the Twegen River and watch Eoforwic burn. The sight didn't make him unhappy—not in the least. On that side of the river, Algarvian soldiers were fighting and dying and using up uncounted eggs and behemoths and sorely needed sacks of cinnabar for their dragons—and none of it cost him so much as a single soldier.

General Gurmun was looking east, too, through a spyglass. Lowering it, he said, "I've never been one to have much use for delay, but I've got to admit that just sitting here serves us pretty well right now."

"It does, doesn't it?" Rathar agreed. "I was thinking the same thing, as a matter of fact. King Swemmel is shrewd, no doubt about it."

"That he is," Gurmun said enthusiastically. "The redheads could be fighting *us* street by street in Eoforwic. Can you imagine how expensive that would be? Instead, they're fighting the Forthwegians. It saves lots of wear and tear on us, and it gets rid of troublemakers we would have had to worry about later on."

"True enough." Rathar suspected—no, he was certain—the Forthwegians didn't think of themselves as troublemakers. In their own minds, they were surely patriots. Of course, what they were in their own minds mattered only so much to Rathar. He had to look at them as his sovereign would.

Gurmun asked, "Do you know what the king plans to do here in Forthweg? He's not going to let that son of a whore of a Penda come back and king it, is he?"

"His Majesty has not told me what he plans for Forthweg," Rathar said carefully. "The only order he has given me in that regard is to make no settlement on my own. He holds everything in his own hands."

"As a king should do." Gurmun was one of Swemmel's men in a way even Rathar wasn't: he'd been a boy, not a man, when the king came to power, and had no standards of comparison. Whatever Swemmel decided was automatically right for him.

And Marshal Rathar dared not show he disagreed. Even if

Gurmun didn't betray him in the hope of becoming Marshal of Unkerlant in his place, someone else was liable to. Unkerlant—especially Unkerlant under King Swemmel—ran on betrayals and denunciations.

"What would you do here if you were king?" Gurmun asked.

Watch my back, Rathar thought. Aloud, he answered, "I'm not king. I don't want to be king. How about you, Gurmun? What would *you* do?" *How do you like the boot on the other foot, Gurmun?*

"Me? I don't know anything about running a kingdom. I don't much care, either," Gurmun answered, as any Unkerlanter who wanted to live to a ripe old age had to do. "All I want is the chance to let my behemoths loose and smash on through the Algarvians again." He pointed across the river once more. "And I can see my odds of doing that will be better later on than they are right now." He wasn't smooth as a courtier, but he got the job done: he didn't criticize Swemmel and he didn't show ambition, at least not of the dangerous sort.

"You'll get your wish, I expect," Rathar said. "We've got that bridgehead over the Twegen north of Eoforwic, and the other one south of the city. The Algarvians haven't a chance of breaking either one of those, not with the Forthwegians inside Eoforwic keeping them so busy."

"That's right." Gurmun nodded. "And we can really use the lull, to get our supply lines straightened out. We outran everything when we chased the Algarvians out of Unkerlant this summer, and the redheads did a cursed good job of sabotaging the ley lines and burning the fields and planting eggs in the roads as they fell back. Powers above only know how we managed to keep bringing things forward."

"We did it," Rathar said. "That's what matters. I'll tell you something else, too: I'd rather manage moving things forward than moving them back." *I had too much practice doing that the first two years of the war.* He almost said so out loud, but held back. He would have told that to General Vatran, whom he trusted, but not to Gurmun. Gurmun was probably a better soldier—Rathar wondered if even the Algarvians had a finer commander of behemoths—but Vatran knew a confidence when he heard one, while the younger officer didn't.

Strangely, or perhaps not so strangely, Gurmun's thoughts ran on an almost parallel ley line: "Vatran's moving forward down in the south, too. He's into Yanina here and there, isn't he? I bet King Tsavellas is pissing on his pompom shoes."

Picturing that, Rathar laughed out loud. "I wouldn't be a bit surprised."

"And we're giving the Zuwayzin what they deserve," Gurmun added. "They should never have caused us so much trouble the last time we fought them."

"You're probably right," Rathar said. *If the king hadn't insisted on attacking them before we'd made all our preparations, they might not have, either.* That, of course, was one more thing he couldn't say. No one who blamed King Swemmel out loud for any of Unkerlant's shortcomings could look forward to anything save prison or hard labor or, things being as they were in this war, becoming a sacrificial victim. Rathar knew he enjoyed no more immunity from that rule than did the lowliest common soldier in the Unkerlanter army.

Gurmun said, "Pity we've never bothered going up into the mountains of central Ortah and teaching the Ortahoin a proper lesson, too. They deserve it, perching up there and trading with both sides and thinking they can just sit out the whole war."

"No." Now Rathar shook his head. "Concentration, Gurmun. We hit what's troubling us. The Ortahoin aren't going to come down out of their mountains and give us a hard time. We took enough of a bite out of their kingdom to get men through the lowland swamps. We don't need more trouble with them, not with two pushes going against the redheads and another one up in Zuwayza."

"And the war against the Gongs out in the far west," Gurmun added. "Fair enough, lord Marshal. I see your point." Getting Gurmun to admit that to anyone was no small feat.

"The war against the Gongs is like a one-legged fat man walking," Rathar said. "It's not going anywhere any time soon. We've made sure they can't break out of the woods, and they're not really trying any more, either. Their big fight is against the Kuusamans in the islands of the Bothnian Ocean."

"They're losing that one, too," Gurmun said with somber satisfaction.

"Good. If they were winning in the island war, they would have more energy to put into the fight against us," Rathar said. "And the Kuusamans and Lagoans are really running the Algarvians out of Jelgava."

"Of course they are—the cursed Algarvians are fighting us a lot harder than they're fighting the islanders," Gurmun said.

"We owe them more than the Kuusamans and Lagoans do," Rathar said. "They know it, too, and they don't want to pay off. Look at it from their eyes, and their strategy makes pretty good sense."

Gurmun screwed up his face. "I don't want to look at anything from Algarvian eyes. Powers below eat all the redheads."

"Powers below eat 'em, aye," Rathar said. "But sometimes you have to try to see things through their eyes. If you don't, you won't understand what they're trying to do, and you'll have a harder time beating them." That made Gurmun look thoughtful. He did want to beat the Algarvians. Rathar could fault him for a few things, but never for lack of desire.

"The next interesting question—" Gurmun began.

Before he could say what he thought the next interesting question would be, a crystallomancer came running into the headquarters calling, "Marshal Rathar! Marshal Rathar!"

"I'm here," Rathar said. "What in blazes has gone wrong now?" By the young mage's tone, something had.

Sure enough, the fellow said, "Sir, we've just lost two of the bridges into the bridgehead south of Eoforwic. We almost lost the third one, too."

"What?" Rathar and Gurmun said together, in identical tones of angry disbelief. Rathar went on, "How the demon did the redheads get so fornicating lucky?"

"Sir, it wasn't luck," the crystallomancer said. "They've got some new sorcery that's letting them really aim some of the eggs they drop from dragons. The people down at the bridgehead don't know just how they're doing it, but they've watched eggs swerve in midair and land on the bridges or right by them in the river."

Marshal Rathar spent the next little while cursing Algarvian ingenuity. Then he turned to General Gurmun and said, "We have to let Addanz know about this. If the redheads can figure out a way to steer dropping eggs, our mages can figure out a way to stop them."

"They'd better be able to, anyhow," Gurmun said. "If they can't, King Swemmel will find himself a new archmage in one demon of a hurry, and Addanz will likely find himself down in the cinnabar mines in the Mamming Hills: the king'll squeeze *some* use out of him, anyhow."

Rathar reckoned the commander of behemoths almost surely right. Swemmel had a low tolerance for failure. Swemmel, come to that, had a low tolerance for almost everything. Rathar and Gurmun followed the crystallomancer down the street to the house where he and his comrades worked. With Rathar in overall command of all of Unkerlant's fighting fronts, the crystallomancers didn't fit into the house where he worked and slept.

When Addanz's image appeared in a crystal, Rathar explained what had happened. The Archmage of Unkerlant nodded. "I have heard somewhat of this from the Kuusamans," he said. "Apparently, even Mezentio's men have trouble doing what they do. Only a handful of their mages are capable of such rapid kinetic sorcery. It may prove a nuisance, but no worse."

"If they knock down our last route into that bridgehead, it'll be a lot worse than a nuisance," Rathar growled. "And if you know what Mezentio's mages are up to, why aren't you trying to stop it?"

"We have already begun work on countermeasures," Archmage Addanz said. "But these things do take a certain amount of time, and—" He blinked. "Powers above, what was that?"

Rathar didn't answer him. *That* had been an egg bursting close by, close enough to startle him into biting his tongue. He tasted blood. He and General Gurmun dashed out of the crystallomancers' headquarters, leaving it to the mages to break the etheric connection. Rathar needed only an instant to see what had happened: an egg had burst squarely on the building where he'd been living.

"Was that one of their steered eggs?" Gurmun asked.

"How should I know?" Rathar trotted toward his headquarters. "Let's see if anyone's left alive in there.

"They don't want *you* left alive," Gurmun said.

"That's all right," Rathar told him. "I don't want them left alive, either—and I'm going to get my wish."

Seventeen

Summer was fading fast in the Naantali district. Fernao had watched that happen before. Setubal, the capital of Lagoas and his home town, didn't have the best weather in the world. Not even the most ardent Lagoan patriot could have claimed otherwise—not when, in peacetime, COME TO BALMY BALVI! broadsheets sprouted like mushrooms on walls and fences every autumn. But even Setubal looked subtropical when measured against the wastelands of southeastern Kuusamo.

Even before nights turned longer than days, the grass started going from green to yellow. Birds began flying north, first by ones and twos and then in enormous flocks. More and more clouds boiled up from the south, so that even when it was daylight, gloom held sway more often than not.

The worsening weather perfectly fit Fernao's mood. The rattle and scrape and bang of hammers and saws and chisels and other tools as Kuusaman construction crews raced to repair the hostel after the Algarvians dropped their steerable egg on it did little to improve his spirits, either.

"Don't worry about a thing," Ilmarinen told him at supper one evening. "If they aren't ready before the snow starts falling, I'm sure all of us Kuusaman mages know the ancient art of building snow houses. We'd be happy to teach it to you, so you can stay as warm and cheerful as we do."

"Thank you so much." Fernao cast about for a word in Kuusaman, didn't find it, and switched to classical Kaunian: "Can you quantify exactly how warm and cheerful you will be?"

"Oh, of course," Ilmarinen said. "Can you provide me with an appropriation to investigate it with all the latest sorcerous techniques?"

Fernao took a tiny copper bit from his belt pouch. "Here you are."

"Excellent!" Ilmarinen scooped up the coin. "You may expect your answer in about ten thousand years."

He laughed uproariously. Fernao laughed, too. Glum or not, he couldn't help it. Ilmarinen worked hard at being outrageous, and was good at what he did.

"What's funny?" Pekka asked as she sat down at the table with them. Fernao explained. Pekka gave Ilmarinen a severe look. "Snow houses, indeed," she said. "When was the last time you made a snow house or herded reindeer like our ancestors?"

"Day before yesterday," he answered, as seriously as if it were true.

Noise from down the hall covered Fernao's snort and Pekka's cough. She said, "I'll tell you what worries me: all those carpenters. I'm sure the Algarvians will have tried to put spies among them."

"Hard for an Algarvian to look like a Kuusaman," Fernao said. That gave him an excuse to look at her and to admire the way she looked. When the steerable egg burst by the hostel, all he'd worried about was whether she was all right. The sorcery they were working on hadn't mattered a bit.

But Pekka and Ilmarinen both shook their heads. "Plenty of masking sorceries," Pekka said.

"A good many of them used against the Algarvians here and there," Ilmarinen added, speaking with considerable authority. He had knowledge and sources for knowledge at which Fernao couldn't begin to guess. "Wouldn't be too surprising if they tried to get some of their own back."

"There are ways to look behind such masks, I'm sure," Fernao said.

"Oh, aye." Ilmarinen spoke with authority again. "Anything one mage can figure out how to make, another mage can figure out how to break."

Pekka gave her order to a serving girl even as she nodded. "That's right. It leaves me with two worries on my mind: that Mezentio's mages haven't done something particularly clever that we don't notice, and that we do our checks on all the workmen and don't let any slip past unexamined."

Fernao called for a mug of ale. When it came, he sipped slowly. The ale gave him an excuse to pick at his supper. Ilmarinen, on the other hand, ate as if he were stoking a roaring fire. Rising from his seat just as the girl brought Pekka's food, he leered down at Fernao. "Don't do anything I wouldn't enjoy," he said, and went off whistling.

"He's a nuisance," Fernao said.

One of Pekka's eyebrows quirked upward. "You just noticed?" she said, and applied herself to her chop.

Well, you got what you wanted, Fernao thought. *You're alone with her, or as alone as you can be inside the refectory with a lot of other people eating, too. Now what are you going to say?*

He didn't say anything. He couldn't say anything. He felt as callow and nervous as he had when a youth calling on a girl for the first time. He just sat there, still picking at his food, sipping the ale, and enjoying her company as much as he could. After a bit, she started talking shop. He had no trouble doing that, save for the occasional word that, like *quantify*, came out in classical Kaunian because he couldn't come up with it in Kuusaman.

He called for more ale and for a mouth-puckeringly tart gooseberry pastry so he wouldn't have to get up and leave as Ilmarinen had. Then he left the pastry half eaten when Pekka finished her supper faster than he'd expected. Getting to his feet in a hurry wasn't easy or comfortable, but he did it anyway.

Pekka noticed, of course. "Are you following me?" she asked, sounding somewhere between amused and alarmed.

"I can't very well leave the refectory without following you," he answered, which had the twin advantages of being true and not requiring him to say *aye*.

It also got a smile from Pekka, who said, "All right."

But Fernao, suddenly bold, went on, "Will you come back to my chamber with me?"

"What? Why?" Now Pekka definitely sounded alarmed. "Are you planning on stopping more scandal? Remember what happened the last time. We just started some—and made our lives more . . . complicated."

"I know," Fernao said. By then, they were out in the hall, away from the crowd inside the eating chamber. "Come or not, however you like. I'm not going to try to molest you. I think you know that much. If you don't, you'd better not come."

He limped on toward his chamber. He still hadn't got used to limping. He didn't know why—he was going to limp for the rest of his life—but he hadn't. He looked down at his feet and at the rubber tip to his cane. He didn't want to look over his shoulder to see whether Pekka was following—part of him didn't want to, anyhow. But he couldn't keep his eyes from sliding toward where she would be if she was . . . and she was. He breathed a silent sigh of relief, then wondered if he should have. He was, he knew, liable to make things worse, not better.

After opening the door to the bare little room, he stood aside to let Pekka in before him. "Sit down," he said, shutting the door behind them. "Make yourself comfortable."

Pekka didn't. She stood there in the middle of the floor like a nervous bird that would fly away the instant it saw the slightest motion. The comparison, Fernao feared, was liable to be all too apt.

"What is it?" Pekka asked in tones as brittle as her stance. "What did you need to bring me here to say? Should we have anything to say to each other that we can't say where everyone can hear?"

"I don't know. By the powers above, I don't." But Fernao remembered how they'd clung after the Algarvian egg burst by the hostel, when each had feared the other dead. He took a deep breath and went on in a rush: "By the powers above, though, I do know that I love you. I've never felt like this about any other woman before, and I'm not interested in feeling like this about any other woman ever again. There. That's all."

Pekka turned and took a long step toward the door. Fernao thought she was going to flee on the instant. If she did . . . What would he do if she did? *Get drunk and stay drunk for a week* was the first thing that came to mind.

But she stopped and turned back so suddenly, it was more like a whirl. Her face was as pale as he'd ever seen it. "Why did you have to go and say a thing like that?" she demanded, and she sounded furious.

"Because it's the truth, curse it," Fernao answered stubbornly, hopelessly. "Because I didn't care whether I lived when that egg came down till I saw you were all right. If that isn't reason enough, what is?" He sounded angry, too, and he was—angry at the world that wouldn't let him have what he wanted most.

Pekka stared at him. She'd gone even whiter, and he hadn't thought she could. Tears glistened in her eyes, as they had after she'd made love with him that first—and only—time. In a tiny voice, hardly more than a whisper, she said, "If I told you I felt the same way, what would you do?"

Fernao's cane almost slipped from his fingers. Having hoped for words like those, he had trouble believing he'd really heard them. He also had trouble coming up with an answer. Almost too late, he realized words weren't what he needed. He did let the cane fall, but only because he'd taken Pekka in his arms. He bent down to her at the same time as she was tilting her face up to him.

Not very much later, and without another word between them, they lay down close together on his bed. They had to lie close together; the bed was too narrow for anything else. Pekka sighed as Fernao went into her. But her eyes were shut. Then, though, with what Fernao thought a deliberate act of will, she opened them and looked up at him from a distance of only a couple of inches. And then, for a little while, Fernao stopped thinking at all.

Afterwards, he wondered if she would bolt from his chamber as she had the first time. They'd surprised themselves by becoming lovers then. This time, they'd known what they were doing. And Pekka understood as much, for she asked, "What are we going to do now?" It was a serious question, not the dismay-filled one she'd asked after they joined before.

"Whatever you like," he answered. "I know you're the one with the hard choices to make. You need to know I'd be glad to marry you and live with you in Kajaani or Setubal or wherever you please, if that's what you want to do. I hope it is."

"I don't know," Pekka said. "Right now, I have no idea what I'm going to do. I have to th—"

Fernao knew what he was going to do right then, and he did it: he kissed her. That not only kept her from talking, it kept her—and him—from thinking for some time longer. He hadn't known he could make love twice in such quick succession, not in his mid-thirties and not after the battering his body had taken.

But, no matter how pleasantly worn he and Pekka were after gasping their way to delight for a second time, Pekka asked her question over again: "What are we going to do now?"

"We'll just have to see," Fernao said. Pekka frowned thoughtfully, then nodded.

Colonel Sabrino had never been in Yanina before. When the war against Unkerlant began, he'd been stationed in the north, flying out of Forthweg. He wished with all his heart he weren't in Yanina now. Had the Algarvians and Yaninans and Grelzers and the soldiers from Plegmund's Brigade and the Phalanx of Valmiera been able to halt King Swemmel's latest bludgeon of an assault, he wouldn't have been in Yanina. As things were . . .

As things were, the tattered remnants of his wing of dragon-fliers and the equally ragged remains of Major Scoufas' were flying out of a makeshift dragon farm on the outskirts of the town of Kastritsi, north and west of Patras, King Tsavellas' capital. The Unkerlanters had paused only a couple of miles outside of Kastritsi; the people there fled east as fast as they could go, on foot or in wagons or on unicorns and horses and donkeys. They clogged the roads, making it harder for the soldiers trying to hold back Swemmel's men to get where they needed to go.

Some of the men fleeing Kastritsi should have been in Tsavellas' army. Some of them, almost without a doubt, were in Tsavellas' army, but had somehow got their hands on civilian clothes.

When Sabrino remarked on that, Captain Orosio nodded. "Next thing'll be, they'll start running without bothering to take their uniforms off first." He spat. "It won't be long, I bet."

"I wish I thought you were wrong," Sabrino said.

"So what in blazes are we going to do about it?" the squadron commander asked.

Before answering, Sabrino looked toward the center of Kastritsi. The taller buildings—those still standing, anyway—sported strangely painted onion domes that reminded him he was in a foreign kingdom. He sighed. "I don't think we *can* do anything about it except to go on fighting the Unkerlanters as hard as we can for as long as we can. Have you got any better ideas?"

Orosio sighed, too, and spat again. "I was hoping you did, sir. You've been right a lot of times before."

"What if I have?" Sabrino said. "How much good has it done me? How much good has it done Algarve?"

Orosio had no reply for that. Since Sabrino didn't, either, he didn't see how he could blame the younger man. From over by the tents where the dragonfliers slept—when they slept—a Yaninan waved to him. He waved back, polite as usual. Then the Yaninan waved again, more urgently this time. Captain Orosio said, "Sir, I think he wants you."

"I think he does, too," Sabrino said with another sigh of his own. "I was hoping he didn't."

"Major Scoufas, he want to see you," the fellow said when Sabrino went over to him.

"Does he?" Sabrino said, and the Yaninan dipped his head in his kingdom's gesture of agreement. Sabrino headed for Scoufas' tent. He had nothing against the Yaninan officer. Scoufas made a good dragonflier and a good wing commander. It wasn't his fault that most of his kingdom's fighting men were unenthusiastic and that the kingdom lacked many of the tools it needed to do a proper job of fighting.

As often happened with commanders, Scoufas was busy with paperwork when Count Sabrino ducked into his tent. Scoufas shoved the leaves of paper aside with every sign of relief. "I propose that we fly forth and attack the Unkerlanters threatening Kastritsi," he said.

"You do?" Sabrino said in some surprise. In all the time he'd been associated with the Yaninans over in the Duchy of Grelz, he'd never heard such words from any of them. Scoufas flew more than bravely enough, but he hadn't been aggressive in seeking out missions.

But now the Yaninan dipped his head. "Aye. We must drive the barbarous invaders from the soil of my kingdom."

If your countrymen had fought harder in Unkerlant, those barbarous invaders might not be on the soil of your kingdom now. But what point to saying that to Scoufas? He couldn't change what had already happened, any more than Sabrino himself could.

And, as far as Sabrino was concerned, helping Scoufas defend a Yaninan town now made it less likely that he'd have to try to keep the Unkerlanters from overrunning an Algarvian town some time in the not too indefinite future. The mere thought was enough to make him nervously glance eastward.

Scoufas not only noticed him doing it but understood why. The Yaninan's chuckle held more sorrow than mirth. "It makes a difference when it is one's own kingdom, does it not?" he said.

"Aye," Sabrino said harshly. "Have we got enough eggs and cinnabar to give the Unkerlanters a proper pounding?"

"Not so much as we would like," Scoufas answered. "Never so much as we would like, is it not so?" He waited for Sabrino to nod, then went on, "But we must do what we can with what we have—is that not so as well?"

"Aye," Sabrino repeated, even more harshly than before. "When do you want to fly?"

"Let the dragon handlers load eggs aboard our dragons. Let them give the beasts what meat they have laced with brimstone and with what cinnabar they can find," the Yaninan wing commander said. "An hour's time should be plenty, would you not agree?"

Sabrino rose and bowed. "I shall be honored to have your company in an hour's time, Major." He bowed again, then strode out of Scoufas' tent and shouted for his own men to ready themselves for a raid.

They came from their tents with an eagerness that still delighted him after five years of fighting. *How can anyone beat us?* he thought proudly. But if that question didn't have an answer, what was he doing fighting here in Yanina and not going after the Unkerlanters in their own kingdom or relaxing back in Trapani following a victorious war?

"Yaninans are a lot happier about fighting now that they're doing it at home, aren't they, Colonel?" one of the dragonfliers said.

"As long as they *are* happy," Sabrino said—again, what point to worrying about how things had been before?

He climbed aboard his dragon while the bushy-mustached Yaninan handler was still feeding it chunks of meat yellow with brimstone or scarlet with cinnabar—too few of the latter, though. Brimstone was easy to come by. Quicksilver . . . He thought about Algarve's failure in the land of the Ice People and his kingdom's failure to reach the Mamming Hills, then realized he was worrying about what had gone before whether he wanted to or not.

With a wave, the handler unchained the dragon from its stake. "Luck to you good," the fellow said in rudimentary Algarvian. Sabrino waved back, then booted the dragon into the air. It rose with a scream of fury and a thunder of wings. Other beasts painted in Algarvian and in Yaninan colors joined it. Between them, they had about forty dragons.

The raid . . . was a raid. Sabrino wondered how many hundred he'd flown in the course of the war. The dragons dropped their eggs on the Unkerlanters busy digging themselves in west of Kastritsi, then swooped low to flame whatever men and beasts they could catch out in the open. Swemmel's soldiers had a good many heavy sticks. A couple of Yaninan dragons tumbled out of the sky. Sabrino didn't see any Algarvian dragons go down. He hoped he hadn't missed anything. *I'll find out after we fly home,* he thought.

His dragon's flame was shorter than it should have been, and faded faster. All the Algarvian and Yaninan animals had the same predicament. Major Scoufas appeared in one of the crystals Sabrino carried. "We have done what we can do, I think," Scoufas said.

"I think you're probably right," Sabrino agreed.

"We have hurt them," Scoufas said.

"No doubt of it," Sabrino said. The raid was a pinprick, a fleabite, nothing more. If it delayed the fall of Kastritsi by so much as an hour, he would have been astonished. Scoufas was no fool. He had to see that, too. But, these days, even delays of less than an hour to the relentless Unkerlanter advance were not to be sneezed at. Sabrino spoke into the crystal attuned to his own squadron leaders. They pulled their men out of the attack and flew back with the Yaninans toward their latest dragon farm.

No Unkerlanter dragons had paid the farm a call while the Algarvians and Yaninans flew on the attack. The bushy-mustached dragon handler chained Sabrino's mount to its stake once more. He waved to Sabrino as the Algarvian wing commander descended from the beast. Sabrino managed a nod in return.

Not too far away, a Yaninan crystallomancer trotted up to Major Scoufas. They put their heads together. After a moment, Scoufas jerked as if stung by a wasp. He said something loud and pungent in Yaninan, then abruptly fell silent. Sabrino wondered what was going on. He shrugged. It looked to be a purely Yaninan concern, and he had plenty of troubles of his own. With a weary sigh—flying dragons was, by rights, a young man's game—he trudged off to his tent.

A few minutes later, Scoufas stuck his head through the flap and said, "May I come in?"

"Of course, Major," Sabrino said in some surprise; he usually visited Scoufas rather than the other way round. "Let me get you something wet and strong."

"I thank you, but no," Scoufas replied. "When I am done, you will not care to drink with me, I fear. I have been honored to fight alongside you, Your Excellency—always remember that."

Sabrino didn't know just what Scoufas meant, but didn't like the sound of it. "Have you been transferred?" That was the most innocuous explanation he could find.

"In a manner of speaking, Colonel—in a manner of speaking," Scoufas replied. "My kingdom, you might say, has been transferred. As of earlier today, I am informed, Yanina finds herself in alliance with King Swemmel of Unkerlant and at war with King Mezentio of Algarve. I am sorry to be the bearer of such news, but it is something you must know."

"It certainly is." It was also one of the best-timed betrayals Sabrino had ever heard of, but that was neither here nor there. Doing his best to gather himself, he asked, "And are you at war with me, Major?"

Scoufas tossed his head. "No. I wish with all my heart that King Tsavellas had not done this. You Algarvians scorn us, I know, but you did not mistreat our kingdom. What Swemmel will do . . . It may be better than what he would have done had he taken Yanina by conquest. So Tsavellas hopes. Me . . ." He shrugged. "I have my doubts, and so you and your men may fly off wherever you would. I will say I am sorry, but I got the order too late to try to stop you. Good luck, Colonel."

Sabrino bowed. "I thank you. You are a gentleman. Would you care to fly with my men? Believe me, you would be most welcome."

"Thank you, but no," Scoufas said. "Whatever else I am, I am a Yaninan."

"I understand, Major." Sabrino bowed again. What he didn't understand was what would happen next—or rather, how anything good for Algarve could possibly happen next.

"It's another fornicating new kingdom," Sidroc said as he tramped through a town somewhere in western Yanina. "If this futtering war ever ends and we get back to fornicating Forthweg, we can set up as fornicating tour guides."

Ceorl barked laughter. "I like that. I'd go on a fornicating tour any day. Best kind of tour to go on, you ask me." He rocked his hips forward and back.

"Where in blazes are we, anyway?" Sergeant Werferth asked.

This wasn't exactly Plegmund's Brigade any more. It was a collection of men who'd got out of the Mandelsloh pocket in one piece: Forthwegians, Grelzers, blonds from the Phalanx of Valmiera, Algarvians, Yaninans. The Algarvians' assumption seemed to be that, since they'd managed it when so many hadn't, nothing could hurt them now. Sidroc hoped the assumption was right.

"All right, maybe I won't make a tour guide after all," he said. "The Unkerlanters use one kind of writing I can't read, and the Yaninans use another one. Wherever it is, it's the arse end of nowhere, and the fornicating Yaninans are welcome to it. So are the Unkerlanters, if anybody wants to know what I think."

He and his comrades had spoken Forthwegian, of course. One of the Yaninan soldiers asked, "What you say?" in Algarvian, the only language the men who fought for King Mezentio had in common—when they had any in common at all. "You say of my country the name many times."

"I wondered what the name of this town was—that's all, Yiannis," Sidroc said.

Yiannis looked as if he suspected it wasn't all, but he didn't challenge Sidroc on it. "Of this town, the name is Kastritsi," he said.

"Miserable place, ain't it?" Ceorl said, but in Forthwegian.

Before Yiannis could ask him what that meant, an Algarvian soldier pointed to the outskirts of town. "Look—there's a bunch of dragons taking off."

"Are those the same bastards who flew over us to give Swemmel's buggers a hard time a while ago?" Sidroc asked.

"Hope so," the redhead answered. "The more the Unkerlanters get hit, the slower they'll come after us."

"They're flying off toward the east, not back toward the Unkerlanters," Sidroc said in disappointed tones.

"Must come from this kingdom, then," Sergeant Werferth said—in Forthwegian. He didn't mention Yanina's name, so Yiannis and his countrymen, none of whom knew a word of Forthwegian, noticed nothing amiss.

People on the streets of Kastritsi stared at the retreating soldiers with big, dark, round, solemn eyes. *If you're retreating, their faces said, the Unkerlanters will come next.* They didn't seem to look forward to meeting King Swemmel's men. A good many of them were getting out of Kastritsi while they could. Sidroc understood that. He wanted to get out of Kastritsi, too.

And he did get out of the town, though the refugees slowed down the couple of regiments' worth of men of which he was a part. He kept looking anxiously up to the sky. If Unkerlanter dragons appeared overhead, the result would be gruesome.

But the difficulty, when it came, came on the road ahead, not from out of the sky. A company of Yaninan soldiers in very clean uniforms that showed they'd seen little action were letting the refugees from Kastritsi—and from other towns farther west—go through, but they spread across the road and the fields to either side when they saw the armed men heading their way.

Their commander, a skinny little captain, stepped forward and held up his hand, palm out, like a constable halting traffic at a busy street corner. He sounded like one, too, when he spoke in Algarvian: "You are to halt. Who of you is the commander?"

That was a pretty good question. Sidroc wasn't sure anyone would, or could, answer it. He and his comrades were almost as much refugees as the people fleeing Kastritsi. He had nothing left but his looks to show he was a Forthwegian—and, for the life of him, he couldn't imagine why Algarvians were kilts. To him, they were miserable, demonically uncomfortable things.

But the rangy Algarvian major who strode out in front of the motley group of men of which Sidroc was a part wore his ragged kilt with panache. "I guess I am," he said. "What's your skirmish line here all about, Captain? It doesn't look what you'd call friendly."

"It is not supposed to be friendly," the Yaninan officer replied. "Yanina is as of today the ally of Unkerlant. Yanina is as of today the enemy of Algarve and of all kingdoms allied with Algarve. You will all of you put your sticks on the grounds and your hands in the air. You are our captives."

"Oh, we are, are we?" the Algarvian officer said, looking down his nose at the captain who'd called for his surrender. The Yaninan dipped his head, plainly confident the redhead would do as he was told. But the Algarvian had other ideas. He turned back to the soldiers he led and shouted, "Come on, boys—let's take 'em! You want to let 'em hand us over to the Unkerlanters?"

He toppled in the next instant, blazed by three Yaninans at the same time. But nobody who'd fought in the west wanted to fall into Unkerlanter hands. And, while Sidroc didn't know about anybody else, he was cursed if he wanted to surrender to a bunch of Yaninans who looked as if they'd never done any real fighting in all their born days. He took a blaze at a Yaninan who made a pretty clear target. The man went down with a howl.

And Sidroc wasn't the only one. The veterans who'd faced everything Swemmel's hordes had thrown at them weren't about to let a handful of Yaninans push them around. Shouting, "Mezentio!" they deployed from column into line and rolled over Tsavellas' men. Some of them did fall, but not very many—the Yaninans who'd been sent out to stop them didn't really seem to believe till too late that they would fight back.

It was all over in a couple of minutes. Of the Yaninans who didn't get blazed, some fled and rather more threw their hands high and gave up. Sidroc laughed as he collected the stick from one of those. "Why did they think *we'd* give up?" he said. "It's all they're good for themselves."

"That may well be why," a blond from the Phalanx of Valmiera said. "But what do we do now that Yanina has turned against us? It is not just this one company. It is the whole cursed kingdom."

Sidroc hadn't thought of that. "Are we going to have to fight our way through this whole cursed kingdom, like you said?"

"Who knows?" The Valmieran shrugged. "I will say this: I would sooner fight Yaninans than Unkerlanters any day." Sidroc nodded. The fellow from the Phalanx might be nothing but a fornicating Kaunian, but he wasn't a stupid fornicating Kaunian.

With the Algarvian major dead, the highest-ranking officer left on his feet was a lieutenant who had to be a couple of years younger than Sidroc. When he called out, "Crystallomancer!" his voice broke and squeaked like a youth's.

Did they have a crystallomancer with them? Sidroc wouldn't have bet on it, but one of the Valmierans stepped forward. "Aye, sir?" he said.

His blond hair seemed to startle the lieutenant, but the officer told him, "See if you can find out where there's a garrison we can attach ourselves to." The man from the Phalanx of Valmiera saluted and went about his business. The Algarvian lieutenant raised his voice—and kept it from cracking: "All you Yaninans who've been with us, you have a choice. You can stay with us and go on fighting Swemmel, or you can lay down your sticks and your packs and walk away from the war right now."

A couple of dozen men who'd fought in Unkerlant did walk away. Sidroc wondered what he would have done had someone offered him the same choice. *I'd stay,* he thought. *Nobody made me sign up for Plegmund's Brigade. I did it myself.* And most of the Yaninans stayed, too.

"We'd better keep an eye on them," Sergeant Werferth murmured in Forthwegian. "No telling what they'll do if they have to keep blazing at their own people."

The crystallomancer said, "Sir, we have forces toward the southeast, about ten miles from here."

"We'll head that way, then," the Algarvian lieutenant said. A moment later, he asked, "Did they say what's going on in Patras? It lies in that direction, too."

"There's fighting there, sir," the crystallomancer replied. "There's fighting all over Yanina, as best I can tell."

"How are we supposed to hold off the Unkerlanters if we've got these Yaninan whoresons nipping our ankles at the same time?" Sidroc asked.

Ceorl said, "We kick 'em in the balls a few times, they'll stop biting."

"Hope so," Sidroc said. Along with his comrades, he started trudging toward that other force loyal to Mezentio. He'd been retreating before. Now he was retreating through hostile country. He knew the difference. Unkerlant had taught it to him.

Movement now could turn into battle without warning. If a couple of regiments of Yaninans came over that low hill . . .

They didn't. Along the road, a few men loyal to Tsavellas blazed at Sidroc and his comrades from whatever cover they could find. Methodically, the Algarvians and Forthwegians and Valmierans and the Yaninans who'd stayed with Mezentio's men hunted them down and killed them.

When they marched through a village, people called out in broken Algarvian: "Save us from Unkerlanters!" They didn't know their sovereign had chosen the strategic moment to change sides.

"You'd better get the blazes out of here," Sidroc called back. "Those bastards will come and eat you for breakfast." Someone translated that into gurgling Yaninan. The villagers exclaimed in horror. Some of them started fleeing east with no more than the clothes on their backs.

"Curse it, keep your fool mouth shut," Sergeant Werferth snapped. "Now those miserable Yaninans will clog the roads for everybody else."

"Sorry, Sergeant." But Sidroc wasn't sorry. He had all he could do to keep from laughing out loud as he left the Yaninan village. He nudged Ceorl. "Didn't they look like a flock of spooked chickens?"

"Sure did," Ceorl said. After another few paces, he added, "You're not such a bad son of a whore after all."

"Thanks. You, too." Sidroc grinned. Ceorl grinned back. In Forthweg, he'd been a ruffian, a robber, probably a murderer. Here, he was a comrade. Sidroc didn't worry about what he did in his spare time. And Ceorl, evidently, had at last forgiven him for not being rough enough.

Just after sunset, they joined up with the Algarvian brigade the crystallomancer had found. Sidroc wasn't far from the lieutenant who led his group when that worthy asked the colonel in charge of the brigade, "Sir, what are we going to do now? What *can* we do now?"

"Fall back," the colonel answered. "There's higher ground farther east. They won't have such an easy time pushing us off it. We *have* to hold there—nothing but Algarve behind." The lieutenant nodded earnestly. Sidroc nodded, too, in a different way. The lieutenant thought everything would be all right once they got to the high ground, wherever it was. Sidroc had done enough retreating by now to doubt whether everything would ever be all right again.

Pekka had had to beg the Seven Princes to get a few days' leave from the sorcerous project in the Naantali district. She'd put Raahe and Alkio jointly in charge while she was away. They were solid and steady, not given to wild adventurism. She'd also advised them to smack Ilmarinen over the head with a rock when and as needed.

Getting from the Naantali district back down to Kajaani was an adventure in and of itself. The carriage ride from the hostel to the nearest ley-line terminal was long and bumpy. Then, thanks to the way the earth's energy grid in that part of the world ran, she had to go around three sides of a rectangle before finally heading south to her home town.

And she did every bit of it with a smile on her face, which wasn't like her. Small inconveniences didn't bother her, while larger ones seemed small. *This is what falling in love does,* she thought. *I remember. I didn't think I'd ever feel this way again. But I do.*

It wasn't that she'd stopped loving Leino. That made what she felt for Fernao seem stranger, but didn't make it go away. Leino was far away, in time and space, while Fernao . . . Her whole body felt warm when she thought about Fernao, though the Kuusaman landscape outside looked as bleak and chilly as it always did in autumn.

The ley-line caravan glided over the last low hills and down toward the harbor of Kajaani. "Coming up on Kajaani," the ticket-taker said as he strode through the cars—as if anyone could doubt where this particular caravan was going. "Coming up on Kajaani, the end of the line," he added—as if anyone seeing the gray, whitecap-flecked ocean ahead could doubt that, either.

Grabbing her carpetbag from the rack above her seat, Pekka was among the first out the door when the caravan halted under the steep roof of the depot. There stood her sister Elimaki, waving. And there beside Elimaki was . . .

"Uto!" Pekka squealed, and her son ran to her and squeezed the breath out of her. "Powers above, how big you've got!" she said.

"I *am* big," he answered. "I'm nine." He picked up the carpetbag she'd dropped to hug him. "I can carry this," he said importantly, and he was right.

Nine, Pekka thought, a little dazed. But he was also right about that, of course. He'd been four when the Derlavaian War started. The world had spent more than half his lifetime tearing itself to pieces.

Pekka had thought she would tear herself to pieces, too, with guilt, when she saw her son. But that didn't happen, either. She still loved him as unreservedly as ever. Aye, seeing him reminded her of Leino. But it wasn't that she didn't love Leino. *It really isn't,* she though, as if someone had insisted that she didn't. She felt as if she loved everybody—except the Algarvians. Them she still hated with a hatred whose cold viciousness astonished her whenever she paused to look at it.

She didn't have to look at it for long, because here came Elimaki behind Uto. "Good to see you again," Pekka's sister said as the two of them embraced and kissed each other on the cheek. "It's been too long. It's always much too long between your visits."

"I'm busy." Pekka mimed exhaustion and falling to pieces to show how busy she was.

Laughing, Elimaki said, "You must be doing something important." When Pekka didn't answer right away, her sister nodded to herself. "I know lots of people who don't talk about what they're doing these days."

"I *can't* talk about what I'm doing," Pekka said.

Elimaki nodded again. "That's what they all say. Come on, let's get up to the houses." They'd lived side by side for years. "It's getting dark."

"Of course it is," Pekka said. Kajaani lay even farther south than the Naantali district, which meant fall and winter here were even darker and gloomier. As they hurried out of the depot, she asked, "How is Olavin?"

It was, she thought, a harmless question. Elimaki's husband wore uniform, aye, but he'd been a banker before the war and was a paymaster nowadays—he came nowhere closer to battle than Yliharma. Pekka was astonished when her sister stopped in her tracks and spoke in a low, toneless voice: "Oh. You must not have got my last letter yet."

"I never get them as fast as you think I should," Pekka answered. "They always read them and scratch things out first. What's happened?"

Voice still flat, Elimaki said, "He's taken up with one of his pretty little clerks, that's what. He wants to leave. Our solicitors are snapping at each other."

"Oh, no!" Pekka exclaimed.

"Oh, aye." Elimaki smiled wryly. "I doubt I'll ever see him again. Right now, I hope I don't. He always thought he was too big for a provincial town like Kajaani. Now he gets to try his luck in the capital, and on someone else, or maybe on a lot of someone elses. He *is* sending me money for the house. He's always been scrupulous about money. Other things . . ." Pekka's sister shrugged. "And how are *you*?"

"I don't know. I think I'm stunned." Pekka had intended to unburden herself to Elimaki. If she couldn't talk about men and life and love with her own sister, with whom could she? The answer to that looked to be, *no one*.

"Uncle Olavin is a louse," Uto said.

Elimaki laughed a harsh laugh. "I've called him a lot worse than that, but I try not to do it where Uto can hear. He picks up enough bad language without learning it from me." Uto looked proud when his aunt said that. Pekka had to stifle a giggle. Uto had always delighted in the mischief he caused.

They took the local ley-line caravan to the stop where Pekka had got out so often on her way home from Kajaani City College. Then they walked up the hill to the lane with her house and Elimaki's beside it. By then, full darkness had fallen. Lights were few and far between. Pekka worried more about slipping and turning an ankle than about footpads. Robbers were few and far between in Kajaani: an advantage to provincial towns, though Kuusamans generally were law-abiding folk.

Elimaki's house lay closer to the opening of the lane than did Pekka's. "Why don't you come in with me?" her sister said. "I'll fix some supper and something for both of us to drink, and we can go on from there."

"That sounds wonderful," Pekka said.

"What's wonderful is to see you," Elimaki answered. "Now I have someone I can let my hair down to." She sighed. "I'm jealous of you and Leino. Isn't that terrible?"

Pekka's ears heated. "Not really." She changed the subject in a hurry: "I'll help in the kitchen."

Elimaki didn't let her do much, but she did fix them both stiff drinks. Uto hung around while the halibut steaks cooked. He stared wide-eyed at his mother all through supper. Elimaki, these days, surely felt more like a mother to him than Pekka. After supper, though, he hurried off to play. Before long, a horrible crash came from a back room. "What was that?" Elimaki called as she and Pekka carried dishes back to the kitchen to wash them.

"Nothing," Uto answered sweetly. Pekka snickered. She knew *that* tone altogether too well.

She and Elimaki had a couple of more drinks while they did the dishes, and they took more brandy out to the parlor. Eventually, Elimaki called Uto and told him to go to bed. He sent Pekka the look of appeal she knew too well and hadn't seen in too long. "Do I have to, Mother?"

"Is this the time you usually go to sleep?" Pekka asked. *Powers above! I don't even know!* Reluctantly, Uto nodded—Elimaki would give him the lie if he did anything else. "Then you do," Pekka told him. "But come give me a kiss first." He ran to her. They clung to each other. Then, with less fuss than she'd expected, he went off to the back of the house. Pekka glanced over to Elimaki. "He's growing up." She emptied her glass.

"Aye—when he feels like it," her sister said. "He's probably reading under the covers for a while. Sometimes I let him get away with that." Elimaki drained her glass, too, then poured it full again and filled Pekka's with it. "You haven't said two words about yourself since you got off the caravan car."

"Well . . ." Discretion warred with brandy. For the moment, discretion won. Pekka said, "There are a lot of things I can't talk about." She could hear the beginning of a slur in her words. Brandy hadn't lost by much.

"I know *that*," Elimaki said impatiently. "I don't care about what you *do*. I wouldn't understand most of it anyway—I'm no mage. I want to know how you *are*."

"Do you?" Pekka said. Her sister nodded, the motion exaggerated enough to show she'd had a good deal to drink, too. "*Do* you?" Pekka repeated. Elimaki nodded again. And Pekka, surprising herself even as the words poured out, told her.

Silence stretched and stretched after she finished. *I shouldn't have done that,* she thought, and blamed the brandy. But it wasn't just the brandy, and she knew it. One of the reasons she'd come home was to talk with Elimaki about Fernao. Now she'd done it. If only Olavin hadn't chosen the most inconvenient possible time to take up with someone else, too.

At last, Elimaki said, "I don't know what to say. I . . . never expected anything like this—from Olavin or from you. Especially from you, I think."

"I didn't really *expect* it, either," Pekka said, and knocked back the brandy Elimaki had poured her. "It just . . . happened. These things do, sometimes."

"I know. I ought to know." Elimaki's face twisted. She paused again, then asked, "What are you going to do? What are you going to tell Leino?"

"I don't know," Pekka answered. "I just don't know. I haven't the faintest idea in the world. I'll cross that ice when I come to it."

"I *didn't* expect it of you," Elimaki said again. "If anybody in the family was going to go off and take a lover, I thought it would be me. Here I was, sitting at home by myself—except for Uto, and that's a pretty big 'except.' But I . . . sat here. I was lonely, but it wasn't that bad. And now this." Her goggle-eyed look also came only in part from the brandy.

"I know. But—" Pekka stopped, unsure how to go on.

Her sister held up a hand. "Never mind. Your face says it all. If I doused every one of the lamps, you'd still glow."

"Does it? Would I?" Pekka asked. Very solemnly indeed, Elimaki nodded. So did Pekka. "Well, it's the truth. It's how I feel. I know it's not the way I'm supposed to feel, but I do."

"I don't know whether to be green with envy of you or to want to hit you over the head with a brick," Elimaki said. "These things usually don't have happy endings, you know."

"Of course I know," Pekka said. "At least we aren't Algarvic people, where they go to knives sometimes instead of solicitors." And then, even before her sister could say anything, she remembered Fernao *was* of Algarvic blood. That gave her something brand new to worry about. *As if I didn't have enough,* she thought.

Behind Garivald—who was getting used to thinking of himself as Fariulf—lay the Twegen River. Behind him also lay a good many artificers frantically repairing the bridges over the Twegen the Algarvians had knocked down with their sorcerously guided eggs. Ahead of him, to the east, were the rest of Forthweg and all the redheads trying to keep his countrymen and him from taking any more of it.

To the north, smoke rose from the burning city of Eoforwic. Garivald supposed the Algarvians could have given this bridgehead even more trouble than they had if they weren't trying to put down the rebellious Forthwegians in their capital.

That didn't mean Mezentio's men were idle here. Garivald wished it would have. Eggs started bursting not far away. They were of the plain, ordinary, unsteered variety, but if one burst in the hole where he crouched it would kill him just as dead as the fanciest product of inventive Algarvian sorcery. The eggs kicked up great, choking clouds of brown dust. Coughing a little, Garivald marveled at that. Down in the Duchy of Grelz, it would have been raining now—the fall mud time—with snow on the way. Here, rain fell mostly in the late fall and winter, and snow was uncommon. So he'd been told, anyhow. He had trouble believing it, but it looked to be true.

"Stay alert!" Lieutenant Andelot shouted. "They like to attack after they plaster us with eggs. They think that's an efficient way to do things. Our job is to show 'em they're wrong."

"That's right," Garivald said. From what he'd seen of Algarvian soldiers, they were alarmingly efficient, but he had to back up his officer. That was part of what being a corporal was about. And he spoke the absolute truth when he added, "We've got to hold on to this bridgehead, no matter what."

A moment later, somebody else let out a frightened yell: "Here they come!"

Garivald quickly looked every which way. There were the kilted Algarvians loping forward. Some of them shouted, "Mezentio!" as they ran. They still acted as much like worldbeaters as they had when they overran his home village of Zossen. True, they'd been driven out of Unkerlant, but that didn't seem to be because they were bad soldiers, only because there weren't quite enough of them to overwhelm the larger kingdom.

Every which way also included behind Garivald. He'd learned as an irregular to know where he would retreat before he had to fall back. He'd had that lesson brutally reinforced in Swemmel's regular army, too. A soldier who didn't think ahead wouldn't get many chances to think at all.

"Mezentio!" Aye, the redheads still knew their business. As soon as the Unkerlanters started blazing at them, some of them dove for cover and blazed back. Others scrambled forward. Then they flopped down in turn, while the troopers in back of them ran past them and toward the Unkerlanter front line.

"Get up there, curse it!" Garivald yelled at a soldier too deep in his hole to fight. "You've got a better chance if you blaze at them, too."

The soldier couldn't have been older than sixteen. He'd had his father yelling at him back in his home village, not an underofficer with all the savage weight of King Swemmel's army behind him. His father, losing his temper, might beat him. A corporal, losing his temper, could do or cause to be done far worse than that. Garivald didn't think he could ever make himself give a man over to the inspectors for sacrifice, but the youngster didn't need to know that.

And his curses did what they were supposed to do: they got the kid up and fighting. He might want to blaze Garivald along with or instead of the Algarvians, but he was blazing at them. Garivald blazed at one of them, too. The fellow kept running, so he must have missed. He cursed again, this time at himself.

He looked back over his shoulder. If the redheads kept coming, he'd have to scurry back toward that next hiding place. He hoped no one else had marked it—it wouldn't hide a pair of men.

Just as he was about to jump out of his hole and fall back, what seemed like all the eggs in the world descended on the Algarvians. The Unkerlanters had moved a lot of egg-tossers into the bridgehead. A crystallomancer must have reached the men who served them, and the efficient way they responded would have warmed King Swemmel's heart—assuming anything could.

Whatever such efficiency would have done to Swemmel's heart, it wreaked havoc on the Algarvians. Their onslaught petered out, smashed under a blizzard of bursts of sorcerous energy. The ground shook under Garivald's feet—not as it would have when one side or the other started sacrificing, but simply because so many eggs were coming down close to him.

"Take that, you whoresons!" Lieutenant Andelot screamed at the redheads. He was only a youngster himself. This probably seemed like a great lark to him.

"We ought to go after the stinking buggers," somebody said.

But, youngster or not, Andelot knew how to follow orders. "No," he said. "For the time being, we're just supposed to hold this bridgehead."

"When do we break out, sir?" the soldier asked.

"When the generals tell us to," Andelot answered. Garivald found himself nodding. Sure enough, that was how things worked.

Once driven off, the Algarvians didn't resume their attack. From what the handful of surviving old-timers Garivald had talked with said, that was a change from the earlier days of the war. Mezentio's men didn't have the reserves of strength they'd once enjoyed. As far as he was concerned, they were quite bad enough as they were.

Andelot came over to him. "What's up, sir?" he asked cautiously. He didn't like drawing official attention to himself.

"Don't worry, Fariulf—you're not in trouble," Andelot said, which did nothing to keep Garivald from worrying. "I just wanted to say you did a good job of handling that fellow who wasn't blazing at the redheads."

"Oh," Garivald said. "Thank you, sir."

"I think you've got the makings of a good soldier—a fine soldier, even," Andelot said. "Would you like to move up in the army? You might be an officer by the time the war ends. Wouldn't surprise me a bit."

Garivald wanted to become an officer about as much as he wanted an extra head. "Sir, I don't have my letters," he said, thinking that would dispose of that.

"I'll teach you, if you like," Andelot offered.

"Would you?" Garivald stared. "Nobody ever said anything like that to me before, sir. My village didn't even have a school. The firstman there could read, and maybe a few other people, but not that many. I'd give a lot, sir, to be able to read and write." *I could write down my songs. I could make them better. I could make them last forever.*

"It would be my pleasure," Andelot said. "The more men who do know how to read and write, the more efficient a kingdom Unkerlant becomes. Wouldn't you say that's so, Corporal?"

"Aye, sir," Garivald replied. New thoughts crowded in on the heels of his first excitement. *If I do write my songs down, I have to be careful. If the inspectors find them, they'll know who I really am. And if they know who I really am, I'm in a lot of trouble.*

He didn't show what he was thinking. Showing your thoughts could and often did prove deadly dangerous in Unkerlant. He did his best to look interested and attentive when Andelot pulled a scrap of paper, a pen, and a bottle of ink from his belt pouch. He wrote something on the paper in big letters. "Here's your name—Fariulf."

"Fariulf," Garivald repeated dutifully, wondering what his real name looked like. He didn't ask. If he ever got the hang of this writing business, he'd figure it out for himself.

"That's right." Andelot smiled and nodded. "It's not hard, re-ally—all the characters always have the same sound, so you just have to remember which sound each character makes. See? You have an 'f' sound at each end of your name."

"Those both say 'f'?" Garivald asked. Andelot nodded. Garivald scratched his head. "Why don't they look the same, then?"

"Ah," Lieutenant Andelot said. "You use *this* form—the royal form, people call it—for the first one because it's the first letter of a name. You'd do the same thing if it were the first letter of a sentence. The rest of the time, you use small letters."

"Why?" Garivald asked.

Andelot started to answer, then stopped, chuckled, and shrugged. He looked very young in that moment. "I don't know why, Corporal. It's just how we do things. It's how we've always done them, so far as I know."

"Oh." Garivald shrugged, too. Rules didn't have to make sense to be rules. Anyone who'd lived under King Swemmel understood that perfectly well. "All right, you make the one kind of mark for—what did you say, sir?"

"For the first letter of a name or the first letter of a sentence," Andelot repeated patiently.

"Thanks. I'll remember now." And Garivald thought he would. Not least because he couldn't read or write, he had a very good memory.

To his surprise, Lieutenant Andelot thrust the pen at him. He recoiled from it, almost as if it were a knife. "Here. Take it," Andelot said. "Write your own name. Go ahead—you can do it. Just copy what I did."

When Garivald held the pen as if it were a knife, Andelot showed him a better way. Brow furrowed in concentration, he made marks on the paper, doing his best to imitate what the officer had written. "There," he said at last. "Does that say . . . Fariulf?" He nearly made the mistake of using his real name. He might get away with that mistake once. On the other hand, he might not.

"Aye, it does." Andelot beamed at him, so he must have done it right. The officer started to write again, then stopped and fumbled in his belt pouch till he found a bigger leaf of paper.

He wrote a lot of characters on it. "These are the royal form an̶ the regular form of all the letters, in the right order. Do yo̶ know the children's rhyme that helps you remember the orde̶ and the way each letter sounds?"

"No, sir," Garivald said simply.

Andelot sighed. "You really must have lived in the back o̶ beyond." Garivald shrugged again. He probably had. Andelo̶ taught him the rhyme, which had a catchy little tune. H̶ learned it quickly enough to please the lieutenant. "That'̶ good," Andelot said. "That's very good. Here, let me give yo̶ more paper. You can have that pen, too, and here's a bottle o̶ ink. Go practice shaping the letters and keep saying the rhym̶ so you know what each one sounds like. In a couple of days, I'̶ show you how to read more things, too."

"Thank you, sir," Garivald said. He went back to his ow̶ hole, his head as full of that children's rhyme as it had eve̶ been with his own songs. He wrote the alphabet several times̶ reciting the rhyme as he wielded the pen. Then—first lookin̶ around to make sure no one could see him—he wrote *Gari vald* as best he could, being certain to use the royal form o̶ the G.

And then he crumpled up that leaf of paper and threw it i̶ the closest fire. He let out a small sigh of relief as he watched ̶ burn. In Swemmel's kingdom, no one could be too careful. Far̶ iulf he was, and Fariulf he would have to remain.

Istvan raised an axe and brought it down on a chunk of fire̶ wood. The chunk split into two smaller chunks. The Kuusama̶ guards who watched the wood-cutting detail stayed ver̶ alert—axes were real weapons. A few feet from Istvan, Ku̶ was chopping away, too.

"Anyone can tell you didn't grow up cutting wood," Istva̶ said.

"I do it well enough." Kun was touchy about everything̶ That had got him into trouble with the guards at the captives̶ camp a couple of times. It would have been worse trouble if h̶ hadn't managed to talk his way out of most of it.

"I didn't say you didn't," Istvan answered.

"I'll say that," Szonyi told Kun with a grin. "You don't cut as much wood as the sergeant or I do, not even close."

"You're both twice my size," Kun said—an exaggeration, but not an enormous one: by Gyongyosian standards, he *was* on the scrawny side.

Even so, Istvan shook his head. "We'd still do more, even if we were your size or you were ours. Anybody can see that. You waste motion."

"If I were an Unkerlanter, you'd complain I wasn't efficient enough," Kun said.

"If you were an Unkerlanter, you'd still be a lousy woodcutter," Szonyi said. "By the stars, you'd be a lousy woodcutter if you were an Algarvian."

"Algarvians," Kun said, and chopped away at the wood scattered before him with great spirit if not with great efficiency.

"They're strange people." Szonyi paused for a moment to wipe sweat from his face with a tunic sleeve. Like most early autumn days on the island of Obuda, this one was cool and misty, but cutting wood was plenty of work to keep a man warm. "Even the one who speaks our language is strange, and the other three . . ." He rolled his eyes. "They're even worse."

"Makes you wonder why we ever allied with them," Istvan said, leaning on his axe. "They're . . . foreign."

Kun laughed. "Of course they're foreign. They're *foreigners*, by the stars. Did you expect them to be just like us?"

Actually, Istvan *had* expected something like that. The only foreigners with whom he'd had any experience up to now were Unkerlanter and Kuusaman enemies—and trying to kill one another hadn't proved the best way to strike up an acquaintance—and the natives of Obuda, whom he reckoned contemptible because they bowed down to whoever occupied their island. He said, "I expected them to be more like us than they are, I'll tell you that."

"Why?" Kun asked.

"Because we're on the same side, of course," Istvan answered. Szonyi nodded vigorous agreement.

"We're on the same side as the naked black Zuwayzin, too," Kun said. "Do you think they'll be just like us?"

Istvan had trouble believing there really were people with black skins who ran around with no clothes on all the time. It sounded like one of the stories big boys told their little brothers so those little brothers would look like fools when they repeated them to their parents. He said, "I've never seen a Zuwayzi, and neither have you. And we weren't talking about them. We were talking about Algarvians."

"Aye, but you were saying that foreigners shouldn't—" Kun began.

"No to talk!" a guard shouted in bad Gyongyosian. "To work! To chop!"

With something close to relief, Istvan went back to cutting wood. Kun had a way of twisting things till they seemed upside down and inside out. The former mage's apprentice got back to work, too, but he didn't stop talking. *He never does,* Istvan thought, which wasn't quite fair. Kun continued, "Foreigners shouldn't be different from us if we're going to ally with them. I think that's a silly notion."

"No to talk!" the Kuusaman guard yelled again. This time, Kun did shut up—for a while.

After what seemed like forever, the wood-chopping detail finished its work. The Kuusamans carefully counted the axes before sending the captives back to their barracks. Istvan didn't know how anyone could hope to sneak an axe away, but the guards took no chances.

In the barracks, Captain Frigyes and Borsos the dowser and the Algarvian who spoke Gyongyosian—his name was Norandino, which struck Istvan as a thoroughly barbarous appellation—had their heads together. Istvan didn't like that. Both Frigyes and, from what he'd been able to see, Algarvians in general were much too fond of blood sacrifice and the sorcerous power that sprang from it to suit him.

By the way Frigyes looked up in alarm, he and Borsos and Norandino had been plotting something. Whether it had to do with cutting some large number of Gyongyosian throats here, Istvan didn't know. He hoped he wouldn't ever have to find out.

Norandino said something in questioning tones, too low for

Istvan to make out the words. Frigyes answered a little more loudly: "Oh, aye, they're reliable enough. Nothing to worry about with them."

Istvan knew he should have felt reassured, complimented, even flattered. What he felt instead was something a man not from a self-styled warrior race would unquestionably have called fear. He had too good a notion of what sort of bloody thoughts went through his company commander's mind.

Szonyi and the rest of the woodcutters went to their cots and relaxed without the slightest worry—all save Kun, who caught Istvan's eye. Kun didn't say anything. He hardly changed expression. But Istvan knew they were thinking the same thing, and that it appalled them both.

Norandino's laugh rang out. It filled the barracks hall. How could anyone who talked of slaughter sound so cheerful about it? Istvan didn't know, but the redhead certainly seemed to manage. And it wasn't a laugh of anticipation of someone else's trouble, as might have come from a Gyongyosian. By the sound of it, Norandino knew his own neck might be on the line. He not only knew, he thought that was part of the joke.

Or maybe I'm imagining things, Istvan thought as he lay down on his own cot. He stared up at the boards of the ceiling and tried to make himself believe it. He couldn't. Why would Frigyes and a mage of sorts and an Algarvian talk together, if not for purposes of sorcery and sacrifice?

Reliable. Captain Frigyes thinks I'm reliable. Am I? That he could even ask himself the question left him startled. *If I thought he could really do something to win the war for Gyongyos, I might not feel the same. But he can't hurt anything but Obuda, and the fighting's moved a long way from here.*

Which meant . . . Istvan knew what it meant. He knew, but he shied away from following the thought where it had to lead. He glanced over toward Kun, who sprawled a couple of cots away. Kun was looking in his direction, too. Istvan jerked his eyes away, as if he'd caught the other man doing something disgusting. But he hadn't. The disgust was all in his own mind, with much of it aimed at himself.

Kun didn't shy away from logic. Kun would know the choice perfectly well—would know it and know what to make of it. Either you let your throat be cut—or, if you were lucky, your friends' throats—or you let the Kuusamans know what was brewing. Istvan saw no middle ground.

He'd talked about such matters. Talking about them, he discovered, was one thing. Actually nerving himself to speak to a guard? That was something else again. *If I do it, I can never go back. If I do it, I can probably never set eyes on another Gyongyosian as long as I live.*

But that wasn't it, or wasn't the biggest part of it, anyway. *If I do it, will the stars still shine on me? Or will they cast me into eternal blackness once I die?*

Then Borsos said something loud enough for him—and for the whole barracks—to hear: "No, by the stars! I'll have no part of it!" The dowser sprang to his feet and hurried out of the building.

Istvan let out a loud, long sigh of relief. He didn't care who heard him, not right then he didn't. *The stars be praised,* blazed through his mind. *They've arranged things so I don't have to betray my countrymen. Truly they are as kindly as people say.* Even his cot all at once felt more comfortable than it had.

But he soon discovered the stars intended other things than keeping him happy. Captain Frigyes called, "Come over here a moment, Sergeant Istvan."

"Sir?" Istvan said, his heart sinking. He would sooner have gone into battle again in the trackless forests of western Unkerlant than climb to his feet and walk over to the corner of the barracks hall where Frigyes and Norandino the Algarvian sat.

Captain Frigyes nodded to him in a friendly way, which only worried him more. "Now, Sergeant," the company commander said, "I've been telling Norandino here that you're a man with good sense."

"He has indeed. His praise of you would make the stars blush in the sky," Norandino said. That praise made Istvan blush. So did the redhead's whole manner of speaking. Gyongyosian was a language in which a man said what he meant and had done. The Algarvian turned it into something that sounded flowery and unnatural.

When Istvan merely stood mute, Frigyes pressed ahead: "You've said you know Major Borsos, haven't you?"

He knew perfectly well Istvan had said that. Istvan couldn't deny it now, however much he wanted to. "Aye, sir," he said unhappily, and said no more.

Captain Frigyes beamed at him. "Splendid!" He sounded almost as flowery as Norandino. "Then you won't mind talking him into seeing what's good sense, will you?"

"I don't know, sir," Istvan answered, more unhappily still. "I really don't know what you're talking about, sir." That was a great thumping lie, but how he wished it were the truth!

"We want to do to Kuusamo all we can—is that not true?" Norandino said. "And we see only one way of doing anything at all to Kuusamo on this miserable little island. Is that not also true?" He made everything he said seem not only true but obvious.

Istvan had his doubts about what was true. To him, nothing seemed obvious except that Frigyes was daft. Daft or not, Frigyes was also his superior. And so, instead of saying what he thought, he just shrugged.

Norandino looked disappointed. "Oh, my dear fellow," he began, as if he were Istvan's close kin.

"I'll handle this," Frigyes broke in. He aimed a forefinger at Istvan as if it were a stick. "You swore an oath. Are you ready to live up to it, or not? Answer me straight out, Sergeant."

"Sir, I wasn't a captive then, stowed away where I couldn't do Ekrekek Arpad or Gyongyos any good," Istvan said.

Frigyes eyed him with cold contempt. "Begone, oathbreaker. Believe me, I can find someone else to make Borsos see what needs seeing, do what needs doing. And as for you, Sergeant, as for you . . . May the stars forget you as you have forgotten them." Istvan stumbled away, shame and joy warring in his heart.

Eighteen

A sharp, peremptory knock on the bedchamber door woke Krasta in the middle of the night. "Who is it?" she asked muzzily, though only one person was likely to presume on her so. And even he had his nerve, waking her out of a sound sleep.

Sure enough, Colonel Lurcanio spoke from the hallway: "I am a commercial traveler, milady. Can I interest you in a new laundry soap?"

With a snort, Krasta got out of bed and walked to the door. The waistband of her pyjama trousers was getting tight. Her belly had finally started to bulge. Before long, she would have to start wearing a larger size—*and then do it again and again, until I finally have this baby,* she thought with more than a little annoyance.

She'd opened the door before she realized she could have told Lurcanio to go to the powers below. If he suddenly took it into his head to want her at whatever ghastly hour this was, she was ready to give herself to him, no matter how much she might resent it later. Till she knew him, she'd never imagined a man could intimidate her so. No one else had ever come close.

There he stood in full uniform, from boots to jaunty hat complete with jaunty plume. Instead of taking her in his arms, he swept off the hat and bowed. "Good-bye, my sweet, and as much good fortune to you as you deserve, or perhaps even a little over that. Because of you, I have enjoyed Priekule a good deal more than I thought I would." He bowed again.

Krasta swallowed a yawn instead of yielding to it: another measure of how much of an edge Lurcanio had on her. Her wits were still working slower than they might have, whether she showed the yawn or not. "What do you mean, good-bye?" she asked.

Lurcanio smiled. "What most people mean when they use the word. 'Farewell' is a synonym, I believe." But his amusement slipped then, and he defined himself more precisely: "I mean that I am leaving Priekule. I mean that Algarve is leaving Priekule. Perhaps I will come back one day, if the fortunes of war permit."

"You're . . . leaving?" Krasta said. "Algarve is . . . leaving?" He'd warned her that might happen, but she hadn't believed it, not down deep.

"I said so. It is the truth," Lurcanio answered. "Long before the sun rises, I shall be gone."

"But what am I going to do?" Krasta exclaimed—as usual, she came first in her own thoughts.

Her Algarvian lover shrugged. "I expect you will manage. You have a knack for it—and you are pretty enough to let you get away with a lot that would be intolerable from some other woman." He stepped forward and slid his hand under the waistband of her trousers. Instead of fondling her as he'd done so many times, though, he let his palm rest on her belly. "If by some accident the baby does turn out to be mine, try not to hate it on that account." He brushed his lips across hers, then hurried down the stairs without a backward glance.

Krasta took a step after him, but only one. She recognized futility when it hit her in the face. Lurcanio wouldn't stop for her or for anyone else. She turned around and went to the bedchamber window. A small swarm of carriages waited there. Lurcanio came out and said something in his own language as he got into one. The Algarvian drivers flicked their reins. The carriages rattled away. Krasta watched till the last one vanished into predawn darkness.

How many Algarvians were leaving Priekule now, by carriage and on horse- and unicornback and aboard ley-line caravans gliding west? Thousands? Tens of thousands? Krasta couldn't begin to guess. The question nonetheless had an answer. *All of them.* Lurcanio had said so.

What would Priekule be like without redheads strutting through it? Krasta could hardly imagine. It had been too long. *More than four years,* she thought with sleepy wonder. She lay down again. Of itself, her own hand went where Lurcanio's had lain only moments before.

Only a little bulge under there—no sound at all, of course. No movement, either, or none to speak of. She thought she'd felt the baby stir once or twice, but she wasn't sure. "Why aren't you Valnu's?" she whispered to her belly. "Maybe you *are* Valnu's. He had the first chance that day, after all."

By the time she'd fallen asleep, she was more than halfway to convincing herself the Valmieran viscount *had* to be the baby's father.

Rain on the roof woke her—rain on the roof and the sounds of a raucous celebration downstairs. She muttered something vile under her breath. Since she'd started carrying that baby— Viscount Valnu's baby; of course it was Viscount Valnu's baby—she'd needed all the sleep she could get, and an extra hour besides. She started to shout for Bauska, then checked herself. She could hear her maidservant making a racket along with the rest of the help, and Bauska wasn't likely to hear her.

Muttering more unpleasantries, she got out of bed, threw on some clothes (the trousers weren't stylish, but they weren't tight, either, which counted for more), and emerged from her bedchamber. Having emerged, she slammed the door behind her. That should have been plenty to make the servants downstairs grow quiet on the instant.

It should have, but it didn't. Somebody—was that, could that possibly have been, her driver?—howled out a suggestion for King Mezentio that had to be the foulest thing she'd ever heard in her life, and she'd heard a good deal. A moment later, one of the cooks topped it. Everyone down there roared laughter.

Hearing that laughter, Krasta shivered a little. That laughter didn't hold mirth—or rather, not mirth alone. A hunger for vengeance lived there, too. With the Algarvians gone like so many thieves in the night, where would that hunger feed?

"And the same to the twat upstairs!" someone else yelled, which brought more laughter and several cries of agreement.

Krasta shivered again. She'd just had her question answered for her. She wished she knew who'd shouted that last. She would have dismissed him at once, and with a bad character, too.

A moment later, though, she squared her shoulders and marched down the stairs. Those were *servants* down there, after all, and who of noble blood could take servants quite seriously?

They were sitting—some sprawling—around the big dining-hall table, eating her food and swilling down her ale and brandy. Abrupt silence fell when they saw her standing in the doorway. "Here is the twat upstairs," she said crisply. "Now, what do you intend to do about it?"

That should have cowed them. Before the war, it surely would have. Even now, it almost did—almost, but not quite. After that silence stretched, it tore. One of the women pointed at her and said, "Filthy whore! She's got an Algarvian baby growing in her belly!"

Those weren't roars that rose from the servants now. They were growls—fierce, savage growls. Krasta wondered if she should have left Priekule with Lurcanio. She wondered if he would have taken her. Too late to worry about any of that. If she didn't face down the servants this very minute, she would never get another chance. She might never get a chance to do anything else, ever again.

"Smilgya, you're sacked," she said. "Take whatever you have and go."

"You can't tell me what to do any more," Smilgya screeched, "not when you've been spreading your legs for the redheads all this time. Whore! Traitor!"

There sat Bauska, gulping ale and nodding vigorously. Krasta almost sacked her, too, but came up with something better instead: "How is Brindza this morning, Bauska? And what do you hear from Captain Mosco?"

Bauska flushed scarlet. Her half-Algarvian bastard daughter was almost three years old now. The other servants—some of them, anyhow—stared at her, not at Krasta. They'd come to take Brindza for granted. Suddenly they had to remember her mother had had a redheaded lover, too.

And she wasn't the only one, either. Smiling spitefully,

Krasta said, "How many women here haven't bedded an Algarvian or two? You all know the truth." She didn't know the truth herself, but she'd heard a lot of gossip.

When no one came back with an immediate sharp retort, her smile got wider and more spiteful still. Then, in a shrill voice, Smilgya said, "*I* never did, by the powers above!"

"I believe *that*," Krasta replied with flaying contempt: Smilgya was chunky, fifty-five or so, and homely. She let out a shriek of fury, but some of the other servants—mostly men—laughed at her. Krasta pressed an advantage she knew she might not keep for long: "I told you—you're dismissed. Get out of my house."

Smilgya looked around for support. She didn't see so much as she'd expected. Springing to her feet, she cried, "I wouldn't work for anyone who sucked up to the redheads—who sucked off the redheads—like you did, not any more I wouldn't." She stormed away, adding, "I hope your Algarvian bastard is born with the pox, and I hope you've got it, too."

Krasta set a hand on her belly again. This time, she tried to forget Lurcanio's hand resting there in the middle of the night. "That's not an Algarvian bastard in me," she said. *I hope it's not.* Doing her best to ignore her own thought, she went on rapidly: "It's Viscount Valnu's, and you all know what he did to the redheads, and how they almost killed him for it."

"That's not what you've been saying," Bauska pointed out.

"Well, what if it isn't?" Krasta tossed her head. "Would *you* have told Lurcanio you'd been with another man, and a Valmieran at that? Or told your Captain Mosco, when you were riding his prong? I doubt it very much, my dear."

Bauska looked daggers at her. She didn't care about that. She cared about stopping what felt like a peasant uprising from years gone by. Someone chose that moment to hammer on the front door with the old bronze knocker there. That helped distract the servants, too.

"Be so good as to answer that, Valmiru," Krasta said, almost—but not quite—as imperiously as she might have before the war.

The butler got to his feet. Two or three servants shook their heads. One reached out to try to stop him. Valmiru just shrugged and headed for the door. A moment later, surprise filled his voice as he called back, "It's Viscount Valnu, milady!"

"There, you see?" Krasta said triumphantly. The servants blinked and gaped. Bauska's eyes looked big as saucers. Krasta had hoped it might be Valnu, but hadn't dared expect it. She started to hurry to the front door, but changed her mind and took her time. A gaggle of servitors trailed after her, as if wanting to see the viscount for themselves before believing Valmiru.

Valnu's smile lit up his bony face when Krasta strode into the entry hall. "Hello, sweetheart!" he said, and hurried up to plant a kiss on her mouth. "They're gone at last. Isn't it wonderful?"

"It certainly is," Krasta answered, that seeming a better choice of words than a grudging, *I suppose so.* Asking whether Valnu missed certain handsome Algarvian officers didn't strike her as the best idea at the moment, either. Instead, she set a hand on her belly and said, "I'm so glad you came to see us."

Viscount Valnu's smile only got brighter. "Life is full of such interesting possibilities, isn't it?" he murmured, and slipped an arm around Krasta's waist. The staring servants sighed—relief? disappointment? Krasta couldn't tell. She didn't care, either. *I got away with it,* she thought.

Every time Ealstan came home to her and Saxburh, Vanai praised the powers above. These days, he had to sneak back to their block of flats, for the Algarvians had retaken this part of Eoforwic. While Vanai was about her praises, she squeezed in some gratitude that their block of flats remained standing. Two on the other side of the street were nothing but debris.

"What is the point?" she demanded of him one evening. The flat was a grim, dark place; the Algarvians blazed without hesitation or warning at any light that showed, and the shutters weren't all they might have been. It was also chilly—none of the windows had any glass save a few knifelike shards left in it. When the rains came in earnest . . . She didn't want to think about that. So far, the autumn had stayed dry.

Ealstan spooned up the stew of barley and peas and almonds she'd cooked with wood taken from the ruins across the way.

He'd brought back a couple of jugs of wine; they both sipped from them. The water still wasn't working here. Vanai had to carry water back from a fountain on a street corner a few blocks away.

"We've got to keep trying," Ealstan said stubbornly.

"Why?" Vanai demanded. "Can't Pybba see you've lost? You'll only get more men killed if you go on fighting." *You might get killed yourself,* she thought, and made a gesture older than the Kaunian Empire—or so Brivibas had told her, at any rate—to turn aside the evil omen. *I wouldn't want to go on living if anything happened to you. What would I do without you? How would I go on living? Why would I care to?*

But Ealstan shook his head. She could hardly see the motion, there in the gloom. "We have to go on now, and hope for the best. When the redheads catch us these days, they kill us. They won't let us surrender. If Pybba tried to give up, they'd slaughter all our fighters."

"Oh." Vanai hated the weakness and fear she heard in her own voice, hated them but couldn't help them. She was relieved when Saxburh woke from a nap and started to cry.

As she went to get the baby, though, her husband's voice pursued her: "Now the Forthwegian fighters are starting to understand what being a Kaunian in this kingdom was like. They don't much care for it." He laughed without mirth.

Vanai brought her daughter out to the kitchen. As she undid her tunic so Saxburh could nurse, she said, "Stay here with me, then. Don't go back to it at all. You've done enough—can't you see that?"

"If we can drive the redheads out of Eoforwic ourselves, we have a better chance of dealing with the Unkerlanters afterwards," Ealstan insisted.

"So what?" Vanai said. "So fornicating what?" Even in the darkness, she could see his mouth fall open. She went on, "What difference does it make? Between you and Mezentio's men, you've wrecked the city. It won't be the same for the next fifty years. And the Unkerlanters are going to take it away from you or the Algarvians sooner or later anyhow."

"We have to try," Ealstan said again, and Vanai knew argument was useless. Forthwegian patriots were some of the bravest men on the continent of Derlavai. No one would have quarreled with that. They were also some of the most block-headed men on Derlavai. Vanai expected she would have got quarrels there. But she knew what she knew, and Ealstan gave her all the evidence she needed to prove it.

She thought about seducing him to get him to stay here instead of going back to the fighting. Spinello had taught her everything she ever needed to learn about trading favors for something she wanted. But she'd never done that sort of thing with Ealstan, and the idea of starting sickened her. She hadn't married Ealstan, she hadn't borne his child, to prostitute herself with him.

Besides, and even more to the point, she didn't think it would work. Unlike Spinello, Ealstan wasn't one to change his mind because a woman did or didn't go to bed with him. In fact, the next thing she found that would make him change his mind once he'd made it up would be the first.

Even though it was dark, Saxburh felt like playing once she'd been fed and changed. She'd learned how to roll over not too long before, and would do it again and again, laughing each time. Her joy made Ealstan laugh, too, something Vanai hadn't been able to manage.

Eggs burst, not too far away. Saxburh had heard those roars so often, they hardly bothered her any more. She remained intent on what she'd been doing. Vanai envied her. Unlike the baby, she knew the havoc eggs could wreak.

"By the time this is over, there won't be much left of Eoforwic—you're right about that," Ealstan said.

"Pybba should have thought of that before he raised his rebellion," Vanai answered. Saxburh just kept laughing. The pure glee in the sound made Vanai wish she were four months old, too.

"Who would have thought Mezentio's men would fight back like *this*?" Ealstan said bitterly. "And who would have thought the Unkerlanters would sit quiet on the other side of the Twegen and let the Algarvians smash us?"

"Algarvians are Algarvians," Vanai pointed out. "We've

known for years how they're fighting this war. And the Unkerlanters are no bargain, either, except when you compare them to the redheads."

"True. Every word of it's true." Ealstan slammed his fist, hard, into the palm of his other hand. "But seeing it . . ." He hit himself again, harder yet. Maybe he was hoping he could hurt himself.

"You couldn't have done anything to change the way it happened," Vanai said, guessing what was troubling him. "Pybba wouldn't have listened to you even if you tried. Pybba doesn't listen to anyone but himself."

"Well, *that's* true enough," Ealstan said. "Still—"

"No." Vanai did her best to make her voice firm and unyielding. "You've done everything you could. You've done more than anyone could have expected, including yourself. Sometimes things don't work out the way you wish they would have, and that's all there is to it."

"I wish I could say you were wrong," Ealstan told her. "You don't know how much I wish I could say that."

"Oh, I think I might," Vanai said. He thought about that, then nodded. As if to stop thinking for a little while, he picked up Saxburh and cuddled her. She promptly fell asleep. She seemed to do that faster for Ealstan than she did for Vanai. It sometimes annoyed Vanai—she did most of the work of taking care of the baby, so why should Saxburh go to sleep more easily for Ealstan?

When Ealstan set Saxburh in the cradle, she woke up with a yowl. Vanai, feeling vindicated, scooped her out and rocked her till she quieted down again. It didn't take long; the baby *was* sleepy. Vanai got her back into the cradle without waking her.

Ealstan sighed. So did Vanai. "Let's go to bed," she said. With the lights working, it wouldn't have seemed so late. As things were . . .

As things were, Ealstan chuckled and asked, "How do you mean that?"

Vanai considered. Giving herself to him now wouldn't be the same as doing it in the hope of keeping him from going out to try to kill more Algarvians. *And if we don't do it now, we may not get another chance.* She did her best to suppress that thought, as she did whenever ones like it crossed her mind. After a pause almost surely too short for Ealstan to notice, she said, "However you like. If you'd rather just sleep, that's all right."

He snorted. "I'm so far behind on sleep, I don't think I'll ever get even. Come to think of it, I'm pretty far behind on the other, too." He caught her to him. They hurried into the bedroom, each with an arm around the other's waist.

Afterwards, Vanai lay awake for a while, listening to the sounds of war in Eoforwic. Ealstan sprawled beside her, not moving, hardly seeming to breathe. He didn't usually roll over and go to sleep right after making love, but he didn't usually set his life on the line every time he left the flat, either. Jokes about men who rolled over and fell asleep went back at least to the days of the Kaunian Empire, but Vanai couldn't begrudge Ealstan the rest he needed so badly.

Pybba, on the other hand . . . She wished something unfortunate would happen to Pybba. He couldn't have known ahead of time how things would turn out. Who could? All the same, his miscalculation had brought Eoforwic down in ruins, along with his hopes.

All this death, all this wreckage—and even if they had thrown Mezentio's men out of Eoforwic for good, how much difference would it have made to Swemmel of Unkerlant? Even a copper's worth? Vanai didn't think so. Forthwegian pride had done nothing more than leave a lot of Forthwegians dead.

And the Algarvians are killing any fighters they catch. Have they finally run out of Kaunians? Vanai shivered. She moved closer to Ealstan, for warmth and because she didn't want to be alone even if he was dead to the world. Couldn't Mezentio's men take blonds out of Valmiera and Jelgava? Vanai shrugged. Since the Forthwegians in Eoforwic rose up against the Algarvian occupiers, she'd heard little about how the war was going in other corners of Derlavai. If Ealstan hadn't been close to Pybba, she wouldn't have heard anything at all.

She started to set a hand on Ealstan's shoulder, but quickly drew back before touching him. She'd made the mistake of doing that once, and only once. He might be asleep to the point of unconsciousness, but he woke instantly and struck out, as if someone were trying to kill him. Maybe someone *had* tried to kill him while he was asleep. If so, the redhead hadn't managed it—and Ealstan had never said a word about it to Vanai.

Time was, when I had secrets from you, but you had none from me, Vanai thought. *It's not like that any more.* When they'd first come together, the year or so she had on him had often seemed like four or five. It wasn't like that any more, either. Ealstan was a man, with a man's silences hanging about him. The thought made Vanai, at twenty-one, feel very old indeed.

She fell asleep at last without noticing she'd done it. Saxburh let her sleep through the night. Sometimes the baby did, sometimes she didn't. When Vanai woke, gray, gritty light was sneaking through the slats of the shutters. She rolled toward Ealstan, and discovered he wasn't lying beside her.

She cursed in both classical Kaunian and Forthwegian as she got out of bed. He'd gone off to fight again, and he hadn't even said good-bye. He'd done that before, and it never failed to infuriate her. She went out to the kitchen to build up the fire in the stove.

Ealstan had left a note on the table there. That was something: not enough, but something. *I love you,* he'd written in classical Kaunian. *Because I love you, I will be careful.*

She hoped he wasn't lying to make her feel better. And she wished he didn't love Forthweg quite so much. *A lot of good that wish does me,* she thought, and fought back tears.

"Come on!" Skarnu said. "We're going home, by the powers above. I've been waiting more than four years for this day."

But Merkela, instead of scrambling up into the seat of the worn-out old carriage the Valmierans had scrounged up for them from who could guess where, hung back, little Gedominu in her arms. "I don't know," she said, and Skarnu could indeed hear the doubt in her voice. "I never thought I'd go to Priekule and I'm not so sure I want to."

"Dadadadada!" Gedominu said cheerfully. He might even have known what it meant; he sometimes said, "Mama," too, although, to Merkela's annoyance, less often than the other.

"Don't worry about a thing," Skarnu said. "Priekule's *our* city again, Valmiera's city again, and we're going back to settle accounts with all the traitors and collaborators. You weren't afraid to take on Count Simanu, in the days when the kingdom had hardly any hope at all. Now we finally get to pay my sister back for sleeping with that redhead all these years."

That made Merkela brighten, but less than Skarnu had hoped it would. At last, she came out with what was really bothering her: "When we get to Priekule, you'll be a marquis again, and I'll just be a peasant wench."

"Oh, nonsense," Skarnu said, or something rather earthier than that. "When we get to Priekule, you'll be the woman I'm going to marry and spend the rest of my days with. And if any fancy bitch toting a sandy-haired baby instead of a proper blond"—he reached out and ruffled Gedominu's fine, white-gold hair; the baby squealed with glee—"says anything different, I do believe I'll break her pointy nose."

"That won't make the bluebloods like me any better," Merkela said.

She was probably—almost certainly—right. Skarnu was cursed if he would admit it. And he had a point of his own to make: "You're coming into Priekule with an underground leader. You're coming into Priekule *as* an underground leader. If anybody doesn't like it, blaze her."

That got a smile from Merkela. Rather more to the point, it got her to climb into the carriage. Gedominu tried to throw himself out of her arms. He could crawl and pull himself upright, and thought he could do everything. He was wrong, but he didn't know it. Plenty of people older than ten months had the same problem.

Skarnu flicked the reins. The horse, a gelding almost as decrepit as the carriage it drew, let out a resentful neigh but then got moving. Something felt wrong along the roads leading north toward the capital. Skarnu needed a little while to figure out what it was. When he did, he felt like whooping for joy. All he said was, "No Algarvian patrols!"

"I should hope not," Merkela said.

"I've been hoping not ever since the king surrendered," Skarnu answered. "Now the wish has finally come true."

They did run into a patrol after a while: half a dozen armed Valmierans, most of them looking like farmers, four carrying Algarvian-issue sticks, the other two lighter weapons intended for blazing for the pot, and two unarmed men with hands high. When Skarnu spoke the word *Pavilosta*, he might have unleashed a potent spell. "Pass on, sir," one of the poorly shaven irregulars said. "It's our kingdom again, or most of it is."

"We'll get the rest before too long," Skarnu said confidently, and the other irregulars nodded in unison. After the carriage bumped around a corner, Skarnu turned to Merkela. "I wonder what they were going to do with those couple of captives they had with them."

"Nothing good, I hope." No, there was no compromise in Merkela, not when it came to people who might have collaborated with the redheads. And Skarnu only nodded; when it came to such people, he felt very little compromise inside himself, either.

Getting to Priekule took three days. By the way the horse complained, Skarnu might have made it gallop all the way instead of taking it at the slow walk that seemed to be the beast's only gait this side of a dead stop. Little Gedominu was complaining, too, even more loudly than the horse. He didn't like being held so much. He wanted to get down and make trouble.

Another patrol, this one of men in actual Valmieran uniform, halted the carriage on the southern outskirts of Priekule. Again, Skarnu had no trouble convincing them who and what he was. One of them said, "Oh, aye, sir, we know about you. You're the Marchioness Krasta's brother, isn't that right?"

"That's right," Skarnu agreed sourly. "What about it?"

"Well, sir, if what we hear tell is right, she's friendly with Viscount Valnu," the fellow answered. "Valnu, he's been a big blaze in the underground since dirt, or so they say. Good man to be friendly with, if you ask me—and if that's how things really go."

Not knowing what to say to that, Skarnu didn't say anything. He drove past the checkpoint and on into Priekule. "Friendly with Viscount Valnu?" Merkela said. "With an underground leader?"

Skarnu spread his hands helplessly. "I heard the same thing you did. Who knows? Maybe Lurcanio was lying to me when he said what he said. I wouldn't put it past an Algarvian." He flicked the reins. "Or maybe this fellow didn't know what he was talking about. I can't tell you. All *I* know is, she's been with Lurcanio since the redheads marched in, and she never seemed unhappy about it that I heard."

So I have been given to understand. That was how Lurcanio had answered when Skarnu asked if Krasta's baby was his: not a ringing endorsement of her fidelity. Krasta had collected lovers like beads on a string in the days before the war. Who hadn't, back then? Why would she have changed since? She was constant, even in things like inconstancy.

As they went deeper into Priekule, Merkela's eyes got bigger and bigger. "It's so huge," she said. "I never believed a city could be this size."

She'd thought the provincial towns in which they'd stayed were a match for the capital. Now she was finding out otherwise. Skarnu kept looking around, too; he hadn't been here for a long time. Something was wrong. At last, he put his finger on it: "The Kaunian Column of Victory is gone! You could see it from almost anywhere in the city."

"You already knew the redheads knocked it down," Merkela pointed out.

"I knew," he said, "but I hadn't seen it."

A bonfire blazed on a street corner. Skarnu could still see some of the Algarvian signs burning there: signs that had directed Mezentio's soldiers to theaters and eateries and, no doubt, brothels as well. *No longer,* Skarnu thought. *Never again.*

But then another thought went through his mind. *My sister is a whore, no matter what that fellow said.* He shook his head. *I have no sister.*

A downcast woman who'd been shaved bald walked by. People whistled and jeered at her: "Mattressback!" "Algarvian slut!" "Stinking bitch!" She seemed to shrink in on herself even more, trying to become invisible.

"She deserves worse than that," Merkela said, her voice and eyes cold as the land of the Ice People.

"Maybe she'll get it, too," Skarnu said, which seemed to satisfy her.

After what seemed both a very long time and hardly any time at all, they came to the mansion on the outskirts of town. An Algarvian signpost still stood at the entranceway, directing Mezentio's men, Skarnu supposed, to Colonel Lurcanio and whatever he'd done. But then he forgot about that, for Merkela whispered, "You . . . lived here?"

"Aye," Skarnu answered, and saw the astonishment on her face. "And will again—and so will you, if you want to. If you don't, we'll live somewhere else. But first we have some business to finish." He heard his own grimness.

He hitched the carriage in front of the house and handed Merkela down. Then he strode to the door. She followed, little Gedominu in her arms. He hammered at the door with the knocker.

A maidservant opened. She looked half nervous, half haughty. Haughty won. "What do you want?" she demanded, almost as sharply as Krasta might have.

Skarnu knew what she saw: a weatherbeaten man in the clothes of a farmer, with a peasant woman and a brat in tow. What she didn't see was *him.* "Hello, Bauska," he answered, making his voice milder than he'd first intended. "I want to see my sister." He said the words once more, even if they felt like a lie in his heart.

Bauska's eyes kept widening till they seemed to fill her whole face. "My lord Marquis," she whispered, and dropped a curtsy of the sort Skarnu hadn't seen since the Algarvians overran Valmiera. "Come with me sir, and—?" She looked a question toward his companions.

"Merkela, my fiancée," Skarnu said. "Gedominu, my son and heir."

Bauska's eyes got wider still. Skarnu hadn't thought they could. The servant led him inside. He'd forgotten how big the place was. What had he done with all this space? Merkela's eyes were almost as wide as the maidservant's.

A pretty little girl, perhaps three years old, ran by with a doll under her arm. Pretty, aye—but with hair closer to bronze than to gold, and with cat-green eyes. Merkela hissed something under her breath. Harshly, Skarnu asked, "Is she Krasta's, too?"

"No, my lord," Bauska answered quietly. She went pale first, then red. "She's mine. Her name is Brindza."

Merkela started to snarl something. Skarnu shook his head. "Later," he said. "First things first." A little to his surprise, she nodded. They followed Bauska into a drawing room. There sat Krasta and, to Skarnu's surprise, Viscount Valnu. The man from the patrol had known whereof he spoke after all. And Valnu *was* a big blaze among the underground leaders in Priekule, playing the most dangerous of double games with the redheads.

"Skarnu!" Krasta exclaimed, springing to her feet. She knew him, at any rate. Her belly bulged, just a little. "Welcome home!" She threw her arms around him and kissed him on the cheek. Then she pointed to Merkela. "Who is your . . . friend?"

"My fiancée," Skarnu corrected, and gave Merkela's name again, and Gedominu's. His voice like iron, he went on, "I stayed with my own kind, you see."

Krasta glared at him. He looked back stonily, expecting a tantrum from her and not about to put up with one. But she surprised him. One hand went to that bulging belly; the forefinger of the other pointed at Valnu. "Nothing wrong with the blood of my child, not with him as the father."

"*Him?*" Skarnu's eyes swung to Valnu in astonishment. The fellow with the stick had said friendly, but *that* friendly? "You?"

"So I have been given to understand," Valnu said—the exact same words Lurcanio had used. Where Lurcanio had sounded bedeviled, though, he merely seemed amused.

"But . . . But . . ." Merkela seemed about to burst from the outrage trapped inside her that now, against all expectations, couldn't escape.

"I will add that there have been times when the marchioness proved most useful to those opposing Algarve," Valnu said.

Which means there were also times when she wasn't, Skarnu thought. But, plainly, he couldn't just throw Krasta out of the mansion into the cold, perhaps with her head shaved, as he'd intended doing. She saw as much, too, and looked as smug as a mouse with a hole too deep for the cat's paw. That made him want to slap her all over again. *We'll find out,* he thought, but couldn't help sighing. *We won't find out for quite a while, curse it.*

If Ealstan could have blazed the Algarvian major with his eyes, the man would have fallen over dead. The redhead ignored him and all the lesser Forthwegian rebels who stood behind Pybba. He bowed to Pybba, as he might have bowed to a fellow noble in Trapani. "My superiors have agreed to the terms you propose, sir," he said in good Forthwegian.

"All right," Pybba answered heavily. "All right, powers below eat you. We give over the fight, and you treat the men who surrender as proper captives."

"Better than you deserve, in my opinion," the Algarvian said. "My superiors feel otherwise, however, and so . . ." He shrugged one of his people's theatrical shrugs. "The truce will hold till tomorrow noon. At that time, you shall come forth from your holes—those you have left. Anyone who does not yield himself up to us at noon tomorrow shall be reckoned a bandit, and we shall treat him as one when we catch him." He sliced a thumb across his neck.

They'd been doing that all along. Maybe they'd decided it made the rebels fight harder. If treating the Forthwegians as war captives let Mezentio's men regain their grip on Eoforwic, that must have seemed a worthwhile bargain to them.

"Curse you," Pybba said. The Algarvian only bowed again. Then he turned his back and marched away through the wreckage of the Forthwegian capital.

"It's over," somebody said in a dull voice. "Everything's over."

Pybba shook his head. "It's not over till noon tomorrow, when I get to hand myself to the Algarvian general and thank him kindly for not murdering all of us—only most of us. The rest of you"—he looked from one shabby, filthy, disgruntled Forthwegian to the next—"you can surrender, or you can try and disappear. Of course, the redheads will kill you if you try and disappear and don't quite make it."

"Odds are they'll kill us anyhow," Ealstan said. "The ordinary fighters will probably do all right, but us? Why would the Algarvians want to let us live?"

"I'm not telling anybody what to do, not any more," Pybba said. "Look what that already got us. Maybe I'll see some of you here tomorrow, and maybe I won't." Broad shoulders slumped, he strode off.

"I'll be here with you, if they don't blaze me first," Ealstan called after him. Then, stick in hand, he too left the square where the arrogant Algarvian major—as if there there were any other kind—had delivered the surrender terms his kingdom would deign to accept.

As soon as he was out of sight of his comrades, he gently set the stick on some rubble, then took off his armband and tossed it down on top of the stick. He didn't like lying to Pybba, but a lie here might help cover his trail. If he failed to come in to surrender after saying he would, people might think he'd been killed between now and then. Who wanted to search for a dead man?

Of course, if he wasn't careful, people might be right. The block of flats he shared with Vanai and Saxburh lay in a district the redheads had already reconquered. He still had to get there without drawing their notice. They couldn't cover every inch of Eoforwic . . . could they?

He began to wonder in earnest before he'd gone very far. Like cockroaches and lice and fleas, Algarvian soldiers seemed to be everywhere, and seemed intent on making sure none of the Forthwegian fighters got out of the small part of Eoforwic they still held. The Algarvians had mages and ferociously barking dogs to try to keep their foes penned up.

Mages or no mages, dogs or no dogs, Ealstan wouldn't have worried back in Gromheort. He'd known the town his whole life, and felt sure he could have gone anywhere there without having foreigners notice. But he was a relative stranger in Eoforwic himself. Some of Mezentio's men might have been here as long as he had. He didn't know the secret ways a local would.

And even had he known those ways, how much good would it have done him? Not much was left standing in Eoforwic, and most of what might have been secret was now buried. He didn't want to climb over rubble, so he had to skirt it as best he could.

Somewhere close by, a dog growled a warning. Ealstan froze. He wished he hadn't left his stick behind. Without it, though, he could hope to pass himself as somebody who'd never been a fighter. Then a Forthwegian cried out in fright. The dog snarled and barked. An Algarvian shouted, "Halting!" in accented Forthwegian. "Halting or blazing!"

By the sound of thudding feet, the other Forthwegian didn't halt. By the Algarvian's curses, he missed his blaze. "To me! To me! After the whoreson!" he yelled in his own language. More thudding feet told of other redheads rushing to his aid.

Ealstan huddled against the wreckage of what had been a butcher's shop. There'd been plenty of butchery in Eoforwic since the place went up in flames. Three Algarvian troopers ran right past him. None gave him a second glance, or even a first. They knew he wasn't the man their shouting comrade was after.

Whoever the other fellow was, he led Mezentio's men on a long chase, and one that took them away from Ealstan. Seizing his luck, he hurried toward his block of flats. What better time than when all the redheads nearby were going after someone else?

Before long, I'll be in the part of town they've held for a while, and then they won't pay any attention to me. But that thought had hardly crossed Ealstan's mind before another redhead barked out, "Halting!"

Feet skidding on broken bits of brick, Ealstan did halt. The

Algarvian had a stick aimed straight at him. If he tried to run, he was a dead man. He smiled a broad, foolish smile, trying to look anything but dangerous.

The Algarvian, a plump fellow, came cautiously toward him. Ealstan noticed the redhead wore the uniform of a constable, not a soldier. Some small hope blossomed in him; Mezentio's soldiers had proved much more brutal in Eoforwic than the Algarvian constabulary. The plump redhead tried to say something more in Forthwegian, made a complete hash of it, and, to Ealstan's surprise, started over again in slow, bad, but understandable classical Kaunian: "You following me?"

"Aye, I follow you," Ealstan replied in the same language.

"Good." The Algarvian seemed unaware of the irony of his using the speech of the folk his own people killed. Even so, that he knew enough of it to use kept Ealstan's hope alive. Then the constable gestured with his stick, and Ealstan wondered how long his hope—and he—would live. "What you doing here?" the redhead demanded, hard suspicion in his voice.

"I am going home," Ealstan said, which had the advantage of being literally true. "I mean no one any harm." For the moment, that was true, too.

"Likely telling," the constable sneered. "Why you *out*? You being fighter?"

"No, I am not a fighter," Ealstan said carefully. *But if I'm not a fighter, what* am *I doing out and about?* Inspiration struck, in the form of a couple of worthless toadstools sprouting from the dirt next to the bottom couple of courses of a wall. Moving slowly so as not to alarm the constable, he bent, picked them, and held them out. "I was gathering mushrooms, sir. These are very good. Would you like them?"

"No! Not liking!" The Algarvian made a horrible face. "You Forthwegian crazy. Mushrooms? *Faugh!*" The last was a guttural noise of disgust.

But he didn't call Ealstan a liar. That meant he'd been in Forthweg a while, and knew of the passion Forthwegians—and Kaunians in Forthweg—had for mushrooms, a passion Algarvians emphatically didn't share. "May I go now, sir?" Ealstan asked.

With an elaborate Algarvian shrug, the constable shook his head. "How I knowing you not being a fighter, eh?" he said. Ealstan's heart sank. Then the fellow did a very Algarvian thing: he stuck out his hand, palm up.

Trying not to shout for joy, Ealstan dug into his belt pouch and gave the redhead silver. "This is all I have, sir," he said. It wasn't; he wanted to keep some in reserve in case he had to pay off another venal constable or soldier. But he thought it would do.

And it did. The redhead had a belt pouch, too. The coins vanished into it. "Going on," he told Ealstan.

"I thank you," Ealstan said gravely. He thought he remembered seeing this fellow around Eoforwic for a while, and also thought him a human being, or as close to a human being as an Algarvian constable was likely to come.

By the time another Algarvian noticed him, he was well inside the territory the redheads had retaken. The soldier paid him no particular attention; plenty of Forthwegians trudged through the wreckage of Eoforwic, or else scrabbled through it, looking for whatever they might find.

A couple of Algarvians were pasting broadsheets on walls that hadn't been knocked down. Ealstan hadn't seen these before. They showed King Swemmel as a bleeding hog, with his blood spilling out of Unkerlant and pouring over eastern Derlavai toward Algarve and even the lands beyond. Facing the hog stood an Algarvian with a butcher's apron and an outsized cleaver. The legend read, HELP US STOP THE FLOOD!

He'd seen worse broadsheets. He liked the Unkerlanters only a little better than the Algarvians. Plenty of Forthwegians liked them less than they liked the redheads. Plegmund's Brigade might get some new recruits. Of course, with the Unkerlanters already having overrun half of Forthweg, and with them rampaging forward in the south, too, how much good would a few new Forthwegian footsoldiers do King Mezentio? Not much, or so Ealstan hoped.

An Algarvian colonel, a short, handsome fellow with the jaunty ferocity of a fighting cock, was giving orders to some of the men he led: "Come on, my dears. Don't just stand there now that the fornicating Forthwegians have thrown in the sponge. The Unkerlanters are sitting on their arses just across the Twegen. Pretty soon they'll decide they're done with their holiday and get around to fighting us again. We'd better be ready for them, right?"

"Right, Colonel Spinello," one of the redheads said, in the indulgent tones soldiers used when they were fond of an officer.

"We'd better dig in, then," Spinello said. "We'd better do it deep and tight, as deep and tight as I was into that Kaunian girl of mine back when the war was new." He sighed. His men laughed. Ealstan's hands folded into fists. With a deliberate effort of will, he made them relax. *Don't give yourself away*. The Algarvian colonel kissed his bunched fingertips. "That Vanai, she was a special piece, she was. I trained her myself."

Ealstan stumbled and almost fell, though he hadn't tripped on anything. Mezentio's soldiers laughed, as if they'd heard this colonel's stories a great many times before. They probably had. *I shouldn't have left my stick behind after all*, Ealstan thought. *Even without it, I'll find a way to kill him*. But that vow still left his feet unsteady beneath him, as if he were drunk or stunned. *I am stunned. What do I do when I get home to Vanai? What do I say? What can I do? What can I say?* Good questions, all of them. He had perhaps five minutes to find good answers.

Bembo's belt pouch was nicely heavy with silver these days. As he strutted through the streets of downtown Eoforwic—or what was left of them—he was even acting as a constable again, not as a soldier any more. He should have been happy, or at least happier. He should have been, but he wasn't.

Some of the constables had gone back to business as usual the minute the Forthwegian rebels finally surrendered and marched off to captives' camps—those who hadn't tried fitting back in among the ordinary people of Eoforwic, or the survivors thereof. Up in the tropical continent of Siaulia, there were supposed to be big birds that hid from danger by sticking their heads in the sand. Bembo's complacent comrades reminded him of those big birds.

"They won't look across the river," he told Oraste—he had

his old partner back, for Delminio had been badly wounded at the start of the fighting. "It's going to happen, but they don't want to think about it."

"Shut up," Oraste said. "I don't want to think about it, either."

"But you never want to think about anything." Bembo was still no braver than he had to be, but before his spell as a soldier he would never have dared say anything like that to Oraste. "It's different with those other buggers. They want to forget about the Unkerlanters, and how can we?"

Oraste looked west, toward the Twegen. "We'll fight like mad bastards when they cross the river," he said.

"Of course we will," Bembo agreed. "But how much good will it do us?"

His partner's shrug was not the usual Algarvian production. "How much good has fighting the stinking Unkerlanters done us so far?" Oraste asked bleakly. "Sometimes you go into something and you figure you won't come out the other side, that's all. You're futtering stuck, that's all."

Bembo shivered, though the day was mild enough. He watched soldiers methodically preparing defenses against the attack they too knew was coming. One of the soldiers looked up from his pick-and-shovel work and called, "Hey, constable! When they come, you think they'll pay any attention to which uniform you're wearing?"

His laugh, Bembo thought, was singularly unpleasant. His question was singularly unpleasant, too, especially since the obvious answer was *no*. Bembo stuck his nose in the air. That only made the soldier laugh harder.

Forthwegian civilians with hods hauled rubble from hither to yon under the sticks of Algarvian guards. "They might as well be Kaunians," Bembo remarked.

With another one of those businesslike shrugs, Oraste answered, "Better they get their throats cut than I get mine."

"Better nobody gets his throat cut," Bembo said, but Oraste looked at him as if that were beyond the realm of possibility. Given the sorry state of the world these days, it probably was.

Oraste walked on for a few paces, then nudged him in the ribs. Oraste being who and what he was, the nudge sent Bembo staggering sideways and almost knocked him flat. Oraste grabbed him and held him up. "Come over here with me," he said, steering Bembo away from the Forthwegian laborers.

"Why?" Bembo asked. "Do you want to murder me in privacy?"

"Only sometimes," Oraste said patiently. "Not right now. Now I want to make a bet with you."

"Ah?" That got Bembo's notice, all right. "What do you have in mind?"

Before answering, Oraste looked around to make sure nobody but Bembo was in earshot. Then he said, "Name however much you want, and I'll lay you two to one that none of those Forthwegians who gave up ever comes home again. I figure it serves 'em right if we use 'em just like Kaunians."

"We said we'd treat 'em like war captives," Bembo reminded him.

"I know what we said," his partner answered. "And if you think we'll really do it, put your money where your mouth is."

Bembo thought it over. Oraste suggestively jingled his belt pouch. But Bembo hesitated only a couple of seconds before shaking his head. "Find another sucker, Oraste. I won't touch that one. I think you're too likely to be right."

Oraste snapped his fingers. "There, you see? You're not as dumb as you look, and all this time I thought you were."

"Funny," Bembo said. "Ha, ha. Very funny." He paused. "What do you want to bet that the Unkerlanters are getting rid of all the Forthwegians they don't like, too?"

"I'll bet on it, if you want," Oraste said. "Will you bet against it?"

"Me? Are you crazy?" Bembo shook his head again, even more decisively this time. "That's not a sucker bet. That's an idiot bet."

"Never can tell," Oraste said. "Plenty of idiots running around loose in Algarve. A lot of 'em wear fancier uniforms than we ever will."

"And isn't that the sad and sorry truth?" Bembo agreed. "The way things are these days, I don't care if I ever get promoted. All I want to do is get back to Tricarico in one piece."

"Why not wish for the moon while you're at it?" Oras waved toward the west. "You suppose the Unkerlanters wa any of us to get home?" He seemed to have forgotten saying I didn't want to think about Swemmel's men.

Instead of answering, Bembo just sighed. He didn't suppos anything of the sort. He wished he did. He said, "I never wante to meet those Unkerlanter whoresons up close like this."

"You haven't met 'em up close yet—they're still on the oth side of the Twegen," Oraste said. "Well, most of them are, any way. When they're close enough to yell, 'Swemmel!' and bla at you, that's up close. By all the stories, they do worse tha that if they catch you, too."

Bembo's shiver was no little *frisson* of horror, such as I might have known while hearing a scary story at an evening entertainment with plenty of food and good northern wi around. It was too large, too robust, for that. And it had nothir to do with the weather. It was plain, honest fear. If the Unke lanters caught you, bad things happened. That, to Algarvians the west, was an obvious truth.

And the Unkerlanters did not have to catch Mezentio's me to make bad things happen to them. Bembo grabbed Oraste arm. "Dragons!" he shouted. They both dove for cover as th rock-gray beasts swooped down on Eoforwic from Unkerlant dragon farms on the far side of the river.

"Powers below eat them," Oraste said, his face buried in th dirt. Bembo lay perhaps a foot away from him. Between then some sort of nasty mushroom thrust up from the ground. B mbo was amazed some Forthwegian hadn't picked it and take it off as a prize.

A moment later, as eggs began bursting uncomfortably clo by, he found more urgent things about which to be amaze "The whoresons pretty much left us alone while we were figh ing the Forthwegians here," he said. "Why in blazes are the bothering us now?"

"Of course they left us alone then—we were doing them a f vor," Oraste said. "Now we aren't killing Forthwegians wh might cause 'em trouble further down the ley line, so they don have to bother being nice to us any more."

That exercise in cynicism might have upset Bembo more if he hadn't come to a similar conclusion himself. "We need to get to a shelter," he bawled.

"Go ahead, if you want to," Oraste said. "Me, I think you'll get your stupid self killed if you stand up."

Again, he had a point. Bembo stayed where he was. Enough piles of wreckage lay around to do a good job of shielding him and Oraste unless an egg burst right on top of them. Somebody much too close by started screaming. Bembo couldn't tell if he was Algarvian or Forthwegian. Agony, the constable had discovered, sounded the same in any language.

Bembo rolled from his belly to his back. He saw no dragons, but eggs, more of them than ever, kept bursting all over Eoforwic. "They've got their tossers limbered up, too," he said in dismay.

"Well, if they're going to pound on us, odds are they'll pound on us with everything they've got, eh?" Oraste said.

"There won't be anything left of this place by the time they're through with it," Bembo said. "There wasn't much left of it before they started."

"Aye, we took care of that," Oraste said. "And I'm sure it breaks the Unkerlanters' hearts to knock the capital of Forthweg flat."

"What's that supposed to mean?" Bembo asked, punctuating the question with a yelp as a brick or a stone bounced off his belly. He rolled back over onto his back.

"Don't you remember?" Oraste said. "Back before the Six Years' War, we split Forthweg with the Unkerlanters. Eoforwic used to belong to them. As far as old Swemmel's concerned, there shouldn't ought to be any such thing as a Kingdom of Forthweg."

"Well, there won't be if his men keep doing this to Eoforwic," Bembo said. "Or if there is, there won't be any Forthwegians left alive in it."

"After what they put us through, who'd miss 'em?" Oraste said.

"A point," Bembo said. Then new fear ran through him, fear different from the simple, elementary terror caused by knowing that sorcerous energy might sear him at any moment. The only way he could find to exorcise it was to name it aloud: "You don't suppose Swemmel's men are pounding us like this because they're getting ready to cross the Twegen, do you?"

"How in blazes should I know?" Oraste answered crossly. "If you want to find out something like that, why don't you swim across the river and ask Marshal Rathar? He's over there somewhere."

"Oh, good idea. Really good idea." Bembo's voice dripped sarcasm. "Maybe I should ask for leave again. Then I wouldn't be here when the avalanche came down on our heads."

"Futter you," his partner told him. "Everybody in Gromheort wanted to kill you when you got leave once. If you got it again, somebody *would* up and murder you. And besides, by the time you got to Tricarico, how do you know the stinking Lagoans and Kuusamans wouldn't be holding it?"

"I don't," Bembo admitted. "But if you had to get captured, who'd be your first choice to nab you: one of the islanders or an Unkerlanter?"

"My first choice to capture me? A redheaded gal with big tits," Oraste said. "Second choice'd be a blond wench with big tits. It's all downhill from there."

That wasn't what Bembo had meant, which didn't stop him from laughing. Anything that could make him laugh when the world was coming to pieces all around him was something to be cherished. Only later did it occur to him to wonder just how far his standards had fallen. When it did, he wished it hadn't.

Marshal Rathar, as it happened, was not right across the Twegen River from Eoforwic at that moment. He'd been summoned back to Cottbus, and left the fight in the north in General Gurmun's capable hands. "Don't strike till everything is ready," he'd warned the general of behemoths. "The worst mistakes we've made in this war, we've made by hitting too soon."

"Aye, lord Marshal," Gurmun had said. Rathar had wondered if he could trust the younger man to hold himself in. If King Swemmel ordered Gurmun to attack, he would, whether the situation called for it or not. Gurmun had also said, "I envy you."

He assumed Swemmel was recalling Rathar to confer some new high command on him.

Going through papers as the ley-line caravan glided west, Rathar hoped Gurmun was right. He hoped so, but he had no guarantee of it. For all he knew, the king was summoning him to have him blazed outside the royal palace as a warning to others. You never could tell with Swemmel.

Mile after mile of plain, first Forthwegian and then Unkerlanter, slid past before Rathar's eyes. Every time the ley line took him through or past a village, he winced. No village remained intact. Hardly any buildings remained intact. What the war hadn't wrecked, the Algarvians had often deliberately smashed in their long, slow, stubborn withdrawal toward the east. *If we can't keep it, you won't get any use from it, either,* they seemed to say.

And the villages—the whole ruined landscape—looked the same from early morning, when Rathar left the western suburbs of Eoforwic, till the sun set. It would have gone on looking the same, too, had he been able to see longer. All the way to the suburbs of Cottbus, the devastation would have continued—did continue, though shrouded now in darkness. *How many years, how many generations, will Unkerlant need before she is again what she was?* But that was a question beyond the ken even of marshals.

Rathar's caravan car boasted a couch. He fell asleep on it. An aide shook him awake, saying, "Sir, we're in the capital."

"Are we?" He yawned, stretched, and sat up. The ley-line caravan depot remained dark. No Algarvian dragon could reach Cottbus these days—or so Rathar hoped with every fiber of his being—but the fear remained. Unkerlanters had always feared and suspected and admired the energetic redheads from the east. These past three and a half years, the Algarvians had given them fresh reasons for all three.

Descending from the caravan car gave Rathar another anxious moment. Who would be waiting for him down on the ground? His adjutant, Major Merovec? Or some of Swemmel's hard-eyed, dead-souled guards, there to haul him away to torment or death for some slight the king had imagined? Again, you never could tell.

"Good evening, Marshal." The voice was thin and high an would have been inconsequential, but . . . "We have a new tas for you."

Of all the things Marshal Rathar had expected, that Kin Swemmel himself would meet him at the depot was among th last. He wasted no time in going flat on his belly before his sov ereign. The slates of the floor were chilly. So was the air; au tumn in Cottbus was a different business from the mild day he'd enjoyed outside of Eoforwic.

"Your Majesty!" he cried, and poured out Swemmel's re quired praises, with his forehead knocking the cold stone agai and again. Failure to give the king his due would have been a immediate and thorough a disaster for Rathar—though not fo the kingdom—as losing Cottbus in the first desperate winter o the war.

"Arise," Swemmel said when the ritual was done. Rathar go to his feet. The king went on: "Marshal, we are well pleased i you."

"Thank you, your Majesty," Rathar said. If the king praise him in public, he probably wouldn't get knocked over the head

"Come with us to the palace," Swemmel said. "We have good many things to discuss with you, and they will not wait."

"As you say, your Majesty, so shall it be." Swemmel was notorious insomniac, and if he felt comfortable staying bus half the night, his subjects had to accommodate themselves t his rhythms and his whims. He would not accommodate him self to them. He'd proved that, again and again.

Rathar had wondered if he would ride in the royal carriage Swemmel had granted only a handful of men that privileg throughout his reign; he'd executed about half of them shortl thereafter. Getting a carriage of his own did not unduly upse the marshal.

Back at the palace, King Swemmel said, "In the matter o Eoforwic, you have done as we desire in all particulars."

"Thank you, your Majesty," Rathar said. Had he not done a the king desired, Gurmun would have gone into command i the north long before this. And if Gurmun dared go off and tr things on his own and had something go wrong, none of his past accomplishments was likely to save him from the royal wrath.

But now Swemmel seemed in as benign a mood as Rathar had ever seen him. Even the king's smile held little of the malice that usually informed it. Swemmel said, "That being so, we purpose transferring you to the south, that you may lead our armies there as they drive into Algarve and drive toward Trapani. When you take Mezentio's capital, it is our desire that you leave not a single stone piled upon another. Do we make ourself clear?"

"Aye, your Majesty." Rathar bowed low. "Thank you, your Majesty. Thank you from the bottom of my heart." He'd thanked Swemmel a moment before, too. This time, he really meant it. "Mezentio started this fight. I want to be there when we finish it."

"You shall have your chance, Marshal," the king said. "For all your hesitation early in the campaign, you have served us well since, and we are willing to acknowledge that."

For Swemmel to acknowledge service to anyone else was no small step, as Rathar knew full well. Swemmel was convinced he *was* Unkerlant, and all his officers and servitors merely extensions of his will. Rathar didn't even feel particularly aggrieved at the king's slighting comment. As *he* remembered things, he hadn't been hesitant—Swemmel had been too eager. But he wasn't surprised his sovereign recalled those days differently. Even an ordinary man often remembered things to his own best advantage. How not a king, especially one to whom nobody dared say no?

I dare, every now and again, Rathar thought. *Aye, I dare— and every time I dare, I come away shaking, and with my armpits soaked with the stinking sweat of terror*. Telling Swemmel anything he didn't want to hear was no work for the faint of heart.

"How long?" the king asked suddenly.

"Your Majesty?" Rathar said: whatever King Swemmel was talking about, he hadn't been able to follow the sudden leap.

"How long?" Swemmel repeated in sharp, impatient tones. Then, grudgingly, he explained: "How long till we get to use King Mezentio as we desire? And of how much of our victory will Lagoas and Kuusamo rob us?"

"Your Majesty, I wouldn't even hazard a guess about the first," Rathar replied, which made King Swemmel glare at him. "It does not depend on us alone, you see. It also depends on the Algarvians, as you say, and on our allies. Mezentio, right now, faces choices we never had to make, for which I praise the powers above."

"Never?" Swemmel said. "Not even when we had to choose how much of our kingdom we would yield to the redheads and how much to the Gongs?"

"Not even then," Rathar said. "The Gyongyosians were never—well, hardly ever—more than a nuisance to us. The Algarvians were the deadly threat. But Mezentio faces dreadful danger from both west and east: if we don't move on Trapani, the islanders—and, for all I know, the Jelgavans and the Valmierans—will."

He thought that was obvious. But, by the alarm flaring in Swemmel's eyes, it hadn't been obvious enough. "No!" the king said hoarsely. "They mustn't! They can't! Trapani shall be ours. Ours, do you hear me?" His voice rose to a frightened shout. A bodyguard peered into the audience chamber to make sure he was all right. Cursing, he waved the man away.

Marshal Rathar did his best to calm the king: "As I say, your Majesty, we have only so much control over all this. If Mezentio's men fight us with everything they have but go easy in the east . . ." Had he been King of Algarve, he might have given orders like that. Fighting the Lagoans and Kuusamans remained a polite, civilized business. But the war between Algarve and Unkerlant had seen no quarter asked or given since the moment it began.

"If they steal our victory so . . ." Swemmel's voice was low, low but full of deadly fury. "If they think they can batten on the blood we spill, we shall show them they are wrong even if it takes us a thousand years."

Rathar wasn't worried about what would happen a thousand years from now; he couldn't do anything about that. What would happen in the next few days, the next few weeks, the next few months, was his province. He said, "Your Majesty, always remember: the Algarvians are our greatest danger. Once we crush them, we can worry about other things. Until we crush them, we have to keep them first in our thoughts."

"A thousand years," Swemmel muttered. But then, to Rathar's vast relief, he nodded. "Algarve first, aye. But we do not forget anything else. Lagoas and Kuusamo may steal some of our glory, but we shall take it back."

"When the time comes, your Majesty," Rathar said soothingly. Then he changed the subject: "Er, your Majesty—is it true the islanders have some new strong sorcery, of a different sort from what the redheads—and we—have been using? The reports I've received haven't been clear." He hoped it was true; he loathed the murderous magecraft the Algarvians had devised and Unkerlant had had to copy.

"We are not surprised the reports have been unclear," the king said with a scornful sniff. "We doubt whether Archmage Addanz understands everything he hears of these matters. We often doubt whether he understands anything he hears of these matters, come to that. There is some new sorcery, and it has been used in Jelgava and perhaps on the sea. Past that, we know little—but we are working to learn more."

"Good," Rathar said. Worried about everyone around him, Swemmel had built up a highly efficient corps of spies.

"Not so very good," Swemmel grumbled. "Addanz should have seen to this some time ago, without our urging." Rathar only shrugged. Addanz was a fine courtier, but no great shakes as a mage. Expecting him to act like what he wasn't asked too much. After a moment, Swemmel went on, "You should also know that Hajjaj of Zuwayza has come to Cottbus."

"Has he?" Rathar said. "Aye, your Majesty, you're right—I *should* know that. For what purpose has he come?"

"For what purpose would you think?" King Swemmel demanded. "To yield himself to us, of course."

Nineteen

Hajjaj hated coming to Cottbus for any number of reasons. He disliked having to wear clothes. He really disliked going out in weather cold enough to make wearing clothes a good idea. Most of all, though, he disliked having to come to beg for mercy for his defeated kingdom.

"So good to see you again, your Excellency," said Ansovald, who had been King Swemmel's minister to Zuwayza and was now . . . what? The man who delivered Swemmel's terms to Hajjaj, certainly. Past that, the Zuwayzi foreign minister didn't know and preferred not to guess.

"Always a pleasure," Hajjaj lied. As far as he was concerned, Ansovald was even more boorish than most Unkerlanters.

"Funny we're both speaking Algarvian, isn't it?" Ansovald said now. His laugh showed large, yellow teeth. "Pretty soon we'll squash the redheads flat, and nobody will need to speak their miserable language any more."

"I assure you, the irony was not lost on me, either," Hajjaj said. "But, unfortunately, my Unkerlanter has never been fluent." That was true, though Unkerlant had held Zuwayza throughout his youth and young manhood.

Ansovald grunted. "Your folks probably thought it was beneath 'em to have you learn." That was also true, though Hajjaj, unlike his host, was too polite to say any such thing. Ansovald went on, "Fat lot of good your Algarvian will do you from here on out."

"You may be right," Hajjaj said in tones as chilly as he could make them. "Shall we get down to business?"

"That's what you're here for—to get the business." Ansovald laughed. Hajjaj managed something an inattentive man might have reckoned a smile. But the Unkerlanter wasn't wrong. He was crude, but he wasn't wrong. Swemmel could dictate terms to Zuwayza. He could, and he would.

"Go ahead," Hajjaj said. Outside, there was frost in the gutters. Here in this stuffy chamber of the royal palace, sweat ran down his face. That had only a little to do with the Unkerlanter-style tunic he wore. As if to make up for the cold in which they lived, Unkerlanters heated their buildings well past what even a Zuwayzi thought the point of comfort.

"I have here a list of conditions, prepared for me by His Majesty, King Swemmel himself," Ansovald declared. He took a leaf of paper from his belt pouch, unfolded it, and studied it portentously.

"Go ahead," Hajjaj repeated. He knew he sounded weary. He felt weary, down to the very core of his being. He'd hoped for more than four years that this day would never come. He'd feared for two years that it would. Now it was here, and he had to endure it.

"Item," Ansovald said. "Henceforward, the border between Unkerlant and Zuwayza shall be that which was established by treaty here in Cottbus at the end of the last war between our two kingdoms."

"On behalf of King Shazli, I accept," Hajjaj said at once. He tried not to show how relieved he was. Both he and his king had feared the Unkerlanters would use the victories they'd won against Zuwayza to extinguish the kingdom altogether. Anything short of that was, by Unkerlanter standards, generosity.

"Item," Ansovald went on, inexorable as a landslide. "For the rest of the war against Algarve, and for fifteen years afterwards, Unkerlant shall freely be able to move ships into and out of the ports on the east coast of Zuwayza, and shall freely be able to draw any necessary supplies from those ports."

"I accept," Hajjaj said again, reflecting that it could have been worse. "Your admirals should bear in mind that our ports there are small. They do not overflow with supplies."

"That's your worry, not ours," Ansovald told him. Hajjaj returned another of those almost-smiles. Ansovald continued, "Item: Zuwayza shall give up her alliance with Algarve and enter into alliance with Unkerlant against King Mezentio and all who fight alongside him."

"I accept," Hajjaj said once more. Again, he'd expected nothing less.

"Item," Ansovald said. "Zuwayzi soldiers shall capture, disarm, and turn over to Unkerlant all Algarvian soldiers, sailors, and dragonfliers now in your kingdom."

"We shall do everything we can in that regard," Hajjaj said. "You must understand, though, that Mezentio's soldiers are resisting my countrymen by force of arms even as we speak." Much of that was an elaborate charade to let the Algarvians safely withdraw from Zuwayza. Hajjaj knew as much, and also knew Ansovald and Swemmel had better never find out.

Ansovald's sniff said he had his suspicions, but he did no more than sniff. He proceeded. "Item: Zuwayza shall henceforth, in her dealings with other kingdoms, consult with Unkerlant wherever necessary, and shall bear Unkerlant's interests in mind at all times."

Hajjaj couldn't smile at that. King Swemmel was imposing a protectorate after all. Still, though, it was a partial, relatively polite, protectorate. He wasn't setting Ansovald up in Bishah as governor of a new—or rather, old—Unkerlanter province. *And*, Hajjaj told himself, *we never can forget our big southern neighbor, however much we wish we could.* "I accept," he said. He knew he sounded wounded, but he couldn't do anything about that.

"Item," Ansovald went on. "For the damage Zuwayza has done to Unkerlant, you shall pay an indemnity of seventy million Unkerlanter thals, in silver or in kind, in the space of three years after signing this agreement."

Once more, Hajjaj said what he had to say: "I accept." That would beggar the kingdom. It would beggar it, aye, but wouldn't quite break it. Someone had done some very precise calculating there. Silence fell. Hajjaj looked across the table at Ansovald. "What else, your Excellency?"

Ansovald refolded the paper and set it on the tabletop. "Those are King Swemmel's requirements for peace with Zuwayza."

Is that all? Hajjaj didn't say it, though he came undiplomatically close. Swemmel could have done far worse. He'd expected Swemmel to do far worse. His suspicion kindled. Why hadn't Swemmel done worse? He couldn't ask Ansovald. The only thing that occurred to him was that Swemmel wanted to fight Algarve without distractions, and so granted Zuwayza relatively—but only relatively—mild terms.

"I shall advise King Shazli to agree to these terms," Hajjaj said. "They are not too high a price for us to pay for leaving this war."

"You should have thought of that before you got into it," Ansovald said.

"No doubt," Hajjaj said politely. "Life would be simpler if we could know such things ahead of time." He paused, then added, "I do have one question for you."

"Go ahead," Ansovald said. "But if you think his Majesty will change anything in there, you can think again."

"I wouldn't dream of imagining such a thing," Hajjaj said, and meant it. "But there were once some broadsheets scattered about that spoke of a Reformed Principality of Zuwayza under a certain Prince Mustanjid. Do I gather from what I see here that King Swemmel no longer supports any such entity, whatever it may have been?" *A threat to overthrow Shazli, that's what it was.*

"Did you hear it mentioned anywhere in these terms?" Ansovald asked.

"I did not," Hajjaj admitted.

"Then acknowledging it is not required of your kingdom," Ansovald told him. Hajjaj nodded and said no more. Up in northern Unkerlant or southern, occupied, Zuwayza, the Zuwayzi noble who'd kissed King Swemmel's foot—or some other portion of Swemmel's anatomy—was probably feeling ill-used right now: the Unkerlanters wouldn't install him as King, or even Reformed Prince, of Zuwayza after all. Hajjaj was not prepared to waste much sympathy on Mustanjid.

"May I have access to a crystallomancer, to tell King Shazli your terms before I sign them?" he asked.

"If you insist," Ansovald said. "But I thought you came here as a plenipotentiary, with full power to make agreements on your own."

"I did come here so. I do have that power," Hajjaj said. "But King Shazli is my sovereign, as King Swemmel is yours. Would you do anything without letting your sovereign know you were going to do it?"

"No." For a moment, stark fear glinted in Ansovald's eyes. Hajjaj was not afraid of Shazli; he liked the bright young man who ruled Zuwayza, as he'd liked Shazli's father before him. But he'd thought he knew what Unkerlanters thought of their king, and what sort of power Swemmel enjoyed in this great, broad land. Now he saw he was right, and the seeing saddened him. Ansovald needed to gather himself before he could say, "It shall be as you wish. You may speak to your king."

When things happened in Unkerlant, they happened with a furious energy that almost kept a stranger from noticing how often they did not happen at all. Not five minutes after Hajjaj had made his request, a crystallomancer stood beside him and—after a brief colloquy with Ansovald in Unkerlanter—spoke to him in halting Algarvian: "Your king, Excellency."

"I see. Thank you." Hajjaj sank down on a stool before the crystal that held Shazli's image. "Your Majesty, let me give you the terms they will impose on us," he said, switching to Zuwayzi.

"Go ahead," Shazli answered in the same language. He stiffened ever so slightly, like a man bracing himself for a blow.

Hajjaj went through them one by one. Shazli asked a few questions; he answered them. When he was finished, he said, "Your Majesty, unless you order me not to do so, I shall accept these terms. I do not think we can do anything to improve them, and they are not so harsh as they might have been." More than that he would not say, not when Swemmel surely had someone who spoke Zuwayzi listening to this conversation.

"They are not light, either," Shazli said, which was also true. From a different kingdom, they might even have been reckoned onerous. But Swemmel was willing to leave Shazli on the throne and Zuwayza a kingdom in its own right. Had he chosen to go further, he could have. With a sigh, Shazli said, "I agree. Things being as they are, we must accept. Go ahead, your Excellency."

"Thank you, your Majesty," Hajjaj said. He turned to Ansovald and came back to the Algarvian they shared: "The king agrees, as I was sure he would. The terms are acceptable to Zuwayza."

In a different kingdom, the ceremony would have been more elaborate. Men from the leading news sheets would have crowded in to watch Hajjaj surrender. Here, what went into the news sheets came straight from Swemmel and his ministers anyway. Hajjaj signed the new treaty in a barren little palace antechamber, and had to remind Ansovald to get him a second copy so he could take it back to Bishah.

After he signed, he did get supper: an enormous plate of fatty boiled pork, boiled cabbage, and stewed parsnips. Ansovald got the same sort of supper, and consumed it with relish, washing it down with several mugs of ale. *Food for a cold kingdom*, Hajjaj thought. He ate what he could. It wasn't badly prepared, but ran far from the direction his tastes usually took.

An enormous soft mattress with a prince's ransom of wool blankets and fur coverlets was a bed for a cold kingdom, too. No matter how strange and foreign it felt to Hajjaj, though, he slept well that night. *My kingdom will live.* How could he toss and turn, with the relief that thought brought uppermost in his mind?

Colonel Sabrino had not seen such a great wild melee of foot-soldiers and, above all, of behemoths since the great battles in the Durrwangen bulge more than a year earlier. Now, though, the Unkerlanters and Algarvians were fighting east of Patras, between the Yaninan capital and the border between Yanina and Algarve. Swemmel's men had broken through the Algarvian line with a great force of behemoths—whereupon the Algarvians at either end of the breakthrough, responding as smartly as they might have back in the days when they seemed to have the world on a string, fought toward one another and trapped the Unkerlanters who'd been overbold.

But whether the Unkerlanters would stay trapped was a different question. Peering down from his dragon, Sabrino shook his head in sour wonder. How many behemoths did Swemmel's men have around the town of Mavromouni? Too many—he was certain of that. Had the trap really closed on them, or were they part of a trap closing on his countrymen?

Sabrino whacked his dragon with the goad. The beast screamed. It swung its head toward him on the end of its long, scaly neck. He whacked it again, harder. No matter what it thought, it wasn't going to flame him out of the harness. He whacked it once more, and it dove toward the ground. The rest of his wing, what was left of it, followed.

Wind howled by him, a cold, nasty wind. The behemoths below swelled as if by sorcery. Before long, he saw that some of them had Yaninans aboard, not Unkerlanters. His lips drew apart in a mirthless grin. "You whoresons won't get any more use out of them than we did," he predicted.

However much he was tempted to attack the Yaninans for betraying Algarve, he didn't. Without the Unkerlanters to stiffen them and give them the courage they would surely never find on their own, King Tsavellas' men were no great threat. They never had been, and they never would be. The Unkerlanters, on the other hand . . .

Sabrino chose his behemoth, and steered toward its tail. King Swemmel's men aboard it had a moment to see horror diving on them, a moment in which to try to swing their personal sticks his way. One of them even got the chance to blaze, though wildly. Then Sabrino tapped the dragon on the side of the neck.

It was always glad to get the command to flame. Fire gushed from its jaws, engulfing the Unkerlanters and the behemoth they rode. Sabrino had had to wait till the dragon was almost on top of the behemoth before letting it flame. Algarve was desperately short of quicksilver these days, and without it dragonfire lost much of its heat and distance. That didn't matter so much against behemoths, which had no hope of outrunning flame even at short range. Against Unkerlanter dragons, though, it was one more disadvantage to set beside a crushing disadvantage in numbers.

Against which, Algarve has . . . what? Sabrino wondered as the dragon clawed its way back up into the air again. Experience came to mind. He, for instance, had been flying dragons and commanding this wing since the day war began. But so many dragonfliers were dead, and their replacements raw as any Unkerlanters.

They're so young, Sabrino thought. It wasn't that they were young enough to be his sons. Some of them were young enough to be his grandsons, he having fought in the Six Years' War. *They're so young, and so brave. They're braver than I am—powers above know that's true. They go up there not knowing anything, and knowing they don't know anything. But they go up anyway, with a smile, sometimes even with a song. I couldn't do that, not for anything.*

Here came a swarm of Unkerlanter dragons, all in the dingy rock-gray paint that made them so hard to see, especially against autumn clouds. The men who flew them were better at what they did than they had been when the war was new. The Unkerlanters used many more crystals than they had in those days, and responded to trouble much more quickly. It made fighting a war against them look altogether too much like work.

But they held formation as rigidly as if they'd been glued together. That was how they'd been trained: to follow their leader and do as he did. Some few of them outgrew it and became pretty good dragonfliers. More, though, never learned. Sabrino wasted no pity on them. If they survived his lessons, they would pick up something. He hoped they didn't.

"Melee!" he shouted into his crystal. "Break apart and melee!"

Against good dragonfliers in formation, the order would have been suicidal: break up a smaller force to oppose a larger, better-disciplined one? Madness, nothing but madness.

The Unkerlanters, though, weren't good dragonfliers: this wasn't a wing of freelancers, of the skilled fliers the Algarvians called Swemmel's falcons. These were just the men who'd been closest to the battle by Mavromouni. And if you could rely on any one thing from such men, you could rely on their holding formation too bloody long.

Sure enough, when the Algarvians started swooping at their tails and up from below at their dragons' bellies, they didn't break out of their box till several of them had already tumbled from the sky. Sabrino had seen that time and again. If they'd just broken up and put two or three dragons on every one of his as they could have, he would have had a much harder time of it. But they didn't. They wouldn't. They never did.

They paid for their rigidity, too, as they usually did. By the time Sabrino ordered his wing back toward its latest makeshift dragon farm, he'd counted nine Unkerlanter dragons slain. He'd lost three of his own followers. The only thing troubling him was that, even at three losses for one, the foe could afford it better than he.

Down fluttered his dragons, some of them burned, all of them weary, to the dragon farm in what had probably been some Yaninan peasant's turnip field. Dragon handlers trotted forward to secure the beasts to their iron stakes and tend to their wounds and feed them whatever meat they'd managed to scrounge from the surrounding countryside. The handlers were all Algarvians. Yaninan handlers, nowadays, tended only Yaninan dragons, and Yaninan dragons flew alongside the rock-gray beasts of Unkerlant.

Sabrino wondered how Major Scoufas fared these days. Were it not for Scoufas, he would probably have been languishing in a captives' camp. He wished the Yaninan officer no ill— but if they met in the air, he would do his best to kill him.

Can I? The question was more interesting than he would have liked. Scoufas made a first-rate dragonflier, no doubt about it. He would be flying a fresher dragon, and one brim full of brimstone and quicksilver. Sabrino kicked at the muddy ground, angry at himself. *If you don't think you can win every time you go up, you'd do better staying on the ground.*

That was an obvious truth. Another obvious truth was that he couldn't afford to do any such thing. He kicked at the wet dirt again. No Algarvian could afford to do anything but whatever he was best at that might hold back the Unkerlanter tide, and to keep doing it till he either got killed or he collapsed from exhaustion. Sabrino knew he wasn't far from either.

A road ran not far from the dragon farm. Some Yaninans fled east along it. They couldn't stomach the Unkerlanter alliance, no matter what King Tsavellas might have to say about it. But others moved west, something Sabrino hadn't seen before. Maybe they lived farther east, and were hoping to avoid long battles in their own neighborhoods. Or maybe they hated Algarvians as much as their countrymen hated Unkerlanters. Some Yaninans did.

Being the wing commander, Sabrino got the abandoned farmhouse instead of a tent. With his old bones, he was glad to have the comfort of four walls around him, even beat-up, shabby walls.

He lit a couple of big tallow candles. They filled the one-room farmhouse with the stink of hot fat. By their flickering light, he started to write a report on the fight his wing had just been through. *How many reports have I written in this war? Too bloody many, that's certain sure.*

And then another, even less happy, thought occurred to him. *How many of them have done any bloody good?* He didn't know the answer there, not in numbers, but he knew what he needed to know. *Not many. Not enough—that's certain sure, too.*

He wondered why he bothered. Would anyone in Trapani care if he fell silent? Someone might—his silence could give a superior who wanted to sack him the excuse he needed to do it. That thought alone was plenty to keep Sabrino stubbornly writing. He didn't make things easy for the foe. Why should he for his alleged friends?

A sentry knocked on the door and said, "Someone to see you, sir."

"I don't want to see anyone," Sabrino answered, not looking up.

"I think you should, sir," the sentry said.

That made Sabrino raise an eyebrow. It also roused his curiosity. He stuck his pen into the bottle of ink, got to his feet, and went to open the door. There stood the sentry. And there behind him, in a common soldier's cloak and boots, stood King Mezentio. "What in blazes are you doing here?" Sabrino asked harshly.

"Seeing how things fare in the field," the King of Algarve answered. "And that should be, 'What in blazes are you doing here, your Majesty?' May I come in?"

"Aye." Numbly, Sabrino stood aside. Mezentio walked in and closed the door behind him. Sabrino said, "I have some spirits, if you want any."

"No, thank you, your Excellency." Mezentio took off his hat and cocked his bald head to one side. "Who knows? You might poison them."

Sabrino shook his head. "I wouldn't go that far. I might say 'I told you so.' I cursed well did tell you so, your Majesty, and you, powers below eat you, you wouldn't listen to me."

"And do you think it would have made a counterfeit copper's worth of difference if I had?" Mezentio retorted. "We had no chance to take Cottbus without doing what we did, and we couldn't whip Unkerlant unless we took Cottbus. And so—"

"So what?" Sabrino said. If Mezentio felt like executing him for the lese majesty of interrupting, he didn't much care. "So fornicating what? We did it, and we still didn't take fornicating Cottbus, and how many Kaunians and Unkerlanters are dead now who'd be alive if we'd left well enough alone? How many tens of thousands?"

Mezentio shrugged. "I don't know. I don't care. The Kaunians have been our deadly foes since time out of mind. They deserve whatever happened to them. If they all had a single neck I would have been rid of every one of them at the same time. may yet manage that."

"You would do better to make peace," Sabrino said. "How many Lagoans and Kuusamans think our name is a stench in the nostrils of civilization these days? All of them, or near enough."

"Who will make peace with me now? What sort of peace would it be?" Mezentio asked, two questions for which Sabrino had no good answers. The king went on: "Unfortunately, you are in large measure correct about the islanders, and as for Swemmel of Unkerlant—you know the answer there as well as I do. And so I shall triumph or I shall die, and Algarve with me." He glared at Sabrino. "And you, your Excellency, you shall remain a colonel till one of those or the other happens. I wondered if you'd changed your ways, but I see that was another wasted hope."

Sabrino laughed. King Mezentio glared harder than ever. Laughing still, Sabrino said, "Why am I not surprised, your Majesty?"

Rain spattered the surface of the Twegen River. Blowing in from out of the west, it spattered Colonel Spinello's face, too. As he looked across from the ruins of Eoforwic to the Unkerlanter emplacements on the other side of the river, Spinello didn't mind the rain so much. Were he down in the south of Unkerlant, it would long since have turned to sleet and snow.

What he minded was the feeling he needed eyes in the back of his head. The Forthwegians who'd fought so long and hard had surrendered, aye—or most of them had. But some still blazed at the Algarvians in Eoforwic whenever they saw a chance. Spinello's brigade took a casualty or two from snipers almost every day.

He looked back over his shoulder. Hanging there from a balcony was the corpse of a Forthwegian his men had caught a couple of days before. Along with the noose, the fellow had a placard tied round his neck. THIS IS WHAT YOU GET IF YOU BLAZE AT AN ALGARVIAN, it warned in Algarvian, classical Kaunian, and presumably Forthwegian, although Spinello couldn't read that last.

That kind of warning would have deterred him. Some Forthwegians, though, were willing, even eager, to kill Algarvians regardless of whether it cost them their lives. It usually did, and painfully, but they were still hard to guard against.

He peered across the Twegen again. The river wasn't very wide. Had the Unkerlanters wanted to force a crossing, they probably could have done it. Instead, they seemed content for the time being to pound Eoforwic to pieces while they built up

their forces. Some of them were walking along the riverbank a
openly as if they were back in their own kingdom.

"Crystallomancer!" Spinello shouted in some annoyance. He
had to shout it more than once, which annoyed him further.

"Here, sir," a smooth-cheeked youngster said at last.

Spinello shook his head. The youth looked like an appren
tice, not a real soldier. But he would have to do. "Connect me to
our egg-tossers," Spinello said. "Those whoresons over there
need to learn some respect for us."

"Aye, sir." The crystallomancer did make the etheric connec
tion with commendable speed. "Go ahead, sir."

"Thank you." Spinello stared into the crystal at the image o
a gruff officer who might have fought in the Six Years' War. He
quickly explained what he wanted.

"Aye, we can do that," the veteran said. "Can't have those
bastards think they rule the roost even if they do, eh?" He ges
tured sharply, Spinello supposed to his own crystallomancer
Spinello's crystal flared and then went inert.

A few minutes later, eggs began bursting on the east side o
the Twegen. The rain kept Spinello from seeing as much as he
would have liked, but Swemmel's soldiers wouldn't go for thei
afternoon stroll along the riverbank any more. He was sure o
that. They'd hide in holes the way he did, the ones not too
seared by sorcerous energy to worry about hiding ever again.

All that might have been true. But the Unkerlanters also took
revenge. Spinello wondered how many egg-tossers they had
there on the other side of the Twegen. Plenty to knock down big
chunks of Eoforwic that had somehow stayed standing through
the Forthwegian uprising. Plenty to stir around the chunks that
had already fallen down and to make big chunks into little ones

And plenty to make Spinello laugh, there in his hole with his
face pressed to the earth and with his heart pounding from fear
he couldn't quell. The Unkerlanters could have pounded Eofor
wic just as hard while the Algarvians were crushing the upris
ing. They could have, but they hadn't. *And why should they
have?* he wondered. *We were doing their dirty work for them.
Now they have to do their own.*

The other obvious implication there was that Swemmel's

soldiers thought they could overrun Eoforwic whenever they chose. He'd been fighting them for three years. He had the nasty feeling they knew what they were about.

What does that say about Algarve? he thought at the ground quivered beneath him like an animal in pain. *Does it say we're going to lose the war?* If he looked at things rationally, he couldn't see how it would say anything else. But war wasn't altogether a rational business. He'd seen enough of it to know that, too. *If our secret sorceries come to fruition, or even if the Lagoans and Kuusamans get sick of staying allied to that madman of a Swemmel . . .*

It could happen. Many stranger things had happened. Being something of a student of history, Spinello knew as much. Lagoas and Kuusamo were civilized kingdoms. Why would they stay in harness with a barbarian maniac like Swemmel, especially when they were all fighting against another civilized kingdom like Algarve?

Kaunians. The word tolled in his mouth like an iron bell, seeming louder than all the eggs bursting around and behind him. But then he shook his head. Lagoans and Kuusamans weren't Kaunian folk. Lagoans were Algarvic, with blood ties to Algarve and Sibiu. Why should they care what happened to blonds? They'd fought plenty of wars against Kaunian Valmiera.

They don't want Algarve lord of all Derlavai. That made Spinello laugh, too, though he didn't really find it funny. *So they help Swemmel against us, and* Unkerlant *becomes lord of all Derlavai. What good does that do them?*

He laughed again. *That's the next war. It isn't this one. Who worries about tomorrow when he's fighting to stay alive today?*

The Algarvians were fighting to stay alive today, fighting in a way Lagoas and Kuusamo weren't—and having less luck with it. Somewhere not far away from Spinello, someone started screaming. He cursed. The scream had words, and some of them he recognized as Algarvian. He wouldn't have cared much what happened to a Forthwegian, but a countryman was a countryman.

Before he thought about what he was doing, he popped out

of his hole and ran toward the screams. One of his troopers was doing the same thing. "Get down, Colonel!" the soldier yelled, his voice coming to Spinello by fits and starts through the roar of the bursting eggs.

"Shut up," Spinello said. The soldier didn't argue. Spinello almost wished he would have. *I've got a ribbon with my wound badge,* he thought. *Do I really want another one?* He might easily get killed, too, but he refused even to think about that. He couldn't do anything about it, anyhow.

You could *dive into a hole, fool,* the rational part of his mind insisted. But then he spotted the wounded Algarvian and loped toward him. The trooper followed. It was, he saw as he stooped beside the hurt man, the crystallomancer who'd put him in touch with the egg-tossers.

"Belly," the trooper said, glancing at the wound. "That's not so good."

"I know." Spinello didn't want to look at it. "Here, son." He gave the crystallomancer a long draught of opium-laced spirits. It wasn't much, but it was the best he could do. When he started to put a dressing on the wound, the crystallomancer, only half conscious, tried to fight him off.

The trooper grabbed the wounded man's hands. "We're going to have to get him to the healers," he said as Spinello worked.

Spinello tapped his wound badge. "My pals didn't let me down when I got hurt. Time to pay them back." The common soldier only nodded. He wore a wound badge, too, and already had two ribbons under it.

When they lifted the crystallomancer, he shrieked like a cursed soul. Then, mercifully, he did pass out. They half carried, half dragged him back to a battered building—more battered now than Spinello remembered it—where healers were hard at work. The place smelled of smoke and unwashed men and the butcher-shop odor of blood and the latrine stink of pierced entrails. Spinello did his best to hide his shudder. He'd been in places like this before, when he was the one who suffered. The smells made his body remember, and remember too well.

"Hey, quacks!" the trooper said, perhaps hiding his own unease with bravado. "We've got another one for you to practice on."

A harried healer hurried over. He took one look at the crimsoned, soaking bandages and winced. "Belly wound, eh? We can't do much with that here. We'll have to put him on ice and ship him back to Algarve. Maybe they can help him back there, maybe not. He'll have some kind of chance, anyway."

With a nod, Spinello said, "That's about what I thought." A dragon had flown him out of Sulingen after a sniper put a beam through the right side of his chest. Now he could take a more detached interest in the proceedings.

A couple of eggs burst close enough to make the ground shake under his feet. Irritably, the healer said, "Don't they ever run out of those cursed things?"

Almost on cue, the pounding of Eoforwic eased. "Who knows?" Spinello said in glad surprise. "Maybe they do."

"Not bloody likely." The healer put on a pair of long, thick, obviously insulated gloves. He called for a colleague, who did the same thing. The two men lifted the crystallomancer and set him down in a box that looked something like a coffin and something like a rest crate. Without the gloves, the spell inside the box would have sorcerously frozen their hands and arms in short order, too. The healer muttered a charm over the box. Then he scrawled on the outside a diagnosis in the much-abbreviated classical Kaunian medical men used. With a nod to Spinello, he said, "We'll get him out of here. What happens after that is in the hands of the powers above."

"I hope he comes through all right," Spinello said. "We'll need all the mages of any sort we can get our hands on."

"I wish I could say you were wrong," the healer answered. "When we start using our secret sorceries—"

"Aye, by the powers above!" Spinello broke in eagerly. "You're a sorcerer yourself. How soon do you think that will be?"

"I don't know," the healer said. "I wish I did. But only Mezentio and, I suppose, a few of our first-rank mages could tell you for certain. I will say this, though—it had better be soon."

"It certainly should," Spinello said. "We've lost everything we ever got in Unkerlant, and so many men to go with that. We're practically back to the point where we were when we started fighting Swemmel. And the east ... ." He didn't want to think about the east. He didn't want to think about the Unkerlanters' not being checked here in the west, either—they were only gathering themselves for the next leap forward.

"All true, every word of it." The healer sounded glum. "But that's not the worst. The worst is, where are we going to get the blonds to make the secret sorceries work?"

"I don't know," Spinello answered. "I wish I did. We can start grabbing ordinary Forthwegians, I suppose—or Yaninans, those filthy traitors."

On that gloomy note, he took his leave. He saw some ordinary Forthwegians going through the ruins of Eoforwic. Every so often, one of them would stoop and put something in a basket. *Gathering mushrooms*, he thought, and made a face at the very idea. Algarvians didn't eat mushrooms. As far as Spinello was concerned, people who did deserved whatever happened to them.

Snow already lay thick on the ground in the Naantali district. Pekka wasn't surprised; it would be snowing down in Kajaani, too, and Kajaani had the sea to moderate its climate. Some of the mages from the northern, more temperate parts of Kuusamo and Lagoas complained about the weather. They couldn't do anything about it—what mage could?—but that didn't stop them from complaining.

"Me, I've come to like it better this time of year," Fernao said. "You can go outside without the mosquitoes' eating you alive."

"It's only weather," Pekka said, ignoring snowstorms in mid-autumn with the ease of someone who took hard winters for granted. "What I have to complain about isn't the snow. It's *those*."

She pointed first to one of the heavy sticks now emplaced around the hostel and the blockhouse, then to another and another. When she looked up to the sky, she caught a glimpse of a patrolling dragon through a break in the clouds overhead. The dragon was painted in a pattern of sky blue and sea green, the colors of Kuusamo.

"We have a saying in Lagoas." Fernao paused, probably translating it into Kuusaman from his own language. "Trying to make soup after the dog has stolen the bone."

"Exactly," Pekka said. "How are the Algarvians going to reach us now? They've left most of Valmiera. Their dragons can't possibly fly here from the lands they still hold. And none of these things were in place when that cursed dragon *did* attack us."

Fernao took her hand. She squeezed his. When Leino came home, she would have a lot of things to worry about, a lot of choices to make. She knew as much. Meanwhile, she enjoyed each day—and each night—as if tomorrow would never come. Later? What was later?

Slowly, Fernao said, "Saying what the Algarvians can't possibly do worries me a little. They've already done too many things nobody thought they could do."

"Too many things nobody thought they *would* do," Pekka said, which wasn't quite the same thing. "Too many things nobody thought anyone would do."

Now Fernao squeezed her hand. "What we've done here has gone a long way toward keeping people from doing things like that again. That's mostly thanks to you, you know, to you and your experiments."

Pekka shook her head. "Master Siuntio is the one who really deserves the credit. And Master Ilmarinen. I just did the work. They were the ones who saw I'd stumbled onto something important and figured out what it meant."

"You don't give yourself enough credit," Fernao said. "You never have."

"Nonsense," Pekka said, and then, "I got a letter from my sister this morning."

She'd wanted to change the subject, and she succeeded. Fernao walked along in silence for a little while, kicking up snow at every step. At last, he asked, "And what does she have to say?"

"Nothing too much," Pekka answered. "Olavin's solicitors paid a call on her. She wasn't very happy about that."

"I believe it." In Fernao's long, pale Lagoan face, his slanted eyes were usually a reminder that he had a little Kuusaman blood in him, too. Now, though, they just made his expression harder to read. After a few more silent paces, he said, "Are we going to have to worry about that one of these days?"

Pekka had forced the future out of her purview. Now Fernao brought it back. She wished he hadn't. "I don't know," she said. "I just don't know." She kicked up some snow of her own—kicked it at Fernao, in fact. "Let's go back to the hostel." She turned and started off without waiting to see whether he followed.

He did, and went up the steps only a pace behind her. "Whatever happens, we'll see it through," he said.

"What else can we do?" she said, wishing he would keep quiet. Weren't men supposed to be the ones who didn't want to commit themselves? That didn't fit Fernao. He wanted to run away with her. She was the one full of doubts, full of complications. She sighed. Why couldn't things be simpler?

Going into the hostel certainly made things no simpler. There stood Ilmarinen, just inside the front entrance. He had been talking with a couple of the workmen still busy repairing the hostel after the Algarvian attack. But when he saw Pekka and Fernao together, he broke off and came over to them. "And what were the two of you doing out there?" he purred.

By the way he said it, the question could have only one possible answer. But Pekka replied, "Don't be silly. It's much too cold outside for *that*."

Ilmarinen looked disappointed. Fernao asked him, "And what have you been doing in here?"

"Aye, what *have* you been doing?" Pekka echoed. "Have you finished the calculations I asked you for the other day?"

To her surprise, Ilmarinen nodded. "They're finished, all right."

"And?" Pekka asked when he said no more.

"And it's just what we thought it was," the master mage answered grimly. "Did you think the calculations would show it wouldn't work? Not bloody likely, not after we've spent all this time tearing up the landscape around here."

"You don't sound happy," Fernao observed.

Though much the shorter of the two, Ilmarinen contrived to look down his nose at Fernao. "Should I? What the Algarvians visited on Yliharma, now we can visit on Trapani. Shall I throw my hat in the air? Shall I shout huzzah? Now we can match the barbarians in barbarism. Huzzah indeed!"

"Better that we be able to match them than that we *not* be able to match them," Pekka said. "That's the assumption we've been working on."

"No." Ilmarinen shook his head. "The assumption we've been working on is that they had better not be able to match our new sorcery. And they bloody well can't, not so far as we can tell. But that we use what we have for the same purposes as they use what they have . . ." He shook his head again. "No, by the powers above."

"We can do many more things with ours," Fernao said. "Once the war is over, it will turn the world upside down. But for now . . ." He shrugged. "For now, we do what needs doing, and that means beating Algarve."

"They're using it the right way up in Jelgava, throwing the Algarvians' spells back in their faces," Ilmarinen said. "Mezentio's mages deserve that, and so do his soldiers. But the other? No." He sounded very certain.

"How is it any different from sending dragons over their cities to drop eggs on them?" Pekka asked.

"That's just war," Ilmarinen said. "Everybody does it. The other—you wouldn't, we wouldn't, just be hurting a city if that ever happened, and you know it."

Pekka grimaced. He wasn't wrong, however much she wished he were. But she didn't think she was wrong, either, as she answered, "We have to do what needs doing."

"Do we?" Ilmarinen said. "Don't you suppose the Algarvian mages say the same old thing—the same old lie—just before their soldiers start blazing Kaunians, or however they go about killing them to get their life energy?"

"That's not fair," Pekka said. "We're not killing anyone to get the energy for our magecraft."

"No, that's true—we're not. And so what?" Ilmarinen said. "If we use it the way you have in mind, we'll be killing plenty on the other end."

"That's different," Fernao said. "If you can't get a man to listen to you, you hit him. If he hits you, you get a club. If he hits you with a club, you get a sword. If he hits you with a sword, you get a stick. If he blazes at you with a stick, you go after him with a behemoth, and so on."

"I don't like thinking of myself as a murderer," Ilmarinen said. "I'll do it, mind you, but I don't like it."

"Think of the Algarvians as murderers, then," Pekka said. "They are, you know. Even Master Siuntio thought this fight was worth making—and Mezentio's mages killed him, remember."

"I'm not likely to forget, not when they came so bloody close to killing me, too," Ilmarinen replied. "But I'm sick of war. I'm sick of killing. Aren't you?"

"Of course I am," Pekka said. "But the fastest way to win it is the way Fernao said: to knock the Algarvians down till they can't get up any more. Do you truly think anything else would do the job?"

"I'm not surprised you agree with him," Ilmarinen said, and then laughed. "Ah, there—I've gone and made you angry. I wonder why."

"You've made me angry, all right," Pekka said tightly. "And I'll tell you why: because you didn't try to answer my question, that's why. You just took a cheap blaze at me. Now answer, if you'd be so kind. *Do* you think anything else would do the job, or not?"

This time, Ilmarinen hesitated before speaking. Even so, he didn't quite answer her question. What he said was, "There's more to you than meets the eye. Do you know that?"

"I don't much care," Pekka said. "I'm going to ask you a third time, and I expect a straight answer. Can we beat the Algarvians and the Gyongyosians any other way than by knocking them flat?"

Asking Ilmarinen for a straight answer could easily prove as frustrating as asking a toddler to stop making a nuisance of himself. Pekka didn't get one now, either. The master mage smiled at her till she wanted to punch him in the teeth. He said, "I'll give you the calculations tonight." Then, irrepressible, he leered. "I'll just slide them under the door, so I'll be sure not to interrupt anything." With a sweet, carnivorous smile, he strode away.

Pekka glared after him. Fernao set a hand on her shoulder. "The more he gets you angry, the more he wins. That's what he's after, you know."

"No." Pekka shook her head. "You're close, but you're not quite right. The more he drives me crazy, the more he wins. He's good at it, too. He's been driving everyone crazy for the past fifty years."

"Well, then, don't worry about him," Fernao said.

She laughed as mockingly as Ilmarinen had. "Tell the sun not to come up tomorrow, as long as you're in a mood to give advice."

She wondered if that might anger Fernao. Instead, he answered soberly: "I've been where the sun sometimes doesn't come up for weeks—the land of the Ice People. It can happen. And you can ignore Ilmarinen."

"It's not easy," she said, and then seized his hand. "Come to my room. If anything will help me do it, that will." Had she ever been so blunt with Leino? She had trouble remembering. In any case, right now she wanted to forget.

Ilmarinen *did* slide papers under her door, and chose a very distracting moment to do it, too. A little while later, Fernao said, "I wonder if he did that on purpose."

He ran his hand along her flank. The distraction hadn't ruined things. Pekka felt sated and lazy—too lazy to get up and get the papers on the instant. She said, "He could tell by sorcery if he wanted to badly enough, but I don't think he would bother. I hope he wouldn't bother."

"I hope you're right," Fernao answered. "Are you going to see what the calculations say?"

"Eventually," Pekka said. "Part of me wants to know, but the rest, the rest"—she confessed to Fernao what she would never have told anyone else—"wonders if Ilmarinen isn't absolutely right, though I wouldn't tell him that in a thousand years, not when we have to do this come what may." She felt a little better when Fernao leaned over and kissed her, but much better when he nodded to show he felt the same way.

The Unkerlanter mage nodded to Leudast. "There you are, Lieutenant," the fellow said. "All your flesh is the same age again."

Leudast tried the leg that had been wounded. Without a doubt, it felt worse than it had before the sorcerer cast his spell. But he could still use it. He nodded. "Thanks," he said. "The fellow who helped heal my wound by aging it warned me to make sure I got rid of the spell once it had served its purpose."

"I believe that," the wizard said. After a moment's thoughtful hesitation, he went on, "Do you mind if I ask you something?"

"Go ahead." Leudast had a pretty good idea of what was coming.

And, sure enough, the wizard said, "How did your healer decide to use that particular charm on you? Very often, we reserve it for, ah, special cases."

"What do you mean, special cases?" Leudast asked in turn. The mage didn't answer. But Leudast had little trouble drawing his own conclusions. It had to mean something like, *people more important than a lieutenant with a peasant accent*. He said, "Marshal Rathar personally promoted me."

That had impressed the healer who'd treated him. It impressed this mage, too. He said, "No wonder the man used it with you, then."

Not what you know—who you know. Leudast had had that thought before. Anybody could become a sergeant. Going that far was easy, if you were a good soldier—and if the Algarvians didn't kill you, of course. He'd been pretty lucky, getting away with only two wounds. He wondered how many Unkerlanter soldiers who'd started the war with the redheads were still in it. Then he wondered how many of them had become officers. He'd been lucky in more than staying alive, and he knew it.

"You're ready to go, Lieutenant." Now that the sorcerer knew Leudast knew Marshal Rathar—or at least that Rathar knew him—he was noticeably more polite.

"Thanks very much." Leudast used a little politeness himself. He strode out of the Yaninan farmhouse the regimental healer was using, out into a rain that was beginning to.freeze. His leg *did* hurt a good deal more than it had before he'd had the other wizard's spell removed. He limped a little. He didn't care. He'd already waited longer than he should have to get rid of that magic. Over the next month, he knew exactly how much the limb would improve.

And I know I won't get killed in the next month, too, he thought. Had he been about to die, his leg would have told him of it. *I can be as reckless as I want on the field. The Algarvians can't touch me. For a month, I've got a charmed life.*

But was that really true? What would happen if, say, he picked up a stick right now and blazed out his own brains? He'd be dead, and his leg wouldn't have warned him about it.

He shook his head to clear it. Thinking about such things was as likely to make that head ache as drinking too deep from a jar of spirits. He laughed under his breath. It wasn't nearly so much fun, either.

His company occupied the rest of the village, or what was left of it. The Algarvians had made a stand here a few days before, and most of the huts—actually, the houses were a good deal finer than those in peasant villages in Unkerlant—had either burned or gone up in bursts of sorcerous energy in the nasty process of forcing them out. The ones who hadn't got out still lay here and there; no one had bothered burying the corpses. Only the chilly weather kept the stink from being worse than it was.

Some of the men who couldn't fit into the handful of houses still boasting walls and roofs kept dry in tents plundered from the redheads. The rest made do with their greatcoats and stout felt boots. The Unkerlanter army did issue those to everyone, even if Swemmel's men might not get tents or, for that matter, much in the way of food.

But, regardless of.whether Swemmel's quartermasters got

supplies to them, the soldiers had no trouble keeping themselves fed. Brass pots bubbled over fires the rain made smoky but couldn't douse. Even the men who had only greatcoats seemed contented enough. One thing Unkerlanters knew was how to take care of themselves in the cold and rain.

Once upon a time, Leudast had assumed everybody all over the world knew such things. The trouble the redheads had in the snow the first winter of the war taught him otherwise. So did the fancy food and shelters he and his comrades kept taking from dead Algarvians. How could anyone who needed so much help to fight a war in bad weather seriously expect to win it?

Trying without much luck not to limp on his injured leg, Leudast went over to one of the stewpots and took out his mess tin. A cook with the hood to his greatcoat protecting his face ladled the tin full. "There you go, sir," he said. His voice was curiously neutral; Leudast hadn't been with the company long enough to have created much of an impression for good or ill.

"Thanks," he said now, and dug in with a tin spoon. The stew was hot, which felt good. It had barley and oats and some rather nasty vegetables—the Yaninans ate things Unkerlanters didn't—and bits of meat. Prodding one of those with his spoon, Leudast asked, "Do I want to know what this is?"

"Could be cursed near anything, sir," the cook answered. "There's chunks of two, three different beasts in the pots these days: behemoth and horse and unicorn, maybe even some real pork, too, but I'm not sure about that."

"I won't worry about it," Leudast said. "Whatever it is, it'll keep me going—and it doesn't taste too bad." The cook beamed when he added that.

Eggs started bursting, not very far to the east. As always, the Algarvians fought hard over every inch of ground they yielded. They counterattacked whenever they saw the chance. It was as if they were saying to the Unkerlanters, *If you think you can beat us, you're going to have to pay the price.*

The ground shook under Leudast's feet. For a moment, he thought the eggs accounted for that, but then somebody said, "More behemoths coming in."

He looked back toward the west, toward Unkerlant. Sure

enough, the big, burly beasts were plenty to make the ground tremble. "What's it like up ahead?" one of the men on the lead behemoth called as the beasts squelched forward.

"What do you think it's going to be like?" Leudast answered. "There are redheads up there, and they won't kiss you when they see you."

"We'll kiss them, by the powers above." The fellow riding the behemoth leaned over to pat the heavy stick mounted on the beast's armored back. "We'll kiss them with this. We'll kiss anybody who gets in our way, you bet we will."

"Good. They deserve it." Leudast paused, then asked, "Have you had any trouble from the Yaninans?"

"Not much. They'd be sorry if they gave us any, I'll tell you that," the man on the behemoth said. "Some of 'em like us better than Mezentio's whoresons, and that's fine. Some of 'em like the Algarvians better, I expect, but they haven't had the nerve to show it, and they'd better not. The army is on our side."

Leudast snorted. "Aye, I've heard the same thing. And it'll do us just as much good as it ever did the Algarvians."

"It can soak up some casualties," the behemoth crewman said. "Better the Yaninans than us."

"You're right about that. We've paid our share and then some," Leudast said. The fellow on the behemoth nodded and waved. The beast trudged forward. Its big feet came out of the mud, one after another, with heavy squelching sounds despite the snowshoes that spread its weight. The whole long column of behemoths followed. By the time they all went through, the road was a river of ooze stinking of behemoth dung.

One of Leudast's men said, "There'll be another big fight coming up pretty soon. They don't move behemoths forward unless they mean it."

"You're probably right," Leudast answered. "Only thing we can do about it is try and whip the redheads and not get hurt too bad ourselves."

"That would be good." The soldier didn't sound as if he thought it were very likely to happen, though. Had Leudast been the stuffy sort of officer, he would have given the man a hard time and lectured him about efficiency. Since he'd never been able to stand that kind of officer before getting promoted himself, he kept his mouth shut.

Before long, the regimental commander—himself only a captain—came into the village with orders: "We go forward this afternoon."

"Aye, sir." Leudast nodded. "I thought as much when the behemoths came through earlier in the day."

"You're no fool, are you?" the captain said—his name was Drogden.

"There's plenty who'd tell you otherwise, sir," Leudast said, and got a laugh from Drogden before going on, "My guess is, I've just seen a lot of war."

"Our whole kingdom has seen a lot of war, and my guess is that we've got a good deal more to see yet before the redheads are licked," Captain Drogden said.

"My guess is, that's a pretty good guess," Leudast said.

Drogden nodded. He was an older man, close to forty, weather-beaten enough to show he'd seen a lot of war, too. Maybe he was a jumped-up sergeant like Leudast, or maybe he'd spent a long, long time as a lieutenant. "Aye, the Algarvians have no quit in 'em," he said. "That's plain enough. But still and all, things'll be different once we finally go and break into Algarve."

His voice held an odd anticipation. "Different how, sir?" Leudast asked.

"I'll tell you how," the regimental commander said. "We get to pay those whoresons back for everything they did to Unkerlant when their peckers were up, that's how. We can burn their farms pretty cursed soon. We can wreck their villages. Our mages can tear up their ley line. And, speaking of peckers up, we can throw their women down on the ground and do what we want with them."

Leudast grunted. He knew the Algarvians had done such things in the Unkerlanter territory they'd overrun. "Powers above, I've never even seen a redheaded woman before," he said.

"Neither have I. But if we don't get blazed, I expect we're

going to. It should be fun." With a leer, Drogden slapped him on the back. "Spread the word through your company. It'll give the men something extra to fight for."

Most of his troopers, Leudast discovered, had already had that thought for themselves. Some looked forward to it. But one man said, "Far as I'm concerned, we should just kill all the Algarvians, the men and the women both. Then we won't have to worry about 'em ever again." Leudast couldn't deny that that notion held more than a little appeal for him, too.

When the attack went in that afternoon, the Unkerlanters pushed forward for a couple of miles without much trouble. Then they came to the Skamandros River, which the rain had made too wide and swift to ford, and discovered that the redheads had wrecked all the bridges over it. They also discovered that the Algarvians had a demon of a lot of well-concealed egg-tossers on the far bank. "What now?" Leudast asked when he saw Captain Drogden again.

"Now we wait for the artificers to make some new bridges, or else for our dragons and egg-tossers to smash up the redheads and give us some kind of chance to cross," Drogden answered. "Don't know what else we can do."

"It's not so bad, sir," Leudast said. "We're moving forward, and that counts for more than anything else."

Sidroc hadn't liked Unkerlanters, and they weren't that much different from Forthwegians. Now that the Algarvian army was forced back into Yanina, and Plegmund's Brigade with it, he discovered that he really didn't like Yaninans.

"Where's your food?" he demanded of a skinny villager with cold, dark eyes and a big gray mustache. He said it in Forthwegian, and then in Algarvian. The Yaninan looked back at him, shrugged, and spread his hands as if to say he didn't understand.

"Blaze the son of a whore," Ceorl suggested. "That'll teach him."

"It won't do us any good, though," Sidroc said. "Here, watch me be as efficient as an Unkerlanter. Go inside the house there and bring out this bastard's wife. Don't get rough with her or anything, but bring her."

Ceorl laughed. "I'll do it. I think I know what you've got in mind."

In he went. The Yaninan villager looked alarmed. He looked a lot more alarmed when the woman cried out. But when he took a step toward the house, Sidroc aimed his stick at the fellow's face. "Don't even think about it, pal," he said. Either the words or the gesture got through; the Yaninan froze, though his mouth twisted in a snarl of hate.

Out came Ceorl, manhandling a graying woman about half his size. Sidroc knew no Yaninan, but he was sure she was calling Ceorl everything she could. Ceorl realized that, too. "I hope the old shitter stays clammed up," he said. "I'd enjoy doing in this bitch."

"We'll find out in a minute." Sidroc switched back to Algarvian: "One more time, pal. Where is the food? She'll be sorry if you keep quiet."

Looking daggers at him, the Yaninan answered in pretty good Algarvian of his own: "Dig under the water barrel." He looked as if he wanted to say a good deal more than that, but he bit it back. That was one of the wiser things he'd ever done.

"No." Sidroc gestured. "You dig, pal. And you had better come up with some good stuff, too."

He went into the house with the Yaninan, and watched the skinny old man dig up the dirt floor. What came out was plenty to satisfy him: hams and sausages, all securely wrapped to keep them safe while they were out of sight. At his delighted exclamation, Ceorl came in to see, too. "Well, all right," the ruffian said enthusiastically. "I guess we let the old whore live."

"You see?" Sidroc said to the Yaninan. "You just saved your wife."

"But the two of you, this is too much for you," the man with the gray mustache said.

"We've got friends." Sidroc grabbed a long string of sausages. "Come on, Ceorl. Lend a hand."

Between them, they did a good job of plundering the peasants' larder. When they showed their comrades what they'd got, they were the heroes of the moment. "Haven't eaten this well since we got out of Forthweg," Sergeant Werferth said. He was exaggerating, but not by a great deal.

Sudaku, the blond from the Phalanx of Valmiera who'd broken out of the Mandelsloh pocket with the men of Plegmund's Brigade, nodded. "Good food," he said in Algarvian. He was eating enough for two himself.

"If we had more spirits, we'd have more spirits," Ceorl said, and laughed loudly at his own wit. Sidroc chuckled, too. He wasn't going to let a fellow Forthwegian down, not even a son of a whore like Ceorl.

Werferth said, "Maybe you ought to go shake down that Yaninan of yours again. If he hid the food under the water barrel, he's probably got a distillery on the roof."

"I would not be a bit surprised," Sidroc said—in Algarvian, so the men who weren't Forthwegians but had attached themselves to the now motley unit could understand. He nodded to Ceorl. "What do you say we go have a look?"

"Probably find that ugly bastard and his uglier woman drunk and screwing their brains out." Ceorl started to heave himself to his feet.

Before he got upright, eggs started landing not far away. He threw himself flat. So did Sidroc. So did all the men who'd been sharing the booty they'd found. Veterans knew better than to stay on their feet, or even sitting, when the Unkerlanters started getting frisky.

More of the eggs landed west of the Yaninan village than square on it. That cheered Sidroc, but not for long. A couple of minutes later, Algarvians—and a few Forthwegians, and a couple of the Valmieran Kaunians who'd taken service with King Mezentio—came running back from their forward positions. In the din, he needed a little while to catch what they were shouting. When he did, he wished he hadn't; it was, "Behemoths! Unkerlanter behemoths!"

Sergeant Werferth stuck his head up in the hope of spotting an Algarvian officer—or perhaps in the hope of not spotting one. When he didn't, he spoke in Algarvian: "I am in charge here. We are going to get over that river east of the village as quick as we can. We have no hope of fighting their behemoths without some of our own."

That was a bitter truth the men of Plegmund's Brigade and the Algarvians had learned in too many encounters throughout eastern Unkerlant. Sidroc said, "Once we're over the bridge"— he hoped their was a bridge; he'd swum one stream to escape Swemmel's soldiers, and didn't want to have to try it again— "we'd better wreck it, to keep the enemy from getting a foothold on the other side."

"Sounds good to me," Ceorl said. Sergeant Werferth only shrugged. He'd always paid more attention to the proper rules of soldiering and less to what would save his own neck than made Sidroc comfortable.

But he was the one who'd ordered the retreat. He didn't expect his men to do the impossible; too many of them had died trying. Sidroc's boots squelched through mud. That would slow the behemoths down, too, even if it wouldn't slow them down so much as he would have liked.

"Here! Over here!" That was an Algarvian voice, and one full of the authority the redheads effortlessly assumed. "Here is the crossing of the Skamandros. We shall pass over it, hold it open as long as we can, and then destroy it to keep the Unkerlanters from following."

"There, you see?" Sidroc said cheerfully. "I ought to be an officer."

"You ought to get a good kick in the slats." Ceorl also sounded cheerful, as if he would have enjoyed delivering the kick. All things considered, he probably would have.

The bridge, when they reached it, was wooden and narrow: a miserable, rickety piece of work, like a lot of the things Sidroc had seen in Yanina. "Behemoths would have a demon of a time crossing on this," he said as he started across it himself.

"Don't want footsoldiers crossing, either," Werferth said. "Swemmel's whoresons are downright nasty when it comes to grabbing bridgeheads." He was, without a doubt, right about that. Sidroc sighed with relief when he stepped into the mud on the far bank. The Unkerlanters would be a while crossing, anyhow.

A couple of Algarvian mages stood on the eastern bank of the Skamandros. One said to the other, "We'll give it a few minutes more and then bring down the bridge. We don't want to let the Unkerlanters get close enough to try a counterspell and stop us."

"That's the truth," the other wizard said. "I've still got hopes of living to get old and gray and crotchety. A few behemoths in the wrong place don't do those plans any good."

They both laughed. Algarvians took pride in absurdity. Sidroc didn't. He was just glad he'd got over the river before the redheads sorcerously smashed the bridge.

"To me!" called the Algarvian officer who'd known where the crossing was. "There's a village ahead. We can shelter in it."

"Who knows?" Sidroc said. "Maybe the stinking Yaninans will have more hams buried under the water barrel. Here's hoping." Marching made him weary, as it always did, but he wasn't hungry. That in itself made a pleasant novelty.

He hadn't gone far before a rending crash behind him announced the demise of the bridge. If Swemmel's sorcerers had tried a counterspell, it hadn't worked. Sergeant Werferth said, "Keep moving, boys. The sooner we get to this village, wherever it is, the happier we'll be."

The village wasn't far ahead. Yapping dogs announced its presence before the road came out from among a grove of fruit trees and let Sidroc see it. He'd had the same thing happen more than once back in Unkerlant.

"Keep moving," the Algarvian officer commanded, leading from the front as his kind usually did. "We're going to dig in here. We're going to stop the Unkerlanters in their tracks." As his kind usually did, he sounded utterly certain of that. What difference did it make that powers-above-only-knew-how-many similar declarations had been wrong before?

Sidroc knew what difference it made. "We'd cursed well better stop Swemmel's bastards," he said. "We haven't got a lot of room left to play around with." He scowled at the village ahead, and at the dogs trying to nerve themselves for a run at the soldiers tramping up the road towards them.

"We've got to keep trying, no matter what," Sergeant Werferth said. "If we don't, we're cooked, on account of—" He suddenly stopped talking. He suddenly stopped walking, too, crumpling down to the roadway as if he were a marionette with cut strings. He twitched a couple of times and lay still.

"He's dead," Ceorl said in slow wonder. "I fornicating can't believe it. I was fornicating sure he'd outlive every fornicating one of us."

That thought had gone through Sidroc's mind, too. Now only anger filled him. He pointed ahead. "The beam came from that first house there. I saw it. Now we pay back the bastard who did it."

"Now we pay back the whole fornicating village," said Sudaku, the man from the Phalanx of Valmiera. *He might be only a Kaunian,* Sidroc thought, *but he's a pretty cursed good soldier.*

A low growl ran through the men—Forthwegians, Kaunians, and Algarvians. Everyone who'd known Werferth had liked him. And he was one of their own, and a civilian sniper had blazed him. They shook themselves out into a skirmish line and advanced on the village at a purposeful trot. Most of the dogs in front of it fled, yelping in dismay. The soldiers blazed the ones that didn't.

Another beam winked at them from that farmhouse window. This time, it didn't hit anybody. A couple of soldiers blazed back, while others moved toward the farmhouse. Along with the rest, Sidroc trotted into the village. "Out!" he shouted in Algarvian. "Out! Out! Out!" A dozen, a score, of voices took up the cry. A couple of men even knew how to say it in Yaninan.

Confused and frightened-looking villagers started coming forth. Sidroc blazed the first one he saw, a woman a few years older than he was. She fell with a shriek. The rest of the Yaninans cried out in horror. Then their yells turned to agony, too, for all the men who fought for Mezentio started blazing at them. It was vengeance swift and sure, vengeance a hundred-fold for the soldier their countryman had slain.

Afterwards, Sidroc remembered the massacre in red fragments. An old man with no teeth yammering in mushy terror, mouth open very wide, till Sidroc's beam blew out the back of his head. A young man charging the soldiers but falling before he could use his fists, the only weapons he had. A young woman running and then twisting every which way as three beams caught her at once. A fat grandmother standing and dying so she almost blocked the doorway to her house. The little girl who came out when the grandmother's body didn't block the doorway well enough, and who died a moment later, too.

It didn't take long, the massacre. "They had it coming," Sidroc said. A few Yaninans still writhed and moaned. Most lay where they had fallen.

"Of course they had it coming," the young Algarvian officer said. "Now dig in. I don't know how long the line of the Ska-mandros will hold the Unkerlanters. Not long enough, curse it." He was likely right about that. Sidroc got to work.

Twenty

Somewhere not far ahead, the Algarvians waited. Leino knew it. Some time soon, they would try to strike back. The Kuusaman mage didn't know that, not for a fact, but he felt it in his boots. Mezentio's men had already yielded half of Jelgava—more than half, farther to the south. If they were going to hold the armies of Kuusamo and Lagoas away from their own border, they would have to strike back soon.

He started to say as much to Xavega, but she picked that moment to look up from the grimoire she was studying and announce, "It's too hot in here."

"Well, so it is," Leino said. "You could always go outside the tent for some air."

"It will be too hot out there, too." Even in clean, abstract classical Kaunian, Xavega had no trouble sounding querulous. "This is autumn. The weather should be changing."

"It has changed," Leino said. Xavega shook her head, sending copper curls flying, but he went on, "It was much too hot. Now it is only too hot. Jelgava is a warm kingdom, much warmer than either Kuusamo or Lagoas."

"Disgusting," Xavega said. "I am always as sweaty as if we had just finished making love." She put the grimoire aside and glanced over at him. "Since I am already sweaty, shall we?" Without waiting for an answer, she started undoing the toggles of her tunic.

Leino went to her. Everything they had that was worth keeping, they had in bed: here in this tent, in a couple of narrow, lumpy, uncomfortable cots. He stroked her. She *was* sweaty. In short order, so was he. He might have been bloody, too; her nails had scored his back.

Afterwards, she dressed quickly—no lazing in the afterglow. And she went back to studying the grimoire with the same dour intensity. After a few minutes, she looked up and said, "This is the strangest sorcery I have ever had to learn."

"I think it is fascinating," Leino said. And, whenever he studied that sorcery, he saw Pekka's handprints all through it. She hadn't said much about what she was doing; ever since the war started, she'd been very close-mouthed about her work. But everything Leino saw in these spells corresponded to the little hints he'd got from her. He understood now why she'd kept so quiet. "This is a cleaner way to get more out of sorcery than the Algarvians do with all their murders. What could be better than that?"

"I will tell you what could be better," Xavega answered at once. "The spells could be in Lagoan, or even in classical Kaunian. Because they are in Kuusaman, I have to learn them phonetically, and I do not see how anyone pronounces your language."

"I have no trouble with it," Leino said, laughing. "Now, the sneezes and sounds through your nose that go into Lagoan—I think no sensible language should have those."

"Lagoan is a beautiful language," Xavega said. "Lagoan is the most beautiful language in the world. Only Sibian and Algarvian even come close."

You think so because they're Algarvic languages, too, Leino thought. He didn't raise the issue with Xavega. Some things simply weren't worth arguing about. Before he could find some safe way of steering them away from the beauty or lack of some in Lagoan, a soldier outside did it for him by calling out in Kuusaman: "You wizards decent in there?"

How noisy had Xavega been? Leino hadn't paid close attention to that. Doing his best not to sound embarrassed, he answered, "Aye. What needs doing?"

The soldier stuck his head into the tent. Xavega squawked; she hadn't followed the brief conversation. Still speaking Kuusaman, the soldier said, "Sorry to bother you, but we've got a Jelgavan here. He speaks some classical Kaunian. Can you translate?"

"Aye, I'll do that," Leino replied in Kuusaman. He translated the exchange for Xavega, then added, "Unless you would rather?"

"No, you go ahead," she said. "You would have to translate for me if I did it. This way, I can keep studying here. You see how efficient I am—just like our allies to the west." By her expression, she didn't mean that as a compliment to the Unkerlanters.

"Fair enough," Leino said: no point discussing what he thought or didn't think of King Swemmel and Swemmel's kingdom, not right now. He returned to Kuusaman, telling the officer, "Take me to this Jelgavan, then."

The blond proved bigger and younger than he'd expected. "Hail. I am Talsu son of Traku," he said, and then had to stop and think. As the officer had said, he knew some classical Kaunian, but he wasn't fluent in it, as an educated man would have been. After that pause, he went on, "Algarvian line am— uh, is—before the town of Skrunda, aye?"

"Of course," Leino answered. And it was indeed *of course*; the islanders had been tapping at that line for most of a week, but hadn't yet found a weak spot. Then he realized why the Jelgavan might have come, so he asked, "Do you know a way through it?"

Talsu son of Traku nodded. "I do. I am living in Skrunda all of mine life. I am—*was*—in army of King Donalitu's. Now I am irregular hereabouts."

He could make himself understood, even if his grammar left something to be desired. But . . . Leino said, "Did not the irregulars in these parts suffer a great blow not long ago?"

"That am truth," Talsu said grimly. "We not can to fight much. But I am knowing the of the barbarians position. I am knowing way past it. Men can to go. Behemothses can to go." He murdered conjugations, declensions, and syntax.

Leino didn't care. He liked what he was hearing, regardless of how it was phrased. When he translated for the Kuusaman officer, that worthy's smile said he liked it pretty well, too. He said, "Tell this fellow we'll find him an officer or two who can follow Kaunian, and he can lead them, and they can lead our men. We'll flank those fornicating Algarvians right out of their boots."

When Leino translated that quite literally, Talsu's pale eyes lit up with a fierce fire. "Let us bring woe to the barbarians," he declared, and then, with a grin that made him look even younger than he was, "Hortatory subjunctive. I remember how to make."

"Good," Leino said, not smiling so broadly as he would have liked. "Right now, I think remembering how to make trouble for the Algarvians is more important."

"Even so," Talsu agreed. When he stuck to stock phrases, he did well enough.

"I will come with you until we find a combat officer with whom you can talk," Leino said. "I am only a mage. I fear I am not worth much in the field."

"If you can stop the of the barbarians sorcery, you are worth of much," Talsu said. "You can to save many of Kaunians blood."

After Leino turned that into Kuusaman, the officer who'd got him nodded and said, "He's right." Leino nodded, too; he couldn't very well disagree. The officer continued, "Well, let's find some more overeducated types who call tell what this fellow's going on about."

"It would be handy if more of us spoke Jelgavan," Leino said.

"It'd be even handier if this bastard spoke Kuusaman," the officer said. "Come on with me. I have two or three fellows I can ask." He had to go through five men before finding two who could handle classical Kaunian tolerably well. When he did, he gave Leino half a bow. "I think you can get back to whatever you were doing before, sir." His eyes twinkled. "Maybe you'll be ready to do it again."

"That would be nice," Leino said dryly, "but I don't think I'd better. If you do go and outflank Mezentio's men, they won't stop at anything to push you back. I don't know what that means as far as fighting goes, but I know just what it means when you talk about magecraft. I think Xavega and I ought to be ready to try to block it."

"You're right." The officer's lips skinned back from his teeth in what looked like a smile but wasn't. "Here's hoping you don't have to do what you're ready to try."

"Please to translate?" Talsu said. Leino pretended he hadn't heard. The Jelgavan already knew what the Algarvians might do. Leino didn't feel like talking about it. He knew what he and Xavega were supposed to do if Mezentio's men did start their sorcery—*start murdering blonds,* he glossed mentally. But he'd never tried the counterspells, and didn't care to dwell on that, or even to admit it. Confidence counted for a great deal in a mage.

When he got back to the tent, he found Xavega so deeply immersed in the grimoire, she hardly noticed his return. That pleased him; they both needed to be ready to do what they could against the Algarvians. After a while, she did glance up from the book. "What did the Jelgavan want?" she inquired. Leino explained. Xavega nodded. "Let us hope he can do what he says he can."

"Hortatory subjunctive," Leino murmured. She looked puzzled. This time, he didn't explain. Instead, he said, "If we do look like flanking them, they are liable to start killing people. When they do, we shall feel them. We cannot help but feel them. And we shall have to try to stop them and turn their accursed sorcery back on them."

That made Xavega turn serious on the instant. She said, "You are right, of course. I think, the first time, you had better do the incanting. Draw on me for power; I will give you everything I have. But I am not positive I can cast a proper spell in Kuusaman."

"Let it be as you say," Leino replied. "If you are not positive you can, you should not try, not when you would be going into the teeth of the Algarvians' conjuration."

"My thought exactly," Xavega said. "Thank you for seeing things the same way and not reckoning me a coward."

What an Algarvic notion, Leino thought. *We Kuusamans mostly have better sense than to try something we know is beyond us.* Aloud, he said, "Anyone would have—everyone does have—good reason to worry about what Mezentio's mages are doing."

To his surprise, she kissed him. "Not many Lagoan men would be so understanding," she said. She was probably right, too. Lagoans, as he'd thought only a little while before, were cousins to the Algarvians, and if any folk in this war had tried something beyond their power, it was the one Mezentio led.

With soft, muffled calls and the clank of armor on behemoths and their crewmen, a good-sized force of Kuusaman soldiers left the camp, heading west. Leino hoped Talsu knew what he was talking about. He also hoped Talsu wasn't leading his countrymen into a trap. Some few Jelgavans loathed King Donalitu enough to stay loyal to Mezentio no matter what his men did to blonds.

Then Leino stopped caring about politics, for Xavega kissed him again, more emphatically this time. Telling the Kuusaman officer he wouldn't yield to temptation was one thing. But he and Xavega had both started getting undressed once more when they suddenly froze, him with her nipple between his thumb and forefinger. "*Curse* the Algarvians!" he said, his reasons now intimate along with the wider-ranging ones of the war. But that heaviness in the air, almost palpable to a sorcerer, meant Mezentio's mages were murdering more Kaunians.

"Now we find out what we can do," Xavega said, "aside from *that*, I mean." She let her hand rest affectionately on his crotch for a moment, but then grabbed her tunic and started closing it once more.

Probably just as well that she is, Leino thought. *I can't afford to be distracted, not now, not trying an important spell for the first time.* Gathering himself, he began the charm he was sure his wife had helped shape. He tasted the irony once more, then set it aside—he had no time for it now. It too was a distraction.

So was Xavega, coming up behind him and setting a hand on his shoulder as he incanted. But she was a necessary distraction. Here with the magecraft, she gave unstintingly of herself, more than she did in bed. He felt power flowing from her into him as he chanted and made his passes. And he felt the powers within both of them building as he shaped the spell, building into a sorcerous lance he could aim at the redheads, could use to oppose the darker power they were unleashing.

Could—and did. With a groan almost like the one he would have made at the end with Xavega, he loosed the force pent up inside him. And he felt it strike home, felt it pierce the enemy's own potent magecraft. Whatever they'd been doing with their murderous magic, it was ruined now—and so, he thought, were the wizards who'd attempted it.

Xavega felt the same thing. Eyes shining, she turned him toward her and kissed him. "We did it!" she exclaimed. Leino's answering nod was dizzy for more reasons than one. How much had the conjuration taken out of him. Not *too* much, he hoped. Xavega dropped to her knees. "Where were we?" she asked, looking up at him with eyes full of mischief. They hadn't been quite *there*, but it seemed to Leino as good a place as any, and far better than most. He set a hand on the back of her head, urging her on.

"This way," Talsu said to one of the Kuusaman officers who spoke about as much classical Kaunian as he did. "Do you to see? No barbarians here. Some on *that* side of hills, others on *this* side, but none here. They not to know of way through here."

"I see," the dark little slant-eyed man replied. "This is good. If we get through, this is very good. I think now that we get through." He spoke in his own oddly rhythmic language to his countrymen. A couple of them answered in the same speech. Talsu understood not a word of it, but he still would have guessed the Kuusamans were pleased with the way things were going.

"We give the Algarvians right up the—" The Kuusaman officer used a phrase Talsu hadn't heard before. He didn't even know whether the last couple of words were Kuusaman or classical Kaunian. He didn't care very much, either. Whatever language they were in, he got the message. He laughed out loud. He liked it, too.

He led the Kuusamans on the winding track past Skrunda. The Algarvians probably didn't even know it was there. They couldn't find out everything about the kingdom they'd occupied, and they wouldn't have needed to do any fighting here since the earliest days of their invasion, if then. Plenty of people could have told the Kuusamans and Lagoans about it. Talsu happened to be the one who had.

If the Kuusamans get in behind Skrunda, the redheads will have to pull back, he thought. *And if they pull back, they'll leave my family alone after that. They'll have to, because they won't be able to reach them. Powers above grant that everyone is still safe. They wouldn't have done anything to them . . . would they?*

I'll find out. Once the Algarvians are gone, I'll find out. That's what the Kuusamans and the Lagoans are good for: driving out Mezentio's men. We couldn't do it for ourselves, but it's still going to get done.

"There." He pointed for the Kuusaman officer. "Do you to see? You are gone by Skrunda now. No Algarvian positions here. No barbarians here. Your men can to go ahead."

"I see," the foreigner said. Except for Algarvians, he was among the first foreigners Talsu had ever dealt with. He called out to his own men, and to the behemoths with them. Then he slapped Talsu on the back. He had to reach up to do it; he was a head shorter than the Jelgavan, and so were most of his countrymen. He was short beside Algarvians, too. But with a stick in his hands, what size he was didn't matter much. He grinned and repeated himself: "Right up the—"

"Aye," Talsu said fiercely.

The Kuusaman called out again in his own language. His men and behemoths went forward without the slightest hesitation. They shared that trait with the Algarvians: when they found an opening, they swarmed to take advantage of it. Talsu didn't think any part of the Jelgavan army had ever moved so fast during this war. That was a good reason why there was no Jelgavan army any more, unless King Donalitu was reconstituting one in the lands the Lagoan and Kuusaman armies had regained for him.

From where Talsu stood, he could see a long way into the flat country west of Skrunda. He could see where the Algarvians suddenly realized a dagger had been thrust through their defenses. And he could see the Kuusamans rushing past the redheads' handful of pickets, giving them enough attention to keep them from slowing things down and not a copper more. That was another lesson Mezentio's men had taught, another lesson the Jelgavans hadn't learned.

"What are you going to do about that, you stinking whoresons?" Talsu said, almost hugging himself with glee. "How do you like it when it happens to you?"

But then, almost as soon as the words were out of his mouth, the ground quivered under his feet like an animal in pain. He cried out in horror and in fear. The Algarvians wasted no time hitting back, either, and he knew just how they were doing it: with the life blood of Kaunians.

What would, what could, the Kuusamans do about that? He waited for disaster to strike them, as it had struck the band of irregulars of which he'd been a part after they did too good a job of harassing the redheads.

Talsu waited, but that didn't happen. What did happen was a flash of light somewhere off to the west, almost at the edge of his vision. And after that, he felt no more of the sorcery that had wrecked his comrades in the steeper hills to the south.

What *had* the Kuusamans done? The first fellow he'd talked to, the one who'd spoken classical Kaunian really well, had worn a mage's badge. Had he had something to do with whatever had just happened? *How should I know?* Talsu wondered. It didn't really matter, anyhow. What mattered was that the redheads' magic had failed them.

Did the Kuusamans here even know what their sorcerers had

done? Talsu doubted it. That didn't really matter, either. The redheads in these parts hadn't been able to stop their foes through force of magecraft. Now they would have to try through force of arms. *And I don't think they've got the force of arms to do it, not when their flank's been turned.*

He wasn't, he didn't have to be, part of the battle for Skrunda and the surrounding territory. Watching it unfold without risk to him was a rare luxury, like expensive wine or extra-soft wool for a pair of trousers. A steady stream of Kuusaman soldiers slogged past him, heading into the fight. He waved to the men of each company. They were doing his kingdom an enormous favor. He wondered if they thought of it that way, or whether they were as resigned to doing as they were told as he had been during his army days. The latter, he would have bet.

Dragons flew low overhead, dragons hard to spot because they were painted in Kuusaman sky blue and sea green. No Algarvian dragons that he saw rose to challenge them. He hadn't seen many Algarvian dragons here in Jelgava, not at any time and especially not the past year or so. *Where are they?* he thought. *Defending Algarve itself, I suppose, and trying to hold back the Unkerlanters. But Mezentio's soldiers in these parts are paying a big price because the redheads don't have enough.* That left him something less than brokenhearted.

He trudged forward, sticking to the fields by the side of the track so the advancing Kuusamans would get the benefit of the best ground. Before he'd gone very far, he passed a crater in the ground and a corpse with nastily mangled legs. He gulped. Even if the Algarvians didn't have soldiers covering this route, they'd buried eggs in the ground to slow up an enemy advance. Half a mile farther on lay a dead behemoth with its right hind leg only a bloody mess. Talsu gulped again.

Here came some kilted Algarvians back toward him. They weren't part of a counterattack. None of them carried a stick, and all of them held their hands high over their heads. They were captives, herded along by a couple of bowlegged little Kuusamans. When Jelgava fell, a handful of Algarvians had taken a battalion's worth of Talsu's countrymen into captivity. Now they were tasting the humiliation they'd dished out. Some of them looked weary. More had that beaten-dog grin of relief at being alive.

Going down onto lower ground meant Talsu couldn't see Skrunda any more. But he knew where it lay, and made for it without hesitation. He kept peering northwest, for fear he'd see a great column of greasy black smoke rising into the sky. That would mean the redheads were fighting there, or else that they'd fired the town to help cover their retreat. He hoped they would do no such thing, but knew he couldn't be sure what they might try.

To the Kuusamans, he was just one more civilian now. He did his best to stay out of their way, too. Some of them were liable to blaze first and ask questions later.

Then the road rose and let him see his home town again. He felt like cheering—it looked more or less intact. He hurried toward it with the eagerness of a lover rushing toward his beloved. And he was rushing toward his beloved, too, for Gailisa was there—or he hoped with all his heart she was.

He trudged into Skrunda an hour or so later. The first thing he saw was two Jelgavan bodies hanging from lampposts. The placards tied round their necks said, THEY FOUGHT AGAINST ALGARVE. Neither of them was anybody Talsu knew well. He let out a silent sigh of relief at that.

He made for the grocer's shop his father-in-law ran. Maybe Gailisa would be there. If she wasn't, her father would surely know where she was—and he would know about Talsu's mother and father and sister, too.

But the grocer's shop wasn't there any more. Talsu stared in startled dismay. He'd been away from Skrunda for a couple of months now. How many times had dragons come over the town and dropped eggs on it? In one of those visits, the grocer's shop had gone up in flames, as his own family's tailor's shop had earlier. Now he had to hurry toward the tent city on the west side of town, where refugees like his family had been staying. Maybe he could find Gailisa's father there, too.

Maybe Gailisa's father and Gailisa herself had been in the grocer's shop when eggs fell on and around it. Talsu tried not to think about that.

A couple of people who knew him nodded cautiously as he hurried past them. A couple of others turned their backs. Some folk in Skrunda still thought the Algarvians had let him out of their dungeon because he'd betrayed his countrymen for them. There was very little truth in that, but how could he prove it?

He was about the plunge into the tent city and make for the tent where he'd been sheltering before he had to flee when someone called his name: "Talsu!"

"Ausra!" he said, whirling toward his sister, recognizing her voice even before he saw her. She threw herself into his arms. He squeezed the breath out of her and kissed her on the cheek. "Are you all right? Is Gailisa? Are Father and Mother?"

"Aye, we're all fine," she answered, and he kissed her again, harder this time. But she went on, "Gailisa's father . . ."

"Oh, powers above!" Talsu said. "I saw the shop on the way here. He didn't get out?"

Ausra shook here head. "I'm afraid not. Gailisa's taken it pretty hard."

"I believe that," Talsu said, though he'd always thought of his father-in-law as a plump, not particularly good-natured nonentity, one of the least interesting people he'd ever known. "When did it happen? The ruins looked pretty fresh."

"Just last week," his sister told him. He ground his teeth. Ausra took his arm. "But come on. I don't think the redheads are looking for you any more."

"I didn't see any Algarvians in town," Talsu said, "and I think Skrunda is as good as free, because the Kuusamans have broken through beyond the town, and the redheads will have to pull back or be trapped."

"How do you know that?" Ausra asked.

"Because I showed the Kuusamans the route they could use to break through," Talsu answered proudly. This time, Ausra kissed him.

That was nice, but the looks on the faces of Traku and Laitsina and, best of all, Gailisa were finer still a couple of minutes later. And kissing his wife was ever so much finer than kissing his sister. "You're home!" Gailisa said. "You're safe!" She started to laugh and cry at the same time.

"I'm home. I'm safe," he agreed. "And we're free. We're rid of the redheads for good."

"Here you go, Sergeant," Kun said as he and Istvan cut wood together in the captives' camp on Obuda. "You might want these." He took a few sickly-green leaves from his pocket and held them out to Istvan.

"Oh, I might, might I?" Istvan didn't take the rather wilted leaves. "Stars above, why?"

Kun leaned closer and spoke in a hissing whisper: "Because they'll give you a good two-day dose of the galloping shits, that's why."

Istvan gaped at him. "Are you out of your mind? Why would I want a dose of the shits? They're too stinking easy to get here anyway, the kind of slop the slanteyes feed us."

"Will you take the accursed weeds before the guards start giving us the fishy stares?" Kun snapped. Startled—Kun didn't usually sound so vehement—Istvan did stick the leaves in his own pocket and go back to chopping. Kun started swinging his axe again, too. Nodding, he said, "That's more like it."

"More like what?" Istvan said plaintively. "I still haven't got the faintest idea what under the light of the stars you're talking about."

Corporal Kun rolled his eyes, as he had a habit of doing when sorely tried. "You're such a natural-born innocent, who can guess how you've managed to live this long? But if you've got any sense at all, you'll chew those leaves tonight right around suppertime." His axe bit into a chunk of pine. Chips flew. He smote again. The chunk split in two.

"I'm not going to do any such thing till you tell me why and have it make sense," Istvan said stubbornly.

That only made Kun roll his eyes again. "Just as you say, then." He was most dangerous when most exquisitely polite. "Tonight, you've got yourself a choice. You can leak out your arsehole and go into the infirmary and feel better in a couple of days, or else you can leak out of a cut throat and not feel better ever again. That's it. Depending on how you choose, it may be the last choice you ever get to make."

"Oh!" No matter how naive Istvan was, he couldn't very well misunderstand that. He attacked the chunk of pine in front of him with more violence than it really needed. "They're going to do it tonight?"

"No, I just want to give you the shits," Kun replied. "That way, when you get over them, you can come back and beat the stuffing out of me. I really enjoy having people beat the stuffing out of me, especially when they're twice my size."

"You have leaves of your own?" Istvan asked.

"Of course not," the former mage's apprentice said. "I really enjoy having my own throat cut, too, so I gave you all the leaves I had."

Istvan's ears heated. Maybe Kun didn't deliberately treat him as if he were an idiot. On the other hand, maybe Kun did, too—and maybe he'd earned it with that particular question. But he didn't worry about it for long. He asked, "Did you give Szonyi some of these precious leaves, too?"

If he'd hit the wood harder than he had to, Kun splintered the piece in front of him with his next couple of blows. At last, he answered, "I tried to give him some, but he wouldn't let me. He'd rather take his chances with Captain Frigyes. You can, too, if you think he and the Algarvians and Major Borsos will really do anything worthwhile."

Istvan wished he thought that. Dying for Gyongyos . . . What could be more fitting for a warrior from a warrior race? But he wouldn't be dying for Gyongyos here; he was too mournfully sure of that. He would be dying for Captain Frigyes, for no one and nothing else. Even if Frigyes and Borsos and the redheads made a sorcery to blast the island of Obuda down to the bottom of the Bothnian Ocean, how much would that help Gyongyos and Ekrekek Arpad in the war against Kuusamo? Not very much, not so far as Istvan could see.

"Never mind," he said. Now that it came down to the sticking point, he couldn't stomach betraying his countrymen's plot to the Kuusamans, but he didn't want to be part of it, either. Escaping with a sore belly seemed a better way out of the dilemma than most. "I just wish you could have got Szonyi to see sense."

"So do I," Kun told him. "But he's not in the mood to listen. And he told me, 'Don't waste the sergeant's time, getting him to nag me, either. I know what I'm doing.' I don't think he does, but . . ." He shrugged.

"I'm glad you tried," Istvan said. He also resolved to try to talk to Szonyi himself, no matter what the trooper had told Kun. Wood-chopping seemed to take forever. At last, the guards released the labor detail. Istvan hurried off to try to find his long-time comrade.

But Szonyi wouldn't talk to him, not about that. "I've made up my mind," was all he would say. "I'd rather go out giving the enemy one more lick than spend the rest of my days rotting away here on Obuda."

Istvan found no good reply to that. He finally set his hand on Szonyi's shoulder and said, "May the stars enfold you in their light forevermore, then."

"May it be so." Szonyi gave him an anxious glance. "You and Kun won't betray us, will you? I know you've talked about it."

"No, by the stars, neither one of us," Istvan said. "May they leave us in eternal darkness if I lie. I just don't think you'll do as much as Captain Frigyes thinks you will."

"I think you're wrong, Sergeant." Szonyi turned away. Istvan started to argue some more, then saw it would do no good. He walked off, shaking his head.

When he saw Kun a few minutes later, the one-time mage's apprentice raised a questioning eyebrow. Istvan shook his head. Kun sighed and shrugged.

Along with their suppers, both of them ate the leaves. Istvan had expected, or at least hoped for, a little leisure before they acted and a little dignity while they were working. He got neither. The effect put him in mind of having an egg burst in the middle of his guts. Both he and Kun raced for the latrines at a dead run. Kun's face was pale as milk. Istvan had no doubt he looked the same way.

Neither of them made it to the slit trenches. They both had to yank down their leggings and squat in the middle of the compound while guards cursed them in Kuusaman and Gyongyosian. Istvan stayed on the ground, clutching at his belly. Kun tried to get to his feet, then sank down again. "Must be something we ate," he moaned. That was true, too, if not quite in the way he meant it.

The guards had to drag them to the infirmary. They threw them onto cots in a room of their own and gave them chamber pots. That suited Istvan perfectly. He spent a lot of unpleasant time squatting over his as night replaced day.

"When?" he asked Kun when they chanced to be squatting side by side.

"I don't know," Kun answered. "We'll find out when it happens. In the meantime, shut up." That was doubtless good advice. Istvan tried to tell his guts the same thing. They wouldn't listen to him.

At some point that evening, Istvan asked, "What time is it now?" Since things had started for him, he'd lost a good deal of interest in the outside world, but that still mattered.

Not to Kun, not at the moment. "I don't know, and I don't care," he grunted. That he was squatting again no doubt made him even shorter with questions than he would have been otherwise. After a bit, he added, "And I already told you to shut up. Who knows who's liable to be listening?"

Istvan guessed—and it was only a guess—he fell into an exhausted sleep somewhere around midnight. He knew he hadn't been asleep very long before getting jolted awake by a short, sharp earthquake. He dove under his bed, as he would have done back in his home valley, and hoped the roof wouldn't come down on his head.

Although Kun came from Gyorvar, he knew enough to dive under his cot, too; most of Gyongyos was earthquake country. Through the roar of the ground and the shudder of the infirmary all around them, he shouted, "This isn't just a regular earthquake."

"So what?" Istvan shouted back. "That doesn't mean it can't kill us." Kun didn't answer that. Istvan concluded that, for once, he'd outargued his clever comrade.

Even after the ground stopped shaking, rending and tearing noises went on and on, most of them from outside the captives' camp. Kun stayed right where he was. Istvan started to come out, but seeing Kun on his belly made him decide not going anywhere might be a good idea. Kun said, "Well, they managed to get the spell to work, no doubt about it."

"So they did," Istvan said. "Now, what have they done with it? If they've done enough . . ." *If they've done enough, maybe I should have let them cut my throat. Maybe the stars will turn away from my spirit and leave it in eternal darkness. Am I accursed for cowardice?*

Kun said, "We won't find out till morning at the earliest." If he felt the least bit guilty about remaining alive where his comrades had perished, he showed no sign that Istvan could see.

And a Gyongyosian captive in the next chamber of the infirmary proved him wrong a moment later, calling, "By the stars, half the walls have fallen down!"

"We could escape!" Istvan exclaimed.

"Go ahead," Kun said. "If you want to skulk through the woods up on the slopes of Mount Sorong till the Kuusamans hunt you down with dogs, go right ahead. Me, I don't see much point to it. If I thought we could get back to an island we still held, or even one where we were still fighting, that'd be different. As things are . . ." He shook his head. "No, thanks."

That made more sense than Istvan wished it would have. Some of his countrymen thought otherwise. Outside the infirmary, booted feet pounded across dirt toward what had been the palisade. A Kuusaman shouted in bad Gyongyosian: "To halt! To halt or to blaze!" Those feet kept running. A moment later, a shriek rang out, and then another one. After that, Istvan heard no more running feet inside the captives' camp.

And then, a few minutes later—after he and Kun had cautiously emerged from their shelter—he did. All the shouting this time was in Kuusaman, which he didn't understand. "The slanteyes will have found the bodies," Kun said.

"Do you know that, or are you just guessing?" Istvan asked. It did strike him as a good guess.

"I can understand some of what they're saying," Kun answered. "Not a lot—Kuusaman is a peculiar language, if anyone wants to know what I think: much worse than Unkerlanter—but enough."

All Istvan had ever learned of either were such phrases as,

Hands high! and *Come out of there!* "I'll take your word for it," he said.

A Kuusaman guard charged into their chamber, stick at the ready. He looked at them, saw they were where they were supposed to be and not making trouble, and relaxed a little. Sounding innocent, Kun asked, "What happened?"

"Magic," the guard answered. "Bad magic. Many to be dead." His Gyongyosian was halting but understandable. "To kill themselves to make magic. Bad. Very bad." Shaking his head, he backed out of the room.

Istvan sniffed. "I smell smoke."

"Aye, something's burning," Kun agreed. He sniffed, too. "Not close, I don't think. Nothing we have to worry about." He paused, then went on, "That guard was right, you know. It *was* bad magic, and I don't care that our allies used it first."

"Neither do I," Istvan said, and did his best to believe he was telling the truth.

When the sun rose, he peered eagerly out the window. Sure enough, most of the walls were down, but the Kuusamans had posted an armed man every ten feet or so to prevent escapes. The ley-line depot was also wrecked, and the smoke, he found, came from the direction of the port the Kuusamans had built: he could see as much through the gaps in what had been the palisade. But he could also see that the Kuusamans remained in firm control of the island of Obuda, regardless of what Frigyes and Borsos and the redheads and—most important—Szonyi and the other Gyongyosians who'd laid down their lives had done.

"It was a waste of magic," he said, and would have felt vindicated if he hadn't felt so bad.

"Halt!" Garivald called. "What are you doing?" Seeing any movement was enough to make him swing his stick toward it.

What he saw in the bridgehead by Eoforwic wasn't an Algarvian soldier, but a gray-bearded Forthwegian with a stooped back. When the old man smiled a placating smile, he showed a mouth full of bad teeth. "Nothing, sir," he said. "I'm only . . . mushrooms."

Garivald didn't know the missing word, but had no trouble

figuring out what it meant. Even a Grelzer could follow bits and pieces of Forthwegian, just as the locals could understand a little of what he said. "Come with me," he commanded. "Come with me to my lieutenant."

"Why?" the Forthwegian asked. His smile got wider. He said something else. Garivald couldn't understand it, but could make a good guess—probably something like, *I wasn't doing any harm.*

He shrugged. "Come," he repeated. "Orders. All civilians to be questioned when they're found where they're not supposed to be."

"Only mushrooms," the Forthwegian said. He held up his basket, then held it out to Garivald. "I'll give them to you."

"No." Garivald liked mushrooms, but not so much as the locals did—certainly not enough to let himself be bribed with them. "Come along right now, or you'll be sorry."

Muttering under his breath, the old man came. None of what he said sounded like a compliment. As they went deeper into the bridgehead, he spoke a few words Garivald could understand: "Need to piss."

"Later." With a stick in his hand, Garivald could afford to be heartless.

But the old man whined, "Need to *piss*," again with such dramatic urgency that Garivald relented. He pointed to a stout tree somehow still standing despite all the eggs that had landed on the bridgehead.

The old man disappeared behind it. Perhaps a heartbeat slower than it should have, that roused Garivald's suspicions. "Hey! What are you doing back there?" he barked, and hurried over to find out for himself. The old man wasn't standing there easing himself. He was loping toward a fallen tree not far away, keeping the still-standing one between himself and where Garivald had been. "Halt!" Garivald shouted again.

The old man ran harder than ever. Nobody, though, nobody could outrun a beam. Garivald's caught him in the middle of the back just as he was about to dive behind the tree trunk. He shrieked and went over on his face.

He was still moving feebly when Garivald trotted up to him.

With a glare, he said something Garivald couldn't understand: the blood running from his mouth garbled it. Whatever it was, it didn't sound like Forthwegian. Garivald wished he hadn't blazed to kill—but that, he'd found, was almost always what a soldier intended to do. He hadn't thought of doing anything else till much too late.

With a last unintelligible mumble, the old man died. Garivald knew the exact instant life left his body, for his looks changed in that instant. Suddenly, he no longer looked like a Forthwegian, but like an Algarvian who'd let his beard grow out, as Forthwegians were in the habit of doing.

"Magic!" Garivald exclaimed. His hands twisted in the sign Grelzers used when they ran across magecraft where they didn't expect to. In an abstract way, he admired the redhead's thoroughgoing imposture. It wasn't just the beard: the fellow had spoken good, maybe perfect, Forthwegian, and had even acted as if he liked mushrooms, which Mezentio's men weren't in the habit of doing.

"What have you got, Corporal?" somebody called from behind Garivald: an Unkerlanter. *At least, I think he's an Unkerlanter*, Garivald thought dizzily. Nothing in the world seemed so certain as it had a moment before.

"What have I got?" he echoed. "I've got a spy, that's what. Go fetch Lieutenant Andelot right away. He needs to see this, and to hear about it, too." The Unkerlanter soldier's eyes widened. He took off at a run. Garivald was only a corporal, but common soldiers obeyed him as if he were Marshal Rathar. Of course, he had to obey sergeants and real officers the same way, while Rathar had to obey only the king, with everyone else in Unkerlant obeying him. *The marshal has it easy*, Garivald thought.

Andelot came trotting back with the trooper. "A spy?" he said, and stared down at the dead Algarvian. "How in blazes did he get so far inside our lines, Fariulf?"

"Because he looked just like a fornicating Forthwegian till I blazed him, sir," Garivald answered, and explained what had happened.

"I've heard of such sorcery," Andelot said when he was finished. "Some of the Kaunians here in Forthweg used it to keep the redheads from finding them and killing them. But this is the first time I've heard that the Algarvians are using it to try to make themselves look harmless while they come snooping around."

"I hadn't heard of it at all, sir," Garivald said. "Like I told you, I was taking this fellow back to you so you could question him—he wasn't supposed to be inside the perimeter."

"He must have thought we had a wizard waiting to test him," Andelot said. "He panicked, and got himself killed, *and* gave the game away. If he looked like an old Forthwegian, probably I would have just cursed him and told him to make himself scarce. I wouldn't have guessed he was anything but what he seemed to be."

"I sure didn't, sir," Garivald said. "I was never so surprised in my life as when I saw him change as soon as he died."

"But you did what you were supposed to do by bringing him in," Lieutenant Andelot said. "And you did what you were supposed to do by blazing him when he tried to escape. No one could possibly have asked for more from you, Sergeant Fariulf."

"Serge . . ." Garivald saluted. "Thank you very much, sir!" He didn't much want to be promoted. The higher he rose, the more likely people were to take a long look at him, a look he couldn't afford. But he would also draw long looks if he seemed unhappy about getting a higher rank.

"You're welcome. You've earned it. Eventually, your pay will show that you're getting it, too." Andelot made a wry face. The men who gave out money in the Unkerlanter army plainly didn't think efficiency was anything they had to worry about. "Do you think you could write me a report of everything that happened here, Sergeant?"

"*Write* you a report?" Garivald was more alarmed than he had been when he saw the sorcerously disguised Algarvian trying to get away from him. "Sir, you only showed me my letters a few weeks ago. How in blazes am I supposed to write a report?"

"Just write down what happened, the same as if you were telling it to me," the company commander answered. "Don't worry about your spelling, or anything fancy like that. You would be amazed at how many men who went to good schools can't spell some simple words to keep the powers below from eating them. Believe me, you would. I won't care about that, I promise. But you are the eyewitness. I want the facts down on paper in your words, not mine."

"I'll try, sir," Garivald said dubiously. He pointed to the Algarvian's body. "What do we do with that?"

"Leave him here," Andelot answered. "I'll want a mage to look at him just the way he is. I don't know if he'll be able to learn anything, but I want to give him a chance."

"All right, sir. That makes sense," Garivald said.

"Get some paper, Sergeant—I'll give you some if you can't find it anywhere else—and go write that report," Andelot told him. "Get everything down while it's still fresh in your mind. Don't leave anything out. Maybe it'll help if you pretend you're talking to me instead of writing."

"Maybe." Garivald knew he still didn't sound convinced. He did have to get paper from the lieutenant. Once he got it, he sat apart from his men and started to work. He wrote awkwardly, as a child might have. That annoyed him. It also made his writing harder to read, he knew. He guessed at the spelling of about every other word, and found he had to imitate a conversational style, as Andelot had suggested: it was the only one within his grasp. He couldn't very well imitate other things he'd read, because he hadn't read anything to speak of.

At last, after what seemed like forever and was in fact two leaves of paper, he finished. When he brought Lieutenant Andelot the report, he trembled even more than he had when first going into battle. No man relishes the feeling that he's just made a fool of himself. He had to force his voice to steadiness to say, "Here you are, sir."

"Thank you, Sergeant," Andelot replied. His mention of Garivald's new rank made Garivald feel better and more nervous at the same time. "Let's see what we've got here." He began to read, then looked up and nodded. "You make your letters very clearly."

"You're too kind," Garivald muttered. He had the feeling that was the kind of compliment you got when no others seem to present themselves.

And, sure enough, Andelot said, "Anyone would know, though, that you haven't had much in the way of formal schooling."

"I haven't had any, sir, and you know it," Garivald said.

"Well, so I do." Andelot kept reading. He put down the first leaf and methodically worked his way through the second. When he finished that one, too, he glanced up at the nervously waiting Garivald. He tapped the report with his index finger. "This isn't at all what I expected, Sergeant."

"I'm sorry, sir," Garivald said. "I did the best I could."

Andelot looked surprised. "Sorry? Powers above, what for? Do you think I meant you did a bad job? . . . Oh, I see you do. No, no, no, Sergeant—just the opposite, in fact. This is splendid work. Except for the spelling—which you can't help, of course—I would be sure you'd been writing reports for years." He shook his head. "No, that's not true. I would think you'd been writing romances or poems, not reports. Reports aren't made to be interesting, and most of them aren't. This, though"—he tapped again—"this makes me feel it happened to me, not to you. Only a real storyteller, a born storyteller, has that gift. You've got it."

"I—I don't know what to say, sir," Garivald said. *Maybe I really can write down my songs, or write new ones.* That would have been a safer ambition in almost any other kingdom besides Unkerlant, but he had it even so.

"You don't need to say anything," Andelot told him. "You do need to know that I'm going to have you write more reports whenever you happen to need to. That will give you good practice writing, and I'll have the fun of reading them."

He had to mean it. He wouldn't say something like that just to make Garivald feel good. Real officers didn't much care how underofficers felt. Why should they? They could tell underofficers what to do, and what else mattered? Garivald said, "I'll try it again, sir, but I don't want the kind of surprise that stinking redhead gave me."

"I don't blame you a bit, Fariulf," Andelot said. "The cursed Algarvians have given us too many surprises, all through this fight. That's the way Algarvians are. They always come up with new things. But we gave them a surprise, too, you know. We did—we stodgy old Unkerlanters."

"We did?" Garivald asked in honest amazement. "What kind of surprise?"

"We didn't fall over and die when they hit us, and they thought we would," Andelot said. "The Forthwegians did, and the Sibs, and the Valmierans, and the Jelgavans—and they chased the Lagoans right off the mainland of Derlavai with their tails between their legs. But they hit us, and we kept hitting back—and look where we are now."

Garivald didn't particularly want to be in a bridgehead in the middle of Forthweg. Even so, though, he nodded. Andelot had a point.

Fernao plowed through a Kuusaman news sheet as he ate an omelette for breakfast. By now, after a couple of years reading Kuusaman, he took it almost as much for granted as he did Lagoan. Some of the mages from his kingdom grumbled about it, but Lagoans always grumbled whenever they had to pay more attention to Kuusamo and its ways than they wanted to.

"Anything interesting?" Ilmarinen asked from across the table. He was working his way through a plate of smoked salmon and onions and capers and pickled cucumbers.

"I don't know about interesting, but this report on something that went wrong on the island of Obuda is strange," Fernao answered. He passed the sheet to Ilmarinen, who put on spectacles to read it. "It sounds like something happened there that was too big to ignore, and bigger than the writer really wanted to admit."

"Oh. That." The Kuusaman master mage's voice went hard and flat. "I know about that." Fernao believed him; he knew all sorts of things he had no business knowing. "Some of the people who ran our captives' camp for the Gongs made a big mistake there. Most of them are too dead to court-martial now, but we would if we could. Stupidity is usually its own punishment. It was here."

"Now you're going to have to tell me, you know," Fernao said.

"Or else what?" But Ilmarinen was grinning. He loved to gossip, and made no bones about it. After an odorous bite of salmon and onions, he went on, "Well, for one thing, they let some sort of mage get in with the ordinary captives."

"Uh-oh," Fernao said.

"Uh-oh, indeed," Ilmarinen agreed. "And then they put some Algarvian leviathan-riders into the camp, too. And, just in case you haven't heard, the Gongs have figured out how to work the sorceries that make me hope Algarve and Unkerlant end up destroying each other—but we're never that lucky, are we?"

"Er—no," Fernao said. "From what I know of the Gyongyosians, that surprises me. They're warriors, aye, but not murderers."

"You're right. They aren't murderers—not that kind of murderers, anyhow. But so what?" Ilmarinen paused for another bite. Fernao remembered to eat, too. The Kuusaman master mage continued, "They're warriors, sure enough—and they volunteer, they really and truly do volunteer, to put their necks to the knife for the greater glory of Gyongyos and for the stars that don't give a fart about them."

"Oh." Fernao wished he hadn't started eating again. "And that's what happened on Obuda?"

"That's what happened on Obuda, all right," Ilmarinen said. "Smashed things up pretty well—about like a real earthquake, say." He shrugged. "Now we're putting the pieces back together, and we won't let it happen again. A bad nuisance, but only a nuisance."

"And a lot of dead Gyongyosians," Fernao said. "Dead for nothing."

Ilmarinen nodded. "For nothing much, anyhow. I gather the officer who led this thought doing something was better than sitting around doing nothing and waiting for the war to end. Only goes to show that sometimes sitting around isn't so bad."

"You should have thought of that before you went to the blockhouse by yourself," Fernao said.

After impressive deliberation, Ilmarinen made a face at him. "If we were all as smart as we knew how to make everyone else . . . very likely the world would be as much of a mess as it is right now."

"Aye, very likely." Fernao had wondered if the old man

would be able to get an aphorism out of his cynical start. He'd had his doubts when Ilmarinen paused there, but the theoretical sorcerer had come through. "Are you ready for the experiment tomorrow?"

"I am always ready for experiments," Ilmarinen answered. "Sometimes, unfortunately, experiments are not ready for me." He popped more onions and capers and soft pink-orange fish into his mouth. "I tell you this: I'd a hundred times sooner experiment than stand in front of a chamber full of eager second-raters and tell them what I know."

"I rather like to teach," Fernao said.

"I haven't minded teaching *you*," Ilmarinen said; Fernao realized only later the size of the compliment he'd got. The old man went on, "But these people who want it spelled out and have to have it that way because they can't see it if it isn't . . . They'd make a lovely rock garden, don't you think? Don't *they* think? They don't, and that's the trouble."

Fernao finished his own breakfast and went off to teach a class of mages—mostly Lagoans, with a few Kuusamans to fill out the twenty. Sure enough, the questions he got were of the sort Ilmarinen disliked: "Show me how these two verses work." "What does this formula mean?" "Do we really need to know that?"

"No, you don't really need to know that," he answered, his own temper fraying. "If you want to kill yourself when you try this spell, go ahead and forget it."

"You're not being very helpful," complained the woman who'd asked the question.

"You're not being very imaginative," Fernao said. "Would I have talked about this if you didn't need to know it?"

"Well, you never can tell," the woman said.

Later, Fernao did some complaining of his own to Pekka: "I wanted to pound my head against the wall. We've made this as simple as we can. Have we really made it simple enough for the people who'll have to use it? *Can* we make it simple enough for these people to use it?"

Instead of giving him the sympathy he craved, she annoyed him by laughing. "I've spent years trying to pound sorcery into the heads of people who don't much want to learn it," he said. "The ones we have here are pretty bright."

"Powers above help our kingdoms!" he exploded.

"I hope they will. I hope they do," she answered, and he found nothing to say to that. Then she added, "They must be looking out for me. Otherwise, how would I have met you?"

Fernao's annoyance evaporated. His ears heated. That must have been visible from the outside as well as palpable from within, for Pekka giggled. Fernao bowed. "You do me too much credit, I think."

Pekka shook her head. "I don't think so," she answered. "If I did, would you make me so happy?" Before his head swelled to the point where her chamber couldn't hold it, she added, "If I didn't think so, would I have let my life get so complicated when I didn't intend to?"

He found nothing to say to that, either. His life wasn't complicated. His life had been complicated before they found themselves together, because he'd wanted to be with her when she hadn't wanted to be with him. Now, as far as he was concerned, everything was fine. Of course, he wasn't torn in two directions at once. However much he wished Pekka weren't, he knew she was.

They lay close together on her narrow bed after making love that night when she suddenly said, "It's snowing."

"How can you tell?" he asked.

"The way the air feels—all still and quiet," she said, and turned on the bedside lamp. "There—you see?" Sure enough, the light showed snowflakes softly striking the double-glass window that helped hold cold at bay.

"It doesn't have to be still and quiet for snow," Fernao said. "Down in the land of the Ice People, it blows like this." He held his forearm parallel to the mattress. Then he added, "And I'd sooner look at you than at snow any day." Pekka kissed him. He gathered her in. Before too long, he sighed. "Ten years ago, I could have promised you twice in a row. Now I have to be lucky for that—not that I'm not lucky, you understand."

"Don't worry about it," Pekka said. "The holding is fine, too, all by itself." She reached out to turn off the lamp. They fell asleep in each other's arms—and woke up a couple of hours later, Fernao with an arm asleep, Pekka with a leg that seemed dead below the knee. As they untangled themselves and Fernao got into his clothes to go back to his own room, he yawned and thought, *So much for romance.*

Something closer to romance came the next day, when they rode out to the blockhouse under furs in a sleigh, as they'd done when they first began experimenting down in the Naatali district. He'd been conscious of Pekka as an attractive woman even then. Now . . . If his hands wandered a bit, and if hers did, the furs kept the driver from noticing.

But when they and the other theoretical sorcerers got down from the sleighs and went into the blockhouse, Pekka was all business. "You know what we're going to try today," she said. "We're going to use the energy from the sorcery we've developed to touch off a landslide and close off a pass in the Bratanu Mountains, to make the Algarvians have a harder time moving men and supplies from their kingdom east into Jelgava. I don't think anyone has ever projected so much sorcerous power so far and so precisely in the history of the world."

That's bound to be true, Fernao thought. *It's a demon of a long way from here to the border between Jelgava and Algarve.* Some of the excitement of what they'd been doing came back to him. Making everything cut and dried so people with no spark, no flair, of their own could use it had drained away a lot of that excitement. He was glad to feel it return; he'd wondered if it would.

"I begin," Pekka said, and chanted the ritual phrases Kuusamans used before every conjuration. Fernao had snickered behind his hand when he first heard them. He'd heard them so many times by now, magecraft undertaken without them would have felt strange, unnatural.

He'd only half understood them when he first heard them. He'd understood hardly anything of the Kuusaman cantrips that followed. He did these days. He wouldn't have wanted to try drafting an original spell in Kuusaman, but he had no trouble following one now. If anything went wrong, he knew much more than he had about how to repair it.

Ilmarinen and Piilis joined the incantation. So did Raahe and Alkio. Fernao felt the power build. Part of it was his, flowing from him through Pekka, whose hand he held. It put him in mind of pleasure building when they made love. But when his eyes flicked her way, her face was serious, intent, nothing at all like the way she looked when the two of them were alone. She didn't glance at him. She kept on chanting, doing what she had to do. *That's all any of us are doing,* he thought. *What else is there?*

If not for the world's energy grid more commonly used in traveling along ley lines, they never could have located the mountain pass so precisely. An alert Algarvian mage somewhere between the Naantali district and the pass might have detected the sorcery when at last it burst forth. He might have detected it, but that would have done him no good. By the time he knew it was there, he would have been far too late to stop it.

Fernao felt the spell seize the stones and the already-drifted snow along the sides of the pass, felt it seize them and jerk them and send them crashing down onto the road and the ley line at the bottom. Mezentio's mages might have achieved the same effect by killing a camp full of Kaunians, but never from this range: never, probably, from a quarter of this range. And this spell was clean—no murder attached to it.

Afterwards, all the mages sighed. Now Fernao could squeeze Pekka's hand without distracting her. She smiled and nodded. "We did it," she said. "I could feel that we did it."

"Aye." Fernao nodded, too. "The Algarvians will have harder work now in Jelgava." *And it's likelier your husband will come through safe. Should I be happy about that? Aye, curse it, I should. Leino's not my enemy. He's fighting my enemies.* He kept his face straight. He *didn't* want Pekka to know what he was thinking there. *We do have to be civilized about these things . . . curse it.*

Ever since she'd spied Spinello stalking through the wreckage of Eoforwic, Vanai had known she would try to kill him if she ever saw even the slightest chance. She hadn't known how badly she needed to go looking for that chance till the day be-

fore Pybba's rebels surrendered to the Algarvians, the day the
redheads agreed to treat the Forthwegians as proper war captives instead of butchering them for bandits.

Ealstan had slipped out of the pocket Pybba's men still held.
He'd slipped into and out of that pocket a good many times before then. Vanai had always hated it, but she couldn't deny he
knew what he was doing. And, when he'd come home full of
gloom, she'd thought she understood. However foolish she
reckoned Forthwegian patriotism, Ealstan felt it in his heart, in
his belly, just as she felt her own Kaunianity.

But she hadn't understood, or hadn't understood everything,
even if she'd thought she had. She'd found that out a couple of
hours later, after putting Saxburh down for a nap. Ealstan, by
then, had gone through a good deal of the wine in the flat. She
hadn't even worried about that, though Kaunians often sneered
at Forthwegians for drunkenness. She'd long since seen Ealstan
didn't let wine and spirits rule him, and that day he'd had more
sorrows to drown than usual.

He'd also had more sorrows to drown than she knew. He'd
looked up from the mug when she walked into the kitchen,
looked up from it and—voice not blurry in the least, he'd asked,
"Did you ever run across a redhead named Spinello?"

The question had crashed into her like a lightning bolt from a
clear sky. Her face must have given her away, for she'd seen his
mouth tighten. After that, what point to lying? "Aye," she'd answered quietly. "Back in Oyngestun. How did you know?"

Maybe that hadn't been the perfect question, for it had made
him gulp down all the wine left in his mug. "I heard him . . .
mention your name talking to his men. How could he know I
speak Algarvian?"

Mentioning her name undoubtedly meant going into obscene
detail over all the things he'd made her do back there in her
home village. With a sigh, Vanai had said, "He wanted to get
my grandfather to collaborate with the redheads. That would
have meant something in scholarly circles. You saw him once,
when he was out looking at an imperial Kaunian site with my
grandfather and me."

"I remember," Ealstan had said. He'd hesitated then; Vanai

gave him credit for it. But he'd gone on: "He wanted something else from you."

Vanai had nodded. *What else could I have done?* she wondered. *Nothing. Nothing at all.* "My grandfather said no," she'd told Ealstan. "He kept saying no. You met him. You have some small idea what a stubborn man he was. And so Spinello threw him into a labor gang. He wasn't young. He'd never done work like that in his life. It was killing him. I watched it happen for a little while. I couldn't stand it. Whatever else he was, he was the only kin I had left in the world. And so I . . ." Up till then, she'd managed to sound as cool, as detached, as if she were talking about building a fence. But the last few words came out in a ragged gulp as tears spilled down her cheeks: "I made a bargain with Spinello."

She'd stood there waiting once she got it out. What would Ealstan do? Slowly, he'd climbed to his feet. *Is he going out the door?* she remembered thinking. *Will he come back? Will he even look back? Will he hit me? This once, I could bear it without hating him afterwards.*

He'd come toward her. She remembered bracing herself, too. Then he'd put his arms around her and switched from the Forthwegian they'd been speaking to his slow, clear, classical Kaunian: "Brivibas, I think, was luckier in you than he realized—perhaps luckier than he deserved. And may the powers below eat that Spinello."

Vanai really had burst into tears then, and buried her face in the hollow of his shoulder. They were very nearly of a height; she hadn't had to stand on tiptoe to do it. She remembered whispering, "Thank you," over and over again, but she still wasn't sure if she'd said it loud enough for Ealstan to hear.

But she was sure what he'd said before she looked up again: "May the powers below have some help eating that Spinello." He'd sounded thoroughly grim.

He'd sounded so grim, in fact, that he'd terrified her. She'd thought about killing Spinello. He'd sounded as if he intended to march out right that minute and do it. And so she'd clung to him and exclaimed, "No! He's not worth the risk of you. By the powers above, he *isn't*, Ealstan! And besides, before long the Unkerlanters are bound to do it for us."

"They haven't done it yet," he'd grumbled. But he hadn't gone charging out of the flat then, and, so far as Vanai knew, he hadn't tried stalking Spinello since. She hoped that meant he'd listened to her as well as hearing her. She hoped so, but she wasn't sure. He hadn't seemed any different with her after that dreadful day, and he hadn't seemed any different with Saxburh, either. Vanai dared take that for a good sign.

Even so, she knew that, if she was going to try to get rid of Spinello, sooner was definitely better. Ealstan, she feared, would also try—and even if he succeeded, he was all too likely to get caught. If he did try, he would pick the most obvious, most direct way. Vanai knew him too well to have any doubts on that score. But what Algarvian would pay any particular attention to a Forthwegian woman? Vanai wasn't standing by a mirror to see her own smile, but suspected it showed a lot of pointed teeth. Every now and then, being Thelberge to the world had its advantages.

But being anyone in Eoforwic these days also had its disadvantages, and they were many and large. Few Unkerlanter eggs had burst close to the block of flats, but that didn't mean Swemmel's soldiers couldn't start lobbing them this way whenever they chose. Staying in Eoforwic meant living with danger.

Staying in Eoforwic also meant living with hunger. Not a lot of food came into the Forthwegian capital, and the redheads kept more than their share of what did. People haunted the markets. They also pocked through the wreckage that made up so much of the city, looking for jars of olives and for smoked or salted meat and for wine and, most of all, for rest crates filled with sorcerously preserved food. Find one of those—and get it home without having it stolen—and you might eat well for a long time. Find silver or jewelry and you could pay the piratical prices in the markets.

And, as happened every fall, people hunted mushrooms over every inch of bare ground in Eoforwic. Sometimes Vanai would go out with Ealstan and they would pass the baby back and forth. No matter how dismal things were, Saxburh could make

Ealstan smile. "If it weren't for mushrooms, you wouldn't be here," he would tell her. She hadn't the faintest idea what he was talking about, but she always gurgled with delight when he talked to her.

And sometimes Vanai would take Saxburh out by herself. Nobody in shattered Eoforwic seemed to need bookkeepers, but there were plenty of day-laborer jobs, and Ealstan took them without complaint, especially when he got paid in food instead of silver. Plenty of Forthwegian women took them, too, but Vanai couldn't. Even if she'd had someone to take care of Saxburh, she didn't dare stay out in public for the long shifts such work required. If her sorcerous disguise wore off . . . She didn't want to think about that.

No one kept track of a mushroom hunter's hours, though. Head down, the baby in the crook of her arm or sometimes in a cloth harness she'd made from scraps of old clothes, she eyed damp ground in the park where she'd first shown herself to the world as Thelberge—where, in fact, Ealstan had given her the name she'd used ever since.

Sometimes she had good luck, sometimes not so good. More people were harvesting a lot less space than had been true around Gromheort and Oyngestun. But mushrooms weren't like gold or silver—getting some out of the ground today didn't mean more wouldn't spring up tomorrow. You couldn't live on mushrooms alone, but they did help. And they made barley— often stale barley, sometimes moldy barley—much more bearable and less monotonous than it would have been without them.

Paying close attention to small patches of ground helped Vanai keep from noticing how ravaged the park was. Sometimes, though, as when a score of new craters from bursting eggs pocked its face like some ghastly disease, she couldn't help it. Ealstan was along with her that morning. With a sad sigh, she said, "This place was shabby when you brought me here a couple of years ago. Now—now it's like looking at a corpse."

"A murdered corpse," he agreed. "But if we'd been here when those eggs came down, we'd've been the ones who got murdered."

"Maybe," Vanai said. "But maybe not, too. I've had to jump into craters a few times when the Unkerlanters started tossing eggs across the river, or when their dragons came over the city. It's just something we need to do these days, that's all." She wondered what her former self from Oyngestun—her self from before the war—would have made of that calm, matter-of-fact statement. She would have reckoned it madness. She was sure of that. What else could it possibly be?

But why, if it were madness, was Ealstan soberly nodding? "I've had to do the same thing myself," he answered, and showed his teeth in a mirthless grin. "Life in the big city. It isn't even what irks me these days. You know what is?"

"Tell me," Vanai said, but then she stopped listening because she'd seen some meadow mushrooms peeping out from the edge of a clump of woods. She hurried over, picked them, and put them in her basket. "I'm sorry. *Now* tell me."

"You know about Plegmund's Brigade? Everybody knows about Plegmund's Brigade," he said, and Vanai nodded. Ealstan muttered something under his breath about his cousin Sidroc, then got back to things at hand: "The Algarvians have cooked up something like that for Forthwegian women now, powers below eat them."

"For women?" Vanai said. "Do they give them sticks?"

"No, no." He shook his head. "They call them Hilde's Helpers—you know, after Plegmund's queen. And what Hilde's Helpers do is, they cook and they bake like maniacs, and then they give the redheads everything they make. They just ignore Forthwegian laborers—I've seen that, too, curse them. I heard one of them say the Algarvians deserve the best of everything because they're defending us from Swemmel's savages."

"Do people really believe that? Can people really believe that?" Vanai asked.

"This gal did," Ealstan said. He held Saxburh up in front of his face. "She didn't even know as much as you do. She didn't come close." Saxburh laughed.

Vanai didn't. No Kaunian, of course, could prefer Algarvians to Unkerlanters. But, even now, some Forthwegians evidently could. *Fools,* she thought. But there were also Forthwegians who preferred the Algarvians not in spite of what they'd done to the Kaunians of Forthweg but because of it.

She saw some of Hilde's Helpers a couple of days later. They wore blue-and-white armbands—Forthwegian colors—and, sure enough, carried baskets and trays of food. They all looked well fed themselves, too. Vanai quietly cursed them. And, had they known what she was, they would have cursed her.

She hoped Unkerlanter dragons would raid Eoforwic while Hilde's Helpers were serving Algarvian soldiers. If that wasn't poetic justice, what was? "They would deserve it," she told Saxburh. The baby smiled, showing a new tooth that had cost Vanai an almost sleepless night. Babies didn't argue, except when you wanted them to go to bed.

And then Vanai smiled, too, and kissed Saxburh. Her daughter laughed out loud. A moment later, so did Vanai. She knew what she needed to do. She knew how to do it. "I'll have to get another basket," she said, "a little one. A special one. And I'll need a bit of luck. But do you know what, sweetheart? For once in my life, I won't need much." Saxburh grinned, as if proud of that new tooth. So did Vanai.

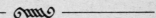

Look for

OUT OF THE DARKNESS

By HARRY TURTLEDOVE

Now available
from Tom Doherty Associates

Turn the page for a preview!

Ealstan intended to kill an Algarvian officer. Had the young Forthwegian not been fussy about which redhead he killed, or had he not cared whether he lived or died in the doing, he would have had an easier time of it. But, with a wife and daughter to think about, he wanted to get away with it if he could. He'd even promised Vanai he wouldn't do anything foolish. He regretted that promise now, but he'd always been honorable to the point of stubbornness, so he still felt himself bound by it.

And he wanted to rid the world of one of Mezentio's men in particular. Oh, he would have been delighted to see all of them dead, but he especially wanted to be the means by which this one died. *Considering what the whoreson did to Vanai, and made her do for him, who could blame me?*

But, like a lot of rhetorical questions, that one had an obvious, unrhetorical answer: *all the other Algarvians in Eoforwic.* The Algarvians ruled the capital of Forthweg with a mailed fist these days. Ealstan had been part of the uprising that almost threw them out of Eoforwic. As in most things, though, almost wasn't good enough; he counted himself lucky to remain among the living.

Saxburh smiled and gurgled at him from her cradle as he walked by. The baby seemed proud of cutting a new tooth. Ealstan was glad she'd finally done it, too. She'd been fussy and noisy for several nights before it broke through. Ealstan yawned; he and Vanai had lost sleep because of that.

His wife was in the kitchen, building up the fire to boil barley for porridge. "I'm off," Ealstan said. "No work for a bookkeeper in Eoforwic these days, but plenty for someone with a strong back."

Vanai gave him a knotted cloth. "Here's cheese and olives

and an onion," she said. "I only wish it were more."

"It'll do," he said. "I'm not starving." He told the truth. He was hungry, but everyone in Eoforwic except some—not all—of the Algarvians was hungry these days. He still had his strength. To do a laborer's work, he needed it, too. Wagging a finger at her, he added, "Make sure you've got enough for yourself. You're nursing the baby."

"Don't worry about me," Vanai said. "I'll do fine, and so will Saxburh." She leaned toward him to kiss him goodbye.

As their lips brushed, her face changed—literally. Her eyes went from brown to blue-gray, her skin from swarthy to pale, her nose from proud and hooked to short and straight. Her hair stayed dark, but that was because it was dyed—he could see the golden roots, which he hadn't been able to do a moment before. She seemed suddenly taller and slimmer, too: not stubby and broad-shouldered like most Forthwegians, including Ealstan himself.

He finished the kiss. Nothing, as far as he was concerned, was more important than that. Then he said, "Your masking spell just slipped."

Her mouth twisted in annoyance. Then she shrugged. "I knew I was going to have to renew it pretty soon, anyhow. As long as it happens inside the flat, it's not so bad."

"Not bad at all," Ealstan said, and gave her another kiss. As she smiled, he went on, "I like the way you look just fine, regardless of whether you seem like a Forthwegian or a Kaunian. You know that."

Vanai nodded, but her smile slipped instead of getting bigger as he'd hoped. "Not many do," she said. "Most Forthwegians have no use for me, and the Algarvians would cut my throat to use my life energy against Unkerlant if they saw me the way I really am. I suppose there are other Kaunians here, but how would I know? If they want to stay alive, they have to stay hidden, the same as I do."

Ealstan remembered the golden roots he'd seen. "You should dye your hair again, too. It's growing out."

"Aye, I know. I'll take care of it," Vanai promised. One way

the Algarvians checked to see whether someone was a sorcerously disguised Kaunian was by pulling out a few hairs and
seeing if they turned yellow when removed from the suspect's
scalp. Ordinary hair dye countered that. The Algarvians being
who and what they were, thoroughness in such matters paid off;
Vanai kept the hair between her legs dark, too.

Carrying his meager lunch, Ealstan went downstairs and out
onto the street. The two blocks of flats across from his own
were only piles of rubble these days. The Algarvians had
smashed both of them during the Forthwegian uprising. Ealstan
thanked the powers above that his own building had survived. It
was, he knew, only luck.

A Forthwegian man in a threadbare knee-length tunic scrabbled through the wreckage across the street, looking for wood
or whatever else he could find. He stared up in alarm at Ealstan,
his mouth a wide circle of fright in the midst of his shaggy gray
beard and mustache. Ealstan waved; like everyone else in Eoforwic, he'd spent his share of time guddling through ruins, too.
The shaggy man relaxed and waved back.

Not a lot of people were on the streets: only a handful, compared to the days before the uprising and before the latest Unkerlanter advance stalled—or was allowed to stall?—in
Eoforwic's suburbs on the west bank of the Twegen River. Ealstan cocked his head to one side. He didn't hear many eggs
bursting. King Swemmel's soldiers, there on the far bank of the
Twegen, were taking it easy on Eoforwic today.

His boots squelched in mud. Fall and winter were the rainy
season in Eoforwic, as in the rest of Forthweg. *At least I won't
have to worry much about snow, the way the Unkerlanters
would if they were back home,* Ealstan thought.

He spotted a mushroom, pale against the dark dirt of another
muddy patch, and stooped to pick it. Like all Forthwegians, like
all the Kaunians in Forthweg—and emphatically unlike the Algarvian occupiers—he was wild for mushrooms of all sorts. He
suddenly shook his head and straightened up. He was wild for
mushrooms of almost all sorts. This one, though, could stay
where it was. He knew a destroying power when he saw one.

His father Hestan, back in Gromheort, had used direct and of
ten painful methods to make sure he could tell a good mush
room from a poisonous one.

I wish the redheads liked mushrooms, he thought. *Maybe on
of them would pick that one and kill himself.*

Algarvians directed Forthwegians hauling rubble to shore u
the defenses against the Unkerlanter attack everyone in the cit
knew was coming. Forthwegian women in armbands of blu
and white—Hilde's Helpers, they called themselves—brough
food to the redheads, but not to their countrymen, who wer
working harder. Ealstan scowled at the women. They were th
female equivalent of the men of Plegmund's Brigade: Forthwe
gians who fought for King Mezentio of Algarve. His cousi
Sidroc fought in Plegmund's Brigade if he hadn't been kille
yet. Ealstan hoped he had.

Instead of joining the Forthwegian laborers as he often did
Ealstan turned away toward the center of town. He hadn't bee
there for a while: not since he and a couple of other Forthwe
gians teamed up to assassinate an Algarvian official. They'
worn Algarvian uniforms to do it, and they'd been otherwis
disguised, too.

Back then, the redheads had held only a slender corridor int
the heart of Eoforwic—but enough, curse them, to use to brin
in reinforcements. Now the whole city was theirs again . . . a
least, until such time as the Unkerlanters chose to try to ru
them out. Ealstan had a demon of a time finding the particula
abandoned building he was looking for. "It has to be aroun
here somewhere," he muttered. But where? Eoforwic had take
quite a pounding since he'd last come to these parts.

If this doesn't work, I'll think of something else, he told him
self. Still, this had to be his best chance. *There* was the build
ing: farther into Eoforwic than he'd recalled. It didn't loo
much worse than it had when he and his pals ducked into it t
change from Algarvian tunics and kilts to Forthwegian-styl
long tunics. Ealstan ducked inside. The next obvious questio
was whether anyone had stolen the uniforms he and his com
rades had abandoned.

Why would anybody? he wondered. Forthwegians didn'

wouldn't, wear kilts, any more than their Unkerlanter cousins would. Ealstan didn't think anybody could get much for selling the clothes. And so, with a little luck . . .

He felt like shouting when he saw the uniforms still lying where they'd been thrown when he and his friends got rid of them. He picked up the one he'd worn. It was muddier and grimier than it had been: rain and dirt and dust had had their way with it. But a lot of Algarvians in Eoforwic these days wore uniforms that had known better years. Ealstan held it up and nodded. He could get away with it.

He pulled his own tunic off over his head, then got into the Algarvian clothes. The high, tight collar was as uncomfortable as he remembered. His tunic went into the pack. He took from his belt pouch first a small stick, then a length of dark brown yarn and another of red. He twisted them together and began a chant in classical Kaunian. His spell that would temporarily disguise him as an Algarvian was modeled after the one Vanai had created to let her—and other Kaunians—look like the Forthwegian majority and keep Mezentio's men from seizing them.

When Ealstan looked at himself, he could see no change. Even a mirror wouldn't have helped. That was the sorcery's drawback. Only someone else could tell you if it had worked— and you found out the hard way if it wore off at the wrong time. He plucked at his beard. It was shaggier than Algarvians usually wore theirs. They often went in for side whiskers and imperials and waxed mustachios. But a lot of them were more unkempt than they had been, too. He thought he could get by with the impersonation—provided the spell had worked.

Only one way to learn, he thought again. He strode out of the building. He hadn't gone more than half a block before two Algarvian troopers walked by. They both saluted. One said, "Good morning, Lieutenant." Ealstan returned the salute without answering. He spoke some Algarvian, but with a sonorous Forthwegian accent.

He shrugged—then shrugged again, turning it into a production, as Algarvians were wont to do with any gesture. He'd passed the test. Now he had several hours in which to hunt down that son of a whore of a Spinello. The stick he carried was more likely to be a robber's weapon than a constable's or an officer's, but that didn't matter so much these days, either. If a stick blazed, Mezentio's men would use it.

Algarvian soldiers saluted him. He saluted officers. Forthwegians gave him sullen looks. No one paid much attention to him. He hurried west toward the riverfront, looking like a man on important business. And so he was: that was where he'd seen Spinello. He could lure the redhead away, blaze him, and then use a counterspell to turn back into his proper self in moments.

He could . . . if he could find Spinello. The fellow stood out in a crowd. He was a bantam rooster of a man, always crowing, always bragging. But he wasn't where Ealstan had hoped and expected him to be. Had the Unkerlanters killed him? *How would I ever know?* Ealstan thought. *I want to make sure he's dead. And who has a better right to kill him than I do?*

"Where's the old man?" one redheaded footsoldier asked another.

"Colonel Spinello?" the other soldier returned. The first man nodded. Ealstan pricked up his ears. The second Algarvian said, "He went over to one of the officers' brothels by the palace, the lucky bastard. Said he had a meeting somewhere later on, so he might as well have some fun first. If it's anything important, you could hunt him up, I bet."

"Nah." The first redhead made a dismissive gesture. "He asked me to let him know how my sister was doing—she got hurt when those stinking Kuusamans dropped eggs on Trapani. My father writes that she'll pull through. I'll tell him when I see him, that's all."

"That's good," the second soldier said. "Glad to hear it."

Ealstan turned away in frustration. He wouldn't get Spinello today. Braving an Algarvian officers' brothel was beyond him, even if murder wasn't. He also found himself surprised to learn Spinello cared about his men and their families. But then he thought, *Well, why shouldn't he? It's not as if they were Kaunians.*

Vanai splashed hot water, very hot water, water as hot as she could stand it, onto her face again and again, especially around her mouth. Then she rubbed and rubbed and rubbed at her lips with the roughest, scratchiest towel she had. Finally, when she'd rubbed her mouth bloody, she gave up. She could still feel Spinello's lips on hers even after all that.

But then she snatched Saxburh out of her cradle and danced around the flat with the baby in her arms. Saxburh liked that; she squealed with glee. "It was worth it. By the powers above, it *was* worth it!" Her little daughter wouldn't have argued for the world. She was having the time of her life. She squealed again.

"Do you know what I did?" Vanai said. "Do you have any *idea* what I did?" Saxburh had no idea. She chortled anyhow. Still dancing, ignoring the sandpapered state of her lips, Vanai went on, "I put four death caps in his stew. Not one, not two, not three. Four. Four death caps could kill a troop of behemoths, let alone one fornicating Algarvian." She kept right on dancing. Saxburh kept right on laughing.

Fornicating Algarvian is right, Vanai thought savagely. Her mouth was sore, but she didn't care. *I'd've put my lips on his prong to get him to take that bowl of stew. Powers below eat him, why not? It's not as if he didn't make me do it before. Teach me tricks, will you? See how you'll like the one I just taught you!*

Spinello, without a doubt, felt fine right now. That was one of the things that made death caps and their close cousins, the destroying powers, so deadly. People who ate them didn't feel anything wrong for several hours, sometimes even for a couple of days. By then it was far too late for them to puke up what they'd eaten. The poison stayed inside them, working, and no healer or mage had ever found a cure for it. Soon enough, Spinello would know what she'd done.

"Isn't that fine?" Vanai asked Saxburh. "Isn't that just the most splendid thing you ever heard in all your days?" The baby didn't have many days, but, by the way she gurgled and wriggled with glee, it might have been.

All Forthwegians hunted mushrooms whenever they got the chance. In that, if in few other things, the Kaunians in Forthweg agreed with their neighbors. No one—not even Algarvian soldiers, not any more—paid much attention to people walking with their heads down, eyes on the ground. And who was likely to notice what sort of mushrooms went into a basket? One thing Vanai's grandfather had taught her was how to tell the poisonous from the safe. Everyone in Forthweg learned those lessons. This once, Vanai had chosen to stand them on their head.

"And so you too have some measure of revenge, my grandfather," she whispered in classical Kaunian. Brivibas would never have approved of her saying any such thing to him in mere Forthwegian.

Saxburh's eyes—they would be dark like Ealstan's, for they were already darkening from the blue of almost all newborns' eyes—widened. She could hear that the sounds of this language were different from those of the Forthwegian Vanai and Ealstan usually spoke.

"I will teach you this tongue, too," Vanai told her daughter, still in classical Kaunian. "I do not know if you will thank me for it. This is a tongue whose speakers have more than their share of trouble, more than their share of woe. But it is as much yours as Forthwegian, and you should learn it. What do you think of that?"

"Dada!" Saxburh said.

Vanai laughed. "No, you silly thing, I'm your mama," she said, falling back into Forthwegian without noticing she'd done it till after the words passed her lips. Saxburh babbled more cheerful nonsense, none of which sounded like either Forthwegian or classical Kaunian. Then she screwed up her face and grunted.

Knowing what that meant even before she caught the smell, Vanai squatted down, laid Saxburh on the floor, and cleaned her bottom. Saxburh even thought that was funny, where she often fussed over it. Vanai laughed, too, but she had to work to keep the corners of her mouth turned up. She wouldn't have used Forthwegian so much before she started disguising herself. It really was as if Thelberge, the Forthwegian semblance she had to wear, were gaining at the expense of Vanai, the Kaunian reality within.

Even if the Algarvians lose the war, even if the Unkerlanter drive them out of Forthweg, what will it be like for the blond left alive here? Will they—will we—go on wearing sorcerou disguises and speaking Forthwegian because it's easier, be cause the Forthwegians—the real Forthwegians—won't hat us so much then? If we do, what happens to the Kaunianity, th sense of ourselves as something special and apart, that we've kept alive ever since the Empire fell?

She cursed softly. She had no answer for that. She wondered if anyone else did, if anyone else could. If not, even if the Algarvians lost the Derlavaian War, wouldn't they have won a great battle in their endless struggle against the Kaunians who'd been civilized while they still painted themselves strange colors and ran naked through their native forests throwing spears?

The familiar coded knock Ealstan used interrupted her gloomy reverie. She snatched up Saxburh and hurried to unbar the door. Ealstan gave her a kiss. Then he wrinkled his nose. "I know what you've been doing," he said. He kissed Saxburh. "And I know what *you've* been doing, too." He took her from Vanai and rocked her in his arms. "Aye, I do. You can't fool me. I know just what you've been doing."

"She can't help it," Vanai said. "And it's something everybody else does, too."

"I should hope so," Ealstan answered. "Otherwise, we'd all burst like eggs, and who would clean up after us then?" Vanai hadn't thought of it like that. When she did, she giggled. Ealstan went on, "And what did you do with your morning?"

Before Vanai realized she would, she answered, "While Saxburh was taking a nap, I put on a blue-and-white armband and went out and pretended I was one of Hilde's Helpers."

"Powers above, you're joking!" Ealstan exclaimed. "Don't say things like that, or you'll make me drop the baby." He mimed doing just that, which made Vanai start and made Saxburh laugh.

Vanai said, "I really did. And do you want to know why?"

Ealstan studied her to make sure she wasn't kidding him.

What he saw on her face must have satisfied him, for he replied, "I'd love to know why. The only reason that occurs to me right now is that you've gone crazy, and I don't think that's right."

"No." Vanai said that in Forthwegian, but then switched to classical Kaunian. "I wore the armband because I wanted to give a certain officer of the redheaded barbarians a special dish—and I did it."

"A special dish?" Ealstan echoed in his own slow, thoughtful classical Kaunian. "What kind of—? Oh!" He didn't need long to figure out what she meant. His eyes glowed. "How special was it?"

"Four death caps," she answered proudly.

"Four?" He blinked. "That would kill anybody ten times over."

"Aye. I know." Vanai wished she could have killed Spinello ten times over. "I hope he enjoyed them, too. People who eat them say they're supposed to be tasty."

"I've heard the same thing," Ealstan answered, falling back into Forthwegian. "Not something I ever wanted to find out for myself." He carefully set Saxburh in her little seat, then came back and took Vanai in his arms. "You told me not to take chances, and then you went and did this? I ought to beat you, the way Forthwegian husbands are supposed to."

"It wasn't so risky for me as it would have been for you," she answered. "I just gave him the food, took back the bowl, and went on my way. He still feels fine—I'm sure of it—but pretty soon he won't. What was I to him? Just another Forthwegian." *Just another wench,* she thought, remembering the feel of his lips on hers. *But the last wench, the very last.*

"It's a good thing you did get the bowl—and the spoon, too, I hope," Ealstan said. Vanai nodded. He went on, "If you hadn't, the Algarvian mages could have used the law of contagion to trace them back to you."

"I know. I thought of that. It's the reason I waited for them." Vanai didn't tell Ealstan about the couple of quizzical looks Spinello had sent her while he ate her tasty dish of death. Had he half recognized, or wondered if he recognized, her voice? Back in Oyngestun, they'd always spoken classical Kaunian.

Here, of course, Vanai had used what scraps of Algarvian she had. That, and the difference in her looks, had kept Spinello from figuring out who she was.

"Well, the son of a whore is gone now, even if he hasn't figured it out yet. Four death caps?" Ealstan whistled. "You could have killed off half the redheads in Eoforwic with four death caps. Pity you couldn't have found some way to do it."

"It is, isn't it?" Vanai said. "But I got rid of the one I most wanted dead." That was as much as she'd ever said since Ealstan found out about Spinello.

Ealstan nodded now. "I believe that," he said, and let it go. He'd never pushed her for details, for which she was grateful.

Saxburh started to cry. Ealstan joggled her, but this time it didn't restore her smile. "Give her to me. I think she's getting fussy," Vanai said. "She's been up for a while now." *And I've been dancing with her, dancing because of what I just did to Spinello. And I still feel like dancing, by the powers above.*

She sat down on the couch and undid the toggles that held her tunic closed. Ealstan reached out and gently cupped her left breast as she bared it. "I know it's not for me right now," he said, "but maybe later?"

"Maybe," she said. By her tone, it probably meant aye. As Saxburh settled in and began to nurse, Vanai wondered why that should be so. Wouldn't seeing Spinello have soured her on men and anything to do with men? Till she first gave herself to Ealstan, she'd thought the Algarvian had soured her on lovemaking forever. Now . . . *Now I just fed him four death caps, and I want to celebrate.* "Come on, sweetheart," she crooned to Saxburh. "You're getting sleepy, aren't you?"

Ealstan, who'd gone into the kitchen, heard that and laughed. He came back with a couple of mugs of something that wasn't water. He gave Vanai one. "Here. Shall we drink to . . . to freedom!"

"To freedom!" Vanai echoed, and raised the cup to her lips. Plum brandy slid hot down her throat. She glanced toward Saxburh. Sometimes the baby was interested in what her mother ate and drank. Not now, though. Saxburh's eyes started to slide shut. Vanai's nipple slid out of the baby's mouth. Hoisting her daughter to her shoulder, Vanai got a sleepy burp from her, then rocked her till she fell asleep. Saxburh didn't wake up when she set her in the cradle, either.

Her tunic still hanging open, Vanai turned back to Ealstan. "What were you saying about later?"